Terence

Terence'S Comedies

Terence

Terence'S Comedies

ISBN/EAN: 9783744792653

Printed in Europe, USA, Canada, Australia, Japan

Cover: Foto ©Andreas Hilbeck / pixelio.de

More available books at **www.hansebooks.com**

TERENCE's
COMEDIES,

TRANSLATED into ENGLISH PROSE,
As near as the Propriety of the Two LANGUAGES will admit.

Together with the

Original Latin from the Best EDITIONS.
WHEREIN

The WORDS of the LATIN TEXT are ranged in their GRAMMATICAL
ORDER; the ELLIPSES carefully supplied; the OBSERVATIONS of the most Valuable
COMMENTATORS, both antient and modern, represented; and the BEAUTIES of the
ORIGINAL explained in a new and concise Manner.

With NOTES pointing out the CONNEXION of the several SCENES, and an INDEX
CRITICAL and PHRASEOLOGICAL.

The WHOLE adapted to the Capacities of YOUTH at School, as well as of PRIVATE
GENTLEMEN.

In TWO VOLUMES.

By S. PATRICK, LL. D.
Editor of AINSWORTH's Dictionary, and HEDERICUS's Lexicon.

The THIRD EDITION.

VOL. I.

To which is prefixed the LIFE of TERENCE, with some Account of the DRAMATIC
POETRY of the Antients.

LONDON:
Printed for EDWARD and CHARLES DILLY in the Poultry.
M, DCC, LXVII.

TO

Norton Powlet, *Esq*;

The following EDITION

OF

TERENCE

IS INSCRIBED;

As a Testimony of the Esteem and Gratitude

OF

His much Obliged, and

Most Obedient

Humble Servant,

The TRANSLATOR.

TO THE

READER.

AS the Education of Youth is a thing of the last Importance to Society, so every Endeavour to render it more easy, or advantageous, has a just Claim to be well received. The first Years of Life are usually spent in acquiring a Knowledge of the Greek and Latin Tongues, especially the latter. And indeed, as that is now become in a manner the Language of learned Men, and all Discoveries in Arts and Sciences, intended to be universal, and of common Benefit to Mankind, are for the most part communicated to the World in that Language; it is impossible to make any considerable Advances in human Learning, till that Key and Inlet (as I may call it) to the Sciences, is first obtained. It must be owned indeed, that the Study of Words, however necessary, is dry and unentertaining: And it is for this Reason, that so many Attempts have been made to render it easy; that the Mind, by a swift Progress, may the sooner arrive at the solid Advantages to be reap'd from it, and be encouraged to proceed with Chearfulness, from a Fore-taste of the ample Recompence it is soon like to meet with.

In studying a dead Language, there are two Things that principally demand our Attention. First, the Words themselves, with their proper and natural Sig-

nifications:

nifications: And then the Peculiarities of the Tongue, those particular Modes of Speech, which distinguish it from all others, and arise chiefly from the Manner of ranging and connecting the Words. And here let it be observed, that this last cannot be attained to any Degree of Exactness, without a competent Knowledge of the Genius, Manners, and Characters of the People whose Language we study. It is evident, that these have a great Influence upon Discourse, and, as the original Writers of any Nation must be supposed to allude frequently to the Modes, Customs, and Institutions of their Country; a full and distinct Comprehension of these cannot but greatly tend to facilitate the Understanding of antient Authors.

Hence it is easy to collect, that whoever undertakes to explain an antient Greek or Latin Writer, with a View to render him serviceable in the Education of Youth, must propose to himself these two Things: First, a just and accurate Translation, fully expressive of the Meaning of the Original; and moreover to accompany this with such Illustrations and Remarks, as may not only serve to remove grammatical Difficulties, but also to throw a Light upon Passages, that by reason of some Allusion to Customs, Places, or Events, must otherwise prove an unsurmountable Obstacle in the way of Beginners. Nor let any one think this last a Matter of small Consequence, as if these obscure Places of an Author might be passed over without Concern. Young Minds are fond of Instruction. When by proper Helps, they have got the better of any seeming Difficulty that lay in their way, it adds wonderfully to their Alacrity, and makes them pursue their Studies with great Spirit and Keenness. Whereas, when all their Endeavours are ineffectual, when they find it impossible to get over the Rubs and Hindrances they meet with, they begin to be discouraged, their Eagerness by degrees slackens

and

and abates; and 'tis well if this Difguſt does not at laſt
ſettle in a fixed Averſion, never to be overcome.

Having thus given the Reader ſome Account of the
principal View I had in undertaking a Work of this Kind,
it will be now proper to ſay ſomething of the Manner in
which I have endeavoured to execute it. Terence I conſidered was an Author very fit to be put into the Hands of
thoſe, who have as yet made no great Advances in the Latin Tongue, and want to improve themſelves farther.
For, beſides a Delicacy and Purity of Language, peculiar
to this Author, there is ſomething ſo agreeable in his Manner, as bids fair to captivate the Mind, and conquer that
Reluctance one naturally feels to the Study of bare Words,
barren of Entertainment; beſides, his Plays are a Picture
of the Times in which he wrote. In them real Life is
repreſented, real Characters are introduced, and his Scenes
are the very Language and Converſation of that Age; ſo
that in reading Terence, one may be ſaid to learn Latin
by converſing with the old Romans: But then it is well
known, that the Style of Converſation is generally ſhort and
conciſe, and ſtrictly connected with the Manners and Cuſtoms
of the People; for Speech conveys our Thoughts with Eaſe,
and in few Words; and hence the Phraſes and Sentences
that moſt frequently occur in common Diſcourſe, are by
degrees pared of all Superfluities, and oft leave a great
deal for the Mind to ſupply, which Uſe and Cuſtom renders eaſy. 'Tis thus, that Ellipſes creep into Language,
and a peculiar Force and Emphaſis is ſtamp'd upon ſome
Words, which though obvious to the Natives, is not to be
comprehended by Strangers, without great Attention and
Care.

These then are ſome of the Difficulties, that we are naturally to expect to meet with, in ſuch a Writer as Terence, and to remove them is the principal Aim of the
following Work. And firſt, becauſe our Author is full of
Ellipſes, ſome of them too very perplexing ones; and that

his

his Words are often ranged in a manner very different from that of other antient Latin Writers, so as to occasion no small Obscurity to a Learner; along with the Latin Text are here given the Words themselves, in the grammatical Order, where all the Ellipses are carefully supplied, and where the Reader will often find that a Sentence otherwise unintelligible, is rendered easy and perspicuous, sometimes by the Addition of a single Word. Opposite to the Latin *Text you have a Translation, made with all the Care and Exactness possible, and in which no Pains have been spared, to bring it as near to the Original, as the Propriety of Language will admit. Not that I pretend to have copied the* Latin *Word for Word; that were impossible, nor indeed is there any Necessity for it. The Thing chiefly wanted, is to come at the Author's real Meaning; and, if possible, convey to the Mind the same Set of Ideas, which his Expressions were design'd to excite. This Point once gained, it will be easy by the Help of the Order of Construction, to apply them to the Words of the Original.*

But I considered, that when all this was done, many Places must still appear obscure to a young Reader, from his Ignorance of the Manners and Customs of the Antients, from Allusions to Events and Places to him unknown, and from a remarkable Peculiarity of Construction, or Conciseness of Expression, frequent with our Author. For this Reason I found it would be necessary to compile a Set of Notes, in which these several Difficulties might be obviated, and all the needful Helps for understanding our Poet set before the Reader in one View. This put me upon consulting the Commentators (especially Donatus, Dacier, Eugraphius, *and* Bentley, *who have succeeded best in explaining our Author) and selecting from them whatever I judged would be useful, either to illustrate an obscure Passage, or convey the Author's Meaning fully and clearly to the Mind of the Reader. But I soon found it would be necessary to carry* my Remarks farther than they had done. They have none of them wrote with a sufficient Condescension to the Capacities of Youth, and are for the most part very defective in pointing out the Beauties of the Poet, especially those that regard the Design and Conduct of the Play. As it is of great Importance to Youth, to have their Taste formed betimes to Correctness and Propriety, I have enlarged particularly on this Article, and connected the various Scenes by a short Introduction to each, in which the Situation of the several Persons concerned is described, and the Progress of the Plot examined. This I flatter myself will be of great use to the Reader, by enabling him to see more distinctly into the Beauties of the Original, and to comprehend that admirable Artifice and Propriety in conducting the different Characters, for which Terence is so justly celebrated. It is evident, that as at the Beginning of every Scene, a particular Account is given of the several Persons introduced, with what Passions they come accompanied, what are their Hopes, Fears, Expectations, and Designs; the Reader must be greatly assisted in judging how far the Characters are well kept up, and whether the Speech and Behaviour of each Person suits his particular Circumstances.

Thus far I thought necessary to say, to prevent Mistakes with regard to the following Work. It is not intended as an elegant Translation, nor for Proficients in the Language, but may be of some service in removing the Difficulties, that are apt to startle young Beginners, at their first Entrance upon these Studies. The Design at least is good; how far it is well executed, the Publick must judge. I shall only add, that to make this Work the more correct and useful, the Latin was printed from the justly celebrated Cambridge Copy, yet not without taking notice of such Alterations and Amendments for the better as have been since made in subsequent Editions. There is

moreover

moreover added a critical and phrafeological Index, in
which the particular Proverbs and Phrafes in the Latin
are rendred by others analogous to them in our Language,
which could not often be done in the Verfion, without breaking in upon the principal Defign.   And in fine, that nothing which could any way conduce to a better Underftanding of our Author might be wanting, I have prefixed a
fhort Account of his Life, with Remarks upon his Genius,
Character, and Writings, and the Rife and Progrefs of
Dramatick Poetry among the Ancients.

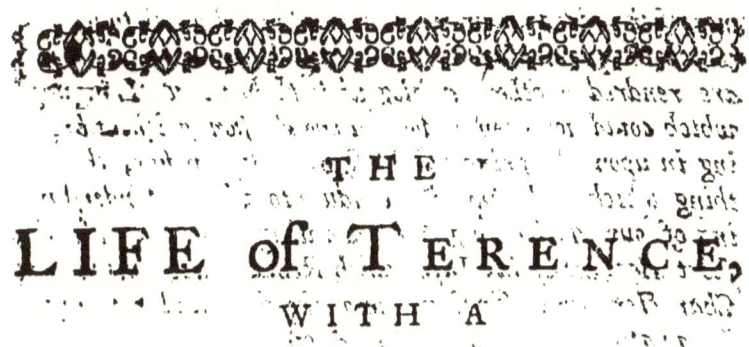

THE
LIFE of TERENCE,

WITH A

CHARACTER of his WRITINGS,

And some ACCOUNT of Antient

DRAMATICK POETRY.

THERE is nothing does a Nation or People greater Honour, than to excel in the Liberal Arts, and to produce Writers of Genius and Character, whose Works are not only the Admiration of the Age in which they live, but by their real Merit lay claim to Immortality. Whether we look into the History of former Ages, or examine what passes in the present, we shall find, that not Extent of Dominion, numerous Armies, or the Splendour of a Court, chiefly distinguish a Kingdom, or State ; but the Wisdom of their Chiefs, their Improvements in Arts and Sciences, and the Monuments of Wit and Genius they leave behind them. An Empire may indeed flourish for an Age, extend its Dominion far and wide, and spread the Knowledge of its Name to the most distant Nations. But we know from Experience, that their Duration is short, Time and Chance hurry them to a Period, and they must be at last indebted for all their Glory, and the Figure they make in the Eye of Posterity, to the Merit of their Poets, Orators, and Historians. *Persia*, an Empire once so potent and extensive, had scarce been known to the present Age, but for the Wars that broke out between it and *Greece*. Even *Cyrus*, a Name renowned in History, owes all his Reputation and Fame, to the incomparable Pen of *Xenophon*.

It is but just therefore, that we pay a kind of Veneration to the Memory of Men, who have rendered States illustrious, and to
whose

whose Labours we are in a great measure indebted, for our Superiority over the many barbarous Nations that surround us. It is a Misfortune indeed that Writers, who serve as Lights to guide us through past Ages, and have conferred Immortality on others, should for the most part be but little known themselves. Antiquity, by an inexcusable Neglect, has left the Lives and Fortunes of many of them in Obscurity. We scarce know their real Names, Place of Birth, or even the Times in which they lived. But few have been ambitious of the Glory, of handing down to Posterity an Account of Men, whose Lives were spent mostly in Retirement, and who, avoiding publick Transactions, and the Concerns of States, afforded but little Scope wherein to display the Talents of an Orator, or Historian. The present Age, however, seems disposed to make them some amends. We are fond of every Hint that can serve to retrieve the Memory of those, whose Writings are our daily Entertainment; and by searching into their own Works, as well as those of their Contemporaries, are often enabled to make up a tolerable Account of them.

This is what I shall now attempt, with regard to our Poet, who, though universally admired in his Writings, is but little known as to himself. For *Suetonius*, who is the only remaining Author of Antiquity, that wrote purposely the Life of *Terence*, is so very short and concise in his Relation, that no great Information can be gathered from him. His Account however, imperfect as it is, must be the Foundation of what is said in the following Pages; and it is with Regret I mention it to the Reader, that very little can be added to his Relation, save here and there a few Illustrations: so lame and defective are ancient Monuments, in what regards the Life of this Poet.

According to the most general Account, he was a Native of *Africa*, and born at *Carthage*. His Parents are utterly unknown, though, if we judge from the Merits of the Son, the Respect that seems to have been paid him even in Slavery, and the early Proofs he gave, under these disadvantageous Circumstances, of an aspiring Soul, it seems but reasonable to conclude, that they were of Distinction. We know that he flourished between the Times of the first and second *Punick* Wars; and as his Death is fixed to the five hundred and ninety-fourth Year of *Rome*, under the Consulship of *Cn. Cornelius Dolabella*, and *M. Fulvius*, nine Years before the breaking out of the third *Punick* War, when he was in his thirty-fifth Year, he must of course have been born in the five hundred and sixtieth Year of the City, eight Years after the Conclusion of the second.

How, being a Native of *Carthage*, he came to fall into the hands of *Terentius Lucanus* a *Roman* Senator; as at that time the *Romans* were at peace with the *Carthaginians*, and had but little Commerce with *Africa*, is not so easy to determine. We are
told

told indeed, by the Historians of those Times, that during the whole Interval between the second and third *Punick* Wars, the *Carthaginians* were engaged in almost continual Broils with the *African* Nations around them, and especially the *Numidians.* It is not unlikely therefore, that *Terence* may have been made a Captive, in some Rencounter between the Troops of that Republick, and those of *Masanissa* King of *Numidia.* The *Romans* sent Deputies three several times to terminate these Differences; and upon one of these Occasions might *Terence* become the Slave of a *Roman* Senator. If it may be allowed me to offer a Conjecture of my own, I think it not improbable, that our Poet might be a Present from *Masanissa* to one of the Deputies, perhaps, this very *Lucanus.* For as that Prince had been highly serviceable to the *Romans* in the second *Punick* War, and had reason to expect great things from their Friendship; it is not to be supposed, but he would be very assiduous in making his Court to the Ambassadors, and might make an offer of this young Captive to one of them, who, as being a Youth of promising Aspect, he probably fancied would be no unacceptable Present. This too accounts naturally for the particular Care *Lucanus* took of his Education, and his granting him his Freedom so early, before he could have rendred any Service to his Master, capable of meriting so high a Recompence. For that Senator, who had received him as an honourable Present from the King, knowing him, perhaps, to be of a good Family, and observing in him early Marks of a bright Genius, took a pleasure in cultivating these natural Talents, and soon restored him to his Liberty, agreeable to that Generosity and Nobleness of Soul, of which we meet with so many Instances among the ancient *Romans.*

But by whatever Accident he came to be a Slave at *Rome*, it is universally agreed, that he received his Liberty very early. Being therefore Master of himself, and his own Actions, and having naturally, a fine Genius, which had been improved by the best Education *Rome* at that time could afford; he applied himself to the Study of Dramatick Poetry, chiefly Comedy, and soon acquired a Reputation, superiour to that of all his Contemporaries. Learning indeed was as yet but in its Infancy among the *Romans*; they were rather a warlike than a polite People: and if we look back into their first Beginnings, the Frame and Constitution of their Government, and Situation in regard to the neighbouring States, it will soon appear, that the Exercise of Arms, not the Study of Arts and Sciences, must be their first Employment. But having by degrees subjected the Nations around them, extended their Conquests, not only over all *Italy*, but even into *Sicily* and *Spain*, and humbled *Carthage*, their most potent and formidable Rival; some time was given them to breathe, and having less to fear from abroad, they were more at liberty to cultivate the peaceful Arts at home.

At

At this time too began their Intercourse with *Greece*, and their Acquaintance with the Writings of that Nation, soon enabled them to make considerable Advances in all kinds of Learning. Dramatick Poetry was what most hit their Taste at first, and, as soon after the Conclusion of the second *Punick* War, it began to be in great request, *Terence* found here the greatest Encouragement for his Application.

But in order to form a right Judgment of our Author, and of the Merit of his Writings, compared with what remains of other Poets, who flourished before or after him, it will be necessary to look back into the Origin of Dramatick Poetry, its several Stages of Improvement in *Greece*, and the Condition *Terence* found it in at *Rome*, when he first applied to that Study. By this means we shall have a clear View of his Advantages and Disadvantages, see how far he contributed to the Reformation of Taste among the *Romans*, and by knowing what Alterations in regard to Learning and Genius happened at *Rome*, during the Interval between him and *Plautus*, be enabled to decide with more Justice, as to the Merit of their respective Compositions.

It is generally allowed, that Poetry had its Rise from the Festivals appointed in honour of the Gods. Hence, in the Beginning it consisted wholly of Songs and Hymns in praise of some particular Deity. In time, Men began to mingle the Praises of their Heroes and Benefactors with those of the Gods, and proceeded at last to the Licentiousness of filling their Poems with biting Satires, which they sung to one another at their drunken Meetings. The Poets that followed, who were indeed the Divines and Philosophers of those Times, finding in the People so strong a Desire after these Feasts and Shows, and the Impossibility of bringing them back to their first Simplicity, bethought themselves of another Method of remedying this Disorder. They resolved to take advantage of the People's Inclination, and give them Lessons of Instruction, disguised under the Mask of Pleasure. Thus, *Hesiod* sung the Genealogy of the Gods in Verse, and taught that all things are managed and conducted by their Interposition and Care. Even the Works that turned upon different Subjects, decided the Events they related, by the Ministration of Divinities. They taught Mankind to consider the Gods as the Authors of whatever happens in Nature. *Homer* and the other Poets every where represent them as the sole Arbiters of our Destinies. It is by them our Courage is either exalted or depressed; they give or deprive us of Prudence; dispense Success and Victory; and occasion Repulse and Defeat. Nothing great or heroick is executed, without the secret or visible Assistance of some Divinity. And of all the Truths they inculcate, they present none more frequently to our View, and establish none with more Care, than that Valour and Wisdom are of no avail without the Aid of Providence.

Among

Among the various Kinds of Poetry, the Epick and Dramatick chiefly claim our Notice, whether we confider the Noblenefs of the Defign, or the Excellency of the Moral and Inftruction. *Homer* was the firft that invented, or finifhed an Epick Poem ; for he found out the Unity of the Subject, the Manners, the Characters, and the Fable. But this Poem could only affect Cuftoms, and was not moving enough to correct the Paffions. There wanted a Poem, which by imitating our Actions might work in our Spirits a more ready and fenfible Effect. 'Twas this, which gave occafion for Tragedy, and banifhed all Satyrs. Thus, was Poetry entirely purged from all the Diforders its Corruption had brought into it.

Thefpis is confidered as the Inventor of Tragedy. It is eafy to judge how grofs and imperfect it was in its beginning. He fmeared the Faces of his Actors with Lees of Wine, and carried them from Village to Village in a Cart, from which they reprefented their Pieces. He lived in the time of *Solon*. That wife Legiflator being prefent one Day at one of thofe Reprefentations, cried out, ftriking the Ground with his Stick. *I am very much afraid, that thefe poetical Fictions, and ingenious Fancies, will foon have a fhare in our publick and private Affairs.* In fact, thefe Entertainments had fuch Applaufe, and took fo greatly among the People, that *Solon,* fearing they might tend to debauch their Minds, and divert them too much from their ufual Labours, thought fit to reftrain them by Law. But this was the Effect of a too hafty Judgment. Succeeding Magiftrates obferving, that thefe Diverfions were not only an agreeable Relaxation to the People, but, if under proper Regulations, might tend greatly to their Improvement, and the Reformation of Tafte and Manners, encouraged Dramatick Writers, and applied Part of the publick Money to the Decorations of the Theatre. This gave new Life and Vigour to the Poets; for finding their Art in fo great Efteem, they applied themfelves to cultivate and bring it to Perfection. *Æfchylus* was the firft that improved Tragedy, and brought it into Efteem. He gave his Actors Mafks, more decent Dreffes, the high-heel'd Boot, or Bufkin, called *Cothurnus,* and built them a little Theatre. His Manner of Writing is noble, and even fublime ; his Elocution lofty, and foaring often to Bombaft.

In a publick Difpute of the Tragick Poets, inftituted upon account of the Bones of *Thefeus,* which *Cimon* had brought to *Athens,* the Prize was adjudged to *Sophocles.* The Grief of *Æfchylus* was fo great, upon feeing himfelf deprived, by a young Poet, of the Glory he had fo long poffeffed, of being the moft excellent in the Theatre, that he could not bear to ftay in *Athens* any longer. He left it, and retir'd to *Sicily,* to the Court of King *Hiero,* where he died in a very fingular manner. As he lay afleep in the Country, with his bald Head uncovered, an Eagle taking it for a Stone,

let

let fall a heavy Tortoise upon it, which killed him. Of fourscore and ten Tragedies which he composed, some say, only twenty-eight, and others, no more than thirteen carried the Prize. *Sophocles* and *Euripides*, who succeeded him, appeared at the same time; and rendred the *Athenian* Stage very illustrious by Tragedies equally admirable, though very different in their Style. The first was great, lofty, and sublime: the other tender, pathetick; and abounding with excellent Maxims for the Manners and Conduct of human Life. The Judgment of the Publick was divided in respect to them; nor have the Criticks either of former, or our own Times, been able to decide to which the Preference is due. *Tragœdias primus in lucem protulit Æschylus (says Quintilian) sublimis, gravis, & grandiloquus, sæpe usque ad vitium. Longè clarius illustraverunt hoc opus Sophocles atque Euripides: quorum in dispari dicendi vi, uter sit poeta melior, inter plurimos quæritur.* Instit. Lib. x. cap. 1.

This short Account of the Rise and Advancement of Tragedy is exactly agreeable to what *Horace* says of it in his Art of Poetry, where, recommending to his Countrymen the Wits of *Greece*, as the Sources whence they might derive the best Rules for this kind of Composition, he briefly mentions the various Authors of that Nation, who had succeeded best in cultivating it.

> *Ignotum tragicæ genus invenisse camœnæ,*
> *Dicitur, & plaustris vexisse poemata Thespis,*
> *Quæ canerent agerentque, peruncti fæcibus ora.*
> *Post hunc personæ pallæque repertor honestæ,*
> *Æschylus, & modicis instravit pulpita tignis,*
> *Et docuit magnumque loqui, nitique cothurno.*
> *Successit vetus his comœdia, non sine multa:*
> *Laude: sed in vitiam libertas excidit, & vim;*
> *Dignam lege regi: lex est accepta, chorusque*
> *Turpiter obticuit, sublato jure nocendi.*

Thespis is said to have first invented a kind of Tragedy till then unknown to the *Greeks*, and to have carried about his Actors on Carts, who played and sung their Pieces, having their Faces stained with Lees of Wine. *Æschylus* afterwards added the Tragick Mask; found out a decent Dress, and built a Stage; taught them to speak with Dignity, and accompany all with just Action. The old comedy appeared next with great Applause; but licentious Liberty degenerating into Abuse and open Insolence, that required to be suppressed by Law; Laws were accordingly enacted, and the Chorus shamefully ceased, when it had lost its Power to hurt.

From what *Horace* here says we further learn, that Comedy did not begin to be cultivated in *Greece*, till after Tragedy had undergone all its Changes, and was come to its last Perfection. And

in

in this his Account exactly agrees with what *Ariſtotle* has ſaid upon the ſame Subject. Indeed, if we reflect upon the different Genius of theſe two Species of Writing, we ſhall ſoon be ſenſible that it muſt neceſſarily ſo happen. For Dramatick Poetry being, as we have already obſerved, an Imitation of Men and their Actions; the Characters of Heroes, as moſt ſtriking, moſt noble, and moſt worthy of Attention, would naturally offer themſelves firſt; and when the Poets had ſucceeded in ſome meaſure herein, others we may ſuppoſe would ariſe, who by introducing Characters of a lower Stamp, and a juſt Repreſentation of common Life, might flatter themſelves to pleaſe, and acquire ſome Reputation. But to enter a little more deeply into the Subject, let us go back to *Homer*, whom we may juſtly ſtyle the Father of the *Grecian* Poetry; for his Writings, if examined with care, will be found to contain the Seeds and firſt Sketches of all the ſeveral Kinds that appeared afterwards. We are told by *Ariſtotle*, that Poetry, after it had diſengaged itſelf from the Rudeneſs of the firſt Ages, and began to have ſome Shape and Form of its own, affected chiefly the ſublime and aſtoniſhing Part, and quitted the natural and eaſy way of Expreſſion, for that which is moſt unlike to Humanity or ordinary Uſe. This was ſoon carried to an unnatural Exceſs, inſomuch that the real Propriety and Likeneſs of Character was neglected, the Marvellous was introduced in Deſcription, and the Language and Expreſſion run into Bombaſt. Till *Homer*, a Genius too mighty to be borne away by the prevailing Current of bad Taſte, aroſe, and by turning his Thoughts to the Truth of Characters, the Beauty of Order, and the ſimple Imitation of Nature, introduced a manner of Writing unknown to all that went before him. His Poems juſtly deſerve the Name of Dramatick, his Characters, as is well obſerved by a great Writer, being wrought to a Likeneſs beyond what any ſucceeding Maſters were ever able to deſcribe. Nor are his Works, which are ſo full of Action, any other than an artful Series or Chain of Dialogues, which turn upon one remarkable Cataſtrophe or Event. He deſcribes no Qualities or Virtues, cenſures no Manners, makes no Encomium, nor gives Characters himſelf, but brings his Actors ſtill in View. 'Tis they who ſhew themſelves. 'Tis they who ſpeak in ſuch a manner, as diſtinguiſhes them in all things from all others, and makes them ever like themſelves. Their different Compoſitions and Allays ſo juſtly made, and equally carried on, through every Particle of the Action, give more Inſtruction than all the Comments and Gloſſes in the World. The Poet, inſtead of giving himſelf thoſe dictating and maſterly Airs of Wiſdom, makes hardly any Figure at all, and is ſcarce diſcoverable in his Poem. This is being truly a Maſter. He paints ſo as to need no Inſcription over his Figures, to tell us what they are, or what he intends by them. A few Words let fall on any ſlight Occaſion, from any of the Parties he introduces, are ſufficient to denote their Manners and diſtinct

Character. From a Finger or a Toe he can reprefent to our Thoughts the Frame and Fafhion of a whole Body. He wants no other Help of Art, to perfonate his Heroes, and make them living. There was no more left for Tragedy to do after him, than to erect a Stage, and draw his Dialogues and Characters into Scenes; turning in the fame manner upon one fingle Action, or Event, with that regard to Place and Time, which was fuitable to a real Spectacle. Even Comedy itfelf was adjudged to this great Mafter, it being derived from thofe Parodies, or Mock-Humours, of which he had given the Specimen in a concealed fort of Raillery intermixed with the Sublime.

Thus we are indebted to *Homer*, not only for Epic, but alfo Dramatic Poetry: For all that was done by fucceeding Poets, was only to copy his Manner, and improve upon the Sketches he had given. Tragedy, as the Author above quoted obferves, came firft, and took what was moft folemn and fublime. In this Part the Poets fucceeded fooner than in Comedy, or the facetious Kind; as was natural indeed to fuppofe, fince this was in reality the eafieft Manner of the two, and capable of being brought the fooneft to Perfection, as *Ariftotle*, the grand Critick of Antiquity, fufficiently informs us. And 'tis highly worth remarking, what this mighty Genius, and Judge of Arts, declares concerning Tragedy, that whatever Idea might be formed of the utmoft Perfection of this kind of Poem, it could in Practice rife no higher, than it had been already carried in his Time; having at length (fays he) attained its Ends, and being apparently confummate in itfelf. The Event proved, how true a Prophet, as well as Critick, this great Man was. For it appeared, that Tragedy being raifed to its Height by *Sophocles* and *Euripides*, and no room left for further Excellency or Emulation, there was no more Tragick Poets befides thefe endured after the Author's Time. Tragedy, I fay, finifhed its Courfe under *Euripides:* whom, tho' our great Author criticizes with the utmoft feverity in his Poeticks; yet he plainly enough confeffes that he carried the Style of Tragedy to its full Height and Dignity. For as to the Reformation which that Poet made, in the ufe of the fublime and figurative Speech in general; fee what our difcerning Author fays in his Rhetoricks: where he ftrives to fhew the Impertinence and Naufeoufnefs of the florid Speakers, and fuch as underftood not the Ufe of the fimple and natural Manner. " The " juft Mafters, and right Managers of the Poetick, or high Style, " fhould learn (fays he) how to conceal the Manner as much as " poffible." But for Comedy, it feems 'twas ftill in hand, and went on improving to the fecond and third degree. It had indeed been already in fome manner reduced; but, as he plainly infinuates, it lay yet unfinifhed; notwithftanding the witty Labours of an *Ariftophanes*, and the other Comick Poets of the firft Manner, who had flourifhed a whole Age before this Critick. As perfect as were thofe Wits in Style and Language; and as fertile in

all

all the Varieties and Turns of Humour; yet the natural and simple, the real Beauty of Composition, the Unity of Design, the Truth of Characters, and the just Imitation of Nature in each particular, were in a manner wholly unknown to them; or, through Petulance or Debauch of Humour, were it seems neglected, and set aside. A *Menander* had not as yet appeared, who arose soon after, to accomplish the Prophecy of our grand Master of Art, and consummate Philologist.

It will be proper to observe here, that the old *Greek* Comedy was of two Kinds. In that properly called the old Comedy, there was nothing feigned in the Subject: the Poets attack'd Vice publickly, without sparing the chief Citizens, or even the Magistrates. In this *Eupolis, Cratinus,* and *Aristophanes* acquired great Reputation. The highest Perfection of what is called *Atticism* was peculiar to it; that is to say, whatever is finest, most elegant and most delicate in Style, to which no other Poetry could come near. It served the *Greeks* instead of Satire. But after the taking of *Athens* by *Lysander*, and the Change of the Government from a *Democracy* to an *Aristocracy*; this Liberty became disagreeable, and Poets were forbid to name the Persons whom they attacked in their Pieces. They therefore feigned Names, but painted the Characters so well, that it was impossible to mistake them: And this was what they called the middle Comedy, which continued till the Time of *Alexander* the Great, who, having totally subjected *Greece*, further restrained the Licentious Humours of the Poets, which was beginning to break out afresh, and gave general Offence. To this last we owe the new Comedy, which was no more than an Imitation of common Life, and where both the Subject and Names were feigned. In this *Menander* shone without a Rival, he not only invented, but excelled all others in it. *Plutarch* prefers him infinitely to *Aristophanes*. He admires an agreeable, refin'd, delicate, lively Spirit of Humour, a Vein of Pleasantry in him, that never departs in the least from the strictest Rules of Probity and good Manners; whereas the bitter and merciless Raillery of *Aristophanes* is excessive Abuse, is Murder in jest, that without the least Reserve tears the Reputation of the most worthy to pieces, and violates all the Laws of Modesty and Decency, with an Impudence that knows no Bounds. *Quintilian* is not afraid to declare, that the Brightness of *Menander*'s Merit had eclipsed and obliterated the Reputation of all the Writers in the same way. *Atque ille quidem omnibus ejusdem operis auctoribus abstulit nomen, & fulgore quodam suæ claritatis tenebras obduxit.* As only a few Fragments of his Writings remain, we are obliged to *Terence* for the Knowledge we have of that renowned Author; for four of our Poet's Plays are expresly copied from the *Greek* Originals of this great Reformer of the *Athenian* Stage. And, it is perhaps, the greatest Praise that can be given him, that *Terence* is allowed by good Judges

to

to have fallen fhort of his Original. *Aulus Gellius* has preferved
fome Paffages of *Menander*, which had been imitated by *Cæcilius*,
an ancient *Latin* Comic Poet of the firft Rank. At the firft reading,
he thought the Verfes of the latter very fine. But he affirms, that
as foon as he compared them with thofe of the *Greek* Poet, their
Beauties entirely difappeared, and they feemed wretched and contemptible. *Menander* was not treated with all the Juftice he deferved during his Life. Of more than an hundred Comedies, which
he brought upon the Stage, only eight carried the Prize. Whether through Intrigue, or Combination againft him, or the bad Tafte
of the Judges, *Philemon*, who undoubtedly deferved only the fecond
Place, was always preferr'd before him.

But to return to the before-cited Author. 'Twas not by Chance
that this Succeffion happened in *Greece*, after the Manner defcribed,
but rather through Neceffity, and from the Reafon and Nature of
Things. For in healthy Bodies, Nature dictates Remedies of her
own, and provides for the Cure of what has happened amifs in
the Growth and Progrefs of a Conftitution. The Affairs of this
free People being in the Increafe, and their Ability and Judgment
every day improving, as Letters and Arts advanced; they would of
courfe find in themfelves a Strength of Nature, which by the Help
of good Ferments, and a wholefome Oppofition of Humours, would
correct in one way, whatever was exceffive, or *peccant* (as Phy-
ficians fay) in another. Thus the florid and over-fanguine Humour of the high Style, was allayed by fomething of a contrary
Nature. The comick Genius was applied, as a kind of Cauftick,
to thofe Exuberances and Fungus's of the fwollen Dialect, and magnificent Manner of Speech. But after a while, when this Remedy
itfelf was found to turn to a Difeafe, as Medicines, we know, grow
corrofive, when the fouler Matters on which they wrought are fufficiently purged, and the Obftructions removed;

> *In vitium libertas excidit, & vim*
> *Dignam lege regi.*——

'Tis a great Error to fuppofe, as fome have done, that the re-
ftraining this licentious Manner of Wit, by Law, was a Violation
of the Liberty of the *Athenian* State, or an Effect meerly of the
Power of Foreigners; whom it little concerned after what manner thefe Citizens treated one another in their Comedies; or what
fort of Wit and Humour they made choice of for their ordinary
Diverfions. If upon a Change of Government, as during the
Ufurpation of the thirty, or when that Nation was humbled at any
time, either by a *Philip*, or an *Alexander*, or an *Antipater*, they
had been forced, againft their Wills, to enact fuch Laws as thefe;
'tis certain they would have foon repealed them, when thofe Terrors
were removed (as they foon were) and the People reftored to their

former

former Liberty. For notwithſtanding what this Nation ſuffered out-
wardly, by ſeveral Shocks received from foreign States; notwith-
ſtanding the Dominion and Power they loſt abroad, they preſerved
the ſame Government at home. And how paſſionately intereſted
they were, in what concerned their Diverſions and publick Spectacles;
how jealous and full of Emulation in what related to their Poëtry,
Wit, Muſick, and other Arts, in which they excell'd all other Nations; is well known to Perſons who have any Comprehenſion of antient Manners, or been the leaſt converſant in Hiſtory.

Nothing therefore could have been the Cauſe of theſe publick
Decrees, and of this gradual Reform in the Commonwealth of
Wit, beſide the real Reform of Taſte and Humour, in the Com-
monwealth or Government itſelf. Inſtead of any Abridgment,
'twas in reality an Increaſe of Liberty, an Enlargement of the
Security of Property, and an Advancement of private Eaſe and per-
ſonal Safety, to provide againſt what was injurious to the good
Name and Reputation of every Citizen. As this Intelligence in
Life and Manners grew greater in that experienced People, ſo the
Reliſh of Wit and Humour would naturally in proportion be more
refined. Thus *Greece* in general grew more and more polite ; and,
as it advanced in this reſpect, was more averſe to the obſcene buf-
fooning Manner. The *Athenians* ſtill went before the reſt, and led
the way in Elegance of every kind. For even their firſt Comedy
was a Refinement upon ſome irregular Attempts which had been
made in that Dramatick Way. And the grand Critick ſhews us,
that in his own Time the *Phallica*, or ſcurrilous and obſcene Farce,
prevail'd ſtill, and had the Countenance of the Magiſtrate in ſome
Cities of *Greece*, who were behind the reſt in this Reform of Taſte
and Manners.

But what is yet a more undeniable Evidence of this natural and
gradual Refinement of Styles and Manners among the Ancients,
particularly in what concerned their Stage, is, that this very Caſe
of Prohibition and Reſtraint happened among the *Romans* themſelves;
where no Effects of foreign Power, or of domeſtick Tyranny can be
pretended. Their *Feſcennin* and *Atellan* Way of Wit, was in early
Days prohibited, and Laws made againſt it for the Publick's ſake,
and in regard to the Welfare of the Community; ſuch Licentiouſ-
neſs having been found in reality contrary to the juſt Liberty of the
People: for ſo *Horace* expreſsly inform us ;

———— *Donec jam ſævus apertam*
In rabiem verti cœpit, jocus & per honeſtas
Ire domus impune minax : doluere cruento
Dente laceſſiti : fuit intactis quoque cura ,
Conditione ſuper communi : quin etiam lex
Pœnaque lata, malo quæ nollet carmine quenquam

Deſcribi :

Describi : vertere modum formidine fustis
Ad bene dicendum delectandumque reducti.

Until at length those bitter *Jests* degenerating into open *Abuse*, attack'd with Impunity the worthiest *Families*. They who felt the bloody Bite, complain'd loudly ; and even they who escaped, could not avoid some Concern for the common *Cause*. In fine, Laws were enacted, and Penalties decreed against such as wounded the Reputation of another by defamatory *Verses*. Fear of Punishment made them change their Tone, they aimed in their Compositions to please and instruct.

In Defence of what I have here advanced, I could, besides the Authority of grave Historians and Chronologists, produce the Testimony of one of the wisest, and most serious of ancient Authors ; whose single Authority would be acknowledged to have equal Force with that of many concurring Writers. He shews us, that this first formed Comedy, and Scheme of ludicrous Wit, was introduced upon the Neck of the Sublime. The familiar airy Muse was privileged as a sort of Counter Pedagogue, against the Pomp and Formality of the most solemn Writers. And, what is highly remarkable, our Author shews us, that in Philosophy itself there happened, almost at the very same time, a like Succession of Wit and Humour; when in opposition to the sublime Philosopher, and afterwards to his grave Disciple and Successor in the Academy, there arose a comic Philosophy, in the Person of another Master, and other Disciples ; who personally, as well as in their Writings, were set in direct Opposition to the former : not as differing in Opinions or Maxims, but in their Style and Manner, in the Turn of Humour, and Method of Instruction.

These are some of the Reflections of the celebrated Author of the Characteristicks, upon the various changes that happened in the Dramatick Poetry of the antient *Greeks*. But it is now time to turn our Eyes towards *Rome*, and take a View of what passed there. As Nature is every where the same, Poetry had much the same Original in *Italy*, as before in *Greece*. She was there too the Daughter of Religion, as we learn from *Horace*, in his Epistle to *Augustus*, and sprang from those Assemblies, which the first Men, being all Shepherds and Labourers, after the Ingathering of the Fruits of the Earth, made in honour of the Gods, to thank them for their Bounty, and make them an Offering of the first Fruits. To these Country Sports was owing the first Rise of the *Fescennine* Rhymes or Verses, so called from *Fescennia* a Town in *Tuscany*, where they were first practised, and from thence brought to *Rome*. They are also often mentioned by antient Writers under the Name of *Saturnian*, because they supposed such to have been in use under *Saturn*. These served the *Romans* instead of theatrical Pieces, near an hundred and twenty Years. The Verses themselves were rude, and almost void of Numbers, as they were extemporaneous, and made by a rustick

illiterate

illiterate People, who knew no other Mafters but Mirth and Wine. They confifted of grofs Raillery, attended with Poftures and Dances, *Hor.* Ep. I. Lib. II.

Fefcennina per hunc inventa licentia morem,
Verfibus alternis opprobria ruftica fudit.

But thefe loofe and irregular Verfes were foon fucceeded by a chafter kind of Poetry, which, though it alfo abounded with pleafant Ridicule, had nothing vicioufly indecent in it. This Poem appeared under the Name of Satyr *(Satura)* from its Variety, and had regular Meafures, that is to fay, regular Mufick and Dances: but obfcene Poftures were banifhed from it. Thefe Satyrs were innocent Farces, in which the Spectators and Actors were indifferently made the Objects of Mirth.

Livius Andronicus found things in this State, when he conceived the Defign of making Comedies and Tragedies in imitation of the *Greeks.* He prefented his firft Tragedy a Year before the Birth of *Ennius,* the firft Year after the firft *Punick* War, and the five hundred and fourteenth of *Rome,* in the Confulfhip of *C. Claudius Cento,* and *M. Sempronius Tuditanus,* about an hundred and fixty Years after the Death of *Sophocles* and *Euripides,* fifty after that of *Menander,* and two hundred and twenty before that of *Virgil.* *Nævius,* encouraged by the Example of *Andronicus,* applied himfelf likewife to the Study of the *Greek* Poets, and about five Years after entertained the Publick with Comedies, as the other had done with Tragedies. Soon after thefe, *Ennius* appeared, and improved the *Roman* Poetry ftill farther. He compofed the Annals of *Rome* in Heroick Verfe, and was at the twelfth Book of that Work, in his fixty-feventh Year. He alfo celebrated the Victories of the firft *Scipio Africanus,* with whom he had contracted a particular Friendfhip, and who always treated him with the higheft Marks of Efteem and Confiderâtion. It is eafy, however, to conceive, that the *Latin* Poetry, in its Infancy, and weak at the time we are fpeaking of, could not have much Beauty and Ornament. It fometimes fhewed Force and Genius, but without Elegance and Grace, and with great Inequality. This *Quintilian,* where he draws *Ennius's* Character, expreffes by an admirable Comparifon: *Ennium ficut facros vetuftate lucos adoremus, in quibus grandia & antiqua robora jam non tantam habent fpeciem, quantam religionem.* "Let us "reverence *Ennius,* fays he, as we do thofe Groves, which Time "has confecrated and made venerable, and of which the great and "ancient Oaks do not ftrike us fo much with their Beauty, as with "a kind of religious Veneration."

I pafs over the Names of feveral Poets who flourifhed about this time, fuch as *Attius, Pacuvius,* and *Cæcilius:* becaufe, though they contributed greatly to the Improvement of the *Roman* Stage, efpecially

cially

cially the laft, yet as none of their Works have had the good Fortune to reach our Times, we can determine lefs with regard to their Merit and Character. It is otherwife with *Plautus,* nineteen of whofe Comedies have efcaped the Injuries of Time, and come down almoft entire to us. It is very probable, that his Works preferved themfelves better than others, becaufe they were more agreeable to the Publick, the Demand for them was greater and more permanent. They were not only acted in the time of *Auguftus*; but, from a Paffage in *Arnobius,* it appears, that they continued to be played in the Reign of *Diocletian,* three hundred Years after the Birth of *Chrift.*

Various Judgments have been paffed on this Poet. His Elocution feems to be generally approved, without doubt in regard to the Purity, Propriety, Energy, Abundance, and even Elegance of his Style. *Varro* fays, that if the Mufes were to fpeak *Latin,* they would borrow the Language of *Plautus. Quintil.* Lib. X. cap. 1. *Licet Varro dicat mufas Plautino fermone locuturas fuiffe, fi Latine loqui vellent.* Such a Praife makes no Exceptions, and leaves us nothing to defire. *Aulus Gellius* fpeaks of him no lefs to his advantage, Lib. VII. cap. 17. *Plautus, homo linguæ atque elegantiæ in verbis Latinæ princeps.* *Horace,* whofe Judgment in this Point ought to have great Weight, does not feem fo favourable to *Plautus.* The Paffage where he cenfures him moft is in his Art of Poetry, *ver.* 270,

At noftri proavi, Plautinos & numeros &
Laudavere fales; nimium patienter utrumque.
Ne dicam ftulte, mirati, fi modo ego & vos
Scimus inurbanum lepide feponere dicto,
Legitimumque fonum digito callemus & arte.

" But our Forefathers were taken with the Jokes and Numbers " of *Plautus,* and admired them with too much Indulgence, not " to call it Stupidity; if it be true that either you or I can diftin-" guifh a genteel from a clownifh Expreffion, and have Ears fine " enough to judge of the Harmony and Beauty of Verfification." This Criticifm feems the more againft *Plautus,* as it argues, that *Horace* was not alone in this Opinion, and that the Court of *Auguftus* had no greater Tafte than he, either for the Verfification or Pleafantries of this Poet.

Horace's Cenfure falls upon two Articles; the Number and Harmony of his Verfes, *Numeros,* and his Raillery, *Sales.* His Judgment ought fure to have great Weight with us, as he was himfelf an excellent Poet, and a candid Critick. But it is not impoffible that, offended by the unjuft Preference given by his Age to the ancient *Latin* Poets againft thofe of their own Times, he may have been a little too exceffive in his Criticifms upon fome Occafions, and on this in particular. But *Horace* does not confine his

Cenfure

Cenſure to the Numbers and Raillery, he ſeems to think alſo that *Plautus* was not very happy in his Characters, Ep. II. Lib. 1. 170.

——— *Aſpice, Plautus,*
Quo pacto pártes tutetur amantis ephebi,
Ut patris attenti, lenonis ut inſiaioſi.

" Reflect only upon *Plautus,* how ill he has ſucceeded in the Cha-
" racters of a young paſſionate Lover, a covetous Father, or a cunning
" Pimp." I know that ſome Commentators ſeem to doubt, whether
this is to be underſtood as a Cenſure, or a Commendation. The beſt
way will be, to examine ſome of his Characters and Plays, and ſee
which ſide theſe incline us too. 'Tis certain that *Plautus,* who ſucceeded ſo well in the intriguing part, and always pleaſed and ſurprized
by his Vivacity, was often unhappy in his Characters. One or two
Inſtances will ſet this Matter in a juſt Light. In the Play called
Pſeudolus, which *Cato* in *Cicero* mentions as a finiſhed Piece, that
perfectly pleaſed the Author, we find the three Characters which
Horace names here, very ill maintained by the Poet. *Calliodorus*
is a young Lover, but his Character is ſo cold and lifeleſs, that he
ſcarcely deſerves the Name. His Father *Simo* does as little to ſupport the Character of *Patris attenti* : for he encourages his Slave
to deceive him, promiſes even a Recompence, and engages to pay
him a round Sum, if he can over-reach the Merchant of the
Slaves, and put into the hands of his Son, the Girl he is enamour'd
with. More Examples of this kind might be given ; look into his
Rudens, and you will find the ſame Remarks may be made. As
to his Verſes, 'tis certain, he was far from being exact, and it
is for that Reaſon he calls them *Numeros inmumeros,* Numbers without Number, in the Epitaph he made for himſelf. He did not
confine himſelf to obſerving the ſame Meaſure, and has jumbled
ſo many different Kinds of Verſe together, that the moſt learned
find it difficult to diſtinguiſh them. It is no leſs certain, that he
has flat, low, and often extravagant Pleaſantries, but at the ſame
time he has ſuch as are fine and delicate. *Cicero* for this Reaſon, who was no bad Judge of what the Ancients called *Urbanity,*
propoſes him as a Model for Raillery. Theſe Faults of *Plautus*
therefore, do not hinder his being an excellent Poet. They are
very happily aton'd for by many fine Qualities, inſomuch that in
the Judgment of ſome Criticks, he diſputes the Prize even with
Terence himſelf. We often meet with fine Maxims in his Plays,
for the Conduct of Life, and Regulation of Manners ; of which we
have a remarkable Example in his *Amphytrion,* in a Speech of *Alc-
mena* to her Huſband, which in a few Lines includes all the Duties
of a wiſe and virtuous Wife.

Non ego illam mihi dotem duco eſſe, quæ dos dicitur :

Sed

Sed pudicitiam, & pudorem, & fedatum cupidinem,
Deûm metum, parentum amorem, & cognatûm concordiam;
Tibi morigera, atque ut munifica fim bonis, profim prolis.

" I do not efteem that a Dowry, which is commonly called fo;
" but Honour, Modefty, Defires fubjected to Reafon, the Fear of
" the Gods, the Love of our Parents, Unity with our Relations,
" Obedience to you, Munificence to the deferving, and to be ufe-
" ful to the Juft." It is not to be diffembled however, that there
are many Paffages in him, contrary to Decency and Purity of
Manners. What *Quintilian* fays of certain dangerous Poems, may
be well applied on this Occafion ; that Youth fhould, if poffible,
be kept entirely ignorant of them, or at leaft, that they fhould
be referved for riper Years, and a Time of Life lefs liable to Corruption. *Amoveantur, fi fieri poteft ; fi minus, certe ad firmius æta-*
tis robur referventur. —— *Cum mores in tuto fuerint, inter præcipua*
legenda erit comœdia.

We have thus taken a fhort View of the *Roman* Dramatick
Poetry, feen it rude and without Shape or Ornament in its Beginning, but polifhing and refining by Degrees, until it had arrived
at a confiderable degree of Perfection under *Plautus.* This advantageous Change was chiefly owing to the Commerce and Acquaintance that began with *Greece,* about the time of the fecond *Punick*
War. For the Poets had then the moft perfect Models in every
kind of Writing, to copy after, and by their Affiduity, and the
Encouragement their firft Attempts met with, arrived, in a very
fhort time, at Chaftity and Correctnefs in their Compofitions ; for
fo *Horace* the great Critick of the *Auguftan* Age informs us, Lib. II,
Ep. 1. 156.

Græcia capta, ferum victorem cepit, & artes
Intulit agrefti Latio. Sic horridus ille
Defluxit numerus Saturnius, & grave virus
Munditiæ pepulere : fed in longum tamen ævum
Manferunt, hodieque manent, veftigia ruris.
Serus enim Græcis admovit acumina chartis,
Et poft Punica bella quietus quærere cepit,
Quid Sophocles, & Thefpis, & Æfchylus utile ferrent :
Tentavit quoque rem fi digne vertere poffet ;
Et placuit fibi, natura fublimis & acer,
Nam fpirat tragicum fatis, & feliciter audet :
Sed turpem putat in fcriptis, metuitque lituram.

" *Greece,* fubdued by the Valour of the *Romans,* triumphed over
" the ftern Conqueror, and introduced a Tafte of the politer Arts
" among the ruftick *Latins.* Thus the harfh Numbers of the *Sa-*
" *turnian* Verfes were foon banifhed, Chaftity and Correctnefs drove
                                                                    " away

" away the deadly Venom: yet the Change was not fo entire,
" but that the Marks of this Rufticity remain'd for a long time
" after, and may ftill in fome Meafure be obferved, even at this
" Day. For it was not till late, that the *Romans* applied to ftudy
" the Writings of the *Greeks:* and, enjoying a little Calm, after
" the firft *Punick* War, were curious to fee what Profit might be
" had from reading of *Sophocles, Thefpis,* and *Æfchylus.* They ef-
" fayed moreover to tranflate fome of their Pieces with Dignity,
" and had no reafon to be difpleafed with the Attempt; for the
" *Romans* are naturally of a lofty and daring Genius, they breathe
" much the Spirit of Tragedy, and are often happy in their Flights;
" but they think Blots fcandalous, and are afhamed to dafh out."
Among all the kinds of *Greek* Poetry, that calculated for the Theatre found the beft Reception at firft, as being a-kin to the Diverfions they had before, and only an Improvement upon them.
As the *Romans* were paffionately fond of thefe Entertainments, the
Magiftrates and great Men could not more effectually make their
Court to the People, than by frequently exhibiting publick Games,
of which Dramatick Shews always made a Part. And therefore
we are not to wonder if Poets applied chiefly to what feemed
to be moft wanted, and was likely to pleafe beft. It was for the
fame Reafon that Comedy was moft cultivated, and made greateft
Advances in thefe early times. For the old Comedy of the *Greeks*
bore a very near Refemblance to the fatirical Sports of the antient
Romans, and therefore would naturally fooneft hit the Tafte of that as
yet rude and unpolifhed People. The Poets at firft contented themfelves with tranflating from the *Greek* Originals, and, as the Scene
was of confequence laid in *Greece,* the Actors wore the *Pallium,*
or Habit of that Nation, whence this kind of Comedy obtained
the Name of *Palliata.* But in a little time their firft Performances
being well received, they ventured to compofe Pieces themfelves,
and laid the Scene in *Rome;* for fo *Horace* fpeaking of the Rife
and Advancement of Dramatick Poetry among the *Romans,* exprefsly tells us, *Art. Poet.* 285.

Nil intentatum noftri liquere poetæ,
Nec minimum meruere decus, veftigia Græca
Aufi deferere, & celebrare domeftica facta,
Vel qui prætextas, vel qui docuere togatas.

" Our Poets made Attempts in every way; nor do they leaft
" deferve Praife, when, difdaining to be beholden to the *Greeks,*
" they have fought a Subject for their Verfe at home, either by
" reprefenting the Manners of the more illuftrious Citizens, or
" a juft Imitation of common Life."

In

In order to form a true Judgment of the *Roman* Comedy, it will
be neceſſary to enter minutely into the Explication of this Paſſage, which is one of the moſt difficult perhaps in *Horace*, occaſioned chiefly by the little light *Latin* Authors give us, in what relates to their Theatrical Pieces. The chief thing is to know whether *Horace* comprehends, in this Account, both Tragedy and Comedy, meaning by *Prætextas* Tragedy, and by *Togatas* Comedy;
or if he only ſpeaks of Comedy, and marks its two principal
Kinds. The firſt ſeems to be the eaſieſt Account, and to ſolve
all Difficulties. But we muſt be determined by the Truth of the
Caſe. The following Paſſage of *Feſtus* will, I hope, ſerve to ſet
this Matter in a clear Light: *Togatarum duplex eſt genus: prætex-
tarum hominum faſtigii ; quæ ſic appellantur, quod togis prætextis rem-
publicam adminiſtrarunt ; tabernariarum quia hominibus excellentibus
etiam humiles permixti.* From this we underſtand, that *Togatæ* was
general, and expreſſed the different Kinds of the *Roman* Comedy,
and that the *Prætextæ* were a particular Kind comprehended under this general Name. They were therefore belonging to the
Togatæ, and conſequently Comedies, for *Tragedies* were never called
Togatæ. Comedies, where the Subject was grave, and the Actors
repreſented the chief Perſons of the State and Magiſtrates, were
called *Prætextæ*, becauſe they were ſuppoſed to be concerned in
the Action, and wore the *Prætexta,* a Robe bordered with Purple.
But Plays, intended only as a Repreſentation of low Life, were
called *Togatæ.* We have none now remaining of either of theſe
Kinds. As their ſubject and Conſtitution were entirely different,
ſo each required a different Genius, and there were Poets particularly famous in each Kind. For Example, *Afranius, Titinius*, and
Quinctius Atta, excelled in pure Comedy, *Comœdia Togata : Pacuvius* and *Accius* in the more ſerious Pieces, *Comœdia Prætexta.*
If it ſhould be objected here, that the two laſt were called Tragick Poets, and the *Prætexta* muſt of conſequence have been Tragedies ; I anſwer, that beſides the Pieces called *Prætexta*, theſe
Poets were Authors of ſeveral Tragedies. *Pacuvius* wrote *An-
chiſes, Antiope, Atalante, Hermione*, &c. *Accius, Achilles, Egiſthus,
Hecuba, Meleager.* It was for this they were called Tragick Poets.
The *Prætextæ* of *Pacuvius*, were his *Paulas* and *Tunicularia* ; thoſe
of *Accius, Brutus,* and *Decius.* By the Names of theſe Pieces, it
is plain that they were of the ſerious Kind, and approached nearly to the Character of Tragedy, tho' they were in fact real Comedies, and of the Kind we have been ſpeaking of.

This was the State of Dramatick Poetry, when *Terence*, that great
Menander of the *Roman* Stage aroſe, and by the Juſtneſs and Superiority
of his Genius, gave it that Elegance of Style, that real Reſemblance of
Nature, that Delicacy of Sentiment, and Politeneſs of Dialogue, which
hitherto it had aimed at, but not attained. For this was the great
and diſtinguiſhing Talent of our Poet, an inimitable Art of expreſ-
ſing

sing the Manners, and copying Nature, with so genuine and unstudied Simplicity, that every body believes himself capable of writing in the same manner; and at the same time such Elegance and Ingenuity, as no body has ever been able to come up to. It is from this Talent, that is to say, this wonderful Art, diffused thoughout the Comedies of *Terence*, which charms and transports without Notice, or any Glitter of Ornament, that *Horace* characterizes this Poet;

Vincere Cæcilius gravitate, Terentius arte.

For with an extreme Purity of Speech, and a simple and natural Style, he unites all the Graces and Delicacy, of which his Language was susceptible, and of all the *Latin* Authors has come the nearest to *Atticism*; that is to say, whatever is finest, most exquisite, and most perfect among the *Greeks*, insomuch that *Quintilian* gives his Writings the Praise of being highly elegant.

But to enter a little more deeply into our Author's Character, and compare it with that of *Plautus* his Predecessor; it is owned that this latter excels in the Vivacity of the Action, and Conduct of the Intrigue; for so *Horace* expresly describes him,

Plautus ad exemplar Siculi properare Epicharmi.

I know there are some Criticks, that interpret this Verse ironically, as if *Horace* meant to accuse *Plautus* of jumbling and precipitating his Fable; but this were to father a very unjust Censure upon that accurate and candid Critick, seeing the Fault implied in it, is very far from being chargeable upon *Plautus*. *Horace* in the Passage here quoted is speaking of the general Opinion that prevailed at *Rome* in his time with regard to the Dramatick Poets, and observes, that though sometimes the People judged amiss, yet often their Criticisms were very just, and that now referred to is an Instance. It was the Character of *Plautus*, that he never lost Sight of his Subject, but without suffering the Spectator to weary, marched with bold Steps to the unravelling. For that is the proper Meaning of *properare*, a Word that admirably expresses the particular Genius of *Plautus*, whose Pieces are full of Action. *Horace* speaking of *Homer* says, *semper ad eventum festinat.* He hastes always to the Event of Things. It might with the same Reason be said, that he there censures *Homer*, as that here he censures *Plautus*, in saying *properat*; for it is just the same. *Epicharmus* was of *Sicily*, and a Disciple of *Pythagoras*; he lived about the time of *Xerxes*, and *Servius Tullius*. He wrote a great Number of Comedies, and several Treatises of Physicks in Verse. We may judge of his Merit, by the Esteem *Plato* expressed for him, who studied his Writings with great Care. He was banished for speaking disrespectfully of the Will of *Hiero*.
We

We have here then the distinguishing Character of *Plautus*, and that wherein I think he is generally allowed to have the Advantage of *Terence*. 'Tis certain this latter has not that Vivacity of Action, and Variety of Incidents, which enflame our Curiosity, and throw the Mind into Impatience to know in what manner the Play will conclude: but, as Madam *Dacier* well observes, the Pleasures he gives his Readers are both more frequent, and more sensible; if he makes us not to wait with impatience for the end of the Adventure, he conducts it in a manner that scarce leaves any thing to be desired: For in every Scene, or rather in every Verse, we meet with things that enchant us, and from which we are loth to part. One may compare *Plautus* to those Romances, that through rugged and thorny Paths, lead us into enchanted Groves, where every thing around us ravishes the Senses. But these enchanted Spots, all equally beautiful, occur at every Step in *Terence*, where a single Scene will agreeably amuse us for a whole day; and I doubt whether any Poet besides *Terence* has found out this valuable Secret.

It is for this Reason that the Antients all agree in giving our Poet that Commendation already quoted from *Horace*;

Vincere Cæcilius gravitate, Terentius arte.

For never had any Writer more Art, although it be concealed with so much Care, that you imagine it Nature herself, without Covering or Disguise. A remarkable Effect of this Art is the great Success of our Poet in painting Life and Manners. He has wrought his Characters to so true a Likeness, that his Scenes seem to be a real Description of the Occurrences of common Life, instead of barely an Imitation of it. And hence *Varro*, speaking of our Poet, says, *In argumentis Cæcilius palmam poscit, in ethesin Terentius.* "In "the Disposition of the Fable *Cæcilius* merits the Prize; *Terence* "in what regards Manners." In reality *Cæcilius* excelled all other Poets, by the Disposition of his Subjects, his Gravity, the Weight of his Sentiments, and the Turn of his Expressions, which were pathetick, and full of Fire. But as to Truth and Justness of Character, and hitting off the real Resemblance of Nature, no one ever equalled *Terence*. To succeed in this part of Poetry, requires a perfect Knowledge of human Nature, of the Passions, their different Degrees of Strength and Influence; in a word, of all the Windings and Turnings of the Heart of Man.

Aristotle observes, that there are different ways of painting Life and Manners. For we may represent Men either worse, or better than the Standard of Nature, or according to the real Truth of Character. It is this last that we expect to meet with in Comedy, and that indeed requires the most masterly Genius: In the other Cases, the Imagination is less confined; it can form an Idea

to

to itfelf, and vary it at pleafure : but here we muft curb a lively
Fancy, and as the Original from what we draw, is full in every
one's View, every Error and falfe Stroke is more liable to be obferved. In this part *Terence* reigns without a Rival ; he always
paints Men as they are, and thus ftands engaged to render a Reafon
for the Figures and Defcriptions he gives, not only to his own, but
to every fucceeding Age.

Another great Advantage of *Terence* over *Plautus* is, that all his
Beauties not only entertain and pleafe the Imagination, but alfo content the Mind ; which two things are in themfelves very different.
Precepts and Sentences of moral Inftruction are rather more neceffary in Comedy than Tragedy. But it is very hard to fucceed
in them, becaufe we ought ever to confine ourfelves within the
Bounds of Simplicity and Nature, which are rather too narrow
and ftinted, for a lively and impetuous Fancy. This is fo true an
Obfervation, that the Sentences of *Plautus* for the moft part are
fuch, as cannot enter into the Commerce of Life, being generally
Romantick, and full of Affectation ; whereas in *Terence* we meet
not with one, but what is perfectly fuited to the Circumftances of the
Perfon who fpeaks, and may at any time with great Propriety
be brought into common ufe. He was fo delicate on this Head,
that when he makes ufe of any Sentence which he had found in
the Writings of a Tragick Poet, he takes great Care to ftrip it of
that Air of Grandeur and Majefty, without which it would have
otherwife but ill fuited Comedy and common Life. There is a fenfible Pleafure in obferving thefe Changes made by our Poet, and
confidering in what manner he warps and tranfpofes a Sentence (to
ufe the Expreffion) without fuffering it to lofe any thing of it's
Beauty.

Wit and Humour are infeparable from Comedy. *Plautus* difcovers himfelf a great Mafter in this refpect, and all Criticks both
ancient and modern commend him for hitting off the truly Ridiculous in his Characters ; his Raillery too is fometimes fine and
delicate, but we muft own it is alfo often low and vulgar. From
the Criticifms of *Horace* we learn, that even in the Court of *Auguftus*, the Humour and Jokes of *Plautus* were look'd upon as rather fit Entertainment for the Mob and vulgar Herd of the People,
than for thofe of a fine and delicate Tafte. But this Deficiency
might perhaps be more the Fault of the Age than of the Poet ;
for he flourifhed foon after the Introduction of the *Greek* Drama,
when the *Romans* had not quite fhaken off their Fondnefs for the
old fatirical Sports, in which a great deal of Petulance and low
Humour, nay of downright Buffoonery and fcurrilous Abufe, prevailed. We are not therefore to wonder that *Plautus* now and
then complies with the Tafte of the Times, and fometimes introduces into his Comedies Scenes of low Wit, as he knew they
would be highly relifhed, and meet with the Applaufe of the People.

When

When *Terence* wrote, the Age was greatly improved, and their Taste
much more delicate and refined. Accordingly his Pleasantries and
Raillery have an infinitely more polite Turn, and are set off with
all the Charms of a chaste and happy Expression. His Plays indeed
are not calculated to excite immoderate, and, as *Homer* calls it,
inextinguishable Laughter; but they give a calm, rational, and uniform Delight, a Joy in which Contentment and Satisfaction reigns,
and which far exceeds that of extravagant Mirth. The one may
be aptly compared to the inward Pleasure we feel in looking at a
Picture, where Nature is perfectly well imitated; the other, to our
Sensation on seeing odd and grotesque Figures, where some vicious
Irregularity, or monstrous Deformity occasions those convulsive Emotions, which the Vulgar mistake for Pleasure. In fine, 'tis the Ridiculous that occasions immoderate Laughter, the Agreeable is of
a Nature more calm and sedate. *Terence* is a perfect Model in this
latter way.

We come now to the Style. *Plautus* is greatly commended for
the Purity and Elegance of his Diction: there is so much Propriety and Justness in his Expression, that many think his Plays the
truest Standard of the *Latin* Language. *Varro* makes no scruple to
prefer his Style, to that of all the other Poets without Exception:
In sermonibus palmam poscit Plautus; and moreover tells us, that
Elius Stilo was wont to maintain, that had the Muses spoke *Latin*,
they would have spoke in the Manner of *Plautus.* But it is more
than probable, that this so favourable Opinion of *Stilo* and *Varro*, proceeded from their Fondness for Antiquity, whose Form and Manner
of speaking was much studied by that Poet. It is not to be denied,
that the Style of *Plautus* is more rich and luxuriant than that
of *Terence*; but then it is far from being so equal, uniform, and
chaste. In some Places it is swelling and bombast, in others too
strong and rampant; whereas that of *Terence* is every where equal
and just, *purcque simillimus amni*. And it may with Reason be said,
that among all the *Latin* Writers we meet with nothing so noble,
so simple, so full of Graces and Charms, so delicate; in fine, nothing
that can be compared to him for the Politeness of his Dialogue.
This is a Truth of which any one will be sensible, who reads
with Attention the Dialogues of *Cicero*; who, though he has endeavoured to vary the Style, so as to suit the Characters of the several Speakers, yet it is easy to discover the Orator in every Sentence: whereas, in *Terence* there is a marvellous Variety, without
deviating from Truth and Nature. And 'tis highly worth remarking, that the more one reads his Comedies, the more beautiful they
appear, and that Persons of the greatest Genius are generally most
charmed with them. *Scaliger* had reason to say, that the Graces
of our Poets are without Number, and that even among the Learned themselves, scarce one in a hundred was able to discover them.
In fact, his Beauties sometimes escape the most quick and piercing
Eyes,

Eyes, for we may fay of every Verfe, what *Tibullus* fays of all the
Actions of his Miftrefs,

Componit furtim, fubfequiturque decor.

It is for this reafon, as *Heinfius* judicioufly obferves, that his Comedies require very able and expert Actors, as there is fcarce a Line
or Word but includes fomething refined and delicate, that ought
to be fupported by juft Action.   But whatever Praifes we of this
Age beftow upon *Terence*, we can fay nothing that approaches near
to the *Elogium* given him in his own Time : for *Afranius*, who
was himfelf a celebrated Comick Poet, and to whom *Horace* gives fo
advantageous a Teftimony,

Dicitur Afrani toga conveniffe Menandro.

acknowledged, and publickly faid that *Terence* had no Equal.

Terentio non fimilem dices quempiam.

So many fine Qualities, by which he excelled all the Poets that
went before him, foon recommended him to the Efteem of the Age
in which he liv'd, and procured him the Friendfhip of fome of the
moft confiderable Men in the City.   There was in particular fo great
an Intimacy and Familiarity, between him and the younger *Scipio
Africanus* and *Lælius*, that a publick Rumour prevailed, and was
even current in the Time of *Suetonius*, that thefe two young No-
blemen affifted him in the Compofition of his Plays.   Nay further,
Suetonius has preferved a Story from *Cornelius Nepos*, that the firft
of *March*, which was the Feaft of the *Roman* Ladies, *Lælius* being
defired by his Wife to fup a little fooner than ordinary, he prayed
her not to difturb him ; and that coming very late to Supper that
Night, he faid he had never compofed any thing with more Pleafure or Succefs; and being afk'd by the Company what it was,
he repeated thefe Verfes of the third Scene of the fourth Act of the
Self-Tormentor,

*Satis pol proterve me Syri promiffa huc induxerunt,
Decem minas quas mibi dare,* &c.

All this may be allowed without any Prejudice to the Reputation of our Poet.   In *Congreve's* Plays, or any other Writer of our
own Nation, we may here and there meet with Lines that their
Friends compofed for them, and yet no one would pretend to fay
on that account, that the Plays were none of theirs.   Thus much
we may gather from the Story of *Cornelius Nepos*, that the Lines,
of which he fpeaks, were thought very elegant and beautiful at

VOL. I.   b   that

that time, and all the Commentators, and Criticks agree in calling
them so still.

Terence himself indeed augmented this Rumour by denying it' but
faintly, as he does in the Prologue to the *Adelphi*, the last of his
Comedies. " As to what those envious Persons say, that he is af-
" sisted in composing his Works by some illustrious Persons, he is
" so far from taking that as the Offence they intended by it, that
" he conceives it the highest Praise which could be given him,
" as it is a Proof that he has the Honour to please those, who
" please this Audience, and the whole *Roman* People; and who in
" Peace, in War, and on all Occasions, have rendered the Com-
" monwealth in general, and every one in particular, the highest and
" most important Services, without either being more shy, or
" more haughty upon that account." We may believe however,
that he only denied this Assistance so negligently, to make his
Court to *Lælius* and *Scipio*, to whom he knew such a Conduct would
not be disagreeable. In reality they might assist him in polishing
his Pieces, and sometimes give him a few Lines they had composed
for their Amusement. To their Assistance and Conversation too,
he may, perhaps, be in some measure indebted for the Purity of
his Style; for it is not likely, that *Terence*, who was an *African*,
and of consequence wrote in a Language foreign to his own, would
neglect the Advantages which the Acquaintance and Friendship
of two such illustrious Natives gave him, in forming his Diction
to Correctness and Propriety. Nor let any one suppose, that more
than this was necessary: *Phædrus*, who wrote in *Latin* with so much
Elegance and Politeness, and has so happily copied the Manner of
Terence, had been also a Slave, and was by Birth a *Thracian*; and
yet no one ever suspected, that he was indebted to others, for that
Purity of Language, which is so conspicuous in his Compositions.
Besides, *Terence* might have been brought young enough to *Rome*,
to forget entirely his own Tongue, and make the *Latin* natural to him.

Six of his Comedies are come down to us. When he sold the
first to the *Ædiles*, it was thought proper that he should read it
beforehand to *Cæcilius*, a Comic Poet as well as himself, and in
great Esteem at *Rome*, when *Terence* first appeared there. Accordingly he went to his House, and found him at Table. He was
brought in, and, as he was very ill drest, a Stool was given him
near *Cæcilius*'s Couch, where he sat down, and began to read.
He had no sooner read some few Verses, than *Cæcilius* invited him
to Supper, and placed him at Table near himself. Judgments are
not always to be formed of Men by their Outsides. A bad Dress
may often cover the most excellent Talents. The *Eunuch*, one of
the six Comedies of *Terence*, was received with such Applause, that
it was acted twice the same Day, Morning and Evening, which,
perhaps, had never happened to any Play before; and a much better
Price was given for it, than had ever been paid for any Comedy

till

till them: for *Terence* had eight thousand Sesterces, that is to say, about fifty Pounds.

Whether *Terence* was for putting an end to the Reproach of publishing the Works of others as his own, or had formed the Design of going to learn the Customs and Manners of the *Greeks* perfectly, in order to represent them the better in his Plays; after having composed the six Comedies still extant, and before he was thirty-five years old, he quitted *Rome*, where he was never seen more. Some say that he died at Sea in his Return from *Greece*, from whence he brought with him an hundred and eight Plays, which he had translated from *Menander*. Others assure us, that he died at the City of *Stymphalus* in *Arcadia*, in the Consulship of *Cn. Cornelius Dolabella*, and *M. Fulvius*, of a disease occasioned by his Grief for having lost the Comedies he had translated, and those he had made himself. He had only one Daughter, who, after his Death, was married to a *Roman* Knight, and to whom he left an House and Garden of twenty Acres upon the *Appian* Way.

Before I conclude this Dissertation, it will be necessary to take Notice of something belonging to the Dramatick Pieces of the Ancients, and which, as they have been now long disused, cannot at all be understood by the modern Representations of that Kind. Of this sort we may reckon up as particularly worth our Observation, the *Buskin*, and the *Sock*, the *Masks*, the *Chorus*, and the *Flutes*. The *Buskin*, *Cothurnus*, is thought to have been a high square Boot, which, by raising the Foot considerably, made the Actors appear larger than the common Size of Men; and such as the Heroes of old Times were supposed to be. It also gave them a slow and majestic Step, such as suited the State and Solemnity of Tragedy. The *Sock* again was a more slight and easy Covering for the Foot, and rather proper to Women; so that their being worn by the Men is thought to have denoted the Inferiority of the Characters in Comedy, as debauched young Sparks, old crazy Misers, Pimps, Parasites, Strumpets, and the like. For that the *Sock* was always accounted scandalous, is evident from *Seneca's* exclaiming against *Caligula*, for sitting to judge upon Life and Death in a rich Pair of Socks adorned with Gold and Silver. The *Mask*, *Persona*, is derived by *Aulus Gellius* from *personare*, to sound through, because their Make was so contrived as to assist the Voice, and render it clearer and fuller, by contracting it into a less Compass. Madam *Dacier* was the first who observed in the Draughts of a famous old Manuscript of our Poet, that the Theatrical Masks of the Ancients were not made like ours, which cover only the Face, but that they came over the whole Head, and had always a sort of Peruke of Hair fastened on them, proper to the Person whom they were to represent. The *Chorus*, was a Company of Actors, as either were present at, or probably might be, so, upon the Stage or Scene where the Business of the Play was transacted. The *Greek* Dramatick Poets were exact

Observers

Obfervers of the Chorus in Tragedy ; but the *Latin* Performances of this kind, which remain under the Name of *Seneca*, as they are faulty in many other refpects, fo particularly are they in the Chorus's : for fometimes they hear all that's faid upon the Stage; fee all that's done; and fpeak very properly to all ; at other times one would think they were blind, deaf, or dumb : we can hardly tell whom they reprefent, how they were drefled, what Reafon brings them on the Stage, or why they are of one Sex more than the other. I fhall not here trouble the Reader with a long Account of the Office of the Chorus, which he will find in *Horace De Art. Poet: V.* 193. but only obferve; that at firft, Comedy had a Chorus as well as Tragedy ; but becaufe of the Licentioufnefs of its Satyr; and the Bitternefs of its Raillery; it was after fome time forbid, as the fame Poet inform us.

And now to bring this Difcourfe (which has already fwelled beyond the Bulk firft intended) to a Conclufion ; we proceed to fpeak of the *Flutes,* a Subject as little underftood; as any in Antiquity, and yet without the Knowledge of them we can make nothing of the Titles prefix'd to our Poet's Comedies. As Madam *Dacier* has given us the moft rational Account of this Matter, I fhall tranfcribe from her what I think neceffary to be faid upon it here. The Performers of the Mufick played always upon two Flutes during the whole time of the Comedy : that which they ftopp'd with the Right Hand, was on that account call'd right-handed ; and that which they ftopp'd with the Left, left-handed. The firft had but a few Holes; and founded a deep Bafe ; the other had a great Number of Holes, and gave a fhriller and fharper Note. When the Muficians play'd on two Flutes of a different Sound, they ufed to fay the Piece was played *Tibiis imparibus,* with unequal Flutes, or *Tibiis dextris & finiftris,* with right and left-handed Flutes. When they played on two Flutes of the fame found, then it was *Tibiis paribus dextris,* if they were right-handed Flutes ; or *finiftris,* if left-handed. Hence; when in the Title of the *Andrian* the Mufick is faid to have been performed *Tibiis paribus dextris & finiftris* ; this is to be underftood of different Reprefentations; where the Flutes were always of the fame kind, but fometimes the one; and fometimes the other ; for, as the fame ingenious Lady conjectures, the Mufick was not guided by the Subject of the Play, but by the Occafion on which it was acted. If at a Funeral Solemnity; the Mufick was performed on right-handed Flutes, as moft grave and folemn ; if on any joyful account; left-handed Flutes were ufed as the moft brifk and airy. But in the great Feftivals of the Gods; that fhared equally of Mirth and Religion; both Kinds were ufed; or elfe by turns, fometimes right-handed, and fometimes left-handed, as is faid in the Title to the *Andrian.*

PUBLII

TERENTII

ANDRIA.

TERENCE's

ANDRIAN.

VOL. I.   B

THE ANDRIAN OF TERENCE WAS EXHIBIT-
ED AT THE MEGALENSIAN GAMES, WHEN
MARCUS FULVIUS, AND MARCUS GLA-
BRIO WERE CURULE ÆDILES. IT WAS
ACTED BY *THE COMPANIES OF* LUCIUS
AMBIVIUS TURPIO, AND LUCIUS ATTILIUS
PRÆ-

ANNOTATIONS.

¹ *Titulus* feu *Didafcalia.* What the *Latins* called *Titulus,* was by the *Greeks* called *Didafcalia,* as much as to fay the *Inftruction* or *Explication.* Thefe introductory Pieces were of great ufe; for they informed the Reader at what Time, upon what Occafion, and under what Magiftrates the Play had been exhibited. If we may credit the *Greek* Scholiafts, thefe Titles were always placed in the Front of Pieces defigned for the Stage; not, indeed, every Performance of this kind, but fuch as were acted at the Celebration of fome remarkable Feaft; as that of *Ceres, Cybele,* or *Bacchus:* and that becaufe thefe only were acted by the Authority of the Magiftrates; for other Plays were commonly publifhed without any Title at all. Madam *Dacier* remarks, that we have no entire Title left us of any Piece, either *Greek* or *Latin,* not even of the Comedies of *Terence.* For no Notice is taken of the Price, that is, of the Money given by the *Ædile* to the Poet for his feveral Plays; and this was what they never failed to mark diftinctly. Nay, they carried this Exactnefs fo far, as to mention the Ho-

nours that had been done the Poet, the Ribbons, Flowers, and Effence that had been prefented to him. It is to be obferved, however, that this was the Practice only in *Greece,* where the Profeffion of a Comedian was accounted honourable, and held in great Efteem : for at *Rome* the Cafe was different, it being looked upon as infamous in the higheft degree.

² *Andria.* The Comedy obtained this Name from *Glycery,* one of the chief Characters in it, who was reputed to be of *Andros,* tho', as afterwards appeared, fhe was really an *Athenian.*

³ *Ludis Megalenfibus.* At the *Megalenfian* Games, or Feaft of *Cybele.* The *Ludi Megalenfes* were Games inftituted in honour of *Cybele,* the great Goddefs, when her Statue was brought from *Peffinum* to *Rome,* with fo much Pomp by *Scipio Nafica.* She was called the Mother of the Gods, being the Daughter of Heaven and Earth, and Wife to *Saturn. Rhea, Ops,* and *Vefta* were alfo Names, by which fhe often went. She was moreover called from the Places where fhe was worfhipped *Dindymene, Berecynthia, Idæa, Phrygia,* &c. Her Priefts
were

ACTA LUDIS MEGALENSIBUS M. FULVIO ET M. GLABRIONE ÆDILIBUS CURULIBUS. EGERUNT L. AMBIVIUS TURPIO, L. ATTILIUS

O R D O.

P. Terentii Andria fuit acta Ludis Megalensibus, Marco Fulvio & Marco Glabrione Ædilibus Curuli-bus. Lucius Ambivius Turpio, & Lucius Attilius

ANNOTATIONS.

were the *Corybantes*, all Eunuchs, who worshipped her by the Sound of Drums, Tabers, Pipes, and Cymbals. This Feast lasted six Days, from the Day before the Nones of *April* to the Ides, that is, from the 8th to the 15th, and was celebrated with all manner of scenical Sports, as we learn from *Ovid*, in the fourth Book of his *Fasti*:

> *Scena sonat, ludique vocant, spectate,*
> *   Quirites.*

" The Stage resounds, the Plays call,
" come, *Romans*, to the public Specta-
" cles."

In the Procession, the Women danced before the Statue of the Goddess, and the Magistrates appeared in all their Robes, whence the Phrase of *Purpura Megalensis*. This was also a solemn Time of Invitation to Entertainments among Friends. They were called *Megalensia*, and *Megalesia*, from μέγας *great*: being, as we have said, instituted in honour of the great Goddess.

⁴ *Ædilibus Curulibus.* The *Ædiles* were at first instituted soon after the *Tribunes*, to assist those Magistrates in the Discharge of some particular Services, the chief of which was the Care of public Edifices,

whence they had their Name. At first they were only two in Number, and elected out of the Commons; but after some time, two more were added out of the Body of the Nobility, and distinguished by the Name of *Curule Ædiles*, because, in public Places, they had the Honour of sitting upon a Chair of Ivory, called by the *Romans Sella Curalis*. *Lipsius* conjectures, that it owed both its Name and Invention to the *Curetes*, a People of the *Sabines*: but the more common Derivation is *à Curru*, because they sat upon it as they rode in their Chariots. They are named here before the Consuls, because it belonged to them to regulate the public Games, and pay the Poets for such of their Plays as were acted upon these Occasions. *Cicero* speaking of them in his second Book of Laws, says:

> *Sunto Ædiles, curatores Urbis, an-*
> *nonæ, ludorumque solennium.*

" Let the *Ædiles* have the Care of
" the City, the Provisions, and sa-
" cred Games."

⁵ *Egerunt L. Ambivius Turpio,* &c. The *Romans* had their Actors ranged into different Companies, each of which had a Master or Head. When

B 2   any

PRÆNESTINUS FLACCUS *THE FREEDMAN*
OF CLAUDIUS COMPOSED THE MUSIC,
WHICH WAS PERFORMED UPON EQUAL
FLUTES, RIGHT AND LEFT HANDED: IT IS
ENTIRELY FROM THE GREEK, AND WAS
PUBLISHED UNDER THE CONSULSHIP OF
MARCUS MARCELLUS, AND CAIUS SULPI-
CIUS.

ʻANNOTATIONS.

any Play was to be acted, the *Ædiles* after buying it of the Poet, gave it to the Master of some Company, who assigned to each Actor the Character which he thought best suited his Genius. When one Company was not sufficient, they often joined two together; or perhaps it might have been acted twice the same Day, or at two different Theatres, by different Sets of Actors. *Lucius Ambivius Turpio,* and *Lucius Attilius Prænestinus* were the Masters of the Companies concerned in the Representation of the *Andrian.*

6 *Modos fecit.* Composed the Music, the same that is often expressed by *modulavit.* For it was the Custom among the *Romans* as well as now, to accompany the Representation of their Stage-Plays with Music, which was generally composed on purpose to suit the Genius of the Play.

7 *Flaccus Claudii.* Flaccus *the Freedman of* Claudius: so we are to understand it, as *Muretus* has very well observed, and not *Flaccus Claudii filius.* For that *Flaccus* must have been either a Slave, or a Freedman, will appear evidently, if we allow ourselves to reflect, that all who mounted the Stage at *Rome* were held infamous. The Pieces only called *Atellanæ* and *Togatæ,* were such as did no dishonour to the Actors. It is for this Reason, that *Laberius,* a Roman Knight, being engaged by *Cæsar* to act some mimic Pieces of his own composing, for a Reward of five hundred *Sestertia,* nearly three thousand eight hundred Pounds, thus elegantly

The

PRÆNESTINUS. MODOS FECIT
FLACCUS CLAUDII, TIBIIS PARI-
BUS, DEXTRIS ET SINISTRIS. ET
EST TOTA GRÆCA. EDITA M.
MARCELLO, C. SULPICIO COSS.

Prænestinus egerunt eam. Flaccus libertus Claudii fecit modos, tibiis paribus dextris & siniftris. Et hæc Comœdia est tota

Græca, edita Marco Marcello, & Caio Sulpicio Consulibus.

ANNOTATIONS.

gantly complained of his unhappy Fate:

Ego bis trecenis annis actis sine nota,
Eques Romanus, lare egressus meo,
Domum revertar mimus; nimirum hoc
*   die*
Uno plus vixi, mihi quam vivendum
*   fuit.*

" After having lived sixty Years
" without Reproach, I leave my
" House, a *Roman* Knight, and re-
" turn an Actor: I have lived this
" one Day longer than I ought to
" have done."

8 *Tibiis paribus dextris & siniftris.*
As this, and all that relates to the Music, that accompanied the *Roman* Stage-Plays, has been fully handled in the Account we have given of their Dramatic Poetry, I shall refer the Reader to what is there said, for Satisfaction in this Point.

9 *Et est tota Græca.* All the Comedies of *Terence* are so, both as the Scene is laid in *Greece*, and as they are translated from *Greek* Originals. See the Notes to the Prologue.

10 *M. Marcello, C. Sulpicio Coss.* *Marcus Claudius Marcellus*, and *C. Sulpicius Gallus*, who were Consuls in the Year of the City 587, the twenty seventh of the Poet's Age, and 166 Years before the Birth of our Saviour.

6

The ARGUMENT *to the* ANDRIAN, *from* MURETUS.

CHREMES *and* Phania *were Brothers, both Citizens of* Athens. Chremes *being under a necessity of going into* Asia, *left* Pasibula, *at that time his only Daughter, to the Care of his Brother. Soon after his Departure, violent civil Wars arising in* Greece, Phania *thought it best to retire from them, and taking the young Girl on shipboard with him, set sail for* Asia, *to find his Brother. A Storm in the mean time arising, he was shipwrecked, and cast upon the Island of* Andros. *There he addressed himself to an* Andrian, *who, though but in low Circumstances, yet entertained him with great Humanity. Not long after this,* Phania *dies. The* Andrian *taking the young Girl under his Protection, changes her Name from* Pasibula *to* Glycery, *and educates her with the same Care as his own Daughter* Chrysis. *In a few Years, he also dies.* Chrysis *finding herself an Orphan, and in danger of Want, taking* Glycery *along with her, sails for* Athens. *Here she endeavoured, for some time, to maintain herself by her Industry, and the Labour of her Hands; but overcome at last by the Solicitations and Promises of the Youth, she takes to the Trade of a Courtezan. Among others that resorted to her, was* Pamphilus *the Son of* Simo, *a Youth of a promising Temper, and not much addicted to Gallantry. Chancing here to see* Glycery, *he fell desperately in love with her; and she receiving only his Addresses, he got her with Child, and afterwards made her a Promise of Marriage.* Chremes, *by this time, had another Daughter, named* Philumena, *who was of Age, and, as* Pamphilus *was a young Man of a very fair Character, desired above all things to marry her to him. For this purpose he comes of his own accord to* Simo, *and concludes the Match. The old Men, without ever communicating their Design to* Pamphilus, *fix upon the Day for consummating the Marriage. While these things are in agitation,* Chrysis *dies. An Accident that followed upon that first brought* Simo *acquainted with his Son's Passion: for going along with him to the Funeral, when* Chrysis *was laid upon the Pile, and fire put to it,* Glycery, *through impatience of Grief, seemed as if she designed to throw herself after her.* Pamphilus *observing it, immediately ran up to her, and endeavoured to prevent her with an Anxiety that plainly discovered his Fondness. The Day after* Chremes *comes to* Simo, *and renounces the Match: declaring that he understood for certain, that* Pamphilus *was married to this Stranger, whom he so called in a way of Reproach, little suspecting in the mean time that she was his own Daughter.* Pamphilus *is overjoyed at the News, and* Simo *as much disconcerted. When the Day that had been appointed for the Marriage-Ceremony was come,* Simo *cunningly resolves to counterfeit the Continuance of the Match, imagining, that by this, he should be able to form a Judgment, how his Son stood affected. For if he shewed any Reluctance, this*

would

M. Ant. Mureti ARGUMENTUM.

*C*HREMES & Phania fratres Athenienses fuerunt. Eorum
Chremes profecturus in Afiam, Pafibulam filiolam, quam tum unicam habebat, fratris fidei credidit. Profecto eo, contigit, ut in Græcia
magni bellorum motus excitarentur, quos fugiens Phania, quum, impofita
fecum in navim puella, ad fratrem iter cepiffet, vi tempeftatis fracta
navi, apud Andrum infulam ejectus eft. Ibi applicat fe ad Andrium
quendam, hominem haud magna in re : a quo tamen benigne humaniterque
exceptus, non ita multo poft moritur. Hofpes Andrius relictæ apud fe
puellæ commutat nomen, et pro Pafibula Glycerium nominat ; quumque per
aliquot annos eam cum filia Chryfide, pari utramque ftudio, educaffet, de-
cedit ipfe quoque de vita. Chryfis, quæ fe & orbam & inopem videret,
abrepta fecum Glycerio, Athenas navigat : ubi quum aliquamdiu vitam
lana telaque toleraffet, ad poftremum, adolefcentum blanditiis & pollici-
tationibus victa, quæftum corpore facero incepit. Ventitabat ad eam inter
cæteros Pamphilus, Simonis filius, probus, & liberali præditus ingenio
adolefcens ; qui non Chryfidis ille quidem, fed ipfius Glycerii mirifico quadam amore percuffus, primus, folufque cum ea rem habuit, fidemque jam
gravidæ dedit, eam fibi uxorem fore. Sufceperat & poftea Chremes aliam filiam, Philumenam nomine, eamque (jam enim nubilis erat) Pamphilo, bona adolefcentis impulfus fama, collocare cupiebat. Quid multa ?
ultro ad Simonem venit, cum eo negotium conficit. Infcio Pamphilo, de
communi fenum fententia, faciendis nuptiis conftituitur dies. Adhuc
hæc erant, quum Chryfis moritur. Ibi primum Simo de filii amore cognovit : nam cum ambo una in funus prodiiffent, accidit, ut, pofita in ignem Chryfide, Glycerium fe, præ doloris impatientia, eodem conjectura videretur. Accurrit Pamphilus, eamque mediam amplexus, ita confolari
cœpit, ut plurimas minimeque dubias totius rei fignificationes daret.
Itaque venit ad Simonem poftridie Chremes, conditionem renunciat : comperiffe fe, Pamphilum peregrinam illam habere in uxoris loco ; nefcius ex
fe natam effe eam, quam ita contumeliæ caufa peregrinam nominaret.
Gaudere, ea re intellecta, Pamphilus ; dolere contra, ac ringi Simo.
Advenit interea dies, qui nuptiis initio fuerat præftitutus. Simo, vete-
ratoria quadam calliditate, fimulandas fibi, ad pertentandum filii animum, nuptias ftatuit : hoc cogitans, fi abnueret filius, veram fibi ob-

jurgandi

would afford sufficient Reason to chide him, which hitherto there could be no just Pretence for ; if otherwise, he hoped that Chremes *might still be prevailed with to let the Match go forward, and thus by the Blessing of Heaven, the Marriage be really concluded. Passing by, therefore, his Son at the Forum, who was quite secure, and never dreamt of his Father's Design, he desires him to go home, and prepare for his Wedding, which was that day to be celebrated. The young Man, struck with this unexpected Speech, and uncertain what Course to follow, is met by* Davus, *a Slave of great Cunning and Dexterity, who by this time understood the whole Project of the old Man, and how* Chremes *stood disposed. There happened to be at that time with* Pamphilus, *one* Charinus, *a Youth greatly enamoured of* Philumena, *who had often in vain essayed to obtain her in Marriage. But hearing that she was that Day to be given to* Pamphilus, *he begs of him in the utmost Despair, that if he had any Regard to his Happiness, he would either decline the Match, or at least defer it for a few days.* Pamphilus, *as much on his own Account, as the young Man's, advises him to take Courage, and leave nothing unattempted to obstruct the Marriage, and that for his part, he also would do all in his power to prevent it.* Davus, *in the mean time, as I have said, coming up, counsels* Charinus, *now full of Hopes, to go about and solicit the old Man's Friends. He afterwards discovers his Suspicions apart to* Pamphilus, *advising him to counterfeit a Compliance with his Father's Will ; For by that means, says he, you will elude the well-laid Snare, and give him no Cause to chide you. Nor is there any ground to fear that the Match may go forward ; for* Chremes, *after having once rejected you, will never again think of offering you his Daughter.* Pamphilus *yields to his Reasons. But this Conduct had a far different Effect from what was expected ; for* Chremes *after some entreaty from* Simo *complies, and thus the Marriage is like to go forward. By good hap* Glycery *was that very Day brought to bed of a Son.* Davus, *being able to think of no other likely Way to disturb the Marriage, causes* Glycery's *Maid to lay the Child before* Simo's *Gate.* Chremes *happening to come upon her at that Juncture, and understanding that the Child belonged to* Pamphilus, *again refuses to give his Daughter. This raises a prodigious Stir, till, as good Luck would have it,* Crito *an Andrian arrives, who being nearest akin to* Chrysis, *had come to* Athens, *to look after the Inheritance, which she had left. By his means* Chremes *comes to know, that* Glycery *was the same with his Daughter* Pasibula. *Thus all ending joyfully,* Pamphilus *obtains* Glycery, *and* Charinus Philumena.*

PER-

jurgandi illius caufam fore, quæ ad eum diem nulla fatis jufta fuerat: fin annueret, facile fe, quod vellet, a Chremete impetraturum, atque ita veras nuptias, diis adjuvantibus, factum iri. Præteriens igitur apud forum, fecuro jam, & nihil tale metuenti filio; Pamphile, inquit, abi domum, ac deos comprecare; uxor tibi ducenda hodie eft. Hoc dicto, velut improvifo quadam jaculo, fauciatus adolefcens, quit ageret, aut quid confilii caperet, nefciebat: quum ad eum Davus, vafro admodum ac verfuto ingenio fervus, animadverfa fenis aftutia, accurrit. Erat tum una cum Pamphilo Charinus, qui adolefcens miro quodam amore Philumenæ incenfus, fruftra fæpe tentatis illius nuptiis, ad poftremum audito eam eo die nupturam Pamphilo, in fummam defperationem, adductus, cum. orabat, fi fe falvum vellet, ut vel eam ne duceret, vel faltem nuptiis dies aliquot produceret. Pamphilus eum fua quidem caufa bono effe animo, atque omnia ad impediendas nuptias moliri jubebat: fe, quantum in fe effet, effecturum, ea ut ne. daretur. fibi. Adveniens, ut dixi, Davus, Charinum, jam fpei plenum, abire ad ambiendos fenis amicos jubet: deinde feorfim Pamphilo conjecturas fuas aperit, perfuadetque, ut patri dicat, fe paratum effe uxorem ducere; nam eo pacto, inquit, & patri omnem jurgandi occafionem præcideris, & non erit tamen verendum, ne nuptiæ fiant: nunquam enim Chremes tibi, femel repudiato, filium fuam iterum commiffurus eft. Hæc ita de fervi confilio acta, longe aliter cecidere, ut putabatur: exorat enim Chremetem Simo. Ita res in verarum nuptiarum difcrimen adducitur. Forte eo ipfo die Glycerium, exactis temporibus, puerum peperit: cum puerum Davus, quum aliter nuptias difturbare non poffet, præ foribus ædium Simonis ab. ancilla collocandum curat. In eum quum incidiffet Chremes, & e Pamphilo natum effe cognoffet, rurfum abducit animum a nuptiis. Turbæ maxime concitantur: donec advenit Crito Andrius, qui, quod Chryfidi genere proximus fuiffet, ad cernendam illius hæreditatem Athenas venerat. Ejus interventu Chremes filiam agnofcit. Ita, fumma omnium lætitia, Charino Philumena, Glycerium Pamphilo nubit.

D R A-

PERSONS *of the* PLAY.

The PROLOGUE. So the Actor was called that repeated the Prologue, commonly the Master of the Company.

SIMO, the Father of *Pamphilus.*

PAMPHILUS, in love with *Glycery.*

SOSIA, *Simo's* Freedman.

DAVUS, Servant to *Pamphilus.*

CHREMES, the Father of *Glycery* and *Philumena.*

GLYCERY, in love with *Pamphilus.*

CHARINUS, in love with *Philumena.*

BYRRIA, Servant to *Charinus.*

CRITO, an *Andrian.*

DROMO, Servant to *Simo.*

MYSIS, *Glycery's* Maid.

LESBIA, a Midwife.

ARCHILIS, an old Woman.

SERVANTS, returning with *Simo* from the Market.

SCENE *ATHENS.*

The

DRAMATIS PERSONÆ.

PROLOGUS.

SIMO, *Pater Pamphili.*

PAMPHILUS, *Amator Glycerii.*

SOSIA, *Libertus Simonis.*

DAVUS, *Servus Pamphili.*

CHREMES, *Pater Glycerii & Philumenæ.*

GLYCERIUM, *Amica Pamphili.*

CHARINUS, *Amator Philumenæ.*

BYRRHIA, *Servius Charini.*

CRITO, *Hofpes ex Andro.*

DROMO, *Servus Simonis.*

MYSIS, *Ancilla Glycerii.*

LESBIA, *Obftetrix.*

ARCHILIS, *Anus.*

SERVI, *Simonem è foro redeuntem comitantes.*

SCENA ATHENÆ.

PRO-

The PROLOGUE.

ARGUMENT.

The Design of this Prologue is to dispose the People in favour of the new Poet, and raise their Contempt against the old, and to convince them, that the Author, though chargeable with some few Faults, was yet a Writer of great Modesty.

WHEN our Poet first applied his Thoughts to writing Comedies; he imagined his only Aim should be, to make his Plays agreeable and diverting to the People. But he finds that Things have fallen out very differently, and that he is obliged to lose Time in writing of Prologues, not such as explain the Subject of the Plot, but to refute the Cavils of an old malicious Bard. Now, pray only hear what it is they so mightily blame. *Menander* wrote the *Andrian* and *Perinthian.* He that knows either one of these Pieces, knows both, for the Plot in each is the same, though they differ considerably in the Manner and Style. Our Poet owns that he has inserted in his *Andrian*, whatever he found in the *Perinthian* agreeable to his Design, and frankly used it as his own. This they greatly cry out against, and warmly maintain, that Plays ought by no means to be confounded and jumbled together. Verily by this Affectation of Knowledge, they make it plain, that they know nothing at all; for in thus accusing our Poet, they accuse also *Nævius, Plautus,* and *Ennius,* whom he professes to have copied in this
Article,

ANNOTATIONS.

SED qui malevoli veteris poeta. One would be apt to conclude from this that it was not usual at *Rome* to begin their Plays with Prologues, or at least that the Design of them was to give a short Account of the Subject of the Play, that the Audience might be the better able to judge in what manner the Poet had conducted the Plot. *Terence* here complains that he was forced to deviate from the common Method of Prologues, and lose time in defending himself against unjust Calumnies and Reproaches. The old Bard complained of here, was, according to *Donatus,* one *Lucius Lavinius.* But Madam *Dacier,* not being able to recollect any Poet of that Name, changes it into *Luscius Lanuvinus,* against whom *Terence* made the Prologue to his second Comedy.

9 *Menander.* A celebrated *Greek* Poet, the great Improver of the new Comedy. His Plays were written with the utmost Elegance and Politeness, and are allowed by all to have been a perfect Pattern of genteel Comedy; what pity is it, that none of them now remain!

Ibid. *Andriam & Perinthiam.* Two *Greek* Comedies of *Menander,* from which our Poet formed the present one. We have already seen in the Notes to the *Didascalia,* why this Play has obtained the Name of the *Andrian,* and the same Reason holds good with respect to the *Original,* whence it was taken. The *Perinthian* in like manner was so called from a Woman of *Perinthus,* the Capital of *Thrace,* upon the Borders of the *Propontis,* who came to *Athens,* and upon whose Story the Fable of the Play mostly turned.

12 *Oratione ac stylo. Donatus* observes here, that *Oratio* respects the Sense, probably the Manner and Conduct of the Play, and *Stylus* the Words or Language. It appears

PROLOGUS.

ARGUMENTUM.

Omnis hujus Prologi intentio est, ut novo Poetæ veniam paret,
& veteri odium : & ut quam maximè modestum miniméque
errantem Terentium probet.

POETA cùm primùm animum ad scribendum
 Id sibi negotî credidit solum dari, [appulit,
Populo ut placerent, quas fecisset fabulas.
Verum aliter evenire multo intelligit.
Nam in prologis scribundis operam abutitur, 5
Non quî argumentum narret, sed quî malevoli
Veteris poetæ maledictis respondeat.
Nunc, quam rem vitio dent, quæso; animum advortite.
  Menander fecit Andriam & Perinthiam.
Quï utramvis recte norit, ambas noverit. 10
Non ita dissimili sunt argumento : sed tamen
Dissimili oratione sunt factæ ac stylo.
Quæ convenere, in Andriam ex Perinthia
Fatetur transtulisse, atque usum pro suis.
Id isti vituperant factum : atque in co disputant, 15
Contaminari non decere fabulas.
Faciunt næ intellegendo, ut nihil intellegant :
Qui cum hunc accusant, Nævium, Plautum, Ennium

ORDO. *POETA Terentius, cùm primùm appulit, animum ad scribendum comœdius, credidit id negotî solum dari sibi, ut fabulæ, quas fabulas fecisse, placerent populo. Verum intelligit evenire multo aliter : nam abutitur operam in scribendis prologis; non quî narret argumentum, sed quî respondeat maledictis malevoli veteris poetæ. Nunc quæso advertite animum ad eam rem quam dent vitio. Menander fecit Comœdias Andriam*

& Perinthiam. Quï norit utramvis recte, noverit ambas : ita sunt non dissimili argumento : sed tamen sunt factæ dissimili oratione ac stylo. Poeta fatetur se transtulisse ex Perinthia Menandri in suam Andriam, quæ ei convenere, atque usum fuisse his pro suis. Isti vituperant id factum, atque disputant in co, fabulas non decere contaminari. Næ illi intelligendo, faciunt ut intelligant nihil : qui cum accusant hunc, accusant etiam Nævium, Plautum, & Ennium;

ANNOTATIONS.

pears, that these two Plays had a very great Likeness, and that the Plot of each turned upon Stories resembling each other in their Circumstances. Nay, *Donatus* assures us, that the first Scene of the *Perinthian* was conceived in almost the same Words as that of the *Andrian*, but otherwise they were conducted differently.

10 *Contaminari non decere fabulas.* Tan. *Faber*, Madam *Dacier*, and *Farnaby*, all agree in explaining *contaminari* by *misceri* and *confundi*, when two different Things are jumbled together to make one. And this was precisely the Charge laid against our Poet. *Livy*, who seems to have well studied and understood *Terence*, joins the Words *contaminare* and *confundere*, in speaking of the Alliances between the Nobles and the Commons. It is very well observed by Ma-

dam *Dacier*, that those who explain it *pollui*, make *Terence* engage in the defence of a very ridiculous Cause, for who can doubt that it was faulty in a Poet to spoil a Play ? The Enemies of *Terence* maintain, *non decere contaminari fabulas* ; *Terence*, on the contrary, maintains *decere contaminari fabulas.* There is therefore a Necessity for affixing a favourable Meaning to *contaminari*. The Etymology of it is thus : from *tango, contango, contagitum, contagimen, contamen, contamine.* This then is the first and original Signification of the Verb *contamino*. But as it is impossible to join several things together into one, without making them cease to be what they were before, hence it came to signify, *to alter, change, or spoil.*

18 *Nævium, Plautum, Ennium,* accusant. *Terence*

Article, and whofe free and unaffected Manner he had rather equal ; than the obfcure formal Correctnefs of thefe *Revilers*. I advife them however to be a little more peaceable for the future, and ceafe thefe Reproaches, left they may come to hear of their own Blunders in their turn.

Hear favourably, attend without Prejudice, and examine into thé Merits of the Piece ; that you may know what Hopes to entertain of his future Plays : whether they will deferve a fair Reprefentation, or to be hiffed off the Stage without hearing.

ANNOTATIONS.

Terence here defends himfelf by the Example of others, who had gone before him, all Poets of great Name and Authority. The Order of Time in which they flourifhed is not here obferved. For *Ennius* was before *Plautus*, but he is mentioned laft, fays *Donatus*, becaufe of greateft Weight and Confideration ; for *Ennius* has been generally efteemed one of the greateft Genius's that *Rome* ever produced. They were all Poets of the firft Rank, had written for the Stage, and taken the fame liberty, for which our Poet was fo feverely cenfured by his Enemies. All their Works are now loft, fave thofe of *Plautus*, who in fome things is allowed to excel even *Terence* himfelf.

20 *Quorum æmulari exoptat negligentiam. Negligentia* is here for the free and unconfined Manner of thefe Poets, both in the Style and Difpofition of their Subjects, without fubjecting themfelves too much to the Slavery of Rules. Madam *Dacier* quotes, from *Cicero de Oratore*, a Paffage which gives great l'ght to this of *Terence*, becaufe he fpeaks exprefsly of this eafy free Manner of *Ennius*. Ennio *delector, ait quifpiam, quod non difcedit a communi more verborum :* Pacuvio, *inquit alius, omnes apud hunc ornati elaboratique funt verfus, multa apud alterum negligentius.* " I am " ravifhed with *Ennius*, fays one, becaufe " he departs but little from the Manner of " familiar

Accufant : quos hic nofter auctores habet :
Quorum æmulari exoptat neglegentiam   20
Potiùs, quam iftorum obfcuram diligentiam.
Dehinc ut quiefcant porrò moneo, & definant
Maledicere, malefacta ne nofcant fua.
Favete, adefte æquo animo, & rem cognofcite ;
Ut pernofcatis, ecquid fpei fit relliquum,   25
Pofthac quas faciet de integro comœdias,
Spectandæ, an exigendæ fint vobis prius.

*quos hic nofter poe-
ta habet auctores :
quorum exoptat æ-
mulari negligenti-
am, potiùs quam
obfcuram diligen-
tiam iftorum. Porrò
moneo, ut debinc
quiefcant, & defi-
nant maledicere, ne
ipfi nofcant fua ma-
lefacta. Vos fpe-*

*ctatores favete, adefte æquo animo, & cognofcite rem hujus Comœdiæ ; ut pernofcatis ec-
quid fpei fit reliquum de iis quas comædias Poeta faciet pofthac de integro : num fpectandæ
fint a vobis, au prius (potius) exigendæ è fcena.*

A N N O T A T I O N S.

" familiar Difcourfe. I prefer, fays another,
" *Pacuvius* ; his Verfes are fmooth, regu-
" lar, and finely polifhed, whereas *Ennius*
" writes in a carelefs negligent way." This
free Manner agrees very well with Comedy,
and is fometimes even neceffary.

21 *Obfcuram diligentiam. Obfcure formal
Correctnefs.* This arifes from too great an
Attachment to Rules, the Effect of which
is, for the moft part, a ftiff formal Air,
that makes the whole difagreeable and un-
pleafant, yea, often brings Obfcurity and
Confufion.

23 *Malefacta ne nofcant fua.* This was
a Liberty, which the Ancients thought they
had a juft Claim to, if any one attacked
them firft, to make Reprizals ; for fo we
learn from feveral of the Morals of *Phædrus*'s Fables, which may be looked upon as
a Collection of Proverbs, expreffing the
Manners and Sentiments of thofe Times.
Thus, Lib. I. Fab. 26. 1.

*Nulli nocendum, fi quis vero læferit
Mulcandum fimili jure fabella admonet.*
And again, Ibid. V. 12.
Sua quifque exempla debet æquo animo pati.
26 *Faciet de integro comœdias.* Some
Commentators, among whom *Eugraphius*,
refer *de integro* to the manner of his tranflating from the *Greek, cum unam Græcam in
unam Latinam tranftulerit.* Intimating, that
though in the prefent Cafe, he had joined
two together ; yet, afterwards, he would
confine himfelf to one. But the Poet's
Defence, all along, fhews that he was fond
of the Practice, and had no Intention to
give it up ; befides, nothing is more common
than to ufe *de, ab, & ex integro,* inftead of *de
novo.* Virg. Ecl. 4. 5.
Magnus ab integro feclorum nafcitur Ordo.
27 *Exigendæ funt prius. Prius* for *potius. Exigere,* is here to reject or damn ;
explodere, exfibilare, as in the Prologue to
the Stepmother. *Novas qui exactas.* v. 4.

P.

*In this Scene, Simo first shews that great Care ought to be
taken in the Education of Youth, because their Manners are
formed by those with whom they converse : He then opens his
Design to Sosia, of disengaging his Son from his Mistress, by
the Pretence of a Marriage.*

SIMO, SOSIA.

Simo. YOU there, carry these Things in, be gone: *Sosia* come
hither, I want a few Words with you.

Sosia. Imagine them already said ; you'd have these
Things carefully look'd after.

Si. Nay, 'tis quite another Affair.

So. What, pray, can my little Skill be farther useful to you in
than this ?

Si. There's no great need of this Skill of yours, to what I have
now in my Mind : I only want that Fidelity and Secrecy, which I
have always remark'd in you.

So. I wait your Pleasure.

Si. You know what an easy gentle Service you have had with me
from a Child, when I first bought you : I even at last granted you
your Freedom, because you had served well and faithfully : Thus
I made you the best Recompence in my power.

So.

ANNOTATIONS.

[1] VOS *istæc intro auferte.* The Scene
opens with *Simo* returning from the
Forum, followed by some Servants. From
his manner of Address to them, we may
suppose that they were bringing home some
Provisions, which he commands them to
carry in. This Conjecture is rendered extremely probable from the Answer of *Sosia,*
on which Criticks observe that the Verb
curare was proper to Cookery and Dressing.
Madam *Dacier* too tells us, that in an ancient Manuscript, where Figures were prefixed
to each Scene ; that at the Beginning of the
Andrian represents two Slaves entering *Si-*

mo's House, one of whom carries a Bottle ;
and the other some Fishes. There you also
see *Sosia* advancing to *Simo,* and holding a
large Spoon in his Hand, which sufficiently
marks his Office, and that *nempe ut curentur recte hæc,* must be understood as the
Language of Cookery.

Ibid. *Sosia adesdum.* This long Discourse
which *Simo* holds with *Sosia,* is well conceived by the Poet, as it serves to explain
the Fable, and give us such an Insight into
the Plot, as was necessary to make us understand it. The whole too is so contrived,
that we find ourselves insensibly prepossess'd

in

In hac scena Simo imprimis ostendit rectam educationem esse adhibendam, cum sumantur a conversationibus mores : ad postremum etiam aperit, quo consilio se daturum illi uxorem simulare, eumque ab amica avellere statuerit.

SIMO, SOSIA.

VOS istæc intro auferte : abite. Sosia,
Adesdum : paucis te volo. So. dictum puta :
Nempe ut curentur recte hæc. SI. imo iliud.
 So. quid est,
Quod tibi mea ars efficere hôc possit amplius ?
SI. Nihil istac opus est arte ad hanc rem, quam paro : 5
Sed his, quas semper in te intellexi sitas,
Fide & taciturnitate. So. exspecto quid velis.
SI. Ego postquam te emi, à parvulo, ut semper tibi
Apud me justa & clemens fuerit servitus,
Scis : feci, è servo ut esses libertus mihi,   10
Propterea quod serviebas liberaliter.
Quod habui summum precium, persolvi tibi.

ORDO.
SI. VOS, servi, auferte istæc intro : abite. Sosia adesdum : volo alloqui te paucisverbis. So. Puta esse jam dictum : nempe vis ut hæc curentur recte. SI. Imo est aliud. So. Quid est quod mea ars possit efficere tibi amplius hoc ? SI. Est nihil opus istac arte ad hanc rem quam paro : sed opus est his solum virtutibus, quas ego semper intellexi esse sitas in te, nempe fide & taciturnitate. So. Expecto quid velis. SI. Postquam ego emi te à parvulo, scis ut servitus clemens & justa fuerit semper tibi apud me : fecit ut è servo esses libertus mihi, propterea quod serviebas liberaliter. Persolvi tibi summum pretium quod habui.

ANNOTATIONS.

in favour of the chief Persons of the Play, and cannot avoid interesting ourselves in their Fortune ; which is one of the grand Secrets in this way of writing.

² *Dictum puta.* As much as to say, I *understand you before you go any farther, and therefore you may fancy you have told me already.* It was a Phrase always used in this Sense, in common Conversation. Slaves piqued themselves upon being able to understand their Masters at a single Word or Nod.

⁵ *Nihil istac opus est arte---sed iis.* The word *Ars* had a very extensive Signification among the *Romans,* and served to express any

Skill or Knowledge whatever, as here it is applied to Cookery, and the Virtues of Secresy and Fidelity. Hence one that knew nothing, nor was trained up to any Employment, was termed *iners.*

⁹ *Justa & clemens fuerit servitus. Justa servitus* is not here to be understood in the Language of Lawyers as a *just Service,* i. e. *a Service legally acquired :* But an easy moderate Service, where nothing rigorous or hard was demanded. *Justus* is often used in *Latin* Authors for *bonus,* and *injustus* for *crudelis,* or *durus.*

¹⁰ *È servo ut esses libertus mihi. Dona-*

    tus

So. I always, Sir, bear it in mind.

Si. 'Tis what I by no means repent of.

So. I am overjoy'd, *Simo*, if I either have done, or can do any thing to pleafe you; and fincerely thank you, that my Service has been fo well received: But after all, this makes me fomewhat uneafy, for your reminding me in this manner feems to reproach me with a Forgetfulnefs of your Favours: Be but fo good as tell me in one word, what it is you would have me do.

Si. I'll do fo. Firft, then, I'm to tell you in this Affair, that the Marriage you look upon as now concluded, is all mere Pretence.

So. Why do you fo give out then?

Si. You fhall hear the whole matter from the beginning: by this means you'll become acquainted with my Son's Life, fee into my Defign, and underftand what Part I'd have you to act in the Affair: For when he came to be of age, *Sofia*, I allow'd him a freer Way of Life; for how otherwife was it poffible to difcover his Genius and Turn, feeing hitherto Age, Fear, and a Mafter had kept him in awe.

So. It is fo.

Si. As it is natural for almoft all young Men to fet their Minds upon fome one darling Purfuit; as training up of Horfes; or Dogs for Hunting; or reading the Philofophers: he fhew'd an extreme Fondnefs for no one of thefe more than another, and yet ftudied all with moderation. I was overjoy'd.

So. And not without reafon; for I take it to be a very ufeful Maxim in Life, to follow nothing too eagerly.

Si. After this manner was his Life fram'd, to be frank and eafy with

ANNOTATIONS.

tus obferves here, that there is a wonderful Elegance in the addition of *e fervo*, as it ferves the more ftrongly to exprefs the Greatnefs of the Favour he had done him, and is perfectly conformable to the Character of old Men, who love to repeat their good Offices, and enhance the Value of them as much as poffible. We fhall here once for all obferve, that among the *Romans*, fuch as were free of the City, were diftinguifhed into *Ingenui, Libertins,* and *Liberti.* The *Ingenui* were fuch as had been born free, and of Parents that had been always free. The *Libertini* were the Children of fuch as had been made free. *Liberti,* fuch as had been actually made free themfelves.

[13] *Haud muto factum. I don't repent.* For to change from what we have done, always intimates that we are diffatisfied with it.

[16] *Iftbæc commemoratio quafi exprobratio eft,* &c. It was a Saying among the *Greeks: When you receive a Kindnefs, remember it; when you do a Kindnefs, forget.* To re- proach Perfons with the Favours we do them, is cancelling the Obligation at once. The only excufe we can plead in this Cafe, is where the Perfon obliged proves ungrateful; and indeed where paft Kindneffes are repeated, it is always thought to imply, either that we are diffatisfied with the Perfon on whom they were beftowed, or defign to afk fome Favour in our turn. *Sofia* had therefore reafon to be fomewhat uneafy at his Mafter's Manner of talking. Our Poet's Sentiments are always juft, and adapted to the Characters and Circumftances of the Perfons that fpeak.

[19] *Prædico tibi.* There is a particular Emphafis in the word *prædico. Sofia* had faid, *Quin tu uno verbo dic: Simo,* by this, lets him know, that it would require fome time. We are alfo to obferve, that this Verb, befides its common Signification relating to Things future, is alfo often ufed to exprefs what is premifed in Difcourfe. Thus *Cornelius Nepos,* in his Life of *Themiftocles,* Cap. vii. *Cum his collegas fuos Themiftocles*

So. In memoriâ habeo.   Si. haud muto factum.   So.
  gaudeo,
Si tibi quid feci, aut facio, quod placeat, Simo : &,
Id gratum fuiſſe advorſum te, habeo gratiam.   15
Sed mî hoc moleſtum eſt : nam iſtæc cómmemoratio
Quaſi exprobratio eſt immemoris beneficî.
Quin tu uno verbo dic, quid eſt quod me velis.
Si. Ita faciam. hoc primum in hac re prædico tibi,
Quas credis eſſe has, non ſunt veræ nuptiæ.   20
So. Cur ſimulas igitur ? Si. rem omnem à principio
  audies :
Eo pacto & gnati vitam, & conſilium meum
Cognoſces, & quid facere in hac re te velim.
Nam is poſtquam exceſſit ex ephebis, Soſia,
Liberiùs vivendi fuit poteſtas.   nam antea   25
Quî ſcire poſſes, aut ingenium noſcere,
Dum ætas, metus, magiſter prohibebant ? So. ita eſt.
Si. Quod plerique omnes faciunt adoleſcentuli,
Ut animum ad aliquod ſtudium adjungant, aut equos
Alere, aut canes ad venandum, aut ad philoſophos ; 30
Horum ille nihil egregiè præter cætera
Studebat, & tamen omnia hæc mediocriter.
Gaudebam.   So. non injuriâ : nam id arbitror
Adprimè in vita eſſe utile, ut ne quid nimis.
Si. Sic vita erat, facile omnes preferre ac pati :   35

fuit ei poteſtas vivendi liberius. Nam antea, quî poſſes ſcire aut noſcere ingenium ejus, dum ætas, metus, & magiſter prohibebant liberam agendi poteſtatem. So. Ita eſt. Si. Quod plerique omnes adoleſcentuli faciunt, ut adjungant animum ad aliquod ſtudium, aut alere equos, aut canes ad venandum, aut ad philoſophos : ille ſtudebat nihil horum egregiè præter cætera, & tamen ſtudebat omnia hæc mediocriter : gaudebam. So. Non injuriâ : nam arbitror id eſſe apprimè utile in vita ; ut ne quid ſit nimis. Si. Vita ejus erat ſic : faciſè preferre ac pati omnes :

So. Habeo in memoria. Si. Haud muto factum.' So. Gaudeo, ſi feci, aut facio, quid tibi, Simo, quod placeat : & habeo gratiam, id fuiſſe gratum, adverſum te. Sed hoc eſt moleſtum mihi ; nam iſtæc commemoratio eſt quaſi exprobratio immemoris beneficii. Quin dic tu uno verbo, quid eſt quod velis me facere. Si. Faciam ita. Sed prædico hoc primum tibi in hac re, hæ nuptiæ quas credis eſſe veras, non ſunt veræ nuptiæ. So. Cur igitur ſimulas ? Si. Audies omnem rem à principio : eo facto & cognoſces vitam gnati mei, & quid velim te facere in hac re. Nam poſtquam is, Soſia, exceſſit ex ephebis,

---

ANNOTATIONS.

miſtocles juſſit proficiſci : eiſque prædixit, ut ne prius Lacedæmoniorum legatos dimitterent, quam ipſe eſſet remiſſus.
²⁺ *Poſtquam exceſſit ex ephebis. Ephebus* is a word of *Greek* derivation, and ſignifies properly one who has arrived at his fifteenth Year, which was what the *Romans* called the Age of *Puberty. Simo's* Manner of introducing this Account is natural and eaſy, and was neceſſary to let us into the Poet's Deſign. His Obſervations too are extremely juſt, and in Character ; the natural Language of old Age and Experience.
³⁺ *Adprime*, &c.   A Particle of Confirmation. *Ne quid nimis*, a common Proverb, and therefore no way improper in the mouth of a Servant. Theſe general Sentences are for the moſt part Obſervations

drawn from Life itſelf, the very Dictates of Wiſdom, and confirmed to be juſt by long Experience. Their Simplicity and Brevity makes us often overlook the deep Senſe contained in them. The preſent may ſerve as an Inſtance of it, being in nothing different from theſe two celebrated and often quoted Lines of *Horace :*

Eſt modus in rebus, ſunt certi denique fines,
Quos ultra citraque nequit conſiſtere rectum.

" There is a Meaſure in Things, there are
" in ſhort fixed and ſtated Bounds, on either
" ſide of which Virtue cannot be found."
Plato obſerves that the Ancients included their whole Syſtem of Morality in theſe ſhort proverbial Sentences.

with all who were his moſt ordinary Companions ; to addict himſelf wholly to them, and comply with their Humours ; contradict-
ing none, never claiming the Preference to others: thus with eaſe
may one gain Praiſe without Envy, and make ſure of Friends.

So. It was to be ſure a wiſe Courſe ; for as Times now are, Complaiſance gains Friends, whereas Plain-dealing makes us diſagreeable.

Si. Meantime, a certain Woman, about three Years ago, came to
this Neighbourhood from *Andros*, compelled by Poverty, and the
Neglect of her Relations ; of exquiſite Beauty, and in the Flower of
her Age.

So. Alas ! I am much afraid that this *Andrian* bodes ſome Miſchief.

Si. At firſt, indeed, ſhe led a chaſte, frugal, and induſtrious Life,
gaining her Livelihood by the Diſtaff and Loom ; but a Lover addreſſing her with Promiſes to reward her Favours, and the Suit being urged by a ſecond, and a third, as the Mind is naturally averſe to
Labour, and ſtrongly bent upon Pleaſure, ſhe yielded to their Offers,
and at laſt began a Trade of it. By ill luck, ſome of her Gallants,
as often happens in theſe Caſes, carried my Son along with them for
Company's ſake. Surely, thought I with myſelf, he's caught, he has
it. Early next Morning, I watched their Servants coming and going : Hark ye me, my Boy, ſaid I, tell me honeſtly, to whoſe Lot
fell *Chryſis* laſt Night ? for you muſt know, that was the Name
this *Andrian* went by.

So. I underſtand.

Si. Phædrus, they tell me, or *Clinias*, or *Niceratus* ; for all theſe
three

A N N O T A T I O N S.

36 *His ſeſe dedere.* That is, to comply with their Wills, and ſuit himſelf to
their Tempers. The Expreſſion is borrowed from War, when an Army, that has
been defeated, ſurrenders to the Conquerors,
and therefore is ſometimes made to ſignify
an abſolute and ſlaviſh Submiſſion. Whence
Thraſo in the *Eunuch.* Act v. Sc. viii. ver. 2.
*Egone ? ut Thaidi me dedam, et faciam quod
jubeat.* But here the Expreſſion is to be ſof-
tened a little, as importing only a Compliance
from Inclination, and a certain natural Sweetneſs of Diſpoſition.

41 *Obſequium amicos, veritas odium parit.*
Madam *Dacier* very juſtly remarks here,
that when *Simo* ſpeaks of his Son's Complaiſance, he means an honeſt Complaiſance,
remote from Flattery, and that did not inter-
fere with Truth. To ſuppoſe the contrary,
would be to make him blame inſtead of com-
mending his Son. But as Servants are not always capable of entering into theſe nice Differences, *Soſia* takes occaſion from thence
to inveigh againſt the Age, by ſaying that

it was offended with the Truth. Thus he
takes *obſequium*, which properly ſignifies
Sweetneſs of Manners, for a mean ſervile
Flattery ; the moſt hateful and contemptible of all Vices. There is an inimitable
Juſtneſs in all *Terence's* Characters. Whoever has taken any pains to examine the
Manners of low Life, will find that their
Converſation is frequently interlaced with
theſe common and general Reflections, which
they treaſure up, and, as they often include
their whole Stock of Knowledge, are fond
of uttering them on all Occaſions.

47 *Primum hæc pudice vitam.* The Poet
here ſhews an extreme Addreſs in giving the
Character of *Chryſis*. He repreſents her as
not wicked through Inclination, but Neceſſity, after ſhe had for a long Time ſtrug-
gled with her adverſe Fortune. And afterwards, in the Account which *Pamphilus*
gives of his laſt Conference with her, we
are inſenſibly led to form Idea's very much in
her Favour, and forget her Error, or at leaſt
think it in ſome meaſure excuſable, on account

Cum quibus erat eunqua unà, his sese dedere,
Eorum obsequi studiis : advorsus nemini ;
Nunquam præponens se aliis. ita facillimè
Sine invidiâ invenias laudem, & amicos pares.
So. Sapienter vitam instituit : namque hoc tempore 40
Obsequium amicos, veritas odium parit.
Si. Interea mulier quædam abhinc triennium
Ex Andro commigravit huc viciniæ,
Inopiâ & cognatorum neglegentiâ
Coacta, egregiâ formâ, atque ætate integrâ. '45
So. Hei vereor, ne quid Andria apportet mali.
Si. Primum hæc pudicè vitam, parcè ac duriter
Agebat, lanâ ac telâ victum quæritans.
Sed postquam amans accessit, precium pollicens,
Unus, & item alter ; ita ut ingenium est omnium 50
Hominum à labore proclive ad lubidinem ;
Accepit conditionem : dein quæstum occipit.
Qui tum illam amabant, fortè, ita ut sit, filium
Perduxere illuc secum, ut unà esset, meum.
Egomet continuò mecum : Certe captus est : 55
Habet. observabam manè illorum servulos
Venientes, aut abeuntes : rogitabam, Heus puer,
Dic sodes, quis herì Chrysidem habuit? nam Andriæ
Illi id erat nomen. So. teneo. Si. Phædrum, aut Cli-
niam

cum quibus cunque erat unà, dedere sese his, obsequi studiis eorum : adversus nemini ; nunquam præponens se aliis ; ita facillime inve- nias laudem sine in- vidiâ, & pares amicos. So. Insti- tuit vitam sapien- ter : namque hoc tempore obsequium parit amicos, veri- tas parit odium. Si. Interia ciciter tri- ennium abhinc, mu- lier quædam com- migravit ex insula Andro huc viciniæ, coactâ inopiâ & negligentiâ cogna- torum, formâ egre- giâ atque integra ætate. So. Hei! ve- reor ne hæc Andria apportet quid ma- li. Si. Hæc pri- mum agebat vitam pudicè, parcè, ac duriter ; quæritans victum lanâ ac telâ ; sed postquam unus

& item alter amans accessit pollicens pretium, ita ut ingenium omnium hominum est proclive ad labore ad libidinem ; illa accepit conditionem : deinde occipit quæstum. Hi qui tum amabant illam, forte, ut sæpe sit, perduxere filium meum illuc secum, ut esset unà. Egomet cogitavi continuo mecum, Certe captus est, habet vulnus. Observabam manè servulos illorum venientes, aut abeuntes, rogi- tabam illos : Heus puer, dic sodes, quis habuit Chrysidem herì ? nam id erat nomen illi Andriæ. So. Teneo. Si. Dicebant Phædrum, aut Cliniam,

ANNOTATIONS.

count of her other good Qualities. All this was necessary to prevent our receiving any disadvantageous Impression of *Glycery*, who passed for her Sister, but was afterwards to be the Daughter of *Chremes*, and Wife of *Pamphilus*.

55 *Captus est, habet.* Expressions bor- rowed from the Combats of the Gladiators in the *Circus*. When any Person received a remarkable Wound, either his Adversary, or the People used to cry out *habet*, or *hoc habet*. Again, the *Retiarius*, who was al- ways matched with the *Secutor*, was dressed in a short Coat, having a *Fuscina* or Trident in his Left-hand, and a Net in his right, with which he endeavoured to entangle his Adversary, and then with his Trident might easily dispatch him. If, in throwing his Net, he happened to be successful, and found his Adversary fairly in his power, the com-

mon Cry was *Captus est*. His Antagonist, as we have already observed, was always the *Secutor*, and so called, because, if the *Re- tiarius* should happen to fail in casting his Net, his only Safety lay in flight ; so that in this Case he ply'd his Heels as fast as he could about the Place of Combat, till he had got his Net in order for a second Throw : In the mean time, this *Secutor*, or Follower pursued him, and endeavoured to prevent his Design. He was armed with a Buckler, and a Helmet, whereon was the Picture of a Fish, in allusion to the Net of his Adversary. His Weapon was a Scyme- tar, or *Falx supina*.

53 *Dic sodes.* Instead of *dic si audes*, and means the same as in our Language, *pray tell me*, or tell me honestly. *Cicero, Orator.*
45. *Libenter etiam copulando verba junge- bunt, ut sodes pro si audes, sis pro si vis.*

C 3

61. *Symbo-*

three were at that time her profeſt Lovers. Ay, but what then did *Pamphilus?* What? why he ſup'd, and paid his Club. I was overjoy'd. In like manner I enquired again another day; ſtill I found that nothing fell to the ſhare of *Pamphilus.* By this time I thought him ſufficiently tried, and a great Example of Moderation; for he who encounters with Men of this Temper, and yet has not his Mind infected by their Vices, may ſafely be truſted with the Manage-ment of himſelf. As I was thus pleaſed with his Behaviour, ſo all my Neighbours began to compliment me upon it, and praiſe my good Fortune, in having a Son of ſo promiſing a Diſpoſition. What need of many Words? *Chremes,* encouraged by this Report, came of his own accord to offer his only Daughter in Marriage, with a large Portion, the Propoſal pleaſed me, I agreed to it, and this is the Day appointed for the Wedding.

So. What hinders it then from now being conſummated?

Si. You ſhall hear. A few Days after, while theſe Things are yet unſettled, *Chryſis,* this Neighbour of ours, dies.

So. O happy Chance! you pleaſe me much: to ſay truth, I dreaded ſome Miſchief from this *Chryſis.*

Si. My Son, upon this, went frequently thither, with thoſe who had been Lovers of *Chryſis,* and join'd with them in the Care of her Funeral; he appear'd too ſomewhat dejected, and would now and then drop a few Tears. I own it gave me Pleaſure, for thus I thought with myſelf: Ha, to be ſo much concern'd at her Death upon ſo ſlight an Acquaintance! What, if he had loved her himſelf? In what manner would he grieve for me, who am his Father? I fondly believed that theſe were all Marks of a humane Temper, and compaſſionate Mind. But, why do I thus make a long Story of it? I myſelf too, to humour him, went out to the Funeral, far from ſuſpecting any harm.

So. Hah! What is it you ſay?

Si. You ſhall know. The Body is brought out, we move for-ward with it. Meanwhile, amongſt the Women, who were there pre-ſent, I chanced to caſt my Eye upon a young Creature of an Air—

So. Good perhaps.

Si. And of a Look, *Soſia,* ſo full of Modeſty and Sweetneſs,
that

ANNOTATIONS.

61 *Symbolam dedit. Symbola* is a Word ori-g'nally *Greek,* and of the ſame ſignification with the *Latin, Collatio.* It was commonly uſed for a Man's *Club,* or Share of a Reck-oning.

66 *Cum ingeniis conflictatur ejuſmodi.* There is a particular Emphaſis and Force in the Word *conflictatur.* It marks the Shock of ſeveral ſolid Bodies meeting toge-ther from oppoſite Directions, and endea-vouring to overpower each other's Motion: and ſerves admirably well to expreſs here all the Aſſaults which a good natured Diſ-

poſition muſt ſuſtain in commerce with de-praved Tempers.

75 *Deſpondi. Donatus* diſtinguiſhes be-tween *ſpondere* and *deſpondere,* making the firſt proper to him who aſked another in Marriage for his Son or Daughter, and the other to him who promiſed. But we don't find that the *Latin* Writers make any ſuch nice Diſtinction. *Deſponderé;* for the moſt part, ſignifies no more than to promiſe frank-ly; the Prepoſition *de* increaſing commonly the Signification of the Verb, to which it is join'd.   80 *Una*

Dicebant, aut Niceratum. nam hi tres tum fimul   60
Amabant. Eho, quid Pamphilus? Quid? fymbolam
Dedit, cœnavit. gaudebam. item alio die
Quærebam : comperiebam nihil ad Pamphilum
Quidquam attinere. enimvero fpeétatum fatis
Putabam, & magnum exemplum continentiæ.   65
Nam qui cum ingeniis confliétatur ejufmodi,
Neque commoveter animus in câ re tamen,
Scias poffe habere jam ipfum fuæ vitæ modum.
Cùm id mihi placebat, tum uno ore omnes omnia
Bona dicere, & laudare fortunas meas,   70
Qui gnatum haberem tali ingenio præditum.
Quid verbis opus eft ? hac famâ impulfus Chremes
Ultro ad me venit, unicam gnatam fuam
Cum dote fummâ filio uxorem ut daret.
Placuit, defpondi : his nuptiis diétus eft dies.   75
So. Quid obftat, cur non veræ fiant? Si. audies.
Ferè in diebus paucis, quibus hæc aéta funt,
Chryfis vicina hæc moritur. So. ô faétum bene !
Beafti : metui à Chryfide. Si. ibi tum filius
Cum illis, qui amabant Chryfidem, unà aderat fre-
    quens :   80
Curabat unà funus: triftis interim,
Nonnunquam conlacrumabat. placuit tum id mihi.
Sic cogitabam : Hem, hic, parvæ confuetudinis
Causâ, mortem hujus tam fert familiariter :
Quid fi ipfe amaffet ? quid mihi hic faciet patri ?   85
Hæc ego putabam effe omnia humani ingeni
Manfuetique animi officia. quid multis moror ?
Egomet quoque ejus causâ in funus prodeo
Nil fufpicans etiam mali. So. hem, quid eft ? Si. fcies.
Effertur. imus. interea inter mulieres,   90
Quæ ibi aderant, fortè unam afpicio adolefcentulam,
Formâ.—So. bonâ fortaffe. Si. & voltu, Sofia,

aut Niceratum; nam bi tres fimul tum amabant illam: Eho dixi, quid Pamphilus fecit ? Quid ? refpondebant, dedit fymbolam, cœnavit : gaudebam, quærebam item alio die : comperiebam nihil quidquam attinere ad Pamphilum. Enimvero putabam cum fpeétatum fatis, & effe magnum exemplum continentiæ ; nam qui confliétatur cum ingeniis ejufmodi, neque tamen animus ejus commovetur in eâ re, fcias ipfum poffe jam habere modum fuæ vitæ. Cum id placebat mihi, tum omnes vicini cœperunt uno ore dicere omnia bona, & laudare meas fortunas, qui haberem gnatum præditum tali ingenio. Quid opus eft verbis ? Chromes, impulfus hac fama, venit ultro ad me, ut daret unicam fuam gnatam uxorem filio cum fumma dote: hæc propofitio placuit mihi, defpondi filium: hic dies diétu eft nuptiis. So. Quid obftat igitur, cur nuptiæ

non fiant veræ ? Si. Audies. Ferè in paucis diebus quibus hæc funt aéta, Chryfis hæc vicina moritur. So. O bene faétum ! beafti me, metui aliquid mali à Chryfide. Si. Tum filius meus aderat frequens ibi, una cum illis qui amebant Chryfidem, curabat funus ejus unà cum illis, interim triftis, nonnunquam collacrimabat. Id tum placuit mihi, cogitabam fic : Hem, hic fert mortem hujus Andriæ tam familiariter, causâ parvæ confuetudinis : quid fi ipfe amaffet ? quid hic faciet mihi patri ? Ego putabam hæc omnia effe officia humani ingenii, marfuetique animi. Quid moror te multis verbis ? Egomet quoque prodes in funus ejus causâ, fufpicans etiam nihil mali. So. Hem, quid eft ? Si. Scies. Mortua effertur. Imus ; interea inter mulieres, quæ aderant ibi, afpicio forte unam adolefcentulam, formâ. So. Fortaffe bonâ. Si. Et voltu, Sofia.

ANNOTATIONS.

80 *Una aderat frequens. Frequens*, fays Donatus, *ut miles apud figna.* The Word is borrowed from the Military Art among the Romans, where *frequentes* was ufed of Soldiers that were always at their Colours.

84 *Tam fert familiariter. Familiariter*, with fo much *Concern.* The old Man means,

that his Son appeared as much dejeéted at *Chryfis's* Death, who was but flightly known to him, as if fhe had long been his familiar Acquaintance, or one of the fame Family with him.

92 *Et voltu, Sofia, &c.* The Poet here very artfully reprefents the old Man, as ftruck

that nothing could exceed it. As she seemed to be much more dejected than any of the rest, and had something in her Appearance
far more graceful and becoming; I went up to the Servants, to enquire who she was. They told me, that she was the Sister of *Chrysis*.
The thing immediately struck me: Nay, nay, think I with myself,
here then is the whole Business, *'tis easy to guess* whence these Tears,
and why all this seeming Compassion.

So. How I tremble to think where all this may end!

Si. Meantime, the Funeral proceeds, we follow, and arrive at the
Sepulchre; the Body is laid upon the Pile; the Company weeps:
then this Sister, I was speaking of, ran up to the Fire very imprudently, and even not without manifest Danger. It was then, that
Pamphilus, in his Fright, discovered the Love he had hitherto so well
dissembled and concealed. He runs up to her, catches her in his
Arms, My *Glycery*, says he, what are you doing? Why would you
thus destroy yourself? when she, all in Tears, fell back upon him
with an Air of tender Familiarity, that made it easy to guess at their
former Love.

So. What do you tell me!

Si. I return home angry, and in great discontent, nor was there
a sufficient Pretence for chiding him. He might say to me; What
have I done, Father? What's my Offence, or wherein am I worthy
of blame? I prevented a Girl from throwing herself into the Flames,
I saved her Life. The Defence is good.

So. You judge right; for if you quarrel with a Man, for saving
another's Life, how would you behave to him, who is guilty of
Violence or Injustice?

Si. Chremes comes to me next day, crying out against this indecent Behaviour of my Son, and telling me he understood for certain,
that this Stranger was his Wife. I positively assured him there was
nothing in it; he insisted there was. In fine, I parted with him in
such

ANNOTATIONS.

struck with the Form and Appearance of
Glycery, that having no other Objection to
her, but her being a Stranger of uncertain
Birth; as soon as that was removed, he
might without hesitation agree to the Match.
Venustus signifies, properly, beautiful or graceful, from *Venus*.

96 *Honesta & liberali*. *Honestus* is often
used, especially by the Poets, instead of
pulcher, decorus. So *Virg. Geor.* II, 391. of
Bacchus:

Et quocunque Deus circum caput agit ho-
nestum

h. e. *Pulchrum. Liberali*, i. e. *qualis*
decet virgines liberas, & honeste educatas.
Thus a Marriage betwixt two, who were
both free and Citizens, is afterwards called,

Conjugium liberale. Pedisequæ, Maids that
followed her on Foot, from *pes* and *se-*
quor.

109 *Rejecit se in cum, flens, quam famili-*
ariter. The word *familiariter*, in the Original, conveys a stronger Idea, than *famili-*
arly in our Language: for which reason, to
give the Poet's full meaning, I have rendred it; *With an Air of tender Familiarity*.
For that *familiariter* often implies Tenderness and Concern, is plain from what we
have said above, on *hujus mortem tam fert fa-*
miliariter.

110 *Quid ais!* *Sosia* here interrupts
the old Man with an Air of Astonishment,
as surprized at what he told him. There
ought, therefore, to follow a Point of Admiration,

Adeo modefto, adeo venufto, ut nihil fuprà,
Quia tum mihi lamentari præter cæteras
Vifa eft, & quia erat formâ præter cæteras   95
Honeftâ & liberali ; accedo ad pedifequas :
Quæ fit, rogo. fororem effe aiunt Chryfidis.
Percuffit illico animum.   At at, hoc illud eft,
Hinc illæ lacrumæ, hæc illa eft mifericordia.   99
So. Quàm timeo quorfum evadas. Si. funus interim
Procedit : fequimur : ad fepulcrum venimus.
In ignem impofita eft. fletur. interea hæc foror,
Quam dixi, ad flammam acceffit imprudentiùs,
Sati' cum periclo. ibi tum exanimatus Pamphilus
Bene diffimulatum amorem & celatum indicat.   105
Accurrit : mediam mulierem complectitur :
Mea Glycerium, inquit, quid agis ? cur te is perditum ?
Tum illa, ut confuetum facilè amorem cerneres,
Rejecit fe in eum, flens, quàm familiariter.
So. Quid ais ? Si. redeo inde iratus, atque ægrè ferens.
Nec fatis ad abjurgandum caufæ. diceret,   111
Quid feci ? quid commerui aut peccavi, pater ?
Quæ fefe voluit in ignem injicere, prohibui,
Servavi. honefta oratio eft. So. rectè putas :
Nam fi illum objurges, vitæ qui auxilium tulit ;   115
Quid facias illi, qui dederit damnum, aut malum ?
Si. Venit Chremes poftridiè ad me, clamitans,
Indignum facinus, comperiffe Pamphilum
Pro uxore habere hanc perigrinam. ego illud fedulò
Negare factum. ille inftat factum. denique   120

Adeo modefto, adeo venufto, ut nihil poffit concipi fuprà. Quia tum eft vifa mihi lamentari præter cæteras, & quia erat formâ honeftâ & liberali præter cæteras ; accedo ad pedifequas, rogo quæ fit : aiunt eam effe fororem Chryfidis. Illico percuffit animum. At at, cogitabam mihi, hoc eft illud, hinc funt illæ lacrumæ. hæc eft illa mifericordia. So. Quàm timeo quorfum evadas. Si. Interim funus procedit : nos fequimur ; venimus ad fepulchrum, mortua eft impofita in ignem : fletur. Interea hæc foror Chryfidis, quam dixi, acceffit imprudentius ad flammam cum fatis periclo. Tum ibi Pamphilus exanimatus indicat amorem fuum hucufque bene diffimulatum & celatum ; accurrit, complectitur mediam mulierem. Inquit, Mea Glycerium, quid agis ? cur is perditum te ? tum illa flens, rejecit fe in eum quam familiariter, ut facile cerneres eorum confuetum amorem. So. Quid ais ? Si. Redeo inde iratus, atque ferens ægrè, nec erat fatis caufæ ad objurgandum : diceret, Quid feci, pater ? quid commerui aut peccavi ? quæ voluit injicere fefe in ignem, prohibui eam, fervavi. Oratio eft honefte. So. Putas rectè : nam fi objurges illum, qui tulit auxilium vitæ, quid facias illi, qui dederit damnum aut malum ? Si. Poftridiè Chremes venit ad me, clamitans indignum facinus ! fe comperiffe Pamphilum habere hanc peregrinam pro uxore. Ego cæpi fedulo negare illud effe factum, ille inftat effe factum. denique,

---

ANNOTATIONS.

miration, not of Interrogation, as fome have inconfiderately marked it.

111 *Nec fatis ad objurgandum caufæ.* Simo admirably well fupports the Character of a Father, anxious and concerned for his Son, but willing to act tenderly, and not chide him, without fufficient Grounds. He does not in the leaft doubt of his having fome Engagement with this Stranger ; yet forefees that he can make a good Defence. He did no more than an Office of common Humanity, and it would be unreasonable to accufe him rafhly on that account, or infer too much from it.

118 *Indignum facinus, comperiffe.* Commentators difagree in their Opinions, how this Sentence ought to be explained. Some join *indignum facinus* with *comperiffe*; Chremes *venit clamitans fe comperiffe indignum facinus,* viz. *Pamphilum habere,* &c. But Donatus, with reafon, rejects this, and obferves, that *indignum facinus* ought to come after *clamitans,* and be diftinguifhed from what follows, by a Point of Admiration thus : *Poftridie Chremes venit ad me clamitans, indignum facinus ! comperiffe Pamphilum habere hanc peregrinam pro uxore.* This laft is the Senfe, that I have chofen to follow,

ſuch manner, as to be ſenſible he no longer intended to marry his Daughter to *Pamphilus*.

So. Did not you, upon this, chide your Son ?

Si. I did not think there was yet ſufficient Cauſe to find. fault.

So. How pray ?

Si. You, Father (might he ſay) have fixed the Period of all theſe Levities, the time draws near, when I muſt ſuit myſelf to the Humour of another; allow me then for the preſent to live a little after my own Taſte.

So. What pretence is therefore left on which to chide him ?

Si. If upon account of his Love he refuſes to marry, this Inſtance of Diſobedience gives me firſt an Opportunity to ſhew my Reſentment. And now my preſent Project is, by this pretended Wedding, to find juſt Cauſe of being angry with him, if he refuſes to agree to it. At the ſame time, that Raſcal *Davus*, if he has any Plot in his Head, let him now put it in execution, when his Tricks can avail nothing : nor do I queſtion, but he'll do all the miſchief in his power, more with a deſign to vex me, than to pleaſe my Son.

So. Why ſo ?

Si. Do you aſk ? a wicked Heart always ſuggeſts wicked Projects. But if I can diſcover any thing of it—yet what need of ſo many Words ? but if it happens, as I would have it, that *Pamphilus* makes no Objection, it then only remains, that I gain over *Chremes*, and all, I hope, will go well. Now, your buſineſs is, to ſupport well this Pretence of the Wedding, to terrify *Davus*, to watch my Son, what he does, and what Counſels they take together.

So. Enough; I'll take care. Let us now go in.

Si.

ANNOTATIONS.

as agreeing better to the Character of *Chremes*, who, thereby, is made to ſpeak with the Concern of a Father-in-Law, for this ill Behaviour of *Pamphilus*.

[122] *Non tu ibi gnatum?* Scil. *objurgaſti.* This is one of thoſe Ellipſes, which are owing to an Exceſs of any Paſſion, as Joy or Grief, that hurries on one's Speech, and will not let them attend to Exactneſs. It, moreover, here implies, that *Sofia* was now almoſt convinced of *Pamphilus*'s Attachment to this Stranger. *Simo* again, to ſhew that he would not be angry with his Son, till he had Juſtice on his ſide ; replies, that even this was not a ſufficient Cauſe of chiding him, and adds the reaſon.

[124] *Tute ipſe bis rebus.* The Father here foreſees, what Defence his Son will make, and owns it to be ſuch as leaves no room for finding fault. We have ſeen above, that when he came to be of Age, *Simo* left him to follow his own Inclinations. His En-

gagement with the *Andrian*, eſpecially as he managed it with ſo much Secreſy and Caution, was a Conſequence of that Liberty, and he might even plead, that he had uſed it with diſcretion, if when Circumſtances altered, and a Wife was offered, he was willing to change his Behaviour, and ſuit it to his State of Life.

[130] *Et nunc id operam do.* *Simo* here lets *Sofia* more particularly into his Deſign, and communicates the Project he had formed to come to the Knowledge of his Son's Sentiments, and find a Pretence of chiding him. If his Attachment to the Stranger prevailed ſo far as to make him averſe to Marriage, there was then ſufficient ground to find fault. But as *Chremes* had gone back in his Propoſal, there was no Opportunity left of forming a Judgment. To remedy this, *Simo* pretends, as if the Wedding ſtill went forward, and wanted *Sofia* to ſecond him in that Deſign. If he found *Pamphilus* averſe,

Ita tum difcedo ab illo, ut qui fe filiam
Neget daturum.   So. non tu ibi gnatum ? Si. ne hæc
    quidem
Sati' vehemens caufa ad objurgandum.   So. qui,
    cedo ?
Si. Tute ipfe his rebus finem præfcripfti, pater,
Prope adeft, cùm alieno more vivendum eft mihi : 125
Sine nunc meo me vivere interea modo.
So. Qui igitur relictus eft objurgandi locus ?
Si. Si propter amorem uxorem nolit ducere,
Ea primum ab illo animadvertenda injuria eft.
Et nunc id operam do, ut per falfas nuptias   130
Vera objurgandi caufa fit, fi deneget:
Simul, fceleratus Davus fi quid confilî
Habet, ut confumat nunc, cùm nihil obfint doli.
Quem ego credo manibus pedibufque obnixè omnia
Facturum; magis id adeo, mihi ut incommodet, 135
Quàm ut obfequatur gnato.   So. quapropter ? Si.
    rogas ?
Mala mens, malus animus. quem quidem ego fi fen-
    fero—
Sed quid opu'ft verbis ? fin eveniat, quod volo,
In Pamphilo ut nihil fit moræ : reftat Chremes,
Qui mihi exorandus eft, & fpero confore.   140
Nunc tuum eft officium, has bene ut adfimules nu-
    ptias .
Perterrefacias Davum ; obferves filium,
Quid agat, quid cum illo confilii captet.   So. fat
    eft :

Ita tum difcedo ab illo, ut qui neget fe daturum filiam Pamphilo. Sô. An non tu ibi objurgafti gnatum? Si. Ne hæc quidem fuit caufa fatis vehemens ad objurgandum. So. Qui, cedo? Si. Diceret, Tute ipfe, pater, præfcripfifti finem his rebus; tempus prope adeft, cùm vivendum eft mihi alieno more; interea fine me vivere nunc meo modo. So. Igitur qui locus objurgandi eft relictus? Si. Si propter amorem nolit ducere uxorem, ea injuria eft primum animadvertenda ab illo. Et nunc do operam ad id, ut per falfas nuptias fit vera caufa objurgandi, fi deneget: Simul fceleratus Davus, fi habet quid confili, ut confumat nunc, cùm doli nihil obfint; quem ego credo fa-

dibufque: id adeo magis ut incommodet mihi, quam ut obfequatur gnato. So. Quapropter ita, cenfes? Si. Rogas? mala mens, malus animus; quem quidem fi ego fenferò-----Sed quid opus eft verbis? fin eveniat, quod volo, ut fit nihil moræ in Pamphilo; Chremes reftat, qui eft exorandus mihi, & fpero confore. Nunc tuum officium eft, ut bene adfimules has nuptias, ut perterrefacias Davum, obferves filium, quid agat, quid confili capiet cùm illo. So Sat eft,

ANNOTATIONS.

averfe, he knew the Danger, and muft take
Meafures accordingly : if, otherwife, there
was hope, that *Chremes* might ftill be prevailed with to comply.

133 *Ut confumat nunc. Confumere confilia,*
implies the bending all one's Care to the
Accomplifhment of a Project, and leaving
nothing unattempted, that 'tis thought may
conduce to it. Thus, *Cicero Fam.* 6. 14.
*Me fcito omnem meum laborem, omnem ope-
ram, curam, ftudium .In tua falute confumere.*

137 *Mala mens, malus animus. A wick-*

ed Heart always fuggefts wicked Projects.
This I take to be the true Senfe of the
Phrafe made ufe of by the Poet. *Animus,*
the Heart conceives wicked Defigns': *Mens,*
the Mind devifes the Means of reducing
them to practice. The one regards the
thing itfelf, the other, the Execution. The
Conclufion of this Speech is wonderfully in
Character. Nothing could more happily
defcribe the Manner of old Age, than thofe
Paufes, Interruptions, and fudden Tranfitions
from one Thought to another, which the
Poet artfully puts into *Simo's* mouth.

Si. Do you go firſt, I'll follow. (*To himſelf.*) There is no doubt but my Son will refuſe to marry; for ſo *Davus* ſeemed to appre-hend, but juſt now, when he heard that the Match was to be. But here he comes.

ANNOTATIONS.

¹⁴³ *Non dubium eſt,* &c. *Simo* having communicated his Deſign to *Soſia*; and giv-en him the proper Inſtructions, his Pre- | ſence was no longer neceſſary. He is, there-fore, diſmiſſed, and the old Man ſuppoſed to remain alone upon the Stage, conjecturing with

---

ACT I. SCENE II.

ARGUMENT.

The old Man endeavours to find out his Son's Intrigue, con-tinues the Pretence of the Wedding, and threatens Davus, if he finds him guilty of any Artifice to obſtruct it.

DAVUS, SIMO.

Davus. (*TO himſelf, not perceiving* Simo.) I was wondering, if this Buſineſs ſhould go off ſo, and always feared where this unuſual Lenity of my Maſter would end, who, after he knew that *Chremes* would not give his Daughter in Marriage to *Pamphilus*, never mentioned it to any of us, nor ſeemed in the leaſt offended at it.

Simo. (*Aſide, over-hearing him.*) But now he will, and that I be-lieve pretty much to your coſt.

Dav. (*Still to himſelf.*) Here was his Project, To ſuffer us to be led away by a falſe Joy, without ever dreaming of his Deſigns; that full of Hopes, and imagining we had nothing more to fear, he might catch us unawares, and leave us no time to plot againſt the Match. Cunning old Fox !

Si. (*Liſtening.*) What is it the Villain ſays ?

Dav. (*Aſide, diſcovering* Simo.) 'Slif; my Maſter, and I never obſerved it.

Si. *Davus !*

Dav. Hah, what's the matter ?

Si. Come hither.

Dav. (*Softly*) What would this old Fellow have ?

Si.

ANNOTATIONS.

' *Mirabar, hec ſi ſic abiret.* *Davus* here comes upon the Stage, and not | obſerving his Maſter, holds this Diſ-courſe with himſelf. His Character, is that of

Curabo : eamus jam nunc intro. Sɪ. i præ, ſequar.   *curabo. Eamus jam*
Non dubium eſt, quin uxorem nolit filius :   145 *nunc intro. Sɪ. I*
Ita Davum modo timere ſenſi, ubi nuptias   *præ, ſequar. Non*
Futuras eſſe audivit. ſed ipſe exit foras.   *eſt dubium, quin*
    filius nolit ducere
    uxorem, ita enim

modò ſenſi Davum timere, ubi audivit nuptias eſſe futuras, ſed ipſe exit foras.

ANNOTATIONS.

with himſelf, how his Son would behave   Converſation with whom makes the Sub-
on this Occaſion ; till at length, *Davus* ap-   ject of the next Scene.
pearing, interrupts his Meditation : the

ACTUS PRIMI SCENA II.

ARGUMENTUM.

*Filii amorem explorat ſenex, ſimulat futuras nuptias ; minatur
Davo ſi quid fallaciæ nuptiis ſtruat.*

DAVUS, SIMO.

ORDO.

Mɪrabar, hoc ſi ſic abiret : & heri ſemper lenitas,   Dᴀ. **M**ɪrabarſi
   Verebar, quorſum evaderet.   *hoc abi-*
Qui, poſtquam audierat non datum iri filio uxorem ſuo,   *ret ſic : & ſemper ve-*
Nunquam cuiquam noſtrûm verbum fecit, neque id   *rebar quorſum leni-*
   ægrè tulit.   *tas heri evaderet.*
Sɪ. At nunc faciet ; neque, ut opinor, ſine tuo ma-   *Qui poſtquam audi-*
   gno malo.   *Sic*   5 *erat uxorem non da-*
Dᴀ. Id voluit, nos ³ ·nec opinantes duci falſo gaudio :   *tum iri ſuo filio, nun-*
Sperantes jam amoto metu, interea oſcitantes opprimi,   *quam fecit verbum*
Ut ne eſſet ſpatium cogitandi ad diſturbandas nuptiás :   *cuiquam noſtrûm,*
Aſtutè ! Sɪ. carnuſex quæ loquitur ! Dᴀ. herus eſt, ne-   *neque tulit id ægrè.*
   que prævideram.   9 *Sɪ. At faciet nunc ;*
Sɪ.Dave.D. hem, quid eſt? Sɪ. ehodum, ad me. Dᴀ. quid   *neque, ut opinor, ſine*
   tuo magno malo.
   Dᴀ. Voluit id, eus
imo, *ſperantes metu nuptiarum jam amoto ; interea opprimi oſcitantes, ut ne eſſet nobis*
ſpatium (tempus) *cogitandi ad diſturbandas nuptias : aſtute !* Sɪ. *Quæ iſte carnifex loquitur ?*
Dᴀ. *Eſt herus, neque prævideram.* Sɪ. *Dave.* Dᴀ. *Hem, quid eſt ?* Sɪ. *Ehodum ad me.*
Dᴀ. *Quid*

nec opinantes sic,
duci falſo gaudio,

ANNOTATIONS.

of a ſly cunning Slave, wholly devoted to   Lenity of the old Man, and ſuſpects that
Pamphilus, and truſted by him in the Ma-   there is ſome Fallacy at bottom. His Con-
nagement of his private Correſpondence with   cern for *Pamphilus* makes him anxious, if
Glycery. His firſt Appearance here is quite   poſſible, to find it out, that he might be
agreeable to this Notion. He wonders at the   able to counterplot him.

Si. (Partly hearing.)   What are you muttering there, Sirrah, *Dav.* About what?

Si. About what? 'Tis the Town-talk, that my Son's in love.

Dav. No doubt: People trouble themselves much about that.

Si. Do you mind what I say to you?

Dav. Yes, Sir, very attentively.

Si. But to examine now too narrowly into these Affairs, would be the Part of a severe Father, for what is paſt no way concerns me.. While the proper Seaſon for theſe Follies continued, I let him ſatisfy himſelf to the full.   But the preſent time requires a different Way of Life, and different Manners.   I therefore expect, or, if it be proper, I even beg of you, *Davus*, that he may now take up and mend.

Dav. What can all this mean?

Si. Young Men, if they happen to be in love, can't bear that a Wife ſhould be forced upon them.

Dav. So they ſay.

Si. Then if ſuch a one has made choice of a knaviſh Counſeller, he is ſure to give the unſettled Mind a wrong Byaſs, by applying to its weak Side.

Dav. Really, Sir, I don't underſtand you.

Si. No? hah.   [*Angrily.*

Dav. No: I'm only *Davus*, not *Oedipus*.

Si. You would then that I ſpeak plainly what I have further to ſay?

Dav. To be ſure.

Si. If I can find you out contriving any Miſchief, to retard my Son's Marriage, or that you want to ſhew how ſhrewd and cunning you are; be aſſured, *Davus*, that you ſhall be ſoundly laſhed, and ſent to *Bridewel* for Life: with this Condition and Promiſe; that, if I ever releaſe you, I will ſuffer myſelf in your room.   What, do you underſtand me now? Or is not even this to be compre-hended?

                                                        Dav.

ANNOTATIONS.

¹² *Id populus curat ſcilicet.* This Anſwer is founded upon the word *Rumor*, which *Simo* had uſed in ſpeaking of his Son's Love: as if it had been a matter of com-mon Report, and what all the People con-cerned themſelves about. *Davus* too by this artfully avoids giving a direct Reply to what his Maſter had ſaid.

¹³ *Hoccine agis? an non?* This was a Form, when they obſerved that no Atten-tion was given to what they ſaid. For *Simo*, directing his Speech to *Davus*, ſays *Mi-um gnatum rumor eſt amare.* *Davus*, as if he had not heard him, makes no Anſwer to his Maſter, but turning to the Spectators,

ſays, *Id populus curat ſcilicet.* *Simo* per-ceiving that *Davus* made him no Anſwer, ſays angrily, *Hoccine agis, an non?* Do you attend to what I ſay? *Davus*, to pacify him, anſwers, *Ego vero iſtuc.* Madam *Dacier* obſerves on this, that in the beſt Authors, the Pronoun *hic* is often uſed for *meus*, and *iſte* for *tuus.* *Hic* is of the firſt Perſon, and *iſte* of the ſecond. Thus the Queſtion put by *Simo*, *Hoccine agis, an non?* ought not to be rendered as ſome by Miſtake have done: *Do you mind what you ſay?* but, *Do you mind what I ſay?* The Maſter interrogates by *hoc*, and *Davus* anſwers by *iſtuc.* This Remark is not ſo incon-ſiderable

hic volt? SI. quid ais? DA. qua de re? SI. rogas?
Meum gnatum rumor eft amare. DA. id populus cu-
rat fcilicet.
SI. Hoccine agis, an non? DA. ego vero iftuc. SI. fed,
nunc ea me exquirere,
Iniqui patris eft. nam, quod antehac fecit, nihil ad
me attinet.
Dum tempus ad eam rem tulit, fivi animum ut exple-
ret fuum : 14
Nunc hic dies aliam vitam adfert, alios mores poftulat.
Dehinc poftulo, five æquum eft, te oro, Dave, ut redeat
jam in viam.
DA. Hoc quid fit? SI. omnes qui amant, graviter fibi
dari uxorem ferunt.
DA. Ita aiunt. SI. tum fi quis magiftrum cepit ad eam
rem improbum,
Ipfum animum ægrotum ad deteriorem partem ple-
rumque applicat.
DA. Non hercle intelligo. SI. non? hem! DA. non:
Davus fum, non Oedipus.
SI. Nempe ergo apertè vis, quæ reftant, me loqui?
DA. fanè quidem.
SI. Si fenfero hodie, quidquam in his te nuptiis
Fallaciæ conari, quo fiant minùs,
Aut velle in eâ re oftendi, quàm fis callidus;
Verberibus cæfum te in priftinum, Dave, dedam uf-
que ad necem;
Eâ lege atque omine, ut, fi te inde exemerim, egõ pro
te molam.
Quid, hoc intellextin'? an nondum etiam ne hoc qui-

bic volt! SI. Quid ais? DA. De qua re? SI. Rogas? eft rumor meum gnatum amare. DA. Scilicet populus curat id. SI. Agis boccine, an non? DA. Ego vero ago iftuc. SI. Sed eft iniqui patris, me exquirere ea nunc; nam quod fecit antebac, attinet nibil ad me. Dum tempus adolefcentiæ tulit illum ad eam rem, fivi ut expleret fuum animum. Nunc bic dies adfert aliam vitam, poftulat alios mores. Debin, poftulo, five æquum eft, oro te, Dave, ut jam redeat in viam. DA. Quid boc fit? SI. Omnes qui amant, ferunt graviter, uxorem dari fibi. DA. Aiunt ita SI. Tum fi quis cepit improbum magiftrum ad eam rem, plerumque applicat ipfum ægrotum animum ad deteriorem partem. DA. Hercle, non intelligo te. SI. Non? bem! aperte quæ reftant? te. SI. Non? bem!

DA. *Non: fum Davus, non fum Oedipus.* SI. *Nempe ergo, vis me loqui aperte quæ reftant?*
DA. *Sane quidem.* SI. *Si fenfero hodie, te conari quidquam fallaciæ in bis nuptiis, quo minus fiant; aut velle oftendi in ea re, quam sis callidus; Dave, dedam te cæfum verberibus, in piftrinum, ufque ad necem, eâ lege, atque omine, ut, ti exemerim te inde, ego molam pro te. Quid, intellexistine boc? an nondum etiam ne quidem boc?*

ANNOTATIONS.

fiderable as at firft fight it may appear.
21 *Davus fum, non Oedipus.* The Story
of *Oedipus*, who folved the Riddle propofed
by the Monfter *Sphinx*, is univerfally known.
Donatus obferves, under this Reply, a nice
and concealed Raillery. *Multiplex contumelia*, fays he, *poteft enim fenem quasi
Sphingem dixiffe, id eft deformem, monftrique
fimilem : poteft etiam inhumanum aut ferum
ut Sphinx.* But this is rather ingenious than
true. *Davus* was unwilling to underftand
what *Simo* faid to him, and therefore endea-
yous, by evafive Anfwers to avoid entringinto
a direct Converfation with him. He therefore pretends that he fpeke in a myfterious

Manner, beyond the reach of his Penetration.
26 *Te in piftrinum, Dave, dedam.* Sent to
Bridewel; literally *to the Grinding-houfe.*
This was the ordinary Punifhment of Slaves,
when they did amifs. They were there employed in grinding Corn, by working the
Mill; a Tafk fo laborious, that Horfes
were commonly ufed in this Service. They
were obliged to labour day and night.
This Prifon was, therefore, of the fame
nature with our *Bridewel*, there being no
other difference, but that Offenders were
condemned to grind Corn in the one, and are
forced to beat Hemp in the other.
27 *Eâ lege atque omine.* This manner of
speaking,

Dav. Oh perfectly well : you have expreſſed yourſelf ſo plainly,
and without circumlocution.

Si. I'll ſuffer myſelf to be deceived in any thing, rather than in this.

Dav. (Jeeringly.) Softly, Sir, ſoftly, I beſeech you.

Si. Do you make a jeſt of it ? I'm not miſtaken in you : but I
warn you, do nothing raſhly, nor think to pretend that you had no
Notice given you.   Take care.

ANNOTATIONS.

ſpeaking is founded upon the Cuſtom of the
Ancients, who in things of conſequence, as
enacting of Laws, or forming of any great
Deſign, always began by taking the Auſpices,
which was held neceſſary to ratify and confirm it. *Lex* properly regards Men, and

the Treaties and Compacts formed among
them. *Omen*, regards the Gods, and our
Engagements to them, *Ea lege atqua omine*,
was, therefore, in a manner, ſwearing by
every thing human and divine.
³⁶ *Ne temere facias.* Some explain *temere :*

ACT I.   SCENE III.

ARGUMENT.

Davus *argues with himſelf, whether he had better aſſiſt* Pamphilus, *or hearken to his Maſter.*

DAVUS.

Davus. VERILY, *Davus*, there is no room for Indolence or Sloth,
as far as I can learn from the old Man's Diſpoſition,
with regard to the Wedding, which, if not artfully provided againſt
will undo either me, or my Maſter.   Nor can I well reſolve what
Part to act : whether I ought to aſſiſt *Pamphilus*, or keep fair with
the old Man.   Should I abandon him, I am in pain for his Life ; if,
again, I aſſiſt him, I dread the other's Threats.   Nor will it be an
eaſy matter to impoſe upon him.   For firſt, he has already diſcovered
ſomewhat of his Son's Love *for this Stranger :* he narrowly watches
me,

ANNOTATIONS.

⁴¹ *Enimvero, Dave,* &c. In this Scene,
Davus remains alone upon the Stage, and
deliberates with himſelf, what he had
beſt do.   On one ſide, his Inclination
leads him to aſſiſt *Pamphilus* ; on the other,
he dreads the Threats of his old Maſter.
This naturally leads his Thoughts to
the Engagements between *Pamphilus* and
Glycery, and the Contrivances they were
falling upon to accompliſh their Deſigns.
By this, the reader is let ſtill farther into

the Circumſtances of the Story, and beginning to intereſt himſelf in the Fate of the
two Lovers, his Impatience to know the final
Event becomes ſtill ſtronger.
    Ibid. *Segnitia neque ſocordia.* Eugra-
phius very judiciouſly diſtinguiſhes the proper meaning of theſe two Words, *Segnitia*
marks a neglect of executing, with dili-
gence, thoſe Expedients, which the Invention ſuggeſted as beſt in the preſent Caſe.
Socordia, again implies, that he ſhould not
be

dem? DA. imo callidè.

Ita apertè ipsam rem modò locutus, nihil circuitione usus es.

SI. Ubivis faciliùs passus sim, quam in hac re, me deludier.

DA. Bona verba quæso. SI. irrides? nihil me fallis sed dico tibi, 30

Ne temerè facias; neque tu hoc dicas tibi non prædictum. cave.

ne facias timere, neque tu dicas hoc non fuisse prædictum tibi. Cave.

DA. *Imò* intelligo *callidè: locutus es modo ipsam rem ita apertè: usus es nihil circuitione.* SI. *Faciliùs sim passus me deludi ubivis, quam in hac re.* DA. *Quæso, da bona verba.* SI. *An irrides? nihil fallis me. Sed dico tibi,*

ANNOTATIONS.

mere: audacter, callide, and observe that it is used in the same sense by *Seneca.* Epist. 19. *Cogita quam multa temere pro pecunia, quam multa laboriosè pro honore tentaveris; aliquid & pro otio audendum est.* And again,

Temeritas, for *Audacia.* Benef. 7. 5. *Nec hoc Alexandri tantum vitium fuit, quem per Liberi Herculisque vestigia felix temeritas egit.* But these scarce come up to the Case in hand.

ACTUS PRIMI SCENA III.

ARGUMENTUM.

Consultat apud se Davus, Pamphilumne adjutet, an potius seni auscultet.

DAVUS.

ENIMVERO, Dave, nihil loci est segnitiæ, neque socordiæ,

Quantùm intellexi modò senis sententiam de nuptiis:

Quæ si non astu providentur, me aut herum pessundabunt.

Nec, quid agam, certum est; Pamphilumne adjutem, an auscultem seni.

Si illum relinquo, ejus vitæ timeo: sin opitulor, hujus minas; 5

Cui verba dare difficile est. primùm jam de amore hoc comperit:

ORDO.

DA. *Enimvero, Dave, est nihil loci segnitiæ, neque socordiæ, quantum modò intellexi sententiam senis de nuptiis: quæ nuptiæ, si non providentur astu, pessundabunt me aut herum Pamphilum. Nec est certem quid agam, adjutemne Pamphilum, an auscultem seri. Si relinquo illum Pamphilum, timeo vitæ ejus: sin opitulor, timeo hujus minas, viz. senis; cui est difficile dare verba. Jam primum comperit de hoc amore:*

ANNOTATIONS.

be careless in deliberating with himself, what Course he had best take. The Root of *Socordia* is *Cor,* whose Compounds are *Concors, Discors, Excors, Vecors,* and *Secors* or *Socors,* that is, *sine Corde.* This last word signifies idle, lazy, negligent, careless, indolent. Thus *Tacitus, socors futuri,* careless of what is to come hereafter. *Quintilian* joins two beautiful Epithets to this Substantive, to express that Indolence of Disposition, which blinds and stupifies the Generality of Parents to the Faults of their Children; *Si non cæca ac sopita parentum secordia est. Tacitus* opposes *Industria* to *Secordia. Languescet alioqui industria, intendetur socordia.*

⁶ *Cui verba dare difficile est. Dare verba*

me, left I should contrive some Fallacy in the Business of the Wedding : if he finds it out, I am undone; or, if the Fancy but takes him, he'll find some Pretence, right or wrong, to send me to the Work-house. To these Mischances, there is this, moreover, to be added : this *Andrian*, whether she be the Wife, or only the Mistress of *Pamphilus*, is with child by him ; and 'tis worth one's while to hear their Assurance, for it is rather the Project of mad People, than of Lovers : whatever is brought into the World, *Boy or Girl*, they have resolved to bring it up. And now they invent I don't know what Story of her being a Citizen of *Athens*. There was formerly, say they, a certain old Man, a Merchant ; he was shipwrecked on the Isle of *Andros*, where he soon after died : *Chrisis*'s Father took then, under his Protection, this young Girl, helpless and destitute. Mere Fables : to me, indeed, it has not the least Air of Probability, yet the Story highly pleases them. But I see *Mysis* coming out from her. Well, I'll hence to the *Forum*, and look for *Pamphilus*, left, perhaps, his Father should surprize him unexpectedly with his Design.

ANNOTATIONS.

ba alicui, is the same as to deceive or impose upon one ; this *Davus*, for several Reasons, which he here enumerates, conjectures would be a very difficult Task. *Donatus* observes upon it, that he does not affirm it to be impossible, from which it might be presumed that he resolved to side with *Pamphilus*.

9 *Quo jure, quaque injuria*. So both ancient MSS. and all the late Editions have it. I cannot, however, pass by here without Notice, the ingenious Emendation of Dr. Bentley. He observes that *quo jure quaque injuria* can by no means subsist in this place ; for that though the Sentence seems to be compleat, yet there is a Word wanting, for that *qua* is necessarily required here, not *quo*. He, therefore, reads it thus : Qua *jure,*

qua me injuria præcipitem in pistrinum dabit. In this manner of ranging a Sentence, the *Latins* never said *qua quaque*, but *qua, qua.* Thus *Cicero, Qua dominus, qua advocati.* And *Livy, Qua paterna injuria, qua sua.* To these Authorities, there may be also this Reason offered for preferring *qua* in both places : Causam ceperit, *qua causa me in pistrinum dabit jure aut injuria.*

14 *Decreverunt tollere.* The word *tollere* signifies properly, to raise or lift from off the Ground. Madam *Dacier* tells us, that it alludes to the Custom of that Age, of laying Children upon the Ground as soon as born. If the Father was willing to educate them, he ordered that they should be taken up : if he said nothing at all, that was a
sign

ACT I. SCENE IV.

ARGUMENT.

The Midwife is called to Glycery *in labour, that by this means an occasion may be offered to* Pamphilus *of meeting with* Mysis.

MYSIS.

Mysis. TO Archilis *within*.) Yes, yes, *Archilis*, I have heard you long ago, you desire that *Lesbia* be immediately brought.
(to

ANNOTATIONS.

1 *Audivi Archilis*, &c.   *Terence*, as *Donatus* observes, frequently makes use of this compendious Manner of carrying on the Plot, that his Persons, in coming out,
speak

Me infensus servat, ne quam faciam nuptiis fallaciam.
Si senserit, perii: aut, si libitum fuerit, causam ce-
   perit;
Quo jure, quaque injuriâ, præcipitem me in pistrinum
   dabit.
Ad hæc mala hoc mî accedit etiam: hæc Andria, 10
Sive ista uxor, sive amica est, gravida è Pamphilo est;
Audireque eorum est operæ precium audaciam:
Nam inceptio est amentium, haud amantium:
Quidquid peperisset, decreverunt tollere:
Et fingunt quandam inter se nunc fallaciam, 15
Civem Atticam esse hanc; Fuit olim quidam senex
Mercator: navem is fregit apud Andrum insulam:
Is obiit mortem. ibi tum hanc ejectam Chrysidis
Patrem recepisse orbam, parvam. fabulæ.
Mihi quidem hercle non fit verisimile: atqui ipsis com-
   mentum placet.
Sed Mysis ab ea egreditur, at ego hinc me ad forum, ut
Conveniam Pamphilum, ne de hac re pater impru-
   dentem opprimat.

insensus servat (ob-servat) me, ne fa-ciam quam falla-ciam in nuptiis. Si senserit, perii; aut, si fuerit libi-tum ei, ceperit cau-sam, quo jure, quo-que injuria, dabit me præcipitem in pistrinum. Hoc e-tiam accedit mihi ad hæc mala: hæc Andria est facta gravida è Pamphi-lo, sive ista est ux-or ejus, sive amica. Estque precium ope-ræ audire audaci-am eorum; nam est inceptio amentium, haud amantium: decreverunt tollere quidquid peperisset: & nunc fingunt quandam fallaciam inter se, nempe

hanc Glycerium esse civem Atticam. Dicunt: Fuit olim quidam senex, mercator: is fregit na-vem apud insulam Andrum: is obiit mortem: ibi tum patrem Chrysidis recipisse hanc ejectam, or-bam, parvam: fabula. Hercle, non fit verisimile mihi quidem: atque commentum placet ipsi. Sed Mysis egreditur ab ea. At ego conferam me hinc ad forum, ut conveniam Pamphilum, ne pa-ter ejus opprimat eum imprudentem de hac re.

ANNOTATIONS.

sign they were to be exposed. This barba-rous Custom continued a long time, till *Plato* at length demonstrated the Enormity of it, and banished it his Commonwealth. It may, perhaps, be of use to observe here, that this alludes to the Custom among the *Greeks,* and not among the *Romans;* for the Reader must all along consider, that though he has in his hands a *Latin* Poet, the Cha-racters are *Grecian.* This Remark is the more necessary here; because *Romulus,* in his Laws, relating to Children, had decreed, that all monstrous Births, and those maimed from the Womb, should be destroyed. However, he had wisely provided at the same time, that this should never be done, till after consulting a Jury of reputable Men, who were to determine, whether the Chil-dren were fitter to live, than to die. Such a Similarity of Customs might easily have led a Reader into the Error here guarded against.

ACTUS PRIMI SCENA IV.

ARGUMENTUM.

Obstetrix accersitur ad Glycerium parturientem, ut hac occasione conveniatur Pamphilus a Myside.

MYSIS.

AUDIVI, Archilis, jamdudum: Lesbiam adduci
   jubes
bet Lesbiam obstetricem adduci.

ORDO.

Mys. A Rebilis, audivi te jamdudum: ju-

ANNOTATIONS.

speak what they are about to do, and at the same time, the Discourse is so con-trived, as to let us know what is doing by others.

(to herself.) Why, truth on't, she's a thoughtless tippling Gossip, and by no means fit to be trusted with a Woman in her first Labour. However, I'll go and bring her. Observe but the Obstinacy of the old Hag, because they are Pot-companions. · Heaven grant my Mistress a good Delivery, and that she may rather miscarry with some other. But whence comes it, that I see *Pamphilus* so strangely disordered! I tremble to think what it may be. I'll stay a little, to know whether the trouble he now seems to be in, threatens any Disaster.

ANNOTATIONS.

² *Temulenta.* That is, one given to Wine, a tippling Gossip; for *Temetum* signifies Wine, and hence a Man sober and moderate in this respect, is called *abstemius.*

Dictum autum Temetum, (says *Donatus*) *ab eo, quia tentet mentem.* Temulenta *vino,* temeraria *naturâ.*

⁴ *Importunitatem spectate aniculæ. Importunitas*

ACT I. SCENE V.

ARGUMENT.

This Scene contains Pamphilus's *Complaint against his Father and* Chremes, *upon hearing of the intended Nuptials, and his firm Resolution to maintain his Pretensions to* Glycery.

PAMPHILUS, MYSIS.

Pamp. TO himself.) Is this a Behaviour or Conduct becoming a reasonable Man? Is this acting like a Father?

Mys. What means this?

Pamp. Heaven and Earth! if this is not ill Usage, what can deserve that Name? He had fixed upon this for the Day of my Wedding, ought I not to have known of it before? Ought it not to have been first communicated to me?

Mys. Wretch that I am, what do I now hear?

Pamp. What can *Chremes* mean, who but so lately refused to give me his Daughter in Marriage? He has changed his Mind, it
would

ANNOTATIONS.

¹ *Hoccine est humanum factum aut inceptum?* *Simo,* after parting from *Davus,* goes to the *Forum,* where meeting with *Pamphilus,* he pretends, according to the Scheme laid open to *Sosia,* that he must that day prepare for his Marriage with *Chremes's* Daughter. *Pamphilus,* disconcerted by a Proposal so sudden and unexpected, deliberates here with himself, what he is to do. *Mysis* is introduced to turn the Scale. At her Appearance, all his former soft and tender Sentiments in respect of *Glycery* revive, and he is confirmed in the Resolution of adhering to her in spite of all Opposition.

² *Proh Deûm atque hominum fide.* This Exclamation, says *Westerhovius,* was usual not only in Cases of great Admiration, but where a Man thought himself used ill and hardly; and as often as he implored those Helps, which are due from one to another, by a natural Obligation. Hence *Fides* is often used for Protection and Patronage. Dr. *Bentley,* upon this Passage, observes that *atque hominum* is wanting in a very noted MS. and that *proh Deûm fidem* is an Expression usual with our Author. According to this, the *proh Deûm atque hominum fidem,* in Verse 12, will come in more elegantly. At
first

Sanè pol illa temulenta eſt mulier, & temeraria,
Nec ſati' digna, cui committas primo partu mulierem :
Tamen eam adducam. importunitatem ſpeĉtate ani-
culæ ;
Quia compotrix ejus eſt. Di date facultatem, obſecro, 5
Huic pariundi, atque illi in aliis potius peccandi lo-
cum.
Sed, quidnam Pamphilum exanimatum video ? vereor
quid ſiet.
Opperiar, ut ſciam, numquidnam hæc turba triſtitiæ
adferat.

Sanè pol illa eſt temulenta mulier, & temeraria, nec ſatis digna, cui committas mulierem in primo partu : tamen adducam eam. Speĉate importunitatem aniculæ ; quia Leſbia eſt compotrix ejus. Dii, obſecro, date huic Glycerio facultatem pariundi, & illi obſtetrici locum peccandi in aliis potius fœminis. Sed quidnam video Pamphilum exanimatum ? vereor quid ſiet. Opperiar, ut ſciam, num hæc turba afferat quidnam triſtitiæ.

ANNOTATIONS.

tunitas is a very expreſſive Term, and ſignifies properly an imprudent Obſtinacy, that
regards neither Time, Place, nor Circumſtances.

ACTUS PRIMI SCENA V.

ARGUMENTUM.

*Continet hæc ſcena querelam Pamphili adverſus patrem & Chre-
metem, cognito nuptiarum conſilio, & deliberationem animum-
que obſtinatum in tuendo Glycerii amore.*

PAMPHILUS, MYSIS.

HOCCINE eſt humanum faĉtum aut ince-
ptum ? hoccine eſt officium patris ?
MYS. Quid illud eſt ?
PA. Pro Deûm atque hominum fidem ! quid eſt, ſi
hoc non contumelia eſt ?
Uxorem decrêrat dare ſeſe mî hodie. nonne oportuit
Præſciſſe me antè ? nonne prius communicatum opor-
tuit ? 5
MY. Miſeram me, quod verbum audio !
PA. Quid Chremes ? qui denegârat, ſe commiſſurum
mihi

ORDO.

PA. Hoccine eſt humanum faĉtum aut inceptum ? hoccine eſt officium patris? MY. Quid eſt illud ? PA. Proh fidem Deûm atque hominum ! quid eſt contumelia, ſi hoc non eſt contumelia ? decreverat ſeſe dare uxorem mihi hodie. Nonne oportuit me præſciſſe hoc antè ? nonne oportuit hoc fuiſſe communicatum mihi prius ? MY. Heu me miſeram, quod verbum audio ! PA. Quid Chremes vult ſibi ? qui denegaverat ſe commiſſurum ſuam gnatam uxorem mihi ;

ANNOTATIONS.

firſt he appeals only to the Gods, afterwards
to Gods and Men.

3 *Uxorem decrêrat.* In this, *Pamphilus*
places the Injury, that his Father had ſo
ſuddenly charged him to prepare for Marriage, not that the Match propoſed could be
thought an Injury ; though we may well
preſume he would have conſidered it as a
great Hardſhip. But he imagines, that had
he known it beforehand, he would have
found ſome Pretence to elude his Father's
Will. Hence he adds, *Nonne oportuit præſciſſe me ante,* &c. *Eugraphius.*

would feem, becaufe he fees me unchangeably the fame. Is he then fo obftinately bent to draw me from *Glycery?* which, indeed, if he can compafs, I'm ruined for ever. Is there, think you, upon Earth a more unfortunate or unhappy Wretch than I? Good Heavens! is there no poffible way for me to fhun this Alliance with *Chremes?* How much have I been abufed and mal-treated? All things were concluded and agreed on. Hah, on a fudden I am caft off, and again fought after. And why, unlefs it is as I fufpect; they certainly rear up fome Monfter, whom as they can force upon nobody elfe, they have recourfe to me.

Myf. This Speech has almoft frightened me out of my Senfes.

Pamp. But what fhall I fay all this while on the part of my Father? How! to refolve upon an Affair of that importance with fo little Forethought? Paffing by me juft now at the Forum, *Pamphilus,* fays he, you are to be married to-day, go home, and make ready. To me it founded, as if he had faid, Go home prefently and hang yourfelf; I was amazed. Do you think that I could utter fo much as one word; or frame any Excufe, however falfe, foolifh, or unjuft? I ftood fpeechlefs. But had I been apprized of it before; fhould any one now afk me, what in this Cafe I would have done? why, I would have done any thing, not to do this *they now urge me to.* But what courfe had I beft take at prefent? So many Cares diftract me, and draw my Mind different ways, Love, Pity for my dear *Glycery,* Importunities to marry. Add to all this, the Reverence due to a Father, who has hitherto with fo much mildnefs indulged me in every thing that Heart could wifh. How then can I refolve to contradict him? Alas! I know not what to choofe. *Myf.*

ANNOTATIONS,

⁷ *Id mutavit, quoniam me immutatum videt.* *Pamphilus* here cannot conceive with himfelf, why *Chremes,* who had refufed to give him his Daughter in Marriage, becaufe he was engaged in an Affair with another, fhould now fo fuddenly change his Mind, tho' he ftill perfifted in that Paffion, which had caufed all the Obftruction. But here a very fenfible Difficulty occurs; for according to all the Rules of pure *Latin, immutare* fignifies to change, and of confequence, *immutatus* can never fignify unchanged. And yet it is plain, that both the Senfe and Truth require it; for *Pamphilus* continued always firmly attached to *Glycery,* nor ever had a Thought of abandoning her. *Tanaquil Faber* has obviated this Difficulty, by making it appear that *immutatus* is here for *immutabilis;* and that compound Adjectives derived from Particles paffive, don't always imply the Reality of the thing, but the Poffibility: that is, to fpeak in the Language of *Grammarians,* they become *Potentials.* Thus to give fome Examples; we meet with *immotus* for *immobilis, invictus* for *invincibilis, invifus* for *invifibilis,*

and thus alfo *immutatus* for *immutabilis. Wefterhovius, Dacier.*

¹⁰ *Invenuftum aut infelicem. Pamphilus* in danger of lofing the Woman he loved, and having one whom he did not love forced upon him, calls himfelf *invenuftus;* that is, one who was unlucky in his Amours, one whom *Venus* did not favour. As, moreover, he could not avoid this Misfortune, without difpleafing his Father, he calls himfelf alfo *infelix,* that being what he accounted a great Unhappinefs.

¹⁵ *Aliquid monftri alunt.* We are to confider *Pamphilus* here as fpeaking in the Violence of Grief and Concern, for finding all his Meafures fo broken. There is nothing more natural, than for a Man in this cafe to fly into extravagant Expreffions, which his more cool Reafon would difapprove. The Poet feems to have been well acquainted with human Nature, and to have underftood perfectly all the Springs and Movements of the Soul. Thofe Sallies of Paffion, that here break from *Pamphilus,* are the real Language of a Heart irritated by Difappointments, and the Misfortune of

feeing

Gnatam fuam uxorem ; id mutavit, quoniam me immutatum videt.

Itane obftinatè operam dat, ut me à Glycerio miferum abftrahat ?

Quod fi fit, pereo funditus, 10

Adeon' hominem invenuftum effe, aut infelicem quenquam, ut ego fum ?

Proh Deûm atque hominum fidem !

Nullon'ego Chremetis pacto affinitatem effugere potero ?

Quot modis contemtus, fpretus ? facta, transfacta omnia. hem,

Repudiatus repetor, quamobrem ? nifi fi id eft, quod
fufpicor : 15

Aliquid monftri alunt : ea quoniam nemini obtrudi
poteft, [metu.

Itur ad me. MY. oratio hæc me miferam exanimavit

PA. Nam quid ego dicam de patre ? ah !

Tantamnerem tam neglegenter agere ? præteriens modò

Mihi apud forum, uxor tibi ducenda eft, Pamphile,
hodie, inquit : para : [fpende te.

Abi domum. id mihi vifus eft dicere, Abi cito, & fu-

Obftupui. cenfen' ullum me verbum potuiffe proloqui ?

Aut ullam caufam, ineptam faltem, falfam, iniquam ?
obmutui.

Quòd fi ego prius id refciffem ; quid facerem, fi quis
nunc me roget ;

Aliquid facerem, ut hoc ne facerem. fed nunc primûm
quid exfequar ? 25

Tot me impediunt curæ, quæ meum animum divor-
fe trahunt :

Amor, mifericordia hujus, nuptiarum folicitatio ;

Tum patris pudor, qui me tam leni paffus eft animo
ufque adhuc,

Quæ meo cunque animo libitum eft, facere : eine ego
ut advorfer ? hei mihi !

Mutavit id confilium, quoniam vi-det me immutatum. Datne operam ita obftinatè, ut ab-ftrahat me miferum à Glycerio ? quod fi fit, pereo fundi-tus. Putetne aliquis quenquam hominem effe adeo invenuftum aut infelicem, ut ego fum ? Proh fi-dem deorum atque hominum ! Poterene ego nullo pacto ef-fugere affinitatem Chremetis ? quot modis fui contem-tus, fpretus ? omnia-funt facta tranf-actaque. Item ! ego repudiatus re-petor. Quamobrem ? nifi fi eft id, quod fufpicor : alunt ali-quid monftri : ea, quoniam poteft ob-trudi nemini, itur ad me. MY. Hæc oratio exanimavit me mi-feram metu. PA. Nam quid ego dicam de patre ? Ah! eum-ne oportuit agere tantum rem tam neg-ligenter ? Modo præ-teriens apud forum, inquit mihi, Pam-phile, uxor eft du-cenda tibi hodie ; para te : abi do-mum ; eft vifus di-cere id mihi ; Abi cito, & fufpende te. Obftupui : cenfefne

me potuiffe proloqui ullum verbum ? aut ullam caufam, ineptam faltem, falfam, iniquam ? obmutui. Quòd fi quis roget me nunc, quid facerem, fi ego refciffem id prius : facerem aliquid, ut ne
facerem hoc. Sed nunc quid exequar primum ? tot curæ impediunt me, quæ trahunt meum animum
diverfè : amor, mifericordia hujus Glycerii, folicitatio nuptiarum ; tum pudor mei patris, qui ufque adhuc eft paffus me tam leni animo, facere quæcunque eft libitum meo animo : egone ut adver-
fer ei ? hei mihi !

ANNOTATIONS.

feeing all its Defigns baffled. It adds too
greatly to the Poet's praife, that all here
flows with a natural Eafe and Simplicity ;
there is nothing forced or overftrained in the
Sentiments.

19 *Apud forum.* Forum fignifies a Place
where Caufes are debated, or where People
met on Affairs of Traffick and Merchan-
dize, and often a common Market-place, in

which laft Senfe it is frequently ufed by Terence. Sometimes too it is taken for a Place
of Exchange, where Money-Matters were
tranfacted. This is evident from a Paffage in the laft Act of Phormio :

----- *Tranfi fodes · ad Forum atque illud
mihi
Argentum rurfum jube refcribi.*

23 *Quod fi ego refciffem,* &c. Commentators

Myf. Hah, I tremble to think what this Irrefolution may turn to. But now 'tis abfolutely neceffary, either that he himfelf fpeak to my Miftrefs, or that I fpeak fomewhat to him about her. While the Mind wavers in Uncertainty, a little matter will turn it either one way or the other.

Pamp. Who fpeaks here ? *Myfis*, Good-morrow.

Myf. O *Pamphilus*, Good-morrow.

Pamp. How does your Miftrefs ?

Myf. How does fhe ? fhe's now in labour, and, moreover, full of anxiety ; becaufe this is the Day fome time ago fixed on for your Wedding : nay, fhe is fomewhat apprehenfive too, left you fhould abandon her.

Pamp. How ! Do you imagine it poffible, that I can entertain fuch a Thought ? Can I fuffer an unfortunate young Creature to be ruined for my fake ? one, who has trufted me with her Life, Honour, and every thing that is dear to her : One, whom I have loved with the Fondnefs and Tendernefs of a Hufband. Shall I, I fay, fuffer a Difpofition, trained up to Chaftity and Virtue, to ftruggle with Want and Neceffity, and ftoop to things below it ? I'll never do it.

Myf. I don't much fear indeed, did it depend only upon yourfelf ; but how can you withftand the Authority of a Father ?

Pamp. Do you then imagine me fo mean, fo ingrateful, fo inhuman, and barbarous, that neither a long Intimacy, Love, nor Honour, can move or engage me to keep my Promife to her ?

Myf. One thing I know, that fhe well deferves you fhould remember her.

Pamp. Remember her : O *Myfis*, *Myfis*, thofe laft Words which *Chryfis* fpoke to me concerning *Glycery*, are even now, at this inftant, written in my Heart. She was juft dying, I remember, when fhe called me ; I went : when ye were withdrawn, and we left by ourfelves, fhe thus begins ; My *Pamphilus*, you fee the Youth and Beauty of this poor Orphan, nor can you be ignorant how little they will avail to the Security, either of her Virtue, or the fmall Fortune, that

ANNOTATIONS.

tators differ much as to the Manner of reading and pointing this Paffage : that which I have followed, is according to the more common Editions. *Wefterbovius*, in his Text has done the fame ; but in his Notes, he tells us, that we ought by all means to read and diftinguifh it thus ;

Quod fi ego refciffem id prius, (quid facerem ? fi quis nunc me roget)

Aliquid, facerem, ut ne hæc facerem.

For after that *Pamphilus* had faid, *Quod fi ego refciffem ad prius* ; he ftops a little, as if loft in Thought. Some one of the Spectators might in the mean time have afked, *quid faceres ?* Humouring, therefore, this Suppofition, he goes on to fay, *Quid facerem ?*

fi quis nunc me roget ? and anfwers at the fame time, *aliquid facerem, ut hoc ne facerem.* That is, I would feign or invent any thing to prevent a Marriage, to which I am fo averfe.

32 *Dum in dubio eft animus, paulo momento.* This is a manner of fpeaking, tranflated from the Balance, when the two Scales equiponderate, in which cafe the leaft Weight added to either of them will deftroy the Equilibrium, and make the Balance incline to that fide where the additional Weight, is put. *Momentum*, as if *Movimentum*, a fmall Motion of the Balance, and hence too the little additional Weight that caufes this Motion. By the fame Derivation, it is made

to

Incertum eſt quid agam. MY. miſera timeo, incertum
   hoc quorſum accidat. 30
Sed nunc peropu' eſt, aut hunc cum ipsâ, aut me ali-
   quid de illâ advorſum hunc loqui,
Dum in dubio eſt animus, paulo momento huc vel il-
   luc impellitur.
PA. Quis hic loquitur? Myſis, ſalve. MY. ô ſalve,
   Pamphile. PA. quid agit? MY. rogas?
Laborat è dolore: atque ex hoc miſera ſolicita eſt die,
Quia olim in hunc ſunt conſtitutæ nuptiæ. tum au-
   tem hoc timet, 35
Ne deſeras ſe. PA. hem, egone iſtuc conari queam?
Ego propter me illam decipi miſeram ſinam?
Quæ mihi ſuum animum atque omnem vitam credidit,
Quam ego animo egregiè caram pro uxore habuerim,
Bene & pudicè eju' doctum atque eductum ſinam 40
Coactum egeſtate ingenium immutarier?
Non faciam. MY. haud verear, ſi in te ſolo ſit ſitum:
Sed vim ut queas ferre. PA. adeon' me ignavum putas?
Adeon' porro ingratum, aut inhumanum, aut ferum,
Ut neque me conſuetudo, neque amor, neque pudor 45
Commoveat: neque commoneat, ut ſervem fidem?
MY. Unum hoc ſcio, meritam eſſe, ut memor eſſes ſui.
PA. Memor eſſem? ô Myſis, Myſis, etiam nunc mihi
Scripta illa dicta ſunt in animo Chryſidis
De Glycerio. jam ferme moriens me vocat: 50
Acceſſi: vos ſemotæ: nos ſoli: incipit:
Mi Pamphile, hujus formam atque ætatem vides:
Nec clam te eſt, quàm illi nunc utræque inutiles
Et ad pudicitiam & ad rem tutandam ſient. 54

doctum atque eductum bene & pudice, inmutari coactum egeſtate? non faciam. MY. Haud ve-
rear, ſi fit ſitum in te ſolo: ſed ut queas ferre vim. PA. Putaſne me adeo ignavum, adeone
porro ingratum, aut inhumanum, aut ferum, ut neque conſuetudo, neque amor, neque pu-
dor commoveat: neque commoneat me, ut ſervem fidem illi? MY. Scio hoc unum, eam eſſe
meritam, ut eſſes memor ſui. PA. Ut eſſem memor? ô Myſis, Myſis, dicta illa Chryſidis de
Glycerio, ſunt etiam nunc ſcripta mihi in animo. Jam ferme moriens vocat me: acceſſi: vos
ſemotæ, nos ſoli, incipit: Mi Pamphile, vides formam atque ætatem hujus, nec eſt clam te
quàm inutiles utræque hæ res nunc ſint illi, & ad tutandum pudicitiam, & ad tutandam rem.

Right margin (italic paraphrase):

Incertum eſt quid agam. MY. Miſera timeo, quorſum hoc incertum acci-dat. Sed nunc per-opus eſt, aut hunc Pamphilum loqui cum ipsâ Glycerio; aut me loqui ali-quid de illâ adver-ſum hunc. Dum animus eſt in du-bio, impellitur pau-lo, momento huc vel illuc. PA. Quis loquitur hic? My-ſis, ſalve. MV. O Pamphile, ſalve. PA. Quid Glyce-rium agit? MY. Rogas? laborat e dolore partûs: at-que miſera eſt ſoli-cita ex hoc die, quia olim nuptiæ tuæ ſunt conſtitutæ in hunc: tum au-tem timet hoc, ne tu deſeras ſe. PA. Hem! egone queam conari iſtuc? egone ſinam illam miſe-ram decipi propter me? quæ credidit ſuum animum atque omnem vitam mihi, quam ego habuerim egregie caram ani-mo pro conjuge, an ſinam ejus ingenium

---

ANNOTATIONS.

to ſtand for the ſmalleſt interval of Time.

++ *Ingratum, aut inhumanum, aut ferum.*
The Obſervation which *Donatus* makes upon
this Paſſage is excellent, and lets the Reader
into all its Beauty. *Mira omnis converſio.*
Non enim dixit: Adeone me obſequentem pa-
tri exiſtimas, adeo gratum, adeo pium, adeo
manſuetum? Thus he all along preſerves the
Character of a Lover, and by theſe paſſio-
n-te and rhetorical Expreſſions makes it appear, as if it would be a Crime of the higheſt
nature, to ſubmit to his Father in this Inſtance.

48 *Etiam nunc mihi ſcripta illa dicta,*
&c. *Pamphilus* is led into this train of Reflection in a very eaſy and natural manner;
and ſuch a Croud of tender paſſionate Ideas
flowing in upon his Soul at once, muſt have
a wonderful Tendency to confirm him in his
Attachment to *Glycery.* The whole is
wrought up with all the Delicacy and Softneſs imaginable, nor is it poſſible to read
it without being ſenſibly touched.

53 *Quàm illi utræque res nunc inutiles,*
&c. *Donatus* obſerves that ſome MSS. read
utiles;

that I may leave her. I, therefore, conjure you by this right Hand ; by that fweetnefs of Temper, which is natural to you, by your fulemn Engagements to her, and her own forlorn helplefs Condition that you never feparate her from you, nor abandon her. If I have always loved you with the Affection due to a Brother ; or fhe prized you above all the World befide, and in every thing made your Will her Law : I bequeath you to her as her Hufband, Friend, Guardian, and Father. I commit all my Fortune to your Care, and entruft you with the Management of it. With thefe Words fhe gave her into my Hand, and a few Moments after expired. I received her, and am refolved to keep her.

Myf. I hope fo indeed.

Pamp. But why are you abfent from her at this time ?

Myf. I go to fetch the Midwife.

Pamp. Make hafte then : But d'ye hear ? Not a Word of the Wedding, left that fhould add to her Illnefs.

Myf. I underftand ye.

ANNOTATIONS.

utiles, and fome Commentators tells us, that this manner of fpeaking is far more expreffive of what is here intended, than the other. *Sane autem* (fays *Wefterbovius*) *ejufmodi locutio inutilitatem maximam defcri-* | *bit.* It is granted, but the Word is always in this Cafe ufed ironically, which would by no means fuit the Earneftnefs and Concern wherewith *Pamphilus* expreffes himfelf on this Occafion.   62 *Hanc*

ACT II. SCENE I.

ARGUMENT.

This Scene expreffes the Anxiety of Charinus, *upon hearing from his Servant* Byrrhia, *that* Pamphilus *was that day to be married to* Philumena, *with whom he was defperately in love. Meeting* Pamphilus, *he begs of him not to wed her.*

CHARINUS, BYRRHIA, PAMPHILUS.

Char. WHAT is it you tell me, *Byrrhia* ? Is fhe to be marry'd to *Pamphilus* to-day ?

Byr. For certain.

Char. How d'ye know ?

Byr. I had it from *Davus* juft now at the *Forum.*

Char. Wretch that I am ! while divided between Hope and Fear,
I bore

ANNOTATIONS.

¹ *Quid ais, Byrrbia ?* We have feen in a former Scene, that *Davus* went to the *Forum* in queft of *Pamphilus,* that he might tell him what had paffed between | him and the old Man. There meeting with *Byrrhia,* he informs him of the intended Marriage. *Charinus,* who was in love with *Philumena,* hearing this from
Byrrhia,

Quod ego te per hanc dextram oro, & ingenium tuum,
Per tuam fidem, perque hujus folitudinem
Te obteſtor, ne abs te hanc fegreges, neu deferas :
Si te in germani fratris dilexi loco,
Sive hæc te folum femper fecit maxumi,
Seu tibi morigera fuit in rebus omnibus,   60
Te iſti virum do, amicum, tutorem, patrem :
Bona noſtra hæc tibi committo, & tuæ mando fidei,
Hanc mi in manum dat: mors continuò ipfam occupat :
Accepi : acceptam fervabo. My. ita fpero quidem. 64
Pa. Sed cur tu ab illâ ? My. obſtetricem accerfo. Pa.
     propera :
Atque audin' ? verbum unum cave de nuptiis,
Ne ad morbum hoc etiam. My. teneo.

Quod ego oro te per hanc dextram, & tuum ingenium, per tuam fidem, perque folitudinem hujus obteſtor te, ne fegreges hanc abs te, neu deferas, eam ; fi dilexi te in loco germani fratris, five hæc puella femper fecit te folum maximi, feu fuit morigera tibi in omnibus rebus. Do te virum, amicum, tutorem, patrem iſti : committa hæc noſtra bonò tibi, &

mando ea tuæ fidei. Dat hanc mihi in manum : mors continuò occupat ipfam. Accepi illam, fervabo acceptam. My. Spero ita quidem. Pa. Sed cur tu abis ab illâ ? My, Accerfo obſtetricem. Pa. Propera : atque audin' ? cave dicas unum verbum de nuptiis, ne hoc etiam accedat ad morbum. My. Teneo.

ANNOTATIONS.

62 *Hanc mihi in manum dat.* Marriage, as *Donatus* tells us, was celebrated *Conventione in manum,* by giving the Hand of the Woman into the Hand of the Man, whence ſhe was ſaid *venire in manum viri. Pamphilus,* therefore, by this, would inſinuate that he had received her as his Wife, and was reſolved to adhere to her as ſuch.

ACTUS II. SCENA I.

ARGUMENTUM.

Solicitudo Charini adolefcentis, qui ex Byrrhia fervo refciverat Pamphilum eo die uxorem ducturum Philumenam, quam ipfe Charinus mifere deperibat. Idem rogat Pamphilum ne ducat.

CHARINUS, BYRRHIA, PAMPHILUS.

QUID ais, Byrrhia ? daturne illa Pamphilo hodie
     nuptum ? By. fic eſt.
Ch. Quî fcis ; By. apud forum modò è Davo audivi.
     Ch. væ mifero mihi !

ORDO.

Ch. QUID ais, Byrrhia ? illane Philumena datur nuptum Pamphilo hodie ? By.

Sic eſt. Ch. Quî fcis ? By. Audivi modò è Davo apud forum. Ch. Væ mifero mihi !

ANNOTATIONS.

Byrrhia, gives riſe to the Converſation in this Scene. *Donatus* informs us, that *Charinus* and *Byrrhia* were not in the original Piece of *Menander,* but added by *Terence,* to render his Play the more compleat, and that the Concluſion might not appear tragical or imperfect, if, when *Pamphilus* came to efpoufe his Miſtreſs, *Philumena* ſhould be left without a Huſband. This Remark to me appears to be of conſiderable Importance.

     à Animus

I bore up as well as I could: but now that Hope is wholly taken away, defponding, and overwhelmed with Anxiety, I am quite ftupified.

Byr. For Heaven's fake, *Charinus*, fince it can't be as you would have it, content yourfelf with what may be.

Char. I can be contented with nothing but *Philumena*.

Byr. Ah, Sir, how much better were it to ftrive to get rid of this Paffion, than to be talking thus, which ferves only to augment your Flame to no purpofe !

Char. All of us, when we are well, find it an eafy matter to give good Counfel to the Sick. Were you in my place, you'd think very differently.

Byr. Well, well ; do as you think beft.

Char. But yonder I fee *Pamphilus* ; I am refolved to try all, rather than perifh quite.

Byr. What is he about now ?

Char. I'll befeech him ; I'll become a fuppliant to him ; I'll acquaint him with my Paffion. I imagine I fhall at leaft prevail with him to defer the Wedding a few days. Meantime, I hope fomething may happen.

Byr. And that fomething, believe me, is juft nothing at all.

Char. What d'ye think, *Byrrhia*, fhall I go to him ?

Byr. Undoubtedly: that if you can obtain nothing, he may know his Wife will find a ready Gallant in you, fhould he marry her.

Char. Go hang yourfelf, you Rafcal, with thefe bafe Sufpicions.

Pamp. O here is *Charinus* ! Sir, your Servant.

Char. O *Pamphilus*, your Servant. I come to you to beg for Hope, Health, Counfel, and Affiftance.

Pamp. Why really *Charinus*, I am in a condition neither to advife nor affift. But what can this be ?

Char. Are you to be marry'd to-day ?

Pamp. So I'm told.

Char. *Pamphilus*, if fo, this day you fee the laft of me.

Pamp. Why fo ?

Char. Alas, I am afraid to mention it ; pray, *Byrrhia*, do you tell him.

Byr. I will.

Pamp. What's the matter.

Byr. He's in love with your defigned Bride.

Pamp. Why really he and I are not of the fame Mind. But hark ye, tell me honeftly, *Charinus*, have you had no nearer Engagements with her ?

Char. Ah *Pamphilus*, none.   *Pamp.*

ANNOTATIONS.

3 *Animus in fpe atque in timore attentus.* This laft Word is very ftrong and expreffive, as it is put here. His Mind was upon the ftretch between Hope and Fear, and attentive to every Circumftance that could leave room for conjecture either one way or another.

4. *Laffus, cura confectus. Laffus,* when by a Difeafe, the Strength and Vigour of Conftitution is impaired. Thus the Mind, by a continued Attention was fo weakened, that it could hold out no longer. *Cura confectus.* The new Acceffion of Sorrow arifing from what he had heard lately, banifhed all future Hope, he funk under the Weight

Ut animus in spe atque in timore usque antehac atten-
tus fuit, [stupet.
Ita, postquam ademta spes est, lassus, curâ confectus
By. Quæso edepol, Charine, quoniam non potest id
fieri, quod vis, 5
Id velis quod possit. Ch. nihil vol● aliud, nisi Philu-
menam.
By. Ah, quanto satius est, te id dare operam, [loqui,
Quî istum amore ex animo amoveas tuo, quàm id
Quo magis libido frustrà incendatur tua !
Ch. Facilè omnes, cùm valemus, recta consilia ægro-
tis damus. 10
Tu si hic sis, aliter sentias. By. age, age, ut lubet.
Ch. sed Pamphilum
Video. omnia experiri certum est priùs, quàm pereo.
By. Quid hic agit ?
Ch. Ipsum hunc orabo: huic supplicabo: amorem huic
narrabo meum.
Credo, impetrabo, ut aliquot saltem nuptiis prodat dies.
Interea fiet aliquid, spero. By. id aliquid nihil est. Ch.
Byrrhia, 15
Quid tibi videtur? adeon' ad eum ? By. quidni ? si nihil
impetres,
Ut te arbitretur sibi paratum moechum, si illam duxerit.
Ch.Abin'hinc in malam rem cum suspicione istac.scelus.
Pa. Charinum video. salve. Ch. ô salve, Pamphile.:
Ad te advenio, spem, salutem, auxilium, consilium ex-
petens, 20
Pa.Nequepolconsilii locumhabeo,neque auxilii copiam.
Sed istuc quidnam est ? Ch. hodie uxorem dulcis? Pa.
aiunt. Ch. Pamphile,
Si id facis, hodie postremùm me vides. Pa. quid ita ?
Ch. hei mihi !
Vereor dicere huic : die quæso, Byrrhia. By. ego di-
cam. Pa. quid est ?
By. Sponsam hic tuam amat. Pa. næ iste haud mecum
sentit. ehodum, dic mihi, 25
Numquidnam amplius tibi cum illâ fuit, Charine ?
Ch. ah Pamphile,

Ut animus usque antebac fuit attentus in spe atque in timore, ita, postquam spes est adempta, animus lassus, confectusque, curâ stupet. By. Quæso edepol, Charine, quoniam id non potest fieri, quod vis, velis id quod possit. Ch. Volo nihil aliud nisi Philumenam. By. Ah, quanto est satius, te dare operam ad id, quî amoveas istum amorem ex tuo animo, quàm loqui id, quo tua libido magis incendatur frustrà ! Ch. Omnes, cùm valemus, facilè damus recta consilia ægrotis ; si tu sis hîc, sentias aliter. By. Age, age, ut lubet. Ch. Sed video Pamphilum. Est certum experiri omnia consilia, priùs quàm pereo. By. Quid hîc agit nunc ? Ch. Orabo ipsum hunc : supplicabo huic : narrabo huic meum amorem. Credo, impetrabo, ut saltem prodat aliquot dies nuptiis. Interea, spero, aliquid fiet. By. Et id aliquid est nibil. Ch. Byrrhia, quid videtur tibi ? adeone ad eum ? By. Quid ni ? ut, si impetres nibil, arbitretur te paratum moechùm sibi, si duxerit il-

lam. Ch. Abin' hinc scelus in malam rem cum istbac suspicione. Pa. Video Charinum : salve. Ch. O Pamphile, salve : advenio ad te, expetens spem, salutem, auxilium, consilium. Pa. Pol, neque habeo locum consilii, neque copiam auxilii ; sed quidnam est istuc ? Ch. An ducis uxorem bodie ? Pa. Aiunt. Ch. Pamphile, si facis id, bodie vides me postremum. Pa. Quid ita ? Ch. Hei mibi, vereor dicere buic ; tu Byrrhia, quæso dic. By. Ego dicam. Pa. Quid est ? By. Hic amat tuam sponsam. Pa. Næ iste haud sentit mecum : ebodum, dic mibi, num quidnam amplius fuit tibi cum illâ, Charine ? Ch. Ab Pampbile,

ANNOTATIONS.

Weight of his Misfortunes, like one wounded beyond a Possibility of Cure.

10 *Facile omnes*, &c. Dacier observes
here, that *Æschylus* was probably the first
vvho

Pamp. I wiſh with all my Soul you had.

Char. Now I intreat you by all that is ſacred in Love and Friend-
ſhip, firſt not to marry her.

Pamp. Poſitively I'll do my Endeavour.

Char. But if you can't grant me this, or the Marriage is to your liking--

Pamp. To my liking !

Char. At leaſt defer it ſome Days, that I may get out of the way,
and not have the mortification of ſeeing it.

Pamp. Hear me then, *Charinus* ; I think it below a Man of Honour to lay claim to an Obligation, where he has done nothing to
merit any.   I am no leſs anxious to avoid this Marriage, than you
to compaſs it.

Char. You reſtore me to Life again.

Pamp. Now, if you can contrive any thing, you or this *Byrrhia*,
plot, beſtir yourſelves, deviſe what you pleaſe ; in a word, ſome how
or other bring it about, that you may have her ; I, on my ſide, will
do all in my power not to have her.

Char. Enough, I am ſatisfied.

Pamp. But ſee, here comes *Davus* in the beſt time in the World ;
for 'tis his Advice that I chiefly rely on.

Char. (*To* Byrrhia.) But you, Sirrah, are good for nothing, unleſs to
tell me what I had better know nothing of.   Don't you get out of
my ſight ?

Byr. That I will, and with great Chearfulneſs.

ANNOTATIONS.

who brought this Sentence upon the Stage, who in one of his Tragedies has, *'Tis eaſy for a Man, who himſelf ſuffers under no Ca-lamities, to adviſe and counſel thoſe who do.* *Terence,* in adopting it, has cloathed in Language ſuited to Comedy.

31 *Ego, Charine, newtiquam officium,* &c. By *homo liber,* we are to underſtand here, not barely a Man, who is not a Slave, but one of Rank and Diſtinction, and in good Eſteem with his Fellow-Citizens. *Cicero,* Lib. I. Office. *Nihil eſt agricultura melius, nihil homine libero dignius.*

38 *Niſi ea, quæ nihil opus ſunt ſciri.* *Dona-tus* refers this to what had before paſſed be-tween *Charinus* and *Eyrrhia* in the Be-ginning of this Scene, and is followed in it by *Boeclerus.* But *Weſterbovius* contradicts this,

---

ACT II.   SCENE II.

ARGUMENT.

Davus *diſcovering that the Marriage was all mere Pretence, ex-ults, and acquaints* Pamphilus, *by what Signs and Conjec-tures he was led to think ſo.*

DAVUS, CHARINUS, PAMPHILUS.

Davus. GOOD Gods, what good News do I bring ! But where
ſhall I meet with *Pamphilus*, that I may eaſe him of the
Fear he is now under, and fill his Heart with Joy ?   .   *Char.*

ANNOTATIONS.

1 *Di boni.* We have ſeen in the laſt Act, that *Davus* went to the *Forum* to find out

Pamphilus, and warn him of his Father's Deſign. Not ſeeing him, he inquires of *Byrrhia,*

Nihil. PA. quàm vcliem ! CH. tunc te per amicitam
& per amorem obfecro,

Principio, ut ne ducas. PA. dabo equidem operam. CH.
fed fi id non potes,   [aliquot dies

Aut tibi nuptiæ hæ funt cordi ; PA. cordi ! CH. faltem

Profer, dum proficifcor aliquò, ne videam. PA. audi

nunc jam :   30

Ego, Charine, neutiquam officium liberi effe hominis
puto,

Cum is nil promereta, poftulare id gratiæ apponi fibi.

Nuptias effugere ego iftas malo, quàm tu adipifcier.

CH. Reddidifti animum. PA. nunc fi quid potes aut tu,
aut hic Byrrhia,

Facite, fingite, invenite, efficite, quî detur tibi :   35

Ego id agam, mihi quî ne detur. CH. fat habeo. PA.
Davum optumè

Video. hujus confilio fretu' fum. CH. at tu hercle haud
quidquam mihi,

Nifi ea, quæ nihil opu' funt fciri. fugin' hinc ? BY.
ego verò ac lubens.

Reddidifti animum. PA. Nunc fi aut tu potes facere quid, aut hic Byrrhia, facite, fingite, invenite, quî Philumena detur tibi : ego agam id, quî ne detur mihi. CH. Habeo fat. PA. Video Davum optimè, nam fretus fum confilio hujus. CH. At tu bercle, Byrrhia, haud dicis quidquam mihi, nifi ea quæ funt nibil opus fciri. Fugin' hinc ? BY. Ego verò fugio ; ac lubens.

ANNOTATIONS.

this, as imagining it was highly neceffary for *Charinus* to know what *Byrrbia* had told him relating to the Marriage of *Philumena*. He therefore fancies that *Byrrbia* was at this time whifpering fome trifle in his Mafter's Ear, which he, taken up with more important Cares, could not attend to. But befides that this would not fo well confort with the Rules of the Drama, there is no Neceffity for fuppofing that *Charinus* fays nothing but what is juft and reasonable ; or perhaps it may refer to *Byrrbia's* diffuading him from addreffing *Pampbilus.*

ACTUS II. SCENA. II.

ARGUMENTUM.

Compertâ nuptiarum fimulatione, Davus exultat, & Pampbilo narrat, quibus conjeɛturis fignifque eam deprebendiffet.

DAVUS, CHARINUS, PAMPHILUS,

DI boni, boni quid porto ! fed ubi inveniam Pamphilum :

Ut metum, in quo nunc eft, adimam, atque expleam animum gaudio ?

metum, in quo nunc eft, atque expleam animum ejus gaudio ?

ORDO.
DA. DII boni· quid bo-ni porto ! fed ubi invcniam Pamphi-lum, ut adimam

ANNOTATIONS.

Byrrbia, and tells him what he had juft then heard of his young Mafter's Marriage, which, upon his meeting *Charinus,* gave Occafion to the immediately preceding Scene. *Davus*

Right column ordo (italic paraphrase):

Nibil. PA: Quàm vellem fuiffet ! CH. Nunc obfecro te per poftram aniicitiam & per meum amorem, principio, ut ne ducas illam. PA. Equidem dubo operam. CH. Sed fi non potes efficere id, aut fi bæ nuptiæ funt tibi cordi ; PA. Cordi ! CH. Saltem profer eas aliquot dies, dum proficifcor aliquo, ne videam. PA. Audi jam nunc. Ego, Charine, neutiquam puto effe officium liberi bominis, cum is promereat nil, poftulare id apponi gratiæ tibi. Ego malo effugere iftas nuptias, quàm tu adipifci eas. CH.

Char. He feems to be pleafed, I don't know with what.

Pamp. O, nothing at all; he has not heard of thefe late Misfortunes.

Dav. Who, I perfuade myfelf, does he but know he is to be married to-day—

Char. D'ye hear him?

Dav. Is looking for me all over the Town in great diftrefs. But where fhall I feek for him? Or which way go to find him?

Char. Do you forbear fpeaking to him?

Dav. Well, I'll be going.

Pamp. *Davus*; foho here, ftay.

Dav. Who can this be, who? O *Pamphilus*, the very Man I look for. What *Charinus* too! fortunately met; I wanted both.

Pamp. *Davus*, I'm undone.

Dav. Do but hear me.

Pamp. I'm abfolutely ruined.

Dav. Pfhaw. I know what you fear.

Char. As for me, I'm in danger of lofing my Quiet for ever.

Dav. I know too what you fear.

Pamp. I'm threatned with a Marriage.

Dav. And I know that too.

Pamp. But this very Day.

Dav. You dun me, although I know all. You, *Pamphilus*, are in pain, left you be compelled to marry her: you, *Charinus*, again are impatient till you marry her.

Char. You have it.

Pamp. The very fame.

Dav. And in this very fame there is no danger: I engage for it.

Pamp. For Heaven's fake, rid me as foon as poffible of my Fears.

Dav. I will do it this Inftant. *Chremes* will not give his Daughter in Marriage to-day.

Pamp. How d'ye know?

Dav. I know it perfectly well. Your Father met me juft now at the *Forum*, and taking me afide, told me he intended you fhould take a Wife to-day; alfo a great deal more, that I have not now time to repeat. I ran to the *Forum*, and made all hafte to find you, that I might tell you of it. Not finding you there, I got upon a Height, and looked about me, but could fee you nowhere. By chance, I there

spy'd

ANNOTATIONS.

Davus ftill at a lofs where to find *Pamphilus*, as he is returning home, begins to fufpect from the Behaviour of *Simo*, that there muft be fome Myftery in the Cafe. Running to *Chremes*, and feeing no Preparations for a Wedding there, he immediately fees into his Mafter's Project, and haftens to *Pamphilus* to acquaint him with it, and free him from the Uneafinefs, which he knew he muft be under upon hearing of the intending Wedding. As he forefaw that this

News muft give his Mafter great Joy, he appears exulting, and with an Air of Triumph.

'3 *Iftue ipfum nibil pericli eft.* *Davus* here would have his Mafter to banifh Fear. and gives the Reafon in brief; *Uxorem tibi jam non dat Chremes.* This is exactly according to the Rules of juft Writing. An Orator ought alway (before he gives a particular Detail, which muft be fuppofed to take up time) to begin by a fhort Account

of

CH. Lætus eſt, neſcio quid. PA. nihil eſt. nondum hæc
   reſcivit mala.   [nuptias,
DA. Quem ego nunc credo, ſi jam audierit ſibi paratas
CH. Audin' tu illum ? DA. toto me oppido exanima-
   tum quærere.   5
Sed ubi quæram ? aut quò nunc primùm intendam ?
   CH. ceſſas alloqui ?
DA. Abeo. PA. Dave, ades, reſiſte. DA. quis homo
   eſt, qui me ? ô Pamphile,   [volo.
Teipſum quæro. euge, ô Charine! ambo opportunè : vos
PA. Dave, perii. DA. quin tu hoc audi. PA. interii.
   DA. quid timeas, ſcio.
CH. Mea quidem hercle certè in dubio vita eſt. DA.
   & quid tu, ſcio.   10
PA. Nuptiæ mihi. DA. & id ſcio. PA. hodie. DA. ob-
   tundis, tametſi intellego.
Id paves, ne ducas tu illam ! tu autem, ut ducas. CH.
   rem tenes.   [me vide
PA. Iſtuc ipſum. DA. atqui iſtuc ipſum, nil pericli eſt :
PA. Obſecro te, quamprimùm hoc me libera miſerum
   metu. DA. hem,
Libero. uxorem tibi jam non dat Chremes. PA. qui
   ſcis ? DA. ſcio.   15
Tuus pater modo me prehendit : ait, tibi uxorem dare
Hodie : item alia multa, quæ, nunc non eſt narran-
   di locus.   [tibi hæc.
Continuò ad te properans, pecurro ad forum, ut dicam
Ubi te non invenio, ibi aſcendo in quendam excelſum
   locum.   19
Circumſpicio : nuſquam. forte ibi hujus video Byrrhiam

paves id, ne ducas illam, tu autem, Charine, paves ut ducas. PA. *Iſtuc ipſum.* DA. *Atqui quod ad iſtuc ipſum nil pericli eſt: vide me.* PA. *Obſecro te, quamprimùm libera me miſerum hoc metu.* DA. *Hem, libero te: Chremes non jam dat gnatam ſuam uxorem tibi.* PA. *Qui ſcis ?* DA. *Scio. Tuus pater modo prehendit me : ait, ſeſe dare uxorem tibi hodie: item alia multa, quæ nunc non eſt locus narrandi. Continuò properans ad te, percurro ad forum, ut dicam hæc tibi. Ubi non invenio te ibi, aſcendo in quendam excelſum locum. Circumſpicio, video te nuſquam. Forte video ibi Byrrhiam ſervum hujus Charini ;*

Right margin note:
CH. Lætus eſt, neſcio ob quid. PA. Nibil eſt, nondum reſcivit hæc noſtra mala. DA. Quem ego nunc credo, ſi jam audiverit nuptias eſſe paratas ſibi. CH. Audin' tu illum ? DA. exanimatum quærere me toto oppido. Sed ubi quæram illum ? aut quò nunc primùm intendam iter ? CH. An ceſſas alloqui ? DA. Abeo. PA. Dave, ades, reſiſte. DA. Quis homo eſt qui vocat me ? O Pamphile, quæro teipſum, euge ô Charine, ambo opportunè adeſtis : vos vos. PA. Dave, perii. DA. Quin audi tu hoc. PA. Interii. DA. Scio quid timeas. CH. Mea vita quidem hercle eſt certè in dubio. DA. Et ſcio quid tu timeas. PA. Nuptiæ parantur mibi. DA. Scio & id. PA. Sed hodie. DA. Obtundis me, tametſi intelligo omnia. Tu, Pamphile,

---

ANNOTATIONS.

of what he intends, that the Matter may be | the better underſtood, and the Reaſons and | Circumſtances he inſiſts upon, have their full | Force. *Pamphilus*'s Impatience would have | been too great not to interrupt *Davus*, had | he taken any other way : but by telling him | in the Beginning, that *Chremes* would not | give him his Daughter, it was natural to aſk | how he came to know it ? Thus we are, in | a very eaſy ſimple manner, let into all the | Particulars of this Diſcovery.

15 *Jam non dat.* *Donatus*'s Obſervation | upon the Particle *jam* is ſomewhat remark-

able. *Bene jam, quod ſi non dixiſſet, intelligeret Pamphilus, vel poſtea Chremetem filiam eſſe daturum. Sed addito jam plena ſecuritas eſt. Jam enim renunciatio eſt perpetuitatis.* But this ſeems to me to be a mere Refinement ; for how *Davus* ſhould pretend to know ſo much of *Chremes*'s Diſpoſition in that Point, is hard to be conceived. Beſides, the Reaſons he brings afterwards from the little Preparations that were making, ſerve only to ſhew that there was to be no Wedding that Day. In fact, the great Perplexity was, that the Marriage being ſo ſudden,

fpy'd *Byrrbia :* I enquire of him; he tells me he had not feen you. This perplexed me : I began to confider with myfelf, what I had beft do. Meantime, as I was returning thence, a Sufpicion rofe in my Mind from the very thing. Hah, fcarce any Provifions extraordinary, my Mafter fad, a Marriage all of a fudden : thefe things don't agree.

Pamp. Well, what of all this?

Dav. Away I ran directly to *Chremes :* when I came there, nothing but Silence before the Door. I was overjoy'd.

Char. Well faid.

Pamp. Go on.

Dav. Here I ftayed fome time; not a Soul was to be feen going in, or coming out: never a Matron: not the leaft Preparation or Hurry in the Houfe; I drew near, and looked in.

Pamp. I underftand you, an admirable Sign!

Dav. Has this the Appearance of a Wedding?

Pamp. I fcarce think it, *Davus.*

Dav. Scarce think it, dy'e fay? you don't take it right; the thing is certain. Nay, more, as I was returning thence, I met *Chremes's* Boy carrying home fome little Fifhes, and a Bunch of Herbs for the old Man's Supper.

Char. I am reftored to Life again to-day by your means, *Davus.*

Dav. For certain not in the leaft.

Char. Why fo? your Mafter is not like to have her.

Dav. Very wife truly: as if becaufe my Mafter is not like to have her, fhe muft of neceffity fall to your Share. Unlefs you beftir yourfelf, folicit the old Man's Friends, and make your Court to them; all this will turn to nothing.

Char. 'Tis good Advice; I'll follow it, altho' I have already more than once been difappointed of this Hope. Adieu.

Rogo: negat vidiffe. mihi molestum. quid agam, cogito.
Redeunti interea ex ipsa re mî incidit fufpicio. hem,
Paululum opfonî, ipfus triftis, de improvifo nuptiæ.
Non cohærent. PA. quorfumnam iftuc? DA. ego me
continuò ad Chremem. ·   · ·   24
Cum illò advenio, folitudo ante oftium. jam id gaudeo.
PA. Rectè dicis, perge. DA. maneo. interea introire
neminem   .౿ː͵ʌΓ·
Video, exire neminem, matronam nullam, in ædibus
Nil ornati, nil tumulti. acceffi, introfpexi. PA. fcio.
Magnum fignum. DA. num videntur convenire hæc
nuptiis?   ˌ ɹˌ   ˌ.ˌ ɩdˌ ˌ   [accipis. 30
PA. Non opinor, Dave. DA. opinor, narras? non rectè
Certa res eft. etiam puerum inde abiens conveni
Chremis,   ˑ ʔ᾿ʋː·   ˑ᾿ˑ᾿ˑˑʕ   ʔ
Olera, & pifciculos minutos ferre obolo in cœnam feni.
CH. Liberatus fum, Dave, hodie tuâ operâ. DA. at nullus
quidem,   [diculum caput!
CH. Quid ita? nempe huic prorfus illam non dat. DA. ri-
Quafi neceffe fit, fi huic non dat, te illam uxorem du-
cere.   ˑ   ·ˑ᾿ʕ᾿ˑˑ   35
Nifi vides, nifi fenis amicos oras, ambis. CH. bene mones.
Ibo: etfi hercle fæpe jam me fpes hæc fruftrata eft. vale.

Rogo eum, negat
fe vidiffe te: hoc
erat molestum mihi:
cogito quid agam.
Interea fufpicio in-
cidit mihi redeunti,
ex ipfâ re. Hem,
paululum opfonii,
ipfe triftis: nuptiæ
de improvifo: hæc
non cohærent. PA.
Quorfumnam ftu?
DA. Continuò ego
confero me ad Chre-
mem, cùm advenio
illâ, folitudo eft
ante oftium, gaudeo
jam propter id.
PA. Dicis rectè,
perge. DA. Ma-
neo. Interea vi-
deo neminem Intro-
ire, neminem exire,
nullam matronam,
nil ornati, nil tu-
multi in ædibus;
acceffi, introfpexi.
PA. Scio; magnum
fignum eft. DA.
Num hæc videntur
convenire nuptiis?

PA. *Non opinor, Dave.* DA. *Opinor, narras? non accipis rectè.* |*Res eft certa: etiam abiens*
inde conveni puerum Chremis, video eum *ferro olera & minutos pifciculos* emptas obolo, feni, in
cœnam. CH. *Dave, fum liberatus hodie tuâ operâ.* DA. *At nullus quidem.* CH. *Quid ita?*
nempe Chremes *prorfus non dat illam huic.* DA. *Ridiculum caput! quafi neceffe fit, fi ille non*
dat eum huic, te ducere illam uxorem: nifi vides, nifi oras amicos fenis, nifi ambis. CH. *Mones*
bene, ibo: etfi hercle hæc fpes fæpe jam fruftrata eft me: vale.   ˑ   ʕ   ˑʕ᾿ʔ(

ANNOTATIONS.

in value equal to one Penny-Farthing one
fixth.

33 *At nullus quidem.* A great many have
ac. *Le Clerc* in his *Art Critica,* rejects both
Readings, and contends for *hac nullus qui-*
dem; that is, *Hac quidem opera mea nullus*
liberatus es; *You are never the better for this*
my Information. *Quafi fubinuat* (adds that
celebrated Critic) *gloriofus fervus peffe fe eum*
liberari, fi id operam dent. But altho' this
muft be allowed ingenious; yet how far it is
true, I am in doubt: for as Bifhop *Hare* well
remarks, nothing can be more remote from
Davus's Intention, than this laft Turn. For
it is not his Defign to make *Charinus* think
highly of him; but folicitous only for *Pam-*
philus, and diftrufting himfelf; he artfully
fets *Charinus* to work, that by his means
too *Pamphilus* might have his Defign fur-

thered as much as poffible. *At,* therefore,
feems to have the beft Pretenfions here, for
it is a Particle of no fixed and certain Signification; but may be differently turned, according to the different Circumftances in
which it is applied: for, to pafs by others, it
is fometimes ufed as an Adverfative, at other
times we find it inftead of *certe.* But in
Dialogue, when it begins the Anfwer, it is
for the moft part an Expletive, and brought
in rather for Ornament, than to help out
the Senfe.

30 *Nifi vides,* &c. This ftill ferves to
confirm what has been obferved in the foregoing Note, and this is the Conftruction,
that even *Donatus* puts upon the Words:
Artificiofe Davus Charinum excitat, ut, fi fieri
poffit, adjuvetur negotium Pamphili, dum ille
fibi providet.

E 2   ACT

ACT II. SCENE III.

ARGUMENT.

Davus *advises* Pamphilus *to pretend to his Father, that he was willing to marry, from which Counsel new Troubles arise.*

PAMPHILUS, DAVUS.

Pamp. WELL, but prithee what can my Father propose by this Pretence of a Wedding?

Dav. I'll tell ye; if he should be angry with you now, because *Chremes* refuses to give you his Daughter, he must tax himself with using you ill, and not without Reason, being as yet uncertain how you stand inclined to the Marriage; but if you should reject the Match, he'll lay all the blame upon you: then there will be Noise and Scolding.

Pamp. What would you advise me to? Shall I bear it all?

Dav. He's your Father, *Pamphilus:* 'tis a delicate Point; besides, this Mistress of yours has no-body to stand by her: he'll easily find some Pretence to expel her the Town.

Pamp. Expel her the Town!

Dav. Ay, and speedily too.

Pamp. Tell me then, *Davus*, what I had best do.

Dav. Say you'll marry her.

Pamp. Hah.

Dav. What's the matter?

Pamp. Shall I say so?

Dav. Why not?

Pamp. I'll never do it.

Dav. Nay, but pray don't refuse.

Pamp. Never think of it.

Dav. Only consider what will follow from it.

Pamp. That I shall be deprived of *Glycery*, and tyed down to the other.

Dav. Far from it: for after this manner, if I mistake not, your Father will address you: *Pamphilus*, 'tis my Will, that you take a Wife to-day. With all my heart, say you: tell me on what Pretence can he chide you? By this means you will render all his Measures, which he thinks so well concerted, without Effect; and that too without any danger to yourself: for it is not once to be doubted,

that

ANNOTATIONS.

¹ *Quid igitur sibi volt pater? Pam-philus* now left alone with *Davus*, and convinced by what he had heard from him, that *Chremes* had no Thoughts of giving him his Daughter, is at a loss to conceive what his Father could mean by such a Pretence. *Davus*, whose Character is that of a shrewd, cunning, penetrating Slave, easily conjectures the true Reason; and gives *Pamphilus* such Advice, as he thinks will serve best to disconcert the old Man.

² *Si id succensat nunc.* The Particle
sub

ACTUS II.   SCENA III.

ARGUMENTUM.

*Confulit Pamphilo Davus, ut dicat patri fe ducturum uxorem,
cujus confilio major oritur perturbatio.*

PAMPHILUS, DAVUS.

ORDO.

QUID igitur fibi volt pater? cur fimulat? DA. ego
   dicam tibi,
Si id fuccenfeat nunc,quia non dat tibi uxoremChremes,
Ipfu' fibi effe injurius videatur : neque id injuriâ;
Priufquam tuum, ut fefe habeat, animum ad nuptia
   perfpexerit.
Sed fi tu negâris ducere, ibi culpam in te transferet : 5
Tum illæ turbæ fient. PA. quid vis? patiar? DA. pa-
   ter eft, Pamphile :   [ctum invenerit
Difficile eft. tum hæc fola eft mulier : dictum ac fa-
Aliquam caufam, quamobrem ejiciat oppido. PA. eji-
   ciat? DA. citò.
PA. Cedo igitur, quid faciam, Dave? DA. dic te du-
   cturum. PA. hem! DA. quid eft?
PA. Ego dicam? DA. cur non? PA. nunquam faciam.
   DA. ne nega.   10
PA. Suadere noli. DA. ex eâ re quid fiat, vide.
PA. Ut ab illâ excludar, huc concludar. DA. non ita eft
Nempe hoc fic effe opinor dicturum patrem :
Ducas volo hodie uxorem. tu, ducam, inquies :
Cedo, quid jurgabit tecum? hìc reddes omnia,   15
Quæ nunc funt certa ei confilia, incerta ut fient,

PA. QUID i-
gitur pa-
ter vult fibi? cur
fimulat? DA. Ego
dicam tibi. Si
nunc fuccenfeat pro-
pter id, quia
Chremes non dat
filiam uxorim tibi,
ipfe videatur fibi
effe injurius : neque
id injuriâ, fi fuc-
cenferet priufquam
perfpexeret tuum a-
nimum, ut habeat
fefe ad nuptias. Sed
fi tu negâris ducere,
ibi transferet cul-
pam in te; tum
illæ turbæ fient.
PA. Quid vis?
Patiarne has tur-
bas? DA. Eft pater,
Pamphile, difficile
eft refiftere ei; tum
hæc mulier eft fola :
dictum ac factum
invenerit aliquam
caufam, quamobrem

ejiciat eam oppido. PA. Ejiciat eam? DA. Imo citò. PA. Cedo igitur, Dave, quid faciam?
DA. Dic te effe ducturum uxorem. PA. Hem! DA. Quid eft? PA. Egone dicam? DA.
Cur non? PA. Nunquam faciam. DA. Ne nega. PA. Noli fuadere mihi. DA. Vide quid
fiat ex tâ re. PA. Ut excludar ab illâ Glycerio, concludar huc cum Philumena. DA. Non
eft ita. Nempe fic opinor patrem tuum effe dicturum hoc: Volo ut ducas hodie uxorem: tu inquies, Ducam: cedo, quid jurgabit tecum? Hic reddes omnia, quæ nunc funt certa ei,
ut fient incerta,

ANNOTATIONS.

fub, when it enters into Compofition, generally denotes a thing that is done privately,
or to one's felf. Such, therefore, who after the Rates fixed by the Cenfors, complained
that they were taxed beyond their Eftate,
were faid properly *fuccenfere*; that is, fays
Wefterbovius, clauculum *recenfere.* Hence, *fuccenfere* is often ufed inftead of *fubirafci, iniquo
animo ferrt, ftomachari,* as here, and afterwards
II. 6. 17. *Eft quid fuccenfet tibi.*

6 *Quid vis? patiar?* There are very
different Opinions as to the meaning of thefe
Words, arifing chiefly from the Variety of
Readings in different Copies. I have endeavoured to fix upon that which agrees beft

with the Anfwer immediately following.
Davus had told him, that if he refufed to
marry, his Father would lay all the blame
upon him, and think he had a right to chide
him feverely. What then would you have
me to do? Shall I bear it all? *Davus* replies, 'Tis your Father, the Cafe is difficult,
nor do you feem to attend to all the Confe-
quences; for tho' perhaps you may think that
you can ftand your Father's Reproaches, yet
he will not probably ftop there, but, finding
you obftinate, endeavour to have *Glycery* ex-
pelled *Athens.*

10 *Ego dicam?* There is a particular
Emphafis upon the Word *ego* here. What
shall

E 3

that *Chremes* has no Intention of giving you his Daughter; nor would I have you hefitate a moment, left perhaps he may change his Mind. Say to your Father, you are ready to obey, that when he would be angry with you, he may find no juft Pretence. For as to what you fondly flatter yourfelf with, I'll eafily fhew the Weaknefs of it. No one will give his Daughter to a Man of fuch unfettled Morals, you fay : but he'll rather find out fome Girl without any Fortune at all, than fuffer you to go on at this rate. But if he fees you take all in good part, he'll become more indifferent, look out for another at his leifure, and who knows what Fortune may do in the mean time ?

Pamp. Do you really think fo ?

Dav. There is not the leaft doubt of it.

Pamp. See that you don't lead me into fome fatal Error.

Dav. Do but make yourfelf eafy.

Pamp. I yield : but Care muft be taken he know nothing of my having a Child by her, for I have promifed to bring it up.

Dav. O extravagant Madnefs !

Pamp. She conjured me to give her this Promife, as a Token I would never abandon her.

Dav. Well, we'll take care : but yonder comes your Father ; let it not appear to him, that you are under any Concern.

ANNOTATIONS.

fhall I fay fo, *I*, who am under fuch folemn Engagements to *Glycery*, I who have no manner of Attachment to *Philumæna*, and who abhor from my Soul Hypocrify and Deceit ?

19 Ne is fuam mutet fententiam. Whom does the Poet mean here by *is*, *Chremes* or *Simo ? Donatus* contends for *Chremes*, and almoft all Commentators are of the fame mind. But as *Wefterbovius* thinks it fhould be underftood of *Simo*, and by that means, gives a quite different Turn to the Paffage, I fhall tranfcribe here what he fays, that it may be compared with the common Interpretation. *Omnino Simo videtur intelligendus, ut fenfus verborum Davi fit :* " Stat " patri tuo fententia te Philumenam ductu- " rum. Ne igitur mutet fuam hanc fen-

" tentiam, & de alia tibi danda cogitet, tu " dices, te ducturum Philumenam illam : " quod facere potes fine omni periculo : ne- " que enim Chremes tibi gnatam daturus " eft. Si vero ita tecum cogitas, mutet " fane pater fuam fententiam, velitque mihi " dare aliam, fatis fcio neminem honeftum " daturum mihi, his moribus prædito, & " Glycerii amoribus irretito gnatam fuam : " ita tibi habe ; patrem tuum non mora- " turum dotem, fed inopem potius inven- " turum, quam finat te porro corrumpi."

Integrum itaque locum ita lego & diftinguo :

------*Nec tu ea caufa muxueris*

Hæc, que facis. Ne is mutet fuam fententiam,

Patri dic velle, ut, quum velit, tibi jure irafci non queat.

Hæc

ACT II. SCENE IV.

ARGUMENT.

Davus *encourages* Pamphilus *not to appear difconcerted before his Father, but to behave with Prefence of Mind.*

SIMO, DAVUS, PAMPHILUS.

Simo. **I** Return again to fee what they are about, or what Project they may now have fallen upon.   *Dav.*

ANNOTATIONS.

1 *Revifo quid agant.* While *Davus* is arguing with *Pamphilus*, *Simo* comes up | with a defign to put the Queftion to his Son. *Davus* fees him at a diftance, and obferving it

Sine omni periclo. nam hocce haud dubium eſt, quin
    Chremes
Tibi non det gnatam : nec tu eâ causâ minueris
Hæc quæ facis, ne is ſuam mutet ſententiam.   19
Patri dic velle : ut, cùm velit tibi jure iraſci, non queat.
Nam quod tu ſperas, propulſabo facilè : uxorem his
    moribus   [pi ſinat.
Dabit nemo. inopem inveniet potius, quàm te corrum-
Sed ſi te æquo animo ferre accipiet, neglegentem feceris.
Aliam otioſus quæret. interea aliquid acciderit boni.
PA. Itan' credis ? DA. haud dubium id quidem eſt. PA.
    vide quo inducas. DA. quin taces ?   25
PA. Dicam. puerum autem ne reſciſcat mihi ex illâ,
    cautio eſt :
Nam pollicitus ſum ſuſcepturum.   DA. ô facinus au-
    dax ! PA. hanc fidem   [darem.
Sibi, me obſecravit, qui ſe ſciret non deſerturum, ut
DA. Curabitur. ſed, pater adeſt. cave te eſſe triſtem ſen-
    tiat.

Sine omni periculo tibi. Nam hocce haud eſt dubium, quin Chremes non det gnatum uxorem tibi: nec tu minueris hæc quæ facis, eâ causâ, ne is mutet ſuam ſententiam. Dic patri te velle ducere : ut cùm velit, non queat iraſci tibi jure. Nam facile propulſabo quod tu ſperas: nempe putas, Nemo dabit uxorem homini prædito his moribus. Inveniet potius inopem, quam ut ſinat te corrumpi. Sed ſi accipiet te ferre id æquo animo, feceris negligentem ; quæret aliam otioſus : interea aliquid boni acciderit. PA. Crediſne ita ? DA. Id quidem haud eſt dubium. PA. Vice quò inducas me. DA. Quin taces ? PA. Dicam. Autem cautio eſt, ne pater reſciſcat eſſe puerum mihi ex illa. Nam pollicitus ſum me ſuſcepturum illum. DA. O audax facinus ! PA. Obſecravit me ut darem hanc fidem ſibi, qui ſciret me non eſſe deſerturum ſe. DA. Curabitur : ſed pater adeſt ; cave ne ſentiat te eſſe triſtem.

ANNOTATIONS.

Hæc opinor expeditiſſima ſunt & planiſſima. I would only obſerve in the general upon this, that as to *Simo*'s Deſign, there ſeems to be no Conſequence depending upon it. *Davus* had already diſcovered, that it was all but Pretence, to learn how his Son was inclined. But as to *Chremes*, *Pamphilus* had good Reaſon to fear. For as he had declined the Match, only becauſe he fancied *Pamphilus* under Engagements to *Glycery* ; ſo there was Danger, if that Suſpicion ſhould once be removed, that *Simo* might prevail upon him to conſent again to the Marriage : whereas, if *Pamphilus* ſtill continued obſtinate, there was no Probability that *Chremes* would hazard his Daughter with a Man of that Character. And this deluding Fancy *Davus* indeavours in the next Sentence to deſtroy.

²⁴ *Interea aliquid acciderit boni.* Becauſe in very diſtreſſing Circumſtances, that ſeem unavoidable, the only Relief is in delay. *Pamphilus*, therefore, yields to *Davus*'s Advice ; but, afterwards foreſeeing another Inconvenience from *Glycery*'s being with Child, and his Promiſe to bring it up, he propoſes that alſo. For altho' *Glycery* was not yet brought to bed ; yet having heard from *Myſis* that ſhe was in Labour, and the Midwife ſent for, he already conſiders himſelf as a Father. *Davus* endeavours to make him eaſy, and concludes with aſſuring him, that all proper Care ſhould be taken.

ACTUS II. SCENA IV.

ARGUMENTUM.

Monet Pamphilum Davus, apud patrem ne titubet ; ſed ut animo præſenti loquatur.

SIMO, DAVUS, PAMPHILUS.

REviſo, quid agant, aut quid captent conſili.

quid conſilii captent.

ORDO.
SI. R*Eviſo quid agant, aut*

ANNOTATIONS.

it to *Pamphilus*, exhorts him to act with Spirit and Reſolution.

2 *Hic*

Dav. He now don't in the leaft doubt, but you'll refufe to marry. He comes plotting ftrongly from fome folitary Corner, and hopes he has contrived a Speech, whereby to difconcert you; be fure, there-fore, to behave with great Prefence of Mind.

Pamp. As well as I can, *Davus.*

Dav. Pamphilus, I fay, believe it for certain, that your Father will not give you one angry Word to-day, if you but fay you'll marry.

ANNOTATIONS.

² *Hic nunc non dubitat.* *Davus* con-jectures this from many Circumftances. When *Simo* firft fpoke of the Wedding, to *Pamphilus*, at the *Forum,* he appeared afto-nifhed, and quite difconcerted; he moreover was not infenfible of his Son's being ftill at-tached to *Glycery,* he alfo fees the concert-ing with *Davus,* whofe Inclinations he was no Stranger to.

³ *Meditatus.* This word properly means, applying one's Thoughts to the making of

Verfes. Hence it is transferred, to fignify any Employment of the Mind, that com-prehends Attention and Forethought. Thus, *Adel.* II. 1. 41.

Nunc vide: utrum vis? Argentum accipere, an caufam meditari tuam?

Phor. II. 1. 12.

Meditari fecum oportet, quo pacto adverfam ærumnam ferant.

⁵ *Qua differat.* *Difturba & in diver-fum ferat,* fays *Donatus,* which indeed is the

---

ACT II. SCENE V.

ARGUMENT.

Simo tries his Son's Difpofition with regard to the Wedding. Pamphilus, by the Perfuafion of Davus, confents. Byrrhia overhearing Pamphilus's Anfwer, is concerned on his Mafter's account.

BYRRHIA, SIMO, DAVUS, PAMPHILUS.

Byrrhia. MY Mafter commanded me, that leaving every thing elfe, I fhould particularly obferve *Pamphilus* to-day, and learn, if poffible, what were his Defigns in regard to the Mar-riage; and 'tis for this Reafon, that feeing his Father walk this way, I now follow him. But here he is himfelf along with *Davus:* Now therefore I'll do the beft I can.

Si. I fee they are both here.

Dav. S't! Mind your Cue.

Si. Pamphilus.

Dav. Look back with an Air of Surprize, as if you had not feen him before.

Pamp. O! Father.   *Dav.*

ANNOTATIONS.

¹ *Herus me, reliĉtis rebus.* We have feen in a former Scene, what paffed between *Charinus* and *Pamphilus.* The former of thefe feems, however, to have had ftill fome Diftruft, and therefore charges his Servant *Byrrhia* to watch him, and, if poffible, learn what paffed between him, and his Father. With this defign he appears in this Scene,

intent to obey his Mafter's Orders. *Reliĉtis rebus,* was a proverbial Expreffion, denoting that a Man, for a time, forgot every other Concern, to attend to what he had in view at prefent. Thus, *Eunuch.* I. 2. 85.

Nonne ubi mihi dixti, cupere te ex Æthiopia Ancillulam, reliĉtis rebus omnibus Quæfivi?

Cicero

DA. Hic nunc non dubitat quin te ducturum neges.
Venit meditatus alicunde ex folo loco:
Orationem fperat inveniffe fe,
Qui differat te : proin' tu fac, apud te ut fcies.   5
PA. Modò ut poffim, Dave. DA. crede, inquam, hoc
   mihi, Pamphile,
Nunquam hodie tecum commutaturum patrem
Unum effe verbum, fi te dices ducere.

Dave. DA. Pampbile, inquam, crede mibi boc; patrem tuum nunquam effe commutaturum unum verbum tecum bodie, fi dices te velle ducere uxorem.

ORDO (right column):
DA. Hic nunc ncn dubitat quin tu neges te ducturum effe uxorem. Venit meditatus alicunde ex folo loco: & fperat fe inveniffe orationem, qui differat te: proin' fac tu, ut fis apud te. PA. Modò; ut poffim,

ANNOTATIONS.

the proper meaning of the word. *Virgil.*
   ------ *Atque arida differt*
   Nubila.
And *Velleius Patereulus* 2. 79. fpeaking of a Fleet. *Vis Africi laceravit ae diffulit. Simo's* Defign, as *Davus* apprehended, was to diftract and difconcert *Pampbilus,* as is plain from what he afterwards fays,
   Proin' tu fac, apud te ut fies.
   7 *Commutaturum patrem. Verba commutare,* is here for *jurgia babere,* a manner of

fpeaking, not fo common, nor do I, indeed, remember to have feen it any where, but in *Terence,* who gives another Example of it in his *Pbormio* IV. 3. 33.
   Tria non commutabitis
   Verba *bodie inter vos.*
That is, fays *Donatus Dabitis atque accipietis,* id eft, *jurgabitis.* And adds. *Ego puto commutare* verba *boc effe, pro bonis dictis mala ingerere; boc eft, iracundiâ in maledicta compelli.*

ACTUS II. SCENA V.

ARGUMENTUM.

Explorat animum filii de nuptiis Simo, cui affentitur Pampbilus impulfus Davi; & Byrrbia beri fui caufa, audito Pamphili refponfo, perturbatur.

BYRRHIA, SIMO, DAVUS, PAMPHILUS.

HERU' me, relictis rebus, juffit Pamphilum
   Hodie obfervare, ut, quid ageret de nuptiis,
Scirem. id propterea nunc hunc venientem fequor:
Ipfum adeo præftò video cum Davo. hoc agam. [phile. 5
SI. Utrumque âdeffe video. DA. hem, ferva. SI. Pam
DA.Quafi de improvifo refpice ad eum. PA.ehem pater.

adeo video ipfum præftò cum Davo. Hcc agam. SI. Video utrumque adeffe. DA. Hem, ferva te. SI. Pampbile. DA. Refpice ad eum quafi de improvifo. PA. Ebem, pater.

ORDO (right column):
BY. HERUS juffit me, relictis rebus aliis, obfervare Pampbilum bodie, ut fcirem quid ageret de nuptiis: propterea id nunc fequor bunc venientem:

ANNOTATIONS.

Cicero ufes the fame Form of fpeaking. *Fam.* 2. 14. *Omnia relinques, fi me amabis, quum tua opera Fabius uti volet.* Again, 12. 14. *Cujus rei tanto in timore fui, ut omnibus rebus relictis, cum paucioribus & minoribus navibus ad illas ire conatus fim.*
   3 *Nunc bunc venientem fequor, Bentley* contends that this Verfe muft certainly be fpurious; for as *Pampbilus,* fays he, has not difappeared fince *Byrrbia* left the Stage, in the fecond Scene of this Act, he could not

fay, *Nunc bunc venientem fequor.* The Authors of the *Terence,* Latin and *Englifh,* in three Volumes, repeat this Remark with Approbation; and add, that if we fuppofe the Line genuine, we muft at the fame time fuppofe *Terence* guilty of a monftrous Abfurdity. But without bringing fo heavy a Charge againft our Poet, we may ftill retain a Verfe, which, as it is to be met with in all Editions, ought not to be too fuddenly rejected, *Hunc* does not here refer to *Pampbilus,*

Dav. Excellent!

Si. 'Tis my Defign, that you take a Wife to-day.

Byr. Now I am in pain on my Mafter's account, as to what An-fwer he may give.

Pamp. Neither in this, nor any thing elfe, will you ever find me backward to obey you.

Byr. Hah!

Dav. He's mute.

Byr. What was it he faid?

Si. You do as becomes you, my Son, when what I demand of you, is thus yielded to with a good Grace.

Dav. Did not I judge right?

Byr. My Mafter, as far as I can perceive, muft go without a Wife.

Si. Go in then, *Pamphilus*, that you may'nt be out of the way, when wanted.

Pamp. I go.

Byr. Is there then no Confidence to be put in Men in any Cafe? Well, I find the old Saying to hold good; *Every Man for himfelf.* I have feen this young Lady, and remember that I faw a moft charm-ing Creature. I can, therefore, the more readily excufe *Pamphilus*, if he had rather fhe flept in his Arms, than in my Mafter's. I'll go, and make my Report, that I may receive as hard Ufage, as are the Tidings which I bring.

A N N O T A T I O N S.

philus, but to *Simo*; and fo plainly too, that I wonder how it could efcape their Notice. *Davus* and *Pamphilus* are both upon the Stage. *Simo* is feen at fome diftance com-ing up to them; *Byrrhia* is clofe behind, who being charged by his Mafter to obferve what paffed between the Father and the Son, watches the old Man's Steps, that he might be prefent at their firft Interview. *And it is for this Reafon, fays he, that I now*

A C T II. S C E N E VI.

A R G U M E N T.

In this Scene, Davus *plays upon* Simo *with great cunning, and, whilft he is in doubt what to think, confirms him in the Be-lief of what he wanted; he artfully combats his Sufpicions, by which the Plot is advanced. Each diftrufts the other, and is afraid of being deceived.*

DAVUS, SIMO.

Davus. I Know that he now thinks I have fome Plot a hatching a-gainft him, and that I ftay here for that very purpofe.

Si. What is *Davus* faying?

Da. Why really nothing at all at prefent.   *Si.*

A N N O T A T I O N S.
¹ *Hic nunc. Pamphilus* is ordered in by his Father; and *Byrrhia* having learned all he wanted to know, goes to acquaint his Mafter with it. *Davus* and *Simo* are, there-fore, left by themfelves. As they diftrufted each other, and it was the Intereft of both

Da. Probe. Si. hodie uxorem ducas, ut dixi, volo.
By. Nunc noftræ parti timeo, quid hic refpondeat.
Pa. Neque iftic, neque alibi tibi erit ufquam in me
   mora. By. hcm!
Da. Obmutuit. By. quid dixit? Si. facis ut te decet, 10
Cùm iftuc, quod poftulo, impetro cum gratiâ.
Da.Sum verus?By.herus,quantum audio,uxore excidit.
Si. I jam nunc intro, ne in morâ, cùm opu' fit, fies.
Pa. Eo. By. nullane in re effe homini cuiquam fidem?
Verum illud verbum eft, volgò quod dici folet,   15
Omnes fibi malle melius effe quàm alteri.
Ego illam vidi virginem : formâ bonâ
Memini videre; quo æquior fum Pamphilo,
Si fe illam in fomnis, quàm illum, amplecti maluit.
Renunciabo, ut pro hoc malo mihi det malum.   20

Da. Probe. Si. Volo ducas hodie uxorem, ut dixi. By. Nunc timeo noftræ parti, quid hic refpondeat. Pa. Neque iftic, neque alibi, erit ufquam mora tibi in me. By. Hem! Da. Obmutuit. By. Quid dixit? Si. Facis ut decet te, cùm impetro iftuc quod poftulo cum gratiâ. Da. Sum ne verus vates? By. Herus meus, quantum audio, excidit uxore. Si. I jam nunc intro, ne fis in morâ, cùm opus fit. Pa. Eo. By. Itane equidem eft? effe fidem cuiquam homini in nulla re? Illud verbum eft verum, quod vulgò folet dici, viz. omnes malle effe melius fibi, quàm alteri. Ego vidi illam virginem : memini videre illam effe bonâ formâ : quo fum æquior Pamphilo, fi maluit fe amplecti illam in fomnis, quàm illum herum meum amplecti eam. Renunciabo hæc illi, ut det mihi malum pro hoc malo.

ANNOTATIONS.

now follow the old Man.* That this is the real meaning appears from what comes immediately after, for as he advanced ftill nearer, perceiving alfo *Davus* and *Pamphilus*, he adds, *Nay, and now I fee alfo Pamphilus himfelf juft at hand, along with* Davus. *I'll mind what I am about. Ipfum adeo præfto video cum Davo. Hoc agam.* Can any

thing be more evident?

12 *Herus, quantum audio,' uxore excidit.* *Excidere uxore,* is an elegant Expreffion as ufed here, to fignify, that a Man is difappointed of the Wife he hoped for. The *Romans* were wont to fay, in the fame manner *excidere lite,* to lofe his Procefs. It is a way of fpeaking borrowed from the *Greeks.*

ACTUS II. SCENA VI.

ARGUMENTUM.

In hac fcena Davus admodum aftute Simonem ludificatur, atque illum dubitantem confirmat, fufpicionem callide avertit, ex quo promovetur epitafis. Tum alter de altero male fufpicatur, & timet falli.

DAVUS, SIMO.

HIC nunc me credit aliquam fibi fallaciam
  Portare, & eâ me hîc reftitiffe gratiâ.   [dem.
Si. Quid Davus narrat? Da. æquè quidquam nunc qui-

ORDO.
Da. HIC Simo nunc credit me portare aliquam fallaciam fibi, & me reftitiffe hîc eâ gratiâ. Si. Quid Davus narrat? Da. Narro æquè quidquam nunc quidem.

ANNOTATIONS.

to difguife their real Sentiments as much as poffible, this gives rife to a very artful Converfation, where the Poet has fucceeded very

happily, in making both fpeak agreeably to their Charaçters.

3 *Æquam quidquam nunc quidem.* Equally my

Si. Nothing? ha.

Dav. Juft nothing.

Si. But I was expecting fomething.

Dav. He is difappointed of his Aim, I fee ; this nettles the Gentleman.

Si. Can you tell me the Truth ?

Dav. Nothing more eafily.

Si. Does not the Marriage give my Son fome Uneafinefs, becaufe of his Engagements with this Stranger ?

Dav. Why. truly none at all ; or if fo, it is only a Concern of two or three Days you know ; and then will ceafe : for he has now thought of the matter as became him.

Si. I commend him.

Dav. While it was permitted by you, and his Youth required it, he loved, but then he did it fecretly, and took care that it fhould not hurt his Reputation, as becomes every difcreet and prudent Man. 'Tis now time for him to marry, and you fee he has his Thoughts wholly upon Matrimony.

Si. Methoughts, however, he looked a little difturbed at it.

Dav. Not on that account, I affure you : but there is fome reafon why he fhould complain of you.

Si. What, pray, is it ?

Dav. A meer trifle.

Si. Well, but what ?

Dav. Nothing.

Si. Nay, but tell me what it is.

Dav. He fays you are too fparing of Expence on this Occafion.

Si. Who, I ?

Dav. Yes, you. My Father, fays he, has fcarce laid out ten Drachms for Provifions ; does this look like a Son's Wedding ? which of my Companions, fays he, fhall I invite to Supper, efpecially at fuch a time as this ? And what may be faid here privately between us ; you are a little too fparing, I don't approve of it.

Si. Hold your prating.

Dav. I've ftung him.

Si. I'll take care that every thing be done as it fhould be. (*To himfelf.*)

What

any thing for the prefent, that is, *nothing at all.* This appears from the Anfwer *Simo* gives immediately after. *Nibilne ? bem. Hem,* is an Interjection, expreffing his Anger againft *Davus,* for pretending that he had faid nothing. *Perizonius* thinks there is a long Ellipfis here, and fupplies it thus : *Nunc quidem æque quidquam narro, ac narro tunc, quando nibil narro.*

· ¹⁴ *Ut virum fortem decet. Vir fortis,* is not here to be interpreted a brave or coura-geous Man, but a difcreet prudent Man, a Man of Spirit and Honour, who values his Reputation.

¹⁶ *Subtriſtis vifus eſt eſſe aliquantulum mibi.* Let us obferve here, how well the Poet has fucceeded in marking the Character of *Pampbilus,* and how judicioufly it is drawn. He did all in his power, not to appear difturbed or forrowful to his Father, and yet he could not wholly conceal his Uneafinefs. It would have offended againft
Pro-

Sɪ. Nihilne ? hem. Dᴀ. nihil prorſus. Sɪ. atqui ex-
ſpectabam quidem.

Dᴀ. Præter ſpem evenit: ſentio: hoc malè habet virum.

Sɪ. Potin' es mihi verum dicere ? Dᴀ. nihil facilius. 6

Sɪ. Num illi moleſtæ quidpiam hæ ſunt nuptiæ,
Hujuſce propter conſuetudinem hoſpitæ ?

Dᴀ. Nihil hercle: aut ſi adeo, bidui eſt, aut tridui
Hæc ſolicitudo: noſtin' ? deinde deſinet :   10
Etenim eam ſecum rem rectâ reputavit viâ

Sɪ. Laudo. Dᴀ. dum licitum eſt illi, dumque ætas tulit,
Amavit : tum id clam. cavit ne unquam infamiæ
Ea res ſibi eſſet, ut virum fortem decet.-

Nunc uxore opus eſt ; animum ad uxorem appulit. 15

Sɪ. Subtriſtis viſu' eſt eſſe aliquantulum mihi.

Dᴀ. Nihil propter hanc rem: ſed eſt, quod ſuccenſet tibi.

Sɪ. Quidnam eſt ? Dᴀ. puerile eſt. Sɪ. quid eſt ? Dᴀ.
. nihil. Sɪ. quin dic, quid eſt ?   [te.

Dᴀ. Ait nimiùm parcè facere ſumtum. Sɪ. mene ? Dᴀ.
Vix, inquit, drachmis eſt opſonatus decem :   20
Num filio videtur uxorem dare ?

Quem, inquit, vocabo ad cœnam meorum æqualium
Potiſſimùm nunc ? &, quod dicendum hîc ſiet,
Tu quoque perparcè nimiùm. non laudo. Sɪ. tace.

Dᴀ. commovi. Sɪ. ego, iſtæc rectè ut fiant, videro. 25

uxore ; appulit animum ad uxorem. Sɪ. *Viſus eſt mihi eſſe aliquantulum ſubtriſtis.* Dᴀ. *Nihil
propter hanc rem ; ſed eſt propter quod ſuccenſet tibi.* Sɪ. *Quidnam eſt.* Dᴀ. *Puerile eſt.* Sɪ. *Quid
eſt ?* Dᴀ. *Nihil.* Sɪ. *Quin dic : quid eſt ?* Dᴀ. *Ait tè facere ſumptum nimium parcè.* Sɪ.
Mene ? Dᴀ. *Ita te. Inquit, pater vix eſt opſonatus decem drachmis : num videtur dare uxorem
filio ? Quem, inquit, meorum æqualium vocabo ad cœnam potiſſimum nunc ? Et quod ſit dicendum
hîc, tu quoque facis ſumptum nimium preparcè. Non laudo.* Sɪ. *Tace.* Dᴀ. *Commovi.* Sɪ. *Ego
videro, ut iſthæc fiant rectè.*

Side margin column:

Sɪ. *Nibilne ? Hem*
Dᴀ. *Nibil prorſus.*
Sɪ. *Atqui quidem
expectabam aliquid.*
Dᴀ. *Evenit illi
præter ſpem ; ſen-
tio ; boc malè ha-
bet virum.* Sɪ.
*Poteſne dicere ve-
rum mibi ?* Dᴀ.
Nibil "eſt facilius.
Sɪ. *Num bæ nu-
ptiæ ſunt quidpiam
moleſtæ illi, propter
conſuetudinem bujuſ-
ce -hoſpitæ ?--*Dᴀ.
*Nibil bercle ; aut ſi
adeo, bæc ſolicitu-
do eſt tantum bidui,
aut tridui : noſtine ?
deinde deſinet : ete-
nim ipſe reputavit
eam rem ſecum rectâ
viâ.* Sɪ. *Laudo eum.*
Dᴀ. *Dum eſt lici-
tum ei, dumque ætas
tulit, amavit : tum
fecit id clam. Ca-
vit ne ea ret un-
quam eſſet infamiæ
ſibi, ut decet virum
fortem. Nunc eſt opus*

ANNOTATIONS.

Probability to ſuppoſe, that a Man ſo much
in love as he, could put on a Countenance
altogether joyful and contented ; nay, it
would have been injurious to his Character,
as it is all along repreſented by the Poet, to
ſuppoſe that he could have acted the Hypo-
crite ſo perfectly. This is the Remark of
Donatus, and ſo juſt, that it would have
been inexcuſable to paſs it by without Notice. His Words are, *Mire ſervatum eſt
in adoleſcente libero* τὸ πρέπον, *& in amatore* τὸ πιθανόν. *Nam & boneſto juveni
non congruebat verſipellis vultus : & in
amatore abſurdum fuerat, ingenuam celare
triſtitiam. Itaque nec ad plenum triſtis fuit,
quia dixit celanda res erat : nec gaudium fuerat, quia ingenium & amoris neceſſitas in
triſtitiam retrabebat.* Theſe uncommonly
delicate Strokes ought to be well ſtudied by

ſuch as write for the Theatre, becauſe they
generally fail moſt in the drawing of Characters. *Dacier.*

  ¹⁸ *Nihil.* *Donatus* ſeems to be in doubt.
here, whether theſe dilatory Anſwers are
deſigned to raiſe the old Man's Curioſity, or
becauſe he had not as yet thought to what he
had beſt aſcribe the Concern which *Simo* had
obſerved *Pampbilus* under, and that he a-
muſes him in this manner, till he could hit
upon ſome ſpecious Pretence. The laſt is
the more probable, and more ſuited to the
Theatre.

  ²⁰ *Vix drachmis opſonatus eſt decem.* The
Attic *drachm* was in Value equal to Nine-
pence of our Money. Some eſtimate it
lower, and make it only Sevenpence-three-
farthings.

²⁶ *Quidnam*

What can be the meaning of all this? What would this old Fox be
at? For if there's any Mifchief going forward; my Life for it, he's
the chief Contriver of it.

ANNOTATIONS.

26 *Quidnam hoc rei eſt ? Quidnam hic vult* | the Artifice. *Donatus* ſeems to think that
veterator ? Davus goes off, and *Simo* is left | it may refer to the Women, whom he faw
here by himſelf, ruminating on what had | coming, and who make their Appearance in
paffed between them. The Notice taken of | the Beginning of the next Act. *Veterator*,
the little Preparation for a Wedding begets | ſays *Donatus*, *eſt vetus in aſtutia, & qui in*
in the old Man ſome Sufpicion, that this | *omni re callidus eſt. Et hi duo verſus often-*
cunning Slave and *Pamphilus* had diſcovered | *dunt, pulſatum eſſe ſenem argumento falſarum*
nuptiarum :

ACT III. SCENE I.

ARGUMENT.

*The old Man is ſtartled by the coming of the Women, and fancy-
ing himſelf deceived by* Davus, *is angry with him.*

MYSIS, SIMO, DAVUS, LESBIA, GLYCERY.

Myſis. VERILY 'tis juſt as you have ſaid, *Lesbia*, ſcarce can you
meet with a Man that's faithful to his Miſtreſs.

Si. This Maid belongs to the *Adrian*, don't ſhe?

Dav. Yes, Sir.

Myſ. But this *Pamphilus* ——

Si. What ſays ſhe?

Myſ. Hath confirmed his Promiſe.

Si. Hah!

Dav. I wiſh that either he was deaf, or ſhe dumb.

Myſ. For he has ordered whatever Child ſhe ſhall be delivered of,
that it be brought up.

Si. O *Jupiter!* What do I hear? all's paſt Recovery, if what ſhe
ſays be true.

Leſ. You ſpeak of a Youth of uncommon Goodneſs.

Myſ. The beſt in the World; but follow me in, that you may'nt
be too late for my Miſtreſs.

Leſ. I follow.

Dav. What Remedy ſhall I now find for this Evil?

Si. What can all this mean? Is he ſo beſotted? with this Stranger?
Ah! Now I know; what a Fool was I not to perceive it before?

Dav.

ANNOTATIONS.

1 *Ita pol quidem*, &c. In the firſt Act, | had deſigned to conceal from him. At firſt
Myſis was ſent to call the Midwife to *Gly-* | he is greatly perplexed, but afterwards
cery, who was in Labour. Juſt at their com- | ſuſpecting that all was but a mere Trick to
ing. *Simo* happened to be ſtanding with | retard the Wedding, he applauds himſelf for
Davus before *Glycery*'s Door, and as their | the Succeſs of his Project, and the Hopes
Converſation run upon *Pamphilus*, and his | he had of being able with Eaſe to defeat all
candid Behaviour, *Simo* overhears them, and | their Meaſures.
by that means comes to know what they | 3 *Ab Andria eſt ancilla hæc : quid nar-*
ras?

Quidnam hoc rei eſt? quidnam hic volt veterator ſibi? | *Quidnam rei eſt hoc?*
Nam ſi hîc mali eſt quidquam, hem illic eſt huic rei caput. | *Quidnam hic ve-*
teraːor vult ſibi?

nam ſi eſt quidquam mali bic, bem; illic eſt caput buic rei.

ANNOTATIONS.

nuptiarum: 'illo argumento quod ait, paulu-
lum opſoni, tanquam ſe illuderet Davus.
Sunt ergo verba, ut diximus, ſecum cogitantis
ſenis, aut de his quæ nunc Davus locutus eſt, aut
de adventu mulierum, quæ in ſcenam veniunt
modo.

²⁷ *Caput. Caput* ſignifies here, the Contriver. In general it expreſſes the Origin and
prime Source of any thing. As in *Virgil*
Æn. xi. 361.

------- O'Latːo caput borum, & cauſa
malorum.

ACTUS III. SCENA I.

ARGUMENTUM.

Terretur mulierum adventu ſenex, & ſe a Davo decipi putat, cui
iraſcitur.

MYSIS, SIMO, DAVUS, LESBIA, GLYCERIUM.

ORDO.

ITA pol quidem res eſt, ut dixti, Lesbia:
Fidelem haud ferme mulieri invenias virum.
SI. Ab Andriâ eſt ancilla hæc. quid narras? DA. ita eſt.
MY. Sed hic Pamphilus. SI. quid dicit? MY. firmavit
fidem. SI. hem.
DA. Utinam aut hic ſurdus, aut hæc muta facta ſit. 5
MY. Nam quod peperiſſet, juſſit tolli. SI. ô Jupiter!
Quid ego audio? actum eſt, ſiquidem hæc vera prædicat.
LE. Bonum ingenium narras adolenſcentis. MY. optu-
mum.
Sed ſequere me intro, ne in morâ illi ſis. LE. ſequor.
DA. quod remedium nunc huic malo inveniam? SI.
quod hoc? 10
Adeon' eſt demens? ex peregrinâ? jam ſcio: ah!

MY. POL qui-
dem, res
eſt ita, ut dixti, Leſ-
bia: ' baud ferma
invenias virum fi-
deſem mulieri. SI.
Hæc ancilla eſt ab
Andriâ, quid nar-
ras? DA. Eſt ita.
MY. Sed hic Pam-
pbilus. 'SI. Quid
dicit? MY. Fir-
mavit ſidem. SI.
Hem. DA. Utinam
ut aut bic ſit factus
ſurdus, aut hæc ſit
facta muta. MY.
Nam juſſit quod pe-
periſſet tolli. SI. O

Jupiter! quod ego audio? actum eſt de nobis, ſiquidem hæc prædicat vera. LE. Narras bonum
ingenium adolːſcentis. MY. Optimum. Sed ſequere me intro, ne ſis in morâ illi. LE. Seguar.
DA. Quod remedium nunc inveniam_buic malo? SI. Quid boc? Eſtne adeo demens? ex peregri-
nâ? Jam ſcio; ah!

ANNOTATIONS.

ras? So we find it in all the printed Editions,
and MSS. of this Author. It is worth while,
however, to take notice of the Alteration
propoſed by Dr. *Bentley.* He thinks the
Sentence ought to be diſtinguiſhed in this
Manner:
Si. *Ab Andria eſt ancilla hæc.* Dav. *Quid*
narras? Si. *Ita eſt.*
Quid narras, are the Words of *Davus,*
not ſo properly implying a Queſtion, as ex-
preſſing his Admiration, how the old Man
came to ſuſpect it, ſeeming to deny, or at

leaſt own it with Reluctance, as in the *Phor-*
mio Act 5. Scene 6. 42.
De. *Ut filius cum illa habitet apud te, hoc*
veſtrum conſilium fuit. Ph. *Quæſo,* quid
narras?
And ſo frequently in other places. *Ita eſt,*
are the Words of *Simo,* ſignifying, that he
is confirmed in his Suſpicions.

¹¹ *Adeon' demens eſt ex peregrina?* There is
a great Emphaſis here in the word *peregrina;*
for what ſeems chiefly to provoke the old
Man's Rage, is to think that his Son, inſtead

Dav. What's this he fays, he has perceived?

Si. Here is the firſt Trick which this Raſcal plays upon me: they pretend that ſhe now lies in, in order to frighten *Chremes* from the Match.

Glyc. *Juno Lucina* help me, ſave me, I beſeech you.

Si. Hy, hy, ſo ſoon! Ridiculous! when ſhe heard that I was
ſtanding before the Door, ſhe made haſte to begin. You ſeem,
Davus, to have taken your Meaſures but indifferently, things don't
appear to be well timed by you.

Dav. How! By me?

Si. What have your Scholars forgot their Leſſons?

Dav. Why, really I don't know what you mean.

Si. Had this Fellow attacked me unprovided in a real Marriage;
how many Tricks would he have play'd me? But now all is at his
peril; I ride ſafe in the Harbour.

ANNOTATIONS.

ſtead of a Citizen of *Athens,* had taken it
into his head to marry a Stranger, but little
known, and whoſe Chaſtity he had probably
no great Opinion of.

¹² *Vix tandem ſenſi ſtolidus.* ,Donatus
obſerves upon this Paſſage, that the Poet,
by a beautiful Moral, ſhews that a ſuſpicious
Man is in no leſs danger of being deceived,
than a Perſon of ſlow Apprehenſion. For
by too great an Acuteneſs and Diſcernment,
he is apt to miſtake. Truth for Artifice.
This the Poet feigns to ariſe from the Event
itſelf, for it is not here *Davus,* who endeavours to impoſe upon the old Man. The Conduct therefore, is the more beautiful, as it is
juſt. It very often happens, that Men who
pretend to know the World, and have ſeen
much of the Diſguiſe and Hypocriſy of it,
are apt in many Caſes to ſee too far, and
ſuſpect Artifice and Deſign, even in thoſe
who are ſcarce capable of it. So that it is,

perhaps, one of the greateſt Secrets of living,
to know when to act openly, and when with
a proper Reſerve.

¹⁵ *Juno Lucina, fer epem.* *Diana* had the
Care of Women in Child-bed, under the
three ſeveral Names of *Juno Lucina,* *Ili-
thyia,* and *Genitalis.* It is for this Reaſon,
that ſhe is ſaid, by the Poets, to be thrice
invoked. Thus *Horace,* in the 22d Ode,
of Book III. addreſſed to this Goddeſs:

Montium cuſtos nemorumque virgo,
Quæ laborantes utero puellas
Ter vocata audis, adimiſque letho,
Diva triformis.

I ſay it is not improbable, that this triple
Invocation implied the addreſſing her by
theſe three ſeveral Names; for we know
it was the Cuſtom of the Ancients, in celebrating the ſacred Solemnities of their
Gods, to invoke them by all the Names,
under which they were known. This is
evident

ACT III. SCENE II.

ARGUMENT.

*The old Man is confirmed in his Error, by the Words of the Mid-
wife to the Maid, and much more by thoſe of* Davus, *who
warns him that things would happen juſt as he himſelf had
projected to conduct them, that by this means he might free
himſelf from all Suſpicion of being concerned in the Plot.*

LESBIA, ARCHILES, SIMO, DAVUS.

Lesbia. HITHERTO, *Archiles,* all the uſual and neceſſary Signs
of Safety appear in *Glycery.* The firſt thing you are now
to

ANNOTATIONS.

¹ *Adhuc Archilis.* *Glycery,* now ſafely
brought to bed; *Leſbia,* as ſhe is coming

out, gives Inſtructions to thoſe within, how
they are to manage. This Behaviour ſerves
only

Vix tandem fenfi ftolidus. DA. quid hic fenfiffe ait ?
SI. Hæc primum adfertur jam mihi ab hoc fallacia.
Hanc fimulant parĕre, quo Chremetem abfterreant.
GL. Juno Lucina, fer opem : ferva me, obfecro.   15
SI. Hui, tam citò ? ridiculum. poftquam ante oftium
Me audivit ftare, approperat: non fat commodĕ
Divifa funt temporibus tibi, Dave, hæc. DA. mihin' ?
SI. Numimmemoresdifcipuli?DA.ego,quidnarresnefcio.
SI. Hiccine, fi me imparatùm in veris nuptiis   20
Adortus effet, quos mihi ludos redderet ? ;
Nunc hujus periclo fit. ego in portu navigo.

ftolidus vix tandem fenfi. DA. Quid hic ait fe fenfiffe ? SI. Jam primum hæc fallacia ad fertur mihi ab hoc Davo. Simulant hanc parcre, quo abfterreant Chremetem. GL. Juno Lucina, fer opem, ferva me, obfecro. SI. Hui, tam citò ? ridiculum. Poftquam audivit me ftare ante oftium, approperat. Dave, hæc non funt fat commodè divifa temporibus tibi. DA. Mihine ? SI. Num difcipuli tui funt immemores ? DA. Ego nefcio quid narres. SI. Hiccine, fi adortus effet me imparatum in veris nuptiis, quos ludos redderet mihi ? nunc fit hujus periclo, ego navigo in portu.

A N N O T A T I O N S.

evident from the Defcription which *Ovid* gives in the Beginning of his fourth Book, of the manner in which the Feftival of *Bacchus* was celebrated at *Thebes*; where we have the feveral Names of that Deity enumerated. *Horace* too, in his fecular Poem, when he invokes *Diana* for her Protection to Women in Child-bed, addreffes her under all the three forementioned Names :

.. *Rite maturos aperire partus*,
    Lenis Ilithyia, tuere matres :
    Sive tu Lucina probas vocari,
        Seu Genitalis.

ɔ 17. *Non fat commodè divifa funt temporibus. Non fatis digefta, & compofita, & diftributa funt per tempora*, fays *Donatus* ; i. e, *confufa funt tibi omnia, nec unumquodque fuo tempore geritur, qui rei praeerit*. This manner of Speaking is borrowed from the Theatre, where Times and Actions muft be fo managed, that every thing may follow in a natural Order, and what ought to come in only in the fifth Act, don't appear in the fecond or third. *Simo*, therefore, reproaches *Davus*, that he had neglected this Rule, in making

Glycery lie in too fpeedily, intimating by that, that he fufpected the whole to be his Contrivance. We find this manner of fpeaking frequently ufed both by Hiftorians and Poets. An Example or two will enable the Reader to comprehend it better. *Juftin* Præfat. *Et quæ hiftorici Græcorum, ut cut commodum cuique fuit, inter fe fegregati occupavere, omiffis quæ fine fructu erant, ea omnia Pompeius divifa temporibus, & feriel rerum digefta compofuit.* Salluft. Catil. 4. 3. *Cætera multitudo conjurationis, fuum quifque negotium exfequeretur, fed ea divifa hæc modo dicebantur.*

In like manner *Horace*, Book I. Ode 36. 6.
    Nulli plura tamen dividet ofcula :
19 *Num immemores difcipuli.* The Difciples here are *Myfis, Lefbia, Glycery*, and *Pamphilus*, by whom he fuppofes the Plot is carried on ; *Davus* is the Mafter, or Contriver of it. In fome Copies we read, *Num immemor es difcipuli* ? referring it to *Pamphilus*, as if he faid, By this ill-patched Plot, you have done no great fervice to your Scholar *Pamphilus*. But the other Reading is evidently the beft.

ACTUS III. SCENA II.

ARGUMENTUM.

Confirmatur in errore fenex, verbis obftetricis ad ancillam, & multo magis Davi, qui prædicit fore quæ ipfe facturus erat, ut a fe fufpicionem fallaciæ avertat.

LESBIA, ARCHILIS, SIMO, DAVUS.   ORDO.

A Dhuc, Archilis, quæ adfolent, quæque oportet
   Signa ad falutem effe, omnia huic effe video.

Lesbia. Adhuc Archilis, video effe huic Glycerio, omnia figna quæ adfolent, quæque oportet effe ad falutem.

A N N O T A T I O N S.

only to confirm *Simo* the more in his Sufpicions. *Davus* underftanding his Error, gives

way to it, and artfully turns it fo as to be fubfervient to his Defign.

to do, is to bathe her. Then let her drink of what I prescribed, and in what quantity I ordered. I'll return again in a minute. By *Castor*, *Pamphilus* has got a fine Boy : pray Heaven he may live, as he himself is so sweet a tempered Youth, and one that scorned to wrong this promising young Creature.

Si. Who that knows you would not believe that you was the Contriver of this ?

Dav. What is this then, that I am the Contriver of !

Si. She did not give Orders within doors, about what ought to be done with the lying-in-Woman ; but as soon as she was come out, she bawls from the Street to those in the House : O *Davus !* am I then become thus contemptible to you ? or do you find me a Person fit to be play'd upon in this open manner ? Sure you should have done it a little more artfully, that if I came to find it out, it might seem that I had at least been feared.

Dav. Why, sure he now imposes upon himself, not I.

Si. Didn't I tell you ? Didn't I threaten you not to attempt any thing ? Did it make you afraid ? What end has it served ? Do you imagine, I believe, that this Woman has borne a Child to *Pamphilus ?*

Dav. (*To himself.*) I see his Error, and know what I am to do.

Si. Why don't you speak ?

Dav. What do you talk of believing, as if you had not been told before, that all this was to be.

Si. Did any one tell me of it ?

Dav. How ! Have you of yourself discovered, that all this is but a meer Feint ?

Si. I am then laughed at.

Dav. Nay, 'twas certainly told you ; for otherwise, how came you by this Suspicion ?

Si. How ? Because I knew you.

Dav. As if you would have it that it was done by my Contrivance.

Si. Nay, I'm certain of it.

Dav. You don't yet know well enough, Sir, what kind of Man I am.

Si. I not know you.

Dav. But if I go about to speak a word, you'll presently think that I have a design to deceive you.

Si. And do I think so without reason ?

Dav. For which Cause I dare not now presume to speak a word.

Si.

ANNOTATIONS.

3 *Isthac ut lovet.* It was the Custom in *Greece* for Women, after they were brought to bed, to be put into the Bath. There is a remarkable Passage in *Callimachus*, and another in *Lucian* to this purpose. *Isthac* is a Nominative singular for *ista*. Commentators have been strangely mistaken here. *Dacier.*

5 *Mox ego huc revertor.* The Poet here very naturally makes *Lesbia* imitate the Tone and Manner of Physicians, for *jubere*, *imperare*, and *praecipere*, was exactly their Language, and also a frequent Promise with them, *mox ego huc revertor.*

6 *Per ecastor.* To swear by *Castor* and *Pollux*, was a kind of Oath, held ornamental

Nunc primûm fac, iftæc ut lavet: poft deinde,
Quod juffi ei dari bibere, & quantum imperavi,
Date: mox ego huc revertor. 5
Per ecaftor, fcitus puer eft natus Pamphilo [nio bono:
Deos quæfo, ut fit fuperftes: quandoquidem ipfe eft inge-
Cuinque huic veritus eft optumæ adolefcenti facere in-
juriam.
Si. Vel hoc quis non credat, qui nôrit te, abs te effe ôr-
tum? Da. quidnam id eft? [ræ: 10
Si.Non imperabat coram, quid opus facto effet puerpe-
Sed poftquam egreffa eft, illis, quæ funt intus, clamat
de via. [neus
O Dave, itan' contemnor abs te? aut itane tandem ido-
Tibi videor effe, quem tam aperte fallere incipias dolis?
Saltem accuratè, ut metui videar certè, fi refciverim.
Da. Certè hercle nunc hic fe ipfus fallit, haud ego. Si.
edixin' tibi? 15
Interminatus fum,ne faceres? num veritus? quid retülit?
Credon' tibi hoc nunc, peperiffe hanc è Pamphilô?
Da. Teneo, quid erret: quid ego agam, habeo. Si.
quid taces? [fore.
Da.Quid credas? quafi non tibi renunciata fint hæc fic
Si. Mihin' quifquam? Da. eho, an tute intellexti hoc
adfimulari? Si. irrideor. 20
Da. Renunciatum eft: nam qui iftæc tibi incidit fu-
fpicio? [confilio meo.
Si. Quî? quia te nôram: Da. quafi tu dicas, factum id
Si. Certè enim fcio. Da. non fatis me pernôfti etiam,
qualis fim, Simo. [nuò dari
Si. Egone te? Da: fed, fi quid narrare occœpi, conti-
Tibi verba cenfes. Si. falfô? Da. itaque hercle nihil
jam mutire audeo. 25

Nunc primùm fac, ut ifthæc lavet: deinde poft, date ei bibere, quod juffi dari, & quantùm imperavi: ego revertor huc mox. Per ecaftor, fcitus puer eft natus Pamphilo: quæfo deos ut fit fuperftes, quandoquidem ipfe eft ingenio. bono; cumque veritus eft facere injuriam huic optimæ adolefcenti. Si. Vel quis, qui noverit te, Dave, non credat hoc effe ortùm abs te? Da. Quidnam eft id? Si. Non imperabat coram, quid opus effe facto puerperæ; fed poftquàm eft egreffa, clamat de via, illis, quæ funt intùs. O Dave, itanè contemnor abs te? aut videorne tandem tibi effe ita idoneus, quem incipias fallere dolis tam aparte? faltem debuifti fallere accurate, ut certe videar metui, fi refciverim. Da. Certè hercle, nunc hic ipfe fallit fe, haud ego. Si. Edixine tibi? interminatus ne fum, ne faceres? Num es-

veritus? quid retulit? Credòne tibi hoc nunc, hanc Glycerium peperiffe? Pamphilo? Da. Teneo quid erret, & habeo quid ego agàm. Si. Quid taces? Da. Quid credas? quafi hæc non fint renunciata tibi, fore fic. Si. Quifquamne renunciavit mihi? Da. Eho, an tute iple intellexti hoc. adfimulari? Si. Irrideor. Da. Eft renunciatum: nam qui iftæc fufpicio incidit tibi? Si. Quî? quia noveram te. Da. Quafi tu dicas, id fuiffe fuctum meo confilio. Si. Scio enim certè. Da. Non pernovifti me etiam fatis, qualis fim, Simo. Si. Egone pernovi te? Da. Sed fi ecœpi narrare quid, continuò cenfeo verba dari tibi. Si. An falfo? Da. Itaque hercle, jam audeo mutire nihil.

ANNOTATIONS.

tal to Difcourfe, and frequently ufed by Women,

24 *Continuò dari tibi verba cenfes.* In all the Editions of *Terence*, after thefe Words of *Davus*, *Simo* is made to fay *fulfo*. *Bentley* objects againft this, and afcribes the whole to *Davus* thus:

------ *Continuò dari*
Tibi verba cenfes, falfo; itaque hercle nil
jam mutire audeo.

The Editors of the *Terence*, Latin and English, in three Volumes, are for omitting the word *falfo* altogether; they tell us, that *dare verba*, fignifies to deceive, impofe upon, or equivocate, that *fulfo* is needlefs; and bad when joined with it. As for afcribing it to *Simo*, they think that nothing can be more out of Character; he difcovering all along his opinion of *Davus*, to be that of a fharking fly Knave. But methinks they ought not

Si. I only know one thing, that no body has been brought to bed here.

Dav. Have you found it out ? yet neverthelefs they will by and by bring a Child hither before your door. This I now give you timely Warning of, Mafter, that you may be aware of it, nor afterwards pretend that it was done by the Artifices and Contrivance of *Davus.* I would willingly remove altogether this wrong Opinion you feem to have form'd of me.

Si. But how came you to know this ?

Dav. I have heard fo, and am ftrongly inclin'd to believe it : many Circumftances concur, by which I am led to make this Conjecture. For firft fhe gave out that fhe was with Child by *Pamphilus.* That was found falfe. Now when fhe heard that a Wedding was on foot at home, a Maid is immediately fent to call the Midwife to her, and defire her to bring a Child along with her : for unlefs it could be fo contrived, that you fhould fee a Child, the Marriage would ftill go forward.

Si. What's this you tell me ? When you underftood that fuch was their Defign, why did you not forthwith inform *Pamphilus* of it ?

Dav. And who elfe do you imagine it was, that difengaged him from her but myfelf ? for we all know with what excefs of Paffion he loved her. Now he wifhes for nothing fo much as a Wife. In fine, Sir, leave that bufinefs to my Management. Do you in the mean time go on in making up the Match, as you have begun, and I hope that Heaven will profper it.

Si. Well, now go in, wait there till I come, and get ready whatever you think may be wanted. (*alone*) He has not yet perfuaded me to give entire Credit to him, nor am I fully fatisfied that all he fays is true ; but I don't much regard it. That is of far greater moment to me, which my Son himfelf has promifed. I will now find out *Chremes,* and requeft his Daughter for my Son. If I obtain her, what

A N N O T A T I O N S.

not to be fo rafh in expunging a Word that has fo many Authorities to fupport it. *Falfo,* in *Simo's* mouth, makes very good Senfe, and is very natural, if we confider it as followed with a mark of Interrogation ; *falfo ? Would I wrong you in thinking fo ? Will it be any Injuftice ?* This too, makes *Davus's* Anfwer come in very eafy and natural : *Itaque hercle nibil jam mutire audeo.*

38 *Id ego jam nunc tibi renuncio.* This is very pleafant ; *Davus* here makes ufe of *Simo's* Error to forward his own Defigns, and warns him of what he was himfelf to do, that the old Man might not fufpect his being concerned in a Project which he had feemingly betrayed to him.

39 *Quis igitur eam ab illa abftraxit ?* Simo afks him why he had not warn'd *Pamphilus*

of the Plot that was form'd againft him. He had no good Anfwer to make, for he could not with any face pretend that he had really done fo. He therefore gives it another Turn, and amufes the old Man with an Infinuation that he had drawn off *Pamphilus* from *Glycery.* This was doing more than to warn him, and feem'd to include every thing ; nothing can be conceived more artful and delicate.

44 *Non impulit me,* &c. Thefe are the Words of the old Man deliberating with himfelf, after he had difpatched *Davus.* His Character of Sufpicion and Diftruft is very happily preferv'd all along by the Poet, who by the Word *omnino* lets us fee that he was not as yet perfuaded of every thing. However, he has fet Circumftances in fuch a Light,

Si. Hoc ego scio unum, neminem perperisse hîc. Da.
    intellextin' ?
Sed nihilo fecius mox deferent pueruni huc ante oftium.
Id ego jam nunc tibi renuncio, here, futurum, ut sis
    sciens :   [dolis.
Ne tu hoc mihi pofterius dicas Davi factum confilio, aut
Prorfus à me opinionem hanc tuàm, effe ego amotam
    volo.   30
Si. Unde id scis ? Da. audivi, & credo. multa con-
    currunt fimul,   [è Pamphilo
Quî conjecturam hanc nunc facio. jam primùm hæc se
Gravidam dixit effe. inventum eft falfum. nunc, poft-
    quam videt
Nuptias domi apparrai, miffa eft ancilla illico
Obftetricem accerfitum ad eam, & puerum ut adferret
    fimul.   35
Hoc nifi fit, puerum ut tu videas, nil moventur nuptiæ.
Si. Quid ais ? cùm intellexeras, .
Id confilii capere, cur non dixti extemplò Pamphilo ?
Da. Quis igitur eum ab illâ abftraxit, nifi ego ? nam
    omnes nos quidem
Scimus, quàm miferè hanc amârit. nunc fibi uxorem
    expetit.   40
Poftremò id mihi da negotî. tu tamen idem has nuptias
Perge facere ita, ut facis : & id fpero adjuturos Deos.
Si. Imo abi intrò : ibi me opperire, &, quod parato
    opus eft, para.
Non impulit me, hæc nunc omnino ut crederem.
Atque haud scio, an, quæ dixit, fint vera omnia : 45
Sed parvi pendo. illud mihi multo maxumum eft,
Quod mihi pollicitu' eft ipfus gnatus. nunc Chremem
Conveniam :. orabo gnato uxorem. id fi impetro,

*lum ab ea, nifi ego? Nam omnes nos quidem fcimus, quam miferè amaverit hanc. Nunc
expetit uxorem fibi. Poftremo, da id negotii mibi. Tamen tu idem, perge facere bas nuptias, ita ut facis :· et fpero deos adjuturos id. Si. Imo, abi intro ; opperire me ibi, et
para quod eft opus parato, Non impulit me ut nunc crederem bæc omnino; atque baud fcio an
omnia quæ dixit fint vera ; fed pendo parvi. Illud eft multo maximum mibi, quod ipfe gnatus
eft pollicitus mibi. Nunc conveniam Chremen : Orabo fuam filiam uxorem gnato : fi impetro id,*

Marginal note

Si. Scio boc unum, neminem peperiffe bîc. Da. Intellex-tine ? Sed nibilo fecius, mox defe-rent puerum buc an-te oftium. Ego jam nunc renuncio tibi, bere, id effe futurum, ut fis fciens : ne tu pofterius dicas mibi boc fuiffe factum confilio aut dolis Davis. Ego volo bunc tuam opinio-nem effe prorfus a-motam a me. Si. Unde fcis id ? Da. Audivi, et credo. Multa fimul concur-runt, qui nunc fa-cio banc conjectu-ram. Jam primum bæc dixit fe effe gravidam e Pam-pbilo : hoc inven-tum eft falfum: nunc poftquam videt nu-ptias apparari domi tuæ, illico ancilla eft miffa, accerfitum obftetricem ad eam, et ut adferret pue-rum fimul. Nifi boc fit, ut tu videas puerum, nuptiæ nil moventur. Si. Quid ais ? cum intellex-eras eas capere id confilii, cur non dix-ifti extemplo Pam-pbilo ? Da. Quis igitur abftraxit il-

---

ANNOTATIONS.

Light, that it was impoffible for him with all his Cunning, not to be deceived in what related to *Glycery*'s lying in. Here it very naturally occurs to inquire what could be *Davus*'s Defign in confirming the old Man thus in his Error ? *Donatus* and all the other Commentators tell us, that *Davus* does this to prevent *Simo* from fufpecting him in the Part he intended to act afterwards, and in compliance with that general Opinion have I expreffed myfelf in the Note upon the 28th Verfe of this Scene. But if I may be allowed to give my real Sentiments, he wanted only to hinder the old Man from be-lieving that *Pampbilus* had a Child by *Gly-cery*, nor had he at this time any Appre-henfion of the Part he was afterwards to act. *Pampbilus* fays to *Davus* in the third Scene of the fecond Act, *Puerum autem ne re-fcifcat mibi effe ex illâ cautio eft.* This therefore was the Defign at prefent, to hide all from *Simo*, and *Davus* had undertaken

what have I elfe to do than to conclude the Match this very day?
For after my Son has promifed, there is no doubt but I can compel
him to it, if he fhould refufe. But fee, here comes *Chremes* himfelf,
in the very Nick of Time!

ANNOTATIONS.

the Management of that Affair; but this
new Accident had broken all his Meafures,
and let *Simo* into the Knowledge of what
he wanted of all things to conceal from him.
Something therefore muft be done to avert
this Storm that threatned them: *Quod re-*

medium nunc huic malo inveniam? For that
it could not be with an Eye to what happened afterwards, is evident from this, that
at prefent he had not any fuch Intention.
It was a new Project that he form'd upon a
new Emergence, and which after long tor-
turing

ACT III. SCENE III.

ARGUMENT.

Simo *requefts of* Chremes *that he will give* Pamphilus *his
Daughter in Marriage, and with fome difficulty prevails.*

SIMO, CHREMES.

Simo. CHREMES, your Servant.
　　Chr. Ha, I was juft looking for you,
　Si. And I for you.
　Chr. We are fortunately met. Some Perfons have come and told me
they heard from you, that my Daughter is to be married to your Son
to-day: now I come to fee whether you or they have loft their Senfes.
　Si. Hear me for a moment; and you fhall foon know, what I
would have of you, and what you inquire after.
　Chr. I hear: fpeak what you have a mind.
　Si. I requeft of you, *Chremes*, by the Gods, and by our Friendfhip;
which, begun in our Childhood, has increafed with our Years; by
your only Daughter, and my only Son whom it is now wholly in
your power to reclaim; that you will affift me in this important
Conjuncture; and as the Match was once defign'd, fo that you fuffer
it ftill to go on.
　Chr. Pray don't afk me: as if there were need of Intreaties to obtain this Favour of me. Do you think me now a different Perfon
from what I was when I firft promifed her? If this Marriage is for
their mutual Advantage, let her now be called. But if it will be attended with more Harm than Good to both, I intreat of you to weigh
the matter impartially, as tho' fhe were your Daughter, and *Pamphilus* my Son. 　　　　　　　　　　　　　　　　　　　　*Si.*

ANNOTATIONS.

[1] *Jubeo Chremetem.* Simo now perfuaded
that his Son was difgufted with *Glycery,*
imagines that every thing will go on fmooth-
ly, if he can but obtain *Chremes*'s Confent.
He therefore reprefents the Cafe to him, and
after urging it very earneftly, prevails. This
gives quite a different Turn to Affairs; for
as the Obftacle which *Davus* chiefly relied

upon was removed, all his Meafures are at
once broken, and he expofed to the Refentment of *Pamphilus*, for having urged him to
take a Step that was like to involve him in
fo many Difficulties. Thus the Play becomes more interefting, our Attention is
raifed, and we grow impatient to fee how
the Poet will unravel the Plot.

　　　　　　　　　　　　　　　　　　● Per

Quid aliàs malim, quàm hodie has fieri nuptias?
Nam gnatus quod pollicitu' eſt, haud dubium eſt mihi,
Si nolit, quin eum meritò poſſim cogere. 51
Atque adeo in ipſo tempore eccum ipſum obviàm.

quid malim aliud, quam has nuptias fieri hodie? Nam ſi gnatus nolit præ- ſtare quod eſt pollici- tus, haud eſt dubi-

um mihi, quin poſſim cogere eum meritò. Atque adeo eccum Chremen *ipſum obviam in ipſo tempore.*

A N N O T A T I O N S.

turing his Invention, the hearing by chance | Lover, whom ſhe was in danger of loſing, he
Glycery's Door creak, gave him the firſt | makes him eaſy, and prevents his Reſent-
Hint of. But by amuſing the old Man at | ment from falling heavy upon *Pamphilus*,
preſent with the Conceit that this was only | which ſeems to be what he chiefly aims at in
a Contrivance of *Glycery*'s to regain her | this Caſe.

ACTUS III. SCENA. III.

A R G U M E N T U M.

Simo Chremetem orat, ut filiam ſuam Pamphilo det uxorem, atque id vix exorat.

SIMO, CHREMES.

O R D O.

JUBEO Chremetem. CH. oh, teipſum quærebam,
  SI. & ego te. CH. optatò advenis [filiam
Aliquot me adiere, ex te auditum qui aiebant, hodie
Meam nubere tuo gnato. id viſo, tune, an illi inſaniant.
SI. Auſculta paucis, quid ego te velim ; . & tu, quod
  quæris, ſcies.
CH. Auſculto: loquere, quid velis. 5
SI. Per te Deos oro, & noſtram amicitiam, Chreme,
Quæ incepta à parvis cum ætate accrevit ſimul,
Perque unicam gnatam tuam, & gnatum meum,
Cujus tibi poteſtas ſumma ſervandi datur;
Ut me adjuves in hac re, atque ita, utì nuptiæ 10
Fuerant futuræ, fiant. CH. ah, ne me obſecra:
Quaſi hoc te orando à me impetrare oporteat.
Alium eſſe cenſes nunc me, atque olim, cùm dabam?
Si in rem eſt utrique, ut fiant, accerſi jube.
Sed ſi ex eâ re plus mali eſt, quàm commodi 15
Utrique; id oro te, in commune ut conſulas,
Quaſi illa tua ſit, Pamphilique ego ſim pater.

SI. *JUBEO Chre- metem ſalvere.* CH. *Ob, quærebam teipſum.* SI. *Et ego quærebam te.* CH. *Advenis optatò. A- liquot adiere me, qui aiebant fuiſſe audi- tum ex te, meam fi- liam nubere tuo gna- to hodie. Viſo id, tune, an illi inſani- ant.* SI. *Auſculta paucis verbis, quid ego velim te facere, & tu ſcies quod quæris.* CH. *Au- ſculto: loquere, quid velis.* SI. *Oro te, Chreme, per deos & noſtram amicitiam, quæ incepta à no- bis parvis, accre- vit ſimul cum æ- tate, perque tuam unicam gnatam, &*

meum gnatum, cujus gnati ſervandi ſumma poteſtas nunc datur tibi ; ut adjuves me in hac re, at- que utì nuptiæ fuerant futuræ, ita fiant. CH. *Ah, ne obſecra me, quaſi oporteat te impetrare hoc à me orando. Cenſes me eſſe nunc alium atque fui olim, cum dabam? Si eſt in rem utrique ut nuptiæ fiant, jube accerſi. Sed ſi eſt plus mali quam commodi utrique ex eâ re; oro te id, ut con- ſulas in commodum commune, quaſi illa ſit tua filia, egoque ſim pater* Pamphili.

A N N O T A T I O N S.

⁶ *Per te Deus oro,* &c. A Form of In- | ſtances of this nature, where the Perſon
treaty, where the natural Order of the | who makes the Requeſt has his Mind ear-
Words is changed, and *te* or *vos* interpoſed | neſtly ſet upon it, we are to ſuppoſe that he
betwixt the Propoſition *per* and the Noun | cannot attend to the Manner of placing his
that is joined to it. Thus, *Liv. l.* 23. 9. | Words, and therefore there is a particular
*Per ego te, inquit, fili, quæcunque jura li- | Elegance in this ſeeming Irregularity.
beros jungunt parentibus precor quæſoque. In- | ¹² *Quaſi hoc te orando,* &c. There is

Si. Nay, that's the very thing I mean to do; and 'tis for this Reafon that I fo earnefly defire your Confent; nor would I afk it of you, if the matter itfelf did not require it.

Chr. How require it?

Si. *Glycery* and my Son are at variance.

Chr. I hear you.

Si. So much, that I am in hopes to difengage him from her.

Chr. Stories.

Si. Pofitively it is fo.

Chr. So as I tell you: The falling out of Lovers is the Renewal of Love.

Si. Well, but I intreat you, let us prevent the worft, now that an Opportunity offers, and while his Paffion is cool'd by ill Ufage. Let us give him a Wife before they by their Artifices and diffembled Tears foften his love-fick Mind to Pity. I hope, that by a continued Intimacy, and Union with a Perfon fo agreeable and of equal Rank, he will eafily be able to extricate himfelf from thefe Perplexities.

Chr. So you are willing to believe, but I am of a very different mind; for neither will it be in his power to prove conftant to her, nor can I bear that it fhould be otherwife.

Si. How can you be certain of this, 'till you make trial?

Chr. But to make trial at the hazard of my Daughter's Repofe, is a hard Cafe.

Si. Well, but if the worft fhould happen, which Heaven forbid, all the Inconvenience amounts to this; a Separation: whereas if he is reclaimed, think only what Advantages will follow. In the firft place, you will reftore a loft Son to your Friend; have a defireable Son-in-Law to yourfelf, and a good Hufband to your Daughter.

Chr. What's all this? If you have fo far perfuaded yourfelf, that it may be of fervice to reclaim your Son: I would not have you find in me any Obftacle to your Satisfaction.

Si. It is with Reafon that I have always had the greateft Value for you, *Chremes.*

Chr. But what's this you fay?

Si. What?

Chr. How do you know that they have fallen out?

Si. *Davus* himfelf, who knows all their Secrets, told me of it; and

advifes

ANNOTATIONS.

an inimitable Beauty and Juftnefs in this Anfwer, which *Chremes* gives to *Simo.* Among reafonable Friends, nothing will be demanded by the other, but what is fair and equitable, nor when the Requeft is of that nature will there be need of many Intreaties to obtain it. The Character of *Chremes* is that of a mild peaceable Man, and a good Friend: he weighs maturely every thing he does, and immediately agrees to a Propofal, when he is convinced of its being reafonable. Both thefe Parts of his Character are marked more

strongly towards the End of the Play, where he takes fo much pains to foften *Simo's* Anger, and make him behave mildly and calmly towards his Son and *Crito,* and confent, fo readily to the Marriage between him and *Glycery,* as foon as he underftands that fhe was his own Daughter.

20 *Audio.* This Word is often ufed ironically, and here denotes that *Chremes* gave but little Credit to what *Simo* faid on that head.

23 *Anar-*

SI. Imo ita volo, itaque postulo ut fiat, Chreme :
Neque postulem abs te, ni ipsa res moneat. CH: quid est?
SI. Iræ sunt inter Glycerium & gnatum. CH. audio. 20
SI. Ita magnæ, ut sperem posse avelli. CH. fabulæ.
SI. Profectò sic est. CH. sic hercle, ut dicam tibi :
Amantium iræ amoris integratio est.
SI. Hem, id te oro, ut antè eamus, dum tempus datur,
Dumque ejus lubido occlusa est contumeliis ; 25
Priusquam harum scelera & lacrumæ confictæ dolis
Reducunt animum ægrotum ad misericordiam,
Uxorem demus. spero consuetudine, &
Conjugio liberali devinctum, Chreme,
Dehinc facile ex illis sese emersurum malis. 30
CH. Tibi ita hoc videtur : at ego non posse arbitror,
Neque illum hanc perpetuò habere, nequè me perpeti.
SI. Quî scis ergo istuc, nisi periclum feceris ?
CH. At istuc periclum in filiâ fieri, grave est.
SI. Nempe incommoditas denique huc omnis redit ; 35
Si eveniat, quod Di prohibeant, discessio, at
Si corrigatur, quot commoditates, vide.
Principio amico filium restitueris :
Tibi generum firmum, & filiæ invenies virum.
CH. Quid istìc ? si ita istuc animum induxti esse utile, 40
Nolo tibi ullum commodum in me claudier.
SI. Meritò te semper maxumi feci, Chreme.
CH. Sed quid ais ? SI. quid ? CH. quî scis eos nunc dis-
    cordare inter se ?   [dixit
SI. Ipsu' mihi Davus qui intimu' est eorum consiliis,

non posse fieri ; neque illam habere hanc Philumenam perpetuò, neque me perpeti ut sit.
aliter. SI. Quî ergo scis istuc, nisi feceris periculum ? CH. At est grave, 'istuc pericu-
lum fieri in filia. SI. Nempe omnis incommoditas redit denique huc : discessio, si eveniat,
quod dii prohibeant. At si filius corrigatur, vide quot commoditates sint. Principio restitue-
ris filium amico : invenies firmum generum tibi, & virum filiæ. CH. Quid istìc ? si induxti
animum ita credere, istuc esse utile, nolo ullum commodum claudi tibi in me. SI. Meritò semper
feci te maximi, Chreme. CH. Sed quid ais ? SI. Quid ? CH. Quî scis eos nunc discordare inter
se ? SI. Ipse Davus dixit mihi, qui est intimus consiliis eorum ?

SI. Imo volo ita, postuloque ut fiat ita, Chreme : neque postulem hoc abs te, nisi ipsa res moneat. CH. Quid est ? SI. Iræ sunt inter Glycerium et -meum gnatum. CH. Audio. SI. Ita magnæ, ut sperem eum posse avelli. CH. Fabulæ. SI. Profectò est sic. CH. Hercle sic, ut dicam tibi : Iræ amantium est integratio amoris. SI. Hem, oro id te, ut antè eamus, dum tempus datur, dumque lubido ejus est occlusa contumeliis. Demus Igitur uxorem ei, priusquam scelera harum et lacrimæ confictæ dolis reducunt ejus animum agrotum ad misericordiam. Spero, Chreme, eum fore devinctum consuetudine & conjugio liberali, dehinc facile emersurum sese ex illis malis. CH. Hoc videtur ita tibi : at ego arbitror non posse fieri ; neque illam habere hanc Philumenam perpetuò, neque me perpeti ut sit.

ANNOTATIONS.

23 *Amantium iræ amoris integratio est.*
A Sentence the Truth of which every day
gives fresh Experience of. Some read *Rein-*
tegratio and *Redintegratio,* but the other is
better : *Integrare* is the same as *in integrum*
restituere. Our Poet too in the fourth Act
uses *integrascit* in nearly the same Sense.

29 *Conjugia liberali.* A Marriage with
one that was free and a Citizen. This is
said in opposition to what *Glycery* then appeared to be, whose Parents not being as yet
known, she passed at *Athens* for a Stranger.

32 *Neque me perpeti.* viz. *vagos Pam-*
phili amores. For Fathers had that Power
over their Children, that when a Husband
behaved ill, he might take away his Daugh-

ter from him. *Chremes* therefore means
that he could not think of marrying his
Daughter to a Man who would probably
slight her, and run after a Mistress ; the
Consequence of w ich must be, that he
would soon take her home again to himself.

41 *Ullum commodum in me claudier.* That
is, *occlusum esse, quo minus eo potiri possis.* In
like manner as in the Eunuch, Act I. Sc. 2. S 3.

Nunc ubi meam
Benignitatem sensisti in te claudier.
Bentley hower is dissatisfied with the com-
mon Reading, as thinking it a Manner of
Expression that can't be defended, and there-
fore in both places proposes *interclaudier.*

43 *Quî scis eos nunc discordare inter se ?*
                                        Nothing

advifes me to haften forward the Match as faft as I can. Do you
think he would do it, unlefs he knew that my Son were inclined
the fame way ? Nay, you yourfelf fhall hear prefently what he fays.
Soho, call *Davus* hither ; but O, I fee he comes of himfelf.

ANNOTATIONS.

Nothing can be more natural than this | ftill apprehenfive that all was not as he could
Queftion of *Chremes.* Overcome by the Im- | wifh it, he is willing to know a little farther,
portunities of his Friend, he confents ; but | whether it was certain that the Lovers had
| quarrelled,

ACT III. SCENE IV.

ARGUMENT.

*Davus hastens to urge the Conclufion of the Marriage, though
far from expecting that it was actually fo near. But when
he underftands that the thing was ferioufly defigned, he chides
himfelf for the ill Succefs of his Project.*

DAVUS, SIMO, CHREMES.

Dav. I Was coming to you.
  Si. What's the matter ?
Dav. Why is not the Bride fent for ? it begins to be late.
  Si. Do you hear him ? I have for fome time been diftruftful of you,
Davus, left you fhould take Example by the great erpart of Servants,
and endeavour to over-reach me by your Artifices, becaufe my Son is
in love with this Stranger.
  Dav. Could I, Sir, do any fuch Thing ?
  Si. I fufpected it: and therefore fearing as much, I concealed from
you what I am now going to tell you.
  Dav. What pray ?
  Si. You fhall know ; for I now begin to have fome Confidence in
you.
  Dav. You have then at length difcovered what fort of a Perfon I am.
  Si. There was no Marriage here intended.
  Dav. What, not intended ?
  Si. 'Twas all but a Contrivance, to try how you were inclin'd.
  Dav. What's this you tell me ?
  Si. 'Tis juft fo.
  Dav. See : I could never have fathom'd this Defign ; blefs me, an
artful Contrivance !   *Si.*

ANNOTATIONS.

* *Ad te ibam.* Simo had commanded | *Glycery* were at variance, and that he was
Davus to go in, and have every thing in | now willing to take a Wife. *Davus* not
readinefs for the Marriage. Mean time he | dreaming of what had happened, but fecure
meets with *Chremes,* and partly by Entrea- | that no Wedding was intended, is of him-
ties, partly by his Reafons, prevails upon | felf coming out to have the pleafure of in-
him to let the Match go forward ; and to | fulting *Simo* a little, when to his great
confirm him yet the more, orders *Davus* to | mortification he learns the ill Succefs of his
be called to fatisfy him that *Pampbilus* and | Project, and is thrown into the greateft per-
| plexity

Et is mihi fuadet, nuptias, quantam queam, ut ma- | *Et is fuadet mibi,*
turem.   45 | *ut maturem nupti-*
Num,cenfes, faceret, filium nifi fciret eadem hæcvelle? | *as, quantum queam.*
Tute adeo jam ejus audies verba. heus, evocate huc | *Num, cenfes, faceret*
Atque eccum, video ipfum foras exire.   [Davum. | *ita, nifi fciret fili-*
                                                   | *um meum velle hæc*
                                                   | *eadem ? Adeo jam*

tute ipfe audies verba ejus. Heus evocate Davum huc. Atque eccum, vides ipfum exire
foras.

ANNOTATIONS,

quarrelled, and if the Difference was of that | 48 *Atque eccum.* Eccum *quafi* ecce eum ?
nature as to give Hopes they would not be | for the Ancients frequently ufe eccùm, eccujus,
eafily reconciled. | and ellum inftead of ecce illum, or en illum.

ACTUS III. SCENA IV.

ARGUMENTUM.

Approperat Davus, urgetque nuptias, quas tamen nolit fieri,
Qui ubi cognofcit rem agi feriò, confilium fuum deteftatur.

DAVUS, SIMO, CHREMES.

ORDO.

AD te ibam. SI. quidnam eft? | DA. IBAM ad te,
  DA. Cur non accerfitur? jam advefperafcit. | SI. *Quid-*
SI. audin' tu illum?   [ceres idem, | *nam eft ?* DA. Cur
Ego dudum non nil veritus fum, Dave, abs te, ne fa- | *uxor non accerfi-*
Quod volgus fervorum folet, dolis ut me deluderes, | *tur ? jam advefpe-*
Propterea quòd amat filius. DA. egon' iftuc facerem? | *rafcit.* SI. *Au-*
SI. credidi: 5 | *difne tu illum ?*
Idque adeo metuens vos celavi, quod nunc dicam. | *Ego dudum fum*
  DA. quid? SI. fcies: | *veritus non nil abs*
Nam propemodum habeo tibi jam fidem. DA. tan- | *te, Dave, ne fa-*
  dem agnôfti, qui fiem,   [SI. fed eâ gratiâ | *ceret idem quod vul-*
SI. Non fuerant nuptiæ futuræ. DA. quid? non? | *gus fervorum folet*
Simulavi, vos ut pertentarem. DA. quid ais? SI. fic | *facere, ut deluderes*
  res eft. DA, vide e | *me dolis; propterea*
Nunquam iftuc quivi ego intellegere. vah confilium | *quod filius amai.*
  callidum!   10 | *DA. Egone face-*
                                                   | *rem iftuc?* SI. *Cre-*
                                                   | *didi: adeoque me-*
                                                   | *tuens id, celavi*
                                                   | *vos, quod nunc di-*
                                                   | *cam.* DA. *Quid ?*

SI. *Scies: nam jam propemodum habeo fidem tibi,* DA. *Tandem agnovifti, qui fiem.* SI.
Nuptia non fuerant futuræ. DA. *Quid ? Non futuræ ?* SI. *Sed fimulavi eas eâ gra-*
tiâ, ut pertentarem vos. DA. *Quid ais ?* SI *Res fic eft.* DA. *Vide: ego nunquam*
quivi intelligere iftuc: vah confilium callidum!

ANNOTATIONS.

plexity. He diffembles however his Con- | 4 *Quod volgus fervorum folet.* Simo is
cern as much as poffible before the old Men, | now fatisfied with *Davus,* and therefore
and *Chremes* imagining that all was well, | fpeaks in a fmooth contented Tone, endea-
returns home to give proper Orders. | vouring, as he goes on, to extenuate the Ac-
  3 *Ego dudum. Donatus* obferves upon | cufation, and convince him that the Sufpi-
this that a Speech which begins with the | cion he had of him was natural, from the
Pronoun *ego* always promifes fomething | Circumftances in which they both were.
mighty and important,

Si. Hear me then. No fooner had I ordered you to go in, than I very opportunely met with *Chremes* here.

Dav. (afide) What! Are we then ruin'd?

Si. I repeat to him what you told me juft now.

Dav. (afide) What do I hear?

Si. I requefted of him his Daughter, and with much ado prevail'd.

Dav. (afide) I'm undone.

Si. Hah! What was it you faid?

Dav. I tell you, admirably well managed.

Si. Now there is no delay on his fide.

Chr. I'll go home directly, to give the proper Orders, and then return to inform you what I have done.   [*Exit.*

Si. Now, *Davus*, I requeft of you, as you alone have brought about this Match to-day—

Dav. I alone indeed.

Si. Continue your Endeavours to reclaim my Son.

Dav. That I will, by *Hercules*.

Si. 'Twill be an eafy matter now, while he is difcontented with her.

Dav. Do you make yourfelf perfectly eafy.

Si. Go then; but where is he juft now?

Dav. It is a wonder, if he be not at home.

Si. I'll go to him, and tell him the very fame that I have already told you.

Dav. (Alone.) I am ruin'd. What can hinder me now from being fent directly to *Bridewel?* There is no room left for Prayers and Entreaties; I've now fpoiled all; deceived my Mafter, and forced an *odious* Marriage upon my Mafter's Son. In a word, I have this day brought it about, contrary to his Expectation, and the Inclinations of *Pamphilus.* See what my Artifices have done? Could I have been quiet, no Mifchief would have happened. But hah, yonder he comes! I'm a loft Man. Would to Heaven there were fome Precipice here, whence I might in a moment throw myfelf headlong.

ANNOTATIONS.

[13] *Quidnam audio? Donatus* here tells us, that fome read *quidnam audiam,* and further obferves that *Menander,* of whom *Terence* is a profefs'd Tranflator, has the fame Expreffion. Τί δή ποτ' ἀκύσω. *Bentley* too contends for the fame Reading, the Senfe requiring that the Verb fhould be in the future, not the prefent Tenfe. *What am I going to hear?* For *Simo* had faid: *Narro* Chremeti *quæ tu dudum narrafti mihi,* viz. *Iras effe inter* Glycerium *& filium.* There is nothing in this to ftartle *Davus;* but he had reafon to apprehend what was yet to come, and whether the next Sentence might not inform him that *Chremes* had been prevailed on to give his Daughter.

[14] *Optume inquam factum. Davus* had faid in a low Voice to himfelf, *occidi,* yet fo as to be partly overheard; upon which *Simo* fays with fome earneftnefs; *Hem quid dixit? Davus* anfwers, *optime.* There is a Refemblance of Sound between *occidi* and *optime,* which might eafily deceive the old Man, who had heard but imperfectly; and this is what *Donatus* means, when he fays, *Bene ufus eft παρομοίῳ occidi & optime, ut fimilitudine falleret audientem.* This Similitude could not be preferved in the Tranflation. *Dacier.*

[17] *Ego vero folus. Simo* imagines, that *Davus* fays this, applauding himfelf for what he had done; but we are to underftand it as

faid

SI. Hoc audi. ut hinc te juſſi introire, opportunè hic
fit mihi obviàm. [dudum narraſti mihi.
DA. Hem, numnam periimus? SI. narro huic quæ
DA. Quidnam audio? SI. gnatam ut det oro, vixque
id exoro. DA. occidi.
SI. Hem, quid dixti? DA. optumè inquam factum.
SI. nunc per hunc nulla eſt mora.
CH. Domum modò ibo : ut apparentur, dicam : atque
huc renuncio. 15
SI. Nunc te oro, Dave ; quoniam ſolus mihi effeciſti
has nuptias— [enitere.
DA. Ego verò ſolus. SI. corrigere mihi gnatam porro
DA. Faciam hercle ſedulò. SI. potes nunc, dum ani-
mus irritatus eſt.
DA. Quieſcas. SI. age igitur : ubi nunc eſt ipſus? DA.
mirum, ni domi eſt.
SI. Ibo ad eum, atque eadem hæc, quæ tibi dixi, di-
cam itidem illi. DA. nullus ſum. 20
Quid cauſæ eſt, quin hic in piſtrinum rectà proficiſcar
viâ? X hinc
Nihil eſt preci loci relictum : jam perturbavi omnia :
Herum fefelli : in nuptias conjeci herilem filium :
Feci hodie, ut fierent, inſperante hoc, atque invito
Pamphilo.
Hem aſtutias! quòd ſi quieſſem, nihil eveniſſet mali. 25
Sed eccum : ipſum video : occidi : [tem darem.
Utinam mihi eſſet aliquid hîc, quo nunc me præcipi-

Age igitur : ubi nunc eſt ipſe? DA. Mirum, ni eſt domi. SI. Ibo ad eum, atque dicam itidem illi, hæc eadem quæ dixi tibi. DA. Sum nullus. Quid eſt cauſæ, quin proficiſcar hinc in piſtri-num rectâ viâ? nihil loci eſt relictum preci: jam perturbavi omnia : fefelli herum : conjeci filium herilem in nuptias : feci hodie, ut fierent, hoc hero inſperante, atque Pamphilo invito. Hem aſtutias! Quòd ſi quieſſem, nihil mali eveniſſet. Sed eccum : video ipſum Pamphilum : occidi : utinam aliquid eſſet mihi hîc, quo nunc darem me præcipitem.

Right margin:
SI. Audi hoc. Ut juſſi te introire hinc, bis Chremes obviàm ſit mihi opportunè. DA. Hem : numnam periimus? SI. Narro huic, quæ tu narraſti mihi dudum. DA. Quidnam audio? SI. Oro ut det gnatam, vixque exoro id. DA. Occidi. SI. Hem, quid dixiſti? DA. Inquam, optimè factum. SI. Nunc eſt nulla mora per hunc Chremetem. CH. Ibo domum modò : dicam ut nuptiæ apparentur : atque renuncio huc. SI. Nunc, Dave, oro te ; quoniam tu ſolus effeciſti has nuptias mihi—— DA. Ego verò ſolus effeci eas. SI. Porro enitere corrigere gnatum mihi. DA. Hercle Faciam ſedulò. SI. Nunc potes, dum animus ejus eſt irritatus. DA. Quieſcas. SI.

ſaid in rage, and chiding himſelf, *I alone indeed, in ſpite of all my Cunning to prevent it.*
18 *Faciam hercle ſedulo.* This is to be
underſtood in the ſame manner as the Expreſſion in the foregoing Note, conceived by
Simo as an Aſſent to what he deſired, but
meant by *Davus* quite the contrary.
19 *Ubi nunc eſt ipſus?* The ſuſpicious old
Man ſuddenly ſtarts this Queſtion, in order,
if poſſible, to ſurprize *Davus;* but he is too

cunning to be ſo eaſily catched. He remembers, that he had told his Maſter, that *Glycery* and *Pamphilus* had quarrelled, and therefore anſwers, as if he made no queſtion of
his being at home. *Donatus.*
20 *Nullus ſum.* Theſe are the Words of
Davus to himſelf, reflecting upon what he
had to expect; when *Pamphilus* ſhould come
to know what Misfortune his ill-timed Advice had brought upon him.

ACTUS

ACT III. SCENE V.

ARGUMENT.

Pamphilus *expostulates with* Davus, *that by his ill-timed Advice, he had forced this Marriage upon him.*

PAMPHILUS, DAVUS.

Pamphilus. WHERE is that Villain, who has undone me?
 Dav. I'm ruin'd.

Pamp. Nay, I own that I deserved no other, in being so indolent and void of Counsel. What? trust myself and Fortune to the Management of a wretched Slave? I have the due Reward of my Folly, but he shall never escape without feeling the Weight of my Resentment.

Dav. If I can but get off clear this once, I know for certain, I shall never hereafter be in danger.

Pamp. For what shall I say now to my Father? Shall I refuse to conclude the Match, who but just now so frankly promised my Consent? With what Face can I dare to do so? nor can I think what Course to follow.

Dav. Nor I; and yet all my Wits are at work. I'll pretend, however, to have hit upon an Expedient, that by this means I may avert, if but for a little, the Evil that threatens me.

Pamp. O!

Dav. I am discovered.

Pamp. Come hither, good Sirrah; what Excuse now? Do you see to what perplexity I am reduced by your wretched Advice?

Dav. But I'll soon extricate you.

Pamp. You'll extricate me!

Dav. Assuredly, *Pamphilus.*

Pamp. Without doubt, as you have done already.

Dav. I hope a little better.

Pamp. O! Rascal; do you fancy that I'll any more trust you? Can you set to rights an Affair desperate and lost? Hah, whom have I so blindly trusted? One, who from a Situation the most calm and undisturbed in the World, has this day forced me on a hateful Marriage.

ANNOTATIONS.

[1] *Ubi illic scelus est?* Towards the end of the last Scene, *Simo* leaves *Davus*, to go and meet *Pamphilus*, and tell him what had passed between him and *Chremes*. *Pamphilus* is no sooner informed of it, than full of rage he comes out to look for *Davus*, and vent his Fury upon him. Accordingly he appears upon the Stage looking round him, and enquiring, *Ubi illic scelus est, qui me perdidit?* *Davus* endeavours to soften him, and assures him that he will contrive some Project to extricate him from the present Difficulty.

[3] *Futili.* The Etymology of this Word is given at large by the old Scholiast upon *Statius, Theb.* 8. 297.

------ *Nec futile mæstis*
Id visum Danais.

Futile *vas, est quoddam fato ore, fundo angusto, quo utebantur in sacris Vestæ, quia aqua in sacris Vestæ in terra non ponitur,*

ACTUS III. SCENA V.

ARGUMENTUM.

Expoſtulat cum Davo Pamphilus, quod ſe in nuptias ſuo conſilio conjecerit.

PAMPHILUS, DAVUS.

UBI illic ſcelus eſt, qui me perdidit? DA. perii.
PA. atque hoc confiteor [conſili
Jure obtigiſſe, quandoquidem tam iners, tam nulli
Sum. ſervon' fortunas meas me commiſiſſe futili?
Ergo precium ob ſtultitiam fero: ſed inultum id nun-
quam à me auferet.
DA. Poſthac incolumem ſat ſcio fore me, nunc ſi evi-
to hoc malum. 5
PA. Nam quid ego nunc dicam patri? negabon' velle
me, modò [deam?
Qui ſum pollicitus ducere? quâ fiduciâ id facere au-
Nec, quid me nunc faciam, ſcio. DA. nec de me
equidem; atque id ago ſedulò.
Dicam aliquid jam inventurum, ut huic malo aliquam
producam moram. PA. oh.
DA. Viſus ſum. PA. ehodum, bone vir, quid ais? vi-
den' me conſiliis tuis 10
Miſerum impeditum eſſe? DA. at jam expediam. PA.
expedies? DA. certè, Pamphile.
PA. Nempe ut modò. DA. imo, melius ſpero. PA. oh,
tibi ego ut credam, furcifer? [fretu' ſum,
Tu rem impeditam & perditam reſtituas? hem, quo
Qui me hodie ex tranquilliſſimâ re conjeciſti in nuptias.

ORDO.
PA. UBI eſt il-
lic ſcelus
qui. perdidit me?
DA. Perii. PA.
Atque confiteor hoc
obtigiſſe mibi jure;
quandoquidem ſum
tam iners, tam nulli
conſilii. Mene opor-
tuit -commiſiſſe meas
fortunas futili ſervo?
Ergo fero precium
ob ſtultitiam: ſed
nunquam auferet id
inultum à me. DA.
Sat ſcio me fore
poſtbac incolumem,
ſi nunc devito boc
malum. PA. Nam
quid ego dicam nunc
patri? Negabone me
velle, qui modò ſum
pollicitus ducere au-
orem? Quâ fiduciâ
audeam facere id?
Nec ſcio quid nunc
faciam de me: DA.
Nec ego equidem
ſcio quid faciam de
me: atque ago id ſe-
dulò; dicam me jam
inventurum aliquid, ut producam aliquam moram huic malo. PA. Oh! DA. Sum viſus. PA.
Ebodum, bone vir, quid ais? Videſne me miſerum eſſe impeditum tuis conſiliis? DA. At jam expediam. PA. Expedies? DA. Certè, Pamphile. PA. Nempe ut modò. DA. Imo, ſpero melius.
PA. Oh! ut ego credam tibi, furcifer? Tu reſtituas rem impeditam & perditam? Hem, quo
ſum fretus? te, qui conjeciſti me hodie ex tranquilliſſimâ re in nuptias.

ANNOTATIONS.

tur, quod ſi fiat, piaculum eſt. Ideo excogita-
tum eſt vas, quod ſtare non poſſet, ſed ſi poſitum,
ſtatim funderetur. Unde & homo commiſſa non
retinens, futilis dicitur, contra non futilis bonus in conſiliis. Vas futile, was a kind of Veſſel,
with a broad Mouth, and a narrow bottom, and
commonly uſed in celebrating the Rites of Veſta,
becauſe in celebrating her Solemnities, it was
accounted a Profanation to ſet the Water upon
the ground. Therefore a Veſſel was contrived
of ſuch a make, that the Prieſt was under a

neceſſity of bolding it in his band the whole
time of the Sacrifice, becauſe if be ſhould ſet it
down, as it could not ſtand, the Water muſt
immediately be ſpilt. Hence alſo a Man that
could not keep the Secrets truſted to him, is ſometimes called futiles.
¹¹ Impeditum eſſe. Impeditus is properly
ſaid of one who has his Feet bound, ſo that
he cannot walk. Expedire is of a contrary
ſignification.

15 Quid

riage. Did not I tell you, that this would be the Consequence?

Dav. You did.

Pamp. What do you then deserve?

Dav. The Gallows: but give me leave to come a little to my-self, I'll soon find a Remedy.

Pamp. Alas! why havn't I time to punish you as I could wish? For the present Moment allows me only to look after myself, not to take my revenge of you.

ANNOTATIONS.

15 *Quid meritus?* DA. *Crucem.* This Question, and the Answer given to it, is founded upon a Custom among the Athenians, who in the Case of a Person convicted of a Capital Crime, never at first condemned him to any express Punishment, until they had put the Question to himself, what he thought he deserved. They, in order to ex-cite Compassion, often condemned themselves to a severer Punishment than they deserved, and by this means, the Minds of their Judges being softened, they were sometimes wholly acquainted. *Aristophanes,* in one of his Comedies, has a Passage exactly the same with this. *Ran.* 1044. Τί παθεῖν φησις ἄξιος εἶναι; ΔΙ. Τεθνάναι. *Quo supplicio dignum*

ACT IV. SCENE I.

ARGUMENT.

Charinus *in danger of losing his Mistress, expostulates with* Pamphilus *for Breach of Promise.*

CHARINUS, PAMPHILUS, DAVUS.

Charinus. **I**S this a thing to be believed or related, that any Person should be possessed with so untoward a Soul, as to rejoice at the Misfortunes of others, and build all their Hopes of Success upon their Ruin? Ah! Can such a thing really be? Yes, these are undoubtedly the worst and most dangerous of all Men, who are ashamed of giving a downright Refusal, but when the time of Performance comes, finding themselves hard pressed, are necessarily obliged to take off the Mask; they are afraid, and yet the thing itself obliges them to deny. On these Occasions, they observe no bounds in their Language, are awed by no Shame. What are you? What are you to me? Why should I resign my Pretensions to you? pray remember that Charity begins at home. But if you ask, where is Sincerity and Honour? they are not

ANNOTATIONS.

1 *Haccine est credibile,* &c. This Scene begins with the Complaints of *Charinus,* who accuses *Pamphilus* of Breach of Promise. *Byrrhia,* who, in a former Scene, had been sent to overhear what passed between *Pamphilus,* and his Father, not knowing with what View *Pamphilus* had seemingly consented to the Proposal of a Wedding, carries his Mistake to *Charinus,* and reports that *Pamphilus* was, by his own Consent, to be that day married to *Philumena.* Cha-rinus, not as yet undeceived, comes upon the Stage, inveighing severely against *Pamphilus,* as having acted dishonourably. After they meet, *Charinus* is so full of Reproaches and Resentment, that its some time before they come to a right Understanding. But when the thing is fully known, both lay the blame of all upon *Davus,* who defends himself in the best manner he can, and promises by some Artifice to make all easy.

5 *Idne est verum?* *Charinus* astonished at

An non dixi hoc effe futurum? DA. dixti. PA. quid
  meritus? DA. crucem.   15
Sed fine paululum ad me redeam: jam aliquid difpiciam. PA. hei mihi,   [ut volo:
Cùm non habeo fpatium, ut de te fumam fupplicium,
Namque hoc tempus, præcavere mihi me, haud te
  ulcifci, finit.

An non dixi hoc effe futurum? DA. Dixifli. PA. Quid es meritus? DA. Crucem. Sed fine me paululum ut ad me redeam: jam difpiciam aliquid. PA. Hei mibi; cùm non habeo fpatium, ut fumam fupplicium de te, ut volo: namque hoc tempus, tantum finit me præcavere mibi, haud ulcifci te.

ANNOTATIONS.

dignum te dicis? BA. *Morte.*
  18 *Sinit.* This Word does not refer to *præcavere,* but only to *ulcifci.* And in general, where two Verbs are wanted, whereof one denies, the other affirms, or one commands, and the other forbids, the firft is for the moft part omitted. We have an

Example of the very fame kind in *Phædrus,* Book IV. *Fab.* 17. 31.
  Non veto dimitti, verum cruciari fame.
Where we are to fupply *jubeo.* The Sentence, therefore, compleat is thus: *Namque hoc tempus præcavere mibi me monet, haud te ulcifci finit.*

ACTUS IV. SCENA I.

ARGUMENTUM:

Periclitatur Charinus de amica, & cum Pamphilo expoftulat de foluta fide.

CHARINUS, PAMPHILUS, DAVUS.

HOCCINE credibile eft, aut memorabile,
  Tanta vecordia innata cuiquam ut fiet,
Ut malis gaudeant, atque ex incommodis
Alterius fua comparent ut commoda? ah;   4
Idne eft verum? imo id genus eft hominum peffumum,
In denegando modo queis pudor eft paululum;
Poft ubi jam tempus eft promiffa perfici,
Tum coacti neceffariò fe aperiunt, & timent:
Et tamen res cogit denegare. ibi
Tum impudentiffima eorum oratio eft: 10
Quis tu es? quis mihi es? cur meam tibi? heus,
Proxumus fum egomet mihi. attamen, ubi fides;
Si roges, nihil pudet. hîc, ubi opus eft,

ORDO.

CH. *Occine eft credibile, aut memorabile, ut tanta vecordia fi et innata cuiquam; ut gaudeant malis, atque ut comparent fuæ commoda ex incommodis alterius? Ah, eftne id verum? Imo, id eft poffumum genus hominum, quibus paululum pudor modò adeft in denegando; poft ubi eft tempus jam promiffa perfici, tum coacti, neceffariò aperiunt fe, et timent, & tamen res cogit eos denegare. Ibi tum, eratio eorum eft impudentiffima: Quis es tu? quis es mibi? Cur dem meam rem tibi? Heus, egomet fum proximus mibi. Attamen fi roges, ubi fides? pudet eos nibil. Hic ubi eft ofus vereri,*

ANNOTATIONS.

at this Bafenefs of Behaviour, feems here to doubt with himfelf, whether it be poffible that there can be fuch a Race of Men as he had found *Pamphilus* to be.
  6 *Queis pudor eft paululum.* It is natural for *Charinus* to tax that in others as a great Crime, by which he had been a great Suf-

ferer. *Pamphilus*'s falfe Modefty, as he imagined it, in not refufing to refign *Philumena* to him, had made him fecure, fo that he had taken no Meafures for himfelf, or to thwart the Defigns of his Rival.
  13 *Ilic, ubi opus eft, non verentur.* When a Promife is afked of them, they are afham'd

not in the leaſt aſhamed. They are not at all concerned in this Caſe, where they ought to be ſo; but they have a great deal in the other, where it is not neceſſary. But what ſhall I do? Shall I go find him out, and reproach him with this injurious Treatment? Shall I vent all the ill-natur'd Language I can againſt him? But perhaps ſome one will ſay, *You'll get nothing by it.* A great deal: I ſhall at leaſt give him ſome Diſturbance, and gratify my own Reſentment.

Pamp. Charinus; unleſs the Gods ſome how befriend us, I have, by my Imprudence, ruined both you and myſelf.

Char. Yes, no doubt by your Imprudence? You have then at laſt found an Excuſe. You have finely kept your Promiſe indeed!

Pamp. What do you mean by this *at laſt?*

Char. Do you think to deceive me a ſecond time by theſe fine Speeches?

Pamp. What can be the meaning of all this?

Char. After I had told you that I was in love, it ſeems you took a fancy to her likewiſe. Unhappy Wretch, thus to judge of another Man's Heart by own!

Pamp. You are under ſome Miſtake.

Char. Did not your Joy appear compleat enough, without tantalizing an unhappy Lover, and feeding him with falſe Hopes? You may take her.

Pamp. I may take her! Ah, little do you know in what perplexities I am involved, and how much Anxiety this Raſcal here has bred me by his pernicious Counſels.

Char. What is there ſo wonderful in that, if he takes example by you?

Pamp. You would hardly talk in this manner, if you rightly underſtood either me, or my Paſſion.

Char. I know, you have had ſome Words with your Father on this Subjeſt, and he is now angry with you, nor could by any means prevail upon you to-day to conſent to the Marriage.

Pamp. Nay, to ſhew you how little you are acquainted with my preſent Troubles; this Match was not deſigned for me, nor did any body dream of giving me at this time a Wife.

Char. I know, you are forced by your own Conſent.

Pamp. Hold, you don't yet comprehend me.   *Char.*

ANNOTATIONS.

to refuſe, and this is the time when they ought not to be aſhamed; for we may boldly refuſe another, what cannot be granted without an Inconvenience to ourſelves. But when the time comes, that they ought to make good their Promiſes, there they are not aſhamed of breaking their Word, and 'tis then, if ever, that they ought to be aſhamed. For altho' they might with a good Grace have refuſed the Favour when aſked, yet after a Promiſe is made, it ought to be ſacred. *Terence* has manifeſtly borrowed this from a Paſſage of the firſt Scene of the ſecond Aſt of the *Epidicus* of *Plautus.*

> *Plerique homines, quos, cum nibil reſert,*
>   *pudet: ubi pudendum eſt,*
> *Ibi eos deſerit pudor, quum uſus eſt ut*
>   *pudeat.*

[16] *Mala ingeram multa. Mala,* a Word commonly uſed by the *Latins,* inſtead of *probra* or *convicia.* So *Plautus Bacchid.* IV. 8. 34.

> *Ut tibi mala multa ingeram.*

[18] *Niſi quid dii reſpiciunt.* The Gods
    ·   were

Non verentur : illîc, ubi nihil opus eft, ibi verentur.
Sed quid agam? adeamne ad eum, & cum eo injuriam
  hanc expoftulem? 15
Mala ingeram multa? atque aliquis dicat, nihil pro-
  moveris. . . . [geffero.
Multum. moleftus certè ei fuero, atque animo morem
PA. Charine, & me & te imprudens, nifi quid Dii
  refpiciunt, perdidi. . [vifti fidem.
CH. Itane, imprudens? tandem inventa eft caufa: fol-
PA. Quî tandem? CH. etiam nunc me ducere iftis
  dictis poftulas? 20
PA. Quid iftuc eft? CH. poftquam me amare dixi,
  complacita eft tibi. . [ctavi meo!
Heu me miferum, cùm tuùm animum ex animo fpe-
PA. Falfu' es. CH. non tibi fatis effe hoc vifum foli-
  dum eft gaudium, , . .
Nifi me lactaffes amantem, & falsâ fpe produceres?
Habeas. PA. habeam? ah, nefcis quantis in malis ver-
  fer mifer, . . 25
Quantafque hic fuis confiliis mihi confecit folicitudines
Meus carnufex. CH. quid iftuc tàm mirum, de te fi
  exemplum capit? . . . . [meum.
PA. Haud iftuc dicas, fi cognôris vel me, vel amorem
CH. Scio, cum patre altercafti dudum, & is nunc pro-
  pterea tibi 29
Succenfet, nec te quivit hodie cogere, illam ut duceres.
PA. Imo etiam, quo tu minùs fcis aerumnas meas, . .
Hæ nuptiæ non apparabantur mihi; . . .
Nec poftulabat nunc quifquam uxorem dare.
CH. Scio : tu coactus tuâ voluntate es. PA. mane ; 34

beas eam. PA. Habeam? Ah, nefcis in quantis malis ego mifer verfer, quantafque folicitudines hic meus carnifex confecit mihi fuis confiliis. CH. Quid eft iftue tam mirum, fi capit exemplum de te? PA. Haud dicas iftuc, fi cognoveris vel me, vel meum amorem. CH. Scio, altercafti dudum cum patre, & propterea is nunc fuccenfet tibi, nec quivit cogere te hodie, ut ducere illam. PA. Imo etiam, ut fentias quo tu minùs fcis meas ærumnas, hæ nuptiæ non appara-gantur mibi, nec quifquam nunc poftulabat dare uxorem mibi. CH. Scio : tu es coactus tuâ voluntate. PA. Mane :

ANNOTATIONS.

were faid *refpicere homines*, when they were favourable ; hence *fortuna refpiciens*, figni-fies profperous or propitious Fortune. For the Gods were fuppofed to look down upon Men for Favour and Protection ; whereas, when they turned away from them, it was in token of Averfion.

19 *Solvifti fidem. Solvere fidem*, is to difcharge one's Promife by Performance, and to be underftood here ironically, as im-plying exprefsly the contrary of what *Cha-rinus* meant.

20 *Quî tandem. Pamphilus* infifts upon the word *tandem*, at *laft*, and with reafon,

because it is an injurious Word, and may juftly give Offence : for it marks an Ex-cufe found after Breach of Promife, and therefore falfe. A real Excufe precedes the Action; as being the Caufe of it, but a falfe one is found after it, and ferves only for Pretence. *Dacier.*

31 *Quo tu minus fcis ærumnas meas.* This *quo tu minus*, has very much puzzled Commentators. *Donatus* thinks *quo* is here for *quod*, and fupplies *audi* or *accipe*, explain-ing it *quod* or *quoniam minus fcis*, &c. But Madam *Dacier* contends that *quo* is an Ab-lative, to which *id* is underftood. *Id quo minus*

G 2

Char. I know well enough, that you are juft upon marrying her.

Pamp. Why do you rack me? only hear. He never gave over teazing me, to fay to my Father, that I'd marry her; begging, entreating; until at length he forced a Promife from me.

Char. Who was it did this?

Pamp. Davus.

Char. Davus?

Pamp. Davus has ruin'd all.

Char. Why?

Pamp. I can't tell; only that the Gods have been angry with me, to make me give ear to fuch a Rafcal.

Char. Is this your doing, *Davus?*

Dav. 'Tis my doing.

Char. Hah, what fay'ft thou, Villain? May the Gods bring you to the End which you deferve. Tell me, had all his Enemies combin'd to force him to this Marriage, what other Counfel could they have given him but this?

Dav. I have miffed of my Aim, but don't defpair.

Char. I know it.

Dav. We have not fucceeded in this, let us make trial of another Method; unlefs perhaps you think that becaufe it fail'd the firft time, this Misfortune is not capable of being redrefs'd.

Pamp. Nay more, I verily believe, that if you fet ferioufly about it, out of one, you will be able to work me into two Weddings.

Dav. Thus much, *Pamphilus,* I owe you as your Servant, to labour for you night and day, with all my Power; yea, even to hazard my Life if it can be of any fervice to you. 'Tis yours, on the other hand, if things fall out otherwife than expected, to forgive. My Endeavours may not be always fuccefsful, but I do my beft. Do you, if you can, contrive fomething better, and difmifs me.

Pamp. I defire nothing more, only reftore me to the Condition in which you found me.

Dav. I will.

Pamp. But it muft be done prefently.

Dav. Hufh! *Glycery's* Door opens.

Pamp. What's that to the purpofe?

Dav. My Wits are at work.

Pamp. What now at length?

Dav. I'll foon give you a Proof of my Skill.

ANNOTATIONS.

minus fcis, as if he had faid, *What you know the leaft of all my Misfortunes.* That is, the only thing you want: to know perfectly my Mifery is, *&c.*

56 *Parum fuccedit quod ago.* 'Tis our part to try and endeavour, but the Event is not always in our power. *Davus* had reafon to think he was ill ufed by *Pamphilus,* who continued to chide him fo much for an Accident, that had fallen out contrary to his Intention.

59 *Concrepuit a Glycerio oftium.* We learn from *Plutarch,* in *Publicola,* that when any one was coming out, he ftruck the Door on the infide, that fuch as were without, might be warned to take care of themfelves, and ftand out of the way, left they might be hurt. The Doors of the *Romans,* on the contrary,

Nondum ſcis. CH. ſcio equidem illam ducturum eſſe te.
PA. Cur me enecas ? hoc audi, nunquam deſtitit
Inſtare, ut dicerem, eſſe ducturum, patri :
Suadere, orare, uſque adeo, donec perpulit.
CH. Quis homo iſtuc ? PA. Davos. CH. Davos ? PA.
Davos omnia.
CH. Quamobrem ? PA. neſcio : niſi mihi Deos ſatis 40
Scio fuiſſe iratos, qui auſcultaverim.
CH. Factum eſt hoc, Dave ? DA. factum eſt. CH,
hem, quid ais, ſcelus ?
At tibi Dî dignum factis exitium duint.
Eho, dic mihi, ſi omnes hunc conjectum in nuptias
Inimici vellent, quod, ni hoc, conſilium darent ? 45
DA. Deceptus ſum, at non defatigatus. CH. ſcio.
DA. Hac non ſucceſſit, aliâ aggrediemur viâ :
Niſi id putas, quia primò proceſſit parum,
Non poſſe jam ad ſalutem converti hoc malum.
PA. Imo etiam : nam ſati' credo, ſi advigilaveris, 50
Ex unis geminas mihi conficies nuptias.
DA. Ego, Pamphile, hoc tibi pro ſervitio debeo,
Conari manibus, pedibus, nocteſque & dies
Capitis periculum adire ; dum proſim tibi:
Tuum'ſt, ſi quid præter ſpem evenit, mî ignoſcere. 55
Parum ſuccedit quod ago ; at facio ſedulò.
Vel melius tute reperi, me miſſum face.
PA. Cupio. reſtitue in quem me accepiſti locum.
DA. Faciam. PA. at jam hoc opus eſt. DA. hem, ſt,
mane : crepuit à Glycerio oſtium.
PA. Nihil ad te. DA. quæro. PA. hem, nunccine de-
mum ? DA. at jab hoc tibi inventum dabo. 60

primò, hoc malum non poſſe jam converti ad ſalutem. PA. Imo etiam : nam credo ſatis, ſi advigilaveris, conficies geminas nuptias mihi ex unis. DA. Pamphile, ego debeo hoc tibi pro ſervitio, conari manibus, pedibus, nocteſque & dies, adire periculum capitis, cum proſim tibi. Eſt tuum officium, ſi quid evenit præter ſpem, ignoſcere mihi ; quod ſuccedit ſorte parum, at facio ſedulò. Vel tute reperi aliquid melius, & fac me miſſum. PA. Cupio : reſtitue me in quem locum accepiſti. DA. Faciam. PA. At jam hoc eſt opus. DA. Hem, ſt, mane : oſtium concrepuit à Glycerio. PA. Hoc eſt nihil ad te. DA. Quæro conſilium. PA. Hem, nuncne demum? DA. At jam dabo hoc inventum tibi.

ANNOTATIONS.

contrary, opened on the inſide, as appears, from *Pliny*, Book XXXVI. Ch. 15. But the creaking meant here, is more probably that of the Door itſelf upon the Hinges, to prevent which in the Night-time, it was uſual for Lovers, to pour Wine or Water upon them. Thus, *Plautus Curc. I.* 1. 88.

PH. *Agite, bibite, feſtivæ fores ; potate : fite mihi volentes propitiæ.*
And again. I. 3. 1.
Placide egredere, & ſonitam prohibe forium, & crepitum cardinum.

Ne, quod hic agimus, herus percipiat fieri, mea Planeſium.
Mane, ſuffundam aquulam. PA. *Viden, ut anus tremula medicinam facit.*
Eapſe merum condidicit bibere, foribus dat aquam, quam bibant.
60 *Nihil ad te.* What's that to the pur-poſe ? This is the proper Senſe of the Words. *Pamphilus* would have *Davus* to think of nothing, but what regards himſelf, and find ſome Expedient to extricate him from his preſent Troubles ; whereas he imagines by this, that he wanted only to gain time.

ACT

ACT IV. SCENE II.

ARGUMENT.

Glycery *is in fear of loſing* Pamphilus, *having heard that he was that day to be married, and on that account had or-dered* Myſis *to bring* Pamphilus *to her ;* Myſis *meeting him,' confirms him in his Reſolution of continuing faithful to* Gly-cery, *and* Davus *prepares for ſome new Project.*

MYSIS, PAMPHILUS, CHARINUS, DAVUS.

Myſ. I'LL inſtantly ſee to find out your *Pamphilus* for you, where-ever he may be, and bring him along with me to you; do you only, my dear Soul, ceaſe fretting and tormenting yourſelf in this manner.

Pamp. Myſis !

Myſ. What's that—? O *Pamphilus,* we are fortunately met.

Pamp. What's the matter?

Myſ. My Miſtreſs charg'd me to entreat you, if you have any Love for her, to come to her preſently, for ſhe wants of all things to ſee you.

Pamp. Ah ! I'm undone : Misfortunes come one upon the neck of another. *(to Davus)* That we ſhould now be plunged into ſo many Anxieties by your perverſe Counſel ! for I am therefore call'd, be-cauſe ſhe has heard of the Preparations for the Wedding.

Char. In reſpect of which, how well and quiet might we have been, had this Raſcal been but eaſy.

Dav. Well done : as if he were not mad enough of himſelf, you make him ſtill worſe.

Myſ. And in reality that is the very thing ; and 'tis for this reaſon that ſhe is now, poor Soul, in ſo much Diſtreſs.

Pamp. Myſis, I ſwear to you by all the Gods, that I will never a-bandon her, not if I were ſure to draw upon myſelf the Hatred of all the World. I have deſir'd her above all others, my Deſires are granted ; our Humours agree : away with all thoſe who would divide us, nothing but Death ſhall be able to ſeparate me from her.

Myſ.

ANNOTATIONS.

¹ *Jam ubi ubi erit,* In this Scene, *My-ſis* comes out from *Glycery,* who knowing that this was the day, that had been agreed upon for *Pamphilus's* Marriage with *Philu-mena,* is full of Anxiety, and impatient to ſee him, that ſhe may be ſatisfied of every thing from himſelf. The ſight of *Myſis* renews, in *Pamphilus,* his Tenderneſs and Remembrance of *Glycery,* and produces a ſolemn Promiſe, that no Conſideration ſhall be able to make him abandon her. This Appearance of *Myſis,* and mention of *Gly-* cery to *Pamphilus,* in his preſent Perplexity, is finely imagined by the Poet, that the Lover may be rouzed, and confirmed in his Reſo-lution of adhering to his Miſtreſs, notwith-ſtanding the Promiſe he had made to his Father. And becauſe *Myſis* herſelf was ſcarcely ſufficient to bear him up againſt ſo preſſing a Difficulty, it is ſo contrived, that he is carried to *Glycery* herſelf.

⁵ *Hoc malum integraſcit.* Intelligit inte-grationem amoris, & ſolicitudinis de nuptiis, *Integraſcit* for *integratur : quod ad integrum redit,*

ACTUS IV. SCENA II.

ARGUMENTUM.

Glycerium in difcrimen venit amittendi Pamphilum, quem acce-
perat eo die uxorem ducturum. Ea gratia Myfidem jufferat
accerfere Pamphilum. Hæc ancilla interim illius animum erga
Glycerium confirmat, & ad novum confilium fe parat Davus.

MYSIS, PAMPHILUS, CHARINUS, DAVUS.

ORDO.

JAM, ubi ubi erit, inventum tibi curabo, & me-
   cum adductum   [cerare.
Tuum Pamphilum : tu modò, anime mi, noli te ma-
PA. Myfis. MY. quid eft? hem Pamphile, optumè
   mihi te offers. PA. quid eft ?
MY. Orare juffit, fi fe ames, hera, jam ut ad fefe ve-
   nias :   [grafcit. 5
Videre ait te cupere. PA. vah, perii. hoc malum inte-
Siccine me, atque illam operâ tuâ nunc miferos foli-
   citarier ?
Nam idcirco accerfor, nuptias quòd mî apparari fenfit.
CH. Quibu' quidem quàm facile poterat quiefci, fi hic
   quieffet.   [MY. atque edepol,
DA. Age, fi hic non infanit fatis fuâ fponte, inftiga.
Ea res eft; proptereaque nunc mifera in mœrore eft.
   PA. Myfis,   10
Per omnes tibi adjuro Deos, nunquam eam me defer-
   turum :   [homines.
Non, fi capiundos mihi fciam effe inimicos omnes
Hanc mihi expetivi, contigit : conveniunt mores : va-
   leant   [adimet nemo.
Qui inter nos difcidium volunt : hanc, nifi mors, m

ORDO.

MY. JAM curabo tuum Pamphilum, ubi ubi erit, effe inventum tibi, & adductum mecum : tu modò, mi anime, noli te macerare te. PA. Myfis. MY. Quid eft ? hem Pamphile, offers te mihi optime. PA. Quid eft ? MY. Hera juffit me orare te, fi ames fe, ut jam venias ad fefe : ait fe cupere videre te. PA. Vah, perii. Hoc malum integrafcit. Siccine oportet me atque illam nunc miferos folicitari tuâ operâ, Dave ? nam idcirco accerfor, quòd fenfit, nuptias apparari mihi. CH. Quibus nuptiis quidem quàm facile poterat quiefci, fi hic Davus quieviffet.

DA. *Age, fi hic non infanit fatis fuâ fponte, inftiga cum.* MY. *Atque edepol ea eft res ; proptereaque nunc mifera eft in mœrore.* PA. *Myfis, adjuro tibi per omnes Deos, me nunquam deferturum eam : non fi fciam omnes homines effe capiundos inimicos mihi. Expetivi hanc mihi, contigit : mores conveniunt : omnes valeant qui volunt difcidium inter nos : nema adimet hanc mihi nifi mors.*

ANNOTATIONS.

redit, quod repetitur, quod inftauratur. Thus,
Virg. Georg. 4. 514.

------ *Ramoque fedens miferabile carmen*
   Integrat.

  9 *Age, fi hic non infanit fatis fua fponte, infti-*
ga. Altho' *Davus* had born with patience the
Anger of *Pamphilus*, yet it was not to be
fuppofed, that he would bear with the fame
Calmnefs the Behaviour of *Charinus*, who
inftead of foftening his Mafter, only provoked him more againft him. He therefore
checks him here, to make him fenfible,

that he ought to act otherwife,

  12 *Non, fi capiundos mibi fciam effe ini-*
micos omnes bomines. This is to be fuppofed fpoken with Warmth and Earneftnefs,
and marks ftrongly *Pamphilus*'s Paffion.
Yet in all this Heat and Excefs of Concern,
he ftill preferves a Decency, which ought
not to efcape our Notice. It is his Father,
whom he has chiefly in his eye here ; for
as to others, he had but little reafon to apprehend any thing from them. But as it
would have looked harfh and unnatural to
                              name

Myf. I begin to revive.

Pamp. Apollo never gave a truer Anfwer than this. If I could contrive that my Father fhould not imagine it owing to me. that this
Marriage was broke off, I would fain have it fo : but if that can't be,
I'll take the Method that moft directly offers, and let him believe
that I am the Hindrance. What think ye of me now.?

Char. That you are unhappy equally as I am.

Dav. I'm contriving an Expedient.

Char. (*to Pamphilus.*) Then you have Courage.

Pamp. I know your fine Defign.

Dav. Nay, reft fatisfied, it fhall be effectual.

Pamp. But it is wanted prefently.

Dav. Well, and I have it prefently.

Char. What is it ?

Dav. Don't miftake ; it is for my Mafter, and not for you.

Char. Enough, I'm fatisfied.

Pamp. Well, tell me then what you're to do ?

Dav. I doubt whether the whole Day will anfwer for my Project :
don't then fancy that I have leifure to give you a long Account of it:
get out of my way therefore, for ye but hinder me.

Pamp. I'll go fee *Glycery.*

Dav. (*to Charinus.*) And you, where do you go ?

Char. Would you have me tell you the very Truth ?

Dav. To be fure (*afide.*) He begins a long Speech of it.

Char. What will become of me !

Dav. Ridiculous ! are you not contented that I reprieve you a
whole Day, by putting off the Marriage to him ?

Char. But yet, *Davus.*

Dav. What then ?

Char. That I may marry her.

Dav. Foolifh !

Char. Be fure come to me, if you can think of any thing.

Dav. Why fhould I come ? I can do nothing.

Char. But if you can————

Dav. Well, well, I'll come.

Char. If you can, I fhall be at home.

Dav.

ANNOTATIONS.

name him in particular, he expreffes himfelf in general Terms of all Mankind. His
Father is chiefly meant, but not mentioned.
This is what *Donatus* obferves ; *Mira vera-
cundia : omnes homines maluit dicere, ut in
his quoque parentes fignificaret, quam aperte
dicere* patrem, *cujus metu promifit nuptias.*

    ¹⁹ *Quis vidsor ?* CH. *Mifer æque atque
ego.* DA. *Confilium quæro.* CH. *Fortis.*
This Paffage is not eafy to unravel. *Donatus* fancies that *Pamphilus* wanted to be

complimented by *Charinus,* upon his Courage and Firmnefs. *Guyetus* gives the fame
turn to the Words, and to make the Senfe
more apparent, difpofes them thus ; *Quis
vidsor ?* CH. *Fortis ; at mifer æque atque
ego.* DA. *Confilium quæro. Tanaquil Faber* was the firft who corrected it from *Donatus, at tu fortis es,* for thefe are his Words,
*Mifer æque atque ego, bene atque ego, quia
hic amore vexatur, & intulit paredoxen, nam
volebat*

My. Refipifco. Pa. non Apollinis magi' verum, at-
que hoc, refponfum eft.   15
Si poterit fieri, ut ne pater per me ftetiffe credat,
Quo mi ùs hæ fierent nuptiæ, volo. fed fi id non po-
   terit ;
Id faciam, in proclivi quod eft, per me ftetiffe ut credat.
Quis videor? Ch. mifer æque atque ego. Da. confi-
   lium quæro. Ch. fortis.
Pa. Scio quid conere. Da. hoc ego tibi profectò ef-
   fectum reddam.   20
Pa. Jam hoc opus eft. Da. quin jam habeo. Ch.
   quid eit? Da. huic, non tibi, habeo; ne erres.
Ch. Sat habeo. Pa. quid facies, cedo? Da. dies hic
   mi ut fati' fit, vercor,   [dum credas.
Ad agendum: ne vacuum effe me nunc ad narran-
Proinde hinc vos amolimini : nam mi impedimento eftis.
Pa. Ego hanc vifam. Da. quid tu? quò hinc te agis?
   Ch. verum vis dicam? Da. imo etiam :   25
Narrationis incipit mihi initium. Ch. quid me fiet?
Da. Eho tu impudens, non fatis habes, quod tibi die-
   culam addo,   [men. Da. quid ergo?
Quantum huic promoveo nuptias? Ch. Dave, atta-
Ch. Ut ducam. Da. ridiculum. Ch. huc face ad me
   venias, fiquid poteris.
Da. Quid veniam? nihil habeo. Ch. attamen, fi
   quid. Da. age, veniam. Ch. fi quid,   30

My. Refipifco. Pa. Refponfum, Apollonis non eft magis verum quam hoc. Si poterit fieri, ut pater ua credat ftetiffe per me, quo minus hæ nuptiæ fierent, vo-lo id : fed fi id non poterit fieri, faciam id quod eft in proclivi, ut credat eas ftetiffe per me. Quis videor? Ch. Mifor æque atque ego. Da. Quæro confilium. Ch. Es fortis. Pa. Scio quid conere. Da. Profecto ego reddam hoc effectum tibi. Pa. Eft opus hic jam. Da. Quin habeo jam. Ch. Quid eft? Da. Ha-beo huic, non tibi, ne erres. Ch. Ha-beo fat. Pa. Cedo, quid facies? Da. Vereor ut hic dies fit fatis mihi ad agendum : ne credas me nunc effe vacu-um ad narrandum. Proinde vos amoli-

mini, nam eftis impedimento mibi. Pa. Ego vifam banc. Da. Quid tu? quò agis te
binc? Ch. Vis ut dicam verum? Da. Imo etiam: incipit initium narrationis mibi. Ch.
Quid fiet de me? Da. Eho tu impudens, non babes fatis quod addo dieculam tibi, quantum
promoveo nuptias buic? Ch. Attamen, Dave. Da. Quid ergo? Ch. Ut ducam. Da.
Ridiculum. Ch. Face ut venias buc ad me, fi poteris quid. Da. Propter quid veniam?
babeo nibil. Ch. Attamen, fi habueris quid. Da. Age veniam. Ch. Si habueris quid ;

ANNOTATIONS.

*volebat Pampbilus fibi dici, at tu fortis es,
quod illi tamen mox dicetur.* This is undoubtedly the true Reading ; *Cbarinus* wants
to encourage *Pampbilus* in this Refolution,
of not forfaking *Glycery,* becaufe that gave
the faireft Profpect of advancing his own
Affair.

   20 *Scio quid conere. I know ; doubtlefs a
fine Expedient.* He means that this fine
Project, he was fo bufy in contriving, would
probably only bring new Incumbrances upon
him, as he had faid before, *ex unis geminas
mibi efficies nuptias.*

   2c *Imo etiam: narrationis incipit miki
initium.* There is fome difficulty in thefe
Words ; what feems moft probable, is this :

Davus pleafed, that *Pampbilus* was gone,
and willing to remove *Cbarinus* alfo out of
the way, afks: *Quid tu? Quo' hinc te a-
gis?* But he now, that *Pampbilus* was abfent, thinking a fine Opportunity was offered of difcourfing with *Davus* upon the
Subject of his Love, begins as if he meant
to make a long Speech : *Verum vis dicam?*
To which *Davus* replies : *Imo etiam: narrationis incipit mibi initium.* The firft part,
imo etiam, is addreffed to *Cbarinus* ; the reft
he fays turning about to the fpectators,
Cbarinus being fuppofed not to hear it ; nor
was *Davus,* at prefent, in a humour to attend to a long Story.

   27 *Eho tu impudens. Proprie,* fays Do-
   - - - nato,

Dav. Wait for me a little, *Mysis*, 'till I come out again.
Myс. For what?
Dav. There's a Necessity for it.
Myс. Make haste then.
Dav. I tell you I'll be here again in a Minute.

ANNOTATIONS.

tatus Charino dixit impudens, *quasi insolita* | *Davum sibi moram præstitam Pamphili nupti-*
& multa poscenti : quippe qui & sponsam alie- | *arum.*
nam petere ausus sit, & non satis babeat, per

ACT IV. SCENE III.

ARGUMENT.

Myсis *remains alone upon the Stage, and complains of the Inconstancy of human Affairs.*

MYSIS.

Mysis. IS there then nothing that a Person can call his own ! Good
Heavens ! I considered this *Pamphilus* as my Mistress's chief
Good ; her Friend, Lover, and Husband, ready to serve her upon
all Occasions, And yet what Anxiety, poor Soul, does she now
suffer on his account ? Indeed her present Trouble is much greater
than all her former Satisfaction. But I see *Davus* coming out from
her, Hah, my good Man, pray what's this you have got ? Where
do you carry the Child ?

ANNOTATIONS.

[a] *Nilne esse proprium cuiquam ?* *Davus,* | fore passed. In the midst of those her Cogi-
at the End of the last Scene, steps into *Gly-* | tations, she is interrupted by *Davus,* whom
cery's, and leaves *Mysis* alone upon the | she sees coming out with the Child in his
Stage, who falls into a train of Reflections, | Arms.
that naturally offers from what had just be- | Ibid, *Proprium.* By *proprium,* the An-
| cients,

ACT IV. SCENE IV.

ARGUMENT.

Davus *instructs* Mysis *to lay the Child before his Master's Door,
to frighten* Chremes *from giving his Daughter to* Pamphilus.

DAVUS, MYSIS.

Davus. NOW, *Mysis*, I stand in need of your prompt Cunning and
Address to help me in the present Case.
Myс. What Project now ?
Dav. Take this Child from me quickly, and lay him before our
Door.
Myс. What, on the Ground ?   *Dav.*

ANNOTATIONS.

[a] *Mysis nunc opus est tua mibi,* &c. *Davus* | his Arms, designing to lay it before his
comes out from *Glycery* with the Child in | Master's Door, that when *Chremes* came to
| hear

Domi ero. DA. Tu, Myfis, dum exeo, parumper me
opperire hic.   [DA. jam, inquam, hic adero.
MY. Quapropter? Da. ita facto eft opus. MY. matura.

ero domi. DA. *Tu,*
Myfis, opperire me
parumper hic, dum
exeo. MY. *Qua-*
propter? DA. *Ita eft opus-facto.* MY. *Matura.* DA. *Inquam, adero hic jam,*

ACTUS IV. SCENA III.

ARGUMENTUM.

Manet fola in fcena Myfis, & de rerum inconftantia queritur.
MYSIS.

ORDO.

NILNE effe proprium cuiquam? Divoftram fidem!
  Summum bonum effe heræ putabam hunc Pam-
philu'm,
Amicum, amatorem, virum, in quovis loco
Paratum : verum ex eo nunc mifera quem capit
Dolorem? facile hîc plus mali eft, quam illîc boni. 5
Sed Davus exit. mi homo, quid iftuc, obfecro, eft?
Quò portas puerum?

MY. Nilne ef-
fe pro-
prium cuiquam ho-
mini? Dii veftram
fidem! Putabam
hunc Pamphilum ef-
fe fummum bonum
heræ, amicum, ama-
torem, virum para-
tum in quovis loco:
verum quem dolorem

nunc illa mifera capit ex eo? facile eft plus mali hic, quam boni illic. Sed Davus exit. Mi
homo, obfecro quid iftuc eft? Quo portas puerum?

ANNOTATIONS.

cients, for the moft part, meant *perpetuum.*
Thus, *Virg. Æn.* vi. 872.
  Propria hæc fi dona fuiffent.
There is nothing, therefore, which we can
claim the property of in this fenfe; for
whatever can be taken from us, is not properly our own. Wifdom, Prudence, Virtue,
are in the power of none to deprive us of,
but the Gifts of Fortune are precarious.

ACTUS IV. SCENA IV.

ARGUMENTUM.
Davus mandat Myfidi ut apponat puerum ante januam heri fui,
quo Chremes deterreatur a dando filium fuam Pamphilo.

DAVUS, MYSIS.

ORDO.

MYSIS, nunc opus eft tuâ   [aftutiâ.
  Mihi ad hanc rem expromtâ memoriâ atque
MY. Quidnam incepturus? DA. accipe à me hûnc ociùs,
Atque ante noftram januam appone. MY. obfecro,

DA. MYSIS,
nunc eft
opus mihi tuâ ex-
promta memoriâ at-
que aftutiâ ad hanc
rem. MY. Quidnam

es incepturus? DA. *Accipe ociùs hunc puerum a me, atque appone ante neftrum januam.* MY.
Obfecro,

ANNOTATIONS.

hear of it, he might be deter'd from giving
his Daughter. But forefeeing that *Simo*
would fufpect him as the Contriver of the
Plot, and might, if he fhould deny it, require his Oath as a Satisfaction; he begs
of *Myfis* that fhe would expofe the Child;
which, after rallying him a little upon
his religious Scrupulofity, fhe confents to
do.

  Ibid. *Expromta aftutia,* &c.   *Malitia*
(as fome read it, inftead of *memoria*) is
here to be interpreted *Calliditas*, and like
a Cun-

Dav. Take some Herbs from the Altar there, and strew them under him—

Myf. But why don't you do it yourself?

Dav. That if my Master should put me to my Oath, whether I laid the Child there, or no, I may do it with a safe Conscience.

Myf. I understand: you are become wonderfully scrupulous all of a sudden. Give me the Child.

Dav. Quickly then, that you may know what I further want with you. O *Jupiter!*

Myf. What's the matter now?

Dav. I see the Bride's Father coming this way; my first Design must now be drop'd.

Myf. I can't conceive what you mean.

Dav. I'll make as if I came this way here from the Right-hand; do you your best to humour my Discourse, and say nothing but what is to the purpose.

Myf. I can't in the least comprehend what you're about; but if my help is wanted in any thing, or you see farther than I can, I'll stay, rather than be a Hindrance to your Designs.

ANNOTATIONS.

a Cunning as was exerted with Promptness and Address. A great many, however, contend that the true reading is *memoria*, and seem to have a good deal of Reason on their side. By *memoria*, if that reading is received here, we are to understand Judgment, and such a Presence of Mind as is not easily disconcerted, but has always proper Answers at Command.

5 *Ex ara hinc sume verbenas tibi.* Scaliger the elder observes upon one' of *Plautus's* Plays, that in the Representation of theatrical Pieces, there was commonly an Altar upon the Stage. When a Tragedy was acted, the Altar was upon the Right-hand, and consecrated to *Bacchus*; but where the Play was a Comedy, it was upon the Left-hand, and sacred to *Apollo.* But Madam *Dacier*

ACT IV. SCENE V.

ARGUMENT.

Chremes *spying the Child laid before* Simo's *Door, is deterred from the Marriage.* Davus *quarrels with* Myfis, *who, not understanding his Design, or how to promote his Artifice, takes all seriously, and is provok'd at him.*

CHREMES, MYSIS, DAVUS.

Chr. AFTER preparing every thing necessary for my Daughter's Marriage, I return, that I may order her to be sent for. But what's this here? A Child, as I live. Woman, did you lay this Child here?

Myf. Where is he now?

Chr. Don't you answer me?

Myf. He's not to be seen. Alas? Wretch that I am, the Fellow has left me, and is gone.   *Dav.*

ANNOTATIONS.

1 *Revertor, postquam.* Towards the end of the last Scene, *Chremes* came unexpected-ly upon *Davus* and *Myfis*, before they had finished the Project they were about. This
obliges

Humíne? DA. ex ará hinc fume verbenas tibi,　5
Atque eas fubfterne. MY. quamobrem id tute non facis?
DA. Quia, fi forte opu' fit ad herum jurandum mihi
Non appofuiffe, ut liquidò poffim.　MY. intellego.
Nova nunc religio in te iftæc inceffit. cedo.
DA. Move ociùs te, ut, quid agam, porro intellegas.　10
Proh Jupiter! MY. quid? DA. fponfæ pater intervenit
Repudio quod confilium primùm intenderam.　[terá.
MY. Nefcio quid narres. DA. ego quoque hinc ab dex-
Venire me adfimulabo. tu, ut fubfervias
Orationi, utcunque opu' fit, verbis, vide.　15
MY. Ego, quid agas, nihil intellego: fed, fi quid eft,
Quod mea opera opus fit vobis, aut tu plus vides,
Manebo, ne quid voftrum remorer commodum.

eft? DA. Pater fponfæ intervenit. Repudio confilium, quod primum intenderam. MY. Nefcio quid narres. DA. Ego affimulabo me venire hinc quoque ab dextera parte : tu vide ut fubfervias meæ orationi verbis, utcunque fit opus. MY. Ego intelligo nihil quid agas : fed fi, eft quid, quod fcit opus mea opera vobis, aut tu vides plus quam ego, manebo, ne quid remorer veftrum commodum.

ANNOTATIONS.

Dacier with good Reafon maintains, that thefe Altars have no relation to what is here tranfacted in the Play. For we are to re-gard the prefent Adventure as a thing that happened in the Street, and it would offend againft the Rules of Probability to fuppofe, that the Altar here referred to, was one of thofe theatrical Altars. At *Athens* every Houfe had an Altar proper to itfelf, juft by the Door that opened into the Street, which was covered with frefh Herbs every Day. It is doubtlefs of one of thefe Altars that *Terence* fpeaks here. *Verbenæ* a Word ufed to ex-prefs all kinds of Herbs and Leaves ufed in covering of Altars.

ACTUS IV. SCENA V.

ARGUMENTUM.

Confpecto ante ædes Simonis puero, Chremes à nuptiis abfterretur. Jurgat cum ancilla Davus, quæ, ob confilii ipfius ignorantiam, fallaciæ non fubfervit, fed omnia fexio refpondet.

CHREMES, MYSIS, DAVUS.

R Evertor, poftquam, quæ opus fuere ad nuptias
Gnatæ, paravi, ut jubeam accerfi. fed quid hoc?
Puer hercle eft. mulier, tun' appofuifti hunc? MY. ubi
Illic eft? CH. non mihi refpondes? MY. hem, nufquam
eft. væ miferæ mihi,

puer. Mulier, tunc appofuifti hunc? MY. Ubi eft illic Davus? CH. Non refpondes mibi? MY. Hem Davus eft nufquam. Væ miferæ mibi,

ANNOTATIONS.

obliges *Davus* to alter his Meafures, who leaves *Myfis* abruptly, giving her no more than a very general Intimation of his De-sign. He meant to come upon her as one intirely ignorant of the Child's being there, and after making her declare, that it belong'd

Dav. Good Heavens! What a Buſtle there is at the *Forum?*
What Confuſion, Noiſe, and Mobbing? And then Proviſion is very
dear. (*To himſelf.*) Faith, I don't know what elſe to ſay.

Myſ. How, pray, came you to leave me here alone?

Dav. What Story is this now? Hey, hey, *Myſis*, whence comes
this Child? Who brought it hither!

Myſ. Are you in your Senſes, to aſk me ſuch a Queſtion?

Dav. Whom elſe ſhould I aſk then, when I ſee nobody here but
you?

Chr. I wonder whence it ſhould come.

Dav. Do you, then, give me no Anſwer to what I aſk?

Myſ. Au?

Dav. (*ſoftly to her.*) Come a little here to the Right-hand.

Myſ. (*ſoftly to him.*) You rave: Didn't you yourſelf?

Dav. (*ſoftly to her.*) For your Life ſay not a word, but in anſwer
to what I aſk.

Myſ. You confound me.

Dav. Whence this Child, I ſay? (*ſoftly to her.*) Speak out di-
ſtinctly!

Myſ. From us.

Dav. Ha! ha! ha! But ought one to wonder that a Strumpet acts
impudently?

Chr. As far as I can find, this Girl belongs to the *Andrian.*

Dav. Do we appear then ſo proper to be made your Dupes, and
have theſe Tricks play'd upon us?

Chr. I came in the critical Minute.

Dav. Make haſte, I ſay, to take away the Child from the Door.
(*ſoftly to her.*) Stay; ſtir not an Inch from the Place where you are.

Myſ. A Curſe for ever upon you, you frighten me ſo much.

Dav. Is it to you I ſpeak, or not?

Myſ. What would you have?

Dav. What do you ſtill aſk? Tell me whoſe Child is this you
have brought hither? Speak.

Myſ. As if you did'nt know.

Dav. Away with what I know; do you tell me what I aſk.

Myſ. 'Tis yours.

Dav. Which of ours?

Myſ. *Pamphilus*'s.

Dav. Hah! What? *Pamphilus*'s!

Myſ. Why, is it not?

Chr. It is with Reaſon I was always averſe to this Match.

Dav. Oh! intolerable Confidence.

Myſ. Why do you bawl out ſo?

Dav. Did'nt I ſee this Child brought to you yeſterday in the
Evening?   *Myſ.*

A N N O T A T I O N S.

long'd to *Pamphilus,* quarrel with her, and   moſt likely way to alarm *Chremes,* without
accuſe her of Falſhood. This ſeem'd the   giving any Suſpicion of their having con-
                                                 certed

Reliquit me homo, atque abiit. DA. Dî voſtram fidem, 5
Quid turbæ eſt apud forum? quid illîc hominum litigant?
Tum annona cara eſt. quid dicam aliud, neſcio.
MY. Cur tu, obſecro, hic me ſolam? DA. hem, quæ
  hæc eſt fabula?
Eho, Myſis, puer hic unde eſt? quiſve huc attulit?
MY. Satin' ſanus, qui me id rogites? DA. quem
  ego igitur rogem, 10
Qui hîc neminem alium videam? CH. miror, unde ſit.
DA. Dicturan' quod rogo? MY. au. DA. concede ad
  dexteram.
MY. Deliras. non tute ipſe? DA. verbum ſi mihi
Unum, præterquam quod te rogo, faxis, cave—
MY. Male dicis. DA. unde eſt? dic clarè. MY. à nobis
DA. ha, ha, hæ. 15
Mirum vero, impudenter mulier ſi facit!
CH. Ab Andriâ eſt ancilla hæc, quantum intellego.
DA. Adcon' videmur vobis eſſe idonei,
In quibus ſic illudatis? CH. veni in tempore.
DA. Propera adeo puerum tollere hinc ab januâ. 20
Mane: cave quoquam ex iſtoc exceſſis loco.
MY. Dii te eradicent: ta me miſeram territas. [rogas?
DA. Tibi ego dico, an non? MY. quid vis? DA. at etiam
Cedo, cujum puerum hîc appoſuiſti, dic mihi.
MY. Tu neſcis? DA. mitte id, quod ſcio: dic quod
  rogo. 25
MY. Veſtri. DA. cujus veſtri? MY. Pamphili. DA.
  hem, quid Pamphili? [nuptias.
MY. Eho, an non eſt? CH. rectè ego ſemper fugi has
DA. O facinus animadvertendum! MY. Quid clamitas?
DA. Quemne ego herì vidi ad vos adferri veſperi?

homo reliquit me, atque abiit. Dii veſtram fidem, quid turbæ eſt apud forum? quid hominum litagant illic? tum annona eſt cara. Neſcio quid aliud dicam. MY. Obſecro, cur tu reliquiſti me ſolam hîc? DA. Hem, quæ fabula eſt hæc? Eho, Myſis, unde eſt hic puer? quiſve attulit eum huc? MY. Eſne ſatis ſanus, qui rogites me id? DA. Quem ego rogem igitur, qui videam neminem alium hîc? CH. Miror, unde ſit. DA. Eſne dictura quod rogo? MY. Au. DA. Concede ad dexteram. MY. Deliras: nonne tute ipſe attuliſti eum huc? DA. Cave; ſi faxis unum verbum mihi, præterquàm quod rogo— MY. Dicis male. DA. Unde eſt? Dic clare. MY. A nobis. DA. Ha! ba! bæ! Eſt vero mirum, ſi mulier meretrix facit impudenter! CH. Hæc ancilla eſt ab Andria, quantum intelligo. DA. Videmurne vobis eſſe adeo idonei, in quibus illudatis ſic? CH. Veni in tempore. DA. Propera adeo tollere puerum hinc ab janua. Mane: cave exceſſeris quoquam ex iſtoc loco. MY. Dii eradicente te: ita territas me miſeram! DA. Dico ego tibi, an non? MY. Quid vis? DA. At etiam rogas? Cedo, cujum puerum appoſuiſti hic, dic mihi. MY. An tu neſcis? DA. Omitte id quod ſcio, dic quod rogo. MY. Eſt veſtri. DA. Cujus veſtri? MY. Pamphili. DA. Hem, quid Pamphili? MY. Eho, an non eſt? CH. Recte ego ſemper fugi has nuptias. DA. O facinus animadvertendum! MY. Quid clamitas? DA. Diciſne illum eſſe puerum Pamphili, quem ego vidi afferri ad vos herì veſperi?

ANNOTATIONS.

certed it among themſelves. *Myſis* not perfectly acquainted with the Plot, and amazed at *Davus*'s Behaviour, is at a loſs how to anſwer, and would have diſcovered all, had not *Davus*, by Nods and Winks, made her in part to underſtand him. At laſt all ends ſucceſsfully, and to the'r Wiſh.

20 *Propera adeo puerum*, &c. He here pretends to command *Myſis* to take away the Child from the Door, but afterwards, in a low Voice, charges her not to ſtir. For *Chremes* had not yet heard all that *Davus* wanted him to know. He had learn'd only yet, that the Child was expoſed by Command of *Glycery*, not that it belong'd to *Pamphilus*. He therefore afterwards frames a Queſtion, to have this alſo told before *Chremes*.

Myf. O impudent Wretch!

Dav. 'Tis true I faw *Canthara* with a great Bundle in her Lap.

Myf. Thank Heaven that fome reputable Women were prefent at her Labour.

Dav. Nay, 'tis plain fhe little knows the Perfon on whofe account all this is done. *Chremes,* fay they, if he fees a Child laid before the Door, will not give his Daughter to *Pamphilus;* whereas in truth he'll fo much the rather give her.

Chr. By *Hercules,* but he won't, though.

Dav. Now therefore, that you may know better, unlefs you prefently take away the Child, I'll tumble it into the Middle of the Street, and roll you after it into the Kennel.

Myf. The Man, I believe, has loft his Senfes.

Dav. One Story brings on another. I now hear it whifper'd, that fhe is a Citizen of *Athens.*

Chr. Hah!

Dav. And that he will be obliged by the Laws to marry her.

Myf. Au! For Heaven's fake, is fhe not a Citizen?

Chr. I was like to have fallen unawares into a comical kind of Scrape.

Dav. Who's this fpeaks? O! *Chremes,* you're come in good time: Do but hear.

Chr. I have already heard all.

Dav. What! Heard all!

Chr. I have heard it, I tell you, from the beginning.

Dav. Have you heard then? Why thefe are all mere Fictions: She ought to be taken hence to the Rack. This is *Chremes* himfelf: Don't think you now trifle with *Davus.*

Myf. Unhappy that I am; indeed, Sir, I have not faid one word of Falfhood.

Chr. I know the whole Affair. Is *Simo* within?

Dav. He is.

Myf. Don't touch me, Villain: If I don't tell all to *Glycery*—

Dav. Phoh, Fool, you don't know what is done.

Myf. How fhould I know?   *Dav.*

ANNOTATIONS.

30 *Vidi Cantharam fubfarcinatam.* Donatus and Madam Dacier obferve here, that Davus does his Part with a great peal of Addrefs. Before he had faid, *Quemne ego heri vidi ad vos adferri vefperi?* Here he fays, I faw *Cantharida* with a Bundle in her Lap. But where was the Neceffity that this Bundle fhould be a Child? He makes ufe of this weak Argument, only with a defign, the better to impofe upon the old Man, who, upon hearing fo frivolous a Defence, would be but the more confirmed in the Notion, that the Child really belong'd to Pampbilus. *Et hoc dicit, ut leviter redarguat. Myfidem, non ut vincatur,* fays Donatus.

31 *Cum in pariundo aliquot adfuerunt liberæ.* To accommodate this to our Manners, we muft tranflate it *creditable Women; Women of Character and Fafhion;* but at the fame time it is to be obferved, that the Word literally means free Women, Women who were Citizens of *Athens;* for none but fuch were allowed to appear as Witneffes. This appears from what *Geta* fays towards the End of the Firft Act of the *Phormio. Sirvum*
Le—

MY. O hominem audacem! DA. verum. vidi Can-
tharam ·   30
Subfarcinatam. MY. Diis pol habeo gratias,
Cùm in pariundo aliquot adfuerunt liberæ.
DA. Næ illa illum haud novit, cujus causâ hæc incipit.
Chremes, si positum puerum ante ædes viderit,
Suam gnatam non dabit : tanto hercle magis dabit. 35
CH. Non hercle faciet. DA. nunc adeo, ut tu sis sciens,
Ni puerum tollis, jamjam ego hunc mediam in viam
Provolvam, teque ibidem pervolvam in luto.
MY. Tu pol, homo, non es sobrius. DA. fallacia
Alia aliam trudit. jam susurrari audio,   40
Civem Atticam esse hanc: CH. hem: DA coactus legibus
Eam uxorem ducet. MY. au, obsecro, an non civis est?
CH. Jocularium in malum insciens penè incidi.
DA. Quis hîc loquitur? ô Chreme, per tempus advenis:
Ausculta. CH. audivi jam omnia. DA. anne tu omnia? 45
CH. Audivi, inquam, à principio. DA. audistin' ob-
secro? hem
Scelera: hanc jam oportet in cruciatum hinc abripi.
Hic ille est: non te credas Davum ludere.
MY. Me miseram: nihil pol falsi dixi, mi senex.
CH. Novi omnem rem. est Simo intus? DA. est. 50
MY. Ne me attingas, sceleste. si pol Glycerio non om-
nia hæc—
DA. Eho inepta, nescis quid sit actum. MY. quî sciam?

MY. O hominem audacem! DA. Est vérum Vidi Cantharam subfarcinatam. MY. Pol habeo gratias Diis, cum aliquot liberæ adfuerunt in pariundo. DA. Næ illa haud novit illum, cujus causa incipit hæc. Chremes, si viderit puerum positum ante ædes, non dabit suam gnatam Pamphilo: hercle dabit eam tanto magis. CH. Hercle non faciet. DA. Nunc adeo, at tu sis sciens, nisi tollis purum, ego jam provolvam hunc in mediam viam, pervolvamque te ibidem in luto. MY. Pol, tu homo non es sobrius. DA. Alia fallacia trudit aliam. Jam audio susurrari hanc esse civem Atticam. CH. Hem. DA Pamphilus coactus legibus, ducem eam uxorem. MY. Au, obsecro, an non est civis? CH. Pene incidi insciens in jocularium: malum. DA. Quis loquitur hîc? O Chreme, advenis per tempus: auscultò. CH. Jam audivi omnia. DA. Anne tu audivisti omnia hæc? CH. Inquam, audivi omnia a principio. DA Obsecro, audivistine? hem scelera: oportet hanc jam abripi hinc in cruciatum. Hic est ille Chremes: non credas te ludere Davum. MY. Me miseram: pol, mi senex, dixi nihil falsi. CH. Novi rem omnem. Est Simo intus? DA. Est. MY. Scelěste, ne attingas me. Pol si non renunciem hæc omnia Glycerio.---DA. Eho inepta, nescis quid fit actum. MY. Qui sciam?

ANNOTATIONS.

hominem causam orare leges non sinunt, neque testimonii dictio est. The Laws don't allow a Servant to plead, nor is his Evidence taken.

41 *Civem Atticam esse hanc.* This is artfully brought in, and discovers a World of Cunning. The sly Knave knew that nothing was more likely to alarm *Chremes*, and deter him from the Match, than the Apprehension of *Glycery*'s being a Citizen; for the Law obliged whoever had debauched a free-born *Athenian* Virgin to marry her.

47 *Hanc jam oportet in cruciatum hinc abripi.* *Davus* means, that every thing *Myfis* had said was false, and that she ought to be put to the Torture, to oblige her to confess, and vindicate *Pamphilus* from these unjust Aspersions; for it was a common way at *Athens* to force the Truth from Slaves by Torture.

Thus in the *Step Mother*, where *Bacchis* is endeavouring to clear *Pamphilus* from the unjust Suspicions he lay under to his Father and Father-in-law, imagining they might give but little Credit to what she said, offers her Slaves to be put to the Torture.

48 *Hic ille est*, &c. This *Davus* says, pointing with his Finger at *Chremes*, as intimating, that he found she but little regarded what he said; but that she was now before a Man of Power and Influence, who could have her severely questioned, if she dar'd to advance any Falshood.

50 *Ne me attingas scelefte.* *Chremes* now disappears to go and talk with *Simo.* *Davus* and *Myfis* are therefore left by themselves upon the Stage. He was sensible that *Myfis* had not thoroughly understood his Design; for it appears by her Answers, that she thought

Dav. This is the Bride's Father; there was no other way of let-ing him know thofe things we defired he fhould know.

Myf. But you fhould have told me of it before.

Dav. Do you think there is no difference between what Nature prompts us to fay in fuch a fudden Surprife, and what's done by Pre-meditation and Concert?

ANNOTATIONS.

thought he was in earneft in whatever he faid. We are therefore to fuppofe him advanc-ing with a complaifant, mild Air to unde-ceive her, while fhe, provok'd at the ima- | gin'd ill ufage fhe had met with, bids him keep at a diftance, and threatens to complain to *Glycery.*

55 *Paulum intereffe cenfes?* In fact, the Differ-

ACT IV. SCENE VI.

ARGUMENT.

Crito *coming from* Andros *to* Athens, *inquires after* Glycery, *and whether fhe had yet found her Parents. Hearing that fhe had not found them, he is vexed, becaufe he forefees that fhe will prove an Obftacle to his being declared the Heir of* Chryfis.

CRITO, MYSIS, DAVUS.

Crito. I Am told that *Chryfis* liv'd in this Street, who chofe rather to amafs Riches here with Infamy, than to live poor, but honeftly in her own Country. By her Death her Effects, of right, belong to me. But I fee fome Perfons there, of whom I may enquire. Your Servant.

Myf. Blefs me, who's this I fee? Is not this *Crito, Chryfis's* Cou-fin-german? It is he.

Cri. O, *Myfis,* your Servant.

Myf. Your Servant, *Crito.*

Cri. Is then *Chryfis?* Hah!

Myf. She has indeed left us very difconfolate.

Cri. How is it with you? How do you live here? Well enough?

Myf. We! As well as we may, fince we can't as we would.

Cri. How is *Glycery?* has fhe yet found her Parents?

Myf.

ANNOTATIONS.

1 *In hac habitaffe platea.* In this Scene a new Perfon appears, by whofe means the Plot comes afterwards to be unravelled. This Perfon is *Crito,* Coufin to *Chryfis.* As he was her neareft Kinfman, and had heard at *Andros* of her Death, he comes to *Athens,* to look after her Inheritance, which by Law fell to him. He is therefore introduced here fpeaking in fuch a manner, as gives us to underftand who he is, and the Reafon of his coming to *Athens.* I am apt to think, that the Fifth Act ought to begin here, though in moft Editions it is made | the laft Scene of the Fourth, probably be-caufe *Myfis* and *Davus* are fuppofed not to have difappeared, but that *Crito* enters the Street, as they are ftanding talking together, after the Departure of *Chremes.*

4 *Ejus morte ea ad me lege redierunt bona.* The Character of *Crito* is that of a worthy good Man, which appears at once, by what he fays in relation to *Chryfis.* For though he was her Heir at Law, and came to take poffeffion of what fhe had left, he is not fo far blinded by Intereft, as not to condemn her for preferring Riches got with Infamy

to

Dᴀ. Hic focer eſt. alio pacto haud poterat fieri,
Ut ſciret hæc, quæ volumus. Mʏ. hem, prædiceres.
Dᴀ. Paulum intereſſe cenſes, ex animo omnia,　　55
Ut fert natura, facias, an de induſtria?

Dᴀ. *Hic eſt focer.*
Haud poterit fieri
alio pacto, ut ſciret
bæc, quæ volumus.
Mʏ. *Hem prædi-*
ceres mihi. Dᴀ. *Cen-*
ſis intereſſe paulum, num *ſaeias omnia ex animo, ut fert natura, an de induſtria?*

ANNOTATIONS.

Difference is infinite, and *Davus*, however he might have frightened *Myſis* a little, yet acted with the greateſt Prudence with regard to the main Chance. For what one says naturally and unpremeditated, has by far a greater Air and Appearance of Truth, than what is ſaid, after being beforehand prepared for it.

ACTUS IV. SCENA. VI.

ARGUMENTUM.

Crito veniens ex Andro Athænas, de Glycerio percontatur, an parentes repererit ſuos : audiens non reperiſſe, dolet, quod videat hoc ſibi obſuturum in adeunda hæreditate.

CRITO, MYSIS, DAVUS.

IN hac habitaſſe plateâ dictum eſt Chryſidem,
　Quæ ſeſe inhoneſtè optavit parere hîc divitias
Potiùs, quàm in patriâ honeſtè pauper vivere.
Ejus morte ea ad me lege redierunt bona.
Sed quos percontor, video. ſalvete. Mʏ. obſecro,　5
Quem video? eſtne hic Crito, ſobrinus Chryſidis?
Is eſt. Cʀ. ô Myſis,ſalve. Mʏ. ſalvos ſis,Crito. [perdidit.
Cʀ. Itan' Chryſis? hem. Mʏ. nos quidem pol miſeras
Cʀ. Quid vos? quo pacto hîc ? ſati' ne rectè? Mʏ. nos
ne? ſic
Ut quimus, aiunt ; quando, ut volumus, non licet. 10
Cʀ. Quid Glycerium ? jam hîc ſuos parentes repperit ?

ORDO.

Cʀ. EST *dictum*
　Chryſidem
habitaviſſe in hac
plateâ, quæ optavit
potius ſeſe parere di-
vitias hic inhoneſte,
quam vivere pauper
honeſte in patria.
Ejus morte ea bona
redierunt lege ad
me. Sed video quos
percontor. Salvete.
Mʏ. *Obſecro, quem*
video ? Eſtne his
Crito, ſobrinus Chry-
ſidis? eſt is. Cʀ.
O Myſis, ſolve. Mʏ. *Crito, ſis ſalvus.* Cʀ. *Itan' Chryſis eſt mortua ? Hem.* Mʏ. *Pol quidem perdidit nos miſeras.* Cʀ. *Quid vos agitis ? Quo pacto vivitis hic ?* Mʏ. *Noſne ? ſic ut quimus, ut aiunt, quando non licet vivere, ut volumus.* Cʀ. *Quid Glycerium agit ? jamne repperit ſuos parentes hic ?*

ANNOTATIONS.

to an honourable Poverty. The Paſſage here refers to *Chryſis* having died without making a Will, in which Caſe the neareſt of Kin was legal Heir. For thus *Cicero*, Verr. I. 45. *Minucius quidam mortuus eſt ante iſtum prætorem. Ejus teſtamentum erat nullum. Lege hæreditas ad gentem Minuciam veniebat.* For that is ſaid to be by Law, *quod fit ex præſcripto legis & juris.* Some have made it a Queſtion, to what we are to refer *ea*, whether to *bona*, or *morte*. But this, I think, may be eaſily determined; for tho' the very Word is not uſed before, yet what is equivalent to it, *Crito* makes mention of the Riches ſhe had acquired by her Profeſſion, which Riches fall now to him by Law.

8 *Itane Chryſis ? hem.* This manner of Expreſſion carries in it a great deal of Mildneſs and Tenderneſs. The Ancients avoided as much as poſſible the Mention of any thing that ſounded harſh and ſhocking to Nature ; and, where Neceſſity required it, they endeavoured to ſoften it as far as they could.

10 *Ut quimus, aiunt.* This, from the manner in which it is here ſaid, appears to have been a Proverb. It ſerves as an Excuſe both for their preſent and paſt Way of Life, and no doubt *Myſis* had it in her Eye to perſuade *Crito*, that Neceſſity, and not Choice, had compell'd *Chryſis* to follow the Way of Life ſhe had betaken herſelf to.

　　　　　is Nunc

Myf. I wifh fhe had,

Cri. What, not yet? I have made but an unlucky Journey of it at that rate; for had I really known that, I had never fet foot hither. She was always call'd and look'd upon as her Sifter, and now poffeffes what belong'd to her: for me a Stranger to engage in a Law-Suit, I may eafily learn from the Example of others, how vain and unprofitable a Tafk it would be. Befides, I queftion not, but by this time fhe has got fome Friend to ftand by her; for fhe was pretty well grown up when fhe left us. They will not fail to call me a Sycophant and Beggar, hunting after Inheritances. Befides, I have no Inclination to ftrip her of what fhe has.

Myf. O excellent Man! Verily, *Crito*, you are juft the fame as ever.

Cri. Lead me to her, fince I am come hither, that I may fee her.

Myf. With all my heart.

Dav. I'll follow them, for I don't much care the old Man fhould fee me at this time.

ANNOTATIONS.

15 *Nunc, me bofpitem lites fequi.* This, as Madam *Dacier* obferves from a marginal Note, in a Manufcript of her Father's, is not to be perfectly underftood, but by thofe who have read *Xenophon's* little Treatife upon the Policy of the *Athenians.* In that we are told, that all the Inhabitants of Cities and Iflands in alliance with the *Athenians* were obliged, in all Claims, to repair to *Athens,* and refer their Caufe to the Decifion of the People, it not being permitted to plead elfewhere. *Crito* therefore had reafon to expect no great Juftice from that Tribunal, who would certainly, he might imagine, prefer

Glycery, the fuppofed Sifter of *Chryfis,* and then living at *Athens,* before him, a new Comer. And this as to the Succefs of the Affair. Then as to the length of the Procefs, fo inconvenient to a Stranger, he had ftill more to fear. The *Athenians* had fo many Affairs of their own, and celebrated fo many Feftivals, that very little Time was left for what related to others, and a Stranger found it next to impoffible to get his Suit ended. But befides the Uncertainty and Length of Time, there was ftill another Inconvenience rather more difagreeable; and that is, he was obliged to make his court
to

ACT V. SCENE I.

ARGUMENT.

Chremes *greatly enraged, by what he had heard from* Davus, *and feen of the Child, intreats* Simo *to think no more of the Marriage.* Simo *endeavours to calm* Chremes's *Refentment, and perfuade him, that thefe were no more than Contrivances of* Glycery *to difturb the Wedding.*

CHREMES, SIMO.

Chremes. ENough, *Simo,* enough hath my Friendfhip towards you been proved, I have run hazard enough? ceafe now therefore your Intreaties: while I ftudied to pleafe you, I almoft fooled away my Daughter's Repofe.   *Si.*

ANNOTATIONS.

1 *Satis jam, fatis.* As *Chremes,* by overhearing the Converfation between *Davus* and *Myfis,* was entirely determined againft the Match, he leaves them with a defign to find

My. Utinam. Cr. an nondum etiam ? haud aufpicatò
  huc me appuli:
Nam pol, fi id fciffem, nunquam huc tetuliffem pedem:
Semper enim dicta eft ejus hæc atque habita eft foror :
Quæ illius fuerunt, poffidet. nunc, me hofpitem 15
Lites fequi, quàm hîc mihi fit facile atque utile,
Aliorum exempla commonent. fimul arbitror,
Jam effe aliquem amicum, & defenforem ei : nam fere
Grandiufcula jam profecta eft illinc. clamitent,
Me fycophantam hæreditatem perfequi,   ·20
Mendicum. tum, ipfam defpoliare non libet.
My. O optume hofpes, pol, Crito, antiquum obtines.
Cr. Duc me ad eam, quando huc veni, ut videam.
    My. maxume.   .
Da. Sequar hos: nolo me in tempore hoc videat fenex:

linc jam fere grandiufcula. Clamitent me fycophantam & mendicum perfequi hæreditatem. Tum non libet defpoliare ipfam. Mv. *O optime hofpes: pol, Crito, obtines antiquum.* Cr. *Duc me ad eam, ut videam, quando veni huc.* Mv. *Maxime.* Da. *Sequar hos : nolo ut fenex videat me in hoc tempore.*

Mr. *Utinam repe-riffet.* Cr. *An non-dum etiam repcrit ? appuli me huc haud. aufpicatò : nam pol, fi fciviffem id, nun-quam tetuliffem pe-dem huc: enim hæc eft femper dicta atque eft habita foror ejus: poffidet ea quæ fue-runt illius: nunc ex-empla aliorum com-monent quam facile: atque utile fit mihi lites, me hofpitem fequi lites. Simul arbitror effe jam aliquem ami-cum & defenforem ei : nam profecta eft il-*

ANNOTATIONS.

to the People, and gain them over by great Largeffes. We are not therefore to wonder if *Crito* was unwilling to engage in a Suit fo long, fo expenfive, and whereof the Succefs was fo uncertain, not to fay worfe. I hope what has been faid will ferve to clear up the Paf-fage, and make it rightly underftood. *Dacier*.
  20 *Sycophantum. Sycophanta* is a Word of *Greek* Derivation and of nearly the fame Import with the *Latin, calumniator,* and was ufed of any one who accufed or profecuted another wrongfully.

24 *Nolo me intempore hoc videat fenex.* *Donatus* is the only Commentator who has fet the Beauty of this Paffage in a true light. *Davus* is unwilling that his Mafter fhould fee him, becaufe he knew that *Chremes* was with him, and he apprehended that *Simo* might oblige him to affure *Chremes*, that *Pamphilus* had entirely broke with *Glycery*, which might perhaps undo all he had hitherto contriv'd to embroil Matters. *Dacier*.

ACTUS V. SCENA I.

ARGUMENTUM.

Chremes vehementer iratus, ob ea quæ audirat ex Davo, quæ-que viderat de puero, Simonem compellat, ut quod jam cæp-tum erat de nuptiis, id prorfus deleretur. Conatur Simo leni-bus verbis iram Chremetis fedare, & probare nititur, mere-tricem ifta omnia effe molitam ad difturbandas nuptias.

CHREMES, SIMO.

SATI'jam, fati', Simo, fpectata erga te amicitia eft mea:
  Sati' pericli cœpi adire : orandi jam finem face.
Dum ftudeo obfequi tibi, penè illufi vitam filiæ.

Ctata : cœpi adire fatis pericli : fac jam firem orandi. Dum ftudeo obfequi tibi, pene illufi vitam filiæ.

ORDO.
Ch. Simo, mea amicitia er-ga te eft fatis jam, fatis inquam fpe-

ANNOTATIONS.

find out *Simo*, and let him know the reafon of his having changed his Mind. Accord-
    ingly, *Chremes* addreffes *Simo* in a tone of Difcontent, as if he thought himfelf in-

                jured

Si. Nay but *Chremes,* I now more than ever intreat and beg of you, that the Favour so long since promised in Words, may be now granted in reality.

Chr. See how unreasonable you are, out of earnestness to effect what you desire : you neither regard the Bounds of Complaisance, nor think what it is you request of your Friend ; for if you allowed your self to reflect, you would sure abate of these injurious Demands.

Si. What Demands ?

Chr. Ah! do you ask? You have importun'd me to give my Daughter to a young Man, whose Affections are already engaged, and who is utterly averse to Marriage ; you'd have me plunge her into a Life of Discord, and wed her to a Husband whom she cannot long retain ; that by her Misery and Sufferings, I may reclaim your Son You have prevail'd : I agreed while the Case would admit of it, but now the matter has taken a different turn ; you must bear it in the best manner you can. They say she is a Citizen of *Athens* ; there is a Child too : pray give us no more trouble.

Si. I conjure you, *Chremes,* by all the Gods, give no credit to these Wretches, whose Interest it is to make him appear in the worst Light possible. All these Stories are forg'd and contriv'd on account of the Marriage ; when the Cause that prompts them to undertake all this is removed, they'll give over.

Chr. You are deceiv'd. I myself overheard *Davus* wrangling with the Maid.

Si. I know it.

Chr. Nay, but in earnest ; when neither of them had any Notion of my being near.

Si. I believe it : and *Davus* not long since warn'd me that this was to happen ; nor do I well know how I came to forget telling you of it to-day, as I intended.

A N N O T A T I O N S.

jured by him, in being urged so much to Intreaties, that *Chremes* will persevere in what what he thought must make his Daughter he had promised.
miserable merely because *Simo* fancied he ⁵ *Vide quam iniquus sis.* *Chremes* had
might, by that means, reform his Son. spoke hitherto only in the general, but here
This gives rise to a very warm and interest- he comes to give the particular Reasons of
ing Conversation, till *Davus* is by chance his Refusal, that *Pamphilus* was so engaged
seen coming out from *Glycery,* which changes to another, that it was no less than giving
the Strain of it quite. up his Daughter to certain Misery to marry
    ⁴ *Imo enim nunc.* *Simo* did not rightly her to him.
apprehend the meaning of the above general ¹⁵ *Per ego te deos oro.* *Simo* still persists
Accusation, and therefore has recourse to in his Endeavours to prevail with *Chremes,*
                                            and

A C T

Sı. Imo enim nunc quam maxumè abs te oro atque
poſtulo, Chreme,
Ut beneficium, verbis initum dudum, nunc re com-
probes.   5
Cн. Vide quam iniquus ſis præ ſtudio. dum efficias id
quod cupis,   [cogitas :
Neque modum benignitatis, neque quid me ores,
Nam ſi cogites, remittas jam me onerare injuriis.
Sı. Quibus ? Cн. ah rogitas ? perpuliſti me, ut homini
adoleſcentulo,
In alio occupato amore, abhorrenti ab re uxoriâ,   10
Filiam darem in ſeditionem, atque incertas nuptias ;
Ejus labore atque ejus dolore gnato ut medicarer tuo.
Impetraſti : incepi, dum res tetulit : nunc non ſert :
feras.   [ſos face.
Illam hinc civem eſſe aiunt : puer eſt natus : nos miſ-
Sı. Per egŏ te Deos oro, ut ne illis animum inducas
credere,   15
Quibus id maxume utile eſt illum eſſe quam deterri-
mum.
Nuptiarum gratiâ hæc ſunt fiĉta atque incepta omnia.
Ubi ea cauſa, quamobrem hæc faciunt, erit adempta
his, deſinent.   [Sı. ſcio. Cн. at
Cн. Erras. cum Davo egomet vidi jurgantem ancillam.
Vero voltu ; cùm, ibi me adeſſe, neuter dum perſen-
ſerat.   20
Sı. Credo ; & id faĉturas, Davus dudum prædixit mihi :
Et neſcio quid tibi ſum oblitus hodie ac volui dicere.

Sı. Imo enim, nunc
quam maximè ero
atque poſtulo 'abs te,
Chreme ; ut compro-
bes beneficium du-
dum initum verbis,
nunc ipſa re. Cн.
Vide quam ſis ini-
quus præ ſtudio ; dum
efficias id quod cu-
pis : neque cogitas
modum benignitatis,
neque quid eres me :
nam ſi cogites, re-
mittas jam onerare
me injuriis.   Sı.
Quibus   injuriis ?
Cн. Ab rogitas ?
Perpuliſti me, ut da-
rem filiam homini
adoleſcentulo, eccu-
pato in alio amore,
& abhorrenti ab re
uxoriâ, in ſeditio-
nem atque incertas
nuptias ; ut medi-
carer tuo gnato,
ejus labore, atque
ejus dolore. Impe-
traſti, incepi dum
res tulit ; nunc
non ſert : feras.
Aiunt illam eſſe ci-
vem hinc : puer eſt,
natus : fac nos miſ-
ſos. Sı. Ego oro te
per Deos, Chreme,

ut ne inducas animum credere illis, quibus id eſt maxime utile, illum Pamphilum eſſe quam deterrimum. Hæc omnia ſunt fiĉta atque incepta gratiâ nuptiarum. Ubi ea cauſa, quamobrem
faciunt hæc, erit adempta, deſinent. Cн. Erras. Egemet vidi ancillam jurgantem cum Davo.
Sı. Scio. Cн. At vero vultu : cum neuter dum (adhuc) perſenſerat me adeſſe ibi. Sı. Credo :
& Davus dudum prædixit mihi eas faĉturas id, & neſcio quid ſum oblitus dicere tibi bodie, ac
volui.

ANNOTATIONS.

and would, if poſſible, perſuade him, as he
himſelf believed, that all was no other than
Pretence to retard the Marriage: his chief
Argument is taken from the Perſons themſelves, and the Intereſt they had in doing
ſo. *Quibus id maxime utile eſt, illum eſſe
quam deterrimum.* But that when once the
Marriage is concluded, all this will naturally ceaſe, becauſe they will find it in vain
to contend any longer.

22 *Et neſcio quid.* Donatus and Boeclerus
have been at a great deal of pains to diſcover
the natural Order of theſe Words, and fill
up the Ellipſes. Donatus makes it, *neſcio
propter quid oblitus ſum dicere tibi bodie,* contra quam *volui.* But it is enough to obſerve
here, that it was a Form commonly uſed,
when what they deſigned to ſay had eſcaped
their Memory.

H 4   ACTUS

ACT V. SCENE II.

ARGUMENT.

Simo, *when he sees* Davus *coming out from* Glycery, *and bearing from him, that there was one come, who affirmed that* Glycery *was a Citizen of* Athens.; *full of Indignation he orders* Davus *to be thrown in Prison.*

DAVUS, CHREMES, SIMO, DROMO.

Davus. WELL, now you may set your Minds at eafe—

Chr. 'Hah ! there's *Davus* for you.

Si. Whence doth he come !

Dav. Thro' my means, and that of this honeft Stranger.

Si. What mifchief is this now?

Dav. I have not in my Life feen a more convenient Man, Time, or Encounter.

Si. Who can this be, he commends fo much?

Dav. The Danger is now all over.

Si. Do I forbear fpeaking to him?

Dav. 'Tis my Mafter ; what fhall I do?

Si. O your Servant, good Sir.

Dav. Ha *Simo,* O our *Chremes,* every thing is now ready within.

Si. No doubt you have taken fine care.

Dav. Send for the Bride when you will.

Si. Very well : that indeed is now the only thing wanting : but do you anfwer me this ; what bufinefs had you in that Houfe ?

Dav. Who, I ?

Si. Yes, you.

Dav. I ?

Si. Yes, you.

Dav. I went in but juft now.

Si. As if I afk'd how long you had been there.

Dav. Along with your Son.

Si. What is my Son there too? I'm on the Rack. Didn't you fay, Rafcal, that they had quarrel'd?   *Dav.*

ANNOTATIONS.

[1] *Animo jam nunc otiofo effe impero. Davus,* at the end of the laft Act, had gone in with *Crito* to *Glycery,* becaufe he did not care to be feen by the old Man. There we are to underftand, that the Converfation had run upon *Glycery's* Parents, and whether fhe had found them. *Crito* relates before *Davus,* the Circumftances of her being fhipwrecked at *Andros,* and the great Probability of her being a Citizen of *Athens.* *Davus* thinking the Proofs indifputable, is reprefented here, as he comes out, giving them Affurance, that all was now perfectly fafe, and things would foon fucceed according to their Wifhes. The Poet conducts with

wonderful Art and Judgment this Appearance of *Davus.* He comes out with an Air of Triumph and Affurance, as now confident, that there was no farther Danger. By this means, his Reverfe of Fortune appears the greater, and more ftrongly touches the Imagination of the Reader.

[2] *Unde egreditur?* This is not fo properly an Interrogation ; for *Simo* could not be ignorant where *Glycery* lived, as he had been at her fuppofed Sifter's Funeral. It is to be conceived, as faid in a way of Admiration, partly mixed with Indignation, as *Donatus* has very judicioufly remarked.

[4] *Omnis res eft jam in vado.* A Proverbial

ACTUS V. SCENA II.

ARGUMENTUM.

Simo, cum vidiſſet Davum egredientem a Glycerio, & cum ex eo audiſſet, veniſſe, qui Glycerium diceret civem eſſe Atticam, ira accenſus, Davum intro raptum conjicit in vincula.

DAVUS, CHREMES, SIMO, DROMO.

ANIMO jam nunc otioſo eſſe impero.—CH. hem
  Davom tibi.   [SI. quid illud mali eſt ?
SI. Unde egreditur ! DA. meo præſidio, atque hoſpitis.
DA. Ego commodiorem hominem, adventum, tem-
  pus non vidi. SI. ſcelus !   [SI. ceſſo alloqui ?
Quen-nam hic laudat ? DA. omnis res eſt jam in vado.
DA. Herus eſt : quid agam ? SI. ô ſalve, bone vir. DA.
  hem Simo, ô noſter Chremes, *Si.*   5
Omnia apparata jam ſunt intus. CH. curaſti probe.
DA. Ubi voles, accerſe. SI. bene ſanè. id enimvero
  hinc nunc abeſt.   [DA. mihin'? SI. ita.
Etiam tu hoc reſpondes, quid iſtîc tibi negotî eſt ?
DA. Mihine? SI. tibi ergo. DA. modò introii. SI.
  quaſi ego, quàm dudum, rogem.
DA. Cum tuo gnato unà. SI. anne eſt intus Pamphi-
  lus ? crucior miſer.   10
Eho, non tu dixti eſſe inter eos inimicitias, carnufex ?

ORDO.

JAM nunc impero vos
eſſe animo otioſo.---
CH. Hem Davum
tibi. SI. Unde e-
greditur ? DA.
meo præſidio, at-
que præſidio hujus
hoſpitis. SI. Quid
mali eſt illud ? DA.
Ego non vidi com-
modiorem hominem,
adventum, & tem-
pus. SI. Scelus !
quennam hic lau-
dat ? DA. Omnis
res eſt jam in vado.
SI. Ceſſo alloqui ?
DA. Eſt herus ;
quid agam? SI. O
ſalve, bone vir. DA.
Ehem Simo, O no-
ſter Chremes. Om-
nia ſunt jam apparata intus. SI. Curaſti probe. DA. Accerſe ſponſam, ubi voles. SI. Bene
ſanè. Enimvero id tantum nunc abeſt hinc. Etiam tu reſpondes hoc, quid negotii eſt tibi iſtic ?
DA. Mihine? SI. Ita. DA. Mihine ? SI. Tibi ergo. DA. Introii modò. SI. Quaſi ego rogem quam dudum fueris ibi. DA. Unà cum tua gnato. SI. Anne eſt Pamphilus intus ? Miſer
crucior. Eho, non tu carnifex dixti inimicitiàs eſſe inter eos ?

ANNOTATIONS.

hial Sentence, denoting the moſt perfect Security. Thus, *Plautus Aul.* iv. 10. 73.
  Hæc propemodum jam eſſe in vado ſalutis res
  videtur.
For though Shelves are dangerous to Sailors,
yet they afford the greateſt Security in ſwim-
ming. *Cicero*, probably alludes to this Proverb, pro Cœl. 21. *Sed quòniam emerſiſſe*
jam à vadis, & ſcopulos prætervecta videtur
oratio mea, perfacilis mibi reliquus curſus oſten-
ditur.
  5 *O noſter Chremes.* I am ſurprized how
Donatus came to fancy that *Davus* by *noſter*
here tacitly inſinuates that *Glycery* was
found to be the Daughter of *Chremes*, for
that does not appear till towards the end of
the fourth Scene, nor could *Davus*, at preſent, have any the leaſt Apprehenſion of it.
As he knew he had been ſeen coming out
from *Glycery*, he means to ſoften them by
this little Piece of Diſſimulation, which is
beſides a proper Introduction to what follows;
Omnia apparata jam ſunt intus, as if he al-

ready conſidered *Chremes* as his young Maſter's
Father-in-Law.
  7 *Id enimvero hinc nunc abeſt.* There
are great Diverſities in Editions here, with
regard to the Reading, ſome making it, *It*
enimvero hinc nunc abeſt ; is, referring to
Pamphilus. Others ; *Id enimvero hic nunc*
abeſt, that is, *enimvero propter id hic Pam-*
philum nunc abeſt. But I am rather inclined
to follow *Donatus*, who takes *abeſt* here for
deeſt, ſo that the Senſe muſt be, *Omnia ita*
ſunt apparata, ut nihil deſit, ut Philu-
mena accerſatur. *Eugraphius* too gives the
ſame turn to the Paſſage : his Words are ;
Hoc enim ſolum jam deeſt, ut ipſa puella de-
beat evocari. We are not, however, to forget that this muſt be underſtood in a way of
Irony.
  8 *Mihin'?* *Davus* here, not knowing
what to anſwer, endeavours to gain time,
partly by Repetitions, partly by evaſive Anſwers.
  10 *Cum tuo gnato unà.* The Poet here
makes

Dav. They have.

Si. Why? is he there then?

Chr. Why do you think? to fcold her a little.

Dav. Nay, *Chremes*, you fhall hear from me an infupportable Piece of Infolence. I know not what old Man has lately arrived, who feems to be a fhrewd refolute Perfon. To look at him, you would take him for a Man of Confequence. There is in his Countenance an Air of Gravity that commands Refpect, and Sincerity and Candour are in his Words.

Si. What's this you bring now?

Dav. Why nothing but what I heard him fay.

Si. What fays he then?

Dav. That he knows *Glycery* to be a Citizen of *Athens*.

Si. Soho, *Dromo*, *Dromo*.

Dav. What's the matter?

Si. Dromo.

Dav. Hear me a moment.

Si. If you add a fingle Word more—*Dromo*

Dav. Hear me, I beg of you.

Dro. Your Pleafure, Sir.

Si. Trufs up this Fellow, and carry him in immediately.

Dro. Whom?

Si. Davus.

Dav. Why?

Si. Becaufe it is my Pleafure: away with him, I fay.

Dav. What have I done?

Si. Away with him.

Dav. If you catch me in a Lie in any one Article, kill me.

Si. I hear nothing. I fhall now make you tremble.

Dav. What, although all I have faid be true?

Si. Although it fhould: take care he is well fecur'd; and, d'ye hear? bind him Hand and Foot. Carry him off. I'll make you fenfible to-day, if I live, what it is to deceive your Mafter, and him to provoke his Father.

Chr. Alas! Don't give way fo much to your Paffion.

Si. O *Chremes!* Where's the Duty of a Son? Don't you pity me? To have fo much Concern upon me for fuch a Son? Well, *Pamphilus*; come out then *Pamphilus*; have you then any Shame left?

ANNOTATIONS.

makes *Davus* fo difconcerted and frightened, that he forgets all his Cunning, and betrays *Pamphilus*. The Fable itfelf required this, for the Poet now wants to come to the unravelling of the Plot. However, to preferve in fome degree *Davus*'s Character of Prefence of Mind, tho' he does not dare to fpeak to his Mafter, he recovers himfelf fomewhat, by turning fuddenly to *Chremes*, and telling him what he had heard from *Crito* the *Andrian*, which, to fet off the more artfully, he does with an Air, as if he gave but little credit to it.

16 *Triftis feveritas.* The word *triftis* is taken fometimes in a favourable Senfe, and here means a grave judicious Severity, free from thofe light and foolifh Tranfports, which Joy, according to the common Acceptation of the word, produces. For true Joy is of the ferious kind, as *Seneca* has well obferved.

DA. Sunt. SI. cur igitur hîc eſt? CH. quid illum cen-
ſes? cum illâ litigat.   [ex me audias.
DA. Imo verò indignum, Chreme, jam facinus faxo
Neſcio qui ſenex modò venit: ellum, confidens, catus:
Cùm faciem videas, videtur eſſe quantivis precî: 15
Triſtis ſeveritas ineſt in voltu, atque in verbis fides.
SI. Quidnam apportas? DA. nil equidem, niſi quod
illum audivi dicere.   [eſſe Atticam.
SI. Quid ait tandem? DA. Glycerium ſe ſcire civem
SI. Hem Dromo, Dromo. DA. quid eſt? SI. Dromo.
DA. audi. SI. verbum ſi addideris—Dromo.
DA. Audi, obſecro. DR. quid vis? SI. ſublimem hunc
intro rape, quantùm potes.   20
DR. Quem? SI. Davum. DA. quamobrem? SI. quia
lubet. rape, inquam. DA. quid feci? SI. rape.
DA. Si quidquam mentitum invenies, occidito. SI. ni-
hil audio.   [verum eſt? SI. tamen.
Ego jam te commotum reddam. DA. tamen etſi hoc
Cura adſervandum vinctum: atque audin'? quadru-
pedem conſtringito.
Age, nunc jam ego pol hodie, ſi vivo, tibi   25
Oſtendam, herum quid ſit pericli fallere, &
Illi, patrem. CH. ah, ne ſævi tantopere. SI. Chreme,
Pietatem gnati! nonne to miſeret mei?
Tantam laborem capere ob talem filium?
Age, Pamphile: exi, Pamphile: ecquid te pudet?   30

DA. Sunt. SI. Cur igitur eſt Lic? CH. Quid cenſes illum agere ibi? litigat cum illâ. DA. Imo verò, Chreme, faxo ut jam audias ex me indignum facinus. Neſcio quid ſenex venit modò; ellum (en illum) confidens, catus; cùm videas faciem; videtur eſſe quantivis pretii: triſtis ſeveritas ineſt iu vultu, atque fides in verbis. SI. Quidnam apportas? DA. Equidem nibil, niſi quod audivi illum dicere. SI. Quid tandem ait? SI. Ait ſe ſcire Glycerium eſſe civem Atticam. SI. Hem Dromo, Dromo. DA. Quid eſt negotii? SI. Dromo. DA. Audi. SI. Si addideris verbum ---Dromo. DA. Obſecro, audi. DR. Quid vis? SI. Rape hunc ſubli-

mem intro, quantum potes. DR. Quem? SI. Davum. DA. Quamobrem? SI. Quia lubet.
Inquam, rape. DA. Quid feci? SI. Rape. DA. Si invenies me mentitum fuiſſe quidquam,
occidito. SI. Audio nibil. Ego jam reddam te commotum. DA. Tamen etſi-bec eſt verum?
SI. Tamen. Cura aſſervandum vinctum: atque audin'? conſtringito eum quadrupedem. Age:
pol ego jam nunc, ſi vivo, oſtendam tibi bodie, quid pericli ſit fallere herum, & illi Pamphilo,
quid pericli ſit fallere patrem. CH. Ab, ne ſævi tantopere. SI. O Chreme, ſpecta pietatem
gnati! nonne miſeret te mei? capere tantum laborem ob talem filium? Age, Pamphile: exi, Pamphile: ecquid pudet te?

ANNOTATIONS.

obſerved. *Severa res eſt verum gaudium.* Cicero, in like manner, Act. I. in Ver. 10. has, *Judix triſtis & integer.*

20 *Sublimem bunc intro rape.* That is, *in ſublime, per altum.* This Expreſſion was uſual, where one was to be hurried away with Violence, ſo as not to be ſuffered to touch the Ground. Plautus elegantly uſes *ſuperbus* in the ſame Senſe. *Ampb.* I. 1. 201.

　　Faciam ego hodie te ſuperbum, niſi hinc abis. So. *Quonam modo?*
ME. *Auferere, non abibis, ſi ego fuſtem ſumſero.*

23 *Ego jam te commotum reddam.* Donatus explains *commotum, citum, celerem,* according to which we muſt ſuppoſe them addreſſed to *Dromo,* who was too ſlow in carrying off *Davus.* But I am apt rather to think that *commotum reddam* is here for *commoveho,* and refers to *Davus,* who, in the Beginning of this Scene, had ſaid, *Animo jam nunc otioſo eſſe imp.ro.*

24 *Quadrupedem conſtringito.* Donatus ſeems at a loſs to think in what ſenſe *Quadrupes* is here to be taken. If for a Slave or Fugitive, as *Virgil* uſes it, the Word *conſtringito* is altogether ſuperfluous, eſpecially as he had ſaid before, *cura adſervandum vinctum.* The meaning therefore, as far as I can judge, is, *Manibus & pedibus conſtringito quaſi quadrupedem, & ne vincula rumpat aufugiatque.* For thus Suetonius, *Ner.* 48. *Atque ita quadrupes per anguſtias effoſſæ cavernæ receptus, in proximam cellam decubuit ſuper lectum medicella culcita, vetere pallio ſtrato inſtructum.* This Cuſtom of binding Hand and Foot, was derived to *Rome* from *Athens,* for there are Examples of it in *Plato.*

ACT

ACT V. SCENE III.

ARGUMENT.

Pamphilus *is seen by his Father, coming out from* Glycery, *and heavily accused. The Son acknowledging his Fault, asks pardon, and subjects himself entirely to his Father's Will.* Chremes *endeavours to pacify his passionate Friend, and at length prevails.*

PAMPHILUS, SIMO, CHREMES.

Pamp. WHO's this that calls me? I'm undone, 'tis my Father.

Si. What say'st thou, of all Men the——

Chr. Ah! rather argue the Case calmly, and leave this ill Language.

Si. As if I could say any thing too harsh against one who has behaved in this manner. What then? do you pretend at length that *Glycery* is a Citizen of *Athens?*

Pamp. So it is reported.

Si. So it is reported! O unparallel'd Impudence! Does he consider what he says? Does he repent of any thing he has done? Does his Countenance betray any Token of Shame? To be so little Master of himself, as without regard either to the Customs and Laws of his Fellow-Citizens, or the Will of his Father; he will yet, in defiance of Infamy and Reproach, set his Heart upon this Stranger.

Pamp. Wretch that I am!

Si. O *Pamphilus;* are you now only sensible of this! Then indeed, then ought you to have perceived it, when you had determined with yourself to gratify your Passion at any price. From that moment might you with justice have dated yourself an unhappy Wretch. But what am I a doing? Why do I torment my self? Why do I fret my self? Why afflict myself in my Old Age for his Folly? Am I to suffer the Punishment of his Errors? E'en let him have her, make his best of her, and pass his Life with her.

Pamp. My Father!

Si. Why, my Father? As if you thought you had any need of such a Father. You have got a Home, a Wife and Children, and all in contradiction to your Father's Will. You have also found out some who pretend that she is a Citizen of *Athens;* I can hold out no longer.

Pamp. Father, will you give me leave to speak a few Words?

Si. What can you have to say?

Chr.

ANNOTATIONS.

[1] *Quis me volt?* Pamphilus, as he comes out from *Glycery*, hearing himself named, and finding that it was his Father, is quite confounded. *Chremes,* in this Scene, endeavours to moderate *Simo's* Anger, and bring him to reason. *Pamphilus* behaves with great Submission, and unable to stand out against his Father's Anger, promises an entire Resignation, but, as he was uneasy to lie under any unjust Suspicions, intreats of his Father, that he would suffer him to clear himself from the Charge of having suborned

Crito ;

ARGUMENTUM.

Evocatur Pamphilus è domo Glycerii, & graviter à patre accusa-
tur : confessus crimen filius, veniam petit, ac se totum pater-
næ subjicit voluntati. Nimis commotum senem placare nititur
Chremes, & tandem exorat.

PAMPHILUS, SIMO, CHREMES.

ORDO.

QUIS me volt? perii, pater est. SI. quid ais, om-
nium? CH. ah!
Rem potiùs ipsam dic, ac mitte male loqui.
SI. Quasi quidquam in hunc jam gravius dici possiet.
Ain' tandem? civis Glycerium est? PA. ita prædicant.
SI. Ita prædicant! ingentem confidentiam!   5
Num cogitat, quid dicat? num facti piget?
Nam ejus color pudoris signum usquam indicat?
Adeon' impotenti esse animo, ut præter civium
Morem, atque legem, & sui volentatem patris,
Tamen hanc habere cupiat cum summo probro?   10
PA. Me miserum! SI. hem, modóne id demum sensti,
Pamphile?
Olim istuc, olim, cùm ita animum induxti tuum,
Quod cuperes, aliquo pacto efficiundum tibi,
Eodem die istuc verbum verè in te accidit.
Sed quid ago? cur me excrucio? cur me macero? 15
Cur meam senectam hujus solicito amentiâ? an
Pro hujus ego ut peccatis supplicium sufferam?
Imo habeat, valeat, vivat cum illâ. PA. mi pater!
SI. Quid, mi pater? quasi tu hujus indigeas patris.
Domus, uxor, liberi inventi, invito patre: 20
Adducti, qui illam civem hinc dicant. viceris.
PA. Pater, licetne pauca? SI. quid dices mihi?

PA. QUIS vult
me? pe-
rii, est pater. SI.
Quid ais omnium in-
digissime? CH. Ab!
Dic potius ipsam
rem, ac mitte male
loqui. SI. Quasi
quidquam gravius
posset dici jam in
hunc. Ain' hoc tan-
dem? Estne Gly-
cerium civis Atti-
ca? PA. Prædi-
cant ita. SI. Præ-
dicant ita! O in-
gentem confidentiam!
Nunc cogitat, quid
dicat? Num piget
facti? Num ejus
color usquam indi-
cat signum pudoris?
Eum-ne esse adeo
impotenti animo, ut
præter morem at-
que legem civium,
& præter veluntta-
tem sui patris, ta-
men cupiat habere
hanc cum summo pro-
bro? PA. Heu me
miserum! SI. Hem:

modone sensisti id demum, Pamphile? Olim istuc, olim inquam istuc verbum verè accidit in te ;
eodem die, cum induxti tuum animum ita, id quod cuperes esse efficiundum tibi aliquot pacto. Sed
quid ago? Cur excrucio me? Cur macero me? Cur solicito meam senectutem amentiâ hujus? An
ut ego sufferam supplicium pro peccatis hujus? Imo habeat, valeat, vivat cum illa. PA. Mi
pater. SI. Quid, mi pater? Quasi tu indigeas hujus patris. Domus, uxor, liberi inventi sunt
tibi, invito patre. Adducti sunt, qui dicant illam esse civem hinc. Viceris. PA. Pater, li-
cetne loqui pauca? SI. Quid dices mihi?

ANNOTATIONS.

Crito; this at last, he obtains through the
Intercession of *Chremes*, by which a way is
laid open for the unravelling of the Plot,
and discovering the *Glycery* Parents.

12 *Olim istuc, olim,* &c. Madam *Dacier*
observes justly upon this Passage, that it is
perfectly fine, and includes a Maxim of the
deepest Philosophy. Men never think themselves unhappy, till the Disasters that are

the necessary Effect of their own Folly
actually come upon them ; whereas, if they
were to judge right, they ought to date
themselves unhappy from the very Moment,
that by their own Choice they have abandoned themselves to those Follies, which un-
avoidably bring these Calamities upon them.
There is a beautiful Passage to this purpose
in *Arrian* upon *Epictetus: You'll say, perhaps,*

Chr. But *Simo*, do, hear him.

Si. I hear him! What shall I hear, *Chremes?*

Chr. But give him leave at least to speak.

Si. Well; let him speak, I give leave.

Pamp. I own to you, Father, that I love her; and if that be a Fault, I own that too. But Father, I subject myself wholly to you: lay any Charge upon me: command me: Would you have me take a Wife? Would you have me abandon her? I'll bear it in the best manner I can. This I only request of you, not to think that this old Man is suborned by me: allow me to clear my self, and bring him here before you.

Si. Bring him here?

Pamp. Allow me, Father.

Chr. He asks but what is reasonable; do, permit him.

Pamp. Let me obtain thus much of you.

Si. I allow it. I could almost agree to any thing, so I find that I have not been deceived by him, *Chremes.*

Chr. A small Punishment will satisfy a Father for a great Offence in his Son.

ANNOTATIONS.

tops, that Paris was then indeed unhappy, when the Greeks sacked the City of Troy, destroyed all with Fire and Sword, extinguished the whole Family of Priam, and led their Wives captive. You are deceived, my Friend. Paris was then most unhappy, when he lost Probity and Honour, when he began to shake off all the Tyes of Decency, and violate the Rights of Hospitality.

In like manner, it was not the Death of Patroclus, that we ought to call the great Misfortune of Achilles: but the Folly of giving himself up to the Dictates of Passion and Resentment, the Weakness of grieving for the Loss of Briseis, and his forgetting that be came to that War, not to indulge himself with a Mistress, but to restore a Wife to her Husband.

²⁵ *Eg*

ACT V.   SCENE IV.

ARGUMENT.

By *means of* Crito *the* Andrian (*whose meeting with* Simo *and* Chremes *is contained in this Scene*) Glycery *is found to be the Daughter of* Chremes, *and given to* Pamphilus. Davus *too is set at liberty.*

CRITO, CHREMES, SIMO, PAMPHILUS.

Crito. FORBEAR intreating: any one of these Reasons are sufficient to prevail with me to do what you ask: either regard to yourself, or that Truth requires it, or because I wish well to *Glycery.*

Chr. Is this *Crito* the *Andrian* that I see? 'tis certainly he.

Cri. Your Servant, *Chremes.*   *Chr.*

ANNOTATIONS.

¹ *Mitte orare.* In this Scene, *Chremes*, by means of *Crito*, comes to know that *Glycery* was his own Daughter, which immediately reconciles *Simo* to his Son's A-

mour, and raises Pamphilus *to the Height of his Wishes. It appears from what Crito says, as he is coming out from* Glycery, *that* Pamphilus *had been requesting of him to do his*

CH. Tamen, Simo, audi. SI. ego audiam? quid au-
diam.
Chreme? CH. at tandem dicat sine. SI. age, dicat, sino.
PA. Ego me amaré hanc fateor. si id peccare est, fa-
teor id quoque.   25
Tibi pater me dedo. quidvis oneris impone: impera.
Vis me uxorem ducere? hanc amittere? ut potero,
feram.   [hunc senem
Hoc modò se obsecro, ut ne credas à me adlegatum
Sine me expurgem, atque illum huc coràm adducam.
SI. adducas? PA. sine, pater.
CH. Æquum postulat: da veniam. PA. sine te hoc
exorem. SI. sino.   30
Quidvis cupio, dum ne ab hoc me falli comperiar,
Chreme.   [patri.
CH. Pro peccato magno paulum supplicii satis est

CH. Tamen, Simo, audi illum. SI. Ego audiam? Quid audiam, Chreme? CH. At tandem sine ut dicat tibi. SI. Age, dicat, sino. PA. Ego fateor me amare hanc. Si id est peccare, fateor id quoque. Pater, dedo me tibi. Impone quidvis oneris: impera: vis me ducere uxorem? vis me amittere hanc? feram, ut potero. Modo obsecro te hoc, ut ne credas hunc senem esse allegatum à me. Sine ut expurgem me, atque adducum illum

huc coram te. SI. Adducas? PA. Pater, sine. CH. Postulat æquum, da veniam illi. PA. Sine ut exorem hoc à te. SI. Sino. Cupio quidvis, Chreme, dum comperiar me ne falli ab hoc. CH. Paulum supplicii est satis patri, pro magno peccato filii.

ANNOTATIONS.

25 *Ego me amare hanc fateor.* Donatus observes, that he does not here name *Glycery*, because he knew that was a Sound, would have been disagreeable to his Father, nor does he call her a Stranger, *hanc peregrinam*, it being a term of Reproach, and he believing her to be a Citizen; but says barely *hanc*, which is more soft, and passes easily. Indeed, the whole Speech is framed with wonderful Judgment. His Disposition naturally good, can't bear his Father's Resentment; and if he promises to sacrifice all to please him, it is yet with such apparent Reluctance, as discovered the Constraint he put upon himself: nor are we to suppose that *Chremes* would be very forward to give his Daughter to a Man, whom he saw forced to marry against his Will. *Et multum valet sub præsentia Chremetis hæc confessio, ad recusandas nuptias,* says *Donatus.*

ACTUS V. SCENA IV.
ARGUMENTUM.

Opera Critonis Andrii (cujus hic cum Simone & Chremete congressus continetur) Glycerium Chremetis filia agnoscitur, & conceditur Pamphilo, & Davus liberatur.

CRITO, CHREMES, SIMO, PAMPHILUS.

MITTE orare. una harum quævis causa me, ut
faciam, monet: [cerio.
Vel tu, vel quòd verum est, vel quòd ipsi cupio Gly-
CH. Andrium ego Critonem video? certè is est. CR.
salvos sis, Chreme.

ORDO.
CR. Mitte orare me. Una quævis causa barum monet, ut faciam: vel tu, vel quod est verum, vel quod cupio ut sit be-

ne ipsi Glycerio. CH. Video ego Critonem Andrium? Certe est is. CR. Chreme, sic salvus.

ANNOTATIONS.

his utmost to convince the old Men, that she was really an *Athenian*; as this required some time, and *Chremes* and *Simo* don't go off the Stage, we must suppose that they

Chr. What could occasion your coming to *Athens*, a thing so very unusual?

Cri. So it has happened, you see; but is this *Simo?*

Chr. The same.

Si. Do you ask for me? Hark ye, Friend; do you say that *Glycery* is a Citizen of *Athens?*

Cri. Do you deny it?

Si. What are you come so well prepar'd?

Cri. About what?

Si. Do you ask? or do you expect to escape unpunished for this? Are you come here to draw in young Gentlemen well educated and without Experience? will you by your fine Speeches and Promises seduce and confirm them in their vain Fancies?

Cri. Are you in your Senses?

Si. And confirm their shameful Intrigues by a lawful Marriage?

Pamp. I'm undone : I fear that this Stranger cannot bear all this ill Usage.

Chr. If, *Simo*, you but knew the Man, you would be far from harbouring such a Suspicion. He's a very worthy Man.

Si. He a worthy Man! what, to come here so very opportunely, on the Day of the Wedding, and never before? Is any Credit to be given to such a Man, *Chremes?*

Pamp. (*aside.*) Were I not afraid of my Father, I could help him out extremely well in this matter.

Si. A Sycophant!

Cri. Hah!

Chr. 'Tis his way, *Crito*; never mind him.

Cri. Let him see to himself. If he persists to say whatever he has a mind to, he shall hear what he perhaps won't so much like. Do I dream of disturbing the Nuptials, or care how they go? Can't you bear your Misfortunes with an equal Mind? For as to what I say, whether it be true or false, may be soon known. A certain *Athenian* some time ago, being shipwreck'd, was cast upon the Isle of *Andros*, and this little Girl along with him : as he was in want

of

ANNOTATIONS.

fill up the Scene with Nods, and proper Gestures.

4 *Insolens.* This Word had undergone several Changes of Signification. Originally it was equivalent to *infuetus, infolitus*, and in that Sense is to be taken here. Those too, who, from being poor, suddenly came to the Possession of great Riches, were called *insolentes* ; and as they were apt to be arrogant and haughty, hence *insolens* is, for the most part, used for a proud arrogant Man. *Cicero, Philip. 9. 6. Mirifice enim Servius Sulpicius majorum continentiam diligebat : hujus seculi insolentiam vituperabat.* And in

his Oration for *Roscius* 8. *Qui in re sua fuisset egentissimus, erat, ut fit, insolens in aliena.*

10 *Meretricios amores nuptiis conglutinas?* That is, do you attempt to confirm, by a lawful Marriage, an Amour that has hitherto been carried on only by stealth and privately? for the Word *conglutino* is used in Cases of strict Friendship, that are united by the strongest Tyes. For so *Cicero, Att. 7. 8. Suspicionem autem æ mihi majorem tua taciturnitas attulerat, quod & tu foles conglutinare amicitias testimonii tui.* And again, in his Treatise *de Senectute* 20. *Ut nervum,*

CH. Quid tu Athenas infolens ? CR. evenit. fed hiccine eſt Simo ?

CH. Hic cſt. SI. men' quæris ? eho, ţu Glycerium hinc civem eſſe ais ?   5

CR. Tu negas ? SI. itane huc paratus advenis ? CR. quare ? SI. rogas ?   ․ [fcentulos,

Tune impunè hæc facias ? tunc hîc homines adole- Imperitos rerum, eductos liberè, in fraudem illicis ? Solicitando, & pollicitando eorum animos lactas ? CR. fanun' es ?

SI. Ac meretricios amores nuptiis conglutinas ?   10

PA. Perii : metuo, ut fubſtèt hofpes. CH. fi, Simo, hunc nôris fatis,

Non ita arbitrere. bonus eſt hic vir. SI. hic vir fit bonus?
Itane adtemperate venit hodie in ipfis nuptiis,
Ut veniret antehac nunquam ? eſt verò huic creden- dum, Chreme ?   ․ ․

PA. Ni metuam patrem, habea pro illâ re, illum quod moneam probè.   15

SI. Sycophanta. CR. hem. CH. fic, Crito, eſt hic·: mitte. CR. videat, qui fiet.   [audiet.

Si mihi pergit, quæ volt, dicere, ea, quæ non volt,
Ego iſtæc moveo, aut curo ? non tu tuum malum æquo animo feres ?

Nam, ego quæ dico, vera; an falfa audieris, jam fciri poteſt.   19

Atticus quidam olim navi fracta ad Andrum ejectus eſt,
Et iſtæc una parva virgo. tum ille egens fortè applicat

quid pro illâ re, quod probè moncam illum. SI. Sycophanta. CH. Hem. CR. Videt qui fiet, fi pergit dicere mihi quæ vult, audiet ea quæ non vult. Ego ne moveo aut curo iſtæc ? Nonne tu feics tuum malum æquo animo ? Nam quod ad ea quæ ego dico, facile fciri ſeteſt, num audieris vera an falfa. Olim quidam Atticus navi fracta eſt ejectus ad Andrum, & iſtæc parva virgo una. Tum ille egens fortè applicat ●

CH. Quid tu info- lens veniſti Athenas ? CR. Evenit: fed CH. Hic eſt. SI. CH. Hic eſt. SI. Quærifne me ? Eho, ais tu Glycerium eſſe civem hinc? CR. Negas tu ? SI. Ad- venifne huc ita para- tus? CR. Quare? SI. Rogas? Tunc facias hæc impunè ? Tune hic illicis, in fraudem, homine a- dolefcentulos, imperi- tos rerum, eductos liberè ? Tunc lactas animos eorum folici- tando, & pollicitan- do? CR. Sanufne es? SI. Ac conglu- tinas amores meretri- cios nuptiis ? PA. Perii ; metuo ut ho- fpes fubſtet. CH. Si, Simo, novù is hunc hominem fatis, non arbitrere ita. Hic eſt vir bonus. SI. Hic fit vir bonus? v- nitne ita attempera e hodie in ipfis nuptiis, ut nunquam veniret antehac ? Eſt verò credendum huic,Ch c- me ? PA. Ni metuam patrem, habeam ali- quid pro illâ re, quod probè moncam illum. Crito: mitte eum. CR. Videat qui fiet, fi pergit dicere mihi quæ vult, audiet ea quæ non vult. Ego ne moveo aut curo iſtæc? Nonne tu feis tuum malum æquo animo ? Nam quod ad ea quæ ego dico, facile fciri ſeteſt, num audieris vera an falfa. Olim quidam Atticus navj fracta eſt ejectus ad Andrum, & iſtæc parva virgo una. Tum ille egens fortè applicat

ANNOTATIONS.

novem, ut ædificium idem deſtruit facillime, qui conſtruxit : fic hominem eadem optime, quæ conglutinavit, natura diſſolvit.

18 Ego iſtæc moveo, aut curo? There is a great Emphaſis to be laid upon the Pro- noun ego. Simo had faid in the fifth Verfe, Tu Glycerium hinc civem eſſe ais ? Tune im- punè hoc facias? Tu homines adolefcentulos, &c. Crito therefore anfwers with an Air of In- dignation, Ego iſtæc moveo, aut curo ?

21 Forte applicat fe primum ad Coryfidis patrem. Applicare was a Term commonly ufed, where one of inferiour Rank had re- courfe to his Patron in any Emergence, and in general expreſſes an Addreſs for Relief in whatever Circumſtances of Diſtreſs, as after

a Shipwreck, in Baniſhment, &c. Hence Cicero employs the Expreſſion, jus applica- tionis, in fpeaking of an exiled Perfon, where he calls it an obfcure and unknown Right. His Words are in his firſt Book de Oratore 39. Qui Romam in exilium veniſſet, cui Romæ exulare jus eſſet, fi fe ad aliquem quaſi patro- num applicaviſſet, inteſtatoque eſſet mor- tuus, nonne in ea cauſa jus applicationis, obfcurum fane & ignotum, patefactum in judicio, atque illuſtratum eſt à patrono ?
‘ A Man who fhould come to Rome; as an
‘ Exile, and be there fuffered to pafs the
‘ whole Time of his Baniſhment ; if he
‘ fhould apply to any Citizen as his Patron,
‘ and afterwards die without making a Will,

of every thing, he chanced to apply firſt to *Chryſis*'s Father.

Si. So: He begins a Tale.

Chr. Let him go on.

Cri. Does he pretend to interrupt me thus ?

Chr. Do you go on.

Cri. This *Chryſis*'s Father, who received him, was a Relation of mine. It was there I heard from himſelf that he was an *Athenian*. He died there.

Chr. His Name ?

Cri. His Name ſo ſuddenly ? *Phania*.

Chr. Hah ! I'm thunder-ſtruck.

Chr. I think indeed that it was *Phania :* one thing I am very certain of, that he ſaid he was of *Rhamnus*.

Chr. O *Jupiter*.

Cri. Many other People in *Andros*, *Chremes*, heard theſe very things I now tell you.

Chr. I heartily wiſh it may be as I hope. But tell me ; what ſaid he of this Girl, did he pretend that ſhe was his own ?

Cri. No.

Chr. Whoſe then ?

Cri. His Brother's

Chr. She's certainly mine

Cri. What d'ye ſay ?

Si. What's this you ſay ?

Pamp. Hearken, *Pamphilus*, hearken.

Si. Why do you believe ſo, *Chremes ?*

Chr. That *Phania* was my Brother.

Si. I know it, and remember him very well.

Chr. He on account of a War which was juſt then breaking out, and expecting to find me in *Aſia*, whither I had gone a little before, left this Place. At the ſame time thought it not ſafe to leave the Child behind him. Since which, this is the firſt time I have heard what happened to him.

Pamp. I am ſcarcely my ſelf, my Mind is ſo diſtracted with Fear, Hope, Joy, and this ſo wonderfully great and unexpected good Fortune.

Si. Nay, I am overjoyed that ſhe proves to be yours for many Reaſons.

Pamp. I believe it, Father.

Chr. But there remains yet one Scruple, *Crito*, which gives me ſome Uneaſineſs.

Pamp. I could almoſt hate you with your Scruples ; you are hunting for a Knot in a Bulruſh.

Cri. What's that pray ?   *Chr.*

' is it not certain that in the Courſe of | ' would be illuſtrated and ſet in a proper
' Pleadings upon this Cauſe, the *jus applica-* | ' Light by the Pleader ?' It is probable that
' *tionis* at preſent obſcure and unknown, | in this Caſe the Patron would have been de-
                                                                                            clared

Primùm ad Chryſidis patrem ſe. SI. fabulam inceptat.
  CH. ſine   [cognatus fuit,
CR. Itane verò obturbat? CH. perge. CR. tum is mihi
Qui eum recepit. ibi ego audivi ex illo, ſeſe eſſe Atti-
  cum.
Is ibi mortuus eſt. CH. ejus nomen? CR. nomen tam
  citò tibi? Phania. CH. hem,   25
Perii. CR. verùm hercle opinor fuiſſe Phaniam. hoc
  certò ſcio,   [hæc, Chremè,
Rhamnuſium ſe aiebat eſſe. CH. ô Jupiter! CR. eadem
Multi alii in Andro tum audivere. CH. utinam id ſit
  quod ſpero. eho, dic mihi,
Quid eam tum? ſuamne eſſe aibat? CR. non. CH.
  cujam igitur? CR. fratris filiam.
CH. Certè mea eſt. CR. quid ais? SI. quid tu? quid
  ais? PA. arrige aures, Pamphile.   30
SI. Quî credis? CH. Phania ille frater meus fuit. SI.
  nòram, & ſcio.   [quens, proficiſcitur.
CH. Is hinc bellum fugiens, meque in Aſiam perſe-
Tum illam hîc relinquere eſt veritus. poſtilla nunc
  primùm audio,
Quid illo ſit factum. PA. vix ſum apud me: ita ani-
  mus commotus eſt metu,   34
Spe, gaudio, mirando hoc tanto, tam repentino bono.
SI. Næ iſtam multimodis tuam inveniri gaudeo. PA.
  credo, pater.   [habet. PA. dignus es
CH. At mihi unus ſcrupulus etiam reſtat, qui me male
Cum tuâ religione odio. nodum in ſcirpo quæris.
  CR. quid iſtud eſt?

ſe primùm ad patrem Chryſidis. SI. Incep-tat fabulam. CH. Sine illum pergere. CR. Itane verò obtur-bat? CR. Perge. CR. Tum is, qui recepit eum, fuit cognatus mihi. Ibi ego audivi ex illo, ſeſe eſſe Atti-cum. Is mortuus eſt ibi. CH. Quid fuit ejus nomen? CR. No-men poſtulas dari tàm citò tibi? Pha-nia. CH. Hem, perii! CR. Verùm hercle opinor nomen fuiſſe Phaniam. Scio hoc certò, aiebat ſe eſſe Rhamnuſium. CH. O Jupiter! CR. Multi alii tum in Andro audivere hæc eadem, Chreme. CH. Utinam id ſit, quod ſcio: eho, dic mibi, quid tum aiebat eam eſſe, ſuamne? CR. Non. CH. Cujam filiam igitur? CR. Aiebat eſſe filiam fratris. CH. Certè eſt mea fi-lia. CR. Quid ais? SI. Quid tu? quid ais? PA. Pamphile, arrige aures. SI. Quî credis? CH. Ille Phania fuit meus fra-

ter. SI. *Noveram illum, & ſcio fuiſſe tuum fratrem.* CH. *Is fugiens bellum, perſequenſque me in Aſiam, proficiſcitur hinc. Tum eſt veritus relinquere illam hîc. Poſt illa tempora nunc primùm audio quid ſit factum de illo.* PA. *Sum vix apud me, animus eſt ita commotus metu, ſpe, gaudio, hoc tanto mirando, tam repentino bono.* SI. *Næ gaudeo iſtam inveniri tuam multimodis.* PA. *Credo, pater.* CH. *At etiam unus ſcrupulus reſtat mihi, qui habet me male.* PA. *Es dignus odio cum tua religione; quæris nodum in ſcirpo.* CR. *Quid eſt iſtud?*

ANNOTATIONS.

clared legal Heir to the Perſon he had received: for it had been provided by the
Laws, that a Man might take poſſeſſion of
the Goods of him whom he had received
into his Houſe.

²² *Fabulat inceptat.* Simo ſpeaks thus in
reference to the Manner of *Crito's* beginning his Relation, *Atticum quidam olim,*
for *olim* was proper to Fables. Thus *Horace,*
Sat. Lib. 2. 6. 79.

- - - - - - - - - *Olim,*
Ruſticus urbanum murem mus paupere ſertur
Accepiſſe cavo, veterem vetus hoſpes amicum.
²⁷ *Rhamnuſium ſe aiebat eſſe.* *Rhamnus*
and ſuch other Placcs often mentioned in

Terence, were maritime Towns of *Attica,*
near to which the more wealthy *Athenians*
had Country-Seats.

³⁷ *At unus ſcrupulus.* *Donatus* derives
ſcrupulus from *ſcrupus* a little Stone, which
in walking, eſpecially if they get into the
Shoe, hurt the Feet very much. But *Nannius* rejects this, deriving it from *ſcriptulum*
the twenty-fourth Part of an Ounce, as if
the Senſe were, that *Chremes,* upon examin-
ing the Proofs, found them of full weight
except one Scruple, which was ſtill wanting,
viz. the Girl's Name not agreeing. But
this laſt is rather ingenious than ſolid.

³⁸ *Nodum in ſcirpo quæris. Scirpus,* ſays
       I 2   *Donatus,*

Chr. The Name don't anfwer.

Cri. She had indeed another when a Little-one.

Chr. What was it, *Crito?* Can you remember it?

Cri. That's what I now want.

Pamp. Shall I fuffer his bad Memory to ftand in the way of my Happinefs, when I have it in my power to remedy my felf at once? I will not. Hark ye *Chremes,* the Name you afk for is *Pafibula.*

Cri. The very fame.

Chr. That's it.

Pamp. I have heard it from herfelf a thoufand times.

Si. I believe, *Chremes,* you are fatisfied we all rejoice at this Difcovery.

Chr. As I hope for the Favour of the Gods, I do.

Pam. What remains now to be done, Father?

Si. The thing itfelf has already brought me to agree to it.

Pamp. Excellent Father! *Chremes* will never oppofe my enjoying my Wife, in like manner as I have already done.

Chr. The beft Reafon in the World, unlefs your Father is of another Mind.

Pamp. What fay you to it?

Si. I agree.

Chr. Her Portion, *Pamphilus,* is ten Talents.

Pamp. I'm fatisfy'd.

Chr. I'll haften to my Daughter: here, *Crito,* come along with me, for I doubt whether at this Diftance of Time fhe will know me.

Si. Why don't you order her to be fent for hither?

Pamp. Well thought! I'll give that Charge to *Davus.*

Si. He can't.

Pamp. Why?

Si. Becaufe he has fomething to think of, that more nearly concerns himfelf.

Pamp. What?

Si. He's bound.

Pamp. Father, it was not well done to bind him.

Si. But I ordered it fhould be well done.

Pamp. Pray command that he be unbound.   *Si.*

ANNOTATIONS.

Donatus, paluftris res, & leviffima. Lucilius in primo, Nodum in fcirpo infane facere vulgus. *Eft autem fcirpus fine nodo, & levis junci fpecies.*

45 *Jamdudum.* This does not here refer to Time, but to th Meafure and Degree of the Thing, and is equivalent to *fatis fuperque.* We meet with frequent Inftances of its being ufed in this Senfe. Thus in the Eunuch, Act 3. Sc. 1. 57.

Quando illud, qued tu das, expectat, atque amat,

Jamdudum te amat: jamdudum illi facile fit Quod dileat.

47 *Nempe.* *Si. fcilicet. Guyetus* in explaining this Paffage fancies that *Simo* in giving his Anfwer held out a little Bag of Money, as if he meant *id fcilicet fubvolo,* i. e. *Nummos volo.* But this is mere Conjecture, nor is there any thing in the Words that leads us to think he meant to fpeak of her Portion. *Pamphilus* had faid: Chremes *will eafily agree to let me have my Wife, as I have already enjoyed her.* Chremes replies, *The beft Reafon in the World, unlefs your Father is of another mind.* Pamphilus *then turns to his Father to know his Intentions.*

Nempe,

Cн. Nomen non convenit. Cr. fuit hercle aliud huic parvæ. Cн. quod, Crito?

Numquid meminifti? Cr. id quæro. Pa. egone hujus memoriam patiar meæ   40

Voluptati obftare, cùm ego poffim in hac re medicari mihi?   [Cr. ipfa eft. Cн. ea eft.

Non patiar. heus Chreme: quod quæris, Pafibula eft.

Pa. Ex ipsâ millies audivi. Si. omnes nos gaudere hoc, Chreme,   [quid reftat, pater.?

Te credo credere. Cн. ita me Dii ament, credo. Pa.

Si. Jamdudum res reduxit me ipfa in gratiam. Pa. ô lepidum patrem!   45

De uxore ita, ut poffedi, nihil mutat Chremes. Cн. caufa optuma eft: [dos, Pamphile, eft

Nifi quid pater aliud ait. Pa. nempe. Si. fcilicet. Cн. Decem talenta. Pa. accipio. Cн. propero ad filiam. eho mecum, Crito: [huc transferri jubes?

Nam illam me credo haud noffe. Si. cur non illam

Pa. Rectè admones. Davo ego iftuc dedam jam nego- ti. Si. non poteft.   50

Pa. Quî? Si. quia habet aliud magis ex fefe, & ma- jus. Pa. quidnam? Si. vinctus eft.

Pa. Pater, non rectè vinctus eft. Si. haud ita juffi. Pa. jube folvi, obfecro.

Pa. Nempe. Si. Scilicet. Cн. Pamphile, dos eft decem talenta. Pa. Accipio. Cн. Propero ad filiam: eho Crito, veni mecum; nam credo illam haud noffe me. Si. Cur non jubes illam tranf- ferri huc? Pa. Admones rectè. Ego jam dedam iftuc negoti Davo. Si. Davus non poteft. Pa. Quî? Si. Quia habet aliud negotium majus, & magis ex fefe. Pa. Quidnam? Si. Eft vinctus. Pa. Pater, non eft rectè vinctus. Si. Haud juffi vinci rectum ita. Pa. Obfecro, jube eum folvi.

ANNOTATIONS.

Nempe, quid dicis? What fay you to it? Simo anfwers, *Scilicet, the very fame,* I agree. Upon which Chremes finding all Parties had confented, names her Portion.

Ibid. *Dos, Pamphile, eft decem talenta.* As Commentators have generally neglected com- puting the true Value of ancient Sums, or at leaft have not done it with any tolerable Ac- curacy, I fhall here once for all take notice of the different Coins mentioned in *Terence,* and give at the fame time their true Efti- mation. We are to obferve therefore, that though the Plays are written in *Latin,* yet as the Scene is at *Athens,* both the Names and Value of the feveral Pieces of Money mentioned, are *Attic.* The loweft Coin in ufe at *Athens* was the *Obolus,* which was of Brafs, and equal in Value to a Penny-far- thing and one-fixth of our Money. Six Obo- li were equal to a Drachm, the loweft filver Coin in ufe, in Value Seven-pence-Three- farthings. An hundred Drachms make a

Mina, three Pounds four Shillings and Seven- pence. Sixty Mina's a Talent, one Hundred Ninety-three Pounds fifteen Shillings: Ten Talents therefore were equal to one Thou- fand nine Hundred and thirty-feven Pounds, ten Shillings of our Money; a very handfome Fortune in thofe Days.

50 *Davo ego iftuc dedam jam negoti.* I believe it will be hard to meet with another Inftance of the Verb *dedere,* in the Senfe which it bears here. The common Rule of Speech was *dare iftuc negoti* and not *dedere iftuc negoti:* for *dare* and *dedere* are Terms very different in Signification. *Terence* 'tis probable hazarded this Word to avoid ufing *dabo;* and the too great Conformity of Sound there would have been between that and the proper Name *Davo;* for *Davo iftuc dabo,* in the fame Verfe, muft have founded harfh and uncouth to the Ear. *Dacier.*

52 *Haud ita juffi.* The Underftanding of this Verfe depends upon attending to the Ambi-

Cн. Nomen non convenit. Cr. Fuit hercle aliud nomen huic parvæ virgini. Cн. Quod nomen, Crito? numquid me- minifti? Cr. Quæro id. Pa. Egone pa- tiar memoriam hujus obftare meæ volupta- ti, cùm ego poffim me- dicari mihi in hac re? Non patiar. Heus Chreme, nomen quod quæris eft Pafi- bula. Cr. Eft ipfa. Cн. Ea eft. Pa. Audivi millies ex ip- fa. Si. Credo, Chreme, te credere nos omnes gaudere ob hoc. Cн. Ita dii ament me, cre- do. Pa. Quid reftat, pater? Si. Res ipfa jamdudum reduxit me in gratiam. Pa. O lepidum patrem! Chremes mutat nibil de poffidenda uxore, ita ut poffedi. Cн. Caufa eft optima, nifi pater ait quid aliud.

Si. Well, let it be fo then.

Pamp. But immediately.

Si. I'm going in.

Pamp. O fortunate and happy Day !

ANNOTATIONS.

Ambiguity of the Word *recté*. For *Pam-* | anfwers him jokingly, *Non recbes, fed ut qua-*
philus meant the fame by it as if he had | *drupes vinctus eft*; and therefore fays; *baud ita*
faid, *non jufté vinctus eft*, but the Old Man | *jufti*; for we know his Command was *Qua-*
　　　　　　　　　　　　　　　　　　　 | *drupe-*

ACT V. SCENE V.

ARGUMENT.

Charinus *here comes upon the Stage, that he may learn from* Pamphilus, *what had happened:* Pamphilus *exults in his Felicity.*

PAMPHILUS, CHARINUS.

Char. I Come to fee what *Pamphilus* is doing, and here he is.

Pamp. Some may perhaps imagine that I don't believe what I now fay to be true, but at prefent I am at leaft willing to think it is true : I therefore hold the Gods to be immortal, becaufe they enjoy Pleafures which they can call their own. For I have now purchafed Immortality, if no Mifchance comes in to difturb my Joy. But whom fhall I chiefly wifh for at this time, to tell him of my good Fortune ?

Char. What Matter of Joy is this now ?

Pamp. I fee *Davus* : there is not in the World a Perfon I'd rather meet; becaufe I know of none that will rejoice more at my Happinefs.

ANNOTATIONS.

[1] *Provifo, quid agat Pamphilus.* At the End of the laft Scene *Simo* retires to give Orders for fetting *Davus* at liberty. *Pamphilus* in the mean time is expreffing his Joy for the good Fortune that had befallen him, and *Charinus* coming in the mean time, over-hears all.

[3] *Ego vitam deorum propterea fempiternam effe arbitror.* *Epicurus* faid that the Gods were immortal, becaufe they were exempt from all Cares, Dangers, and Misfortunes; but *Terence* here gives another Reafon, which expreffes better the Joy of *Pamphilus* : for he fays, that their Immortality proceeds from
　　　　　　　　　　　　　　　　　　 the

ACT V. SCENE VI.

ARGUMENT.

Davus *releafed, is in queft of* Pamphilus, *and meeting with him, both relate what had happened to them.* Charinus *overhearing that* Pamphilus *was to marry* Glycery, *rejoices; and takes Meafures for obtaining* Philumena.

DAVUS, PAMPHILUS, CHARINUS.

Davus. WHERE can this *Pamphilus* be ?

Pamp. Davus !

Dav. Who's that ?　　　　　　　　　　　　　　　　*Pamp.*

ANNOTATIONS.

[1] *Pamphilus ubinam He eft ?* *Davus* is now fet at liberty, and comes out looking | round him for *Pamphilus* : when they meet, he is informed of all that happened, and *Cha-*
　　　　　　　　　　　　　　　　　　 rinus

Si. Age, fiat. Pa. at matura. Si. eo intro. Pa. ò faustum & felicem diem.

Si. *Age fiat.*	
At matura.	Si.
Eo intro.	Pa. O

faustum & felicem diem.

ANNOTATIONS.

drupidem constringito. Donatus remarks, that this shews the Complaisance and Frankness of *Simo* to his Son, and how easily he grant-ed the Pardon that was ask'd for *Davus*, as already talking of him in a jesting Way.

ACTUS V. SCENA V.

ARGUMENTUM.

Charinis hic prodit in scenam, ut quæ acta suntè Pamphilo sciat: & Pamphilus de felicitate, quæ sibi obtigit, exultat.

CHARINUS, PAMPHILUS.

PRoviso, quid agat Pamphilus; atque eccum. PA. aliquis forsan me putet [verum lubet.
Non hoc putare verum : at mihi nunc sic esse hoc
Ego vitam Deorum propterea sempiternam esse arbitror, [mortalitas
Quòd voluptates eorum propriæ sunt. nam mihi imParta est, si nulla huic ægritudo gaudio intercesserit. 5
Sed quem ego potissimùm exoptem nunc mihi, cui hæc narrem, dari? [quem mallem, omnium :
Ch. Quid illuc gaudî est? Pa. Davom video. nemo est,
Nam hunc scio mea solidè solum gavisurum gaudia.

ORDO.

Ch. PRoviso quid Pamphilus agat : atque eccum. Pa. Forsan aliquis putet me non putare hoc esse verum : at nunc sic lubet mihi hoc esse verum. Ego arbitror vitam deorum esse propterea sempiternam, quod voluptates eorum sunt propriæ. Nam immortalitas est parta mibi, si nulla ægritudo intercesserit huic gaudio. Sed quem ego exoptem dari mibi potissimùm nunc, cui narrem hæc? Ch. Quid gaudii est illud? Pa. Video Davum. Est nemo omnium hominum, quem mallem videre : nam scio hunc solum gavisurum solidè propter meà gaudia.

ANNOTATIONS.

the Solidity and Duration of their Pleasures. The Precaution which *Pamphilus* takes in the Beginning of this Speech, *some may perhaps imagine*, was necessary to excuse the Liberty which in the Excess of his Joy he takes of giving a different Reason for the Immortality of the Gods, from that which the Philosophers before him had assign'd, and especially *Epicurus*, whose Memory was yet fresh, and his Sentiments generally received.

+ *Voluptates eorum propriæ sunt.* Perpetuæ, sempiternæ, quæ non sunt accommodatæ ad tempus, ac mutæ. See what we have said above Act 4. Scene 3. *Nibi:ne esse proprium cuiquam?*

ACTUS V. SCENA VI.

ARGUMENTUM.

Davus revinctus quærit ubinam si Pamphilus : eo invento, uterque de fortunis suis recenset. Supervenit Charinus, audit Pamphilum ducturum, quam amarat, Glycerium. Id gaudet, & ad Philumenæ nuptias accingitur.

DAVUS, PAMPHILUS, CHARINUS.

PAmphilus ubinam hic est? Pa. Dave! Da. quis

ORDO.

Da. UBinam est hic Pamphilus? Pa. Dave! Da. Quis

ANNOTATIONS.

*i*nus being present, enters into the Conversation, by which all is cleared up, and the Play concludes happily for the several Persons concerned in it.

Pamp. 'Tis I.

Dav. O *Pamphilus.*

Pamp. You don't know what has happen'd to me.

Dav. No really : but I know what has happen'd to myself.

Pamp. And I too.

Dav. 'Tis according to the common run of human Things, that you should hear of my Mishap, before I hear of your good Fortune.

Pamp. My *Glycery* has found her Parents.

Dav. Well done!

Char. Hah!

Pamp. Her Father's an intimate Friend of ours.

Dav. Who?

Pamp. *Chremes.*

Dav. Excellent!

Pamp. Nor is there now any Hindrance to my marrying her.

Char. Does he dream, I wonder, what he would wish to happen when awake?

Pamp. Then as for the Boy, *Davus.*

Dav. Ah say no more; he's Heav'ns distinguished Favourite.

Cha. I'm in a fair way! if this be true; I'll go speak to him.

Pamp. Who's this? *Charinus!* you come in the luckiest Time in the World.

Char. You're a happy Man.

Pamp. What have you heard any thing?

Char. I have heard all. Well, think of me now in your Prosperity. *Chremes* is yours, and I know he'll do whatever you desire.

Pamp. I'll remember you. And because it is too long to wait his coming out, follow me this way, for he is now with *Glycery.* Do you, *Davus,* run home, and make haste to send somebody to conduct her hence. Why do you stand? What do you linger for?

Dav. I'm a going. *(Turns to the Spectators.)* Don't wait their coming out: the Marriage will be concluded within, and whatever else remains, will be transacted within doors. One Clap, and farewel.

ANNOTATIONS.

7 *Num ille somniat ea, quæ vigilans voluit?* *Charinus* says this here, because we are very apt to dream of things that have before much engaged our Thoughts; for so *Lucretius,* Lib. 4. Ver. 959.

Et cui quisque fere studio devinctus adhæret,
Aut quibus in rebus multum sumus ante
morati,
Atque in qua ratione fuit contenta magis
mens;
In somnis ea 'em plerumque videmur abire.

It is probable that this Passage gave *Virgil* the Idea of that fine Line;

Credimus? An qui amant ipsi sibi somnia
fingunt? Ecl. 8. 108.

17 *Intus transfigetur, si quid est, quod restet.* This Passage has been evidently mistaken by the greater part of Commentators; which is the more surprizing, as *Donatus* might have easily guarded them against the Error. They have separated the Words *si quid est, quod restet,* from *intus transfigetur,* to join them with *plaudite.* 'If there is any thing further wanting, it is, Gentlemen, that you give us your Applause.' But that is by no means what the Poet would be understood to say, who intends: *si quid est, quod restet, illud intus transfigetur.* 'Whatever else remains, will be transacted within doors.' In fact there were yet a great many

homo'ft? PA. ego fum. DA. ô Pamphile.

PA. Nefcis quid mihi obtigerit. DA. certè: fed, quid mihi obtigerit, fcio. [fim nactus mali,

PA. Et quidem ego. DA. more hominum evenit, ut quod Priùs refcifceres tu, quàm ego, tibi quod evenit boni.

PA. Mea Glycerium fuos parentes reperit. DA. ô factum bene. 5

CH. Hem. PA. pater amicus fummus nobis. DA. quis? PA. Chremes. DA. narras probè.

PA. Nec mora ulla eft, quin jam uxorem ducam. CH. num ille fomniat [ah, define:

Ea, quæ vigilans voluit? PA. tum de puero, Dave? DA.

Solus eft, quem diligunt Dî. CH. falvus fum, fi hæc vera funt.

Conloquar. PA. quis homo eft? Charine, in tempore ipfo mî advenis. 10

CH. Bene factum. PA. hem, audifti? CH. omnia. age, me in tuis fecundis refpice, [omnia.

Tuus eft nunc Chremes. facturum, quæ voles, fcio

PA. Memini: atque adeo longum eft, nos illum ex-fpectare, dum exeat. [abi domum,

Sequere hac me intus ad Glycerium nunc. tu, Dave,

Propere accerfe, hinc qui auferant eam. quid ftas? quid ceffas? DA. eo. 15

Ne exfpectetis, dum exeant huc: intus defpondebitur

Intus tranfigetur, fi quid eft, quod reftet. Plaudite.

CALLIOPIUS RECENSUI.

homo eft? PA. Ego fum. DA. O Pamphile. PA. Nefcis quid obtigerit fcio quid obtigerit mihi. PA. Et quidem ego. DA. Evenit more hominum, ut tu priùs refcifceres quod mali ego fum nactus, quàm ego refcifcerem illud boni quod evenit tibi. PA. Mea Glycerium reperit fuos parentes. DA. O bene factum. CH. Hem, PA, Pater ejus, eft fummus amicus nobis. DA. Quis? PA. Chremes. DA. Narras probè. PA. Nec eft ulla mora, quin jam ducam eam uxorem. CH. Num ille fomniat ea, quæ vigilans voluit? PA. Tum, Dave, de puero. DA. Ah, define: eft folus quem dii diligunt. CH. Sum falvus, fi hæc funt vera. Colloquar. PA. Quis homo eft? Charine, advenis mihi in ipfo tempore. CH. Bene factum.

PA. Hem audiviſti? CH. Audivo omnia. Age, refpice me in tuis rebus fecundis. Chremes eft nunc tuus. Scio eum effe facturum omnia, quæ volet. PA. Memini: atque eft adeo longum. nos expectare illum, dum exeat. Sequere me hac intus ad Glycerium nunc. Tu, Dave, abi domum. Propere accerfe aliquos, qui auferant eam Glycerium hinc. Quid ftas? DA. Eo. Spectatores: ne expectetis, dum exeant huc: defpondebitur intus: fi eft quid, quod reſtet, tranfigetur intus. Plaudite.

ANNOTATIONS.

many things to be done: the Marriage of Charinus: and the deciding the Pretenfions of Cito, but thefe could not be brought upon the Scene, becaufe the Spectators are not fufficiently interefted in them, and therefore they muft have made the Action appear languifhing.

Ibid. Plaudite. Almoft all ancient Copies have Ω before plaudite here, and before vos valete & plaudite in other Plays. Learned Men are not agreed as to what muft have been intended by it. Some are of opinion, that inftead of Omega, it was at firft o o, which might eafily by degrees degenerate into ω; and that thefe two o o ftood for ὅλος ὄχλος, the whole Troop or Company of Players, by which we are made to underftand,

that plaudite was faid by all the Comedians together. But this has not any probable Foundation, nay we know that plaudite was not faid by the whole Company, but moft commonly by the Actor who fpoke laft, or the Chorus. I fhould rather be apt to think, that if Omega is to be interpreted in any fuch manner as this, it may be defigned for the firft Letter of Ωδὸς, which is Greek for Cantor, who, as we learn from Horace, was the Perfon that at the End of the Play demanded the Applaufe of the Audience; for fo in his Art of Poetry, Ver. 154.

Si plauforis eges aulæa manentis, & ufque Seffuri, donec cantor, Vos plaudite, dicat.

But it is more likely that Omega was added by Tranfcribers and ſtands for Finis: for as

Alpha

ANNOTATIONS.

Alpha the firſt Letter of the *Greek* Alphabet was often uſed to mark the Beginning of a Work, ſo *Omega* the laſt, mark'd the End.

After *plaudite* we meet in all the ancient Copies of *Terence* with theſe Words, *Calliopius recenſui*, and ſome have fancied that this *Calliopius* was one of the Actors. This is the Reaſon that even in the firſt Editions of *Terence*, we ſee the Figure of *Calliopius* among thoſe of the other Comedians, but we muſt excuſe this Error in an Age which ſeems to have had but little Light into theſe Matters. Theſe two Words *Calliopius recenſui*, as Madam *Dacier* has well obſerv'd, ſignify, I *Calliopius* have reviewed and corrected this Piece. And this comes from the Manner of ancient Critics, who reviewed Manuſcripts with Care. When they had read over and corrected any Work, they always put their Name at the End of it. We have a remarkable Proof of this in the Funeral Oration which *Ariſtides* the Orator made upon his Preceptor *Alexander*, where he ſays, among other things, that in all the Books which he had read over and corrected, we ſee at the End his Name and that of his Country: *and indeed ſays, he has left behind him this Teſtimony of his Love for his Country; for after putting his own Name at the End of a Work, he always took care to add alſo that of his Country.* That is, this *Alexander* was not contented with putting *Alexander recenſui;* but he put *Alexander Cutiæus recenſui.*

P U B-

PUBLII
TERENTII
EUNUCHUS.

TERENCE's
EUNUCH.

TERENCE's
EUNUCH.

The TITLE.

THIS COMEDY WAS EXHIBITED AT THE ME-
GALENSIAN GAMES, WHEN L. POSTHUMIUS
ALBINUS, AND L. CORNELIUS MERULA
WERE CURULE ÆDILES. IT WAS ACTED
BY THE COMPANIES OF L. AMBIVIUS TUR-
PIO, AND L. ATTILIUS PRÆNESTINUS. FLAC-
CUS THE FREEDMAN OF CLAUDIUS COM-
POSED THE MUSIC, WHICH WAS PERFORM-
ED ON TWO RIGHT-HANDED FLUTES. IT
IS FROM THE GREEK OF MENANDER, AND
WAS ACTED TWICE, UNDER THE CONSUL-
SHIP OF M. VALERIUS, AND C. FANNIUS.

ANNOTATIONS.

What we have said upon the Title to the *Andrian*, will serve sufficiently for all the other Titles of *Terence's* Plays. We may take notice here however, that by some neglect of Transcribers, the Price which the *Ædiles* paid for this Comedy is omitted in the Title; for we are told expresly by *Suetonius*, that it was anciently marked in it. His Words are; *Eunuchus quidem bis die acta est, meruitque pretium quanta nulla antea cujusdam comœdia, id est, octo millia nummùm, propterea summa quoque titulo adscribitur.* "The *Eunuch* was "acted twice in one Day, and the "Poet received a greater Sum for "it, than had ever before been given "for any Comedy, for they allowed "him eight thousand Sesterces, and "on this account, the Sum was "marked in the Title." *Dacier.*

[1] *Tibiis duabis dextris.* To understand this, we must refer the Reader to what is said in the Beginning of this Work, concerning the Music of the *Roman* Stage. I have only to observe here, that *Donatus* tells us, the Music was performed *Tibiis duabus, dextra & sinistra.* But if there be any thing in this, it must be understood only of the first Representation, for afterwards they made use of two equal Flutes.

[2] *Græca Menandru. Menandru* is here a *Greek* Genitive, instead of *Menandrou,* Μενάνδρε.

[3] *Acta II.* We learn from *Donatus,* that this Play was acted thrice. *Hæc edita tertium est, & pronunciata Terentii Eunuchus, quippe jam adulta commendatione poetæ, ac meritus ingenii notioribus populo.* "This Piece "was represented thrice, and entitled "the

P. TERENTII
EUNUCHUS.

TITULUS feu DIDASCALIA.

ACTA LUDIS MEGALENSIBUS, L. POSTHUMIO ALBINO, L. CORNELIO MERULA ÆDILIBUS CURULIBUS. EGERE L. AMBIVIUS TURPIO, L. ATTILIUS PRÆNESTINUS. MODULAVIT FLACCUS CLAUDII, TIBIIS DUABUS DEXTRIS¹. GRÆCA MENANDRU². ACTA II³. M. VALERIO, C. FANNIO COSS⁴.

Menandru, acta II. M. Valerio, C. Fannio Confulibus.

ORDO. Hæc Comœdia fuit *acta Ludis Megalenfibus, L. Pofthumio Albino, L. Cornelio Merula, Ædilibus Curulibus. L. Ambivius Turpio, L. Attilius, Prænestinus egere. Flaccus libertus Claudii modulavit, tibiis duabus, dextris.* Eft *Græca*

ANNOTATIONS.

" the *Eunuch* of *Terence*, the Reputation of the Poet being very high, and his Merit generally known to the People." One is, therefore at a lofs to know how *Acta* II. came to be inferted in the Title. There is certainly fomething wanting here, and to compleat the Senfe, we muft read *Acta* II. *die acta bis die.* That it was play'd twice in one Day. And this agrees with what *Suetonius* fays in the forecited Paffage: *Eunuchus quidem bis die acta est.* The Paffage, however, quoted from *Donatus*, acquaints us with a Circumftance very fingular, and worthy of Notice: that in publifhing and entitling the Plays of a new Poet, who was but little known, and whofe Reputation was not yet eftablifhed, the Name of the Comedy was put firft, and after that the Name of the Poet: thus *Andria Terentii*, that the Play might ferve to make the Poet known. But when the Author was generally approved, and his Reputation fettled, in publifhing or entitling his Pieces, they put his own Name before that of the Play, as in this Inftance, *Terentii Eunuchus. Dacier.*

⁴ *M. Valerio, C. Fannio Cofs.* That is, in the Year of *Rome* 592 and 160 before the Birth of *Chrift*, five Years after the firft Reprefentation of the *Andrian. Donatus* obferves, that there runs thro' this whole Piece a remarkable Equality of Genius, that he every where diverts us with his Pleafantries, nor difcovers in any part that his Fund of Entertainment was drained.

Th⁰

The ARGUMENT to the EUNUCH, from MURETUS.

A Certain Citizen of Athens had a Daughter whose Name was Pamphilia, and a Son called Chremes. Pamphilia while yet but an Infant was carried off from Sunium by a Band of Robbers, who sold her to a Rhodian Merchant: He carrying her to Rhodes, made a Present of her to a Courtezan, whom he was at that time very much in love with. She, after receiving the Girl, brought her up with the same Care and Tenderness, as her own Daughter Thais, insomuch that every body look'd upon them as real Sisters. Thais, who was somewhat older, being now arrived at the Age, when she might render herself agreeable to the Men, following, as for the most part happens, her Mother's way of Life, came to Athens in company with a Stranger, who, dying after some time, left her his Heiress. Mean time a Soldier, by Name Thraso, falls in love with her, who, after he had cohabited with her for some time, set out for Caria. During this Period, Thais's Mother was dead, and her Brother had exposed Pamphila to Sale, hoping, that as she was a great Beauty, and perfectly skill'd in Musick, he might dispose of her to good Advantage. It happened, that at this very time Thais's Lover, the Soldier, was at Rhodes; who, knowing nothing of what we have above related, bought her, that he might present her to his Mistress at his return to Athens. Thais, after the Departure of the Soldier, had aim'd at securing another Lover, and attached to her Phædria an Athenian Youth, the Son of Laches. She had moreover got some Hints with regard to Pamphila, and having conversed several times with her Brother Chremes, imagined she had pretty good Reason to believe that the Girl, who had been educated with her at home, was that young Man's sister. They therefore earnestly desired that she might have it in her power to restore Pamphila to her Relations, and by that means both do a good Office to the Girl, and secure her own Fortune by the Patronage of her Relations. The Soldier returns, but hearing of her Engagements with Phædria, resolves not to present her with the Girl, unless he is first discarded. Thais is at a loss what Course to take, for she lov'd Phædria from her Soul, but imagines that to recover Pamphila, she ought to stick at nothing. At length, hoping with her self, that she might easily justify her Conduct to him whom she had offended; to please the Soldier, she excludes Phædria. Next day sending for him, who was greatly offended at her Behaviour, she endeavours to clear herself, and after many Intreaties prevails with him to let Thraso seemingly have the preference, for the Space only of two Days; assuring him, that as soon as she was in possession of the Girl, she would throw him off altogether. Phædria, that he might bear this two Days Absence with less Regret, resolves to go into the Country, and recommends to Parmeno to carry to Thais, the Eunuch and Ethiopian Girl, whom he had bought for her.

Mean

M. Ant. Mureti ARGUMENTUM.

*C*IVIS quidam *Atheniensis filiam, cui Pamphilæ, & filium, cui
Chremeti nomen erat, habuit. Ex iis Pamphilam, adhuc
infantulam prædones rapuere e Sunio, & mercatori cuidam Rhodio
vendidere: qui, Rhodum advectam, meretrici quam amabat, dono dedit. Hæc acceptam puellam pari cura ac studio, cum Thaide filia
cœpit educare: nemo ut esset, qui non utrumque ex ipsa genitam esse ar-
bitraretur. Thais, quæ grandiuscula erat, quum ad eam ætatem per-
venisset, ut viris placere posset, maternam, ut fit, vivendi rationem in-
secuta, cum hospite quodam Athenas venit, qui eam postea moriens
hæredem reliquit. Interea miles, Thraso nomine, ad eam adjecit
animum: quumque cum ea per aliquod tempus consuevisset, in Cariam
profectus est. Thaidis mater per eos dies vitam morte commutaverat,
fraterque ipsius Pamphilam venalem proposuerat, sperans eam, quod &
formosa esset, & fidibus sciret, præclare a se venditum ire. Forte accidit, ut eo ipso tempore Thaidis amator miles esset Rhodi: qui, harum omnium rerum inscius, Pamphilam emit; ut esset, quod amicæ, A-
thenas reversus, dono daret. Thais, profecto milite, aliam conditionem quæsierat, adjunxeratque sibi Phædriam, adolescentem Atheniensem,
Lachetis filium. Inaudiverat interem etiam aliquid de Pamphilia, jamque cum fratre ipsius Chremete, aliquoties collocuta, eo pervenerat, ut
non dubiis indiciis intelligeret, sororem illius esse, quæ secum in maternis
ædibus educata foret. Summopere cupiebat igitur occasionem sibi aliquam
dari, qua Pamphilam suis restitueret, eodemque facto, & puellam
summo afficeret beneficio, & propinquorum illius amicitia fortunas
constabiliret suas. Redit miles: sed, quum cognosset de amore Phædriæ, puellam se, nisi eo repulso, negat daturum. Thais, quid ageret,
nescire: nam & Phædriam amabat ex animo, & Pamphilæ recipiendæ
gratia quidvis sibi faciundum putabat: tandem, quum sperarat, se
postea facile consilium suum ei ipsi, cujus animum offenderat probatu-
ram; Phædriam, ut militi gratificaretur, excludit. Postridie, accer-
sito ei, atque ægre ferenti, tandem se purgat, multisque precibus ab eo
impetrat, ut, per biduum, priores partem habere Thrasonem sineret:
ubi primum eripuisset puellam, nihil sibi cum illo amplius fore. Phædria, ut hujus bidui molestiam æquiore animo ferret, rus sibi abeun-
dum esse statuit: itaque abiens, mandat Parmenoni, ut Eunuchum &
Æthiopissam, ad Thaidem, cui eos emerat, duceret. Pamphilam, quum*

ex

Mean time as Pamphila *is conducted from* Thraso's *House to* Thais, *she is accidentally seen by* Chærea, Phædria's *younger Brother, who is so violently smitten with her, that he values not what he does, if he can but enjoy her ; nor could be at ease, 'till he had prevailed with* Parmeno *to lead him to* Thais *in the Eunuch's Dress. To conclude,* Thais *having gone to sup with the Soldier,* Chærea *in the mean time ravishes* Pamphila. *This occasions a world of Disturbance, 'till at length the whole Affair being cleared up,* Thais *is received under the Protection of* Laches, *and* Pamphila *being acknowledged by her Relations,* Chærea *marries her.* Thraso, *who had long been the Dupe of all Parties, is at length by means of* Gnatho *his Parasite, admitted to share of the Courtezan's Favours.*

The

ex ædibus Thrafonis ad Thaidem deduceretur, confpicatus in via Phæ-driæ frater natu minor Chærea, ita ejus amore flagrare cœpit, nihil ut penfi haberet, dum ea potiretur: neque prius conquievit, quam ejus res caufa, ad Thaidem pro Eunucho deductus eft. Quid plura? Thaide ad cœnam cum milite profecta, virgini a Chærea per vim vitium offer-tur. Turbæ undique miferabiles, donec, tota re patefacta, Thais a Lachete in fidem & clientelam recipitur. Chærea agnitam Pamphilam ducit uxorem. Thrafo diu illufus, tandem in amoris meretricii partem, Gnathonis parafiti opera, admittitur.

K   PER-

PERSONS *of the* PLAY.

The Speaker of the PROLOGUE.

PHÆDRIA, a young Gentleman, the Son of *Laches*, in love with *Thais*.

PARMENO, Servant to *Phædria*.

THAIS, a Courtezan.

GNATHO, a Parasite.

CHÆREA, the younger Brother of *Phædria*, in love with *Pamphila*.

THRASO, a Soldier, Rival to *Phædria*.

PYTHIAS, Maid to *Thais*.

CHREMES, a young Gentleman, Brother to *Pamphila*.

ANTIPHO, a young Gentleman, *Chærea*'s Friend.

DORIAS, Maid to *Thais*.

DORUS, an *Eunuch*.

SANGA, one of *Thraso*'s Subalterns.

SOPHRONA, *Pamphila*'s Nurse.

LACHES, an old Man, the Father of *Phædria* and *Chærea*.

MUTES.

SIMALIO,
DONAX, } Subalterns of *Thraso*.
SYRISCUS,

PAMPHILA, a young Lady, the Sister of *Chremes*.

The

DRAMATIS PERSONÆ.

PROLOGUS.
PHÆDRIA, *adolescens, Lachetis filius, & amater Thaidis.*
PARMENO, *servus Phædriæ.*
THAIS, *meretrix.*
GNATHO, *parasitus*
CHÆREA, *adolescens, amator Pamphilæ, & frater Phædriæ.*
THRASO, *miles, rivalis Phædriæ.*
PYTHIAS, *ancilla Thaidis.*
CHREMES, *adolescens, frater Pamphilæ.*
ANTIPHO, *adolescens, amicus Chæreæ.*
DORIAS, *ancilla Thaidis.*
DORUS, *eunuchus.*
SANGA, *servus Thrasonis.*
SOPHRONA, *nutrix Pamphilæ.*
LACHES, *senex, pater Phædriæ & Chæreæ.*

PERSONÆ MUTÆ.

SIMALIO,
DONAX, } *Thrasonis servi.*
SYRISCUS,
PAMPHILA, *adolescentula, Chremetis soror.*

            PRO-

The PROLOGUE.

ARGUMENT.

He inveighs according to his usual manner against his Adver-
sary; whom, by enumerating some of his Errors, he exposes
to the greatest Ridicule and Contempt. He afterwards de-
fends the Poet from the Charge of having stolen the greatest
part of his Fable from Nævius *and* Plautus. *Finally, he*
begs the Attention of the Spectators, during the Representation
of the Play.

IF there is in the World a Man, who makes it his Study to please
all Persons of Worth, and give Offence to none, among these
our Poet boldly professes his Name. At the same time if any
one thinks that I have spoken against him in too free and severe a
manner, let him reflect that it is only an Answer, and not an Attack, as he gave the first Offence : who, though a faithful translator,
yet by ill contriving the Scenes, has, out of excellent *Greek* Plays,
made but very sorry *Latin* ones. This same Poet lately gave us *the*
Apparition

ANNOTATIONS.

¹ *Bonis quam plurimis.* As this Prologue has very much engaged the Attention of Commentators, and the Explications
they give of several Passages in it differ considerably, I shall enlarge the more in my Observations, that the Reader may have a clear
View of the several Opinions, and by that
means be the better enabled to examine
them, and judge for himself. In the Passage now referred to, *Eugraphius* separates
the Words, understanding them thus : *Pla-*
cere bonis potius, quam plurimis, sive malis ;
because Men of Worth are generally few in
comparison of those of a contrary Character.
But there does not seem any Necessity for so
nice a Division here : besides, by reading the
Words jointly *quamplurimis bonis,* they
stand the better in opposition to those that
follow, *minime multos lædere* ; where by the
by we may observe, that to render the *An-*
tithesis more compleat, some think we ought
to supply *malos* here. *Placere quamplurimis*
bonis, & lædere minime multos malos. Although I have not affected a strictly literal
Translation of these Words, I have yet
taken care to preserve the *Antithesis* in its
full Force.
⁴ *Tum si quis.* This is to be understood
of the same *Luscus Lavinius,* against whom
the Prologue to the *Andrian* was writ. As
he still persisted in his Rivalship, and did all

in his power to discredit our Poet, he seems
in this Prologue to have given in some measure a loose to his Resentment ; insomuch,
that it is easy to discover, through the whole
of it, the Anxiety of the Author for his
new Play.
⁷ *Qui bene vertendo, & easdem scribendo*
male. Here Interpreters have been strangely perplexed, and each strenuously maintains
his own Sense. Some think that by *bene*
vertere, we are to understand his Choice of
Originals, as if he commonly picked out the
best Plays, but murdered them in the
Translation ; which seems to receive some
Countenance from the next Verse : *Ex*
Græcis bonis Latinas fecit non bonas. This
Interpretation is favoured by *Eugraphius,*
who says, *bene vertit, de Græco in Latinum :*
male scribit, male verba componit. Guyetus
and *Boeclerus* read, *Qui male vertendo,* &c.
Donatus, and after him, Madam *Dacier,*
contend that *bene* is to be understood here
valde ; but by this, *bene* and *male* are opposed to one another only in sound, than
which nothing can be more flat, or unworthy
of *Terence.* Whatever Difficulty may appear in these Words now, I persuade myself, that it is owing wholly to our Ignorance
of Persons and Things, and that, at the time
when this Prologue was recited, they were
understood by all ; for no Writer seems to
h. v.

PROLOGUS.

ARGUMENTUM.

Invehitur suo more in adversarium, quem, quibusdam erratis ipsius commemorandis, in quam maximum potest odium atque invidiam adducit. Deinde poetam defendit, ab eo furti insimulatum; qui dicebat hanc fabulam ex Nævio & Plauto magna ex parte ablatam esse. Tandem attentionem postulat ad fabulam agendam.

SI quisquam est, qui placere se studeat bonis
  Quam plurimis, & minime multos lædere;
  In his poeta hic nomen profitetur suum.
Tum si quis est, qui dictum in se inclementiùs
Existimavit esse, sic existimet,
Responsum, non dictum esse, quia læsit prior,
Qui bene vertendo, & easdem scribendo malè, ex
Græcis bonis Latinas fecit non bonas.

ORDO.
SI est quisquam qui studeat se placere quamplurimis bonis, & lædere minime multos, hic poeta profitetur suum nomen in his. Tum si 5 *est quis, qui existimavit quid esse dictum inclementius in se, existimet sic: illud*

esse responsum, non dictum, quia ille læsit prior, qui bene vertendo fabulas, & scribendo easdem malè, fecit Latinas comœdias non bonas, ex Græcis bonis.

ANNOTATIONS.

have more despised all Affectation of Phrase, than our Poet. Let us see, therefore, whether without turning them into a mere Quibble, we can hit upon any consistent Meaning. *Bentley*, of all that I have seen, seems to bid fairest for it. *Bene vertere*, says he, is to render faithfully, to translate Word for Word from the *Greek*. But *bene vertere* in this Sense, is *male scribere Latinè* for the Genius of the two Languages is very different. *Terence*, on the contrary, took that liberty in translating, that his Plays had a native Air of the Language in which he writ, and did not seem so properly translated from the *Greek*, as originally composed at *Rome*. Whereas *Lavinius Luscus*, by too servile an Adherence to the Original, out of good *Greek* Plays, made but very sorry *Latin* ones. From this Hint, I believe, we may come pretty near to the Sense of this hitherto perplexed Verse. *Lavinius*, by what we may learn from *Terence's* Prologues, was a Poet at this time in considerable Reputation, and as the Comic Poets seldom brought upon the Stage any thing of their own, but employed themselves chiefly in translating from the *Greek*, we may presume he had gained a great Character in this way. But to be able to form some Idea of his Manner, we must have recourse to the Prologue of the *Andrian*. We learn there, that he exclaimed against *Terence*, for throwing two Fables into one; and our Poet speaking of his Manner, and that of his Copiers, calls it *istorum obscuram diligentiam*; from all which we see, that they valued themselves upon the Accuracy of their Translations, and a certain formal Correctness, which our Poet disclaims in the same Prologue. It was probably by boasting of this, that he had obtained the Applause of a People but in the Infancy of Politeness, and whose Taste was not as yet exactly formed. Our Poet would not contradict an Approbation so general, and therefore allows him the Praise of being a faithful Translator, and perhaps that too, more out of Complaisance to the general Voice, than that he really thought he deserved it: but at the same time, when he ventured to add any thing of his own, or change the Disposition of the Plot, *Terence* insinuates, that he was very unhappy in his manner of ranging and disposing the Parts, and spoiled all by his ill Contrivance. That this must be the meaning of *easdem scribendo male*, is plain from what follows; for the Poet immediately proceeds to give an Instance of his preposterous Manner of disposing the Parts of his Play. He had lately given a Translation of the *Phasma* of *Menander*, and in the account of a Suit relating to a Treasure, had contrary to Custom and the Rules of all Courts, brought in the Defendant pleading

K 3   his

Apparition of *Menander*, and in the Story of a Treafure, makes him, from whom the Gold is demanded, firft plead his Title to it, before the Plaintiff, who makes the Demand, declares, on what Pretence he lays claim to his Treafure, or how it came to be lodg'd in his Father's Tomb. Let him not therefore hereafter deceive himfelf, or thus fancy in his own Mind : I now go off with Applaufe, and have executed my Part with Honour, he can object nothing againft me. Again, I advife him not to perfift in this Error, but that he ceafe his Impertinences. I have a great deal more to fay, which I fupprefs at prefent, but which I am determined to produce afterwards, if he goes on to provoke me as he has done already. After the Ædiles had bought the *Eunuch* of *Menander*, which we are now to act before you, he obtained Leave to be prefent at its Rehearfal. When the Magiftrates were come, the Play began. He bawls out, that a Thief, and not a Poet had given that Piece, and that yet he had not deceived them ; for it was an old Play, *viz.* the *Colax* of *Nævius* and *Plautus* ; and that the Characters of both the Soldier and Parafite were taken from thence : If there be any Fault in this, it is a Fault of Ignorance in the Poet, who had no Defign of ftealing from another. That it is fo, you yourfelves will foon be able to judge. The *Colax* is a Play of *Menander* ; in this there is a Parafite

Colax,

A N N O T A T I O N S.

his Title to it, before the Plaintiff had explained his Pretenfions, and opened the Grounds of his Demand. We are, therefore, carefully to diftinguifh between *bene vertere*, and *bene fcribere*. He may be faid *bene vertere*, who does the Office of a faithful Tranflator, keeps near to his Author, and renders his Senfe juftly. But *bene fcribere* is quite a different thing, and refpects the Difpofition and Contrivance in thofe Liberties, which the Poets of that Age often took, of altering the Form of the Original, and adding fometimes entire Scenes of their own.

9 *Idem Mnandri Phafma*, &c. This is the Title of one of *Menander*'s Comedies, the Argument of which is thus given us by Madam *Dacier* : A Woman, who had been privately brought to bed of a Daughter, by one of her Lovers, married afterwards a Man who had a Son by a former Wife. As fhe loved her Daughter tenderly, fhe caufed her to be educated in a Houfe contiguous to her own, and, that fhe might not be wholly deprived of the privilege of feeing her, had an Opening made in the Partition that feparated the two Houfes. This Opening fhe carefully concealed ; and placed an Altar near it, and decked it with Garlands, and green Branches, that it might look like a confecrated Place, whither fhe daily went to her Devotions. The Son, of whom I have

fpoken, obferving his Mother-in-Law one Day, at her pretended Devotion, faw this Daughter, who was it feems an extraordinary Beauty, and whom he took for an Apparition. But, by degrees, coming to the Knowledge of her being but a Mortal, his Paffion for her became fo violent, that it would admit of no Cure, but Marriage.

10 *Atque in Thefauro.* Commentators are here divided in their Sentiments, whether this *Treafure* was a Comedy different from the *Phafma*, or only a Part of it. *Bently* maintains the firft, and gives the Arguments of each, from which he infers, that they had no relation to each other. I am, however, more inclined to follow the other Notion. *Terence* had been fpeaking of his Adverfary's Blunders in the Difpofition of the Parts of his Plays, and mentions the *Apparition* as an Inftance of it, where he had brought in the Story of a Treafure, which he had handled in a manner contrary to all Rules. Unlefs we admit of this Interpretation, one is at a lofs what to think of our Poet's mentioning the *Apparition*, at all, which feems here to be a detached Verfe, without any Defign ; but by confidering it in the Light before-mentioned, the Senfe is full and compleat. I am, therefore, perfuaded that this Incident relating to the Treafure, was not in the Original of *Menander*, but added by the Tranflator, who by his pre-

pofterous

Idem Menandri Phasma nunc nuper dedit,
Atque in Thesauro scripsit, causam dicere   10
Priùs unde petitur, aurum quare sit suum, .
Quàm illic, qui petit, unde is sit thesaurus sibi,
Aut unde in patrium monumentum pervenerit.
Dehinc ne frustretur ipse se, aut sic cogitet ;
Defunctus jam sum, nihil est quod dicat mihi: 15
Is ne erret, moneo, & desinat lacessere : .
Habeo alia multa, quæ nunc condonabitur :
Quæ proferentur post, si perget lædere
Ita, ut facere instituit. nunc quam acturi sumus
Menandri Eunuchum, postquam ædiles emerunt,   20
Perfecit, sibi ut inspiciundi esset copia.
Magistratus cùm ibi adessent, occepta est agi.
Exclamat, furem, non poetam fabulam
Dedisse, & nil dedisse verborum tamen :
Colacem esse Nævî, & Plauti veterem fabulam :   25
Parasiti personam inde ablatam, & militis.
Si id est peccatum, peccatum imprudentiâ est
Poetæ, non quò furtum facere studuerit.
Id ita esse, vos jam judicare poteritis.
Colax Menandri est : in eâ est parasitus Colax,   30

Idem (*Lavinius*) *nunc nuper dedit Phasma Menandri : atque in Thesauro scripsit, eum unde aurum petitur prius dicere causam, quare aurum sit suum, quam illic, qui petit aurum causam dixisset, unde is sit thesaurus sibi, aut unde pervenerit in patrium monumentum. Dehinc, ne ipse frustretur se, aut cogitet sic : Ego sum jam defunctus, est nihil quod dicat mihi. Moneo eum, ne is erret, & u: desinat lacessere me. Habeo multa alia, quæ condonabuntur nunc, sed quæ proferentur post, si perget lædere ita, ut instituit facere. Nam postquam ædiles emerunt Eunuchum Menandri,*

quam sumus acturi nunc, perfecit ut esset sibi copia inspiciundi eam. Cum magistratus adessent ibi, comœdia est occepta agi. Exclamat furem, non poetam dedisse fabulam, & tamen dedisse nil verborum; esse nempe veterem fabulam, viz. Colacem Nævii & Plauti, personam parasiti & militis esse ablatam inde. Si id est peccatum, peccatum est imprudentiâ poetæ, non quo studuerit facere furtum ; & vos jam poteritis judicare id esse ita. Colax est comœdia Menandri ; in eâ est Colax parasitus.

ANNOTATIONS.

posterous Management gave a Proof, with how little Judgment he conducted, when he ventured to depart from his Author. Madam *Dacier*, who gives this Passage the same turn that I have done, thus explains the Incident of *the Treasure: Luscius* had brought into his Play a Story of a Treasure, which had been concealed in the Tomb of the young Gentleman's Father, mentioned in the preceding Remark. The Field in which this Tomb was, had been bought by an old Man. Once, when the young Man sent to offer Libations to his Father, the Servant coming to the Tomb, could not open it, and was obliged to seek help of the old Man, who had bought the Field. When it was opened they found a Treasure concealed in it, which the old Man seized, pretending that he had put it there, during the Wars. The young Man opposed this, and demanded back the Money. In the Comedy was to be seen the Pleadings of both Parties, and the Defendant was brought in first, arguing the Case. The two first Lines of his Plea are still preserved to us by an old Scholiast, and I think first quoted by Dr. *Bentley.*

Athenienses : bellum cum Rhodiensibus
Quod fuerit, quid ego prædicem ?

What may have led some into the Mistake of thinking, that *the Treasure* was the Name of a distinct Piece, is, that in the Prologue to the *Trinummus* of *Plautus*, there is mention made of a Comedy called, *The Treasure.* But that Piece was written by *Philemo*, not *Menander.*

Huic nomen Græce est Thesauro fabulæ :
Philemo scripsit, Plautus vertit barbare.

24 *Nil dedisse verborum tamen.* The most general Meaning given to these Words is, that the Poet had not deceived them, because in stealing the greatest Part of his Play from *Nævius* and *Plautus*, the Audience would be better entertained, than if the Piece had been wholly his own. But *Bentley* rather thinks it a Joke of *Luscius* upon the Poet ; *Sententia est,* says he, *fabulam dedisse, quod ipsum est quodammodo verba dare, fallere : & verba tamen non dedisse, nempe Luscio quo minus deprehenderet furtum factum ex Colace Plauti.*

25 *Colacem esse Nævi, & Plauti,* The Text and Version are here according to the common Reading, but *Bentley* observes that the

Colax, and a vain-boasting Soldier: the Poet does not deny that he introduced these Characters into his *Eunuch* from the *Greek*; but then he positively denies that he ever knew of those Plays being rendred into *Latin*. But if it is not permitted us to give the same Characters, that have been given by others before us, how comes it that we are allowed to represent Slaves running *in great Haste*, to paint virtuous Matrons, jilting Whores, a guzzling Parasite or vainglorious Soldier, to shew a Child exposed, an old Man deceived by a knavish Servant, or to set before you Love, Hatred, Suspicions? In fine, nothing can be said now, that may not have been said before. Wherefore it is but just that you know thus much, and pardon modern Poets, if they take the same Liberties which the Ancients have taken before them. Observe therefore, and attend with Silence, that you may be able to form a right Judgment of our Poet's *Eunuch*.

ANNOTATIONS.

the *Colax* of *Nævius* is no where mentioned, the *Colax* of *Plautus* is cited by *Nonius Marcellus*. *Nævius* was before *Plautus*, and therefore could not write in conjunction with him, and the mention that was supposed to be made in the last Age of the *Colax* of *Nævius*, by *Nonius* and *Priscian*, is found by more ancient Copies to belong to *Nævius*. Besides, if *Terence* borrowed the Characters of the *Parasite* and Soldier from *Plautus* and *Nævius*; *Plautus* must have borrowed from *Nævius*, so that the Accusation will carry along with it also an Apology. He therefore proposes to correct the Passage thus:
  Colacem esse nempe, *Plauti veterem fabulam:*
  Parasiti personam inde ablatam & militis.
Colax is a *Greek* Word, signifying a Flatterer, whence that Name was sometimes given to Plays, and the *Parasite*, who made the chief Character in it.
  33 *Eas fabulas factas prius Latinas scisse sese, id vero pernegat.* It seems almost in-

credible, that *Terence* should be ignorant of these two Plays, writ by *Nævius* and *Plautus*; but our Wonder will abate, when we reflect that all the Learning of that time, was confined to Manuscripts, which as they were but few in number, and not common, could not be in the hands of many People. Besides, as it was not then so general a Custom to collect, into one Volume, all the Works of the same Poet, one might see some of his Pieces, without seeing the whole.
  35 *Quod si personis ifdem uti aliis non licet.* The chief Difficulty of this Passage consists in the word *aliis*, whether it is to come in after *licet*; *Quod si non licet aliis poetis*, or to be joined with *isdem*; *uti isdem aliis*, for *uti iisdem ac alii utuntur*. I incline rather to the last.
  36 *Qui magi' licet currentes servos scribere.* In fact, the Characters of a *Parasite*, or a Soldier, are as common and well known as those of a Slave, an honest Matron, a Courtezan,

Et Miles gloriofus : eas fe non negat
Perfonas tranftuliffe in Eunuchum fuam
Ex Græcâ : fed eas fabulas factas prius
Latinas fciffe fefe, id verò pernegat.
Quòd fi perfonis ifdem uti aliis non licet : — 35
Qui magi' licet currentes fervos fcribere,
Bonu macronas facere, meretrices malas,
Parafitum edacem, gloriofum militem,
Puerum fupponi, falli per fervum fenem,
Amare, odiffe, fufpicari ? denique 40
Nullum eft jam dictum , quod non fit dictum priùs.
Quare æquum eft vos cognofcere, atque ignofcere,
Quæ veteres factitarunt, fi faciunt novi.
Date operam, & cum filentio animadvortite,
Ut pernofcatis, quid fibi Eunuchus velit. 45

fe, fufpicari ? Denique, nullum eft jam dictum, quod non fit dictum prius. Quare æquum eft vos cognofcere atque ignofcere, fi novi poetæ faciunt ea, quæ veteres factitarunt. Date operam, & animadvertite cum filentio, ut pernofcatis quid Eunuchus velit fibi.

& Miles gloriofus Poeta non negat fe tranftuliffe eas perfonas ex Græca fabula in fuam Eunuchum ; fed fefe fciviffe eas fabulas fuiffe factas. Latinè prius, vero pernegat id. Quod fi non licet uti iifdem perfonis aliis ; qui magis licet fcribere fervos currentes, facere bonas matronas, malas meretrices, edacem pa- rafitum, militem glo- riofum, puerum fup- poni, fenem falli per fervum, amare, odif-

ANNOTATIONS.

Courtezan, or an old Man. If therefore a Poet is not allowed to give thefe Characters, becaufe others have painted them before him, he muft be alfo forbid to bring on the Stage the Paffions defcribed in other Pieces, for the Paffions are the fame in all Ages, and unchangeable as the Characters. Terence fays this, to make it appear, that a Poet may refemble another, in defcribing the fame Character or Paffion, without taking any thing from him, or even without having feen them.

41 *Nullum eft jam dictum, quod non fit dictum prius.* The Poet's Reafoning here is what Philofophers call *reductio ad abfurdum.* By a Paffage of Saint Jerome we learn that *Donatus* confidered this, as if *Terence* had expreffed himfelf angry with the Poets who wrote before, and had ftolen all his Cha- racters. *Pereant qui ante nos noftra dixerunt.* But this is a Miftake ; *Terence* does not here

teftify the leaft Chagrin againft thofe who had given the fame Characters before him. On the contrary, he would have it under- ftood, that we have the fame Liberty of imi- tating Characters that have been given before, as of ufing the fame Letters, Names, Words, or Numbers ; and that if one fcruples to fol- low common and general Idea's, he muft alfo refolve not to write at all, becaufe it is as difficult to invent new Characters, as to fay what has not been faid before. *Dacier.*

44 *Date operam.* A manner of fpeaking taken from the Procedure in Courts, and at the *Forum* ; for when the Judges were bufy, and intent upon any Caufe, they were then faid properly *operam dare.* Cic. Verr. 2. 29. *M. Petilium, equitem Romanum, quem habe- bat in confilio, jubet operam dare, quod rei privatæ judex effet.* From this it came to be applied in any Cafe, where a diligent Attention was required.

TERENCE's

T E R E N C E's
E U N U C H.

ACT I. SCENE I.

ARGUMENT.

Phædria, *enraged that he had been deny'd Admittance, delibe-rates with his Servant* Parmeno, *whether he should now go to* Thais, *who had sent for him of her own accord.*

PHÆDRIA, PARMENO.

Phædria. WHAT shall I therefore do ? Shall I not go ? not even now, when she sends for me of her own ac-cord? Or shall I rather resolve with myself, no lon-ger to bear the Insults of those Jilts ? She shut me out, and now recalls me; Shall I therefore return ? not, if she were to beg it on her Knees.

Parm. If indeed you can keep this Resolution, nothing is better, or more worthy a manly Spirit ; but if you shall once begin, and not continue firmly the same, and, when you cannot any longer bear her Absence, come to her of your own accord, when nobody desires it, and before a Peace is made; discovering thereby, that you love her, and cannot bear to be at varience with her ; all is over, you may do any thing, and are ruined past Redemption : she'll use you at pleasure, when she finds you so irrecoverably her Slave.

Phæd. Do you therefore, before it is too late, consider again, and again, with yourself.

Parm. Master, what absolutely rejects all Measure and Rule, can-not possibly be managed according to Measure or Rule. Love is ne-cessarily subjected to a long Train of Evils, Affronts, Suspicions, Quarrels,

ANNOTATIONS.

¹ *Quid igitur faciam ?* The Scene re-presents *Phædria* deliberating with himself, and consulting with *Parmeno* how to behave. *Thraso*, when in *Caria*, had bought *Pamphila* with a Design to present her to *Thais* at his return ; but, hearing of her Engagements with *Phædria*, resolved to part with her up-on no other Terms but those of renouncing all Commerce with that Youth. *Thais*, who desired above all Things to have *Pamphila* in her possession, had the Day before, to please the Soldier, deny'd *Phædria* Admit-tance. But fearing he might take it ill, sends for him now, to explain her Reasons, and be reconcil'd. *Phædria*, who was alto-gether a Stranger to her Motives, is intro-duc'd here as standing before her Door, and so full of Resentment for her Behaviour the former Night, that he resolves not to go in to her, though sent for.

⁵ *Siquidem hercle possis.* Horace in the third Satire of his second Book has given a Copy of this whole Passage with some Va-riations. As the Reader may be pleased to see

P. TERENTII

EUNUCHUS.

ACTUS I. SCENA I.

ARGUMENTUM.

Phædria iratus, quod exclusus fuerit, cum servo Parmenone deliberat, utrum a Thaide nunc accersitus, ire ad eam debeat.

PHÆDRIA, PARMENO.

ORDO.

QUID igitur faciam? non eam? ne nunc quidem.
  Cùm accersor ultro? an potiùs ita me comparem,
Non perpeti meretricum contumelias?
Exclusit, revocat. redeam? non, si me obsecret.
PA. Siquidem hercle possis, nil prius, neque fortius : 5
Verùm si incipies, neque pertendes gnaviter,
Atque, ubi pati non poteris, cùm nemo expetet,
Infectâ pace, ultro ad eam venies, indicans
Te amare, & ferre non posse; actum est ilicet,
Peristi: eludet, ubi te victum senserit. 10
PH. Proin tu, dum est tempus, etiam atque etiam cogita.
PA. Here, quæ res in se neque consilium neque modum
Habet ullum, eam consilio regere non potes.
In amore hæc omnia insunt vitia, injuriæ,
Suspiciones, inimicitiæ, induciæ, 15

PH. *Quid faciam igitur? an non eam? ne nunc quidem, cum accersor abilla ultro? An potius ita comparem me, non perpeti contumelias meretricum? exclusit, revocat. Redeam? Non si obsecret me.* PA. *Hercle, siquidem possis facere hoc, nil est prius, neque fortius : verum si incipies, neque pertendes gnaviter, atque ubi non poteris pati absentiam ejus, venies ad eam ultro,*

nemo expetet, indicans te amare, & non posse ferre absentiam; actum est, ilicet, peristi: eludet, ubi senserit te victum. PH. Proin tu cogita etiam atque etiam, dum est tempus. PA. Here, quæ res neque habet consilium neque ullum modum in se, non potes regere eam consilio. Omnia hæc vitia insunt in amore, injuriæ, suspiciones, inimicitiæ, induciæ,

ANNOTATIONS.

see his Imitation, I shall here transcribe it intire. He is exposing the Folly of Lovers, and compares them to Children, who, when out of humour, refuse the Apples offered to them if you urge it; but if you cease your Importunities, are impatient to have them; he then goes on :

  Exclusus qui distat? agit ubi secum, eat, an non,
  Quo rediturus erat non arcessitus; & læret
  Invisis foribus: nec nunc, cum me vocet
  ultro.

Accedam? an potius mediter finire dolores?
Exclusit; revocat: redeam? Non, si obsecret, cece
Servus non paulo sapientior: O here, quæ res
Nec modum habet, neque consilium, ratione
  modoque [bellum,
Tractari non vult. In amore hæc sunt mala :
Pax rursum. Hæc si quis tempestatis prope
  ritu
Mobilia, & cæca fluitantia sorte, laboret
Reddere certa sibi; nihilo plus explicet, ac si
Insanire paret certa ratione modoque.

How

Quarrels, Parleys, War, and again Peace. If you pretend to fix by Reafon things fo fluctuating and uncertain, you act much as wifely, as if you aimed at running mad with Reafon. And as to what you now are revolving with yourfelf, in the Heat of your Refentment; Shall I go to her? who hath prefered him? who hath difcarded me? who would not admit me laft Night? leave me only to myfelf; I'll die firft; fhe fhall fee what a Man I am. All thefe great Refolves one hypocritical Tear, difficultly fqueezed from her Eyes with much rubbing, will diffipate, and you will be the firft to accufe yourfelf, and give her what Satisfaction fhe afks.

Phæd. O fcandalous Meannefs! For now I know both that fhe is a Wretch, and I myfelf the moft miferable of Men. I am weary of my Folly, and yet a flave to Love, and knowing, fenfible, forewarned, and with Eyes open, I rufh on to my Ruin: nor can refolve what to do.

Parm. What fhould you do? but redeem yourfelf from Slavery, on the eafieft Terms you can. If that cannot be, yet at any Price; and ceafe to afflict yourfelf.

Phæd. Do you counfel me thus?

Par. If you are wife: nor add other Troubles to thofe which Love brings with it, and what are infeparable from it, bear with Firmnefs. But here fhe comes herfelf, the Flood that ravages our Fields; for what ought to fall to our fhare, fhe carries off.

ANNOTATIONS.

'How much differs this from the Cafe of a difcarded Lover, when he hovers round the hated Doors, and argues with himfelf, whether he fhall return when defired, whence he could not bear to be abfent, if uninvited? Shall I return now that fhe calls me back, or fhall I not rather refolve to put an end to all my Griefs? She has ufed me ill, and now relents; fhall I therefore return? No, if fhe were to beg it on her Knees. On this appears a Servant, a much better Head-piece than his Mafter: O Sir, what abfolutely rejects all Meafure and Rule, ought not to be managed according to Meafure or Rule. A conftant Change of Fortune, and alternate Succeffion of War and Peace, are the infeparable Companions of Love. He that endeavours to render fix'd and fteady, Things moveable as a Tempeft, and fluctuating under the Direction of blind Fate, will do much as wifely, as if he aim'd at running mad with Reafon.'

Horace differs in nothing from *Terence*, but in the Image he gives of a Tempeft, to explain the more agreeably the Word *incerta* of the Original.

20 *Egone illam? quæ illum? quæ me? quæ non? &c.* Thefe Words mark ftrongly the Refentment and Indignation of *Phædria*, for they are full of Ellipfes, than which nothing is more common in the Mouth of an angry Perfon. *Prifcian* Inftit. Lib 17. thus fupplies them: *Egone illam* dignor (an dignor) adventu meo? *Quæ illum* præpofuit mihi? *Quæ me* fprevit? *Quæ non* fufcepit heri? For one who fpeaks with himfelf, and in the Earneftnefs of Grief, cannot be fuppofed to attend to his Words, and often paffes fuddenly from one Thought to another, *Virgil* in like manner, *Æn.* 1. 139.

Quos ego --- Sed motos præftat componere fluctus.

25 *Indignum facinus. Phædria* was too fenfible of his own Weaknefs not to be convinced, that what his Servant faid was true

ACT

Bellum, pax rurſum. incerta hæc ſi tu poſtules
Ratione certa facere, nihilo plus agas,
Quàm ſi des operam, ut cum ratione inſanias.
Et quod nunc tute tecum iratus cogitas :
Egone illam? quæ illum? quæ me? quæ non? ſine
   modo :
Mori me malim : ſentiet qui vir ſiem.   21
Hæc verba unâ mehercle falſâ lacrumulâ,
Quam, oculos terendo miſere, vix vi expreſſerit,
Reſtinguet ; & te ultro accuſabit : & ei dabis
Ultro ſupplicium. PH. indignum facinus ! nunc ego &
Illam ſceleſtam eſſe, & me miſerum ſentio :   26
Et tædet : & amore ardeo : & prudens, ſciens,
Vivus, videnſque pereo : nec, quid agam, ſcio.
PA. Quid agas? niſi ut te redimas captum quam queas
Minimo. ſi nequeas paululo, at quanti queas :   30
Et ne te adflictes. PH. itane ſuades ? PA. ſi ſapis:
Neque, præterquam quas ipſe amor moleſtias
Habet, addas : & illas, quas habet, rectè feras.
Sed ecca ipſa egreditur, noſtri fundi calamitas :
Nam quod nos capere oportet, hæc intercipit.   35

bellum, rurſum pax. Si tu poſtules facere hæc incerta eſſe certa ratione, agas nihilo plus, quam ſi des operam, ut inſanias cum ratione. Et quod nunc tute iratus cogitas tecum, nempe: egone adeam illam? quæ prætulit illum Thraſonem? quæ ſprevit me? quæ non admiſit me ? ſine me modo : malim me mori : ſentiet qui vir ſiem. Mehercule una falſa lacrimula, quam vix expreſſerit vi terendo miſere oculos, reſtinguet hæc verba; & ultro accuſabit te, & ultro dabis ſupplicium ei. PH. O indignum facinus ! Nunc ego ſentio, & illam eſſe ſceleſtam, & me eſſe miſerum :

& tædet me illius, & ardeo amore, & prudens, ſciens, vivus, videnſque pereo : nec ſcio quid agam. PA. Quid agas? niſi ut redimas te captum, quam minimo pretio queas : ſi nequeas paululo, at quanti queas ; & ut ne adflictes te. PH. Suadeſne ita? PA. Si ſapis: neque addas alias moleſtias, præterquam quas moleſtias ipſe amor habet : & feras rectè illas, quas habet. Sed ecca ipſa egreditur, calamitas noſtri fundi : nam hæc intercipit id, quod oportet nos capere.

ANNOTATIONS.

true. He ſees his Miſery, and yet has not Courage to attempt his Liberty. Never were the Effects of Love better painted than in this Scene: we ſee how it enervates the Mind, begets Irreſolution, and deprives a Man entirely of the maſtery of himſelf.

34 *Noſtri fundi calamitas.* Calamitas is a Word of Huſbandry, and ſignifies properly a Storm of Hail which beats down the Corn. It comes originally from *Calamus,* becauſe, as *Donatus* ſays, *comminuat calamum, hoc eſt, culmum ac ſegetem.* Cicero uſes it in the ſame Senſe in one of his Orations againſt *Verres* 1. 38. *Per omnes partes provinciæ te, tanquam aliquam calamitoſam tempeſtatem, peſtemque pervaſiſſe demonſtro.* The Allegory

is extremely elegant, and founded upon what was often the Caſe with inconſiderate Lovers ; that they ſpent their whole Eſtates and Fortunes upon theſe Courtezans. *Plautus* expreſſes himſelf ſtill more ſtrongly, *Epid.* 11. 2. 42.

  Quaſi non fundis exornatæ multæ incedant
     per vias.

h. e. *emni pretio fundorum ab amatoribus venditorum.*

35 *Hæc intercipit.* Donatus and ſome others after him, explain *intercipere* as if it were here for *totum capere.* But it ſeems rather here to imply a taking what had been deſtin'd to another, in which ſenſe Letters are commonly ſaid to be *intercepted.*

ACT I. SCENE II.

ARGUMENT.

Thais *excuses herself to* Phædria *for excluding him the Night before, which naturally introduces an account of the Subject of the Play. At last she obtains of him to give the Soldier seemingly the preference for two Days.*

THAIS, PHÆDRIA, PARMENO.

Thais. WHAT an unhappy Creature am I! and how much I fear that *Phædria* may have taken it ill, or otherwise than I intended, that he was not admitted yesterday!

Phæd. I tremble, *Parmeno*, and shake all over, at the very sight of her.

Par. Have a good Heart: draw near to this Fire, you'll soon find it hot enough.

Tha. Who's this that speaks? What was you here, my *Phædria?* Why do you stand here? Why didn't you enter directly?.

Par. But not a Word of his being shut out.

Tha. Why are you silent?

Phæd. No doubt, because these Doors are always open to me, or because I am first in Favour.

Tha. Let these Things pass.

Phæd. Why pass? O *Thais, Thais,* I wish we loved one another upon more equal Terms, and that so it were, either that this might affect you as sensibly as it affects me, or that I might regard this your Behaviour with Indifference.

Tha. Don't, I beg of you, torment yourself, my dearest Soul, my *Phædria.* It was not because I lov'd, or held any one dearer to me than yourself that I did it; but such was the Case, there was a Necessity for doing it.

Par.

ANNOTATIONS.

[1] *Miseram me!* We have seen that *Thais,* uneasy left *Phædria,* not knowing her Design, might take it ill that he had not been admitted the Night before, had sent for him to acquaint him with her Reasons. *Phædria,* tho' an ardent Lover, was too much discontented to make the first Advances, and therefore though he had come to the Door, he could not yet resolve to enter. *Thais* wondering what kept him so long, and fearing left her late Behaviour had by his mistaking it provok'd him too much, is introduc'd here as expressing her Concern on that account. At last perceiving *Phædria,* she calls to him, and kindly chides him for not coming directly. This gives rise to a Conversation upon what had lately happened, wherein *Thais* lets him into the Secret of her pretended Complaisance for the Soldier, and begs his Assistance for the obtaining of *Pamphila* from him. *Phædria* at first suspecting that it was all Artifice, rejects her Proposal with Indignation, but after some time, softened by her soothing Insinuations, he complies and resolves to go into the Country till the time agreed on is expired.

[5] *Accede ad ignem hunc.* Eugraphius thinks this ought not to be explain'd metaphorically, but literally, and observes from *Menander* that Courtezans had commonly just by their Gate an Altar sacred to *Venus,* on which they daily sacrifice; and that therefore *accede ad ignem* means the same as *accede ad aram,* which *Parmeno* says in a jesting way to his Master. But whatever may be said in Defence of this Notion, I am more inclined to follow *Donatus,* who explains *ignis* of *Thais* herself; nothing being

ACTUS I. SCENA II.

ARGUMENTUM.

Phædriæ purgat se Thais de exclusione, & per occasionem narrat argumentum fabulæ. Tandem ab ipso impetrat aliquot dies militi ut concedat.

THAIS, PHÆDRIA, PARMENO.

O R D O.

Mlferam me ! veréor ne illud graviùs Phædria
    Tulerit, neve aliorfum, atque ego feci acceperit,
Quòd herì intromiffus non eft. PH. totus, Parmeno,
Tremo horreoque, poftquam afpexi hanc. PA. bono
    animo es :
Accede ad ignem hunc, jam calefces plus fatis.   5
TH. Quis hìc loquitur ? hem, tun' hìc eras, mi
    Phædria ?
Quid hìc ftabas ? cur non rectà introibas ? PA. cæterùm
De exclufione verbum nullum. TH. quid taces ?
PH. Sane quia verò hæ mihi patent femper fores,
Aut qui Tum apud te primus. TH. miffa iftæc face. 10
PH. Quid, miffa ? ô Thais, Thais, utinam effet mihi
Pars æqua amoris tecum ; ac pariter fieret,
Ut aut hoc tibi doleret itidem, ut mihi dolet :
Aut ego iftuc abs te factum nihili penderem.
TH. Ne crucia te, obfecro, anime mi, mi Phædria. 15
Non pol, quò quenquam plus amem, aut plus diligam,
Eo feci ; fed ita erat res : faciundum fuit.

TH. HEU *me miferam,* veréor ne Phædria tulerit illud gravius, neve, acceperit aliorfum atque ego feci, quod non eft intromiffus heri. PH. Parmeno, totus tremo horreoque, poftquam afpexi hanc Thaidem. PA. Es bono animo : accede ad hunc ignem, jam calefces plus fatis. TH. Quis loquitur hic ? Hem tune eras hic mi Phædria ? quid ftabas hic ? Cur non introibas rectà ? PA. Cæterum nullum verbum de exclufione. TH. Quid taces ? PH. Sanè quia verò hæ fores femper patent mihi, aut quia fum primus apud te. TH. Fac iftæc miffa. PH. Quid miffa ? O Thais, Thais, utinam effet mihi æqua pars amoris tecum ; ac pariter fieret, aut ut hoc doleret tibi itidem, ut dolet mihi : aut ut ego nihili penderem iftuc factum abs te. TH. Obfecro, mi anime Phædria, ne crucia te. Ʀel non feci eo, quo amem quenquam plus, aut diligam plus : fed res erat ita, fuit faciundum.

ANNOTATIONS.

being more common with Lovers than to call their Miftreffes *ignes.* Thus *Virg. Eccl.* 3. 66.
   At mibi fefe offert ultro meus ignis Amyntas.
  6 *Quis bic loquitur ?* It will better agree to the Genius of Comedy, if we fuppofe that *Thais* only pretends here not to have feen *Phædria* before ; for it will not only perfectly correfpond with her Character as a Courtezan, but give greater Weight to what fhe had faid before.
  12 *Ac pariter fieret.* This *pariter fieret* is a metaphor taken from a fett of Horfes ; they are faid to draw equally, *pariter,* when they are of the fame Strength, and march with an equal Pace. It was probably from this that *Horace* took that Idea, *Ode* 35. Book 1. of
   - - - - - *Amici,*
   Ferre jugum pariter dolofi.
fpeaking of thofe falfe Friends, who make

court to us in Profperity, but abandon us in Adverfity, as not able to bear up with equal Courage under the Yoke of Hardfhips.
  15 *Anime mi, mi Phædria.* Mi is the Vocative of the Pronoun *meus,* and is repeated here with an air of foothing Flattery. *Terence* would have us confider this as a Word peculiar to *Thais,* for which Reafon he brings it in fo often. *Tune bic eras, mi Phædria ? Ne crucia te, anime mi, mi Phædria.* We muft fuppofe this faid in a Voice of tender Softnefs, and with a Look and Gefture as if fhe herfelf fuffered by his Uneafinefs.
  16 *Plus amem, aut plus diligam.* The Words *amare* and *diligere* are of different Signification ; and among the beft Writers, the firft feems to imply more than the laft. *Cicero, Fam.* 9. 14. *Quis erat, cui putares ad eum amarem, quem erga te diabolam poff.*

             a. 4. ti

Par. I believe it, poor Soul, as often happens, you shut him out thro' pure Love and Kindness.

Tha. Is this the way you use me, *Parmeno?* Well, well. But my *Phædria,* hear why I sent for you at this time.

Phæd. Say on then.

Tha. But tell me this first : can this Fellow keep a Secret ?

Par. Meaning me ? the best in the World. But heark ; upon these Conditions I engage my Fidelity. Whatever I hear that is true, I am silent, and keep secret the best of any Man : but if false, or vain, or fantastical, it is out immediately : I am full of Holes, it runs from me on every side. If therefore you would have me keep it secret, speak nothing but the Truth.

Tha. My Mother was of *Samos* ; she liv'd at *Rhodes.*

Par. Well, this may be kept secret.

Tha. There a certain Merchant made her a Present of a young Girl, stolen here from *Attica.*

Phæd. What, a Citizen ?

Tha. I believe so, but can't say for certain : she herself told her Father's and Mother's Name : but as to her Country, and other Signs, she neither knew them, nor indeed would her Youth admit of such Knowledge. The Merchant who presented her added ; that he had heard from the Pirates, of whom he bought her, that she was carried off from *Sunium.* My Mother, after she received her, began to teach her every thing very carefully, and educate her in the same manner as if she had been her own Daughter. Most People believed her to be my Sister. Meantime I left *Rhodes,* and came here in company with that Stranger, who was the only Person I had then any Engagements with, and who left me all that I now possess.

Par. Both these Articles are false : they must out.

Tha. Why that ?

Par. Because neither was you satisfy'd with one, nor was he the only Giver ; for this Gentleman too has brought a pretty considerable Share.

Tha. It is so : but let me come to the Point : mean while the Soldier, who had begun to take a liking to me, is obliged to go into
Caria ;

ANNOTATIONS.

aliquid accedere ? tantum accessit, ut mibi nume denique amare videar, antea dilexisse. Amare, answers to *Love* in our Language, and implies an Affection grounded on what is engaging and promises Pleasure. *Diligere* is to *esteem,* to value a Man on account of his Virtue, Learning, or other Qualifications that constitute what we properly call Merit. In order to make them answer right here, we must interpret *amare* to *favour,* to *wish well to,* and *diligere* to *prefer,* to *have in any degree of Esteem.*

[24] *Sin falsum, aut vanum, aut fictum est.*

We have here three several Degrees of Falshood specified. *Falsum* is what is absolutely false, without carrying in it any shadow of Truth. *Vanum* imports what is vain and ridiculously exaggerated. *Fictum* what is feign'd with Address, and has an appearance of Truth. Hence *Donatus : Falsum loqui, mendacis est : fictum callidi, vanum stulti.*

[27] *Samia mibi mater fuit : ea habitabat Rhodi. Thais* avoids saying directly that her Mother was a Courtezan, and yet her Discourse implies as much ; for Women who liv'd in any place different from the in
.nich

PA. Credo, ut fit, mifera præ amore exclufifti hunc foras.

TH. Siccine agis, Parmeno? age. fed, huc quâ gratiâ
Te accerfi juffi, aufculta. PH. fiat. TH. dic mihi   20
Hoc primùm, potin' eft hic tacere? PA. egone? op-
tumè.

Verùm heus tu. lege hac tibi meam adftringo fidem:
Quæ vera audivi, taceo, & contineo optumè:
Sin falfum, aut vanum, aut fictum eft, continuò pa-
lam eft.

Plenus rimarum fum, hac atque illâc perfluo.   25
Proin tu, taceri fi vis, vera dicito.

TH. Samia mihi mater fuit: ea habitabat Rhodi.
PA. Poteft taceri hoc. TH. ibi tùm matri parvolam
Puellam dono quidam mèrcator dedit,
Ex Atticâ hinc abreptam. PH. civemne? TH. arbitror:
Certum non fcimus: matris nomen & patris   31
Dicebat ipfa: patriam & figna cætera
Neque fcibat, neque per ætatem etiam potuerat.
Mercator hoc addebat, è prædonibus,
Unde emerat, fe audiffe, abreptam è Sunio.   35
Mater ubi accepit, cœpit ftudiosè omnia
Docere, educere, ita uti fi effet filia.
Sororem plerique effe credebant meam.
Ego cum illo, quo cum tum uno rem habebam, hofpite
Abii huc, qui mihi reliquit hæc, quæ habeo, omnia. 40
PA. Utrumque hoc falfum eft: effluet. TH. quî iftuc?
PA. quia
Neque tu uno eras contenta, neque folus dedit:
Nam hic quoque bonam magnamque partem ad te
attulit.
TH. Ita eft. fed fine me pervènire, quò volo.
Interea miles, qui me amare occèperat,   45

bus, unde emerat, illam fuiffe abreptam e Sunio. Mater, ubi accepit, cœpit docere eam omnia ftu-
diofe, & educere, ita uti fi effet fua filia. Plerique credebant illam effe fororem meam. Ego abii
huc cum illo hofpite, cum quo uno tum habebam rem, & qui reliquit mihi omnia hæc, quæ habeo.
PA. Utrumque hoc eft falfum: effluet. TH. Qui iftuc? PA. Quia neque tu eras contenta uno, neque
folus dedit hæc omnia tibi: nam hic quoque attulit bonam magnamque partem ad te. TH. Eft
ita. Sed fine me pervenire, quo volo. Interea miles, qui occeperat amare me,.

ANNOTATIONS.

which they were born, were feldom regarded for their Chaftity. Hence Courtezans are fo often in Comedy call'd *Strangers.* Hence before in the *Andrian,* Act. 3. Sc. 1.

Adeon' eft demens? ex peregrina?

35 *Abreptam e Sunio. Sunium* was a part of *Attica* upon the Sea-Coaft, hence Ver. 30. we read *ex Attica hinc abreptam. Thais* here proceeds with her Relation, in which fhe takes care to omit no Circumftance by

which fhe might give a more colourable Pretence for her Earneftnefs to be in poffef-fion of the young Girl. She had been bred up with her from a Child, fhe had been al-ways accounted her Sifter, there was a Pro-bability that fhe was a Citizen of *Athens,* and, if fhe could reftore her to her Relations, fhe might thereby fecure to herfelf fome powerful Friends in a Place where fhe was a Stranger, and might be eafily oppref'd with-out

PA. Credo, ut fæpe fit, tu mifera exclu-fifti hunc foras præ amore. TH. Siccine agis, Parmeno? age. Sed aufculta quâ gratiâ juffi te accerfi. huc. PH. Fiat. TH. dic b. c mihi pri-mum. Potefne hic Parmeno tacere? PH. Egone? Optime. Verum heus tu, ad-ftringo meam fidem tibi hac lege: taceo & contineo optime ea quæ vera audivi; fin quid eft falfum, aut vanum, aut fic-tum, continuo eft pa-lam: fum plenus ri-marum, perfluo hac atque illac. Proin tu dicito vera, fi vis ea taceri. TH. Mulier Samia fuit mater mi-hi: ea habitabat Rhodi. PH. Hic po-teft taceri. TH. Ibi tum quidam mercator dedit parvulam puel-lam, abreptam hinc ex Attica, matri meæ dono. PH. Civemne? TH. Arbitror; non fcimus certum: ipfa dicebat nomen patris & matris: fed neque fciebat patriam & cætera figna, neque etiam potuerat fcire per ætatem. Merca-tor addebat hoc: fe audiviffe e prædoni-

Caria; it was during this time that I came acquainted with you. You yourfelf know how dear you have been to me, and how frankly I truft you with my moft fecret Defigns.

Phæd. *Parmeno* fure will never keep this.

Par. O, is that to be doubted of?

Tha. Mind what I am faying, pray: My Mother is lately dead there; her Brother is fomewhat covetoufly inclin'd. He finding this Girl of an agrecable Prefence, and fkill'd in Mufick, expecting fhe would fetch a good Price, offers her to fale, and foon found a Chap; for by good chance this Friend of mine was there, who bought her as a Prefent for me, not knowing or fufpecting any thing of what I have now told you. He is now come; but when he heard of my Engagements alfo with you, he feigns a thoufand Excufes for not giving her. He fays, that if he could be fure of having always the firft degree of Favour with me, and did not fear, that as foon as I had received her, I would abandon him, he would frankly give her; but that's what he apprehends. But as far as I can conjecture, he has taken a Liking to the Virgin himfelf.

Phæd. Is there nothing more between them?

Tha. Nothing: for I have enquir'd. Now, my *Phædria*, there are many Reafons why I could wifh to have this Girl. Firft, becaufe fhe was thought to be my Sifter. Moreover, that I may reftore and give her back to her Relations. I am here fingle, and have no Creature, neither Friend nor Kinfman, to protect me. 'Tis for this Reafon, *Phædria*, that I want to fecure fome Friends by my good Offices. Help me, pray, in this Defign, that I may the more eafily accomplifh it. Suffer him to have feemingly the preference with me for thefe few Days. Do you anfwer nothing?

Phæd. Wretch! Can I make any anfwer to fuch Propofals as thefe?   *Par.*

ANNOTATIONS.

out fome fuch Support. It is probable that *Thais* forefaw *Phædria's* Sufpicions, and therefore is at all this pains, and fums up her Reafons at the End of her Speech to prevent them.

46 *Te interea loci cognovi.* It is artful in the Poet to make the Soldier the prior Lover, by which *Thais* is at liberty to plead for this Indulgence with a better Grace. For fhe fays that fhe knew not *Phædria* till afterwards, during the Soldier's Abfence. As therefore *Phædria* was a Rival of fhorter ftanding than the Soldier, this laft had greateft reafon to complain, not *Phædria*; nor was it an unreafonable Demand, that, each holding his proper Rank with her, the Soldier fhould be preferr'd to a Lover not known till long after him. And all this, even without regarding the Defign of obtaining the Virgin, pleads ftrongly for *Thrafo* againft *Phædria*.

But obferve the Artfulnefs of the Courtezan, as fhe made a Demand which fhe knew muft be ungrateful to her Lover, how careful fhe is to foften the matter, and perfuade him that he is far more dear to her than the other. *Tute fcis poft illa, quam intimum babeam te. Donatus.*

Ibid. *Cariam. Caria* was a Region of *Afia* minor upon the Sea-Coaft, oppofite to *Rhodes.*

55 *Hic meus amicus.* As fhe is now fpeaking of his Kindnefs and Civility to her, fhe does not ufe the Word *miles*, but *amicus*, a Title that he feem'd to merit from her. This is ftill fet in a clearer Light by what follows. *Emit* (fays fhe) *eam dono mihi, imprudens harum rerum ignarufque omnium.* By this is infinuated with how much greater Earneftnefs and Pleafure he would have done it, had he known all. It carries moreover the flattering Idea of her imparting her fecrets

In Cariam eft profectus. te interea loci   *⁄*
Cognovi. tute fcis, poftilla quàm intumum
Habeam te, & mea confilia ut tibi credam omnia.
Pн. Ne hoc quidem tacebit Parmeno. Pa. oh, du-
 biumne id eft ?
Tн. Hoc agite, amabo. mater mea illîc mortua eft 5c
Nuper. ejus frater aliquantum ad rem eft avidior./
Is, ubi hanc formâ videt honeftâ virginem,
Et fidibus fcire, precium fperans, illico
Producit, vendit. forte fortunâ adfuit   *•*
Hic meus amicus : emit eam dono mihi,   55
Imprudens harum rerum ignarufque omnium.
Is venit : poftquam fenfit me tecum quoque
Rem habere, fingit caufas, ne det; fedulò :
Ait fi fidem habeat, 'fe iri præpofitum tibi
Apud me, ac non id metuat, ne, ubi eam acceperim,
Sefe relinquam, velle fe illam mihi dare ;   61
Verùm id vereri. fed, ego quantum fufpicor,
Ad virginem animum adjecit. Pн. etiamne amplius ?
Tн. Nil: nam quæfivi. nunc ego eam, mi Phædria,
Multæ funt caufæ, quamobrem cupiam abducere 65
Primùm, quòd foror eft dicta : præterea, ut fuis
Reftituam ac reddam. fola fum : habeo hîc neminem,
Neque amicum, neque cognatum; quamobrem, Phæ-
Cupio aliquos parere amicos beneficio meo.   [dria,
Id, amabo, adjuta me, quo id fiat faciliùs.   70
Sine illum priores partes hofce aliquot dies
Apud me habere. nihil refpondes ? Pн. peffima !
Egon' quidquam cum iftis factis tibi refpondeam ?

fufpicor, adji it arimum ad virginem. Pн. *Eftne etiam amplus ?* Tн. *Nil: nam quæfivi.*
Nunc, mi Phædria, juat multæ caufæ, quamobrem ego'cupiam abducere eam. Primum quad eft
dicta foror : proterea, ut reftituam u reddam fuis. Sem fola ; habeo llc neminem, neque amicum,
neque cognatum. Quamobrem, Phædria, cupio parere aliquot amicos meo beneficio. Amabo, adjuta
me ad id, quo i fiat facilius. Sine illum habere priores partes apud me hofce aliquot dies. Re-
fpondes nihil ? Pн. *Peffima ! Egone refpondeam quidquam tibi cum iftis factis ?*

ANNOTATIONS.

erats to *Phædria,* and acquainting him with
Things that his Rival was a Stranger to.
  63 *Etiamne amplus ? Is there nothing more ?*
has nothing eft pafs'd between them ? This is
undoubtedly 'the Senfe of the Words, as
appears from *Tha's* Anfwer. *Pamphilus*
makes ufe of the fame Terms in the *An-*
drian, when he demands of *Charinus,*
 Nam quidnam amplius tibi cum illa fuit,
   Charine ?
And the Precaution which *Terence* takes
here, was very neceffary in the Conduct of
the Plot, to prevent the Spectators from
having any Sufpicions to the difadvantage
of that Girl.
  67 *Habeo hic neminem, neque amicum.*

Donatus here diftinguifhes betwixt a *Lover*
and a *Friend.* A Lover is only for a time,
a Friend is what we expect fhould cont'nue
firm and conftant to us. But it is probable
fhe means here what the Ancients call'd a
Patron, one who would defend her in cafe of
Oppreffion. The Youth durft not undertake the Defence of Women of this Character, becaufe it expofed them to difhonourably
Sufpicions, and would have drawn upon
them the Refentment of their Parents.
  71 *Priores partes.* A manner of fpeaking
tranflated from the Theatre, where the
Parts affign'd to the different Actors, according to their Rank, were call'd *primæ,*
fecundæ, tertia.

Par. Well faid, Mafter of mine, I commend you : he's touched at laft, you're a Man.

Phæ. But I little dream'd to what all this tended. A young Girl was carried off from this Place ; my Mother brought her up with the fame Care as if fhe had been her Daughter ; fhe was reckoned my Sifter ; I want much to have her, that I may reftore her to her Relations. All this tedious Recital in fine comes to this: I am excluded, he is receiv'd. Why fo ? unlefs becaufe you love him more than me; and fear this young Girl now brought over, left fhe fhould fupplant you with a Lover of fuch Importance.

Tha. Do I fear fuch a Thing?

Phæ. Tell me then what elfe can give you all this Anxiety? Is he the only one that makes you Prefents ? Did you ever find my Bounty fail you ? Didn't I, when you faid you wanted an *Ethiopian* Girl for a Slave, forgetting every thing elfe, go in fearch of one ? You faid too, that you fhould like to have an Eunuch, becaufe thefe are ufed only by Women of Fafhion. I found one. Yefterday I gave threefcore Pounds for the two. Ill-treated by you as I was, I yet thought of thefe. For this my Good-nature you ufe me with Contempt.

Tha. Why do you talk in this manner, *Phædria?* Although I paffionately defire to have this Girl, and think it could eafily be done in the way I mention : yet rather than make you my Enemy, I'll do whatever you defire.

Phæd. I wifh that Word were fincere, and came from your Heart : *Rather than make you my Enemy* ; could I believe that fpoken fincerely, I would fubmit to any Thing.

Par. He yields, vanquifhed by a fingle Word, how foon ?

Tha. I not fpeak fincerely, and from the Heart ! What did you ever defire of me even in jeft, that you have not obtain'd ? I cannot prevail with you to grant me only two Days.

Phæd. If indeed it were only two Days : but is there no Danger of their becoming twenty Days ?

Tha. Indeed no more than two Days, or—

Phæd. Or ! I hear nothing.

Tha. It fhall not be. Let me only obtain this Favour of you.

Phæd. Well, it muft be as you will have it.

Tha. I defervedly love you : This is kind.   *Phæd.*

A N N O T A T I O N S.

35 *Nonne, ubi mihi dixti cupere te ex Æ- thiopia ancillulam ?* It is impoffible to doubt that *Terence* has painted, in the ftrongeft Colours, the Manners of the Times in which *Menander* flourifhed ; for it was a prevailing Folly of that Age to difcover a particular Vanity in being ferved by Slaves from *Ethiopia. Theophraftus,* the Difciple of *Ariftotle,* and of confequence co-temporary with *Menander,* who was born the very Year in which *Ariftotle* died, to ridicule a vain Man, whofe Character he draws, among other Follies, does not fail to take notice of his Fondnefs of being followed by an *Ethiopian* Slave. Such therefore was the Vanity of this Courtezan, who wanted an *Ethiopian* Slave, becaufe it was the Fafhion among People of Diftinction. This Humour paffed from the *Greeks* to the *Romans,* and from the *Romans* it has come down to our own times. The Ridicule of *Theophraftus, Menander,* and *Terence,* falls as heavily upon us, as upon the Times in which they lived. *Dacier.*

38 *Quia folæ utuntur his reginæ. Divites,* according to *Donatus,* which Explication is
cen-

PA. Eu noster! laudo. tandem perdoluit: vir es.
PH. Haud ego nescibam, quorsum tu ires. parvola 75
Hinc est abrepta: eduxit mater pro suâ:
Soror est dicta: cupio abducere, ut reddam suis.
Nempe omnia hæc nunc verba huc redeunt denique:
Ego excludor, ille recipitur. quâ gratiâ,   79
Nisi illum plus amas, quàm me, & istam nunc times,
Quæ advecta est; ne illum talem præripiat tibi?
TH. Ego id timeo? PH. quid te ergo aliud solicitat,
Num solus ille dona dat? nuncubi meam   [cedo?
Benignitatem sensisti in te claudier?
Nonne, ubi mihi dixti cupere te ex Æthiopiâ   85
Ancillulam, relictis rebus omnibus,
Quæsivi? porro eunuchúm dixti velle te,   r
Quia solæ utuntur his reginæ. repperi.
Herì minas viginti pro ambobus dedi:
Tamen contemtus abs te, hæc habui in memoriâ: 90
Ob hæc facta abs te spernor. TH: quid istic, Phædria?
Quanquam illam cupio abducere, atque hac re arbitror
Id fieri posse maxumè; verum tamen,
Potiùs quàm te inimicum habeam, faciam utì jusseris.
PH. Utinam istuc verbum ex animo ac verè diceres, 95
Potiùs quàm te inimicum habeam. si istuc crederem
Sincerè dici, quidvis possem perpeti.
PA. Labascit, victus uno verbo, quàm citò!
TH. Ego non ex animo misera dico? quam joco
Rem voluisti à me tandem, quin perfeceris?   100
Ego impetrare nequeo hoc abs te, biduum.
Sa tem ut concedas solum. PH. siquidem biduum.
Verù n ne fiant isti viginti dies.   [moror.
TH. Profectò non plus biduum, aut.—PH. aut? nihil.
TH. Non fiet. hoc modò sine te exorem. PH. scilicet 105
Faciundum est, quod vis. TH. meritò te amo. bene facis.

Phædria? Quanquam cupio abducere illam virginem, atque arbitror id posse fieri maxime hac re;
verum tamen, potius quam habeam te inimicum, faciam uti jusseris. PH. Utinam diceres istuc ver-
bum ex animo ac vere: (potius quam habeam te inimicum) si crederem istuc dici sincere, possem per-
peti quidvis. PA. Quam cito herus labascit, victus uno verbo! TH. An non ego misera dico hæc
ex animo? Quam rem tand m voluisti a me etiam joco, quin perfeceris? Ego nequeo impetrare hoc
abs te, ut concedas saltim duum biduum. PH. Siquidem biduum solum. Verum vereor ne isti dies
fiant viginti. TH. Profectò non plus quam biduum, aut.-----PH. Aut! moror nihil. TH.
non f. t. Modò sine ut exorem hoc te. PH. Scilicet est faciundum, quod vis. TH. Merito
amo te. Facis bene.

ANNOTATIONS.

censured by *Boeclerus.* But I can't conceive what Sense there would be in this Courtezan's Arrogance, if none but Queens, properly so called, used them, and not Matrons of Distinction at *Athens.*

Ibid. *Repperi.* A Word more expressive than *emi.* It is worth while to observe how careful the Poet is in the Choice of apt and proper Words. For speaking of the Eunuch and *Ethiopian* Girl, he makes use of *quæsivi* in the one case, and *repperi* in the other; as implying that they were not to be had without a great deal of Pains and Trouble.

94 *Faciam uti jusseris.* This is far from being a voluntary Offer in *Thais*, nor are

Phæd. I'll go into the Country, and there do Penance thefe two Days: fo it is refolved, for *Thais* muft be humoured. You, *Parmeno*, fee that thefe two Slaves be carried to her.

Par. Yes, Sir.

Phæd. For thefe two Days then, *Thais*, farewel.

Tha. My *Phædria*, adieu. Is there any thing elfe you defire of me?

Phæd. I! what can I defire? But that all the time you are in Company with this Soldier, your heart may be elfewhere; that you love me Day and Night; defire to be with me; dream of me, expect to fee me with Impatience; think of me; hope to be with me foon, delight yourfelf with the Remembrance of me; have your Mind wholly fixed on me; in fine, that your Heart be wholly mine, as mine is altogether yours.

Tha. How uneafy am I, left perhaps he may give but little Credit to what I fay, and judge of my Difpofition from that of other Women? I, who am beft acquainted with my own Mind, know this for certain, that I have neither feigned any Falfhood, nor love any Creature more fondly than this *Phædria*; and whatever I have done in the prefent cafe, is all purely for the fake of the Virgin: for I flatter myfelf, that I have now found her Brother, a young Gentleman of confiderable Rank. He appointed this Day to be at my Houfe, I'll ftep in, and wait his coming.

ANNOTATIONS.

we to fuppofe it faid with an Air of Frank-nefs. It is a mere Artifice. For becaufe by perfifting fhe could not obtain what fhe wanted, by this feeming Submiffion fhe flyly draws on *Phædria* to be lefs obftinate in denying her Requeft. And this manner we find to be fo prevailing, that he was unable to refift it. For nothing is more common, than that what you deny with Obftinacy to one who pretends to force you to it, you'll readily grant, if he is fubmiffive and yielding.

117 *Me miferam!* We ought here to obferve the great Addrefs and Judgment of the Poet, in not making *Thais* fpeak of the Girl's Brother till after *Phædria* and *Parmeno* are gone. By this he is left at liberty to conduct the Plot according to his firft Intention; and *Parmeno* hears nothing that might hinder him from giving *Coæxca* the Advice we meet with in the Sequel. For it is not likely he would have dared to act in that manner, had he known for certain, that

---

ACT II. SCENE I.

ARGUMENT.

Phædria, about to go into the Country, recommends it to his Servant to carry the Prefents to Thais, and fays many things foolifhly, Parmeno mean while rallying a little; who wonders at this great Change in his Mafter, occafioned by the Violence of his Paffion.

PHÆDRIA, PARMENO.

Phæd. SEE that you do as I ordered, let thefe Slaves be carried to *Thais*. *Par.* I will.   *Phæd.*

ANNOTATIONS.

1 *Fac ita, ut juffi, &c.* In this Scene we have *Phædria* giving Orders to his Servant *Parmeno*, about the Eunuch and *Ethiopian Girl* he intended as a Prefent for *Thais*.

After

PH. Rus ibo : ibi hoc me macerabo biduum :
Ita facere certum eſt : mos gerundu' eſt Thaidi.
Tu, Parmeno, huc fac illi adducantur. PA. maxumè.
PH. In hoc biduum, Thais, vale. TH. mi Phædria, 110
Et tu. numquid vis aliud ? PH. egone quid velim ?
Cum milite iſto præſens, abſens ut ſies :
Dies noctesque me ames : me deſideres :
Me ſomnies : me exſpectes : de me cogites :
Me ſperes : me te oblectes : mecum tota ſis :   115
Meus fac ſis poſtremò animus, quandò ego ſum tuus.
TH. Me miſeram ! forſitan hic mihi parum habeat fi-
dem,
Atque ex aliarum ingeniis nunc me judicet.
Ego pol, quæ mihi ſum conſcia, hoc certò ſcio,
Neque me finxiſſe falſi quidquam, neque meo   120
Cordi eſſe quenquam cariorem hoc Phædriâ :
Et quidquid hujus feci, cauſâ virginis
Feci : nam me ejus fratrem ſpero propemodum
Jam repperiſſe, adoleſcentem adeo nobilem : &
Is hodie venturum ad me conſtituit domum.   125
Concedam hinc intro, atque exſpectabo, dum venit.

beat parvam fidem mihi, atque judicet me ex ingeniis aliarum mulierum. Ego pol, quæ ſum con-
ſcia mihi, ſcio hoc certò, me neque fixiſſe quidquuim falſi, neque quenquam eſſe cariorem meo cordi
bac Phædria : & quicquid hujus rei feci, feci cauſâ virginis : nam ſpero me jam propemodum re-
periſſe fratrem ejus, adeo nobilem adoleſcentem : & is conſtituit ſeſe venturum hodie in meam do-
mum ad me. Concedam hinc intro, atque expectabo, dum venit.

ORDO (side column):

PH. Ibo rus : ibi ma-
cerabo me hoc bidu-
um : eſt certum mihi
facere ita : mos eſt
gerendus Thaidi. Tu,
Parmeno, fac ut illi
ancillula & eunu-
chus adducantur huc.
PA. Maxime. PH.
Thais, vale in hoc
biduum. TH. Mi
Phædria & tu vale.
Numquid vis aliud ?
PH. Egone ve-
lim quid aliud ? Ve-
l'm ut tu præſens
cum iſto milite ſis ab-
ſens : ut ames me dies
noctéſque : ut deſi-
deres me : ſomnies de
me : expectes me : co-
gites de me : ſperes me :
oblectes te me : ſis tota
mecum poſtremo fac
ut ſis meus animus,
quando ego ſum tuus.
TH. Me miſeram !
forſitan hic nunc ha-

ANNOTATIONS.

that the Girl was a Citizen of *Athens*, and that *Thais* had come to the Knowledge of her Relations.

118 A'que ex aliorum ingeniis nunc me ju-dicet. *Terence* by this makes his Readers ſenſible that he had found the Secret of bringing new Characters upon the Stage, no leſs natural than thoſe already given, and which muſt be more agreeable to a diſcreet Mind.

125 Et is hodie venturum ad me conſtituit do-mum. *Terence* puts this Diſcourſe into *Thais*'s Mouth, to prepare us for the Appearance of *Chremes* in the third Scene of the third Act, where he is introduced as one that had already had ſome Converſation with this Cour-tezan, and jealous that ſhe had ſome De-ſign upon him.

ACTUS II. SCENA I.

ARGUMENTUM.

Rus conceſſurus Phædria, mancipiorum deductionem ad Thai-
dem ſervo mandat, & multa ridicule loquitur ; illudente in-
terim Parmenone, qui heri ſui mutationem ob nimium amorem
admiratur.

PHÆDRIA, PARMENO.

ORDO.

FAC ita, ut juſſi, deducantur iſti. PA. faciam. PH.
at diligenter

cantur. PA. Faciam. PH. At diligenter.

*F*AC *ita ut juſſi :*
iſti, eunuchus
& ancillula dedu-

ANNOTATIONS.

After recommending this to him in the warmeſt manner, he propoſes himſelf to go | into the Country, where he would continue till the two Days agreed upon between him

Phæd. But with Care, then.

Par. It fhall be done,

Phæd. But quickly.

Par. It fhall be done.

Phæd. Have I recommended this enough to you?

Par. Ah! to afk fuch a Queftion? As if it was indeed a hard matter, I heartily wifh you was as fure of gaining fomething confiderable, as you are of lofing thefe two Slaves.

Phæd. Nay, I lofe what is far dearer to me; I lofe myfelf too; don't be fo mightily concerned about this Trifle.

Par. Not at all: nay, I'll do your Bufinefs effectually; but have you any farther Commands?

Phæd. Set off this our Prefent with all the Eloquence you can, and omit nothing in your Power to drive away this Rival.

Par. Pfhaw! I fhould have thought of that without your telling me.

Phæd. I'll go into the Country, and there ftay,

Par. So I reckon.

Phæd. But heark ye.

Par. What would you fay?

Phæd. Do you really fancy, that I can keep to my Refolution, and hold out without returning in the mean time?

Parm. Who you? Indeed I don't think fo. For either you'll return immediately, or want of Sleep will drive you hither by Night.

Phæd. I'll labour till I'm tir'd, that I may Sleep in fpite of myfelf.

Parm. Nay, you'll do more, you'll lie awake, tired as you are.

Phæd. Ah! 'tis a Joke, *Parmeno*, I muft fee to get the better of this unaccountable Weaknefs of Mind; I indulge myfelf too much. D'ye think then, that I could not live without her, if it were needful even for three whole Days?

Parm. What, live without her three whole Days! take care what you fay.

Phæd. I am refolved to do fo.

Par.

A N N O T A T I O N S.

and; *Thais* were expired. *Parmeno*, who was no ftranger to his Weaknefs 'in this refpect, and knew how little he was able to keep fuch a Refolution, freely tells him his Mind. *Phædria*, confcious that there was but too great Reafon to fufpect his Steadinefs in this Inftance, confirms himfelf in his firft Refolution, and to fhew *Parmeno*, that he was ftill able to exert the Man when he pleafed, departs firmly, purpofing to remain in the Country for three whole Days.

3 *Ah! rogitare? quafi difficile fiet.* This Anfwer is to be fuppofed made with Earneftnefs, and an Air of Countenance that fpeaks *Parmeno* to be under a good deal of Concern. It grieves him to fee his Mafter fo anxious, and giving fuch particular Orders about a Thing that was the eafieft in the World to manage; for this plainly intimated, that his Paffion was come to fuch a Height, as muft be very uneafy to himfelf, and would fcarce admit of a Cure.

13 *Aut mox noctu te adiget horfum infomnia.* The common reading is *adigent.* But if we confider attentively what follows, it is apparent that the Poet here wrote *adiget*, and that *infomnia* is to be underftood here, *want of Sleep,* or *lying awake;* for in this fenfe *Phædria* takes it, as is plain from the Anfwer he gives: *Opus faciam, ut defatiger ufque, ingratiis ut dormiam.* And *Parmeno* not

P. TERENTII EUNUCHUS. 153

Pa. Fiet. Ph. at maturè. Pa. fiet. Ph. fatin' hoc
  mandatum eſt tibi ?
Pa. Ah, rogitare ? quaſi difficile fiet. utinam
Tam aliquid facile invenire poſſis, Phædria,
Hoc quàm peribit. Ph. ego quoque unà pereo, quod
  mî eſt carius.   5
Ne iſtuc tam iniquo patiare animo. Pa. minimè: quin
Effectum dabo ſed numquid aliud imperas ?
Ph. Munus noſtrum ornato verbis, quod poteris : &
Iſtum æmulum, quod poteris, ab eâ pellito.
Pa. Au, memini, tametſi nullus moneas. Ph. ego
  rus ibo, atque ibi manebo.   10
Pa. Cenſeo. Ph. ſed heus tu. Pa. Quid vis ? Ph. cen-
  ſen' poſſe me obfirmare &
Perpeti, ne redeam interea ?. Pa. tene ? non hercle
  arbitror :   [ſum inſomnia.
Nam aut jam revertere, aut mox noctu te adiget hor-
Ph. Opus faciam, ut defatiger uſque, ingratiis ut dor-
  miam.   [cis, Parmeno.
Pa. Vigilabis laſſus : hoc plùs facies. Ph. ah, nil di-
Ejiciunda hercle hæs mollities animi. nimis me in-
  dulgeo.   [triduum ? Pa. hui !
Tandem ego non illâ caream, ſi ſit opus, vel totum
Univorſum triduum ! vide quid agas. Ph. ſtet ſententia.

non arbitror. Nam aut revertere jam, aut inſomnia mox adiget te horſum noctu. Ph. Faciam opus, uſque ut defatiger, ut dormiam ingratiis. Pa. Vigilabis laſſus ; facies hoc plus. Ph. Ah, dicis nil, Parmeno, hercle hæc mollities animi eſt ejicienda : indulgeo me nimis. Non ego caream illâ tandem, ſi opus ſite vel totum triduum ? Ph. Hui ! Univorſum triduum ! Vide quid agas. Pa. Sententia ſtat.

Pa. Fiet. Ph. at ma-turè. Pa. fiet. Ph. Eſtne hoc ſatis man-datum tibi ? Pa. Ah, pergis rogitare? qua-ſi fiet difficile. uti-nam, Phædria, poſſis invenire aliquid tam facile, quam hoc peri-bit. Ph. Ego quoque pereo unâ, quod eſt carius mibi : ne pa-tiare iſtuc tam ini-quo animo. Pa. Minime : quin dabo effectum quod jubes. Sed numquid imperas aliud ? Ph. Ornato noſtrum munus verbis, quod poteris, & pelli-to iſtum æmulum ab ea quod poteris. Pa. Au, memini, tametſi tu nullus moneas. Ph. Ego ibo rus, atque manebo ibi. Pa. Cenſeo. Ph. Sed heus tu. Pa. Quid vis ? Ph. Cenſeſne me poſſe obfirmare & perpeti, ne redeam interea ? Pa. Tene? Hercle

ANNOTATIONS.

not believing t' at even that would be ſuffi-cient, immediately replies ; *vigilabis laſſus.*

14 *Opus faciam.* This is to be underſtood of labouring in the Country, for among the *Greeks* and *Romans* the Study of Agriculture was long held in the higheſt Eſteem, nor did Men of the firſt Rank in the State diſdain to apply themſelves to it. *Cicero* gives a noble Commendation of it, in his Treatiſe *de Offi-ciis,* Lib. I. 42. *Omnium autem rerum, ex quibus al quid acquiritur, nihil eſt agricultura melius, nihil uberius, nihil dulcius, nihil homine libero dign'us.*

15 *Vigilabis laſſus ; hoc plus facies. Phæ-dria* had ſaid *opus faciam, ut defatiger uſque.* *Parmeno* ſmiles at this, as knowing it would avail but little to compoſe his Mind. *True, you will work till you are wearied, but wea-ried as you ſhall be, you will lie awake ; which is doing ſtill more than barely working.* There-fore he adds, *facies hoc plus :* h. e. *facies tan-ta plus.*

17 *Tandem ego non illa caream.* He begins here as one who was about to ſay ſomething great and ſurprizing, and indeed to take ſuch a Reſolution as this, muſt appear ſo in the Eyes of a Lover. 'Tis for this reaſon, that in mentioning the Term of Abſence, he calls it *totum triduum,* it being an Inſtance of great Steadineſs and Command of himſelf, when only two Days were required. *Parmeno* too, in his Anſwer, partly to ſignify his Sur-prize, partly in the way of ridicule, calls it *univorſum tridunm.*

18 *Stat ſententia.* This is to be ſuppoſed ſpoken with an Air and Geſture of Tri-umph, and a certain affected Stead neſs of Countenance, as if nothing were capable of ſhaking his Reſolution. Never were the Conflicts of Paſſion, and the weak Efforts of Reaſon, in a Mind where they have got the maſtery, more happily painted than in this Character.

19 Dii

Parm. (*Alone.*) Good Gods! What fort of Difeafe is this? Is it poffible a Man fhould be fo perfectly changed by Love, that you cannot know him to be the fame? No one was lefs guilty of Folly, than this Mafter of mine, nor was any one more difcreet, or more a Mafter of his Paffions. But who can that be coming this way? O! 'tis *Gnatho,* the Soldier's Parafite, he brings along with him the Virgin, as a prefent here; blefs me! a delightful Girl! It will be a great wonder, if I make not but a fcurvey Figure here to-day, with this decrepit *Eunuch* of mine. This Girl exceeds *Thais* herfelf.

ANNOTATIONS.

19 *Dii boni! quid hoc merbi eft?* Thefe are the Words of *Parmeno,* after *Phædria* is gone; reflecting with himfelf, upon what he had obferved in his Mafter. He had known him a Man of Spirit, Prudence, and Firmnefs, apt to give into none of the Follies, and rafh Projects of other young Men of the like Age. He fees him now all Irrefolution

---

ACT II. SCENE II.

ARGUMENT.

Gnatho, at the Soldier's defire, carrying a young Virgin as a Prefent for Thais, talks to himfelf upon the Art of Flattery: meantime coming up with Parmeno, he attacks him brifkly, and rallies him with a great deal of Keennefs.

GNATHO, PARMENO.

Gnatho. IMMORTAL Gods! How much one Man excels another? What a difference there is betwixt an underftanding Man, and a Fool? This Reflection came into my Mind on this occafion. As I was coming along to-day, I met one of my own Quality and Rank, none of your fordid Wretches, but one who had guzzled away his Patrimony, in like manner as I had done. I fee him rough, nafty, fickly, befet with Rags and Years. What for a Drefs is this, fays I? *Becaufe, Wretch that I am, I have fquandered away all I had: hah, to what am I reduced! all my Acquaintance and Friends have abandoned me.* Here I held him in contempt

ANNOTATIONS.

Towards the End of the laft Scene, as *Parmeno* is wondering with himfelf, at the fudden Change which Love had occafioned in his Mafter, he fees *Gnatho,* the Soldier's Parafite, coming up at fome diftance, and bringing along with him *Pamphila,* as a Prefent for *Thais.* This is ftill continued here. The Parafite advances, and is all the way talking to himfelf, and applauding his own Ingenuity, in comparifon of that of many others of the like Condition with himfelf. After fome time he obferves *Parmeno* ftanding before *Thais's* Door, and is pleafed to think that he had the Air of one who expected to meet with but an indifferent Reception. He goes up to him with a Defign to infult him, and have a little Diverfion at his Expence, which produces a very fmart Converfation between them.

¹ *Stulto intelligens quid intereft! Donatus* very ingenioufly remarks here, that the Poet artfully conveys into this Speech of the Parafite feveral fine Strokes of Satire againft the Manners of his own Age. A Man of Modefty, who cannot prevail upon himfelf to ftoop to any Meannefs, is reprefented as a Fool, and left to languifh in Poverty. But a Rogue who will ftick at no Inftance of Bafenefs to accomplifh his Ends, is treated as an underftanding Man, a Man of Ingenuity and Addrefs. *Horace* draws the fame Picture of the *Romans* of his Time, in the fixth

PA. Dii boni! quid hoc morbi eft? adeon' homines
   immutarier
Ex amore, ut non cognoscas eundem effe? hoc nemo
   fuit   20
Minus ineptus, magis feverus quifquam, nec magis
   continens.   [parafitus Gnatho
Sed quis hic eft, qui huc pergit? at at, hic quidem eft
Militis. ducit fecum unà virginem dono huic: papæ!
Facie honeftà. mirum, ni ego me turpiter hodie hic
   dabo
Cum me) decrepito hoc eunucho. hæc fuperat ipfam
   Thaidem.   25

*facie honefta; mirum ni ego dabo me hic turpiter hodie, cum hoc meo decrepito eunucho. Hæc fu-
perat Thaidem ipfam.*

PA. Dii boni! quid morbi eft hoc? boninefne adeo immutarier ex amore, ut non cognofcas aliquem effe eundem? Nemo fuit minus ineptus hoc, nec quifquam magis feverus, nec magis eft hic, qui pergit huc? at at, hic quidem eft Gnatho parafitus militis: ducit unà fecum virginem dono huic; papæ!

ANNOTATIONS.

resolution and Inconfiftency, never continu- | which could produce fo fudden a Change in
ing a moment in the fame Mind, and this | the Temper, and fo totally enfeeble and un-
entirely owing to his Paffion for *Thais*. He | man the Soul.
had, therefore, reafon to call Love a Difeafe, |

ACTUS II.   SCENA II.

ARGUMENTUM.

*Gnatho, ex mandato militis, deducens puèllam ad Thaidem,
factum adulandi inftituit: interea forte in Parmenonem incidit; in quem multa dicacitate illudit, eumque mordacibus
falibus laceffit.*

GNATHO, PARMENO.

DII immortales! homini homo quid præftat! ftulto
   intellegens
Quid intereft! hoc adeo ex hac revenit in mentem mihi:
Conveni hodie adveniens quendam mei loci hinc atque
   ordinis,
Hominem haud impurum, itidem patria qui abligu-
   rierat bona.   4
Video fentum, fqualidum, ægrum, pannis annifque
   obfitum.   [quod habui, perdidi,
Quid iftuc, inquam, ornati eft? Quoniam mifer,
Hem, quò redactus fum! omnes noti me atque amici
   deferunt.

ORDO. GN. DII immortales! homo quid præftat homini! intelligens, quid intereft ftulte! hoc adeo venit in mentem mihi ex hac re: Hodie adveniens conveni quendam hominem mei loci atque ordinis, haud impurum, qui itidem abligurierat patria bona. Video fentum, fqualidum, ægrum, obfitum pan-

*ris annifque. Inquam, Quid ornati eft iftuc? refpondet: Quoniam mifer perdidi id, quod ha-
bui; hem, quò fum redactus, omnes noti atque amici deferunt me.*

ANNOTATIONS.

fixth Satire of his fecond Book, where | which we live, as thofe in which the Poet
Ulyffes and *Tirefias* are introduced, above an | wrote: for who that has the leaft know-
hundred and twenty Years after *Terence.* | ledge of human Life, has not in many In-
This is, indeed, a Misfortune that we find | ftances feen Impudence to get the better of
has been complain'd of in all Ages, and the | Modefty?
Satire is equally applicable to the Times in | 7 *Noti.* This Word is ufed frequently,
                                                               both

tempt compared with myfelf. What, fays I, thou moſt ſlothful and
dulleſt of Mortals, have you then brought yourſelf to that, that not ſo
much as Hope remains? Have you loſt your Underſtanding, as well as
your Eſtate? Don't you ſee me recovered from the ſame Situation?
How freſh my Complexion, how neat, how well-dreſſed, and what a
good plight of Body I am in! I have not any thing of my own, and
yet command whatever I pleaſe; and though I ſeem to have nothing,
yet is nothing wanting. *But I am of that unhappy Temper, that I can
neither bear to be made ridiculous, nor ſubmit to Blows.* How? Do
you imagine that's the way? You're quite miſtaken. Formerly, in
days of yore, a Living was to be got by this means; but this is a new
fetch, of which I pretend to have been the firſt Inventor. There is
a Race of Men, who would be accounted the firſt in every thing,
and are not. Theſe are the Men for my purpoſe. I make court
to them, not to be laughed at, but I am the firſt to laugh at them,
and at the ſame time ſeem to admire their fine Parts. Whatever
they ſay, I praiſe it; if they ſay juſt the contrary again, I praiſe that
too: Does any one deny? I deny: does he affirm? I affirm. In fine,
I have made it a Law with myſelf, to humour them in every thing.
This Method of Gain is now by much the moſt profitable.

Parm. A very ſhrewd Perſon this truly! From Fools he bids fair
to make Men downright mad. [*Aſide.*

Gnat.

ANNOTATIONS.

both in an active and paffive Signification, and ferves to expreſs either thoſe who are known to us, or thoſe to whom we are known. We have a clear Example of its being uſed in this laſt Senſe, in *Phædrus*, Lib. I. Fab. 11.

Virtutis expers verbis jactans gloriam,
Ignotos fallit, notis eſt deriſui.

" A Man who, without any Pretence to Va-
" lour, is yet perpetually boaſting of his
" Bravery, may impoſe upon thoſe who
" know him not, but muſt appear ridiculous
" to thoſe to whom he is known."

10 *Simul conſilium cum re amiſti?* This, as *Donatus* obſerves, is an Interrogation of one blaming and chiding, and does not require an Anſwer. The Parafite thinks his Friend's Plea no Excuſe at all, becauſe, however Fortune might deprive him of his Eſtate, ſhe had no power over his Mind, nor could weaken thoſe Abilities, by which he might, if he would exert himſelf, retrieve his ruined Circumſtances. This Diſtinction we meet with frequently in the Writings of the Ancients. Thus, *Virgil Æn. 2.* when *Sinon* is brought as a Captive before *Priam*, makes him ſay;

------ *Nec, ſi miſerum fortuna Sinonem*
Finxit: vanum etiam mendacemque improbo
finget.

And *Salluſt B. Jug.* 1. *Neque fortuna eget: quippe quæ probitatem, induſtriam, aliaſque bonas artes neque dare, neque eripere cuiquam poteſt.*

13 *Neque ridiculus eſſe, nec plagas pati poſſum.* We are to obſerve here, that there were anciently two kinds of Parafites. One who, on account of their ſmart Sayings, were entertained at the Tables of the Great, to divert the Company, and called commonly *Scurræ, Buffoons.* Another, who earned a Livelihood by ſubmitting to Blows, and all manner of Indignities. Theſe are well deſcribed by *Valerian Scr.* 10. *de Paraſitis: Huic denique manducanti barba vellitur; illi bibenti ſedilia ſubtrahuntur; hic ligno ſciſſili, ille fragili vitro paſcitur.* Theſe, becauſe often ſubjected to the Whip, *Flagrum,* are ſometimes called *flagriones,* and becauſe they ſold their Shoulders to ſuffer Blows, *Plautus* names them *plagipatidæ,* in thoſe celebrated Lines of the *Captives.* Act III. Sc. I. v. 9.

Illicet paraſiticæ arti maximam in malam
crucem:
Ita juventus jam ridiculos inopeſque abs ſe
ſegregat.
Nihil morantur jam Laconas imi ſubſellii
viros,
Plagipatidas, quibus ſunt verba ſine penu
& pecunia.

" We

Hic ego illum contemfi præ me : Quid, homo, inquam,
  ignaviffime,
Itane parafti te, ut fpes nulla reliqua in te fiet tibi?
Simul confilium cum re amîfti? viden' me ex eodem
  ortum loco?   10
Qui color, nitor, veftitus, quæ habitudo eft corporis?
Omnia habeo, neque quidquam habeo : nil cum eft,
  nil defit tamen.
At ego infelix neque ridiculus effe, neque plagas pati
Poffum. Quid? tu his rebus credis fieri? totâ erras viâ.
Olim ifti fuit generi quondam quæftus apud feclum prius.
Hoc novum eft aucupium : ego adeo hanc primus in-
  veni viam.   16
Eft genus hominum, qui effe primos fe omnium rerum
  volunt,   [rideant,
Nec funt. hoc confector : hifce ego non paro me ut
Sed eis ultro arrideo, & corum ingenia admiror fimul :
Quidquid dicunt, laudo : id rurfum fi negant, laudo
  id quoque :   20
Negat quis? nego : ait? aio : poftremo, imperavi ego-
  met mihi,
Omnia affentari. is quæftus nunc eft multo uberrimus.
PA. Scitum hercle hominem! hic homines prorfum ex
  ftultis infanos facit.

Hic ego contemfi illum præ me : Quid, homo ignaviffime inquam; paraftine te ita, ut nulla fpes fiet reliqua tibi in te? amififti confilium fimul cum re? Videfne me erum ex eodem loco? Qui color, nitor, veftitus eft mihi? Quæ eft habitudo corporis? habeo omnia, nec habeo quidquam : cum nil eft mihi, tamen nil defit. Ille inquit: At ego infelix neque poffum effe ridiculus, neque pati plagas. Quid? refpondeo : tu credis fieri his rebus? erras totâ via. Fuit quondam olim quæftus ifti generi, apud prius feculum. Hoc eft novum aucupium : ego adeo primus inveni hanc viam. Eft genus hominum, qui volunt fe effe primos omnium rerum, nec funt : con-

fector hos. Ego paro me hifce, non ut rideant me, fed ultro arrideo eis, & fimul admiror ingenia eorum : laudo quidquid dicunt : fi negant id rurfum, laudo id quoque : quis negat? nego : ait? aio : poftremo, egomet imperavi mihi affentari omnia : is quæftus eft nunc multo uberrimus. PA. Ecce hercle fcitum hominem! hic facit homines ex ftultis prorfum infanos.

ANNOTATIONS.

"We muft bid adieu to the Profeffion of
"Parafites, which is no more of any value.
"The Youth now make little account of
"poor Buffoons, they now no more think
"of brave Lacedemonians, of Men of the
"loweft Couch, of thefe Blow-bearers, who
"have only Words inftead of Meat and
"Money." This poor Wretch tells Gnatho,
that he is fit to be of neither of thefe kinds.
The Parafite, to encourage him, tells him
that thefe are an antiquated Race, now no
more heard of ; and that there was a third
Kind of his Invention, expofed to no ill
Ufage, nor made the Jeft of the Company,
viz. Flatterers, who ftudied to ingratiate
themfelves with Men of Fortune, by humouring them in every thing, and pretending
to admire whatever they faid or did.

13 Olim ifti fuit generi quon'am quæftus
apud fotum prius. Gnatho is not contented
with faying olim, he adds too quondam, and
to imprefs yet more ftrongly his Meaning,
fubious apud fedum prius. Ifti generi fignifies here to Men of that Profeffion, for

genus is often ufed to exprefs any particular
Manner or Method.   Thus, in Phædrus,
Prologue to Book fecond ; Æfopi genus, The
manner of Æfop : and again, Ufus verufto genere, fed rebus novis. "Keeping ftill to the
"ancient manner of Writing, but upon Sub-
"jects wholly new." Dacier.

19 Sed eis ultro arrideo. This Defcription
of the Manner of the Parafites of that Age
feems to have been copied from Eupolis, a
famed Athenian Writer of the old Comedy,
of whom we have ftill a Paffage remaining,
which tranflated is thus ;

Veftes vero mihi duæ funt feftivæ : larum
  induens
Semper alteram in forum erumpo : illicque
  poftquam
Afpicio quempiam virum fatuum, et di-
  vitem, ftatim huic me applico,
Et fi quid forte dives dicat, vehementer
  laudo, & ftupefcens admiror,
Præ me ferens quafi verbis læter.

23 Scitum hercle hominem! Terence, with
great Judgment, introduces often in his So-
                   liloquies

Gnat. (*To himself.*) While we are thus chatting together, we came to the Market, when immediately ran to meet me, with Countenances full of Joy, a whole Troop of Confectioners, Fishmongers, Butchers, Cooks, Sausage-makers, and Fishermen ; to whom, both in my good and bad Fortune, I had been very serviceable, and often am so still. They salute me, invite me to Supper, and express their Joy at my coming. Then the poor hungry Wretch, when he sees me in so great Honour, and what an easy way of living I had got into ; began to intreat, that I would allow him to learn this Art of me. I bid him follow me, that as the Schools of Philosophers take Names from their several Heads, so, if possible, Parasites may, in like manner, be called the Sect of *Gnathonicks.*

Parm. Do you see the Effects of Idleness, and living at another's Expence ? [*Aside.*

Gnat. (*Still to himself.*) But I delay, all this while, carrying this Girl to *Thais,* and inviting her to come to Supper. (*Seeing* Parmeno.) But I see *Parmeno,* our Rival's Servant, standing before *Thais's* Door, with

ANNOTATIONS.

liloquies Persons, who overhear at a distance, and, by throwing in here and there a Sentence, prevent the chief Speaker from appearing tedious.

²⁴ *Ad macellum ubi advenimus.* Various are the Etymologies of this Word, given both by Ancients and Moderns. *Varro* gives this account of it. Lib. 4. *Hæc omnia postquam contracta in unum locum, quæ ad victum pertinebant, & ædificatus locus, appellatum* Macellum, *ut quidam scribunt, quod ibi fuerit ortus ; alii, quod ibi domus fuerit, cui cognomen fuit* Macellus, *quæ ibi publice diruta, e qua ædificium hoc, quod vocatur ab eo* Macellum. Others, among whom *Donatus,* derive it, *à mactandis pecoribus.* But this last Derivation has this Objection against it, that it would answer only to the *Shambles,* whereas both at *Athens* and at *Rome,* as appears by the Catalogue immediately following, the *Macellum* was a Place where all sorts of Provision were sold, and therefore ought to be rendered by our word *Market.* *Donatus* remarks here, that the Poet is guilty of an Error, in transporting to *Athens* what was to be met with only at *Rome,* and this Error he calls *Peccatum comicum, in palliata res Romanas loquitur.* But it may be questioned whether this is, indeed, a Remark of *Donatus.* He was a Person of too much Learning not to know, that at *Athens,* as well as at *Rome,* there was a Place where Dealers in all kinds of Provisions had their Stations, as may still be seen in some of the Comedies of *Aristophanes.* Nay, without having recourse to *Aristophanes,* the *Trinummus* of *Plautus* is also

one of the Pieces called *Palliatæ,* being translated from a *Greek* Original, and in that Play *Plautus* introduces the same Set which *Terence* brings in here. Act II. Scene IV. Verse 6.

Piscator, pistor abstulit, lanii, coqui,
Olitores, myropolæ, aucupes ; confit cito
Quam si tu objicias formicis papaverem.

²⁵ *Cupedinari.* Qui *cupiditatibus populi serviunt : omnes enim qui esculenta & poculenta vendebant, a rebus cupedinis ob alimentum cupedinarii appellabantur.*

²⁶ *Cetarii.* *Genus est piscatorum* (says Non. Marcellinus) *quod majores pisces capit. Dictum ab eo, quod cete in mari sunt majora piscium genera.* Hence, *Horace* Lib. 2. Sat. 5. 44. calls the Ponds and Apparatus for catching the greater kind of Fishes *cetaria.* Ibid. *Lanii.* *Qui laniabant pecus.* Ibid. *Coqui.* Hi *macellum frequentabant, atque inde conducebantur ab iis, qui lautiores epulas apparant.* Plaut. Aul. II. 4. 1.

Postquam obsonavit herus, & conduxit coquos
Tibicinasque hasce, apud forum, edixit mihi,
Ut dispartirem obsonium hic bifariam.

Ibid. *Fartores.* Qui *istia & farcimina faciunt, vel quod aves farcirent, h. e. saginarent, & altiles facerent ; unde iidem aviarii & altiliarii sæpe vocati.* Ibid. *Piscatores.* They differed from the *Cetarii* in this, that they dealt in the smaller kind of Fish, which they sold fresh, and sometimes alive, whereas the others dealt in the larger sort, salted, or preserved in Pickle. Ibid.

Aucupes,

Gn. Dum hæc loquimur, interea loci ad macellum ubi
   advenimus,
Concurrūnt læti mî obviam cupedinarii omnes,   25
Cetarii, lanii, coqui, fartores, piscatores, aucupes,
Quibus & re salvâ & perditâ profueram & prosum sæpe:
Salutant: ad cœnam vocant : adventum gratulantur.
Ille ubi miser, famelicus, videt me esse tanto honore,
Et tam facilè victum quærere ; ibi homo cœpit me
   obsecrare,   30
Ut sibi liceret discere id de me. sectari jussi ,
Si potis est, tanquam philosophorum habent disciplinæ
   ex ipsis
Vocabula, parasiti itidem ut Gnathonici vocentur.
Pa. Viden', otium & cibus quid facit alienus ? Gn. sed
   ego cesso
Ad Thaidem hanc deducere, & rogare ad cœnam ut
   veniat.   35
Sed Parmenonem ante ostium Thaidis tristem video,

Gn. Interea loci, dum loquimur hæc ubi advenimus ad macellum, cupedinarii omnes, cetarii, lanii, coqui, fartores, piscatores, aucupes, quibus & re salvâ, & perdita, profueram, & sæpe prosum, læti, concurrunt obviam mihi; salutant : vocant ad cœnam : gratulantur adventum. Ille miser & famelicus, ubi videt me esse in tanto honore, & quærere victum tam facile, ibi homo cœpit obsecrare me, ut liceret sibi discere id de me. Jussi sectari : ut si est potis, parasiti itidem vocentur Gnathonici, tanquam disciplinæ philosophorum habent vocabula ex ipsis. Pa. Videsne quid otium & cibus alienus facit ? Gn. Sed ego cesso deducere hanc ad Thaidem, & rogare ut veniat ad cœnam. Sed video Parmenonem servum rivalis tristem ante ostium Thaidis.

ANNOTATIONS.

Aucupes. This last Word is rejected by several Commentators, as disagreeing with the Measure of the Verse ; *Donatus* makes no mention of it, and *Tanaquil Faber* contends, that were it retained, it would amount to no more than an Explication of *fartores*, which he imagines to be the same with the *aviarii*. But methinks we ought not to be too rash in rejecting a word that has so many Authorities to support it. *Horace* seems to have had this Passage in his Eye, in these Lines of the third Satire of his second Book, Ver. 226.

> *Hic simul accepit patrimonî mille talenta,*
> *Edicit, piscator uti, pomarius, auceps,*
> *Unguentarius, ac Tusci turba impia vici,.*
> *Cum scurris fartor, cum Velabro omne macellum,*
> *Mane domum veniat.*

" No sooner is he Master of his Patrimony
" of a thousand Talents, than he summons
" the Fishmonger, the Fruitman, the Hunts-
" man, the Perfumer, the whole impious
" Croud of the Tuscan Ward, the Buffoons,
" Poulterers, Dutchers, Cheesemongers, and
" all of that stamp, to attend his Levee
" next Morning."

³¹ *Sectari jussi.* This refers to the manner of the ancient Philosophers, who commonly went, followed by a Croud of their Disciples, called hence *sectatores* and *sectæ.* In time, the Word *Sect* came to signify any

Number of Men, agreeing in the same Philosophical Principles and Tenets. These *Sects* were for the most part denominated from him, who was accounted their first Founder, or at least had made the chief Figure in it, as the *Sect of Platonists*, the *Epicurean Sect*. In allusion to this, the Poet very pleasantly introduces the Parasite contriving to found a new *Sect* upon the Principles of his own Art, which he proposes to entitle the *Sect of Gnathonicks*.

³² *Si potis est.* These Words, as they are here placed, seem very intricate and perplexed, the true Sense and Construction of them is thus : *Ut Parasiti item* (itidem) *vocentur Gnathonici, si potis est* (fieri) *tanquam disciplinæ* (scholæ) *philosophorum habent vocabula ex ipsis* (philosophis.) That *Disciplina* is sometimes used for a School, or Sect of Philosophers, appears from these Words of *Cicero, Fin.* 3. 11. *Præter, enim tres Disciplinas, quæ virtutem a summo bono excludunt; cæteris omnibus philosophis hæc est tuenda sententia.* Moreover, it was usual for Parasites to speak of themselves as formed by Rules, and to consult their Books on some particular Occasions. Thus, *Gelasimus*, in *Plautus, Stich.* II. 2. 75.

> *Ibo intro ad libros, & discam de dictis meliori-*
> *bus.*

And again, III. 2. 1.

> *Libros inspexi, tom consido, quam potest,*
> *Me meum élructurum regem ridiculis meis.*

³⁷ *Rivalis*

with a very dejected Air. All is fafe. The Men, or I miftake, have
a cold Poft of it. I'm refolved to have a little Sport with this
Knave.

Parm. They think, I warrant, that by this Prefent, *Thais* is for
ever theirs.   [*Afide.*

Gnat. Gnatho complements his very dear Friend *Parmeno* with his
beft Wifhes. What are you a doing?

Parm. I'm ftanding.

Gnat. I fee fo : but is there nothing here that you could wifh out
of fight?

Parm. You.

Gnat. I believe it, but nothing elfe?

Parm. Why fo?

Gnat. Becaufe you look melancholy.

Parm. Not in the leaft.

Gnat. Nay, pray don't. But what think you of this Slave?

Parm. Why really fhe's not amifs.

Gnat. (*Turning to the Spectators.*) I have galled the Fellow.

Parm. (*Overhearing.*) How much he is miftaken!   [*Afide.*

Gnat. How will this Prefent, d'ye think, be received by *Thais?*

Parm. I know you mean to fay, that we are difcarded. Hark
yee, Friend, there's a Viciffitude of all Things.

Gnat. Parmeno, I'll fet you at eafe for fix whole Months, that
you may'nt be running conftantly up and down, and fitting up till
day-break. Don't I blefs you much?

Parm. Me! Hugely.

Gnat. So I am wont to do my Friends.

Parm. I commend you.

Gnat. But I detain you; perhaps you was going fomewhere elfe.

Parm. Nowhere in the world.

Gnat. Then give me a little of your Help : fee to procure me Admittance here.

Parm. Very good : at prefent, thefe Doors are open to you, becaufe you bring this Slave.

Gnat. Do you want that I fhould call any one out to you? [*Enters.*

Parm. (*Alone.*) Let but thefe two Days be over, and I'll undertake that you, who are now fo happy as to open thefe Doors with a
touch of your little Finger, fhall often kick them to no purpofe with
your Heels.   *Gnat.*

ANNOTATIONS.

37 *Rivalis fervum.* Rivales were Shepherds, who had Water from the fame Spring
or Brook, *quafi eodem rivo utentes:* hence Eu-
grophius upon this word, *Rivales dicuntur qui
unam amant, vel meretricem, vel amicam; quod
quafi uno rivo amoris utantur.*

Ibid. *Hic homines frigent.* Frigus, and fri-
geo, was a word often ufed in Cafes of loft
Favour, juft as in our Language, we fay a
Man meets with a *cold Reception.* Horace,
Book II. Sat. I. 60.

------ O puer, ut fis
*Vitalis metuo, & majorum ne quis amicus
Frigore te feriat.*
Perf. Sat. I. 108.

------ *Vide, fis, ne majorum tibi forte
Limina trigefcant.*

38 *Nebulonem hunc certum eft ludere.* Nebulo is derived by fome from *nebula,* a Cloud,
denoting a Man of no Value, unftable as a
Cloud, guided neither by Reafon nor Intereft.

Rivalis fervum. falva res eft : nimirum homines frigent.
Nebulonem hunc certum eft ludere. PA. hice hoc mu-
  nere arbitrantur
Suam Thaidem effe. GN. Plurimâ falute Parmenonem
Summum fuum impertit Gnatho. quid agitur? PA. fta-
  tur. GN. video: 40
Numquidnam hic, quod nolis, vides? PA. te. GN. cre-
  do. at numquid aliud? [ne fis. fed quid videtur
PA.Quî dum; GN. quia trifti' es. PA. nihil equidemGN.
Hoc tibi mancupium? PA. non malum hercle. GN. uro
  hominem. PA. ut falfus animi eft!
GN. Quàm hoc munus gratum Thaidi arbitrare effe?
  PA. hoc nunc dicis,
Ejcétos hinc nos. omnium rerum, heus, viciffitudo eft.
GN. Sex ego te totos, Parmeno, hos menfes quietum
  reddam; 46
Nc furfum, deorfum curfites; neve ufque ad lucem
  vigiles. [PA. laudo.
Ecquid beo te? PA. men'? papæ! GN. fic foleo amicos.
GN. Detineo te: fortaffe tu profeétus aliò fueras.
PA. Nufquam. GN. tum tu igitur paululum da mihi
  operæ: fac admittar 50
Ad illam. PA. age, modò nunc tibi patent fores hæ,
  quia iftam ducis.
GN. Numquem evocari hinc vis foras? PA. fine bidu-
  um hoc prætereat;
Qui mihi nunc uno digitulo fores aperis fortunatus,
Næ tu iftas, faxo, calcibus fæpe infultabis fruftra.

ufque ad lucem. Ecquid beo te? PA. Mene? papæ. GN. Sic foleo amicos. PA. Laudo. GN. Detineo te; fortaffe tu fueras profeétus aliò. PA. Nufquam. GN. Tum tu igitur da mibi paulu- lum operæ: fac ut admittar ad illam. PA. Age, modo hæ fores nunc patent tibi, quia ducis iftam. GN. Num vis quem evocari hinc foras? PA. Sine hoc biduum prætereat; tu qui fortu- natus nunc aperis fores mibi uno digitule, næ faxo ut tu fæpe infultabis iftas calcibus fruftra.

Ret eft falva : nimi-
rum homines frigent.
Certum eft ludere hunc
nebulonem. PA. Hice
arbitrantur Thaidem
effe fuam boc munere.
GN. Gnatho imper-
tit Parmenonem fuum
fummum plurimâ fa-
lute. Quid agitur?
PA. Statur. GN.
Video : numquid vi-
des hic, quod nolis?
PA. Video te. GN.
Credo : at numquid
vides aliud? PA.
Quî dum? GN.
Quia es triftis. PA.
Equidem nibil. GN.
Ne fis. Sed quid boc
mancupium videtur
tibi? PA. Hercle
non malum. GN.
Uro bominem. PA.
Ut eft falfus animi!
GN. Quam gratum
arbitrare boc munus
effe Thaidi? PA.
Dicis boc nunc, ros
effe ejeétos hinc. Heus
tu, eft viciffitudo om-
nium rerum. GN.
Parmeno, ego red-
dam te quietum bos
totos fex menfes, ne
curfites furfum, deor-
fum; neve vigiles

ANNOTATIONS.

reft. The Reafon of this Derivation is the fame as that of *tenebrio* from *tenebræ*. *Ne- bulones* and *tenebriones*, are impious and wick- ed Men, who love Darknefs, and hate Light; for fo *Non. Marcellinus* exprefsly, *Nebulones & tenebriones dicuntur, qui mendaciis & aftu- tiis fuis nebulam quandam & tenebras objiciunt.* "By *Nebulones* and *Tenebriones*, are common- "ly underftood Perfons, who endeavour by "Lying and Artifice to throw a Cloud over "things."

40 *Quid agitur?* This whole Addrefs is an Affeétation of Friendfhip, to render the other ridiculous, and the latter Part of it is not fo properly afking a Queftion, as a flat- tering Infinuation of his Concern for him. The proper Meaning therefore of *quid agitur?* here is, *How fare you? How goes the World with you?* But in the Verfion there was a neceffity for rendering them fo, as they might admit of *Parmeno*'s Anfwer; for al- though we are to fuppofe *quid agitur?* to have a fingle Meaning as fpoke by Gnatho, yet *Parmeno* archly renders it ambiguous, by anfwering *Statur*.

43 *Mancupium.* Slaves taken in War, and bought by the State, were called *man- cipia*, probably as being *manu capti.* Hence *mancipium* came to fignify any juft and law- ful Poffeffion, or whatever a Perfon had a Property in, as his Slaves, &c.

52 *Sine biduum hoc prætereat. Parmeno* fays thefe three Lines, while *Gnatho* is go- ing in to *Thais.* He pronounces them flow- ly, and with an Air that demonftrates his Contempt of the Parafite, and his Confi- dence

Gnat. (Coming out.) What are you still here, *Parmeno?* Was you left here to keep Watch, that no private Messenger might pass between the Captain, and the Lady?

Par. Wittily said! but they must be fine Things that can please the Captain. *(Seeing* Chærea.*)* But I see my Master's youngest Son coming this way; I wonder how he came to leave the Port, for he is there, at present, upon Duty. It can be no Trifle, and he seems in a hurry too; I can't guess why he looks about him so earnestly.

ANNOTATIONS.

dence, that he shall soon be able to triumph over him, after which he walks up and down upon the Stage meditating, and making some Guestures, to fill up the Scene, till *Gnatho*

comes out from offering the Present to *Thais.* 59 *Miror, quid ex Piræo abierit.* This was a Port in *Athens,* where the *Athenian* Youth were placed on Duty, by turns, to watch,

---

ACT II. SCENE III.

ARGUMENT.

Chærea, Phædria's *Brother, having lost Sight of the Virgin, whom, as* Gnatho *was leading to* Thais, *he had followed from the Port into the City, being struck with her uncommon Beauty; looks about for her. Afterwards, by* Parmeno's *Advice, he is introduced to* Thais, *in the* Eunuch's *Dress, which soon occasions a great Disturbance.*

CHÆREA, PARMENO.

Chærea. I'M ruin'd! for neither can I see the Virgin any where, nor do I know where I am myself, who have lost Sight of her. Where shall I look for her? Where shall I trace her? Of whom shall I inquire? Or what rout shall I take? I am quite at a loss: this only hope remains, that wherever she is, she can't long be concealed. O charming Creature! From this Moment I banish all other Women from my Heart; I can no longer endure these vulgar every-day Faces.

Par. So: here's another for you, he talks I don't know what about Love too: O unhappy old Man! for this is a Youth, who, if he

ANNOTATIONS.

In this Scene, we have a new Character; a Youth of a rash ungovernable Temper in love. As *Gnatho* was leading *Pamphila* from his Master to *Thais, Chærea,* Phædria's Brother, who was at that time upon Duty at the *Piræus,* chanced to see her, and, suddenly struck with her uncommon Beauty, followed all the Way to the Street, where *Thais* lived, designing, if possible, to find out who she was. But meeting by the Way with *Archidemides,* his Father's Kinsman, while he talks with him, *Gnatho* had delivered the

Girl to *Thais,* and turned another way. *Chærea,* who had now got rid of the Old Man, is introduced here, looking round for *Pamphila,* whom he had lost Sight of. As he is fretting with himself, and venting Imprecations against the Old Man for detaining him, he sees *Parmeno.* A Conversation thereupon arises, by which he is informed of all he wanted to know; and a Project is formed betwixt them, of habiting him in the *Eunuch's* Dress, and presenting him to *Thais* in his stead. *Parmeno* hesitates for some

Gn. Etiam nunc hic ſtas, Parmeno? eho, numnam hic
   relictus cuſtos,   55
Ne quis forte internuncias clàm à milite ad iſtam cur-
   ſitet?
Pa. Facetè dictum ! mira vero, militi quæ placeant.
Sed video herilem filium minorem huc advenire. [nunc.
Miror, quid ex Piræeo abierit : nam ibi cuſtos publice eſt
Non temere eſt : & properans venit : neſcio quid cir-
   cumſpectat.   60

quid abierit ex Piræeo; nam nunc eſt cuſtos ibi publice. Non eſt temere, & venit properans : cir-
cumſpectat neſcio quid.

ANNOTATIONS.

watch, left any Incurſions ſhould be made by Pirates, or other Enemies. As they were not at liberty to leave their Station, but in the moſt urgent Neceſſity, *Parmeno* had | reaſon to appear ſurprized at ſeeing *Chærea*, and very naturally concluded, that it muſt be ſomething of Conſequence which led him that Way.

ACTUS II. SCENA III.

ARGUMENTUM.

Chærea frater Phædriæ, virginem, quam Gnathone deducente, ſecutus erat ex Piræeo in urbem, ob ſingularem ipſius pulchri-tudinem, propter quam in ipſius amorem exarſerat, è con-ſpectu ſuo amiſſam queritur. Deinde conſilio Parmenonis ſub eunuchi habitu ad Thaidem deducitur : unde motus oritur in fabula.

CHÆREA, PARMENO.   ORDO.

OCCIDI.
   Neque virgo eſt uſquam, neque ego, qui illam
     è conſpectu amiſi meo.   [inſiſtam viam?
Ubi quæram? ubi inveſtigem? quem percontor? quam
Incertus ſum : una hæc ſpes eſt; ubi ubi eſt, diu cela-
   ri non poteſt.   4
O faciem pulchram! deleo omnes dehinc ex animo
   mulieres :
Tædet quotidianarum harum formarum. Pa. ecce
   autem alterum ;
Neſcio quid de amore loquitur. ô infortunatum ſenem !

tædet harum quotidianarum formarum. Pa. autem ecce alterum : loquitur neſcio quid de amore.
O infortunatum ſenem !

ANNOTATIONS.

ſome time, but at laſt, in a manner compelled by *Chærca*, conſents.
  5 *Deleo omnes dehinc ex animo mulieres.* The Character of *Chærea* is that of one who is violent in his Paſſions, and will ha-zard any thing to gratify them. The Poet | makes us ſenſible of this, by his manner at his very firſt Appearance, and ſtill more by what *Parmeno* ſays upon over-hearing him. This was neceſſary to prepare us for what is ſoon after to follow.

he once begins, you'll say the other was meer Play and Pastime, in comparison of the wild Projects his Madness will drive him to.

Chær. May all the Gods and Goddesses confound that old Dotard, who stopped me To-day, and me too, who was so great a Fool as to be hindered by him, or thought it worth my while to stay a Moment for him. But I see *Parmeno*; Good-morrow.

Parm. Why so thoughtful? Why in such a Flutter? Where have you been?

Chær. What I? I can neither tell you where I have been, nor where I am going, so wholly am I absent from myself.

Parm. How, pray?

Chær. I'm in Love.

Parm. Hah!

Chær. Now, *Parmeno*, let me see what a Man you are; you know that you have often promised: " *Chærea*, find but some Girl " that you can like, and I'll soon convince you, how useful I can be " to you in these Matters." 'Twas when I was wont to pillage my Father's Pantry, and convey it privately into your little Cell.

Parm. Pshaw, foolish.

Chær. 'Twas even so: now let your Promises appear, in a Case that so well deserves your exerting all your Abilities. The Girl that I speak of, is not like our Town Ladies, whose Mothers endeavour to have them with Shoulders pressed down, and straiten'd Chests, that they may be slender. If one is a little more plump than ordinary, they say she is an Hostess, and stint her in her Meals; so that though she is well formed enough by Nature, by their over and above Care they reduce her to a Bulrush. 'Tis for this Reason, they are so much admired.

Parm. What for a Girl is this of yours?

Chær. A Countenance of quite a new Make.

Parm. Bless me!

Chær. Her Complexion true, her Body sound, and in admirable Plight.

Parm. Her Age?

Chær. Her Age?——Sixteen.

Parm. The very Flower of Youth.

Chær. See you get her for me, whether by Force, Fraud, or Persuasion; 'tis all one to me, so I but enjoy her.

Parm. Well, but whom does this Virgin belong to?

Chær. I know nothing of that.

Parm. Whence came she?

Chær. Just as much.

Parm. Where does she live?   *Chær.*

ANNOTATIONS.

9. *Præut hujus rabies quæ dabis.* *Donatus* remarks here, that the Poet contrives to make *Parmeno* speak in this manner of *Chærea*, that it might appear he was no Novice in Love-matters. And *Terence*, adds he, takes great Care, that it may not seem in-credible, that a Youth, who might be made to pass for a Eunuch, should so suddenly debauch a Virgin. Therefore like a thorow Master, what could not belong to the Age, he refers to the natural Disposition of *Chærea*. For being of a warm Temper, and subjected
to

Hic vero eft, qui fi occeperit, ludum jocumque dices
Fuiffe illum alterum, præut hujus rabies quæ dabit.
CH. Ut illum di deæque feñem perdant, qui me hodie
    remoratus eft ;   10
Meque adeo, qui reftiterim : tum autem qui illum floc-
    ci fecerim.   [quidve alacris ?
Sed eccum Parmenonem. falve. PA. quid tu es triftis,
Unde is ? CH. egone ? nefcio hercle, neque unde eam,
    neque quorfum eam :
Ita prorfus fum oblitus mei.
PA. Quî, quæfo ? CH. amo. PA. ehem ! CH. nunc,
    Parmeno, te oftendes, qui vir fies.   15
Scis te mihi fæpe pollicitum effe : Chærea aliquid inveni
Modò, quod ames : in câ re utilitatem ego faciam ut
    cognofcas meam :   [bam clanculùm.
Cùm in cellulam ad te patris penum omnem congere-
PA. Age, inepte. CH. hoc hercle factum eft. fac fis
    nunc promiffa appareant,
Sive adeo digna res eft, ubi tu nervos intendas tuos. 20
Haud fimilis virgo eft virginum noftrarum : quas ma-
    tres ftudent
Demiffis humeris effe, vincto pectore, ut gracilæ fient.
Si qua eft habitior paulò, pugilem effe aiunt : deducunt
    cibum :
Tametfi bona eft natura, reddunt curaturâ junceas :
Itaque ergo amantur. PA. quid tua iftæc ? CH. nova
    figura oris. PA. papæ !   25
CH. Color verus, corpus folidum, & fucci plenum.
    PA. anni ? CH. fedecim.
PA. Flos ipfe. CH. anc tu mihi vi, clam, precario,
Fac tradas : meâ nil refert, dum potiar modò.
PA. Quid, virgo cuja eft ? CH. nefcio hercle. PA. unde
    eft ? CH. tantundem. PA. ubi habitat ?

virginum noftrarum ; quas matres ftudent effe humeris demiffis, & vincto pectore, ut fient gracilæ ;
fi qua eft paulò habitior, aiunt effe pugilem ; deducunt cibum : tametfi eft bona natura, reddunt
junceas curaturâ. Ergo itaque amantur. PA. Quid eft iftæc tua virgo ? CH. Figura oris nova.
PA. Papæ. CH. Color verus, corpus folidum, & plenum fucci. PA. Anni quot funt ? CH.
Sedecim. PA. Ipfe flos. CH. Fac tu ut tradas banc mihi, vi, clam, precario : nil refert mea,
dummodo potiar. PA. Quid, cuja eft virgo ? CH. Hercle nefcio. PA. Unde eft ? CH. Tan-
tundem fcio. PA. Ubi habitat ?

ANNOTATIONS.

to the Violence of thefe Paffions, before the ufual Time, his Love, when once kindled, can be reftrained within no Bounds.

10 *Ut illum di deæque fenium perdant.* Ut is here for *utinam*, and *feniam* ftronger and more expreffive, than if he had faid *fcnem.* Nor are we to wonder that the Relative *qui* in the Mafculine Gender, follows *fenium*, becaufe the Conftruction is referred to the

Senfe, as in the Prologue to this fame Play, when he fays, *Tranftulit in Eunuchum fuam.* Befides, *fenex* expreffes barely a Man's Age, *fenium* is a Term of Reproach, and wonderfully fuits the difcontented Humour, in which we muft fuppofe *Chærea* at this time to be.

20 *Sive adeo digna res eft.* Thefe Words, whatever fome Commentators may alledge,

Chær. Nor do I know that.

Par. Where did you fee her?

Chær. In the Street.

Par. How came you to lofe fight of her?

Chær. That's what I was ftorming at myfelf about juft now, in coming along: nor do I believe there is in the World a Man, whofe lucky Rencounters turn out all fo unhappy for him.

Par. What Misfortune now?

Chær. I'm undone.

Par. What's the Matter, pray?

Chær. What's the Matter? Do you know *Archidemides* my Father's Kinfman and Companion?

Par. Why not?

Chær. He, while I was in clofe purfuit of the Girl, came full in my way.

Par. Unfeafonable truly.

Chær. Nay, unhappily rather; for lighter Accidents are to be call'd unfeafonable, *Parmeno.* I am ready to fwear that I have not feen him for thefe fix or feven Months paft till now, when I leaft wanted it, and it was leaft neceffary. How? Is there not fomething monftrous in this? What do you fay?

Par. Monftrous, to be fure.

Chær. He comes running to me a good Diftance off; ftooping, trembling, his Lips hanging, groaning: *Hearkye, hearkye,* Chærea, *'tis you I fpeak to. I ftood. Do you know what I wanted with you? Say. I have a Trial comes on To-morrow.* What then? *Be fure to tell your Father that he remember to appear for me early at Court To-morrow.* While he was faying this, a whole Hour was fpent. I afk if he had any thing further. *That's all.* I left him, but in looking round for the Virgin, I found that fhe was juft turned into this our Street.

Par. A thoufand to one but he means the fame that's juft now prefented to *Thais.*   [*Afide.*

Chær. When I came here, fhe was vanifhed.

Par. Had the Virgin any Attendants with her?

Chær. Yes; a Parafite and a Maid.

Par. (*afide*) 'Tis the fame. (*aloud*) Well, you may fet your Mind at reft, all's over.

Chær. You're a thinking of fomething elfe.   *Par.*

ANNOTATIONS.

are to be referred to *Chærea.* The Order and Senfe of them is thus, *Fac, fi vis nunc, five adeo digna res reft, uti ts nervos intendas tuos, ut premiffa apparcent.*

30 *Qua ratione amifsti?* Had not *Chærea* been detained by *Archidemides,* but followed the Virgin, and feen where fhe was carried before he met with *Parmeno,* the Fable muft have been conducted very differently from the manner in which it is now carried on.

Chærea, it is probable, would not have been fo well inftructed in what regarded *Thais,* nor would the Project of his being prefented to the Courtezan in the Eunuch's Drefs, have fo readily occurred.

32 *Cui magis bonæ facilitates.* He means that thofe Accidents in Life, which at firft had the Appearance of being fortunate, turned out the contrary to him, becaufe he had loft Sight of the Virgin. For he accounts it a Happinefs,

Cн. Ne id quidem. Pa. ubi vidifti? Ch. in viâ Pa. qua ratione amififti? (30

Ch. Id equidem adveniens mecum ftomachabar modò: Neque ego quenquam hominem effe arbitror, cui magis bonæ

Felicitates omnes adverfæ fient.

Pa. Quid hoc fceleris eft? Cн. perii. Pa. quid factum eft? Ch. rogas?

Patris cognatum atque æqualem Archidemidem 35 Noftin'? Pa. quidni? Cн. is, dum fequor hanc, fit mihi obviam.

Pa. Incommodè hercle. Cн. imo enimvero infeliciter: Nam incommoda alia funt dicenda, Parmeno.

Illum, liquet mihi dejerare, his menfibus

Sex, feptem prorfum non vidifle proximis, 40 Nifi nunc, cùm minime vellem, minimeque opus fuit: Eho, nonne hoc monftri fimile eft? quid ais? Pa. maxumè.

Cн. Continuò accurrit ad me, quàm longè quidem, Incurvus, tremulus, labiis demiffis, gemens: Heus, heus, tibi dico, Chærea, inquit. Reftiti. 45 Scin' quid ego te volebam? Dic Cras eft mihi Judicium. Quid tum? Ut diligenter nuncies Patri, advocatus manè mihi effe ut meminerit. Dum hæc loquitur, abiit hora. rogo, numquid velit. Recte, inquit. Abeo. cùm huc refpicio ad virginem, Illa fefe interea commodùm huc advorterat 51 In noftram hanc plateam. Pa. mirum, ni hanc dicit, modò ferat.

Huic quæ data eft dono. Ch. huc cùm advenio, nulla Pa. Comites fecuti fcilicet funt virginem?

Cн. Verùm, parafitus cum ancillâ. Pa. ipfa eft: ilicet, Define, jam conclamatum eft. Ch. alias res agis. 56

Cн. Ne quidem id fcio. Pa. Ubi vidifti? fit? Cн. In via. Pa. Qua ratione amififti? Cн. Equidem adveniens mecum ftomachabar id mecum t reque ego arbitror effe quenquam homini, cui omnes bonæ felicitates funt magis adverfæ. Pa. Quid fceleris eft. hoc Cн. Perii. Pa. Quid eft faciam? Cн. Rogas? Noftine Archidemidem cognatum atque æqualem patris? Pa. Quid ni? Cн. Dum fequor hanc, fit obviam mihi. Pa. Hercle incommode. Cн. Imo enimvero non dicenda incommoda. Liquet mihi dejerare, me non vidiffe fex, feptem menfibus his proximis, nifi nunc, minimeque fuit minime quum vellem mihi, opus. Eho, nonne hoc eft monftri fimile? Quid ais? Pa. Maxume. Cн. Accurrit ad me continuo, quam longè quidem, incurvus, tremulus, labiis demiffis, gemens: Heus, Heus, inquit, dico tibi Chærea. Reftiti. Scifne ait quid ego volebam

bam te? Dic, Cras, eft judicium mihi. Quid, tum? Ut diligenter nuncies patri, ut meminerit effe advocatus mihi mane. Dum loquitur hæc, hora abiit. Rogo numquid velit aliud. Inquit, recte abeo. Cum refpicio huc ad virginem, illa interea commodum adverterat fefe huc, in hanc noftram plateam. Pa. Mirum ni dicit hanc quæ modo eft data huic dono. Cн. Cum advenio huc, erat nulla virgo. Pa. Scilicet, an comites funt fecuti virginem? Cн. Verum, parafitus cum ancilla. Pa. Eft ipfa: ilicet, define, jam eft conclamatum. Cн. Agis alias res.

ANNOTATIONS.

Happinefs, that he had feen her, but that was turned again into a Misfortune, by meeting with *Archidemides*.

44 *Incurvus, tremulus*, &c. Thefe Words agree extremely well with the Temper in which we muft fuppofe *Chærea* at prefent. He was provoked at the Old Man for the Misfortune he had occafioned to him, and therefore reprefents him here in the moft difadvantageous Light.

48 *Advocatus*. This Word has a double Signification. It either means a Friend who went with the Perfon indited to Judgment to do him Honour, or be witnefs in his Caufe, but concerned themfelves no otherwife in the Matter; or it fignifies a Pleader.

56 *Jam conclamatum eft*. That is, fays *Donatus, tranfactum ac finitum*. It is a manner of fpeaking tranflated from the Cuftom at Funerals, becaufe as foon as any Perfon

Par. Not at all; I know perfectly well what I fay.

Chær. What do you know her, pray tell me, or have you feen her?

Par. I have feen her, I know her, and can tell where fhe is gone,

Chær. How, my *Parmeno*, do you know her?

Par. I tell you I know her.

Chær. And can you tell where fhe is gone?

Par. She is juft now carried in as a Prefent to *Thais* the Courtezan.

Chær. What confiderable Man can this be, to make fo rich a Prefent?

Par. *Thrafo* the Soldier, *Phædria*'s Rival.

Chær. My Brother muft have but an indifferent time of it, by your account.

Par. Ay, did you but know what a Prefent he has provided in oppofition to this, you might fay fo indeed.

Chær. What is it, pray?

Par. An Eunuch.

Chær. How! the ugly Wretch he bought Yefterday, that meer Sign of a Man?

Par. The very fame.

Chær. The Man will certainly be thruft out of Doors with his fcurvy Prefent: but I did not know that this *Thais* was our Neighbour.

Par. 'Tis but lately.

Chær. What an unhappy Creature I am, never to have feen her neither: but hark ye, is fhe, as they fay, a great Beauty?

Par. She is indeed.

Chær. But not to be compared with my Girl.

Par. That's another Affair.

Chær. Do, pray, *Parmeno*, let me have this Wench.

Par. I'll do my beft, and labour hard to affift you in it. Do you want any thing elfe with me?

Chær. Where are you a-going now?

Par. Home, to conduct thefe Slaves to *Thais*, as your Brother ordered.

Chær. O happy, happy Eunuch, whofe Lot it is to be fent to that Houfe!

Par.

ANNOTATIONS.

Perfon died, it was cuftomary for the Family to fet up a Cry, e ther to bring their Neighbours together, or to awaken the Soul, if perhaps it fhould be lurking in fome Corner of the Body. *Servius* upon *Virgil* gives this Account of the Cuftoms at Funerals ; *Virg.* Æn. 6. 218. Statim igitur quum exfpirarat mortuus, conclamabatur, deinde depenebatur humi, tunçque fupra terram effe

dicebatur ; poftremum quum exportandum effet cadaver, ultimum conclamabatur. Poftremo, quum in ignem imponeretur, ultimum deflebatur.

64 Quidnam, quæfo hercle? Quæfo and hercle, as they are here ufed, ftrongly mark the Curiofity of *Chærea.* It is alfo worth while to obferve in how natural and eafy a manner the Poet conducts us into all the Windings

of

Pa. Istuc equidem ago. Ch. nostin' quæ sit? dic
  mihi: aut
Vidistin'? Pa. vidi, novi: scio quò abducta sit.
Ch. Eho? Parmeno mi, nostin'? Pa. novi. Ch. et
  scis, ubi siet?
Pa. Huc deducta est ad meretricem Thaidem: ei dono
  data est.   60
Ch. Quis is est tam potens cum tanto munere hoc? Pa.
  miles Thraso
Phædriæ rivalis. Ch. duras partes fratris prædicas.
Ph. Imo enim, si scias quod donum huic dono contra
  comparet,
Tum magis id dicas. Ch. quodnam, quæso hercle?
  Pa. eunuchum. Ch. illumne, obsecro,
Inhonestum hominem, quem mercatus est heri; se-
  nem, mulierem?   65
Pa. Istunc ipsum. Ch. homo quatietur certe cum
  dono foràs.
Sed istam Thaidem non scivi nobis vicinam. Pa. haud
  diu est.   [dum, dic mihi,
Ch. Perii. nunquamne etiam me illam vidisse? eho-
Estne, ut fertur, forma? Pa. sane. Ch. at nihil ad
  nostram hanc. Pa. alia res est.
Ch. Obsecro te hercle, Parmeno, fac ut potiar. Pa.
  faciam sedulo, àc   70
Dabo operam, adjuvabo. numquid me aliud? Ch.
  quo nunc is? Pa. domum.   [Thaidem.
Ut mancipia hæc, ita ut jussit frater, deducam ad
Ch. O fortunatum istum eunuchum, qui quidem in
  hanc detur domum!   A

Pa. Equidem ago;
istuc. Ch. Dic mi-
bi, nostine quæ sit,
aut vidistine? Pa.
Vidi, novi, scio quo
est abducta. Ch.
Eho, mi Parmeno,
nostine? Pa. No-
vi. Ch. Et scis ubi
sit? Ch. Deducta
est huc ad meretri-
cem Thaidem; data
est dono ei. Ch.
Quis est is tam po-
tens cum hoc tanto
munere? Pa. Mi-
les Thraso, rivalis
Phædriæ. Ch. Præ-
dicas duras partes
fratris. Pa. Imo
enim, magis dicas id
tum, si scias quod do-
num contra comparet
huic dono. Ch. Quæ-
so hercle quodnam?
Pa. Eunuchum. Ch.
Obsecro illumne inho-
nestum hominem, se-
nem, mulierem, quem
mercatus est heri?
Pa. Istunc ipsum.
Ch. Homo certe qua-
tietur foras cum dono.
Sed non scivi istam
Thaidem esse vici-
nam nobis. Pa. Haud
est diu. Ch. Perii.
Me nunquamne etiam
vidisse illam? Et-
dum, dic mihi, estne

ut fertur forma? Pa. Sane. Ch. At nihil ad hanc nostram. Pa. Alia res est. Ch. Obsecro
te hercle, Parmeno, fac ut potiar. Pa. Faciam sedulo, ac dabo operam, adjuvabo. Numquid
vis me aliud? Ch. Quo is nunc? Pa. Domum, ut deducam hæc mancipia ad Thaidem, ita ut
frater jussit. Ch. O fortunatum istum eunuchum, qui quidem detur in hanc domum!

ANNOTATIONS.

of his Fable; for this Question brings on of course the Mention of the Eunuch, which gives rise to the Project afterwards form'd between *Chærea* and *Parmeno*.

65 *Senim, mulierem.* *Senim* is not here in the common Gender, but the Expression must be supposed to contain a double Reproach: the one from his Age, that he was old, the other from his natural Defect, that he differed but little from a Woman.

67 *Sed istam Thaidem non scivi nobis vici-nam.* The Poet manages here with a great deal of Address. It was necessary for the Project afterwards to be formed, that *Thais* should neither know nor be known to *Chærea*. This the Reader is let into in the most

easy unaffected manner imaginable. *Thais* had but lately come to that Neighbourhood; *Chærea* had heard of her, but did not know her; he complains of this as a Misfortune, because he could not go to see the Girl under pretence of visiting *Thais*: then recollecting what he had heard of this Courtezan, he asks whether she was as beautiful as Report made her. Who that reads all this, would imagine that the whole was no more than an artful Contrivance of the Poet, the better to introduce his Scheme, and not rather a real Representation of human Life?

73 *O fortunatum istum eunuchum.* Here we come to the grand Scheme upon which the Play chiefly turns, which, as *Donatus* observes,

Par. Why fo?

Chær. Do you afk? He will always have in the Houfe with him a Fellow-Servant of exquifite Beauty, converfe with her, dwell under the fame Roof; fometimes eat with her, and fometimes perhaps too, fleep by her.

Par. What if you fhould become this happy Creature?

Chær. How fo, *Parmeno?* fay.

Par. You may take his Clothes.

Chær. His Clothes! Well, and what then?

Par. I can carry you thither, inftead of him.

Chær. I hear you.

Par. I'll pretend that you are he.

Chær. I underftand you.

Par. You may then enjoy all thofe Advantages which you but juft now faid would fall to his lot. You may eat with her, have her Company, touch her, dally with her, and fleep by her, as not one of them knows you, or can tell who you are: befides, your Age and Countenance is fuch, that you may eafily pafs for an Eunuch.

Chær. Spoken like an Oracle. I never knew better Advice given. Come, let's go in directly; drefs me, away with me, lead me to her as faft as poffible.

Par. What do you mean? I was only in jeft.

Chær. Nonfenfe!

Par. I'm ruin'd. Wretch that I am, what's this I have done? Where d'ye thruft me? (*thrufts him.*) You'll beat me down prefently, I tell you ftay.

Chær. Let us go.

Par. Do you ftill perfift?

Chær. I am refolv'd upon it.

Par. Take care that this Project don't prove a little too hot for you.

Chær. Not at all, give me my way.

Par. Ay, but my Bones will pay for all; befides, it is a bafe Action.

Chær. What! do you call it a bafe Action, if I am conveyed into the Houfe of a Courtezan, and return like for like to thofe Jilts who hold us and our Youth in contempt, and cheat and abufe them by every Method they can contrive? Is it bafe, fay you, to play off the fame

ANNOTATIONS.

ferves, is fo managed by the Poet, that it feems rather to offer of itfelf, than to be the Contrivance of *Parmeno*; for it muft have appeared too rafh in a Slave to give *Chærea* fuch Advice.

73 *Capius tu illius veftem. Chærea* is not let into this Project all at once, but by degrees, one Article after another, to awaken his Curiofity, and make him the more eager to enquire after every Particular. By this means the Advice feems rather to be extorted from *Parmeno*, than too forwardly offered, and that Slave has, moreover, the Opportunity of gratifying his own Vanity, by pronouncing it folemnly, and with an Air of Importance.

87 *Quo trudis?* It is ufual in Comedy to make the Reader fenfible, by the Words of fome one of the Speakers, of what cannot be exhibited but upon the Stage, as in the prefent Inftance we underftand from the Words

PA. Quid ita? CH. rogitas? fummâ formâ femper
conſervam domi
Videbit, conloquetur, aderit unà in unis ædibus, 75
Cibum nonnunquam capiet cum eâ, interdum propter
dormiet. [Parmeno?
PA. Quid, ſi nunc tute fortunatus, fias? CH. quâ re,
Reſponde. PA. capias tu illiu' veſtem. CH. veſtem? quid
tum poſtea? [eſſe dicam. CH. intellego
PA. Pro illo te deducam. CH. audio. PA. te illum
PA. Tu illis fruare commodis, quibus tu illum dicebas
modò: 80
Cibum unà capias, adſis, tangas, ludas, propter dormias:
Quandoquidem illarum neque quiſquam te novit, neque
ſcit qui ſcies.
Præterea forma, ætas ipſa eſt, facile ut te pro eunucho
probes. [dari.
CH. Dixiſti pulchre: nunquam vidi melius conſilium
Age, eamus intro nunc jam: orna me, abduc, duc
quantum potes. 85
PA. Quid agis? jocabar equidem. CH. garris. PA.
perii, quid ego egi miſer! [mane.
Quo trudis? perculeris jam tu me. tibi equidem dico,
CH. Eamus. PA. pergin'? CH. certum eſt. PA. vide
ne nimium eſſidem hoc ſit modò. !
CH. Non eſt profecto. ſine. PA. at enim iſtæc in me
cudetur faba. ah,
Flagitium facimus! CH. an id flagitium eſt, ſi in do-
mum meretriciam 90
Deducar, & illis crucibus, quæ nos, noſtramque ado-
leſcentiam [ciant modis,
Habent deſpicatam, & quæ nos ſemper omnibus cru-

*agis? equidem jocabar. CH. Garris. PA. Perii, quid ego miſer egi? Quo trudis? tu jam
perculeris me, dico equidem tibi, mane. CH. Eamus. PA. Pergiſne? CH. Certum eſt. PA.
Vide ne hoc modo conſilium ſit nimis calidum. CH. Profecto non eſt; ſine. PA. At enim iſtæc
faba cudetur in me: Ah, facimus flagitium! CH. An id eſt flagitium, ſi deducar in domum meretriciam, & nunc referam gratiam illis crucibus, quæ habent nos, noſtramque adoleſcentiam deſpicatam, & quæ ſemper cruciant nos omnibus modis,*

ANNOTATIONS.

Words of Parmeno, that Chærea was puſhing
him with his Hand.
Ibid. *Perculeris. Tundendo ad terram dede-
ris, everteris.* For ſo Cicero metaphorically,
Orat. pro domo, 11. *Deſunt, definunt, homines
iiſdem machinis ſperare, me reſtitutum poſſe la-
befactari, quibus antea ſtantem perculerunt.* And
Virgil's Æneid V. 372.

*Victorem Buten immani corpore, qui ſe
Bebrycia veniens Amyci de gente ferebat,
Perculit, & fulva moribundum extendit
arena,*

89 *At enim iſtæc in me cudetur faba.* Various are the Attempts of Commentators to
clear up this proverbial Expreſſion. Pliny
xviii. 27. ſays: *Antiqui fabam peccantibus
in manum cudebant, unde uſus inolevit, fabam pro culpa aut pæna dici.* Some again
derive it from the *Scutica,* a kind of Whip
wherewith Slaves were puniſhed, having
Knots that partly reſembled the Figure of a
Bean. The Scholiaſt upon Perſius was
the firſt who ſtarted this Notion; his Words
are: *Scutica erat quædam corrigia, habens in
ſummitate nodos quoſdam in modum fabæ, ſi-*
milis

same Tricks upon them, that they often play upon us?, Or should
we rather tamely submit to all this? It is but just to deal thus a little
cunningly with her. Which perhaps you'll say every body that hears
will blame: nay, on the contrary, they will all agree, that she is
used as she deserves.

Par. What's all this? If you are so resolved, do it; but don't
afterwards lay the blame upon me.

Chær. I tell you, I will not.

Par. Do you command me, then?

Chær. I command you, I charge you, I oblige you to it, nor will
I ever deny that I compelled you.

Par. Follow me then. Heaven prosper the Design.

ANNOTATIONS.

miles vero cæstuum: de qua Terentius: Hæc faba
cudetur in me, & erat pœna servorum. It were
endless to repeat all that has been said upon
this Subject, and therefore I shall only further
observe, that however Commentators differ as
to the Manner of explaining the Words, yet
they all agree in making the Sense that *Parmeno* was to suffer the Punishment of all.

‒94 *An potius hæc pati?* The Reading here
followed is that most approved, and which we

find to have prevailed in *Donatus*'s Time.
The Construction is a little perplexed and intricate, but the Manner in which I have
translated it, with the *Ordo*, will clear up that,
without any additional Remark here. It is
only necessary to take notice of a Reading
which is in great Esteem with some, and
gives the Passage quite a different Turn.

*An potius hæc patri æquum est fieri, ut a me
ludatur dolis?*

ACT III.   SCENE I.

ARGUMENT.

Gnatho, *after the manner of Parasites, flatters the Soldier in
the vain Opinion he entertained of himself. Thraso believing
all, boasts immoderately of himself and Actions: He then consults
Gnatho, whether he ought to clear himself to* Thais *of the
Suspicion of loving* Pamphila, *or whether he had not better
encourage that Notion, and so return like for like.*

THRASO, GNATHO, PARMENO.

Thr. WAS then *Thais* indeed very thankful for my Present?

Gnat. O! prodigiously so.

Thr. Was she overjoyed, say you?

Gnat. Not so much with the Gift itself, as that you was the Giver:
that, I can assure you, is her great Triumph.   *Parm.*

ANNOTATIONS.

In this Scene we have a lively Representation of the Manner which the Parasites
and Flatterers of those Times took to ingratiate themselves with Men of great Fortunes, and shallow Understandings. As Men
of the least Merit are most apt to be over-
run with Vanity, and fond of being thought
to possess those Talents which they want, so
they are easily made the Dupes of those
who know how to apply to their weak Side.
Gnatho had carried the young Virgin as a
Present from the Soldier to *Thais. Thraso*

and the Parasite are here introduced as now
first meeting after the Delivery of the Present. *Thraso* asks how it had been received,
and *Gnatho* answers in the manner which
he thought would be most agreeable to this
conceited Fool, by blowing up his ridiculous
Vanity. This gives the Soldier an Opportunity of expatiating, and talking magnificently of himself, to all which the Parasite
counterfeits a ready Belief, and hears him
with an Air of seeing Admiration.

² *Irgentei.* Cicero cites this Passage in
his

Nunc referam gratiam, atque eas itidem fallam, ut
   ab illis fallimur?   [tur dolis.
An potiùs hæc pati? æquum est fieri, ut à me luda-
Quod qui rescierint, culpent: illud meritò factum
   omnes putent.   95
PA. Quid istuc? si certum est facere, facias. verùm
   ne post conferas
Culpam in me. CH. non faciam. PA. jubesne? CH.
   jubeo. imo cogo, atque impero.
PA. Nunquam defugiam auctoritatem. CH. sequere.
   PA. Dii vortant bene.

Jubesne? CH. *Jubes, imo cogo, atque impero.* *Nunquam defugiam auctoritatem.* PA. *Dii vertant bene.*

ANNOTATIONS.

Quod qui rescierint, - culpent: illud meritò factum omnes putent.

According to this Reading, the Sentence is to be rendered thus:

‘ Or do you rather think it reasonable
‘ that I should impose upon my Father, and
‘ endeavour by cunning Artifices to over-
‘ reach him? which every body that hears
‘ of it will blame: whereas in the other
‘ Case, all the World will say, that I have
‘ used her as she deserves.’

95 *Nunquam defugiam auctoritatem.* *Nor will I ever deny that I compelled you.* *Defugere auctoritatem* is properly one's not daring to avow himself the Author of what he has done, but throwing the Blame of all upon others. Thus *Plautus*, *Pœn.* 1, 1, 19.

   Si auctoritatem postea defugeris,
   Ubi dissolutus tu sies, ego pendeam.

‘ If you shall afterwards go to say, that
‘ you had no hand in it, when by that
‘ means you shall have escaped yourself,
‘ I shall be left to suffer for all.’ And *Cicero*, in his Oration for *Sulla*, 11. *Itaque attende jam, Torquate, quam ego non defugiam auctoritatem consulatus mei.* The Sense of which is: quam ego non recusam, me auctore dici gesta, quæ in meo consulatu, & oppressione conjurationis gesta sint.

ACTUS III. SCENA I.

ARGUMENTUM.

Gnatho parasitico more, militi sibi stulte blandienti assentatur; assentanti credit Thraso, seque & facta sua immodice jactitat. Consulit item Gnatho, ne miles purget se Thaidi de amore Pamphilæ, imo potius augeat suspicionem, & sic par pari referat.

THRASO, GNATHO, PARMENO.

MAgnas vero agere gratias Thais mihi?
GN. Ingentes. TH. ain' tu, læta est? GN.
non tam ipso quidem
Dono, quàm abs te datùm esse: id vero seriò

 O R D O.

TH. THAIS vero agere (agebatne) magnas gratias mihi? GN. Agebat ingentes. TH. Aisne, est

læta? GN. *Non tam ipso quidem dono, quam esse datùm abs te: vero serio.*

ANNOTATIONS.

his Treatise *de Amicitia* 26; and adds, *Satis erat respondere*, magnas: ingentes, *inquit: semper auget assentator id, quod is, cujus ad voluntatem dicitur, vult esse magnum.* “ It was enough in answer to the “ Soldier's Question to say great; he “ makes it *huge*: for a Flatterer always “ heightens, what he knows the Person whom he aims at cajoling would have to “ be great.” *Lucretius* has a Reflection much to the same Purpose in his sixth Book, V. 677.

   Maxima quæ vidit quisque, hæc ingentia
     fingit.

3 *Quam abs te datam esse.* Nothing can be more flattering or agreeable to a Lover, than

Parm. (to himself) I come out to watch, that when a fit Opportunity offers, I may bring my Presents: but here's the Soldier.

Thr. That indeed is remarkably my Case, to have every thing I do thought agreeable.

Gnat. So I have always observed.

Thr. Even the King of *Persia* expressed himself always mightily pleased with whatever I did; he was not so complaisant to others.

Gnat. A Man of your Wit and Humour often finds means to appropriate to himself the Glory which others have acquired with a World of Toil.

Thr. Right.

Gnat. The King therefore had you always in his Eye.

Thr. The very Thing.

Gnat. To delight himself with you.

Thr. True: trusted me with the Conduct of his Armies, and all the Secrets of State.

Gnat. Strange!

Thr. Then if at any Time he was tired of Company, or over-fatigued with Business; when he wanted to recreate himself a little, as tho'——You understand me?

Gnat. I know: as tho' when he wanted to rid himself of the Misery of a Croud of Attendants.

Thr. You have it: then I was his sole Guest and Companion.

Gnat. Bless me! he is a King, by your account, very delicate in the Choice of his Friends.

Thr. Such is the Temper of the Man: they are but few that can suit his Taste.

Gnat. (Aside.) Nay, not one I believe, if he makes choice of you for a Companion.

Thr. All the Courtiers envy'd me, and privately reviled me: I minded it but little. They envy'd me wretchedly; but one in particular,

A N N O T A T I O N S.

than the Conceit that his Presents are agreeable to his Mistress, chiefly because they come from himself. *Ovid* manages this Thought to great advantage, in several of his Epistles, particularly 17. 71.

Utque ea non spreno ; sic acceptissima semper Munera sunt, ador quæ pretiosa facit.

The Word *triumphat*, which comes in afterwards, is well chosen, because it must sound agreeable in a Soldier's Ears.

7 *Vel rex.* This may be understood of *Darius* the Third, King of the *Persians*, who reign'd in the Time of *Menander*. But as *Pyrrhus* is mentioned in this very Play, Madam *Dacier* thinks it ought rather to be understood of *Seleucus* King of *Asia.*

9 *Labora alieno magnam,* &c. Some will

have it, that *Gnatho* says this, turning from the Soldier to the Spectators, imagining it impossible that the Soldier should be so absolute a Fool, as not to see that this was meer Banter. But there is no Necessity of being so nice; *Terence* meant the Soldier's Character, as sottish in the highest Degree, and that he both heard what *Gnatho* said, and took it seriously, is plain from his Answer, *Habes.* The Word *sal,* which comes in afterwards, is both here, and often by other Authors made to stand for Wit, Acuteness, Humour, &c. Thus, *Horace* Sat. 1. 10. 3. speaking of *Lucilius,* and his Talent of diverting; says,

—— *At idem, quod sale multo Urbem defricuit, charta laudatur eadem.*

And again, in his Art of Poetry, where he

Triumphat. Pa. huc proviso, ut, ubi tempus fiet.
Deducam, fed eccum militem. Th. eft iftuc datum 5
Profecto ut grata ***** fint quæ facio, omnia. [maxumas
Gn. Advorti hercle animum. Th. vel rex femper
Mihi agebat, quidquid feceram : aliis non item.
Gn. Labore alieno magno partam gloriam
Verbis fæpe in fe tranfmovet, qui habet falem, 10
Qui in te eft. Th. Habes. Gn. rex te ergo in ocu-
lis. Th. fcilicet.
Gn. Geftare. Th. verùm, credere omnem exercitum,
Confilia. Gn. mirum. Th. tum ficubi eum fatietas
Hominum, aut negotî fi quando odium ceperat,
Requiefcere ubi volebat, quafi : noftin' ? Gn. fcio. 15
Quafi ubi illam exfpueret miferiam ex animo. Th. tenes.
Tum me convivam folum abducebat fibi. Gn. hui !
Regem elegantem narras. Th. imo fic homo [tror,
Eft perpaucorum hominum. Gn. imo nullorum, arbi-
Si tecum vivit. Th. invidere omnes mihi,. 20
Mordere clanculum : ego non flocci pendere :

lia mihi. Gn. Mirum. Th. Tum ficubi fatietas hominum, aut fi quando odium negoti ceperat
eum, ubi volebat requiefcere, quafi : noftine ? Gn. Scio ; quafi ubi expueret illam miferiam ex
animo. Th. Tenes. Tum abducebat me folum convivam fibi. Gn. Hui, narras regem ele-
gantem. Th. Imo, fic homo eft hominum perpaucorum. Gn. Imo arbitror nullorum, fi vivit
tecum. Th. Omnes invidere mihi : mordere clanculum : ego non flocci pendere :

Marginal column (right side):

triumphat propterid. Pa. *Proviso huc, ut deducam, ubi tempus fit, fed eccum mili-* tem. Th. *Profecto* iftuc eft datum mihi, *ut omnia quæ facio fint grata,* Gn. *Her-cle animum adverti.* Th. *Vel rex, quid-quid feceram, femper agebat maximas gra-tias mihi : non item* alii:. Gn. *Qui ha-bet falem qui eft in te, fæpe tranfmovet ver-bis in fe, gloriam partam magno alio-no labore.* Th. *Ha-bes.* Gn. *Ergo rex femper habuit te in* oculis. Th. *Scilicet.* Gn. *Geftare.* Th. *Verum : credere om-nem exercitum, confi-*

A N N O T A T I O N S.

he cenfures the low Jefts of *Plautus* :
   At noftri proavi Plautinos & numeros &
   Laudavere fales,
15 *Quafi------Noftin.* Donatus's Remark
upon this Paffage, is extremely juft. *Gra-
te expreffit ftulti infantium militis, qui ante
vult intelligi quod fentit, quam ipfe dicat.
Et proprie hoc morale eft ftolidi, five ruditer
fequentis.*
   16 *Illam 'exfpueret miferiam.* Expuere,
fays *Donatus,* is to reject with Difdain. *Nam
expuere,* adds he, *eft extra pus mittere ; pus
enim eft omis humor corpori onerofus.* It is
evident that *Gnatho* means : *When the King
wanted to throw off the Load of Bufinefs, as
troublefome and oppreffive.* But according to
the above Derivation of *Donatus,* it muft
imply, *As fhocking and offenfive to Nature.* An Interpretation, that can by no
means be allowed here, nor indeed does the
word require it, as we frequently find it ufed
by the beft Writers in a favourable Senfe.
Thus *Lucretius* B. II. 1040. *Expuere ex
animo rationem ;* and *Pliny* B. II. Ch. 2. *A
fydere cœleftis ignis expuere.* *Miferia* is
alfo a very proper Word to exprefs the Care,
Anxiety, and Diftraction of Mind infeparable from a Concern in Affairs of State. *Salluft* ufes it in much the fame Senfe, in his

Preface to the *Cataline* War ; *Igitur ubi
animus ex multis miferiis atque periculis re-
quievit.*
   19 *Sic homo eft perpaucorum hominum.*
That is, he is one who admits but few into
a Familiarity with him, one fo delicate, that
few feem to have Merit enough to deferve
his Friendfhip. *Horace* ufes the fame
Phrafe, and in the fame Senfe, in the oth
Satire of his firft Book, fpeaking of *Mæ-
cenas.* Ver. 44. *Paucorum hominum, &
mentis bene fanæ.* The Expreffion may receive fome Light from the following Paffage
of *Cicero,* in his Book *de Fato* : *Allatus eft
forte acipenfer, qui raro capitur, fed eft pifcis,
ut ferunt, in primis nobilis. Cum autem Scipio unum & alterum ex bis, qui eum falutatum
venerant, invitaffit, plurefque etiam invitaturus
videretur, in aurem Pontius, Scipio, inquit,
Vide quid agas, acipenfer ifte paucorum homi-
eft.* " By chance, a Sturgeon was brou
" a Fifh feldom taken, but faid to b
" the fineft Kind. After *Scipio* had invit-
" ed one or two of thofe, who had fome
" to pay their Refpects to him, and feem'd
" defign'd to invite ftill more ; *Pontius*
" whifpers in his Ear, Take care what you
" do, a Sturgeon is not a Fifh for every
" one's eating."

19 *Imo*

ticular, to whom he had given the Care of the *Indian* Elephants. He being one day a little more troublesome than ordinary, Hark ye, said I, *Strato*, are you so fierce and formidable, because you are Lord over the Beasts?

Gnat. Delightfully said, by *Hercules*, and with Judgment: bless me! you must have shocked the Man prodigiously. How did he behave then?

Thr. Mute in an Instant.

Gnat. How could it be otherwise?

Parm. Good Gods! what a wretched and undone Man is this, and what a Villain that other?

Thr. But, *Gnatho*, did I never tell you how severely I once roasted a *Rhodian* at a Feast?

Gnat. Never: but pray tell it me. (*Aside.*) I have heard it more than a thousand times.

Thr. This *Rhodian* Youth, that I speak of, was present at an Entertainment where I was. By chance I had a Girl there; he began to dally with her, and break his Jests upon me. How now, Mr. Impudence, says I; you the Owner of a Park, and want Venison?

Gnat. Ha, ha, ha!

Thr. What's the matter?

Gnat. Wittily, genteelly, elegantly, nothing could exceed it. Was this Saying your own, pray? I thought it was an old one.

Thr. What! Did you ever hear it before?

Gnat. Often, and 'tis in the highest Esteem.

Thr. 'Tis my own.

Gnat. 'Twas a little cruel, however, to use the young Gentleman so, for a thoughtless Forwardness.

Parm.

ANNOTATIONS.

19 *Immo nullorum arbitror.* This Reproach is too severe and open to be uttered in the Soldier's Hearing; and therefore we are to suppose that *Gnatho* turns from the Captain, and addresses them to the Audience. *Donatus*, indeed, observes that the Sense is ambiguous, and that *Thraso* might have understood them as favouring himself: that the King was so much taken with his Wit and Humour, that he could endure no other Company, and despised all the rest of his Courtiers without exception. Some attribute these Words to *Parmeno* overhearing this Conversation, which takes away the Ambiguity, and makes all plain. *Eugraphius*, among others, falls in with this Conjecture.

22 *Illi invidere misere.* This Repetition is well conceived of the Poet, and strongly marks *Thraso*'s Character. He thinks he cannot dwell too much upon a Circumstance, that seems to be to his Advantage, as was that of the Envy of his Fellow-Courtiers

at the great Favour he stood in with the King.

23 *Elephantis quem Indicis præfecerat.* We must observe here, after Madam *Dacier*, that he who had the Charge of the Elephants, was a very considerable Officer, and had a great Number of Servants under him. It was not, therefore, a small matter in *Thraso*, to have had a Dispute with a Man of that Importance. It is not, moreover, a light Boast which he makes here. The Word *Indicis* ought not to be forgot. This vain Fool imagined, that it gave a higher Idea of his Boldness and Courage, and that the Man, who commanded the *Indian* Elephants, must be much more formidable than he who commanded other Elephants, because they were of a larger Size, and commonly reckoned more fierce.

27 *Jugularas hominem. Everteras & mentum reddideras, non secus ac si esset jugulatus.*

28 *Hominem perditum miserumque, & illum*

Illi invidere misere. verùm unus tamen
Impensè, elephantis quem Indicis præfecerat.
Is ubi molestus magis est, Quæso, inquam, Strato,
Eone es ferox, quia habes imperium in belluas? 25
GN. Pulchre mehercle dictum, & sapienter. papæ!
Jugularas hominem. quid ille? TH. mutus illico.
GN. Quidni esset? PA. Dî vostram fidem! hominem
perditum,
Miserumque; & illum sacrilegum! TH. quid? illud,
Gnatho,
Quò pacto Rhodium tetigerim in convivio, 30
Nunquam tibi dixi? GN. nunquam: sed narra, obsecro.
Plus millies jam audivi. TH. unà in convivio
Erat hic, quem dico, Rhodius adolescentulus.
Forte habui scortum: cœpit ad id alludere,
Et me irridere. quid agis, inquam, home impudens? 35
Lepus tute es, & pulpamentum quæris. GN. ha, ha, hæ!
TH. Quid est? GN. facetè, lepidè, lutè, nihil supra.
Tuumne, obsecro te, hoc dictum erat? vetu' credidi.
TH. Audieras? GN. sæpe; & fertur in primis. TH.
meum est.
GN. Dolet dictum imprudenti adolescenti, & libero. 40

illi invidere misere:
verùm tamen ún-s,
quem præfecerat In-
dicis elephantis, im-
pensè: is ubi est ma-
g.s molestus, Quæso,
inquam, Strato, esne
ferox eo, quia habes
imperium in belluas?
GN. Mehercule. pul-
chre dictum, & sa-
pienter. Papæ! ju-
gularas hominem.;
quid dixit ille? TH.
Illico mutus. GN.
Quidni esset? PA.
Dii vostram fidem?
O hominem perditum,
miserumque; & il-
lum sacrilegum! TH.
Quid? nunquamne
tibi illud tibi; Gna-
tho; quo pacto tetige-
rim Rhodium in con-
vivio? GN. Nun-
quam, sed obsecro,
narra: audivi jam
plus millies. TH. Hic
Rhodius adolescentu-
lus, quem dico, erat

una mecum in convivio. Forte habui scortum: cœpit alludere ad id, & irridere me: Homo im-
pudens, inquam, quid agis? tute es lepus, & quæris pulpamentum: GN. Ha, ha, hæ! TH.
Quid est? GN. Facete, lepide, laute, nihil supra. Obsecro te, hoc dictum eratne tuum? credidi
vetus. TH. Audieras? GN. Sæpe, & fertur in primis. TH. Est meum. GN. Dolet hoc fuisse
dictum adolescenti imprudenti & libero.

ANNOTATIONS.

lum sacrilegum. These Words ought to be carefully distinguished; *Hominem perditum miserumque,* belong to the Captain, and *illum sacrilegum,* are to be referred to *Gnatho.*

30 *Rhodium.* The Rhodians were particularly famous, both for their Skill in naval Affairs, and ready Wit. They were, besides, haughty, and impatient of an Affront. It was, therefore, much to the Captain's Honour, to have the better in a Dispute with a *Rhodian.* That we are to understand it so, is evident from the Care which the Soldier afterwards takes to remind us of the Person's being a *Rhodian: Una in convivio erat hic, quem dico, Rhodius, adolescentulus.*

30 *Lepus tute es, & pulpamentum quæris.* This was a proverbial Expression used at that Time. The proper Meaning of it stript of the Figure is, *You are little more than a Woman yourself, and do you want a Mistress.* We taken from *Donatus* and *Vopisius,* that *Livius Andronicus* had inserted it in his Works before *Terence.* Commentators, who pretend to enter into a minute Explication of it, offer many ingenious Conjectures, but they are rather curious than solid, and of a Nature not fit to be mentioned here.

37 *Quid est?* The Parasite had forced a Laugh, the more easily to impose upon *Thraso,* in making him believe that he had now first heard this Story. The Soldier asks, *What's the Matter?* with the Air and Countenance of one who was sure of being commended, and to give *Gnatho* an Opportunity of launching out in his Praises.

40 *Dolet dictum imprudenti adolescenti,* &c. It is not easy to conceive why *Guyetus* is for rejecting this Verse, for it comes in very aptly from *Gnatho,* who means to flatter the Soldier, as one so cutting in his Railleries, that whoever drew his Resentment upon them, deserved heartily to be pitied. *Imprudenti adolescenti,* a forward Youth: or perhaps, *Who little imagined he would be taken up so short, or that he had to do with a Man, who was so great a Master of Wit. Liber,* may signify here, either one who was free-born, a Youth of Quality or

Parm. Confound you, for a Rafcal !

Gnat. How did he behave, pray?

Thr. Quite difconcerted : every Body prefent was ready to die with Laughing; in fhort, they were all afraid of me.

Gnat. And with good Reafon too.

Thr. But hark ye : had I beft clear myfelf to *Thais*, from the Sufpicion of loving this Girl?

Gnat. By no means ; ftudy rather to cherifh it.

Thr. Why fo ?

Gnat. Why fo ? Don't you fee the Reafon at once? if at any Time fhe mentions *Phædria*, or praifes him with a Defign to vex you——

Thr. I underftand.

Gnat. This is the only Way in the World to prevent it: when fhe talks of *Phædria*, do you immediately name *Pamphila* : if at any Time fhe defires that *Phædria* fhould make one among you, do you propofe fending for *Pamphila* to fing : if fhe praifes his Shape, do you, on the contrary, extol hers : in fine, return always like for like, which will not fail to mortify her foundly.

Thr. If, indeed, fhe loved me, this might be a good Scheme, *Gnatho*.

Gnat. Since fhe loves, and is impatient for your Prefents, there is no doubt to be made of her loving you, nor will you find it any difficult Matter to make her uneafy : and fhe'll always be afraid, left in an angry Fit, you may beftow elfewhere the Offerings which fhe now fhares.

Thr. You fay well : but that never came into my Mind.

Gnat. Ridiculous : then you never fet yourfelf to think of it: for if fo, how much better would you have contrived this yourfelf, *Thrafo* ?

ANNOTATIONS.

Rank, or it may imply Freedom of Speech ; for that it is ufed fometimes in that Senfe, appears from *Ovid Metam.* I. 757. Where *Phæton* fpeaking of the Reproaches he had fuffered from *Epaphus*, fays,

——————*Ille ego* liber

Ille ferox tacui.

42 *Rifu omnes, qui aderant, emoriri.* Donatus remarks here, that it was ufual for Comic Poets in drawing ridiculous Characters, to make them exprefs themfelves foolifhly, and fometimes put in their Mouths wrong Words, which People of Underftanding never ufed. Such, he takes the Word *emoriri* here to be, which the Soldier ufes inftead of *mori.* The Remark, in the general, may be juft enough, but his applying it to the Word *emoriri*, was going too far ; for we find it ufed, fometimes, even by the beft Writers. Thus, *Ovid Metam.* XIV. 215.

—— *Mortemque timens, cupidufque moriri.*

I fhould

PA. At te Dî perdant. GN. quid ille, quæſo? TH.
perditus. *
Riſu omnes, qui aderant, emoriri. denique,
Metuebant omnes jam me. GN. non injuriâ.
TH. Sed heus tu, purgon' ego me de iſtac Thaidi,
Quòd eam me amare ſuſpicata eſt? GN. nihil minus:
Imo magis auge ſuſpicionem. TH. cur? GN. rogas? 46
Scin'? ſi quando illa mentionem Phædriæ
Facit, aut ſi laudat, te ut male urat—TH. ſentio.
GN. Id ut ne fiat, hæc res ſola éſt remedio,
Ubi nominabit Phædriam, tu Pamphilam 50
Continuò. ſi quando illa dicet, Phædriam
Intromittamus comiſſatum; Pamphilam
Cantatum provocemus. ſi laudabit hæc
Illius formam; tu hujus contrà. denique
Par pro pari referto, quod eam mordeat. 55
TH. Siquidem me amaret, tum iſtuc prodeſſet, Gnathô.
GN. Quando illud, quod tu das, exſpectat, atque amat,
Jamdudum te amat: jamdudum illi facile fit
Quod doleat. metuet ſemper; quem ipſa nunc capit
Fructum, ne quando iratus tu aliò conferas, 60
TH. Bene dixti. at mihi iſtuc non in mentem venerat.
GN. Ridiculum: non enim cogitaras. cæterùm,
Idem hoc tute meliùs quanto inveniſſes, Thraſo!

laudabit formam illius; tu contra laudabis formam hujus: denique referto par pro pari, quod mordeat eam. TH. Siquidem, Gnatho, amaret me, tum iſtuc prodeſſet. GN. Quando expectat atque amat illud, quod tu das, jamdudum amat te: jamdudum facile ſit illi quod doleat: ſemper metuet, ne quando tu iratus, conferas aliò fructum, quem ipſa nunc capit. TH. Dixti bene, at iſtuc non venerat in mentem mihi. GN. Ridiculum: enim non cogitaras. Cæterùm, Thraſo, quanto melius tute inveniſſes hoc idem!

PA. At Dii perdant te. GN. Quæſo, quid ille reſpondit? TH. Perditus erat. omnes, qui aderant, emoriri riſu; denique, omnes jam metuebant me. GN. Non injuriâ. TH. Sed heus tu, e-gone purgo me Thaidi de iſtac, quod ſuſpicata eſt me amare il-lam? GN. Nihil mi-nus: imo auge magis ſuſpicionem. TH. Cur? GN. Rogas? Sciſne? ſi quando illa facit mentionem Phæ-driæ, aut ſi laudat eam, ut urat temale: TH. Sentio. GN. Hæc res eſt ſola re-medio tibi, ut id ne fiat. Ubi nominabit Phædriam, tu con-tinuo nominabis Pamphilam. Si quan-do illa dicet; Into-mittamus Phædriam comiſſatum; tu dices, Provocemus Pamphi-lam cantatum. Si hæc

ANNOTATIONS.

I ſhould rather incline to the Opinion of thoſe, who think there is an Affectation of Wit in the uſe of this Word, viz. That Thraſo, deſcribing here the Laughter of all preſent, endeavours to give an Example of it, by his manner of telling it, and that he drew out the Word in Pronunciation, ac-companying it with a Laugh: e-mo-ri-ri.

52 Intromittamus comiſſatum. Comiſſatum comes from the Verb comiſſor, or according to others, comeſſor, to revel or make merry.

There are various Conjectures, as to the E-tymology of the Word: the moſt probable is that which derives it from Comus, the God of Reveling and Drunkenneſs. It is enough to obſerve here, that comiſſatio was properly a promiſcuous Company, met together after Supper, to ſpend the Time in Drinking, Dancing, and amorous Toying, which they often continued thro' the greater Part of the Night.

ACTUS

ACT III. SCENE II.

ARGUMENT.

Parmeno *offers the Slaves from* Phædria *in Presence of the Soldier his Rival, who undervalues and foolishly finds Fault with them;* Gnatho *all the while meanly assenting, and insulting* Parmeno. *At last* Thais *goes along with the Soldier to Supper.*

THAIS, THRASO, PARMENO, GNATHO, PYTHIAS.

Thais. I Thought I just now heard the Soldier's Voice, and here he is: welcome, my *Thraso.*

Thr. O my *Thais,* my dearest Creature, how goes it? Don't you love me now for this Music-Girl I have sent you?

Par. (aside) How polite he is! What a fine Address at his first Meeting!

Tha. O extremely, as your Merit demands

Gna. Let us go then to Supper, what do you stand here for?

Par. (aside) There's another for you; one may swear he's begot of his own Body, *so much are they alike.*

Thr. When you will, I am ready.

Par. (to himself.) I'll go up to them, and pretend as if I was just come out.——Are you a going any where, *Thais?*

Tha. O *Parmeno!* you are welcome, I was just a going out.

Par. Where?

Tha. (aside to Parmeno) What? don't you see this Man here?

Par. (aside to Thais) I see, and am vexed.——*(aloud)* Phædria's Presents are ready whenever you please.

Thr. What do we stand for? Why don't we go hence?

Par. Pray, Sir, with your Leave, let us offer the Lady the Presents we have for her; allow us to advance and speak with her.

Thr. Fine Presents, I suppose; scarce to be named with mine.

Par.

ANNOTATIONS.

While *Thraso* and *Gnatho* are discoursing together, as in the former Scene, *Thais* comes to the Door, and chances to hear them. She therefore advances forward to look for the Captain, and upon seeing him, enters into Discourse with him. *Parmeno* still at some Distance overhears all, and thinking it was time now for him to appear, advances as if but just then come out. He afterwards orders the two Slaves to be called out, and presents them. This brings on a Conversation full of Variety, as being managed by Persons of different Characters. These the Poet preserves with wonderful Judgment, so that among so many Speakers, we neither meet with one who says any thing out of Character, nor is there any Confusion in the Discourse.

4 *De fidicina istac?* De is here instead of *propter,* as if he had said propter *fidicinam.*
Ibid. *Quam venuste!* The Reprehension of *Parmeno* here is just; for in Offices of Kindness, it belongs to him who receives to remember, he that gives should seem to forget.
7 *Ex homine hunc natum dicas.* Whatever may be the true Sense of this, it is plainly meant as a Reproach, *dicas Gnathonem ex homine natum esse. Quo homine? Thrasone scilicet: ita sunt stultitia pares.* This is the more common and obvious Explication of this Passage. Some Commentators purposely pass it over, as seeing a Difficulty in it not easy to be solved. *Bentley* is the only one who has endeavoured to go to the Bottom of the Matter. As his Conjecture is very ingenious, and

ACTUS III. SCENA II.

ARGUMENTUM.

Parmeno dona Phædriæ offert, præsente milite rivali, qui ea contemnit, & inepte cavillatur, assentante interim Gnathone, & Parmenoni insultante: tandemque Thais cum milite ad cœnam proficiscitur.

THAIS, THRASO, PARMENO, GNATHO, PYTHIAS.

	ORDO.
AUdire vocem visa sum modò militis : Atque eccum. salve, mi Thraso. THR. ô Thais mea,	TH. VIsa sum modò audire vocem militis, atque eccum: vi Thraso, salve. THR.
Meum suavium, quid agitur ? ecquid nos amas De fidicinâ istac ? PA. quàm venustè ! quod dedit Principium adveniens ! TH. plurimùm merito tuo. 5 GN. Eamus ergo ad cœnam : quid stas ? PA. hem alterum : [moror Ex homine hunc natum dicas. TH. ubi vis, non PA. Adibo, atque adsimulabo, quasi nunc exeam. Ituran', Thais, quopiam es ? TH. ehem, Parmeno, Bene pol fecisti : hodie itura. PA. quò ? TH. quid ? hunc non vides ? 10 PA. video, & me tædet. ubi vis, dona adsunt tibi A Phædriâ. THR. quid stamus ? cur non imus hinc ? PA. Quæso hercle ut liceat, pace quod fiat tuâ, Dare huic quæ volumus, convenire & conloqui. THR. Perpulchra credo dona, haud nostris similia. 15	O mea Thais, meum suavium, quid agitur ? Ecquid amas nos de istac fidicina? PA. Quam venuste! quod dedit principium advenient! TH. Plurimum tuo merito. GN. Ergo eamus ad cœnam ; quid stai? PA.Hem alterum:dicas hunc natum ex isto homine. TH.Ubi vis, non moror. PA. Adibo, atque adsimulabo quasi exeam nunc. Esne itura quopiam, Thais? TH. Ehem, Parmeno, pol fecisti, & tædet me : Dona adsunt tibi a Phædria, ubi vis. THR. Quid stamus? Cur non imus hinc? PA. Quæso hercle, quod fiat pace tua, ut liceat dare huic quæ volumus, convenire & colloqui. THR. Credo, perpulchra dona, haud similia nostris.

ANNOTATIONS.

and supported with a great Air of Probability, I shall transcribe here what he has said upon it. *Ergo Gnatho, provecta satis ætate, quippe qui patria bona jam abligurrierat, dicatur natus esse ex Thrasone juvene ? Si hoc placet, & fautores invenit ; omnia protinus sint alba.* Parmeno inducitur ut homo callidus & discertus, a principio ad finem eas partes tutatur : cum miles beneficium suum amicæ aggerit, & quasi exprobat ; castigat hoc Parmeno, Quod dedit principium adveniens? Cum edax parasitus, ventri deditus, ejusque solius memor, ex illo principium det. Eamus ergo ad cœnam ; quid stas? Nihilne Parmeno apposite, & πρὸς τὴν γαστέρα ; nihil, nisi id frigidum, Qualis herus, talis servus ; qualis rex & præbitor, talis parasitus ? Immo vel Terentii causa melius quid suggeremus :

   GN. Eamus ergo ad cœnam: quid stas?
  PAR. Hem alterum :
    Abdomini hunc natum dicas.

Recte de parasito, qui de ventre solo cogitaret. Cicero in Pisonem, c. 17. Ille gurges atque belluo ; natus abdomini suo, non laudi atque gloriæ. *Trebellius Gallieno*, c. 16. Natus abdomini & voluptatibus, dies ac noctes vino & stupris perdidit orbem terrarum.

¹⁰ *Bene fecisti. Donatus* asks what *Parmeno* had done here to deserve this ? I can't see any Obscurity in these Words of *Thais*. For as she was going out, and at that Time standing in the very Entrance, when she sees *Parmeno* she says, *Bene fecisti, viz.* in coming just now if you wanted to meet with me, for *hodie itura,* I was just a going out ; had you therefore come later, you would not have found me at home.

¹³ *Pace quod fiat tua. Donatus* observes upon this, that there is a particular Elegance in the Choice of the Poet's Words ; because *pax, datio, deditio, conventio, colloquium,* are Words proper to War.

         ¹⁷ *Ex*

Par. The Thing will fpeak for itfelf: Ho, you within there, let thefe come out quickly as I ordered. (*enter the* Ethiopian) Come forward you: this Girl comes as far as from *Ethiopia.*

Thr. She coft, I fuppofe, about eight or nine Pounds.

Gnat. Hardly fo much.

Par. Where are you, *Dorus?* Come hither. There's a Eunuch for you. How handfome he looks, and in the Flower of Youth too?

Tha. As I hope for Mercy, a good-looking Fellow.

Par. What fay you, *Gnatho?* Is there any Thing here to fhow your Contempt of? What fay you, *Thrafo?* They praife him fufficiently by their Silence. Try him in Books, try him in his Exercifes or Mufick; I'll engage him fkill'd in every thing fit for a freeborn Youth to know.

Thr. (afide to Gnatho) For a Need, that Eunuch might ferve a Man well enough even in cold Blood.

Par. And yet the Gentleman who fends you thefe, don't defire that you live only for him, or exclude all others on his account: he is not perpetually relating his Battles, or boafting of his Scars, nor pretends to confine you, as a certain Perfon that fhall be namelefs: but when it will not be troublefome to you, when you give him leave, and are at leifure to fee him; he thinks it enough to be admitted then.

Thr. This Fellow appears to be the Servant of fome wretched beggarly Mafter.

Gnat. For nobody, I'm certain, could bear this Fellow, who had it in his Power to procure another.

Par. Silence, Wretch, who are to me more defpicable than the loweft Dregs of Mankind: for when you have the Meannefs to flatter him here in every thing, there is nothing fo fordid but I think you capable of.

Thr. Do we now go?

Tha. I'll only ftep in with thefe, and leave fome neceffary Orders, then I'll return immediately.

Thr. I'll go before; do you wait for her.

Par. It were unbecoming the Gravity of a General, to be feen walking in the Street with his Miftrefs.

Thr.

ANNOTATIONS.

17 *Ex Æthiopia eft ufque hæc.* This was what *Thais* had earneftly wanted, a Girl from *Ethiopia. Nonne ubi dixti cupere te ex Æthiopia ancillulam? Ufque* expreffes the Diftance whence fhe came, which was no fmall Addition to the Value of the Gift.

23 *Tacent, fatis laudant.* Silence is a kind of Confeffion, efpecially when an Adverfary puts the Queftion to us. There is a remarkable Paffage of *Cicero* to this purpofe, *pro Sext.* 18. *Me vero non* (movebat) *illius*
ſalus, fed etiam certa taciturnitas, in quot illa oratio tam improba conferebatur: qui tum, quanquam ob aliam caufam tacebant, tamen hominibus, omnia timentibus, tacendo loqui, non inficiendo confiteri videbantur.

24 *Liberum.* The whole Emphafis in pronouncing this Sentence, lies upon this Word, which difcovers *Chærea* to have Accomplifhments above his Rank, who tho' he appeared to be no more than a Slave, yet was equally fkill'd in thefe polite Arts, as if he had been born and educated a Citizen. It was the Practice fometimes among the
Ancients

Pa. Res indicabit. heus, jubéte iftos foràs
Exire, quos juffi. ociùs procede tu huc.
Ex Æthiopiâ eft ufque hæc. Thr. hîc funt tres minæ.
Gn. Vix. Pa. ubi tu es, Dore? accede huc..hem eu-
   nuchum tibi :
Quàm liberali facie, quàm ætate integrâ !   20
Th. Ita me Dii ament, honeftus. Pa. quid tu ais,
   Gnatho?   [Thrafo?
Numquid habes, quod contemnas? quid tu autem,
Tacent : fatis laudant. fac periculum in literis,
Fac in palæftrâ, in muficis. quæ liberum
Scire æquom eft adolefcentem, folertem dabo   25
Thr. Ego illum eunuchum, fi opu' fiet, vel fobrius.
Pa. Atque hæc qui mifit, non fibi foli poftulat
Te vivere, & fuâ caufâ excludi cæteros :
Neque pugnas narrat, neque cicatrices fuas
Oftentat, neque tibi obftat ; quod quidam facit.   30
Verùm, ubi moleftum-non erit, ubi tu voles,
Ubi tempus tibi erit, fat habet, fi tum recipitur.
Thr. Apparet fervom hunc effe domini pauperis,
Miferique. Gn. nam hercle nemo poffet, fat fcio,
Qui haberet quî pararet alium, hunc perpeti.   35
Pa. Tace tu, quem ego effe infra infimos omnes puto
Homines. nam, qui huic animum affentari induxeris,
E flamma petere te cibum poffe arbitror.
Thr. Jamne imus? Th. hos priùs introducam, &,
   quæ volo,
Simul imperabo. poftea, continuò exeo.   40
Thr. Ego hinc abeo : tu iftam opperire. Pa. haud
   convenit,
Unà cum amicâ ire imperatorem in via.

Pa. Res indicabit : heus, jubete iftos, quos juffi, exire foras : tu procede huc ociuj. Hæc eft ufque ex Æthiopiâ. Thr. Hic funt tres minæ. Gn. Vix. Pa. Dore, ubi es tu? Accede huc : hem eunuchum tibi : quam liberali facie, quam integra ætate! Th. Ita Dii ament me, eft honeftus. Pa. Quid tu ais, Gnatho? Numquid habes, quod contemnas? Quid tu autem, Thrafo? tacent : laudant fatis. Fac periculum in literis, fac in palæftra, in muficis ; dabo folertem quod ad omnia quæ æquum eft adolefcentem liberum fcire. Th. Ego illum eunuchum vel fobrius, fi opu fiet. Pa. Atque ille, qui mifit hæc non poftulat te vivere fibi foli, & cæteros excludi fua caufa. Neque narrat pugnas : neque effentat fuas cicatrices, neque obftat tibi; quod quidam facit. Verum dam facit, Habet fatis, fi recipitur tum, ubi non erit moleftum, ubi tu vo-

les, ubi erit tempus idoneum tibi. Thr. Apparet hunc effe fervum pauperis miferique domini. Gn. Nam hercle fcio fatis, nemo qui haberet qui (quâ) pararet alium, poffet perpeti hunc. Pa. Tace tu, quem ego puto effe infra omnes infimos homines, nam tu, qui induxeris animum huic, arbitror te poffe petere cibum e flammâ. Thr. Imus ne jam? Th. Introducam hos prius, & fimul imperabo quæ volo : poftea, continuo exeo. Thr. Ego abeo hinc ; tu opperire iftam. Pa. Haud convenit imperatorem ire in viâ unâ cum amita.

ANNOTATIONS.

Ancients to educate Slaves with Care, either that they might fell for the greater Price, or be the more ferviceable to their Mafters. Horat. Lib. 2. Epift. 2. ver. 6.
  Verna minifteriis ad nutus aptus heriles ; Literulis Græcis imbutus, idoneus arti Cuilibet.
26 *Si opus fit vel fobrius.* This, as it is natural enough in the Mouth of a Soldier, fo it muft appear to be ill-judg'd before *Thais,* unlefs we fuppofe that he whifpered it to *Gnatho*; *Thais* being in the mean time fo engaged with *Parmeno,* as not to overhear.

33 *Apparet fervam hunc effe.* The Captain draws this Conjecture from the Complement which *Parmeno* had juft made to *Thais,* it feem'd every way fo humble and fubmif-five. *Thrafo* fancied that a Man of Fortune, who could make Prefents of Value to his Miftrefs, would never behave in that refpectful Manner, for Riches are apt to make the Owner haughty and over-bearing. This was what the Soldier meant, but *Gnatho* the more to mortify *Parmeno,* takes it in another fenfe.
38 *E flamma petere cibum.* The Ancients
                 when

Thr. Why fhould I trouble my felf in talking to you ? *like Mafter,* *like Man.*

Gnat. Ha, ha, he!

Thr. Why do you laugh ?

Gnat. At what you faid juft now, and your fmart Repartee upon the *Rhodian* too, came into my Mind. But I fee *Thais* a coming.

Thr. Do you run before, make hafte, and fee that Things be in readinefs at home.

Gnat. I go.

Tha. *(to* Pythias*)* Be fure now, *Pythias,* to remember carefully what I order you. If *Chremes* happens to come, firft beg of him to ftay; if that does not fuit him, defire him to come again; but if he can't do that, bring him to me.

Pyt. I'll take care.

Tha. What! What elfe had I to fay? O! take particular care of the young Virgin, and fee that you keep at home.

Thr. Let us go then.

Tha. *(to her Attendants)* Do you follow me.

A N N O T A T I O N S.

when they burn'd the Bodies of the dead, commonly threw Bread, &c. into the Funeral Pile, and the greateft Affront that could be offered to any Perfon, was to tell him that he was capable of fnatching thefe from the Middle of the Flames. *E fiamma* is therefore

---

ACT III, SCENE III.

A R G U M E N T.

This Chremes *was the Brother of the Virgin who had been ftolen away.* Thais *had fent for him with no other Defign but to be certain of the Truth, and reftore his Sifter; but he, as being but a mere Ruftic, fancies all was done with a defign to enfnare him. In this Scene we have admirably defcrib'd the Nature of Rufticks, always fufpicious, and averfe to the Arts of foothing.*

C H R E M E S, P Y T H I A S.

Chremes. WHY truly the more I think of it, this *Thais* will certainly play me fome fcurvy Trick, I fee my felf fo cunningly befet by her on every fide. For when firft of all fhe ordered me to be fent for to her (any one may afk, what Bufinefs had you with her? Why really I know of none at all.) After I was come, fhe found a Pretence to keep me. She told me that fhe had been offering

A N N O T A T I O N S.

The Character of the Perfon who appears in this Scene is taken wholly from *Menander,* and is that of a Youth who had almeft always liv'd in the Country, and was very little acquainted with the Ways of the Town. *Thais* had fent for him to be fatisfied whether the Virgin the Soldier had lately brought over as a Prefent for her, was

Thr. Quid tibi ego multa dicam ? domini fimilis es.
Gn. Ha, ha, hæ ! Thr. quid rides ? Gn. iftuc,
quod dixti modo :
Et illud de Rhodio dictum in mentem venit. 45
Sed Thais exit. Thr. abi, præcurre, ut fint domi
Parata. Gn. fiat. Th. diligenter, Pythias,
Fac cures, fi Chremes huc fortè advenerit,
Ut ores, primùm ut maneat : fi id non commodum eft,
Ut redeat : fi id non poterit, ad me adducito.   50
Py. Ita faciam. Th. quid ? quid aliud volui dicere ?
Hem, curate iftam diligenter virginem.
Domi adfitis, facite. Thr. eamus. Th. vos me
fequimini.

Thr. Quid ego di- cam multa tibi ? es fimilis domini. Gn. Ha, ba, bæ! Thr. Quid rides ? Gn. Iftuc, quod dixti modo : et illud dictum de Rbodio venit in mentem. Sed Thais exit. Thr. Abi, præcurre, ut omnia fint parata domi. Gn. Fiat. Th. Pythias, fac curet diligenter, fi Chremes forte advenerit huc, primum ut ores ut maneat : fi id non

commodum eft ei, ut redeat : fi non poterit facere id, adducito eam ad me. Py. Faciam ita. Th. Quid ? Quid aliud volui dicere ? Hem, curate iftam virginem diligentur : facite ut adfitis domi. Thr. Eamus. Th. Vos fequimini me.

ANNOTATIONS.

therefore here inftead of *e rogo. Lucilius* endeavouring to give a Character of one of the moft contemptible Wretches in Nature, fays, *mordicus petere aurum e cæno expediat, e*

flamma cibum. ‘ He could ftoop to fnatch ‘ with his Teeth Gold from Dung, and Meat ‘ from a Funeral Pile.’

ACTUS III. SCENA III.

ARGUMENTUM.

Hic Chremes furreptæ virginis frater erat : cumque Thais nihil aliud cuperet, quam ei fororem reddere : hic, ut eft rufticus, credit ad fe fallendum omnia fieri. Admirabili autem fuavitate defcribitur in hac fcena rufticorum natura, femper temere fufpicax, & blanditiarum averfatrix.

CHREMES, PYTHIAS.

PRofecto, quanto magi’ magifque cogito,
Nimirum dabit hæc Thais mihi magnum malum :
Ita me video ab eâ aftutè labefactarier.
Jam tum, cùm primùm juffit me ad fe accerfier
(Roget quis, quid tibi cum illâ ? ne nôram quidem)
Ubi veni, caufam, ut ibi manerem, repperit :   6

ORDO.

Ch. PRofecto, quanto cogito magis magifque, nimirum bæc Thais dabit mihi magnum malum : video me ita aftute labefactarier ab ea. Jam tum, cum primum juffit me accerfier ad fe (quis roget quid tibi cum illa ? quidem ne noram) ubi veni, repperit caufam, ut manerem ibi ;

ANNOTATIONS.

was his Sifter, as fhe had fome Reafon to fufpect. This obliged her to afk feveral Queftions relating to himfelf, Family, and Fortune. *Chremes* a Ruftick, unacquainted with the Modes of the Town, a Character naturally jealous and fufpicious, fancies all this done with a Defign to draw him into

fome Snare. He is therefore introduced full of this Idea, and contriving with himfelf how he may beft avoid it.

² *Nimirum dabit bæc Thais.* A Perfon fpeaking by himfelf, is allowed to fupprefs many Words which they who overhear him, may eafily from the Train of his Difcourfe
fupply.

offering a Sacrifice, and that she had an Affair of Importance to treat
with me about. I began even then to suspect that all this was done
with no good Design. She sat down by me, put on an Air of Familiarity, and was at pains to find out Discourse to entertain me.
When she had nothing else to say, she asked how long my Father
and Mother had been dead? I answer, a great while. She then enquired whether I had a Seat at *Sunium*, and how far from the Sea?
I fancy she has taken a liking to it, and hopes to cozen me out of
it. At last she questioned me whether I had ever lost a little Sister
thence? whether any body was with her? what she had about her
when lost? and whether there was any one who could know her
again? What can she mean by all these Enquiries, unless perhaps
she thinks to pass herself upon me for this Sister, so long ago lost?
So great is her Assurance. But she, if living, is just sixteen Years
old, and no more: *Thais* is older than I am. She has, moreover
sent again, to beg of me very earnestly to come. Let her either
tell what she wants, or trouble me no more, for verily I will not
come a third Time. Soho! Soho! Who's there within? I am
Chremes. (*Knocks at the Door.*)

Pyt. O! dear Creature.

Chr. I tell you they have a Design upon me.

Pyt. Thais earnestly begs of you to come again To-morrow.

Chr. I'm going into the Country.

Pyt. Let me prevail with you, pray.

Chr. I tell you I can't.

Pyt. But pray stay with us 'till she return.

Chr. Not I really.

Pyt. Why not, dear *Chremes?*

Chr. Get you gone, you Slut.

Pyt. If you are so positive against it, pray be so good as go over
to the Place where my Mistress is.

Chr. I will go.

Pyt. Here, *Dorias*, go shew this Gentleman to the Captain's.

ANNOTATIONS.

supply. This Beginning of *Chremes*, when
the Ellipses are properly fill'd up, must run
in some such manner as this: *Profecto, quanto magis magisque cogito, nimirum* intelligo vel
invenio, quod *hæc Thais dabit mibi magnum
malum. Nimirum* may be here understood as
a Particle of Confirmation, to paint his Jea-
lousy yet the stronger. *Nimirum intelligo* for
sine dubio, pro certo intelligo.

9 *Dolo malo.* With a bad Design. *Dolus a
dolando, i. e. lædendo*, from hurting or grieving any one. But why does the Poet add
malo, says *Donatus?* The following Quotation from *Cicero* will serve to clear up this,
Off. 3. 14. *Sed quid faceret? nondum enim
Aquilius, collega & familiaris meus, protulerat
de dolo malo formulas: in quibus ipsis, cum ex
eo quæreretur,* Quid esset dolus malus? re-
spondebat,

Ait rem divinam feciſſe, & rem feriam
Velle agere mecum. jam tum erat fufpicio,
Dolo malo hæc fieri omnia. ipſa accumbere
Mecum, mihi feſe dare, fermonem quærere.　　10
Ubi friget, huc evaſit, quàm pridem pater
Mihi & mater mortui eſſent. dico, jam diu.
Rus Sunii ecquod habeam, & quàm longe à mari.
Credo ei placere hoc : ſperat ſe à me avellere.
Poſtremò, ecqua inde parva periiſſet ſoror ;　　15
Ecquis cum eà unà ; quid habuiſſet, cùm perit ;
Ecquis eam poſſet noſcere. hæc cur quæritet ?
Niſi ſi illa fortè, quæ olim periit parvola
Soror, hanc ſe intendit eſſe, ut eſt audacia.
Verùm ea, ſi vivit, annos nata eſt ſedecim,　　20
Non major : Thais, ego quàm ſum, majuſcula eſt.
Miſit porro orare, ut venirem, ſeriò.
Aut dicat quid volt, aut moleſta ne ſiet.
Non herclé yeniam tertio. heus, heus ; ecquis hic ?
Ego ſum Chremes. PY. ô capitulum lepidiſſimum !　25
CH. Dico ego mî inſidias fieri ? PY. Thais maxumo
Te orabat opere, ut cras redires. CH. rus eo.
PY. Fac, amabo. CH. non poſſum, inquam. PY. at
　　apud nos hîc mane,　　　　　　　　　[Chremes i
Dum redeat ipſa. CH. nihil minus. PY. cur, mi
CH. Malam in rem hinc ibis ? PY. ſi iſtuc ita certum
　　eſt tibi,
Amabo, ut illuc tranſeas, ubi illa eſt. CH. eo.　　31
PY. Abi, Dorias, citò hunc deduce ad militem.

Ait ſe feciſſe rem di-
vinum, & velle agere
rem ſeriam mecum
jam tum erat fuſpicio,
omnia hæc fieri malo
dolo. Ipſa cœpit ac-
cumbere mecum, dare
ſeſe mibi, quærere
ſermonem. Ubi ſer-
mo friget, evaſit huc,
Quam pridem pater
& mater eſſent mor-
tui. Dico : Jam diu.
Pergit rogare an ha-
beam ecquod rus Su-
nii, & quam longe a
mari. Credo hoc pla-
cere ei, ſperat ſe poſſe
avellere a me. Poſtre-
mo rogat ecqua parva
ſoror periiſſet indè,
ecquis eſſet una cum
ea ; quid habuiſſet
cùm periit ; ecquis
poſſet noſcere eam :
Cur quæritet æc ?
Niſi ſi forte illa in-
tendit ſe eſſe hanc ſo-
rorem, quæ ſoror o-
lim periit parvola ;
ut eſt audacia. Ve-
rum ea, ſi vivit, eſt
nata annos ſedecim,
non major : Thais eſt
majuſcula, quam ego
ſum. Miſit porro o-
rare ſerio, ut veni-

rem. *Aut dicat quid vult, aut ne ſiet meleſta. Hercle non veniam tertio. Heus, heus, ecquis*
hic ? *Ego ſum Chremes. PY. O lepidiſſimum cap'tulum ! CH. Ego dico inſidias fieri mibi.* PY.
Thais orabat te maxumo opere, ut redires cras. CH. Eo rus. PY. Amabo fac. CH. Inquam,
non poſſum. PY. At mane hic apud nos, dum ipſa redeat. CH. Nibil minus. PY. Cur, mi
Chremes? CH. Ibis hinc in malam rem? PY. Si iſtuc eſt ita certum tibi, amabo ut tranſeas illuc,
ubi illa eſt. CH. Eo. PY. Abi, Dorias, deduc hunc cito ad militem.

ANNOTATIONS.

ſpondebat, Cum eſſet aliud ſimulatum, aliud actum. Hoc quidem ſane luculenter, ut ab homine perito definiendi.

10 *Mibi feſe dare, ſermonem quærere. Seſe dare* is here to be underſtood of *Thais*'s Complaiſance, and a certain free and friendly Air which ſhe put on to *Chremes*, as deſigning, by an Act of Generoſity, to ſecure his Patronage and Protection, and therefore endeavours to appear with all the Inſinuation and Softneſs ſhe is capable of. But we muſt remember this Ruſtick's Suſpicions, which make him here give it a different Turn.

Sermonem quærere is properly to exhauſt all the common Topics of Diſcourſe, when we endeavour to find out Converſation to entertain and amuſe thoſe we are in company with.

30 *Malam in rem bint ibis ? Pythias* had ſaid, *Cur, mi Chremes ?* probably at the ſame time touching him with her Hand. This ſerves but to increaſe his Suſpicions, and draws upon her the ſevere Rebuke here refer'd to. As if he had ſaid : *Non manum abſtines, ſceleſta ?*

ACT III. SCENE IV.

ARGUMENT.

Antipho *is brought in, that by means of him the Spectators may know why* Chærea *was absent from the Port, and to prepare for the next Scene.*

ANTIPHO.

Antipho. **Y**Esterday some of us young Fellows met at the Port, that we might sup together this Day at the Club. *Chærea* had the Care of providing the Supper committed to him. Pledges were given. Place and Time were fixed on. The Time is paft, and no Sign of Preparation in the Place appointed. The Man himfelf is no where to be found, nor do I know what to say or guefs. Now the reft of the Company have charged me to look for him: and therefore I'll firft go see if he is at home: But who's this coming out from *Thais?* What? Is it he, or is it not? It is the very fame. What Sort of Man is here? What kind of Drefs is this? What Mifchief is now upon the Wheels? I cannot enough wonder nor conjecture what it means. But whatever it is, I have a mind to watch here at fome Diftance, 'till I can difcover it.

ANNOTATIONS.

' *Antipho* is here artfully introduced by the Poet, that *Chærea*, meeting him as he came out from *Thais*, might give him an Account of what is fuppofed to have been tranfacted behind the Scenes. This is done for the Sake of the Audience, that they might learn by a Recital what the Poet could not with Decency exhibit upon the Stage. -

' *Coimus in Piræum.* There has been a great Difpute upon this Verfe, whether we ought to read *in Piræo* or *in Piræcum*: nor is it yet wholly decided. The true Reading however, as Madam *Dacier* obferves, may be eafily afcertain'd by inconteftable Reafons. If the Youths who had agreed to fup together, were to go from the City to the Port, we ought undoubtedly to read *coimus in Piræum*. But we muft remember that they were at that

---

ACT III. SCENE V.

ARGUMENT.

Chærea *happening to come out from* Thais, *and overjoyed that he had enjoyed the Virgin according to his Defire, relates his good Fortune to* Antipho, *who chanced to meet him, with a World of Pleafure. This Relation of* Chærea *triumphing in his Succefs, is both well conceived, and happily painted.*

CHÆREA, ANTIPHO.

Chærea. **I**S there any body here? Nobody. Does any one follow me hence? not a living Soul. May I not now freely give
                                   vent

ANNOTATIONS.

Chærea, we have feen, had been prefented to *Thais* for the Eunuch, the Project had fucceeded, and he had obtained the full Completion of his Wifhes. He, therefore, comes

ACTUS III. SCENA IV.

ARGUMENTUM.

Inducitur Antipho, ut per occaſionem doceatur ſpectator, cur ex Piræo abierit Chærea, & eſt præparatio ad ſequentum ſcenam.

ANTIPHO.

HERI aliquot adoleſcentuli coiimus in Piræum,
In hunc diem ut de ſymbolis eſſemus. Chæream
ei rei   ʻ   [eſt,
Præfecimus : dati annuli: locus, tempus conſtitutum
Præteriit tempus : quo in loco dictum eſt, parati ni-
hil eſt.
Homo ipſe nuſquam eſt : neque ſcio, quid dicam, aut
quid conjectem.   5
Nunc mihi hoc negotî cæteri dedêre, ut illum quæram.
Ibo ad eum ; viſam, ſi domi eſt. quiſnam hinc à
Thaide exit ?   [qui hic ornatus eſt ?
Is eſt, an non eſt ? ipſu' eſt. quid hoc hominis eſt ?
Quid illud mali eſt ? nequeo ſatis mirari, neque con-
jicere.
Niſi quidquid eſt, procul hinc libet priu', quid ſit,
ſciſcitari.   10

hinc a Thaide ? Eſt it, an non eſt ? eſt ipſe. Quid hoc eſt hominis ? Qui ornatus eſt hic ? Quid eſt illud mali ? Nequeo ſatis mirari, neque conjicere. Niſi quicquid eſt, libet prius ſciſcitari procul hinc, quid ſit.

ORDO

AN. HEri ali-
quot ado-
leſcentuli coiimus in
Piræum, ut eſſemus
(ex repemus) de ſymbolis
in hanc diem. Præ-
fecimus Chæream ei
rei : Annuli ſunt da-
ti : Locus, tempus eſt
conſtitutum. Tempus
præteriit : eſt nihil
parati, in quq loco
eſt dictum. Homo ipſe
eſt nuſquam, neque
ſcio quid dicam, aut
quid conjectem. Nunc
cæteri dedêre hoc ne-
gotii mihi; ut quæ-
ram illum. Ibo ad
eum ; viſam, ſi eſt
domi. Quiſnam exit

ANNOTATIONS.

that Time upon Duty at the Port. *Terence* therefore could not write any other than *coiimus in Piræo*. Nor can the Teſtimony of *Cicero* deſtroy this, who in the third Letter of his ſeventh Book to *Atticus* cites this Verſe, *coiimus in Piræum*; for it may have been either taken from a faulty Copy of *Te-*rence, or may be an Error of ſome one of his own Tranſcribers.

⁸ *Is eſt, an non eſt ?* We are not to won-der, ſays *Donatus*, that *Chærea* was able to deceive *Thais*, when *Antipho*, who was one of his moſt intimate Friends, ſcarce knew him in this Diſguiſe.

ACTUS III. SCENA V.

ARGUMENTUM.

Per occaſionem Chærea a Thaide egrediens, ac nimio perfuſus gaudio, quod amata virgine ad arbitrium potitus fuerit, Antiphoni forte obvio ſuam felicitatem miro affectu narrat quæ exultantis Chæreæ narratio, jucundiſſima eſt & pulcherrima.

CHÆREA, ANTIPHO

NUM quis hîc eſt ? nemo eſt. num quis hinc me
ſequitur ? nemo homo eſt.

Num quis ſequitur me hinc ? Eſt nemo homo

ORDO

CH. NUM eſt
quis ho-
mo hîc ? Eſt nemo.

ANNOTATIONS.

comes out from *Thais*, triumphing in his good Fortune, and uttering his Joy in very extravagant Terms. *Antipho*, at ſome Diſtance, overhears him, and impatient to know

vent to thefe my Joys? O *Jupiter!* now is the time when I could contentedly fuffer myfelf to be killed, left *Life* by fome Difafter fhould blaft my prefent Happinefs. But is there never a curious inquifitive Fellow near, to follow me wherever I go, to deafen and murder me with Queftions? Why fo pleafed? Why fo joyful? Where are you a going? Whence are you come? How came you by this Garb? What can be your Defign? Are you in your Senfes? Or are you ftark mad?

Ant. I'll go up to him, and do him this Favour, which he fo mightily wants. *Chærea,* what is it that makes you fo joyful? What's the meaning of this Drefs? Why fo pleafed? What's your Defign? Are you in your Senfes? Why do you ftare at me? What, not a Word?

Chær. O happy Day! Welcome my Friend! There is not in the World a Man I now could more wifh to meet than you.

Ant. Pray tell me what all this can mean.

Chær. Nay, and I pray you to hear. Do you know the Miftrefs, whom my Brother is fo fond of?

Ant. Yes: I fuppofe you mean *Thais.*

Chær. The very fame.

Ant. So I fancy'd.

Chær. She had a young Girl prefented to her to-day. Why fhould I now defcribe or commend her Face to you, *Antipho,* who know fo well how nice a Judge I am of Beauty? She has charmed me.

Ant. Say you fo?

Chær. I know, did you but fee her, you would fay fhe was the moft agreeable of her Sex. What need of many Words? I fell in love with her. By good Fortune, there was a certain Eunuch at home, whom my Brother had bought for *Thais*; but who had not as yet been

Jamne erumpere hoc licet mihi gaudium? proh Jupiter!
Nunc eſt profecto, interfici cùm perpeti me poſſum,
Ne hoc gaudium contaminet vita ægritudine aliquâ.
Sed neminemne curioſum intervenire nunc mihi,   5
Qui me ſequatur, quoquò eam, rogitando obtundat,
enecet,   [emergam, ubi ſiem
Quid geſtiam, aut quid lætus ſim, quò pergam, unde
Veſtitum hunc nâtus, quid mihi quæram, ſanus ſim
·anne inſaniam?   [le, inibo
An. Adibo, atque ab eo gratiam hanc, quam video vel-
Chærea, quid eſt hoc, ſic geſtis? quid ſibi hic veſtitùs
quærit?   10
Quid eſt, quod lætus ſis? quid tibi vis? ſati' ne ſanus?
quid me
Aſpectas? quid taces? Ch. ô feſtus dies hominis! amice,
Salve: nemo eſt omnium, quem ego magis nunc cupe-
rem quam te.   [ſecro hercle, ut audias.
An. Narra iſtuc, quæſo, quid ſiet. Ch. imo ego te ob-
Noſtin' hanc, quam frater amat? An. novi: nempe,
opinor, Thaidem.   [hodie eſt ei dono data
Ch. Ipſam iſtam. An. ſic commemineram. Ch. quædam
Virgo. quid ego ejus tibi nunc faciem prædicem, aut
laudem, Antipho,   [ctator ſiem?
Cùm ipſum me nôris, quàm elegans formarum ſpe-
In hac commotus ſum. An. ain' tu? Ch. primam di-
·ces, ſcio, ſi videris.
Quid multa verba? amaré cœpi. forte fortunâ domi 20
Quidam erat eunuchus, quem mercatus fuerat frater
Thaidi:

te. An. Quæſo narra, quid iſtuc ſiet. Ch. Imo hercle, ego obſecro te, ut audias. Noſtne
hanc feminam quam frater amat? An. Novi: nempe, opinor, Thaidem. Ch. Iſtam iſſam.
An. Sic commemineram. Ch. Quædam virgo eſt data ei hodie dono. Quid, Antipho, ego nunc
prædicem aut laudem faciem ejus tibi, cum nôris me ipſum, quam ſim elegans ſpectator formarum?
Sum commotus in hac. An. Ain' tu? Ch. Scio, ſi videris, dices illam eſſe primam. Quid
facio multa verba? Cœpi amare: forte fortunâ erat quidam eunuchus domi, quem frater fuerat
mercatus Thaidi;

ANNOTATIONS.

5 Sed neminemne curioſum. All this is extremely natural. In great Emotions of Joy
we are not only apt to expreſs ourſelves in
Terms ſomewhat extravagant, but to wiſh
for the Company of ſome Friend, to whom
we may impart what we feel.

9 Ab eo gratiam hanc inibo. Inire gratiam, is to do a kindneſs to one, and by that
means merit his Favour and Good-will.
Gratiam ab eo inibo, is therefore the ſame as
if he had ſaid, Gratiam ejus mercbor, or ibo
in gratiam ejus. For Terence often puts ab
eo, inſtead of ejus, as in the Andrian: Hæc

primum ab eo animadvertenda injuria eſt.
That is, ejus injuria.

12 O feſtus dies hominis! The Expreſſion
is here ſomewhat remarkable: Feſtus dies
hominis, for homo qui es quaſi feſtus dies. This
manner of ſpeaking, though ſomewhat ſin-
gular, is yet very frequent in ancient Authors.
Thus, Scelus homo; pietas animi; ſententia dia
Catonis; and Plautus juſt as here, Since, amabo, amari te meus feſtus dies.

13 Elegans formarum ſpectator. Theſe
are, perhaps, three the moſt proper Terms
that could have been pitched upon by any
Writer,

been prefented to her. There *Parmeno* our Servant hinted a Projeƈt, which I readily gave into.

Ant. What was it?

Chær. Don't interrupt me, and you'll hear the fooner: that I fhould change Clothes with him, and order myfelf to be carried thither in his ftead.

Ant. What, inftead of the Eunuch?

Chær. The fame.

Ant. What Advantage could you propofe to yourfelf by that?

Chær. Do you afk? that I might fee, hear, and be in Company with her I loved, *Antipho.* Do you think this a flight Motive or Reafon? I was therefore prefented to the Woman, who as foon as fhe received me, joyfully took me home, and committed the Virgin to my Care.

Ant. To whom? To you?

Chær. To me.

Ant. To a fafe Keeper truly!

Chær. She ordered, that not a Man fhould come near her, and that I fhould not ftir from her, but remain with her alone in the inmoft Part of the Houfe. I gave a Nod of Submiffion, looking modeftly upon the Ground.

Ant. Poor Creature!

Chær. I am going out, faid fhe, to Supper, and accordingly went, taking her Maids with her, except a few new Comers, who were left to attend the Virgin. Immediately, they prepare a Bath for her, I urge them to haften. While it is getting ready, the Virgin fits in a private Room, looking at a certain Piƈture, where was reprefented the Manner, in which *Jupiter* is faid to have defcended into *Danae's* Lap, in a Shower of Gold. I likewife begin to look at it; and, finding that he had formerly play'd the like Game, could not but be highly delighted with the Thought: that a God fhould transform himfelf to a Man, and fteal privately through another's Roof, in form of a Shower, to deceive an unfufpeƈting Girl. But what God, faid I, within myfelf? He, who fhakes with his Thunder

the

A N N O T A T I O N S.

Writer, to exprefs *Chærea's* Delicacy in this Point. *Forma* anfwers exaƈtly to our Word a *Beauty.* *Speƈtare* is to *view, examine, or judge of with Attention.* *Elegantes* are thofe who know how to make a right Choice; *eligere bene.* Hence a Style is faid to be *elegant,* where the Terms made Choice of, are the moft proper, and moft emphatically expreffive of the Things. *Elegans & temperatum genus eloquendi.* Suet. Aug. 86.

22 *Summonuit, quod ego arripui. Summonuit: leviter monuit,* and is a very proper Word here, becaufe of *arriptus. i. e. avido amplexus fum,* which comes in afterwards.

And, indeed, as *Donatus* obferves, the whole is well cenceived: becaufe, as it was not fit for an ingenuous Youth to be ready at contriving Projeƈts of this kind, fo when hinted by another, it was plainly the Part of a Lover to embrace it eagerly.

36 *Sufpeƈtant tabulam quandam piƈtam.* This Thought of the Piƈture here is finely imagined by the Poet. The Piƈture itfelf is, indeed, indecent; but then we are to remember it is in the Houfe of a Ccurtezan. It muft, moreover, have given us a very difadvantageous Idea of *Chærea,* to fuppofe that he formed a Defign of debauching the Virgin

Neque is deductus etiam tum ad eam. summonuit me
    Parmeno
Ibi fervus, quod ego arripui. An. quid id eft? Ch.
    tace fis, citiùs audies.   [luc deducier.
Ut veftem cum illo mutem, & pro illo jubeam me il-
An. Pro eunuchon'? Ch. fic eft. An. quid ex eâ re
    tandem ut caperes commodi?   25
Ch. Rogas? viderem, audirem, effem unâ, quacum
    cupiebam, Antipho.   [mulieri.
Num parva caufa, aut parva ratio eft? traditus fum
Illa illico, ubi me accepit, læta vero ad fe abducit do-
    mum,   [fatis tutò tamen.
Commendat virginem. An. cui? tibine? Ch. mihi. An.
Ch. Edicit, ne vir quifquam ad eam adeat; & mihi,
    ne abfcedam, imperat,   30
In interiore parte ut maneam folus cum folâ. adnuo,
Terram intuens modeftè. An. mifer. Ch. ego, inquit,
    ad cœnam hinc eo: [effent, manent
Abducit fecum ancillas: paucæ, quæ circum illam
Novitiæ puellæ. continuo hæc adornant, ut lavet.
Adhortor, properent. dum apparatur, virgo in con-
    clavi fedet,   35
Sufpectans tabulam quandam pictam, ubi inerat pic-
    tura hæc, Jovem   [imbrem aureum.
Quo pacto Danaæ mififfe aiunt quondam in gremium
Egomet quoque id fpectare cœpi. & quia confimilem
    luferat   [bat mihi,
Jam olim ille ludum, impendiò magis animus gaude-
Deum fefe in hominem convertiffe, atque per alienas
    tegulas   40
Veniffe clanculum per impluvium, fucum factum mu-
    lieri.   [cutit.
At quem Deum? Quid templa cœli fumma fonitu con-

neque is etiam tum fuerat deductus ad eam. Ibi Parmeno fervus fummonuit me, quod ego arripui. An. Quid eft id? Ch. Tace fis, (fi vis) audies citiùs. Ut mutem veftem cum illo, & jubeam me deducier illuc pro illo. An. Pro eunuchone? Ch. Eft fic. An. Quid commodi ex ea re? tandem ut caperes. Ch. Rogas? Viderem, audirem, effem una cum i la, quacum cupiebam, Antipho. Num caufa eft parva, aut ratio parva? Sum traditus mulieri. Illa ilico, ubi accepit me, vero læta abducit me domum ad fe: commendat virginem. An. Cui? tibine? Ch. Mibi. An. Satis tutò tamen. Ch. Edicit, ne quifquam vir adeat ad eam, & imperat mihi, ne abfcedam: ut maneam folus cum fola in interiore parte demus: adnuo, intuens terram modefte. An. Mifer. Ch. Inquit: Ego eo hinc ad cœnam abduc t ancillas fecum: paucæ puellæ novitiæ manent, quæ effent circum illam:

continuo hæc adorant hanc, ut lavet: adhortor ut properent; dum apparatur, virgo fedet in conclavi, fufpectans quandam pictam tabulam, ubi hæc pictura inerat, quo pacto aiunt Jovem mififfe quondam aureum imbrem in gremium Danaæ. Egomet quoque cœpi fpectare id: & quia ille jam olim luferat confimilem ludum, animus gaudebat mihi magis impendio, deum convertiffe fefe in hominem, atque veniffe per impluvium clanculum per alienas tegulas, fucum factum mulieri. At quem deum? Qui contutit fumma templa cœli fonitu.

ANNOTATIONS.

Virgin from the Beginning, and fet about it fo cooly. No more is infinuated in the Progrefs of the Play, than that he wanted to fee her, to hear her fpeak, and be in company with her. The accidental Sight of the Picture incites him to that laft forward Step.

37 *Quo pacto Danaæ mififfe aiunt.* Madam *Dacier* ingenioufly remarks upon this, that the Word *aiunt* deferves particular No-

tice, as it marks the Difcretion of the Poet, who, in fpeaking of a Hiftory fo difhonourable to *Jupiter*, does not fay abfolutely, but adds, *as they tell us.*

42 *Qui templa cœli fumma fonitu concutit.* This Sentence is of the fublime Kind, and taken probably from fome ancient Tragick Poet, or from *Ennius*, as *Donatus* rather thinks. It was ufual for Poets to introduce, on fome particular Occafions, thefe Sentences

the lofty Battlements of Heaven. And fhould I, a poor Mortal, fcruple to do the fame? I, indeed, did it, and without hefitation. While I was revolving thefe Things in my Mind, the Virgin, mean time, was called away to bathe : fhe goes, bathes, and returns, after which they laid her on a Couch. I ftand waiting to fee if they had any Orders for me. At laft, one came up and faid : Here *Do-rus*, take this Fan, and while we are bathing, fan her thus. When we have done, you may bathe too, if you have a Mind. I take it very demurely.

Ant. I could have then wifhed to fee that impudent Face of thine, and the aukward Figure fo great a Booby muft make hold-ing a Fan.

Chær. Scarce had fhe done fpeaking, when in a Moment, they all hurried out of the Room, and run to the Bath in a noify Manner, as is ufual, when Mafters are abfent. Meantime, the Virgin falls afleep. I fteal a private Glance thus, with the Corner of my Eye, thro' the Fan ; at the fame Time look round every where, to fee if the Coaft was quite clear : finding all right, I bolted the Door.

Ant. What then ?

Chær. How ! What then, Simpleton ?

Ant. I own it.

Chær. Should I then have let flip an Opportunity fo fairly offered me : fo fine a one too, fo fhort, fo wifh'd for, and fo unexpected ? I muft then, indeed, have been the Eunuch, whofe Difguife I wore.

Ant. Why, truly you're in the right. But meantime, what's done in relation to the Club ?

Chær. All's ready.

Ant. A noble Fellow. But where ? At home ?

Chær. No, at our Freedman's *Difcus*.

Ant. That's a long way off.

Chær. But let us therefore make the greater hafte.

Ant. Change your Clothes.

Chær. Where fhall I change them ? I am perfectly at a Lofs ; for at prefent, I'm an Exile from home. I am afraid, left perhaps my Brother may be within ; and then I'm of my Father, left he fhould be returned out of the Country.

Ant. Go along with me, that's the nigheft Place where you can fhift this Drefs.

Chær. You're right. Let us go then : for I want alfo to confult, with you, what Method I muft take to make this Girl wholly mine.

Ant. Agreed.

ANNOTATIONS.

of the Heroick kind, and they carry in them, when well applied, a fingular Beauty. *Phædrus* gives us an Inftance of it in the Fable of the Weazels and Mice, 4. 5.

Quos immolatos victor avidis dentibus Capacis alvi merfit Tartareo fpecu.

53 *Ego limis fpectio. Limis*, if it is the Nominative fingular, fignifies the fame as *tranfverfus* ;

Ego homuncio hoc non facerem? ego vero illud feci,
ac lubens.~ [virgo. 44.
Dum hæc mecum reputo, accerſitur lavatum intereà
It, lavit, redit: deinde eam in lectum illæ collocant.
Sto expectans, ſi quid mihi imperent. venit una; heus
tu, inquit, Dore, [vamur.
Cape hoc flabellum, ventulum huic ſic facito; dum la-
Ubi nos laverimus, ſi voles, lavato: accipio triſtis.
An. Tum equidem iſtuc os tuum impudens videre ni-
mium vellem, 49
Qui eſſet ſtatus, flabellulum tenere te aſinum tantum
Ch. Vix elocuta eſt hoc, forà ſimul omnes proruunt ſe:
Abeunt lavatum, perſtrepunt, ita ut ſit, domini ubi
abſunt.
Interea ſomnus virginem opprimit. ego limis ſpecto
Sic per flabellum clanculum: ſimul alia circumſpecto,
Satin' explorata ſint. video eſſe: peſſulum oſtio obdo.
An. Quid tum? Ch. quid? quid tum, fatue? An. fa-
teor. Ch. an ego occaſionem 56
Mihi oſtentam tantam, tam brevem, tam optatam, tam
inſperatam,
Amitterem? tum pol ego is eſſem verè, qui affimulabar.
An. Sanè, hercle, ut dicis. ſed interim de ſymbolis quid
actum eſt? [apud libertum Diſcum. 60
Ch. Paratum eſt. An. frugi es. ubi? domin'? Ch. imo
An. Perlonge eſt: ſed tanto ociùs properemus. muta
veſtem. [tuo fratrem;
Ch. Ubi mutem? perii: nam domo exſulo nunc. me-
Ne intus ſit: porro autem, pater ne rure redierit jam.
An. Eamus ad me: ibi proxumum eſt ubi mutes. Ch.
rectè dicis.
Eamus: & de iſtac ſimul, quo pacto porro poſſim 65
Potiri, conſilium volo capere unà tecum, An. fiat.

Ego lemuncio non facerem hoc? Ego vero feci illud, ac lubens. Dum reputo hæc mecum, interea virgo accerſitur lavatum. It, lavit, redit; inde illæ collocant eam in lectum. Sto expectans, ſi imperent quid mihi: una venit; Heus tu, Dore, inquit, cape hoc flabellum, facito ſic ventulum huic, dum laverimur. tu lavato, ſi voles. ego triſtis accipio. An. Tum equidem animum vellem videre iſtuc os tuum impudens, & qui eſſet ſtatus ejus, te tantum aſinum tenere flabellulum. Ch. Vix eſt elocuta hoc, cum omnes ſimul proruunt ſe foràs, abeunt lavatum, perſtrepunt, ita ut ſit, ubi domini abſunt. Interea ſomnus opprimit virginem. Ego ſic ſpecto clanculum per flabellum limis oculis: ſimul circumſpecto alia, ſatiſne ſint explorata; video eſſe: obdo peſſulum oſtio. An. Quid tum? Ch. Quid? Quid tum, fatue? An. Fateor. Ch. An ego amitterem occaſionem tau-

tam, tam brevem, tam optatam, tam inſperatam, oſtentam mihi? Tum pol, ego vere eſſem is, qui affimulabar. An. Sanè, hercle, ut dicis: ſed interim quid eſt actum de ſymbolis? Ch. Eſt paratum. An. Es frugi: ubi? Domine? Ch. Imo apud Diſcum libertum. An. Perlonge eſt: ſed properemus tanto ociùs. Muta veſtem. Ch. Ubi mutem? perii: nam nunc exſulo domo: metuo ſi autem, ne ſit intus: porro autem, ne pater jam redierit rure. An. Eamus ad me: ibi eſt proxumum ubi mutes. Ch. Dicis rectè; eamus: & ſimul volo capere conſilium una tecum de iſtac puellà; quo pacto poſſim porro potiri ea. An. Fiat.

ANNOTATIONS.

tranſverſus; if the Ablative plural, we muſt ſupply oculis. For limis is the ſame as tranſverſus; whence what runs acroſs to one going in or out at a Gate, is called Limen.

When, therefore, Men want to look at any Thing unobſerved, and for that Purpoſe view it not directly, but aſkance, they are ſaid limis aſpicere.

ACTUS

ACT IV. SCENE I.

ARGUMENT.

This Girl, returning from her Miſtreſs to carry home her Jewels, takes occaſion to inform the Spectators of what had paſſed at the Soldier's, viz. the Quarrel between Thais *and* Thraſo, *occaſioned by the coming of* Chremes.

DORIAS.

SO may the Gods bleſs me, as far as I can judge of this Soldier, I am miſerably afraid, leſt the Madman ſhould cauſe ſome Diſturbance To-day, or offer Violence to *Thais.* For when this young Gentleman, *Chremes,* the Virgin's Brother came, ſhe begged of the Captain, that he might be admitted. He took Fire directly, yet durſt not refuſe. *Thais* ſtill inſiſted, that he would invite the Man in, which ſhe did, that ſhe might keep him a little, becauſe it was not now a fit Time for what ſhe wanted to tell him, in regard to his Siſter. He invites him, at laſt, with a cold Air; the Gentleman ſtaid, when immediately my Miſtreſs entered into Diſcourſe with him. The Soldier imagining, that this was a Rival brought before his very Face, wanted, in his turn, to mortify her. Hark ye, Boy, ſays he, go fetch *Pamphila,* that ſhe may divert us. By no means, returned *Thais*; would you have her at a Feaſt? the Soldier ſtill inſiſted, till at laſt it came to a Quarrel. Meantime, my Miſtreſs, unobſerved, ſlips off her Jewels, and gives them to me, that I may carry them off. This, I know perfectly well, is a Sign that ſhe'll get from thence as ſoon as poſſible.

ANNOTATIONS.

In the third Scene of the third Act, Dorias had been ſent along with *Chremes,* to conduct him to *Thais,* who was gone to ſup with the Soldier. *Thais,* who was willing to behave to him with all the Complaiſance in her Power, deſired *Thraſo* to invite him in, to which he at laſt, but with Reluctance, yielded. No ſooner was he ſat down, but wanting to keep him till ſhe ſhould have a fit Opportunity of ſatisfying herſelf, whether he was the Virgin's Brother, ſhe enters familiarly into Converſation with him. The Soldier alarmed at this, as imagining him a Rival brought in on purpoſe to affront him, to mortify *Thais* in his turn, remembring the Advice given him by *Gnatho,* orders *Pamphila* to be ſent for. This occaſions a Quarrel, which as it was like to run high, *Thais* privately pulls off her Jewels, and gives them to her Maid to carry home, deſigning herſelf to withdraw as ſoon as poſſible. *Dorias,* therefore, appears here upon the Stage, with her Miſtreſs's Jewels, and as ſhe is going home, acquaints the Spectators with what had happened at the Captain's behind the Scenes.

11 *Minime gentium : in convivium illam ?* viz. *adducas.* Some read *tun' in convivium illam ?* For it was contrary to the Manners of the *Greeks,* for Women to appear at Table with Strangers ; for ſo *Cicero,* Verr. 1. 26. *Poſteaquam ſatis calere res Rubrio viſa eſt ; Quæſo, inquit, Philedame, cur ad nos filiam tuam non intro vocari jubes? Homo, qui & ſumma gravitate, & jam id ætatis, & parens eſſet, obſtupuit hominis improbi dicto. Inſtare Rubrius. Tum ille, ut aliquid reſponderet, negavit moris eſſe Græcorum, ut in con-*
ſ *[...]*

ACT

Ancilla ab hera rediens, ut aurum ipsius domum referat, hac oc-
casione docet spectatores, quid in convivio militis actum sit:
nempe initium jurgii inter Thaidem & Thrasonem, ob interven-
tum Chremetis.

DORIAS.

ORDO.

ITA me Dii amant, quantùm ego illum vidi, non
nihil timeo miseram,
Ne quam ille hodie insanus turbam faciat, aut vim
Thaidi. [virginis :
Nam postquam iste advenit Chremes, adolescens frater
Militem rogat, ut eum admitti jubeat. ille continuò
irasci. [nem invitet. 5
Neque negare audere. Thais porro instare, ut homi-
Id faciebat retinendi illius causâ : quia, illa quæ cupiebat
De sorore ejus indicare, ad eam rem tempus non erat.
Invitat tristis: mansit. ibi illa cum illo sermonem occipit.
Miles vero sibi putare adductum ante oculos æmulum :
Voluit facere contrà huic ægrè : heus, inquit, puer,
Pamphilam 10
Arcesse, ut delectet hîc nos. illa exclamat, Minimè
gentium.
In convivium illam ? miles tendere. inde ad jurgium.
Interea aurum sibi clàm mulier demit, dat mihi ut
auferam. [scio.
Hoc est signi, ubi primum poterit, se illinc subducet,

ITA Dii ament me,
quantum ego vi-
di illum militem,
misera timeo non ni-
hil, ne ille insanus fa-
ciat quam turbam
hodie, aut vim Thaidi.
Nam postquam iste
Chremes, adolescens,
frater virginis adve-
nit; rogat militem,
ut jubeat eum admit-
ti. Ille continuo cœ-
pit irasci, neque au-
dere negare ; Thais
porro instare, ut in-
vitet hominem. Fa-
ciebat id causâ reti-
nendi illius, quia quæ
illa cupiebat indicare
de sorore ejus, non e-
rat tempus ad eam
rem. Ille tristis in-
vitat : Chremes
mansit : ibi illa oc-
cipit sermonem cum
illa : miles vero cœ-

pit putare æmulum adductum sibi ante oculos : voluit contra facere ægre huic : Heus puer, inquit,
arcesse Pamphilam hic, ut delectet nos : illa exclamat, Minime gentium, arcessas illum in convivium. Miles cœpit tendere : inde ventum est ad jurgium. Interea mulier clam demit aurum sibi,
& dat mihi ut auferam : scio, hoc est signi, ut subducet se illinc, ubi primum poterit.

ANNOTATIONS.

vivio virorum accumberent mulieres. Thais
therefore, would not admit Pamphila to the
Entertainment, lest she might hear Things
offensive to Chastity, in such free Conversation as was usual on those Occasions. For
as she suspected her to be a Citizen, and designed to restore her to her Relations, she
was unwilling that any thing should happen,
which might injure her Reputation.
[13] *Aurum sibi clam mulier demit.* At
Athens, Courtezans were forbid, by Law, to
wear Gold or Jewels. But these Laws were

not very strictly kept. They were also forbid
to have Servants, and yet nothing was more
common than, for the more noted, to have
whole Troops attending them. Some tell us,
that it was usual for them to have their Jewels
carried to the Place where they intended
to appear dressed, and there put them on ;
and when about to return, send them away
again before them : which, if true, explains
the Reason of Thais's Behaviour here ;
though I would rather attribute it to her
Fear, lest the Soldier should use her rudely.

ACTUS

ACT IV. SCENE II.

ARGUMENT.

Phædria *returns from the Country, both to give an Example of the Inconſtancy of Lovers, and that by his Arrival the Hurry of 'that Part of the Play, wherein he is chiefly concerned, may be promoted.*

PHÆDRIA.

A S I was going into the Country, I began (as commonly happens, when the Mind is under any Concern) to think of one Thing after another, and ſaw every Thing in the worſt Light. What need of Words ? while I was muſing thus with myſelf, I inadvertently paſſed by my Country-houſe, and was got a good Way beyond it, before I perceived it, I returned again, but very uneaſy with myſelf. When I came to the Turning that leads to the Houſe, I ſtopt, and began to Reaſon with myſelf: What! Muſt I ſtay here alone two Days without her? What then? 'tis nothing: What! Nothing? If I am deny'd the Privilege of touching her, muſt I be forbid ſeeing her alſo? If the one is not granted me, at leaſt the other ſhall? and in Love the leaſt Enjoyment is ſure better than nothing. With that I deſignedly paſſed the Houſe : but what can this be, that *Pythias* hurries out in ſuch a Fright?

ANNOTATIONS.

ʳ **Phædria**, according to his Reſolution, in the Beginning of the ſecond Act, goes into the Country with a Deſign to remain there three whole Days. But as Lovers are very apt to change, in going along, revolving one thing after another, and finding himſelf very uneaſy at the Thought of being abſent from *Thais*, for ſo long a Time, he wiſely con- cludes, that ſince he cannot have the full Enjoyment of her, at leaſt not to deny him- ſelf, what is actually in his Power. He is, therefore, introduced here, as come back, and talking over, with himſelf, the Reaſons of a Behaviour ſo full of Weakneſs and Ir- reſolution.

¹² *Extrema linea amare, haud nihil eſt.* This

ACT IV. SCENE III.

ARGUMENT.

Pythias *the Maid complaineth of the Eunuch, who, ſhe under- ſtands, had raviſhed the Virgin.* Phædria *coming up, can't believe it. This give riſe to ſome Conjectures concerning the Poſſibility of the Thing, which* Phædria *expreſsly denies. The Diſpute is pleaſant, and has in it a great deal of Humour.*

PYTHIAS, PHÆDRIA, DORIAS.

Pythias. WHERE, Wretch that I am, ſhall I find this aban- doned impious Villain? Where ſhall I look for him? To

ANNOTATIONS.

Chærea, who had been introduced to *Thais* in the Eunuch's Dreſs, had by this Time ac- compliſhed his Deſign upon *Pamphila*, and made his Eſcape. *Pythias* followed by *Do- rias,*

ACTUS IV. SCENA. II.

ARGUMENTUM.

Revertitur rure Phædria, cum ut amatorum inconstantiam cernas, tum ut ejus adventu promoveatur epitasis alterius partis fabulæ.

PHÆDRIA.

DUM rus eo; cœpi egomet mecum inter vias,
Ita ut fit, ubi quid in animo est molestiæ,
Aliam rem ex aliâ cogitare, & ea omnia in
Pejorem partem. quid opu' est verbis? dum hæc puto
Præterii imprudens villam. longe jam abieram, 5
Cum sensi. redeo rursum male vero me habens.
Ubi ad ipsum veni divorticulum, constiti:
Occepi mecum cogitare; Hem, biduum hîc
Manendum est soli sine illâ? quid tum postea?
Nihil est. quid? nihil? si non tangendi copia est, 10
Eho, ne videndi quidem erit? si illud non licet,
Saltem hoc licebit. certe, extremâlin eâ
Amare, haud nihil est. villam prætereo sciens.
Sed quid hoc, quòd timida subitò egreditur Pythias?

ORDO.

Egomet, dum eo rus, cœpi cogitare mecum aliam rem ex alia inter vias, ita ut fit, ubi quid molestiæ est in animo, & rapere ea omnia in pejorem partem. Quid est opus verbis? dum puto hæc, imprudens præterii villam. Abieram jam longe, cum sensi. Redeo rursum, vero habens me male. Ubi veni ad ipsum divorticulum, constiti: occepi cogitare mecum; Hem; an manendum

est mihi soli hic biduum sine illâ? Quid tum postea? Est nihil. Quid? Nihil? Si non est copia tangendi eam, eho, ne quidem erit videndi? Si illud non licet, saltem hoc licebit. Certe, amare extrema linea haud est nihil. Sciens præterco villam. Sed quid est hoc, quid Pythias egreditur subitò timida?

ANNOTATIONS.

This Passage is variously explained by Commentators. The most likely Conjecture is that which makes it a Metaphor drawn from the Courses of Chariots, where in turning round the Goal, he who is nearest, is said *currere in prima linea*; the next him *in secunda*; and so on to the last, who runs *in extrema linea*. This has some Resemblance to the several Degrees of Love, where the lowest Enjoyment is seeing the Person beloved, and what the Poet here calls *amare in extrema linea*.

ACTUS IV. SCENA III.

ARGUMENTUM.

Queritur de eunucho Pythias ancilla, ob stupratam virginem. Superveniens Phædria, factum non credit. Est autem conjecturalis status, an sit ab eunucho vitiata virgo; idque per ἀδύνατον refellit Phædria. Jucunda itaque est concertatio, & plurimum habet voluptatis.

PYTHIAS, PHÆDRIA; DORIAS.

UBI ego illum scelerosum misera atque impium inveniam? aut ubi quæram?

ORDO.

Pr. UBI ego misera inveniam illum scelero-

sum atque impium? aut ubi quæram?

ANNOTATIONS.

ria, who now came to know what had happened, run out in great haste to look for him, and meeting *Phædria*, tells him all; who thinking it impossible, concludes they are drunk,

To have the boldnefs of venturing upon fo daring a Crime ! I'm ruined.

Phæd. I am in Pain to think what this can be.

Pyt. The Villain too, after he had abufed the Virgin, tore all her Clothes, and drag'd her by the Hair.

Phæd. Hah !

Pyt. Were he but now within my reach, how eagerly would I fly at him, and tear out his Eyes with my Nails !

Phæd. I can't think what Difturbance this muft be, that has happened here in my Abfence. I'll go up to her. What's the Matter ? Why in fuch hafte ? Or whom do you look for, *Pythias ?*

Pyt. Hah, *Phædria !* Whom do I look for ? get you hence, as you deferve with your fine Prefents.

Phæd. What's the Matter, pray ?

Pyt. What's the Matter ? the Eunuch that you fent us, what Difturbance has he raifed ? he has debauched the Virgin, which the Soldier made a Prefent of to my Miftrefs.

Phæd. What do you fay !

Pyt. I'm ruin'd.

Phæd. You're drunk fure.

Pyt. Would that all, who wifh me ill, were drunk in the fame Way.

Dor. Ah, my *Pythias,* pray what a monftrous Thing is this ?

Phæd. You're certainly mad : how could a Eunuch do any fuch Thing ?

Pyt. I don't know who he was, but as to what he has done, the Matter is evident. The Virgin herfelf is all in Tears, nor, when you afk what's the Matter, dare fhe to tell you. As for the Gentleman himfelf, he is no where to be feen. Nay, I moreover fufpect that he has carried fomething off with him when he run away.

Phæd. I cannot enough Wonder where the fluggifh Wretch muft have gone fo foon, unlefs, perhaps he is returned home to our Houfe.

Pyt. Pray go fee, whether he be there.

Phæd. I'll let you know immediately.

Dor. Good Heavens ! prithee, my *Pythias,* I have not fo much as heard of fo daring an Action.

Pyt. I have, indeed, heard they are extremely fond of Women, but

. . *A N N O T A T I O N S.*

drunk, or had loft their Senfes. Willing however to examine a little into the Matter, he returns home to fee if he can find the Eunuch, and learn the Caufe of his running away.

4 *Veftem omnem miferæ difcidit.* The Poet conducts here with wonderful Difcretion and Judgment. It appears that *Chærea* had a hard Struggle before he could obtain his Defires of *Pamphila.* Her Garment torn, and

Hair difheveled, were Evidences that fhe did not tamely fubmit to his Embraces. This was neceffary to preferve her Character as a Lady of Virtue and Honour, and leave no Objection to the Marriage, which was afterwards to be concluded between her and *Chærea.* It was likewife well conceived by the Poet to make us fenfible of it by what *Pythias* fays here, rather than by a Relation from *Chærea* himfelf, becaufe that could not have been

Hoccine tam audax facinus facere esse ausum? perii.
PH. hoc quid fit, vereor.   [virginem,
PY. Quin etiam infuper fcelu', poftquam ludificatu' eft
Veftem omnem miferæ difcidit, tum ipfam capillo con-
fcidit.
PH. Hem. PY. qui nunc fi detur mihi,   5
Ut ego unguibus facilè illi in oculos involem venefico?
PH. Nefcio quid profectò, abfente nobis, turbatum eft
domi.   . [Pythias?
Adibo. quid ifluc? quid feftinas? aut quem quæris,
PY. Ehem Phædria, 'egon' quem quæram? i hinc quo
dignu' es cum donis tuis
Tam inlepidis. PH. quid ifluc eft rei?   10
PY. Rogas me? eunuchum quem dedifti nobis, quas
turbas dedit?
Virginem, quam heræ dono dederat miles, vitiavit
PH. quid ais?
PY. Perii. PH. temulenta es. PY. utinam fic fint, qui
mihi male volunt.   [fuit?
DO. Au, obfecro, mea Pythias, quid iflucnam monftri.
PH. Infanis: qui ifluc facere eunuchus potuit? PY.
illum nefcio   '   15
Qui fuerit: hoc, quod fecit, res ipfa indicat.
Virgo ipfa lacrumat, neque, cùm rogites quid fit, au-
det dicere.   [fera fufpicor,
Ille autem bonus vir nufquam apparet, etiam hoc mi-
Aliquid domo abeuntem abftulifle. PH. nequeo mirari
fatis,
Quò ille abire ignavus poffet longius, nifi fi domum 20
Forte ad nos rediit. PY. vife amabo, num fit. PH. jam
faxo, fcies.   [audivi quidem.
DO. Perii, obfecro. tam infandum facinus, mea tu, ne
PY. At pol ego amatores mulierum effe audicram eos
maxumos,

illum aufum efle fuccre hoccine tam audax facinus? perii. PH. Verſor, quid hoc fit. PY. Atque infuper etiam fcelus, poftquam eft ludificatus virginem, difcidit omnem veftem illi miferæ, tum confcidit ipfam capillo. PH. Hem. PY. Qui fi detur nunc mihi, ut ego facile involem unguibus in oculos illi venefico? PH. Profecto nefcio quid eft turbatum domi, nobis (me) abfente. Adibo. Quid iftuc? Quid feftinas, Pythias? aut quem quæris? PY. Ehem Phædria: egone quem quæram? I hinc quo es dignus cum tuis donis tam illepidis. PH. Quid rei eft iftuc? PY. Rogas me? Eunuchus, quem dedifti nobis, quas turbis dedit? vitiavit virginem, quam miles dederat heræ dono. PH. Quid ais? PY. Perii. PH. Es tumulenta. PY. Utinam illi fic fint, qui volunt male mihi. DO. Au, obfecro, mea Pythias,

quidnam monftri fuit iftuc? PH. Infanis: qui eunuchus potuit facere iftuc. PY. Nefcio illum, qui fuerit; res ipfa indicat hoc, quod fecit: ipfa virgo lucrimat: neque, cum rogites quid fit, audet dicere. Ille autem bonus vir apparet nufquam: etiam mifera fufpicor hoc; eum abeuntem abftulifle aliquid domo. PH. Nequeo fatis mirari, quò ille ignavus poffet abire longius, nifi fi forte rediit domum ad nos. PY. Amabo vife, num fit. PH. Faxo fcies jam. DO. Perii. Obfecro tu, mea Pythias, ne quidem audivi facinus tam infandum. PY. At pol ego audivi am eos effe maximos amatores mulierum,

ANNOTATIONS.

been done without entering into a Detail of Particulars, that muft have been very offenfive to chafte and delicate Ears.

7 *Abfente nobis*, for *me abfente*, by the Figure *Synthefis*, regard being had to the Senfe of *nobis*, which is here the fame as *me*; for though *we* for *I* is now the Style of a Prince, it was formerly a fign of Modefty and Humility. We have an Inftance of the fame Form of Speech in *Plautus*, Amph. 2. 2. 194.

Nec nobis præfente aliquis nifi fervos Sofia affuit.

but that they could do nothing. But alas! it never once came into my Mind: for I would certainly have shut him up somewhere, nor trusted him with the Virgin.

ANNOTATIONS.

24 *Verum miseræ non in mentem venerat.* This must either be taken absolutely that she was never apprehensive of any Accident

of this nature, or refer to what is said in the Verse immediately before *Amatores mulierum esse audieram eos maximos.*

ACT IV. SCENE IV.

ARGUMENT.

Phædria *falls upon* Dorus *the Eunuch with a Load of Reproaches, as believing that he had attempted to debauch the Virgin. By this means* Chærea's *Deceit comes to be known.* Phædria, *therefore, fearing* Thais's *Displeasure, whispers to the Eunuch to deny every thing he had said.*

PHÆDRIA; the EUNUCH, PYTHIAS, DORIAS.

Phæd. COME out, Villain: What! are you afraid to come forward, you Runagade? Out, I say, thou sorry Bargain.

Eun. For Heaven's sake!

Phæd. Oh! but see that; how that Rascal distorts his Face! Why are you come back hither? What means this Change of Dress? What Answer do you make? Had I staid but a Moment longer, *Pythias,* I should not have found him at home, he was so well prepared to march off.

Pyt. Have you got the Gentleman, pray?

Phæd. Have him? assuredly.

Pyt. O, well done!

Dor. That is well indeed.

Pyt. Where is he?

Phæd. What! Don't you see him?

Pyt. I see him! Whom, pray?

Phæd. This Rascal here.

Pyt. What Man is this?

Phæd. The same that was brought to your House to-day.

Pyt. I dare assure you, *Phædria,* that not one in our House ever saw this Man before.

Phæd. What! never saw him?

Pyt. Did you, pray, fancy this to be the same that was brought to us?

Phæd. Whom should I fancy him to be, when I had no other to send?

Pyt. Au! This Fellow is not so much as to be compared with him.

ANNOTATIONS.

Phædria going home to look for the Eunuch, finds him; and as he had no Suspicion of the Project that had been form'd between *Chærea* and *Parmeno,* drags him out, fully assured that he was the same *Pythias* meant, and preparing for further Flight, by

Sed nihil poteſſe : verum miſeræ non in mentem venerat :
Nam illum aliquò concluſſem, neque illi commiſiſſem
virginem.　　　　　　　　　　　　　　　　25

ginem illi.

ſed poteſſe nihil: ve-
rum non venerat in
mentem mihi miſe-
ræ . Nam contcluſſ̄
ſemillum aliquò, ne-
i que commiſiſſem vir-

ACTUS IV. SCENA IV.

ARGUMENTUM.

Phædria multis & acerbis convitiis Dorum eunuchum petit, quem
virginem vitiaſſe putat.　Per hunc dolus Chæreæ proditur :
quare veritus Phædria Thaidem, eunuchum ſubmonet, ut, quod
dixerit, neget.

PHÆDRIA, EUNUCHUS, PYTHIAS, DORIAS.

E XI foras, ſceleſte : at etiam reſtitas,　[PH. oh,
Fugitive ? prodi, male conciliate.　Eu. obſecro.
Illud vide, os ut ſibi diſtorſit carnufex !
Quid huc reditio eſt ? quid veſtis mutatio ?
Quid narras ? paulùm ſi ceſſaſſem, Pythia,　　5
Domì non offendiſſem : ita jam adornarat fugam.
Py. Habeſne hominem, amabo? PH. quidni habeam?Py.
ô factum bene !　　　　.　　　[non vides ?
Do. Iſtuc pol vero bene. Py. ubi eſt ? PH. rogitas ?
Py. Videam, obſecro, quem ? PH. hunc ſcilicet. Py.
quis hic eſt homo ? .　　　　　　　　　　9
PH. Qui ad vos deductus hodie eſt. Py. hunc óculis ſuis
Noſtrarum nunquam quiſquam vidit, Phædria.
PH. Non vidit ? Py. an tu hunc credidiſti eſſe, obſecro,
Ad nos deductum ? PH. nam quem ? alium habui nemi-
nem.　Py. au !
Ne comparandus hic quidem ad illum eſt. ille erat

ORDO.
PH. E XI foras
ſceleſte, at
etiam reſtitas, fugi-
tive ? Prodi, male
conciliate. Eu. Ob-
ſecro. PH. Oh vide
illud, ut carnifex diſ-
torſit os ſibi! Quid
eſt reditio huc ?
Quid mutatio veſtis?
Quid narras ? Si,
Pythia, ceſſaviſſem
paulum, non offen-
diſſem eam domi !
ita jam adornarat
fugam. Pv. Ama-
bo, habeſne hominem?
PH. Quidni habeam ?
Pv. O factum bene !
Do. Pol vero iſtuc
eſt bene. Py. Ubi
eſt.? PH. Rogitas ?
nonne vides ? Pv.

Videam ? Obſecro, quem ? PH. Scilicet hunc.　Pv. Quis homo eſt hic ? PH. Homo qui eſt
deductus hodie ad vos.　Py. Nunquam quiſquam noſtratum, Phædria, vidit hunc ſuis oculis.
PH. Non vidit ? Py. Obſecro, an tu credidiſti hunc eſſe deductum ad nos ? PH. Nam quem ?
habui neminem alium. Py. Au ! hic ne quidem eſt comparandus ad illum.　Ille erat

---

ANNOTATIONS.

by the Change of his Dreſs. But when
Pythias ſaw him, and knew nothing of him,
he is perfectly aſtoniſhed. Upon queſtioning
him a little, he comes to know all the
Truth, and is ſtrangely diſconcerted ; but
willing, if poſſible, to bring himſelf off,
makes Dorus again deny every thing he had
ſaid.
　14 *Ne comparandus hic quidem ad illum*
eſt. We have here an Opportunity of ob-

ſerving the Propriety and Elegance of Terence's Expreſſions.　There is a great deal of
difference between *ne comparandus ad illum,*
and *ne comparandus illi,* or cum *illo.* The
firſt denotes an infinite Difference, that will
not admit of any Degree of Compariſon.
The other expreſſes, that there can be no
juſt Compariſon, though they are not in all
reſpects unlike. *Dacier.*

20 *Quem*

him. He had an agreeable Look, and the Air of a Gentleman.

Phæd. Such he feemed to be then, becaufe he had got on a Coat of different Colours; now, when he is without it, you think him ugly.

Pyt. Prithee don't talk, as if the Difference was indeed fo little. There was brought to us to-day a Youth, whom you might look at with pleafure. This Fellow is wrinkled, old, feeble, in the very laft Stage of Life, and has the Colour of a Weazel.

Phæd. 'Sdeath! What a Story is this? You reduce me to that pafs, that I fhan't myfelf be able to know what I have done. Here you, didn't I buy you?

Eun. You did buy me.

Pyt. Well, but bid him anfwer me too.

Phæd. Afk him.

Pyt. Did you come to us to-day? He denies it. But that other came, whom *Parmeno* brought with him, a Youth of about fixteen.

Phæd. But come, refolve me this firft; Where had you thofe Clothes you have now got on? What! are you filent? Will you an- fwer me nothing, Monfter?

Eun. Chærea came.

Phæd. What! my Brother?

Eun. Yes.

Phæd. When?

Eun. To-day.

Phæd. How long ago?

Eun. Juft now.

Phæd. With whom?

Eun. With *Parmeno.*

Phæd. Did you know him before?

Eun. No, Sir, nor ever heard any thing of him.

Phæd. How came you to know then, that he was my Brother?

Eun. Parmeno faid he was: it was he that gave me thefe Clothes.

Phæd. I am ruined!

Eun. He put on mine, after which they both went out together.

Pyt. Do you now believe that I am in my Senfes, and have told you no Falfhood? Are you not now convinced that the Virgin was debauched?

Phæd. Away, Beaft; do you give credit to what he fays?

Pyt. What need of giving credit to him? The thing fpeaks for itfelf.

Phæd. (To Dorus *foftly.)* Come a little this way. D'ye hear! A little nigher ftill. Very well. Tell me this once more: Did *Chærea* take your Clothes from you?   *Eun.*

²⁰ *Quem tu videre, velles, Phædria.* You yourfelf, who are fo good a Judge of Beau- ty. 'Tis worth while to obferve here the Addrefs and Conduct of the Poet, who, to give us the higher Idea of *Chærea's* Beau- ty, has found the Secret of making it be commended by the Perfon in the World who was moft incenfed againft him.

²² *Colore muftelino. Donatus* here ac- cufes *Terence* of not underftanding the *Greek* of *Menander,* who had written, ἔτος ἐπὶ γαλεώτης γέρων Which he ought to have

Honeſtâ facie, & liberali. PH. Ita viſus eſt 15
Dudum, quia variâ veſte exornatus fuit :
Nunc tibi videtur fœdus, quia illam non habet.
PY. Tace, obſecro : quaſi verò paulum interſiet.
Ad nos deductus hodie eſt adoleſcentulus,
Quem tu videre verò velles, Phædria. 20
Hic eſt vetus, vietus, veternoſus, ſenex,
Colore muſtelino. PH. hem, quæ hæc eſt fabula ?
Eò redigis me, ut, quid egerim, egomet neſciam.
Eho tu, emin' ego te ? Eu. emiſti. PY. jube, mihi denuo
Reſpondeat PH. roga. PY. veniſtin' hodie ad nos ?
negat. 25
At ille alter venit annos natus ſedecim, [hi expedi.
Quem ſecum adduxit Parmeno. PH. agedum, hoc mi-
Primùm iſtam, quam habes, unde habes veſtem ? taces ?
Monſtrum hominis, non dicturus. Eu. venit Chærea :
PH. Fraterne ? Eu. ita eſt. PA. quando ? Eu. hodie.
PH. quam dudum ? Eu. modo. 30
PH. Quicum ? Eu. cum Parmenone. PA. noraſne
cum priùs ?
Eu. Non : nec, quis eſſet, unquam audieram dicier.
PY. Unde igitur, meum fratrem eſſe, ſciebas ? Eu.
Parmeno
Dicebat eum eſſe : is dedit mihi hanc. PH. occidi.
Eu. Meam ipſe induit: poſt unà ambo abierunt foras. 35
PY. PH. Jam ſati' credis ſobriam eſſe me, & nil mentitam
tibi ? [nunc, bellua,
Jam ſati' certum eſt, virginem vitiatam eſſe ? PH. age
Credis huic, quod dicat ? PY. quid iſti credam ? res
ipſa indicat.
PH. Concede iſtuc paululum. audin' ? etiam paululum.
ſat eſt. tibi ?
Dic dum hoc rurſum : Chærea tuam veſtem detraxit

ſacie honeſta, & li-
berali. PH. Eſt vi-
ſus ita dudum, quia
fuit exornatus varia
veſte: nunc videtur
fœdus tibi, quia non
habet illam. PY.
Obſecro, tace: quaſi
vero paulum interſit.
Adoleſcentulus eſt de-
ductus hodie ad nos,
quem tu, Phædria,
velles videre. Hic
eſt vetus, vietus, ve-
ternoſus, ſenex colore
muſtelino. PH. Hem,
quæ eſt hæc fabula ?
Redigis me eò, ut
neſciam, quid egomet
egerim. Eho tu, Do-
re, emine ego te ?
Eu. Emiſti. PY.
Jube, ut reſpondeat
denuo mihi. PH. Ro-
ga. PY. Veniſtine
hodie ad nos ? Ne-
gat. At ille alter
natus ſedecim annos,
quem Parmeno ad-
duxit ſecum, venit.
PH. Agedum, expedi
hoc mihi. Primùm,
unde habes iſtam veſ-
tem, quam habes ?
taces ? Monſtrum ho-
minis nonne dictu-
rus es mihi ? Eu.
Chærea venit. PH.
Fraterne ? Eu. Ita
eſt. PH. Quando ?
Eu. Hodie. PH.
Quam dudum ? Eu.
Modo. PH. Quicun.
Eu. Cum Parmenone.

PH. Noraſme eum prius ? Eu. Non : nec unquam audieram dici quis eſſet. PH. Unde igitur
ſciebas illum eſſe meum fratrem ? Eu. Parmeno dicebat eum eſſe; is dedit hanc veſtem mihi. PH.
Occidi. Eu. Ipſe induit meam veſtem ; poſt ambo abierunt una foras. PY. Jam credis me eſſe
ſatis ſobriam, & menitam nil tibi ? Jam eſt ſatis certum, virginem eſſe vitiatam ? PH. Age nunc,
bellua, credis huic, quod dicat ? PY. Quia credam iſti ? Ipſa res indicat. PH. Concede paululum
iſtuc ; audiſne ? Etiam paululum eſt ſatis. Dic dum hic rurſum : Chærea detraxit tuam veſtem
tibi ?

ANNOTATIONS.

have tranſlated *Colore ſtellionino, h. e. ma-cuoſe, lentiginoſo,* like that of the *Stellio,* or Eſt, a Creature ſpotted, and not unlike a Lizard ; and he adds, that this Miſtake is owing to the Poet's confounding γαλῆ, which ſignifies a Weazel, with γαλεώτης, an Eſt, or Lizard. But I am apt to think, that *Donatus* is rather guilty of an Error here, than *Terence,* becauſe both the Senſe ſeems to require his Tranſlation ; and, if we will be determined by *Suidas,* there is no

difference in Signification between the two Words before cited.

24 *Jube, mihi denuo reſpondeat.* This is, as *Cicero* ſays, when, *Contra firmam argumen-tationem, aliam æque firmam aut firmiorem oppo-nimus.* *Pythias* makes this Requeſt to *Phæ-dria,* becauſe it was not allowed to interro-gate a Slave in the preſence of his Maſter, without having firſt obtained Leave from the Maſter himſelf.

33 *Unde igitur, meum fratrem eſſe, ſciebas ?*

It

Eun. He did.

· *Phæd.* And put them on ?

Eun. He did.

Phæd. And was carried out inftead of you ?

Eun. Yes.

Phæd. (aloud) Great *Jupiter !* O wicked, impudent Wretch !

Pyt. Alas ! Will you not even yet believe that we have been moſt bafely abufed !

Phæd. (to Pythias.*)* It were a Wonder, if you did not believe what he fays. *(afide.)* I can't tell what to do. *(foftly to* Dorus.*)* Heaikye, deny all again. *(aloud.)* Is it no poffible to force the Truth from you to-day ? Did you fee my Brother *Chærea ?*

Eun. No.

· *Phæd.* I fee no Confeffion can be had without Blows: follow me this way ; now he fays one thing, and in a moment the contrary. *(foftly to* Dorus.*)* Pretend to beg for Mercy.

Eun. Phædria, I beg of you for Heaven's fake !

Phæd. Get you in this Moment.

Eun. Hey, hoh !

Phæd. (afide.) I could not think how otherwife to bring myfelf cleverly off ; for if fo, there is now fo Remedy. *(aloud.)* Do you think to make game of me in this fort, Rafcal ?   [*Exeunt.*

Pyt. I am as certain as that I live, that this Trick is of *Parmeno*'s Contrivance.

Dor. It is undoubtedly fo.

Pyt. I'll find a way to be even with him before I fleep : But what is to be done now, think you, *Dorias ?*

Dor. Do you mean with regard to the Virgin ?

· *Pyt.* The fame ; whether I had beft conceal, or difcover it ?

Dor. Why, truly if you are wife, feem to know nothing either of the Eunuch or the Girl's Misfortune ; for by that means you'll both get clear of this Perplexity yourfelf, and oblige your Miſtreſs. Say only that *Dorus* is gone.

Pyt. I'll take your Advice.

Dor. But don't I fee *Chremes ? Thais* will be here prefently.

Pyt.

ANNOTATIONS.

It muſt have appeared extremely improbable to *Phædria*, that his Brother could have been there, becaufe he knew him to be upon Duty at the Port, which was confiderably diftant from the City. We are not therefore to wonder that he queftions the Eunuch fo particularly, in order to be fatisfied of the Truth.

⁴¹ *Et pro te huc deductus eſt ?* Palmerius exclaims againft this Reading as abfurd, becaufe, fays he, *Phædria* was now ftanding within his own Houfe, and queftioning the Eunuch ; fo that inftead of *huc*, it

ough It to have been *hinc.* He therefore reads *pro te ductus eſt.* But he ought to have remembered, that in the Beginning of this Scene, *Phædria* comes out, dragging the Eunuch after him ; and if we alfo fuppofe, that as he now fpeaks to *Dorus*, he points with his Finger to *Thais*'s Houfe, nothing will appear more elegant than, *et pro te huc deductus eſt.*

⁴⁹ *Alio pacto. Terence* never fails in his Regard to Morals. *Phædria* was fenfible that this Piece of Diffimulation was contrary to the Rules of ftrict Virtue, and there-

fore

Eu. Factum. Pн. & eâ eſt indutus? Eu. factum. Pн.
& pro te huc deductu' eſt? Eu. ita.   41
Pн. Jupiter magne! ô ſceleſtum, atque audacem ho-
miṇem! Pʏ. væ miḥi!
Etiam nunc non credis indignis nos eſſe irriſas modis?
Pн. Mirum ṇi tu credas quod iſte dicat. quid agam,
neſcio.
Heus tu, negato rurſum. poſſumṇe ego hodie ex te
exſculpere   45
Verum? vidiſtine fratreṃ Chæreaṃ? Eu. non. Pн.
non poteſt   [modò negat.
Sine malo fateri, video. ſequere me hàc. modò ait,
Orà me. Eu. obſecṛo 'ṭe verò, Phædṛia. Pн. i intrò.
Eu. hoi, hei.   [neſcio.
Pн. Alio paẹto honeſtè quo modọ hinc nunc abeaṃ:
Aẹtum eſt ſiquidem. tu me hîc etiam, ṇebulo, ludi-
ficabere?   50
Pʏ. Parmenonis tam ſcio eſſe hanc technam, quàm
me vivere.   [raṃ gṛatiam.
Do. Sic eſt. Pʏ. inveniam pol hodie pareṃ ubi refe-
Sed nuṇc quid facienduṃ ſuades, Dorias? Do. de
iſtac rogas   [Do. tu pol, ſi ſapis,
Virgine? Pʏ. ita: utrum taceamne, an prædicṭṃ?
Quod ſcis neſcis, neqụe de eunucho, neque de vitio
virginis.   35
Hac re, & te omni turbâ evolves, & illi gratum feceris.
Id modo dic, abiſſe Dorum. Pʏ. ita faciam. Do. ſed
videon' Chremem?

Do. Eſt ſic. Pʏ. Pol inveniam hodie, ubi referam param gratiam. Sed quid ſuades faciendum
nunc, Dorias? Do. Rogas de iſtac virgine? Pʏ. Ita: utrum taceamne, an prædicam? Do.
Pol, tu. ſi ſapis, neſcis quod ſcit, neque de eunucho, neque de vitio virginis. Hac re, et evolves
te ex omnia turba, et feceris gratum illi Thaidi. Dic modo id, Dorum abiiſſe. Pʏ. Faciam ita.
Do. Sed videone Chremem?

Marginal column
Eu. Eſt ſuẹtum. Pн.
Et eſt indutus ea?
Eu. Factum eſt. Pн.
E; eſt deductus huc
pro te? Eu. Ita.
Pн. Magne Jupi-
ter! O hominem ſce-
leſtum, atque auda-
cem! Pʏ. Væ mihi!
etiam nunc non cre-
dis nos eſſe irriſas
indignis modis? Pн.
Mirum ni tu credas
quod iſte dicat: ne-
ſcio, quid agam. Heus
tu, negato rurſum;
Poſſumne ego hodie
exſculpere verum ex
te? Vidiſtine fra-
trem Chæream? Eu.
Non. Pн. Video,
non poteſt fateri ſine
malo. Sequere me
hàc. modo ait, modo
negat. Ora me. Eu.
Vero obſecro te, Phæ-
dria. Pн. I intro.
Eu. Hoi, hei. Pн.
Neſcio quo modo alio
pacto nunc abeam
hinc honeſte. Siqui-
dem actum eſt. Tu,
nebulo, etiam ludifi-
cabere me hic? Pʏ.
Tam ſcio hanc eſſe
technam Parmenonis,
quam ſcio me vivere.

ANNOTATIONS.

fore endeavours here to excuſe it. from the
Neceſſity he was under.

56 Et illi gratum ſeceris. The great
Difficulty here is, whom we are to underſtand by illi. Moſt of the Commentators
following Donatus, ſupply virgini. Becauſe
as the Virgin was ſilent herſelf, and ſhewed
her Concern only by her Tears, Dorias
might readily enough conjecture, that it
would be agreeable to her to have the Matter altogether huſhed. Madam Dacier,
with Reaſon, oppoſes this. Pampbila,
ſays ſhe, was too well born to conceal what
had happened to her. Such a Silence would
have, in ſome meaſure, implied a Conſent.
Virtue knows none of theſe Diſguiſes; it
may be unfortunate, but can never be
blameable. It can therefore be only Thais

that Pythias would do a grateful Office to,
in concealing Pampbila's Misfortune; for
ſhe would without doubt be anxious to have
this kept ſecret, till ſhe had brought Chremes to acknowledge her for his Siſter, leſt
if it ſhould be known before, the Diſhonour,
it was likely to bring upon him, might make
him averſe to the Diſcovery. Altho' this is
a natural and eaſy Explication, and what
ſeems to me to have been the real Deſign of
the Poet, yet I cannot forbear taking notice here of the ingenious Conjecture of
Weſterbovius, who ſuppoſes that illi muſt
refer to Phædria. His Words are: Donatus, cumque ſequuti interpretes virginem in-
telligunt. Mihi Phædria videtur intelligendus. Virginem enim occultum non volui
iſſe crimen, teanſeiſſa veſti & lacrymæ ſatis.

F4

Pyt. Why fo?

Dor. Becaufe when I came away, they were almoft come to a downright Quarrel.

Pyt. Carry in thefe Jewels, I fhall learn of him what's the matter.

ANNOTATIONS.

præ fe ferebant. Gratum igitur faciebat | jam in gratiam redierant, ancillæ cum Phæ-
Phædriæ taccudo vitium virgini per fup- | dria, Pythia ultro agnofcente, Parmenoni
pofitum eunuclum fuum oblatum. Sed & | hanc

ACT IV. SCENE V.

ARGUMENT.

Chremes *returns from the Soldier half fuddled. This Scene indeed is defign'd rather for the Entertainment of the Spectators, than to carry on the Plot; and expreffes the Nature and Effects of Drunkennefs, by which the ftrongeft Minds are often weakened, and infenfibly drawn afide to Luxury.*

CHREMES, PYTHIAS.

Chre. HEYday! I am certainly catch'd here: the Wine that I have drunk has the better of me. But while I fat at Table, I feem'd to myfelf fober enough! After I got up, neither Feet nor Head knew how to do their Office.

Pyt. Chremes!

Chre. Who's that? Oh, *Pythias!* how much handfomer you feem to me now, than fome time ago!

Pyt. Why, truly you are much pleafanter.

Chre. 'Tis indeed a true Saying, *Without Wine and good Cheer, Love is but cold Entertainment.* But has not *Thais* been here fome time?

Pyt. What! has fhe already left the Captain?

Chre. O! long ago, a whole Age fince: there was a prodigious Quarrel betwixt them.

Pyt. Did fhe fay nothing that you fhould follow her?

Chre. Nothing, but that fhe gave me a Nod as fhe went out.

Pyt. Well, and was not that enough?

Chre. But I did not know that to be her meaning, until the Captain corrected my Want of Underftanding: for he fairly thruft me out of doors. But here fhe is: I wonder how I came to get before her.

ACT

ANNOTATIONS.

Chremes is introduced here half fuddled, and wondering at the ftrange Effect which Wine had upon him. The Change in his Behaviour is very natural, and gives us the true Picture of one, who having been all his Life-time accuftomed to Sobriety, is unwarily drawn into Excefs.
3 *Neque pes, neque mens fatis fuum officium facit.* This is both a true and natural Defcription of the Effects of drinking. And

Chremes, who had probably never exceeded in this Way before, feeming furpriz'd at what was unufual to him, is extremely well-judged by the Poet. I believe the Reader will not be difpleafed, if to the Account which *Terence* here gives, of what a Man feels within himfelf on thefe Occafions, we add the following poetical Defcription of this Vice from *Lucretius,* III. 475.

Dr-

Thais jam aderit. Py. Quid ita? Do. quia, cùm inde abeo, jam tum inceperat

Turba inter eos. Py. tu aufer aurum hoc: ego scibo ex hoc, quid fiet.

ego sciam ex hoc, quid sit.

	Thais aderit jam.
	Py. Quid ita? Do.
	Quia, cum abeo inde,
	jam tum turba ince-
	perat inter eos. Py.
	Tu aufer hoc aurum:

A N N O T A T I O N S.

Hanc fuisse technam. Adde, quod ne scire oportebat ancillas, an gratum esset virgini celatum crimen, ipsa non rogante ut celaretur. Porro autem æquum era, ut gratum facerent

Phædriæ, quo neminem esse Thaidi cariorem noverant, cuique disciplina videtu fuisse, remunerari ancillas primum; quetis ad uominam adfectaret viam.

ACTUS IV. SCENA V.

ARGUMENTUM.

Revertitur Chremes à milite semipotus. Hæc vero scena magis ad delectationem spectatorum, quam ad argumenti seriem pertinet; exprimitque naturam & effecta ebrietatis, quia sæpe labefactantur obstinati animi, & in luxum solvuntur.

CHREMES, PYTHIAS,

$\qquad\qquad\qquad$ ORDO.

AT at, data hercle verba mihi sunt: vicit vinum quod bibi [sobrius!

At dum accubabam, quàm videbar mihi esse pulchrè

Postquam surrexi, neque pes, neque mens sati' suum officium facit. [nunc formosior

Py. Chremes. Ch. quis est? ehem, Pythias. vah, quanto

Videre, quàm dudum? Py. certe quidem tu pol multo hilarior. 5

Ch. Verbum hercle hoc verum est: Sine Cerere & Libero friget Venus.

Sed Thais multo ante venit? Py. an abiit jam a milite?

Ch. Jamdudum, ætatem. lites factæ sunt inter eos maxumæ. [biens mihi innuit.

Py. Nil dixit, tu ut sequerere sese? Ch. nihil, nisi a-

Py. Eho, nonne id sat erat? Ch. at nesciebam id dicere illam, nisi quia 10

Correxit miles, quod intellexi minu': nam me extrusit foras. [vorterim.

Sed eccam ipsam video: miror, ubi ego huic ante

CH. *AT at, her-*
cle verba
sunt data miki: vi-
num, quod bibi, vicit
me. At dum accu-
babam, quam vide-
bar mihi esse pulchre
sobrius! Postquam
surrexi, neque pes,
neque mens facit satis
suum officium. Py.
Chremes. Ch. Quis
est? ehm, Pythias,
quanto videris sermo-
sior nunc, quam du-
dum? Py. Certe qui-
dem, tu pol videris
multo hilarior. Ch.
Hercle hoc verbum est
verum: Sine Cerere
& Libero Venus fri-
get. Sed Thais venit
multo ante? Py.
An abiit jam à mi-
lite? Ch. Jamdu-

dum, abiit jam ætatem. Maxmæ lites sunt factæ inter eos. Py. Dixit nil, ut tu sequere sese? Ch. Nihil, nisi quod abiens innuit mihi. Py. Eho nonne id erat satis? Ch. At nesciebam illum dicere id, nisi quia miles correxit, quod intellexi minus: nam extrusit me foras. Sed eccam video ipsam: miror ubi ego anteverterim huic.

A N N O T A T I O N S.

Denique, cur hominem, cum vini vis penetravit
Acris, & in venas discessit diditus ardor,
Consequitur gravitas membrorum? præpediuntur
Crura vacillanti? tardescit lingua? madet mens?

Nant oculi? Clamor, singultus, jurgia, gliscunt?
Et jam cætera de genere hoc quæcunque sequuntur?
Cur ea sunt? Nisi quod vehemens violentia vini
Conturbare animam consuevit corpore in ipso?

ACT IV. SCENE VI.

ARGUMENT.

Thais, *returning from the Soldier, is in so great a Passion that she inveighs against him here in his Absence. She endeavours to rouze* Chremes *against him, and prepares herself to oppose him.* Chremes, *a little frightened, wants to go and call some Assistance, but is hindered by* Thais.

THAIS, CHREMES, PYTHIAS.

Thais. I BELIEVE, indeed, he'll be here presently, to carry her off by Force : let him come : but if he touches her with a single Finger, I'll tear his Eyes out in an Instant. I can bear with his Impertinencies and blustering Words, while they are but Words : but if it comes to Action, I'll make him Smart.

Chr. Thais, I have been here a long Time.

Tha. O my *Chremes !* you are the very Person I wanted. Do you know that this Quarrel was on your account, and that the Matter regards you entirely ?

Chr. Regards me ? How ? as if that——

Tha. Because, while I am doing all I can to restore and give you back your Sister, I have suffered this, and a great deal more ill Usage.

Chr. Where is she ?

Tha. At home, with me.

Chr. Hah !

Tha. What's the Matter ? she has been educated in a Manner becoming herself and you.

Chr. What do you tell me ?

Tha. The very Thing as it is. I freely give her to you, nor demand any Thing from you in return.

Chr. The Favour, *Thais*, is allowed to be great, and shall not fail of the Acknowledgments it deserves.

Tha. But take care, *Chremes*, you don't lose her, before you receive her from my Hands. For it is she, whom the Soldier now comes to take away from me by Force. Go, *Pythias*, and bring out the Casket with the Tokens. *Chr.*

ANNOTATIONS.

Thais returns from the Soldier after the Quarrel, and as they had parted without being reconciled, she foresees he will come to force *Pamphila* from her. She resolves, however, to withstand all his Threats, and, being in the mean time accosted by *Chremes*, communicates the whole Matter to him, that, by his Aid she might be the better enabled to make good her Defence. As this Rustick was not much used to Encounters of this nature, she finds it a very troublesome Task to persuade and prepare him for the Onset ; but at last prevails.

[2] *Oculi illico effodientur.* These are the common Menaces of Women, and made use of both by the Writers of Tragedy and Comedy. *Pythias*, a little before, has recourse to the same Method of Revenge :

Ut ego unguibus facile illi in oculos involem venefico ?

[9] *Ehem! Corcmes*, upon hearing *Thais* speak of restoring his Sister, asks, with Impatience,

ACTUS IV. SCENA VI.

ARGUMENTUM:

Thais, à milite rediens; adeo commota eft, ut etiamnum in abfentem invehatur. Adverfus hunc Chremetem confirmat, feque ad pugnam parat, Chremes vero timidus abit, quæfiturus advocatos fibi.

THAIS; CHREMES, PYTHIAS.

CREDO equidem illum jam adfuturum effe, ut illam à me eripiat : fine veniat :
Atqui fi illam digito attigerit uno, oculi illico effodientur. [fica verba,
Ufque adeo egò illiu' ferre poffum ineptias & magni-Verba dum fint. verùm enim, fi ad rem conferentur; vapulabit. [teipfum exfpecto : 5
CH.Thais, egojamdudumhîcadfum.TH.ômì Chreme, Scin' tu turbam hanc propter te effe factam ? & adeo ad te attinere hanc
Omnem rem ! CH; ad me? quî? quafi iftuc.—TH. quia, dum tibi fororem ftudeo [ta paffa.
Reddere, ac reftituere, hæc atque hujufmodi fum mul-CH. Ubi ea eft ? TH. domi apud me. CH. ehem. TH. quid eft ? [TH. id quod res eft. 10
Educta ita, uti teque illaque dignum eft. CH. quid ais ?
Hanc tibi dono do, neque repeto pro illa abs te quidquam precii. [rita es; gratia.
CH; Et habetùr, & referetur, Thais, à me, ita utì me-TH. At enim cave, ne priùs, quàm hanc à me accipias; amittas, Chreme.
Nam hæc ea eft, quam miles à me vi nunc ereptum venit. Abi tu, ciftellam, Pythias, domo effer cum monumentis. 15

ORDO.

TH. *Equidem credo illum jam effe affuturum, ut eripiat illam à me : fine veniat ; atqui fi attigerit illam uno digi-to, oculi ejus effo-dientur illico. Ego poffum ferre ineptias & magnifica verba illius, ufque adeo dum fint verba; verum enim, fi conferentur ad rem, vapulabit. CH.Thais ego adfum hic jamdudum. TH. O mi Chreme, exfpecto teipfum : fcifne tu hanc turbam effe fac-tam propter te? & adeo hanc omnem rem attinere ad te? CH; Ad me? Qui? quafi ego commoverim iftuc.TH.Quia, dum ftudeo reddere ac re-ftituere fororem tibi, fum paffa hæc, atque multa hujufmodi.CH. Ubi ea eft ? TH. Domi apud me. CH. Ehem. TH. Quid*

eft ? educta eft ita, uti eft dignum teque illaque. CH. Quid ais? TH. Id quad res eft. dono tibi, neque repeto quidquam precii pro illa abs te. CH. Gratia & habetur, & referetur, Thais, à me, ita utì es merita. TH. At enim cave, Chreme; ne amittas hanc; priufquàm accipias à me. Nam hæc eft ea, quæ miles nunc venit ereptum à me vi. Abi tu, Pythias; effer ciftellam cum monumentis domo.

ANNOTATIONS.

patience, where fhe is; and upon hearing that fhe was at her Houfe, expreffes himfelf as here quoted, haftily, and with an Air of Concern : for that we are here to confider *ehem* / as an Interjection of Grief and Trouble, is evident from *Thais*'s Anfwer, *Quid eft* ? *educta ita, uti teque illaque dignum eft. Chremes* was concerned, to think that his Sifter was at the Houfe of a Courtezan, as concluding that her Morals muft before this Time have been debauched. *Thais*, to remove this Apprehenfion, affures him that

fhe has been well educated, and will do him no difhonour.

[14] *Quam miles a me vi nunc ereptum venit. Donatus* obferves here, that this is faid, not to alarm *Chremes*, but to prepare him for what was likely to follow, as *Thais* probably fancied him to have more Courage than in the Event it proved. For fhe will foon change her Tone, and fay, *Quicum res tibi eft, peregrinus eft : minus potens quam tu, minus notus, minus amicorum hic habens.*

[15] *Cum monumentis.* This will be un-derftood

Chr. Don't you fee him, *Thais?*

Pyt. Where does it ftand?

Tha. Upon the great Cheft. Do you loiter, odious Wretch?

Chr. Blefs me! What a Body of Forces the Soldier is bringing up againft you?

Tha. How now, my Man, pray are you afraid?

Chr. Pfhaw, I afraid? no Creature alive is lefs fo. ·

Tha. So you had need.

Chr. Ay! I wonder, what kind of Man you take me to be.

Tha. Nay, confider only this, that he, whom you have to do with, is a Foreigner, lefs powerful, lefs known, and hath fewer Friends to fupport him than you.

Chr. I know that: but 'twere foolifh to expofe ourfelves to a Danger we may avoid. I think it better to prevent in time, than to take Revenge of him, after receiving an Injury. Do you go, and make faft the Door within, while I run hence to the *Forum.* I would have fome Friends with us, to affift us in this Tumult.

Tha. Stay.

Chr. 'Tis better indeed to go.

Tha. Stay, I fay.

Chr. Let me go, I'll be back in a Moment.

Tha. There is no need of Affiftance, *Chremes*: fay only that fhe is your Sifter, that you loft her, when a little Girl, but now know her again, and fhew him the Tokens.

Pyt. Here they are.

Tha. Take them: if he fhall offer any Violence, carry him before a Magiftrate; do you underftand me?

Chr. Yes, perfectly.

Tha. See that you fpeak this with Prefence of Mind.

Chr. I will.

Tha. *(to Chremes)* take up your Cloak. *(Afide.)* I'm undone, I have pitched upon a Champion to defend me, that wants one himfelf.

ANNOTATIONS.

derftcod, by knowing that it was the Cuftom of the Ancients, when they expofed their Children, to leave with them fome Pledge or Token of Value, that they might not be altogether deftitute, and have whereby to be afterwards known. This Cuftom is alluded to here.

27 *Volo ego adeffe hic advocatos nebis.* I have already obferved, that *advocatus* has a double Signification; and 'tis Matter of Difpute here, whether *Chremes* means, that he will go and call in fome Friends to his Affiftance, or that he will confult with fome Lawyers. The firft feems to be the moft natural and eafy; yet the fecond is not without Authority, for it was common

for

CH. Viden' tu illum, Thais? PH. ubi fita eft? TH.
in rifco. odiofa, ceffas?
CH. Militem fecum ad te quantas copias adducere?
At at. TH. num formidolofus, obfecro; es, mi homo?
    CH. apage fis.   [minus.
Egon' formidolofus? nemo eft hominum, qui vivat,
TH. Atque ita opu' eft. CH. ah, metuo, qualem tu
    me effe hominem exiftumes.   20
TH. Imo hoc cogitato: quicum restibi eft, peregrinus eft,
Minu' potens quam tu, minu' notus, minus amicorum
    hic habens.   [mittere eft.
CH. Scio iftuc: fed tu quod cavere poffis, ftultum ad-
Malo ego nos profpicere, quàm hunc ulcifci acceptà
    injuriâ.   [tranfcurro ad forum: 25
Tu abi, atque obfera oftium intus, ego dum hinc
Volo ego adeffe hîc advocatos nobis in turbâ hac. TH.
    mane.   [nil opus eft iftis, Chreme:
CH. Melius eft. TH. mane. CH. omitte, jam adéro. TH.
Hoc modò dic, fororem illam tuam effe, & te parvam
    virginem   [TH. cape.
Amififfe, nunc cognôffe: figna oftende. PY. adfunt.
Si vim faciet, in jus ducito hominem: intellextin'?
    CH. probè.   30
TH. Fac animo hæc præfenti dicas. CH. faciam. TH.
    attolle pallium.
Perii; huic ipfi opus patrono eft, quem defenforem paro.

nobis hîc in hac turbâ. TH. Mane. CH. Eft melius. TH. Mane. CH. Omitte, adero jam. TH.
Chreme, eft nihil opus iftis. Dic modò hoc, illam effe tuam fororem, & te amififfe eam parvam vir-
ginem, nunc cognoviffe: oftende figna. PY. Adfunt. TH. Cape. Si faciet vim, ducito hominem
in jus: intellextine? CH. Probè. TH. Fac ut dicas hæc præfenti animo. CH. Faciam. TH.
Attolle pallium. Perii: eft opus patrono huic ipfo, quem paro effe defenforem.

CH. Videfne tu illum, Thais? PY. Ubi eft fita? TH. In rifco. Odiofa, ceffas? CH. Quantas copias video militem adducere fecum ad te? at at. TH. Obfecro, mi homo, num es formidolofus? CH. Apage fis. Egone formidolofus? nemo hominum, qui vivat, eft minus. TH. Atque eft opus ita. CH. Ab metuo, qualem hominem tu exiftimes me effe. TH. Imo cogitato hoc; homo, quicum eft res tibi, eft peregrinus, minus potens quam tu, minus notus, habens minus amicorum hîc. CH. Scio iftuc. Sed eft ftultum admittere, quod tu poffis cavere. Ego malo nos profpicere, quàm ulcifci hunc, injuriâ acceptâ. Tu abi, atque obfera oftium intus, dum ego tranfcurro hinc ad forum. Ego volo advocatos adeffe

ANNOTATIONS.

for Pleaders of Caufes, to walk in the Forum, ready to make an offer of their Service to any who wanted it. There is a
remarkable Paffage to this Purpofe, in Cicero Orat. III. 33. *M. vero Manlium nos
etiam vidimus tranfverfo ambulantem foro:
quod erat infigne, eum, qui id faceret, fa-cere civibus omnibus confilii fui copiam: ad
quos olim & ita ambulantes, & in folio fe-
dentes domi, fic adibatur, non folum ut de
jure civili ad eos, verum etiam de filia collo-
canda, de fundo emendo, de agro colendo, de
omni denique aut officio, aut negotio referretur.*

ACTUS

ACT IV. SCENE VII.

ARGUMENT.

The Soldier, being enraged, comes with a Design to attack Thais's House, and ridiculously affects the General in drawing up his Men; Gnatho, all the while, under the Guise of Flattery, wittily exposing him. At length afraid of engaging, he leaves Thais without effecting his Purpose.

THRASO, GNATHO, SANGA, CHRÉMES, THAIS.

Thraso. HOW, Gnatho? Shall I submit tamely to so gross an Affront? I'll die rather. *Simalio, Donax, Syriscus,* follow me. First, I'll storm the House.

Gnat. Right!

Thr. I'll carry off the Virgin.

Gnat. Excellent!

Thr. Then I'll drub her handsomely.

Gnat. Delightful!

Thr. Donax, do you advance with your Truncheon, to command the main Body. You, *Simalio,* take Charge in the left Wing; you, *Syriscus,* in the right. Bring up the rest. Where is the Centurion *Sanga,* with his Regiment of Black-Guards?

San. Here he is.

Thr. What, miserable Drone, do you propose fighting with a Dish-clout, that you have brought one along with you?

San. Who, I? I knew the Valour of our General, and the Courage of his Soldiers, that this Fray could never end without Bloodshed: and, therefore, brought this to wipe the Wounds.

Thr. Where are the rest?

San. What rest, in the Name of Wonder? *Sannio* is only left to keep guard at home.

Thr. Do you draw up the Troops in Battalia, I'll take up my Station in the Rear, and thence give the Signal to all.

Gnat.

ANNOTATIONS.

This Scene gives the most lively Representation of the conceited and ridiculous Vanity of the Soldier, who calling together his few Slaves, pretends to marshal and draw them up, as if they made a numerous Army, and gives himself all the Airs of a General. The Poet manages this Part with great Address. *Thraso* says nothing, but what might naturally be expected from the Mouth of such a Coxcomb; and yet it is so contrived, that nothing could have more happily tended to make him appear ridiculous. He advances with his Army in a hostile manner, to attack his Mistress; but finding himself vigorously opposed, retires without effect-

ing any thing; *Gnatho* making him believe, that if he took no notice of her, she would soon return of herself to him in a suppliant manner.

¹ *Contumeliam tam insignem in me accipiam?* It appears by this, that *Gnatho,* who was much fonder of the Bottle, than of fighting, was endeavouring, as they came out, to dissuade *Thraso* from the Contest; who enraged, answers, *How? tamely submit to so scandalous an Affront? I'll die rather.*

² *Ubi centurio est Sanga?* The Centurion was an Officer, who had the Command of a hundred Men, commonly thought to be in quality, as our Captains. For the *Roman Legion*

ACTUS IV. SCENA VII.

ARGUMENTUM.

Furens miles accedit ad Thaidis domum oppugnandum ; & ridicule imperatorem agit in inftruenda acie: quem tamen interim Gnatho falfe irridet. Tandem pertimidus, re infecta, relinquit Thaidem.

THRASO, GNATHO, SANGA, CHREMES, THAIS.

HANCCINE ego ut contumeliam tam infignem in me accipiam, Gnatho?
Mori me fatius eft. Simalio, Donax, Syrifce, fequimini.
Primùm ædes expugnabo. GN. rectè. THR. virginem eripiam. GN. probè.
THR. Male mulcabo ipfam. GN. pulchrè. THR. in medium huc agmen cum vecti, Donax ;
Tu, Simalio, in finiftrum cornu; tu, Syrifce, in dexterum.   5
Cedo alios : ubi centurio eft Sanga, & manipulus furum ? SA. eccum, adeft. [huc portes, cogitas?
THR. Quid, ignave ? peniculon' pugnare, qui iftum
SA. Egone? imperatoris virtutem noveram, & vim militum :   [nera.
Sine fanguine hoc fieri non poffe : quî abftergerem vol-
THR. Ubi alii ? SA. qui, malùm, alii ? folus Sannio fervat domì.   10.
THR. Tu hofce inftrue hîc : ego ero poft principia : inde omnibu' fignum dabo.

ORDO.
THR. O Portetne ut ego, Gnatho, accipiam hanc contumeliam tam infignem in me ? fatius eft me mori. Simalio, Donax, Syrifce, fequimini me. Primum expugnabo ædes. GN. Rectè THR. Eripiam virginem. GN. Probè. THR. Mulcabo ipfam male. GN. Pulchrè. THR. Donax, veni huc in medium agmen cum vecti. Tu, Simalio, in finiftrum cornu, tu, Syrifce, in dexterum. Cedo alios : ubi eft Sanga centurio, & manipulus furum? SA. Eccum, adeft. THR. Quid, ignave ? cogitafne pugnare peniculo, qui portes iftum huc ? SA. Egone? noveram virtutem imperatoris, & vim militum :- & hoc non poffe fieri fine fanguine, porto ideo, quî abftergerem vulnera. THR. Ubi alii ? SA. Qui alii, malum? folus Sannio fervat domì. THR. Tu inftrue hofce hîc: ego ero principia : inde dabo fignum omnibus.

ANNOTATIONS.

Legion was divided into ten Cohorts, and each Cohort into three Manipuli, and each Manipulus into three Centuries, or Ordines. He who prefided over one of thefe leffer Divifions was called Centurio. Madam Dacier obferves, that Thrafo, inftead of faying Manipulus baftarorum, vel velitum, vel triariorum: fays haftily and inconfiderately furum, as it were drawn to it by the Force of Truth, for his Gang were, in a manner, a Set of Banditti. Whether this will fatisfy a judicious Reader, I cannot tell : I own I am very much at a Lofs, to think how Terence came to put thefe Words in the Soldier's Mouth ; becaufe, whatever they were in reality, he, 'tis probable, would fpeak of them magnificently. I have, notwithstanding, tranflated it by an Expreffion, equivalent in our Language to that of the Original,

11 *Ego ero poft principia.* This was the Station of greateft Safety in the whole Army. To underftand it right, we muft know that the Romans called Principes or Principia, thofe, who in an Action, fronted the Enemy, and fought in the Van. Behind thefe, were placed the Haftati and Triarii. But in Time, the Order of Battle was changed, and inftead of the Principes, the Haftati were placed firft, and the Principes between them and the Triarii ; yet they ftill retained their firft Name. Thrafo, therefore, plants himfelf here, behind the middle Line of the Army, as being the Place of greateft Safety. For, properly, this was the Front of the Rear-Guard, and the Place leaft expofed : for both the Van, and the middle Battalions of the Army, muft be beaten, before they could reach him. And as on the

one

Gnat. This is being wife indeed : fo foon as he has drawn up his Men, he takes care to fecure a Retreat to himfelf.

Thr. This was always *Pyrrhus*'s Way.

Chr. Do you fee, *Thais*, what he is doing ? without doubt, that was good Advice which I gave you about barricading the Door.

Tha. Indeed, this Fellow, whom you now take for fuch a mighty Hero, is a great Coward. Don't fear.

Thr. What think you of it ?

Gnat. Had you but a Sling now, to batter them here at Diftance under Covert; they'd foon take to flight.

Thr. But look, I fee *Thais* herfelf.

Gnat. When fhall we fall on ?

Thr. Hold : a wife Commander ought to try all Means, before he comes to an open Affault. How d'ye know, but fhe may furren- der without drawing a Sword ?

Gnat. Good Heavens ! What a great Advantage it is to have Wifdom ! I never approach you, but I go away furnifhed with more Knowledge.

Thr. *Thais*, anfwer firft to this.——When I agreed to give you that Virgin, did you not promife that for fo many Days you would receive me only ?

Tha. Well, and what then ?

Thr. Do you afk that, after admitting and entertaining your Gallant before my Face ?——

Tha. What bufinefs have you with him ?

Thr. And privately withdrawing from me in company with him ?

Tha. 'Twas my Pleafure.

Thr. Deliver up *Pamphila*, therefore, immediately, unlefs you'd have her rather taken from you by force.

Chr. She deliver her up to you ? Or will you dare to touch her ? of all Men the——

Gnat. Ha, what are you doing ? hold your Tongue.

Thr.

ANNOTATIONS.

one hand, he was out of Danger from the Enemy's Attack; fo on the other, he was in a Place convenient for an eafy Flight, if that fhould be needful.

23 *Idem hoc jam Pyrrhus fecitavit.* This *Pyrrhus* was King of *Epire*, and one of the moft renowned Generals of Antiquity. There cannot be a greater Teftimony in his favour, than what paffed in a Difcourfe be- tween *Scipio* and *Hannibal*. The *Roman* afking the other, Whom he looked upon as the greateft General ? he anfwered, *Alexan- der*; becaufe, with a handful of Men he routed vaft Armies, and over-run the World. And when the Queftion was again renewed, *Hannibal* named *Pyrrhus*; becaufe, he firft taught Soldiers how to encamp, and fhewed

greater Skill, than any had done before him, in taking of Places, and difpofing of Guards. It was, therefore, no mean Vanity in this conceited Captain, to pretend that he fol- lowed the Example of fo renowned a Gene- ral as *Pyrrhus*.

16 *Quid videtur ?* The Soldier feems here to have fallen from his Courage, and is doubtful what to do. His Character is preferved by the Poet with great Judgment. He is vain, and apt to boaft of Bravery, when Danger is at a Diftance, but in rea- lity, the greateft Coward in the World. This is remarkably exemplified here. At firft he is fierce and untractable, orders his Soldiers to follow him, and threatens to ftorm the Houfe. As he draws nearer, he begins

Gn. Illuc eſt ſapere : ut hoſce inſtruxit, ipſus ſibi cavit
loco.
Thr. Idem hoc jam Pyrrhus factitavit. Ch. viden' tu,
Thais, quam hic rem agit ? [ædibus.
Nimirum conſilium illud rectum eſt de occludendis
Th. Sanè, quod tibi nunc vir videatur eſſe, hic ne-
bulo magnus eſt : 15
Ne metuas. Thr. quid videtur ? Gn. fundam tibi
nunc nimis vellem dari, [fugum.
Ut tu illos procul hinc ex occulto cæderes : facerent
Thr. Sed eccam Thaidem ipſam video. Gn. quam
mox irruimus. Thr. mane.
Omnia priùs experiri, quàm armis, ſapientem decet.
Quî ſcis, an, quæ jubeam, ſine vi faciat ? Gn. Dî
voſtram fidem ! 20
Quanti eſt ſapere ! nunquam accedo, quin abs te abeam
doctior. [do iſtam virginem,
Thr. Thais, primùm hoc mihi reſponde : cùm tibi
Dixtin' hos dies mihi ſoli dare te ? Th. quid tum
poſtea ? [adduxti tuum ?
Thr. Rogitas, quæ mî ante oculos coràm amatorem
Tha. Quid cum illoc agas ? Thr. & cum eo clam te
ſubduxti mihi ? 25
Tha. Libuit. Thr. Pamphilam ergo huc redde, niſi
ſi mavis eripi.
Ch. Tibi illam reddat ? aut tu eam tangas, omnium ?
Gn. ah, quid agis ? tace.

hæc primum : cum do iſtam virginem tibi, dixtine dare te mihi ſoli hos dies ? Tha. Quid tum poſtea ? Thr. rogitas, quæ coràm adduxti tuum amatorum mi, ante oculos ? Tha. Quid agas cum illoc ? Thr. Et ſubduxiſti te mihi clam cum eo ? Tha. Libuit. Thr. Ergo redde Pamphilam huc, niſi ſi mavis illam eripi tibi. Ch. Reddat illam tibi ? aut tu tangas eam, periſſime omnium ? Gn. Ah ! quid agis ? tace.

[margin notes:]
Gn. *Illuc eſt ſapere: ut (poſtquam) inſtruxit hoſce, ipſe cavit ſibi loco.* Thr. *vit ſibi loco.* Thr. *Pyrrhus jam factitavit hoc tdem.* Ch. *Videſne tu, Thais, quam rem hic agit ? nimirum illud conſilium de occludendis ædibus eſt rectum.* Th. *Sanè hic, ob id quod nunc videatur tibi eſſe vir, eſt magnus nebulo: ne metuas.* Thr. *Quid videtur ?* Gn. *Nunc nimis vellem fundam dari tibi, ut cæderes illos procul hinc ex occulto: facerent fugam.* Thr. *Sed eccam video Thaidem ipſam.* Gn. *Quam irruimus mox.* Thr. *Mane. Decet ſapientem experiri omnia priuſquam aliquid agere armis. Qui ſcis an faciat quæ jubeam ſine vi ?* Gn. *Dii voſtram fidem! quanti eſt ſapere! nunquam accedo, quin abeam doctior abs te.* Thr. *Thais, reſponde mihi*

ANNOTATIONS.

begins to think of Safety, and, therefore, places himſelf in a ſecure Station; *Hic ego ſto poſt Principia.* Now, when they are juſt advancing, he is ſtill more doubtful and wavering, and applies to his Paraſite, *Quid videtur ?* In fine, when he is upon the point of engaging, and the Soldiers appear eager for the Combat, he reſtrains them, *Mane,* and reſolves upon peaceable Meaſures; *Omnia prius experiri, quam armis, ſapientem decet.*
Ibid. *Fundam tibi nunc nimis vellem dari.* This Anſwer of the Paraſite is very ſuitable to the Cowardice and Effeminacy, which ſo evidently appeared in the Soldier. Perhaps too, he was not himſelf fond of briſk Meaſures, and, therefore, gives a conformable Advice. A Man, who dareth not engage Hand to Hand, may fight with a Sling, and he that wants Courage for an open

Attack, will under Covert annoy his Enemy. Some make theſe Words to be ſpoken by *Thais* to *Chremes.* She had ſaid, that *Thraſo* was a great Coward, and the more to expreſs her Contempt, both of the General and his Army, pretends that a ſingle Toſs of a Sling would be enough to put them all to flight.
[19] *Omnia prius experiri.* This is, undoubtedly, a wiſe and juſt Saying; but as it comes from the Mouth of a Coxcomb, who was guided more by Fear than Reaſon, it ſerves only the more ſtrongly to mark his Character, and give it a new Air of Ridicule. Juſt ſuch is that of *Plautus, Mil.* I. 1. 63. where the Soldier, admiring his own Beauty, ſays,

Nimia eſt miſeria pulchrum eſſe hominem nimis.

Thr. Pray, Sir, what do you mean? Shan't I touch my own?

Chr. Yours, Scoundrel?

Gnat. Have a Care: you little dream, how great a Man you now affront.

Chr. (to Gnatho) What won't you make off? *(to Thraso)* And you, Sir, do you know what you have to expect? If you begin the least Diſturbance here To-day, I'll make you remember the Time, Place, and Me too, as long as you live.

Gnat. I pity you, who are making ſo great a Man as this your Enemy.

Chr. I'll break your Head for you, if you do not march off the Spot.

Gnat. Say you ſo, you Puppy? What, is that your way?

Thr. Pray, Sir, who are you? What do you want here? Or what Buſineſs have you with this Woman?

Chr. I'll tell you: firſt of all then, I ſay that ſhe is free,

Thr. Ha!

Chr. And a Citizen of *Athens.*

Thr. Hy!

Chr. And my Siſter.

Thr. Good Aſſurance!

Chr. And therefore, Soldier, I now warn you to offer no Violence. *Thais,* I'm going to *Sophrona,* the Nurſe, to bring her here, and ſhew her the Tokens.

Thr. What, do you pretend to forbid me to touch my own?

Chr. I tell you I do forbid it.

Gnat. D'ye hear? he owns himſelf a Thief, that's enough for you.

Thr. Do you ſay this too, *Thais?*

Tha. Seek one that will anſwer you.

Thr. (to Gnatho) What are we to do now?

Gnat. E'en let us return; ſhe'll ſoon be here again, of her own accord, begging for Favour.

Thr. Think you ſo?

Gnat. Yes, for certain: I know the Sex perfectly: when you purſue them, they are coy; but if you neglect them, they'll court you themſelves.

Thr. You judge right.

Gnat. Shall I then diſmiſs the Army?

Thr. Yes, when you will.

Gnat. Sanga, as becomes a gallant Soldier, remember the Kitchen and Fireſide.   *San.*

ANNOTATIONS.

²⁸ *Tuam autem, furcifer? Donatus* conſiders this as a rude unmannerly Speech, coming from a mere Ruſtick, and one that was an utter Stranger to Politeneſs and Civility. Others think it rather ſaid in the Heat of Paſſion and Indignation, for that *Thraſo,* by claiming *Pamphila* as his Pro-perty, made her a Slave, which *Chremes* could not bear.

³⁶ *Os durum!* Almoſt all Commentators agree in explaining this by *impudens,* and we find this to be the Senſe, In which the Words are moſt commonly uſed by ancient Authors, *Cicero pro P. Quint.* 24. *Mihi videri*

THR. Quid tu tibi vis? ego non tangam meam?
CH. tuam autem, furcifer? [non tu hinc abis?
GN. Cave sis, nescis cui maledicas nunc viro. CH.
Scin' tu, ut tibi res se habeat? si quidquam hodie hîc
turbæ cœperis, 30
Faciam, ut hujusloci, dieique meique semper memineris.
GN. Miseret tui me, qui hunc tantum hominem facias
inimicum tibi. [ain' verò, canis?
CH. Diminuam ego caput tuum hodie, nisi abis. GN.
Siccine agis? THR. quis tu homo es? quid tibi vis?
quid cum illâ rei tibi est?
CH. Scibis, principio eam esse dico liberam. THR.
hem? CH. civem Atticam. THR. hui? 35
CH. Meam sororem. THR. os durum! CH. miles,
nunc adeo edico tibi, [phronam
Ne vim facias ullam in illam. Thais, ego eo ad So-
Nutricem, ut eam adducam, & signa ostendam hæc.
THR. tun' me prohibeas,
Meam ne tangam? CH. prohibeo, inquam. GN. au-
din' tu? hic furti se alligat.
Satis hoc tibi est. THR. idem tu hoc ais, Thais?
THA. quære, qui respondeat. 40
THR. Quid nunc agimus? GN. quin redeamus: jam
hæc tibi aderit supplicans [um mulierum:
Ultro. THR. credin'? GN. imo certe. novi ingeni-
Nolunt, ubi velis: ubi nolis, cupiunt ultro. THR. be-
ne putas. [ga, ita utì fortes decet
GN. Jam dimitto exercitum? THR. ubi vis. GN. San-
Milites, domi focique fac vicissim ut memineris 45

THR. Quid tu vis tibi? Non ego tangam meam? CH. Autem tuam, furcifer? GN. Cave sis, nescis cui viro nunc maledicas. CH. Non tu abis hinc? Scisne tu, ut res habeat se tibi? si cœperis quidquam turbæ hic hodie, faciam, ut semper memineris hujus loci, dieique, meique. GN. Miseret me tui, qui facias hunc tantum hominem inimicum tibi. CH. Ego diminuam tuum caput hodie, nisi abis. GN. Aisne verò, canis? Siccine agis? THR. Tu quis homo es? Quid vis tibi? Quid est rei tibi cum illâ? CH. Scies. Principio dico eam esse liberam. THR. Hem! CH. Civem Atticam. THR. Hui! CH. Meam sororem. THR. Os durum! CH. Nunc adeo, miles, edico tibi, ne facias ullam vim in illam. Thais, ego eo ad Sophronam nutricem, ut adducam eam, & ostendam hæc signa.

na. THR. Tune prohibeas me, ne tangam meam? CH. Inquam, prohibebo. GN. Aadisne tu? hic alligat se furti: hoc est satis tibi. THR. Tu, Thais, ais hoc idem? CH. Quære aliquem, qui respondeat. THR. Quid agimus nunc? GN. Quid? quin redeamus: hæc jam ultrò aderit supplicans tibi. THR. Credisne? GN. Imo certe. Novi ingenium mulierum. Nolunt ubi velis; ubi nolis, cupiunt ultro. THR. Putas bene. GN. Demitto jam exercitum? THR. Ubi vis. GN. Sanga, fac ut memineris vicissim domi, focique, ita utì decet milites fortes.

ANNOTATIONS.

videri ore durissimo esse, qui præsente eo (Ro-
scio) gestum agere conaretur. And Ovid
Metam. 5. 451.
——Duri puer oris, & audax.
Madam Dacier, however, thinks that this
by no means expresses what is here intended
by Thraso. Chremes pretending, that Pamphila was free, a Citizen of Athens, and his
Sister, quite astonishes the Captain. To the
first he says bem, to the second hui, and to
the last, which is the greatest of all, Os durum, a hard Bone indeed, a bome Thrust
really!
39 Illic furti se alligat. Gnatho seeks now
an Opportunity of putting an End to the
Quarrel; he was weary of being so long
upon Duty, and wanted to return to Supper. He, therefore, proposes an Expedient,
that the Dispute should cease for the present,
and as Chremes, by refusing to restore to the
Captain what was his Property, had given
sufficient Ground to bring an Action against
him, he thinks it better to stop this military
Quarrel, and have recourse to Law.
45 Domi focique fac vicissim ut memineris.
There is a particular Elegance and Beauty
in this Passage, because of the Ambiguity
of the Expression, and its being turned from
its common Signification, to answer the Purposes of the Parasite. When a General ex-
horted

San. My Mind has long ago been fet upon my Difhes.
Gnat. You are a brave Fellow.
San. Follow me this way.

ANNOTATIONS.

horted his Soldiers to act with Courage and
Refolution, he always put them in mind,
that they were to fight for their Houfes and
Families, *Domi focique fac memineris.* Here
Gnatho makes ufe of it, to make them quit
their Arms, and leave the Field. In his
Mouth,

ACT V.   SCENE I.

ARGUMENT.

Thais *coming to know that the Virgin had been debauched, ex-*
poftulates with her Maid, who defends herfelf by fhewing that
no Blame can belong to her. Chancing to fee Chærea, *fhe is*
overjoyed, as hoping now to be revenged, and all in her Power
inftigates her Miftrefs to it.

THAIS, PYTHIAS.

Thais. DO you ftill perfift, Wretch, to fpeak in this confufed, perplexing manner? *I know: I don't know: he's gone: I've*
heard: I was not there: can't you tell me the Matter plainly, whatever it is? The Girl is all in Tears, her Gown rent, and fpeaks not
a Word. The Eunuch is gone: Why? What has happened? Are
you ftill filent?

Pyt. What Anfwer fhall I give you, Wretch that I am? they fay
he was no Eunuch.

Tha. Who was he then?

Pyt. That *Chærea.*

Tha. What *Chærea?*

Pyt. That young Gentleman, *Phædria*'s Brother.

Tha. What fay'ft thou, Sorcerefs?

Pyt. But I know it for certain.

Tha. What is he to us, pray? How came he here?

Pyt. I can't fay: but that I believe he was in love with *Pam-*
phila.

Tha. Unhappy Wretch that I am, I'm undone, if what you fay
be true; is that what the Girl cries for?

Pyt.

ANNOTATIONS.

Thais, by this time comes to know that
the Virgin had been ravifhed, and enquiring
of *Pythias,* who was willing to palliate
Matters, is anfwered only by Evafions.
Thais, therefore, comes here upon the Stage
in a Paffion with *Pythias,* and chideth her
for her perplexed Replies. At laft after
fome Difcourfe held, *Chærea* difcovers himfelf coming from *Antipho*'s, where he could
not have an Opportunity of changing his
Drefs.

[2] *Scio; nefcio; abiit audivi; ego non*
adfui. It is natural, when one is angry
with another, to repeat Part of what was
laft faid by the Perfon with whom he is angry. *Thais* here inftances in a few Words,
by

Sa. Jamdudum animus eſt in patinis. Gn. frugi es. | Sa. *Animus eſt jam-*
　　Sa. vos me hac ſequimini. | *dudum in patinis.*
　　　　　　　　　　　　　　　　　　　　　　　| Gn. *Es frugi.* Sa.

Vos, ſequimini me bac.

ANNOTATIONS.

Mouth, they are Terms of Cookery, and a |taken notice of, as they ſerve more than any
Burleſque upon the Military Exhortation. |thing elſe to give us an Idea of the Genius
Theſe particular Turns ought always to be | and Manner of *Terence.*

ACTUS V. SCENA I.

ARGUMENTUM.

*Cognito virginis vitio, Thais cum ancilla expoſtulat; quæ ſe
criminis remotione defendit, & interventu Chæreæ lætatur,
ſperans hominem ſe naƈtum ad ulciſcendum, ad quod heram,
quoad poteſt, inſtigat.*

THAIS, PYTHIAS

ORDO

PERGIN', ſceleſta, mecum perplexè loqui?
　Scio, neſcio: abiit: audivi: ego non adfui.
Non tu iſtuc mihi diƈtura aperte es, quidquid eſt?
Virgo conſciſsâ veſte lacrumans obticet,　　　　　4
Eunuchus abiit. quamobrem? quid faƈtum eſt? taces?
Py. Quid tibi ego dicam miſera? illum eunuchum negant
Fuiſſe. Th. quis fuit igitur? Py. iſte Chærea.
Th. Qui Chærea? Py. iſte ephebus frater Phædriæ.
Th. Quid ais, venefica? Py. atqui certo comperi.
Th. Quid is, obſecro, ad nos? quamobrem adduƈtu'
　eſt? Py. neſcio.　　　　　　　　　　　　　　　10
Niſi amaſſe credo Pamphilam. Th. hem, miſera occidi.
Infelix, ſi quidem tu iſtæc vera prædicas.

Th. *Pergiſne, ſce-
leſta, loqui
mecum perplexè?
Scio, neſcio: abiit:
audivi: ego non ad-
fui. Non tu es diƈ-
tura iſtuc mihi, quid-
quid eſt, aperte? vir-
go lacrimans conſciſsâ
veſte obticet, eunuchus
abiit? quamobrem?
Quid eſt faƈtum?
Taces? Py. Quid
ego miſera dicam ti-
bi? Negant eum
fuiſſe eunuchum. Th.
Quis fuit? Py. Iſte
Chærea.*

Th. *Qui Chærea?* Py. *Iſte ephebus frater Phædriæ.* Th. *Quid ais venefica?* Py. *Atqui comperi certo.* Th. *Obſecro, quid is ad nos? Quamobrem eſt adduƈtus?* Py. *Neſcio, niſi credo illum
amaviſſe Pamphilam.* Th. *Hem, miſera occidi,* ſum infelix, ſi quidem tu prædicas iſtæc vera.

ANNOTATIONS.

by which we may be able to judge of the con-
fuſed and perplexed Replies of *Pythias.* *Donatus* ſeems not to have been very happy in
filling up theſe Ellipſes, nor has *Boeclerus,*
who cenſures him, done much better. Let
us, therefore, ſuppoſe *Thais* returning home
from the Captain, to have met the Virgin in
Tears, and with her Garments tore; upon
which, ſuſpeƈting what had happened, ſhe
runs to *Pythias,* to whom ſhe had given the
Care of her, and enquires:

　Th. *Scis tu nullum virum acceſſiſſe ad
eam?* Py. *Scio.*
　Th. *Quæ igitur cauſa lacrumarum & veſtis
conſciſſæ?* Py. Neſcio.
　Th. *Ubi nobis Dorus noſter?* Py. Abiit.

Th. *Qui ſcis abiiſſe Dorum?* Py. Audivi.
Th. *Quare non retraxiſti fugientem?* Py. Ego
non adfui.

This, or ſome ſuch Diſcourſe, we muſt ſuppoſe to have paſſed between *Thais* and *Pythias,* behind the Scenes, which the Poet
has taken care to give us a Hint of, by
making *Thais* repeat part of what *Pythias*
anſwered,

　4 *Lacrimans obticet.* We cannot here
paſs by, without notice, the Remark of *Donatus,* both as it ſerves to gives us ſome Idea
of the Genius of the *Latin* Language, and
alſo ſhews how delicate *Terence* was in the
Choice of his Terms. *Tacexus,* ſays he,
*conſilia: ut Virg. Æn. 2. 94. Nec tacui de-
mo...*

Pyt. I fear it is.

Tha. What fay'ft thou, Wretch? Did I not give particular Charge about her, when I went hence?

Pyt. What could I do? fhe was committed to his Care only, as you had defired.

Tha. You naughty Pack, you fet the Wolf to guard the Sheep. I am quite afhamed to be impofed upon in fo grofs a manner. But what Man is this?

Pyt. Hufh Madam, hufh; all's fafe, we have got the Man himfelf.

Tha. Where is he?

Pyt. There, on the left Hand, don't you fee him?

Tha. I fee.

Pyt. Order him to be feized immediately.

Tha. What can we do to him, Fool?

Pyt. Do to him, fay you? fee, pray, when you look at him, if he has not a World of Impudence. Has he not? And then with what Affurance he comes forward?

ANNOTATIONS.

mens. Reticemus dolores: ut, Ne verere, ne | Phormione, Heu quidnam obtices ?
retice. Obticemus quorum nos pudet, ut in |

ACT V. SCENE II.

ARGUMENT.

Chærea, *as he is returning home, chances to meet* Thais, *and fo had no tolerable Pretence for denying his late Crime.* Thais *expoftulates with him, firft about his flight; then ferioufly about the Rape he had committed. But upon his defire of being married to the Virgin, they are foon reconciled.*

CHÆREA, THAIS, PYTHIAS.

Chærea.(TO himfelf.) With *Antipho,* both Father and Mother were at home, as if on purpofe; fo that there was no poffibility of entering, without being feen by them. Meantime, as I ftood before the Door, a certain Acquaintance came that way. As foon as I faw him, I took to my Heels with all Expedition, and run into an unfrequented Alley; thence again, into an other, and then another: thus did I harafs myfelf to death, in flying to avoid difcovery. (*Seeing Thais.*) But is not this *Thais,* whom I fee? 'tis fhe: I'm at a ftand: What fhall I do? But what is it to me? What can fhe do?

Tha.

ANNOTATIONS.

Chærea had gone along with *Antipho,* that he might put off the Eunuch's Drefs at his Houfe, as being the neareft Place of any Convenience; but as both the old People chanced to be at home; he could not enter without being feen by them. As he ftands deliberating before the Door, he fees an Acquaintance at fome diftance, and willing to avoid

Num id lacrumat virgo? Py. id opinor. Th. quid ais,
Iftuccine interminata fum hinc abiens tibi? [facrilega?
Py. Quid facerem? ita ut tu jûfti, foli credita eft.   15
Th. Scelefta, ovem lupo commîfti. difpudet,
Sic mihi data effe verba. quid illuc hominis eft?
Py. Hera mea, tace, tace, obfecro, falvæ fumus:
Habemus hominem ipfum. Th. ubi is eft? Py. hem ad
     finifteram,   [poteft.   20
Viden'? Th. video. Py. comprehendi jube, quantum
Th. Quid illo faciemus, ftulta? Py. quid faciam, rogas?
Vide amabo, fi non, cùm afpicias, os impudens
Videtur: non eft? tum, quæ ejus confidentia eft?

habemus ipfum hominem. Th. *Ubi eft is?* Py. *Hem, ad finiftram;* videfne? Th. *Video.* Py.
Jube illum comprebendi, quantum poteft. Th. *Quid faciemus de illo, ftulta?* Py. *Rogas, quid
faciam? Amabo vide, fi, cum afpicias, non videtur os impudens: non eft? Tum, quæ eft ejus
confidentia?*

*Num virgo lacrimat
propter id?* Py.
Opinor propter *id?*
Th. *Quid ais facri-
lega? Interminatone
fum iftuc tibi abiens
hinc?* Py. *Quid fa-
cerem? eft credita il-
li foli, ita ut tu juf-
fti.* Th. *Scelefta,
commififti ovem lupo:
difpudet verba effe fic
data mihi. Quid ho-
minis eft illuc?* Py.
*Mea hera, tace, tace,
obfecro: fumus falvæ;*

ACTUS V. SCENA II.

ARGUMENTUM.

*Chærea domum redire cogitans, in Thaidem incidit, & fic nulla il-
li fuit facinoris negandi facultas. Cum eo Thais expoftulat,
joco quidem primum de fuga; deinde ferio de ftupro virginis.
Cæterum ipfi virginem petenti, facile conciliatur.*

CHÆREA, THAIS, PYTHIAS.

APUD Antiphonem uterque, mater, & pater,
     Quafi dedita operâ, domi erant, ut nullo modo
Introire poffem, quin viderent me. interim
Dum ante oftium fto, notus mihi quidam obviàm
Venit. ubi vidi, ego me in pedes, quantùm queo,   5
In angiportum quoddam defertum: inde item
In aliud, inde in aliud. ita miferrimus
Fui fugitando, ne quis me cognofceret.
Sed eftne hæc Thais, quam video? ipfa eft. hæreo.
Quid faciam? quid meâ autem? quid faciet mihi?   10

O R D O.
Ch. U *Terque pa-
ter & ma-
ter, quafi dedita ope-
ra, erant domi apud
Antiphonem ut poffem
introire nullo modo,
quin viderent me.
Interim dum fto ante
oftium, quidam notus
venit obviàm mili.
Ubi vidi illum, ego,
quantum* (velociter)
*queo, confero me in
pedes, in quoddam de-*

*fertum angiportum: inde item in aliud, inde in aliud: ita fui miferrimus fugitando, ne quis cog-
nofceret me. Sed eftne hæc Thais, quam video? eft ipfa: hæreo. Quid faciam? Quid autem
refer meâ? Quid faciet mihi?*

ANNOTATIONS.

avoid him, runs through feveral By-lanes,
until he unwarily ftumbles upon *Thais.* At
firft he is a little ftruck, but recollecting
himfelf, boldly goes up to her. She at firft
addreffes him in a jefting way, mixed with
Raillery; but foon comes to expoftulate with
him ferioufly, upon the Affront he had offered her. He protefting, that Love only
fpurred him on, and that he was refolved

to marry the Girl, they are reconciled.

[1] *Apud Antiphonem.* *Chærea* here gives
the Reafons of his not being able to change
his Drefs. This was neceffary to prevent
the Surprife of the Spectators, for he had
gone off with *Antipho* for that purpofe before, and the Management of the Plot required that *Chærea* fhould yet appear in the
Habit of the Eunuch.

Tha. Let's go to him. O your Servant, good Mr. *Dorus.* Pray tell me : What did you run for it ?

Chær. I did, Madam.

Tha. And are you pleas'd with the Frolick ?

Chær. No.

Tha. Do you expect to escape unpunished ?

Chær. Forgive me but this once, and if you find me in fault again, kill me.

Tha. Did you dread my severity ?

Chær. No.

Tha. What then ?

Chær. I was afraid of *Pythias* here, lest she might accuse me to you.

Tha. What had you done ?

Chær. A small matter,

Pyt. How, Mr. Impudence, a small matter ? Does it then seem a small matter to you, to debauch a Girl, that is a Citizen ?

Chær. I took her for my Fellow-Servant.

Pyt. Your Fellow-Servant ! I can scarce hold from flying at his Hair. Monster ! he has even the Assurance to come and deride us.

Tha. Won't you be gone, you Bedlam ?

Pyt. Why so ? as if there was any danger in doing so to that Wretch, especially as he owns himself to be your Servant.

Tha. Well, but let us have done with this. Indeed, *Chærea*, you have done a thing unworthy of yourself: for, however it may be supposed that I deserve such an Affront, yet it was unbecoming in you to offer it; nor do I now know what Course in the World to take in regard to this Girl. For you have so perfectly broke all my Measures, that it is not now in my Power to restore her to her Relations, as I ought to do, and as was my Design, that I might, *Chærea*, thereby do myself a real Service.

Chær. But now, *Thais*, I hope that there will be a lasting Agreement betwixt us; for the greatest Friendships often arise from something of this kind, and a bad Beginning. What if some God has ordered all this !

Tha. Indeed I take it so, and heartily wish it.·

Chær. Nay, pray do : and be persuaded of one thing, that I did it, not with any design to affront you, but purely out of love to her.

Tha. I know it ;· and am, therefore, the more willing to forgive you. I have too much softness in my Nature, *Chærea*, and too much Knowledge of the World, to be a Stranger to the Power of Love.

Chær. So may the Gods love me, *Thais*, but I am now charmed with you too.

Pyt.

ANNOTATIONS.

11 *Bone vir Dore.* *Thais* was not ignorant that *Chærea* was the Person she now spoke to, but she artfully dissembles it, that she might use him with the more Freedom, as supposing him her Servant.

34 *Sæpe ex hujusmodi re quapiam, & malo principio*

TH. Adeamus. bone vir Dore, falve: dic mihi,
Aufugiftin'? CH. hera, factum. TH. fatin' id tibi placet?
CH. Non. TH. credin' te impune habiturum? CH.
   unam hanc noxiam
Amitte: fi aliam admifero unquam, occidito.
TH. Num meam fævitiam veritus es? CH. non. TH.
   quid igitur?   15
CH. Hanc metui, ne me criminaretur tibi.
TH. Quid feceras? CH. paululum quiddam. PY. eho,
   paululum, impudens?
An paulum hoc effe tibi videtur, virginem
Vitiare civem? CH. confervam effe credidi.
PY. Confervam! vix me contineo, quin involem in 20
Capillum, monftrum! etiam ultro derifum advenit
TH. Abin' hinc, infana? PY. quid ita vero? debeam,
Credo, ifti quidquam furcifero, fi id fecerim;
Præfertim cum fe fervom fateatur tuum.
TH. Miffa hæc faciamus. non te dignum, Chærea, 25
Fecifti: nam fi ego digna hac contumeliâ
Sum maxumè, at tu indignus qui faceres tamen:
Neque, edepol, quid nunc confilii capiam, fcio;
De virgine iftac: ita conturbafti mihi
Rationes omnes, ut eam non poffim fuis,   30
Ita ut æquom fuerát, atque ut ftudui, tradere, ut
Solidum parerem hoc mihi beneficium, Chærea.
CH. At nunc dehinc fpero æternam inter hos gratiam
Fore, Thais. fæpe ex hujufmodi re quapiam, &
Malo principio, magna familiaritas   35
Conflata eft. Quid, fi hoc quifpiam voluit Deus?
TH. Equidem pol in eam partem accipioque & volo.
CH. Imo ita quæfo. unum hoc fcito, contumeliæ
Non me feciffe caufa, fed amoris. TH. fcio:
Et pol propterea nunc magis ignofco tibi,   40
Non adeo inhumano ingenio fum, Chærea,
Neque ita imperita, ut, quid amor valeat, nefciam.
CH. Te quoque jam, Thais, ita me Dî bene ament, amo.

TH. Adeamus. Dore, bone vir, falve: dic mihi, aufugiftine? CH. Hera, factum fuit. TH. Idne placet tibi fatis? CH. Non. TH. Credijne te habiturum impune? CH. Amitte hance unam noxiam: fi unquam admifero aliam, occidito. TH. Num veritus es meam fævitiam? CH. Non. TH. Quid igitur? CH. Metui hanc, ne criminaretur me tibi. TH. Quid feceras? CH. Quidam paululum. PY. Eho, impudens, vis paululum? An hoc videtur tibi effe paulum, vitiare virginem civem? CH. Credidi eam effe confervam. PY. Confervam! vix contineo me, quin involem in capillum: etiam ultro advenit derifum. TH. Abifti hinc, infana? PY. Vero quid ita? credo, debeam quidquam ifti furcifero, fi fecerim id; præfertim cum fateatur fe effe tuum fervum. TH. Faciamus hæc miffa: Chærea, fecifti quid non dignum te: nam fi ego jam maxime digna hac contumeliâ, at tu indignus qui facere. Neque, edepol, fcio quid confilii nunc capiam de iftac virgine: conturbafti

ita omnes rationes mihi, ut non poffim tradere illam fuis, ita ut fuerat æquum, atque ut ftudui, ut hoc parerem folidum beneficium mihi, Chærea. CH. At nunc, Thais, fpero fore dehinc æternam gratiam inter nos. Sæpe ex re quapiam hujufmodi, & malo principio, magnâ familiaritas eft conflata. Quid, fi quifpiam deus voluit hoc? TH. Pol equidem & volo; accipioque in eam partem. CH. Imo quæfo fac ita. Scito hoc unum, me non feciffe caufa contumeliæ, fed amoris. TH. Scio: & propterea pol nunc magis ignofco tibi. Non fum ingenio adeo inhumano, Chærea, neque ita imperita, ut nefciam quid amor valeat. TH. Thais, ita Dii bene ament me, amo te quoque jam.

ANNOTATIONS.

principio, magna familiaritas conflata eft. | one. Livy feems to have had it in view, Lib.
This is a juft Obfervation, whofe Truth | I. 9. Mollirent modo iras, & quibus fere
comes within the Experience of almoft every | corpora dediffet, darent animos. Sæpe ex in-

Pyt. Then, Madam, I forefee, you had need to take care of your felf.

Chær. I would not dare *to offer any thing here.*

Pyt. I would not truft you any where.

Tha. Have done.

Chær. Now, I beg that you will be an Affiftant to me in this Affair. I commit myfelf to you, and entirely confide in your Honour. I defire to have you for my Patronefs, and implore your Help. May I die, if I don't marry her.

Tha. But if your Father————

Chær. Ah, what? he'll confent, I know, if fhe's a Citizen.

Tha. If you will but ftay a little, the Girl's Brother will be here prefently. He is gone to fetch the Nurfe, who had the Care of her when fhe was a Child. You yourfelf fhall be a Witnefs of the Difcovery, *Chærea.*

Chær. I'll ftay, with all my Soul.

Tha. Won't it be better to ftep in, and wait his coming, than to ftand here before the Door?

Chær. With all my Heart.

Pyt. What are you going to do, pray?

Tha. Why fo?

Pyt. Do you afk? Can you think of admitting him into your Houfe, after what has happened?

Tha. Why not?

Pyt. Believe me for once, Madam, he'll again caufe fome new Difturbance.

Tha. Prithee hold thy Tongue.

Pyt. You feem to have but little Knowledge of his daring Temper.

Chær. I'll do no harm indeed, *Pythias.*

Pyt. I'll not believe you, *Chærea*, until I fee that there is really nothing done.

Chær. But *Pythias*, be you my Keeper.

Pyt. I neither dare truft any thing to your keeping, nor keep you myfelf. Away.

Tha. But here's the Brother himfelf, very fortunately.

Chær. I'm undone: for Heaven's fake, *Thais*, let us go in. I would not for the World he fhould fee me in the Street in this Drefs.

Tha. Why, pray? Are you afhamed?

Chær. The very fame.

Pyt. The very fame! But the Virgin——

Tha. Go you before, I follow. Do you, *Pythias*, ftay, to fhew *Chremes* in.

ANNOTATIONS.

juria poftmodum gratiam ortam. The Words of *Romulus*, upon the Rape of the *Sabine* Virgins.

69 *I pra jequor.* It is evident, fays *Do- natus*, why this Courtezan, who was fo well acquainted with the Arts of enfnaring Men, is.

A C T

Py. Tum pol ab istoc tibi, hera, cavendum intellego.
Ch. Non ausim. Py. nihil tibi quidquam credo. Th.
desinas.   45
Ch. Nunc ego te in hac re mihi oro, ut adjutrix sies:
Ego me tuæ commendo & committo fidei :
Te mihi patronam capio, Thais : te obsecro :
Emoriar, si non hanc uxorem duxero.
Th. Tamen si pater—Ch. ah, quid? volet, certo scio, 50
Civis modò hæc sit. Th. paululùm opperirier
Si vis, jam frater ipse hic aderit virginis :
Nutricem arcessitum iit, quæ illam aluit parvolam :
In cognoscendo tute ipse hîc aderis, Chærea.
Ch. Ego vero maneo. Th. visne interea, dum venit, 55
Domi opperiamur potius, quàm hîc ante ostium ?
Ch. Imo percupio. Py. quam tu rem actura, obsecro, es?
Th. Nam quid ita ? Py. rogitas ? hunc tu in ædes
cogitas   [fidei,
Recipere posthac? Th. cur non ? Py. crede hoc mextæ
Dabit hic aliquam pugnam denuo. Th. au, tace, ob-
secro.
Py. Parum perspexisse ejus videre audaciam.   61
Ch. Non faciam, Pythia. Py. non pol, credo, Chærea,
Nisi si commissum non erit. Ch. quin, Pythias,
Tu me servato. Py. neque pol servandum tibi
Quidquam dare ausim, neque te servare, apage te. 65
Th. Optumè adest ipse frater. Ch. perii hercle. obsecro,
Abeamus intro, Thais : nólo me in viâ
Cum hac veste videat. Th. quamobrem tandem ? an
quia pudet ?   [sequor.
Ch. Id ipsum. Py. id ipsum ? virgo vero—Th. i præ,
Tu istic mane, ut Chremem introducas, Pythias. 70

aliquam pugnam denuo. Th. *Au, obsecro, tace.* Py. *Videre parum perspexisse audaciam ejus* Ch. *Pythias, non faciam.* Py. *Pol, Chærea, non credo, nisi si non erit commissum.* Ch. *Quin, Py-*
thias, servato tu me. Py. *Neque pol ausim dare quidquam servandum tibi, neque servare te :*
apage te. Th. *Ipse frater optimè adest.* Ch. *Hercle perii: obsecro, Thais, abeamus intro, nolo quis-*
quam videat me in viâ cum hac veste. Th. *Quamobrem tandem ? An quia pudet te ?* Ch. *Id*
ipsum. Py. *Id ipsum ? vero virgo.---*Th. *I præ, sequor. Tu, Pythias, mane istic, ut intro-*
ducas Chremem.

Py. *Tum pol, hera,*
intelligo, cavendum
est tibi ab istoc. Ch.
Non ausim. Py. *Cre-*
do nihil quidquam ti-
bi. Th. *Desinat.*
Ch. *Nunc ego oro te,*
ut sis adjutrix mihi
in hac re, ego com-
mendo & committo me
tuæ fidei: capio te,
Thais, patronam mi-
hi : obsecro te: emo-
riar, si non duxero
hanc uxorem. Th.
Tamen si pater——
Ch. *Ah, quid? scio*
certo, volet, modò hæc
sit civis. Th. *Si vis*
opperiri paululùm, ipse
frater virginis aderit
hic jam : ivit arcessi-
tum nutricem, quæ
aluit illam parvolam :
tute ipse, Chærea,
aderis hic in cogno-
scendo. Ch. *Ego vero*
maneo. Th. *Visne*
interea opperiamur
domi, dum venit, po-
tius quàm hîc ante
ostium ? Ch. *Imo*
percupio. Py. *Obse-*
cro, quam rem es tu
actura? Th. *Nam*
quid ita ? Py. *Ro-*
gitas? cogitas tu re-
cipere hunc in ædes
posthac ? Th. *Cur*
non ? Py. *Crede hoc*
meæ fidei ; sic dabit

ANNOTATIONS.

is willing that *Chærea* should go in first, while she followed at her leisure. She wanted that *Chærea* should have some private Discourse with the Girl, and an Opportunity of making known his Passion to her ; unless we will rather suppose that *Terence*, who is allowed by all to excel so much in Art and Judgment, makes *Thais* do this without any Reason at all ; for she

neither goes in herself with *Chærea*, nor suffers *Pythias* to go in with him.

70 *Tu istic mane, ut Chremem introducas.* *Pythias* is left here, because she is to be one of the principal Persons in forwarding the Plot : for by her, *Parmeno* is thrown into the Fright, which makes him discover all to the old Man, who rushing in hastily, by his Presence confirms the Wedding.

Q 2   ACTUS

ACT V. SCENE III.
ARGUMENT.

This Scene prepares the Way for the Trick to be put upon Parmeno, *that the Contriver of the late Plot might not be without his share of the Danger.* ·

PYTHIAS, CHREMES, SOPHRONA.

Pythias. **W**HAT? what can I now devise ? What Contrivance
can I think of to be revenged of the Ruffian, for the
Cheat he has put upon us ?·

Chrem. Come, 'move on a little faster, Nurse.

Soph. I do move. ·

Chrem. I see you do; but you don't make any riddance.

Pyt. Have you shew'd the Nurse the Tokens yet ?

Chrem. Yes : all.

Pyt. Pray, what says she ? Does she know them ?

Chrem. Yes, and remembers them perfectly well.

Pyt. That's happy, I protest, for I have a great Regard for that
young Lady. Be pleased to walk in ; for my Mistress has been expecting you some time. But I see that fine Gentleman *Parmeno* walking
this Way. Observe, for Heaven's Sake, how careless he seems! But I
hope I have it now in my Power to torment him to my Heart's Content.
However, I'll first step in to know the Certainty of this Discovery :
then I'll come out again, and frighten the Rascal to some Purpose.

ANNOTATIONS.

Pythias, while she is waiting to introduce
Chremes, contrives with herself, what Stratagem she can hit upon, to be revenged of
Parmeno. Mean time, *Chremes* and the
Nurse come up, and *Pythias* hearing that
the Tokens were remembered, rejoices for
the Sake of the Virgin. ·

3 *Qui hunc supposuit. Supponere* is a very
proper Word here, being used of those who
are forced upon us, without our knowing or
desiring it ; as *subducere* is used in Cases where
any Thing is taken from us contrary to our
Inclination. ·

10 *Vide*

ACT V. SCENE IV.
ARGUMENT.

Parmeno *here glories in his Plot of substituting* Chærea *for the
Eunuch, and by that means giving him an Opportunity of enjoying the Virgin without Loss or Expence. He afterwards
speaks of the general Character of these Courtezans, and their
sordid Meanness, which but the more provokes* Pythias, *who
was already sufficiently angry with him.* ·

PARMENO, PYTHIAS.

Parmeno. **I** COME to see what *Chærea* has done here ; for if he
has managed artfully, good Gods, how great and what
true ,

ANNOTATIONS.

Parmeno comes walking along by himself, happy in the imagined Success of his

Plot. He recounts the many Advantages
that must arise from it to *Chærea,* and the
great

ACTUS V. SCENA III.

ARGUMENTUM.

Præparatio ad Parmenonis ludificationem, ne sceleris auctor sit periculi expers.

PYTHIAS, CHREMES, SOPHRONA.

ORDO.

QUID? quid venire in mentem nunc possit mihi?
   Quidnam, qui referam sacrilego illi gratiam,
Qui hunc supposuit nobis? CH. move vero ociùs
Te nutrix. So. moveo. CH. video, sed nil promoves.
PY. Jamne ostendisti signa nutrici? CH. omnia.   5
PY. Amabo, quid ait? cognoscitne? CH. ac memoriter.
PY. Bene edepol narras : nam illi faveo virgini.
Ite intro : jamdudum hera vos exspectat domi.
Virum bonum eccum Parmenonem incedere
Video. viden' ut otiosus it; si Dis placet,   10
Spero me habere, qui hunc meo excrutiem modo.
Ibo intro, de cognitione ut certum sciam :
Post exibo, atque hunc perterrebo sacrilegum.

bene: nam faveo illi virgini. Ite intro. Hera jamdudum expectat vos domi. Eccum, video virum bo-num Parmenonem incedere : vide ut it otiosus, si placet Diis! Spero me habere qui (quo) excruciem hunc meo modo. Ibo intro, ut sciam certum de cognitione : post exibo, atque perterrebo hunc sacrilegum.

Ordo column text:
PY. *Quid? quid possit venire nunc in mentem mihi? Quidnam, qui referam gratiam illi sacrilego, qui suppo-suit hunc nobis?* CH. *Vero, nutrix, movete ocius.* So. *Moveo.* CH. *Video, sed pro-moves nil.* PY. *Osten-disti jam signa nu-trici?* CH. *Ostendi omnia.* PY. *Amabo, quid ait? Cognoscitne?* CH. *Ac memoriter.* PY. *Edepol narras*

ANNOTATIONS.

10 *Vide ut otiosus it!* This Picture of Par-meno is artfully touched by the Poet : for as it must but the more provoke *Pythias*, to see him so easy and happy, who had lately raised so great a Disturbance in their House ; so this Security and Tranquility in *Parmeno* pre-pares the way to make his after Calamity ap-pear the greater.

ACTUS V. SCENA IV.

ARGUMENTUM.

Hic Parmeno gloriatur Chæream pro eunucho subornasse, ita ut virgine præter sumptum & dispendium potitus sit. Deinde meretricum ingenia & sordes commemorat : quare Pythiam quam non adesse percipit, prius satis commotam, magis irritat.

PARMENO, PYTHIAS.

ORDO.

REVISO, quidnam Chærea hîc rerum gerat.
   Quòd si astu rem tractavit, Di vostram fidem,

quòd si tractavit rem astu, Dii vostram fidem,

PA. *Reviso, quid-nam rerum Chærea gerat hîc :*

ANNOTATIONS.

great Glory that will redound to the Con-triver. All these sanguine Hopes, this whole Solemnity of Preparation, paves the way for his heavier Distress, when *Pythias* informs him of the ill Success of it ; for he is seen to fall from the most raised Expec-tations, into an Abyss of Despair ; and so great is his Fright, that he is driven to make a Discovery to the old Man, which he fore-saw would bring Vengeance upon himself.

true Glory will redound to *Parmeno.* For to fay nothing of my having procured for him the Perfon he loved, without Trouble, Lofs, or Expence, an Amour that might have proved very difficult and coftly in the hands.of a covetous Bawd ; there is alfo this other Advantage, for 'which I think I ought to bear away the Prize, that I have found out the way of bringing a young Man acquainted with the Tempers and Manners of thefe Harlots; that by thus knowing them in time, he may hate them ever after. When they are abroad, nothing can be more clean, neat, or elegant.: When they fup with their Gallants, they are the moft delicate Creatures in Nature. But to fee how nafty, fordid and needy, what fluttifh voracious Creatures they are when by themfelves at home, how greedily they devour the black Bread fteep'd in yefterday's Sauce ! to know all this, I fay, is the fure Prefervation of young Men. ·

Pyt. By *Pollux,* I'll take a fevere Revenge, for what you have here faid and done ; nor fhall you thus impofe upon, and make fport of us for nothing.

ANNOTATIONS.

4 *Quod ei amorem difficillimum & cariffimum.* When *Parmeno* ought to have faid, *Quod ei amorem. difficillimum & cariffimum confeci,* forgetting the firft Part of the Sentence, he paffes immediately to the mention of the Virgin. Had he faid no more than *amorem confeci ; confeci* might have been explained *expedivi, perfeci.* But what are we to underftand by *virginem confeci ?* Does it not look, as if *Parmeno* meant to infult the Virgin upon the Advantage he fancied he had gained ? For this Word was properly ufed of Gladiators, when, being grievoufly wounded, they were obliged to yield. Thus *Cicero* againft *Cataline,* 2. 11. *Gladiatori illi confecto ac faucio.* *Parmeno,* therefore, boafts here, that he had done the Bufinefs effectually, in regard to the Virgin, and that without any Lofs or Expence to his young Mafter *Chærea. Donatus.*

14 *Quæ, cum amatore fuo cum cænant, liguriunt. Ligurire eft captim & quafi fa-* *ftidiofe. cibum capere. Apulei Metam.* 10. *Partes opimas quafque devorabam, & rancidiora feligens, abliguritbam dulcia.* And *Horace* Satire 3. Book I. ver. 80.

> *Si quis cum fervum, patinam qui tollere*
> *juffus,*
> *Semefos pifces, tepidumque ligurierit jus,*
> *In crucis fuffigat.*

13 *Harum videre ingluviem, fordes, inopiam.* So we read in a great many Editions, but thofe of greateft Authority have *illuviem.* And, indeed, the Order and Manner of oppofing things to one another, makes it evidently appear, that this is the true Reading. He had mentioned two things that are decent in Courtezans ; their Cleanlinefs, and Modefty in eating : the firft, when he fays, *Nihil videntur mundius, nec magis compofitum quicquam, nec magis elegans :* the other, *Quæ cum amatore fuo cum cænant, liguriunt.* To which he now anfwers in the very Order, wherein they were named before ;

A C T

Quantum & quàm veram laudem capiet Parmeno !
Nam ut mittam,·quòd ei amorem difficillimum, &
Cariſſimum ab meretrice avarâ ; virginem   5
Quam amabat,. eam confeci ſine moleſtiâ,
Sine ſumtu, ſine diſpendio : tum hoc alterum,
Id vero eſt, quod ego mihi puto palmarium,
Me repperiſſe, quo modo adoleſcentulus
Meretricum .ingenia & mores poſſet noſcere ;   10
Maturè ut cum cognôrit, perpetuo oderit.·
Quæ dum foris ſunt, nihil videtur mundius,
Nec magi' compoſitum quidquam, nec magis elegans :
Quæ, cum amatore ſuo cùm cœnant, liguriunt.
Harum videre inluviem, ſordes, inopiam,   15
Quam inhoneſtæ ſolæ ſint·domi, atque avidæ cibi,
Quo pacto ex jure heſterno panem atrum vorent :
Nôſſe omnia hæc, ſalus eſt adoleſcentulis.
Py. Ego pol te pro iſtis dictis & factis, ſcelus,
Ulciſcar ; ut ne impune in nos inluſeris.   20

magis elegans : quæ, cum cœnant cum ſuo amatore, liguriunt. Videre illuviem, ſordes, inopiam,
harum, quàm inhoneſtæ ſint domi ſolæ, atque avidæ cibi, quo pacto vorcnt panem atrum ex
beſterno jure : eſt ſalus adoleſcentulis nôſſe hæc omnia. Py. Pol ſcelus, ego ulſciſcar te pro iſtis
dictis & factis : ut me illuſeris in nos impune.

Marginal text:

quantam & quàm veram laudem Par-meno capiet ! Nam ut mittam, quòd confeci ei amorem difficilli-mum, & cariſſimum ab avarâ meretrice ; confeci eam virginem, quam amabat, ſine moleſtiâ, ſine ſumtu, ſine diſpendio : tum hoc alterum, vero id eſt, quod ego puto palmarium mibi ; me repperiſſe quo modo adoleſcentulus poſſet noſcere ingenia & mo-res meretricum: ut cùm cognôverit matu-rè, oderit perpetuò. Quæ dum ſunt foris, nibil videtur mundi-us, nec quidquam ma- / gis compoſitum, nec

ANNOTATIONS.

before : to Cleanlineſs, oppoſing *inluviem*, *ſordes*, *inopiam* ; to Modeſty in eating, that voracious Greedineſs, which he deſcribes in theſe two Verſes :

> *Quam inhoneſtæ ſolæ ſint domi, atque avi-*
> *dæ cibi,*
> *Quo pacto ex jure keſterno panem atrum vo-*
> *rent.*

Whereas, if you read *ingluvium*, beſides that the true Antitheſis would not be obſerved, the Poet would be alſo guilty of another Error, in deviating from the Order he had made choice of himſelf, and by paſſing from *Gluttony* to *Sordidneſs* and *Want*, and then re-turning again to *Gluttony*, contrary to all Rule, confound things very different among themſelves. *Bentley.*

19 *Ego pol te.* Terence is wonderfully

happy in·the Conduct of the Play, by con-triving that *Pytbias* ſhould always retain the ſame Animoſity againſt *Parmeno*, and that *Parmeno*, by all he ſays, ſhould ſtill more provoke *Pytbias*, for this is what leads to the unravelling of the Plot. *Pytbias* frightens *Parmeno*, his Fear obliges him to diſcover all to the old Man, upon which he hurrying in to *Thais*, every thing comes ·to be known, and the Marriage is confirmed. All this is extremely natural, inſomuch, that *Donatus* had reaſon to call it *mirum artificium*, and to ſay, *Hæc ergo artificibus & eruditis, cætera ſpectatoribus pocta exbibet.* " Theſe maſterly " Strokes are deſigned for the learned and " ſkilled in Criticiſm, the reſt for the com- " mon Herd of Spectators."

Q 4   ACTUS

232

TERENCE's EUNUCH.
ACT V. SCENE V.
ARGUMENT.

Pythias *cunningly frightens* Parmeno, *and throws him into the greatest Perplexity, that so the old Man, being informed of all by a Discovery from him, may be dispatched in to* Thais, *to confirm the Marriage, and promote the unravelling of the Plot.*

PYTHIAS, PARMENO.

Pythias. E*Ntering.*) Good Gods! What a base Action is this! O unhappy young Man! O wicked *Parmeno*, who brought him hither!

Parm. What's the matter? [*Aside.*

Pyt. (*To herself, aloud.*) I pity him: and therefore left the House in haste, that I might not see it. What a dreadful Example, they say, they are to make of him!

Parm. (*To himself.*) O Heavens! What Disturbance can this be? Am I then ruined? I'll go speak to her. (*to Pythias.*) *Pythias*, what's all this? What was it you said? Whom are they to make an Example of?

Pyt. Do you ask, impudent Wretch? while you endeavoured to put a Trick upon us, you have quite ruined the young Gentleman, whom you brought hither for the Eunuch.

Parm. Why so? Or what has happened, tell me.

Pyt. I'll tell you: do you know that the young Girl, who was presented to my Mistress to-day, is a Citizen, and her Brother a Man of the first Rank?

Parm. I know nothing of it.

Pyt. But so she is found to be. The unhappy Youth has debauched her: this Brother of her's a Man of violent Passions, when he came to know it—

Parm. What did he do?

Pyt. First, he bound him in a most terrible manner.

Parm. Bound him!

Pyt. Nay, even tho' *Thais* earnestly intreated that he would not.

Parm. What do you tell me?

Pyt. Now he threatens him also with the usual Punishment of Adulterers: a thing I never saw in my Life, nor desire to see.

Parm. Has he the Assurance to venture upon so daring an Action?

Pyt. Why so daring?

Parm. What, is not this one of the most daring kind? Who ever

ANNOTATIONS.

Pythias resolved to be revenged of *Parmeno*, for the Trick he had play'd them, contrives to appear surprized; and under great Concern for what was doing within. This naturally startles *Parmeno*, and makes him impatient to know what was the matter.

Pythias, upon this, devises a Story on purpose to frighten him, and does it so effectually, that in his fear, not knowing what to do better, he resolves to discover all to the old Man, in which *Pythias* encourages him, because her Resentment was not yet quite over;

ACTUS V. SCENA V.

ARGUMENTUM.

*Insigni astutia Parmenonem exterret Pythias, & in maximum
perturbationem conjicit, ut ita ipsius indicio certior factus
senex, ad nuptias confirmandas intromittatur; atque ita fabulæ exitus promoveatur.*

PYTHIAS, PARMENO.

PROH Deûm fidem ! facinus fœdum ! ô infelicem
    adolefcentulum !
O fcelestum Parmenonem, qui istum huc adduxit !
    PA. quid est ?   [fugi foras.
PY. Miferet me. itaque, ut ne viderem, mifera huc ef-
Quæ futura exempla dicunt in eum indigna ? PA. ô
    Jupiter !   [istuc, Pythias ? 5
Quæ illæc turba est ? numnam ego perii ? adibo. quid
Quid ais ? in quem exempla fient ? PY. rogitas, auda-
    cissime ?   [fcentulum
Perdidisti istum, quem adduxti pro eunucho, ado-
Dum studes dare verba nobis. PA. quid ita ? aut quid
    factum est ? cedo.   [data est,
PY. Dicam. virginem istam, Thaidi hodie quæ dono
Scis eam civem hinc esse ? & fratrem ejus esse adprimè
    nobilem ?   10
PA. Nescio. PY. atqui fic inventa est. eam iste vitiâ-
    vit mifer.
Ille ubi id refcivit factum frater. violentissimus—
PA. Quidnam fecit ? PY. conligavit primùm eum mife-
    ris modis.   [faceret, Thaide.
PA. Conligavit ? PY. atque equidem orànte, ut ne id
PA. Quid ais ? PY. nunc minitatur porro fefe id, quod
    mœchis folet :   15
Quod ego nunquam vidi fieri, neque velim. PA. quâ
    audaciâ   [non hoc maxumum est ?
Tantum facinus audet ? PY. quid ita tantum ? PA. an

ORDO.

PY. PROH fidem Deûm ! Facinus fœdum ! O infelicem adolefcentu-
lum ! O fceiestum
Parmenonem, qui ad-
duxit istum huc ? PA.
Quid est ? PY. Mi-
feret me adolefcen-
tuli : itaque mifera
effugi huc foras, ut
ne viderem exempla
indigna, quæ dicunt
futura in eum. PA.
O Jupiter ! Quæ est
illæc turba ? Num-
nam ego perii ? adi-
bo. Pythias, quid est
istuc ? Quid ais ? In
quem exempla fient ?
PY. Rogitas, auda-
cissime ? dum studes
dare verba nobis,
perdidisti istum ado-
lefcentulum, quem ad-
duxti pro eunucho.
PA. Quid ita ? Aut
quid est factum ? ce-
do. PY. Dicam. Scis
istam virginem, quæ
est data dono Thaidi
hodie, eam esse ci-
vem hinc, & fra-
trem ejus esse adpri-
me nobilem ? PA.
Nescio. PY. Atqui

est inventa fic: Iste mifer vitiavit eam. Ille frater violentissimus, ubi refcivit id factum.
PA. Quid nam fecit ? PY. Primùm colligavit eum miferis modis. PA. Colligavit ? PY. Atque
equidem Thaide orante, ut ne faceret id. PA. Quid ais ? PY. Nunc minitatur porro fefe facturum id, quod fole! fieri mœchis : quod ego nunquam vidi fieri, neque velim videre. PA. Quâ
audaciâ audet patrare tantum facinus ? PY. Quid ita tantum ? PA. An hoc non est maximum ?

ANNOTATIONS.

over, and fhe had in view to torment him
still farther.

    4 *Quæ futura exempla dicunt in eum in-
digna ?* This, according to the Punctu-
ation, must be differently explained. Some
make a full stop at *foras*, and mark the
Words here referred to, with a Point of
Interrogation. *What a dreadful Example,*

am I told, *they are to make of him ?* Others
have only a Comma after *foras*, without any
mark of Interrogation at the next Sentence;
according to which the Order must be, *Itaque
mifera effugi huc foras, ut ne viderem exempla
indigna, quæ dicunt esse futura in eam.*
Donatus rightly explains *exempla, graves
pœnas, quæ possunt cæteris documento esse.*

    19 *Nefcie.*

ever saw a Man taken and treated as an Adulterer, in a Courtezan's House?

Pyt. I don't know.

Parm. But that you mayn't be ignorant, *Pythias,* I tell and forewarn you, that this is my Master's Son.

Pyt. How! pray, is it he?

Parm. Let, *Thais,* therefore, take care, that no affront be offered him. But, why don't I myself go in?

Pyt. Take care, *Parmeno,* what you do, lest you neither profit him, and ruin yourself into the bargain; for they imagine all that's done here, to be wholly your Contrivance.

Parm. What, unhappy Wretch that I am, shall I therefore do, or how resolve? But oh! I see the old Man returning from the Country. Shall I tell him of it, or not? I'll tell him, by *Jove,* though I know it will bring a heavy Sentence upon myself. But it is absolutely necessary, that he rescue his Son.

Pyt. You are wise. I go in: do you tell him every thing exactly as it has happened.

ANNOTATIONS.

19 *Nescio.* This is artful enough in *Pythias,* who knew that *Parmeno* had reason for what he said, and therefore does not amuse herself in supporting the Equity of the thing, which would at once have made *Parmeno* suspect the Truth of what she said. She

---

ACT V. SCENE VI.

ARGUMENT.

Parmeno deceived by the Cunning of Pythias, *unwarily betrays both himself,* Phædria, *and* Chærea, *and discovers the whole of what had been done, to the old Man returning from the Country.*

LACHES, PARMENO.

Laches. (*TO himself.*) I have this Advantage from my Country-Seat's being so near, that I am never weary either of the Country or the Town; for when I begin to have enough of one, I immediately go to the other. (*seeing Parmeno.*) But is not that our *Parmeno?* 'tis surely he. Whom do you wait for, *Parmeno,* at this Door here?

Parm. Who's that, pray.—O, Sir, I'm overjoyed to see you returned safe to Town. *Lac.*

ANNOTATIONS.

Laches is introduced here, returning from his Country-Seat, and making some Reflections on the Conveniency of its Situation, just in the Neighbourhood of the Town. Seeing *Parmeno,* he goes up to him, who, full of fears for *Chærea,* could not hide his Concern, but discovers it to the old Man, by his Trembling and Confusion. At last, with much ado, he tells him all. *Laches* asto-nished at so many Misfortunes threatning him at once, and angry with *Parmeno,* whom he looked upon as partly a Promoter of his Son's Debaucheries, breaks away in haste to prevent the Mischief that he imagined threatned his Son.

1 *Ex meo propinquo rure.* We have here an old Man approaching peaceably, his Head filled with no Cares, one that suspects no Mischief,

Quis homo pro mœcho unquam vidit in domo me-
    retriciâ   [fciatis, Pythias,
Prehendi quenquam? Py. nefcio. Pa. at ne hoc ne-
Dico, edico vobis, noftrum effe illum herilem filium.
    Py. hem,   20
Obfecro, an is eft? Pa. ne quam in illum Thais vim
    fieri finat.   [de, Parmeno,
Atque adeo autem cur non egomet intro eo? Py. vi-
Quid agas, ne neque illi profis, & tu pereas. nam hoc
    putant,   [tur faciam mifer?
Quidquid factum eft, ex te effe ortum. Pa. quid igi-
Quidve incipiam? ecce autem, rure video redeuntem
    fenem.   25
Dicam huic, an non? dicam hercle; etfi mihi mag-
    num malum
Scio paratum. fed neceffe eft, huic ut fubveniat. Py. fapis.
Ego abe intro: tu ifti narrato omnem ordine rem, ut
    factum fiet.

video fenem redeuntem rure. Dicam huic, an non? hercle dicam, etfi fcio magnum malum effe
paratum mihi. Sed neceffe eft, ut fubveniat huic. Py. Sapis. Ego abeo intro: tu narra ifti
omnem rem, ordine ut fit factum.

Quis homo unquam vidit quenquam prehendi pro mœcho in domo meretriciâ? Py. Nefcio. Pa. At, Pythias, ne nefciatis hoc, dico, edico vobis, illum effe noftrum herilem filium. Py. Hem! obfecro an eft is? Pa. Ne, Thais, finat quam vim fieri in illum. Atque adeo autem cur egomet non eo intro? Py. Parmeno, vide quid agas: ne neque profis illi, & tu pereas. Nam putant hoc, quidquid eft factum, effe ortum ex te. Pa. Mifer, quid igitur faciam? Quidve incipiam? Ecce autem

ANNOTATIONS.

She is content with giving him a bare account of the thing itfelf, without meddling with the Reafons for or againft it, which it did not at all concern her to know.

ACTUS V. SCENA VI.

ARGUMENTUM.

*Parmeno impulfus dolo ancillæ, incaute fe, Phædriam, & Chæ-
ream prodit, & feni in urbem redeunti rem totam, ut gefta
erat, aperit.*

LACHES, PARMENO.

E X meo propinquo rure hoc capio commodi:
    Neque agri, neque orbis odium me unquam per-
    cipit.
Ubi fatias cœpit fieri, commuto locum.
Sed eftne ille nofter Parmeno? & certe ipfus eft.
Quem præftolare, Parmeno, hîc ante oftium?   5
Pa. Quis homo eft? hem, falvum te adveniffe, here,
    gaudeo.

Parmeno, præftolare hîc ante oftium? Pa. Quis homo eft? hem here, gaudeo te adveniffe falvum.

ORDO.
La. Capio hoc commodi ex meo propinquo rure: neque odium urbis, neque agri unquam percipit me. Ubi fatias cœpit fieri, commuto locum. Sed eftne ille nofter Parmeno? & certe eft ipfe. Quem te adveniffe falvum.

ANNOTATIONS.

Mifchief, who thinks of nothing but the Convenience he found in having a Country-Seat fituated fo near the Town. All this is very happily conceived by the Poet, that the good Man may be the more nearly affected with the News, which he is juft going to hear from *Parmeno*. For by this, the fudden Change of his Condition is better perceived, and affects the Audience more ftrongly. *Dacier.*

6 *Quis homo eft?* Parmeno had feen the old Man before, and taken the Refolution
    of

Lac. Whom do you wait for ?

Parm. I'm ruined. My Tongue is tied up by Fear.

Lac. Ha ! What's the matter ? Why do you tremble fo ? Is all right at home ? Pray tell me.

Parm. Firſt, Sir, I'd have you be perſuaded of what is really the Caſe, that whatever has happened here in this Affair, is through no Fault of mine.

Lac. What ?

Parm. You have reaſon to aſk, for I ought to have told it you firſt of all. *Phædria* lately bought a Eunuch, to make a Preſent of to this Woman.

Lac. To what Woman ?

Parm. To *Thais.*

Lac. He bought ! I'm certainly ruin'd : for how much ?

Parm. Sixty Pounds.

Lac. Paſt Recovery.

Parm. Then *Chærea* is in love with a certain Muſic Girl here !

Lac. How ! What ! He in love ? Does he already know what a Harlot is ? Is he come to Town ? One Misfortune upon the back of another.

Parm. Maſter, don't look ſo at me ; it was not by any Advice of mine, that he did it.

Lac. Forbear ſpeaking of yourſelf. If I live, Raſcal, I'll——But firſt give me an Account of this, whatever it be.

Parm. He was carried to this *Thais*, inſtead of the Eunuch.

Lac. Inſtead of the Eunuch, do you ſay ?

Parm. As I tell you : they have ſince ſeized him within for an Adulterer, and bound him.

Lac. Death !

Parm. Mark but the Impudence of theſe Harlots.

Lac. Is there any other Calamity or Misfortune, that you have not yet told me of ?

Parm. That's all.

Lac. Do I delay ruſhing in upon them ?

Parm. I make no doubt, but Judgment will fall heavy upon me for this day's Work, but that the thing was abſolutely unavoidable. However, I am overjoy'd to think that they too will be made to ſuffer ſeverely by my means ; for the old Gentleman has long ſought an Occaſion of making them Examples : now he has found it.

ANNOTATIONS.

of diſcovering all to him. This Queſtion, therefore, cannot be meant for Information, but is merely a Fineſſe, to prevent the old Man from ſuſpecting he had any Artifice againſt him : for a Meeting ſo ſeemingly accidental gives every thing, he ſays, an Air of being natural, and without deſign.

¹⁷ *An in aſtu venit ?* Ἄςυ is a Greek word, the ſame in Signification, as the *Latin Urbs.* At firſt it was proper only to the City of *Athens*, πόλις being always uſed in ſpeaking of other Places, but by degrees Ἄςυ extended its Signification, and came to be uſed indifferently with the other. From Ἄςυ

A C T

LA. Quem præstolare ? PA. perii. lingua hæret metu
LA. hem,
Quid est ? quid trepidas ? fati' ne falvæ ? dic mihi.
PA. Here, primùm te arbitrari id, quod res est, velim :
Quidquid hujus factum est, culpâ non factum est meâ.
LA. Quid ? PA. rectè sanè interrogasti : oportuit 11
Rem prænarrasse me. emit quendam Phædria
Eunuchum, quem dono huic daret. LA. cui? PA.Thaidi
LA. Emit? perii hercle. quanti ? PA. viginti minis.
LA. Actum est. PA. tum quandam fidicinam amat hic
   Chærea.   15
LA. Hem, quid ? amat ? an fcit jam ille, quid mere-
   trix fiet ?
An in aftu venit ? aliud ex alio malum.
PA. Here, ne me fpectés : me impulfore hæc non facit.
LA. Omitte de te dicere. ego te, furcifer,
Si vivo—fed iftuc, quidquid eft, primum expedi. 20
PA. Is pro illo eunucho ad Thaidem hanc deductus eft.
LA. Pro eunuchon'? PA. fic eft. hunc pro mœch‹ poftea
Comprehendére intus, & conftrinxére. LA. occidi.
PA. Audaciam meretriciam fpecta. LA. numquid eft
Aliud mali damnive, quod non dixeris,   25
Reliquum ? PA. tantum eft. LA. ceffo huc intro ir-
   rumpere?   [malum,
PA. Non dubium eft, quin mihi magnum ex hac re fit
Nifi, quia neceffe fuit hoc facere. id gaudeo,
Propter me hifce aliquid effe eventurum mali :
Nam jamdiu aliquam cıufam quærebat fenex,   30
Quamobrem infigne aliquid faceret iis : nunc repperit.

LA. *Quem præftola-*
re ? PA. Perii: lin-
gua hæret præ metu.
LA. Hem, quid eft ?
Quid trepidas ? Res
noftræ falfne funt
falvæ ? dic mihi.
PA. Here, vel.n te
arbitrari primum id,
qi od res eft : quid-
quid hujus eft fac-
um, non eft factum
meâ culpâ. LA.
Quid ? PA. Sane
interrogafti rectè: o-
portuit me prænar-
raffe rem. Phælria
emit quendam eunu-
chum, quem daret
dono huic. LA. Cui ?
PA. Thaidi. LA.
Emit ? hercle perii ?
quanti ? PA. Viginti
minis. LA. Eft ac-
tum. PA. Tum hic
Chærea amat quan-
dam fidicinam. LA.
Hem quid ? Amat ?
An ille jam fcit, quid
meretrix fit ? An ve-
nit in aftu ? aliud
malum ex alio. PA.
Here, ne fpectes me
ita torve, non facit
hæc me impulfore.
LA. Omitte dicere de
te, ego, fi vivo, fur-
cifer, te—fed expedi
primum iftuc, quid-

quid eft. PA. *Is eft deductus ad hanc Thaidem pro illo eunucho.* LA. *Pro eunuchone ?* PA. *Eft*
fic : poftea comprehendére hunc intus pro mœcho, & conftrinxére. LA. *Occidi.* PA. *Specta au-*
daciam meretricum. LA. *Numquid eft aliud mali damnive reliquum, quod non dixeris ?* PA. *Id*
tantum eft. LA. *Ceffo intro irrumpere huc.* PA. *Non eft dubium, quin magnum malum fit mihi*
ex hac re ; nifi, quia neceffe fuit facere hoc. Sed gaudeo propter id ; aliquid mali effe eventurum
hifce propter me. Nam fenex jamdiu quærebat aliquam caufam, quamobrem faceret aliquid infigne
iis : nunc repperit.

ANNOTATIONS.

ĀFυ is derived *aftutus, artful, cunning,* becaufe thofe who live in Cities, have generally a finer Addrefs, and are better Judges
of Mankind, than fuch as have always lived
in the Country.

  24 *Numquid eft aliud mali,* &c. It is not
without reafon, that *Laches* puts this Queftion to *Parmeno,* becaufe it was plain, he
had difcovered all through mere fear, and
againft his will. He might naturally enough
fufpect, therefore, that *Parmeno* had concealed fome things from him, and he thought
it fit, that he fhould know all, that he might
be the better able to prevent whatever Mif-

chief threatned.

  26 *Ceffo huc intro irrumpere ?* The fear and
concern the old Man is in, will eafily account for his fudden Confent to the Marriage. For expecting to fee his Son in fo
great danger, and not knowing but the Mifchief might be already beyond Remedy,
when he found the Virgin a Citizen of
Athens, and of a very confiderable Family,
his Son in love with her, and her Brother
confenting to the Match : this fudden Tran-
fition, from Grief to Joy, difpofed him to
agree frankly to the Propofal.

ACTUS

ACT V. SCENE VII.

ARGUMENT.

Pythias *derides* Parmeno, *for betraying himself, and being imposed upon so easily.*

PYTHIAS, PARMENO.

Pythias. NEVER, I swear did any thing happen to me in Life, that pleased me better, than to see the old Man come hurrying upon us, full of his Mistake. The Jest was all to myself, because I knew what he feared.

Parm. What's the matter now?

Pyt. I am now come out to meet with *Parmeno*, but where in the world can he be?

Parm. She wants me, I perceive.

Pyt. O I see him: I'll go to him.

Parm. What's the matter, Fool? What would you be at? Why do you laugh? What, never have done?

Pyt. O dreadful! I'm perfectly tired with laughing at you.

Parm. Why so?

Pyt. Do you ask? I never saw, nor shall see in my Life, a greater Fool. It is not possible to express what Sport you have made us within. I once thought you a shrewd cunning Fellow. What? should you have presently believed every thing I said? Was you not satisfied with the Crime you had put the young Gentleman upon, but you must also betray him to his Father? For how great do you think was his Confusion, when his Father saw him in that Dress? What? Do you know that you have utterly ruined yourself?

Parm. Ha! What say'st thou, Wretch? Have you lyed to me? Do you laugh at me too? Is it so pleasant then to make a Jest of us, you Jade?

Pyt. The pleasantest in the world.

Parm. If you escape unpunished.

Pyt. True.

Parm. I'll give it you, by *Jove*.

Pyt. I believe it: but good Mr. *Parmeno*, it may require, perhaps,

ANNOTATIONS.

Pythias had not yet taken her full Revenge on *Parmeno*, she was still resolved to torment him further, and for that purpose, owns the Trick she had but just now put upon him; yet withal adds, that being discovered both as the Adviser and Betrayer of the Plot, both had united against him, in a desire of taking vengeance. When *Parmeno*, provoked at this Insult, threatens a severe Revenge, she only laughs at him, and leaves him, as one whose Threats she knew could not affect her.

[10] *At etiam primo callidum ac disertum credidi hominem. Disertus* here is not to be understood *eloquent*, in which Sense it is frequently used by the Poets, but one of quick Discernment, who can't be easily imposed upon or deceived. An ingenious Man can easily prevent, or extricate himself from any Difficulties. Hence, Letters are called *diserta*, when written with a great deal of Wit and Humour. Cicero Fam. l.l. ...

ACTUS V. SCENA VII.

ARGUMENTUM.

*Pythias muliebri cachinno Parmenonem irridet, quod seipsum pro-
diderit, & decipiendum præbuerit.*

PYTHIAS, PARMENO.

NUnquam edepol quidquam jamdiu, quod magi'
   vellem evenire,   [nit errans.
Mi evenit, quàm quòd modò senex intro ad nos ve-
Mihi solæ ridiculo fuit, quæ, quid timeret, scibam
PA. Quid hoc autem est? PY. nunc id prodeo, ut
   conveniam Parmenonem.
Sed ubi, obsecro, est? PA. me quærit hæc. PY. atque
   eccum video. adibo.   5
PA. Quid est, inepta? quid tibi vis? quid rides? per-
   gin'? PY. perii: [PY. rogitas?
Defessa jam sum misera te ridendo. PA. quid ita?
Nunquam pol hominem stultiorem vidi, nec videbo. ah,
Non sati' potest narrari, quos ludos præbueris intus.
At etiam primò callidum ac disertum credidi hominem.
Quid? illicone credere ea, quæ dixi, oportuit te? 11
An pœnitebat flagitii, te auctore quod fecisset
Adolescens, ni miserum insuper etiam patri indicares?
Nam quid illi credis animi tum fuisse, ubi vestem vidit
Illam esse eum indutum pater? quid? jam scis te periisse?
PA. Ehem, quid dixti, pessuma? an mentita es? etiam
   rides?   16
Itan' lepidum tibi visum est, scelus, nos irridere? PY.
   nimiùm.
PA. Siquidem istuc impunè habueris. PY. verùm. PA.
   reddam hercle. PY. credo.
Sed in diem istuc, Parmeno, est fortasse, quod minitare:

ORDO.

PY. EDepol, nun-
   quam quid-
quam evenit mihi
jamdiu, quod magis
vellem evenire, quàm
quòd senex modò in-
tro venit ad nos er-
rans. Fuit ridiculo
mihi soli, quæ scibam,
quid timeret. PA.
Quid autem est hoc?
PY. Nunc prodeo
propter id, ut con-
veniam Parmenonem.
Sed, obsecro, ubi est?
PA. Hæc quærit me.
PY. Atque eccum
video. Adibo. PA.
Quid est, inepta?
Quid vis tibi? Prop-
ter quid rides? Per-
gisne? PY. Perii:
ego misera sum jam
defessa ridendo te.
PA. Quid ita? PY.
Rogitas? Pol nun-
quam vidi, nec vi-
debo hominem stultio-
rem. Ah, non potest
satis narrari, quos
ludos præbueris in-
tus. At etiam primò
credidi te hominem
callidum ac disertum.
Quid? oportuit ne te

credere illico ea, quæ dixi? An pœnitebat flagitii, quod adolescens fecisset, te auctore, ni insuper
etiam indicares eum miserum patri? Nam quid credis tum fuisse animi illi, ubi pater vidit eum
esse indutum illam vestem? Quid? Scis jam te periisse? PA. Ehem, pessuma, quid dixisti? An es
mentita? Etiam rides? Estne visum tibi ita lepidum, o scelesta, irridere nos? PY. Nimium. PA.
Siquidem habueris istuc impune. PY. Verum. PA. Reddam hercle. PY. Credo. Sed istuc, quod
minitare, Parmeno, est fortasse in diem.

ANNOTATIONS.

starchus Homeri versum negat, quem non pro-
bat, sic tu (libet enim mihi jocari) quod disertum non erit, ne putaris meum. " But if,
" as you write me, these Letters were not
" diverting, know that they were not mine;
" for as Aristarchus, when he met with a
" Line he did not like, denied it to be Ho-
" mer's, so would I have you (for there is no

" harm in jesting) to think whatever is
" not witty, not written by me."
12 An pœnitebat flagitii. This is not
to be explained, did you repent? But was
you not contented? For so Cicero Fam. I. 7.
Me meæ (fortunæ) ne nimium pœniteret, tua
virtute perfectum est.

haps, another Day to fulfil these Threats of yours: you'll be hung up directly, for training on a young Gentleman to Crimes, and then betraying him to his Father. Both will join in making an Example of you.

Parm. I'm ruin'd.

Pyt. This is the Reward you have to expect for your Services: Farewel.

Parm. Wretch that I am, I have this Day, like a Rat, betrayed myself to my own Ruin.

ACT V. SCENE VIII.

ARGUMENT.

Thraso *returns to* Thais, *not with hostile Designs as before, but to surrender at Discretion, and profess himself her Slave; in imitation of* Hercules, *upon whom* Omphale *imposed the Task of spinning.*

GNATHO, THRASO.

Gnatho. WHAT now? With what Hope or Design come we hither? What do you intend, *Thraso?*

Thr. Who, I? to surrender myself to *Thais,* and do whatever she would have me.

Gnat. How, Sir?

Thr. Why should I be less submissive here, than *Hercules* formerly was to *Omphale?*

Gnat. The Example charms me. I wish I might see her soundly break your Head with her Slipper: But her Door opens.

Thr. Death! What Mischief now? I never saw this Man before: What can be the Meaning of his coming out in so violent a Hurry?

ANNOTATIONS.

Thraso, impatient to be again reconciled to *Thais,* appears here with a Resolution of professing an entire Submission, referring, in the usual way of his Vanity, to the Example of *Hercules,* whom he proposes as his Pattern.

¹ *Quid nunc? qua spe?* The Reader ought to remember, that this is the very Person, who before, speaking to the Soldier concerning *Thais,* had said *Jamdudum te amat;* and again, *Jam tibi hæc aderit supplicans ultro.* And here you may see the usual End of Flattery; for the same Person, who before had given him Hopes, endea-

vours now to throw him into Despair. It is worth notice too, that *Gnatho* is always drawn away from Table with Reluctance; for before, in the Quarrel, it is evident from *Thraso's* Words, that *Gnatho* followed against his will. *Hanccine ego ut contumeliam tantam, tam insignem in me accipiam, Gnatho? Mori me satius est.* The Parasite, although tended at present yet asks here, *qua spe, aut quo consilio?* that the Audience might also be informed of it.

³ *Qui minus quam Hercules servivit Om-phale.*

Tu jam pendebis, qui ftultum adolefcentulum nobilitas   20
Flagitiis,& eundem indicasi uterque in te exempla edent.
PA: Nullus fum. PY. hic pro illo munere tibi honos
eft habitus; abeo.
PA. Egomet meo indicio mifer, quafi forex, hodie perii.
tibi pro illo munere. abeo. PA. *Egomet mifer, quafi forex, perii hodie meo indicio.*

Tu jam pendebis, qui nobilitas ftultum a-dolefcentulum flagi-tiis, & indicas eun-dem. Uterque edent exempla in te. PA; Sum nullus. PY. Hic bonos eft habitus

---

ACTUS V. SCENA VIII.

ARGUMENTUM.

Redit ad Thaidem Thrafo, non animo bellandi, ut prius, fed ut deditionem faciat, feque illi tradat in fervitutem: idque Her-culis exemplo, qui Omphalæ fervivit in lanificio.

GNATHO, THRASO.

QUID nunc? quâ fpe, au quo confilio huc imus?
quid cœptas, Thrafo?
TH. Egone? ut Thaidi me dedam, & faciam quod ju-
beat. GN. Quid eft?   [exemplum placet.
TH. Quî minu', quàm Hercules fervivit Omphale? GN.
Utinam tibi commitigari videam fandalio caput.
Sed fores crepuerunt ab eâ; TH. perii, quid hoc au-
tem eft mali?   5
Hunc ego nunquam videram etiam. quidnam prope-
rans hinc profilit?

ORDO.
GN. Quid nunc? Quâ fpe, aut quo confilio imus huc? Quid cœptas, Thrafo? TH. Ego-ne? ut dedam me Thaidi, & faciam quod jubest. GN. Quid eft? TH. Quî minus, quàm her-cules fervivit Om-phale? GN. Ex-emplum placet. Uti-nam videam com-

mitigari caput tibi fandalio. Sed fores crepuerunt ab eâ. TH. Perii: autem quid mali eft hoc? ego nunquam etiam videram hunc. Quidnam hic profilit properans.

ANNOTATIONS.

thale. Terence preferves the Character of the Soldier to the laft. If he fpeaks of Sub-miffion to his Miftrefs, he muft do it in terms of War, *ut Thaidi me dedam: that I may furrender at Difcretion.* If he wants to excufe an Action, that has an Appearance of Weaknefs, he muft do it from fome great Example. Juft fo, in marfhalling his Army, he pretended to follow the renowned Pyrr-bus. . Omphale was a Queen of *Lydia,* with whom *Hercules* falling in love, fhe impofed upon him the tafk of working in Wool, and herfelf changed the Spindle, Diftaff, and other female Weapons, for his Arrows, Club, and Lion's Skin.

4 *Utinam tibi commitigari videam fanda.io caput.* There was probably, fometimes, reprefented upon the *Athenian* Stage, a Co-medy of the Loves of *Omphale* and *Hercules,* in which that Hero was feen fpinning of Wool, and his Miftrefs fitting by, and beat-ing him with her Slipper, when he did wrong.

ACT V. SCENE IX.

ARGUMENT.

Chærea *is overjoyed with the Assurance of having* Pamphila *to Wife with his Father's Consent, and at length breaks out in Commendation of* Thais.

CHÆREA, PARMENO, GNATHO, THRASO.

Chærea. O My Countrymen! Is there, in the world, a Creature happier than myself? not one for certain : for 'tis plain, that the Gods have manifested all their Power in me, on whom so many Blessings are bestowed at once.

Parm. How comes he to be so joyful?

Chær. O my *Parmeno!* the Contriver, Beginner, and Compleater of all my Joys: do you know how happy I am? Do you know that my *Pamphila* is found to be a Citizen of *Athens?*

Parm. I have heard it.

Chær. Do you know that she is my Bride?

Parm. Good News, as I hope for Heaven.

Gnat. (*To Thraso.*) Do you hear, Sir, what he says?

Chær. Besides, I have this to give me Joy, that my Brother *Phædria's* Mistress is secured to him. We are now become one Family. *Thais* has begged my Father's Patronage, and put herself wholly under his Care and Protection.

Parm. Thais is, therefore, wholly your Brother's.

Chær. Wholly.

Parm. This then is also another Reason for our Joy, that the Soldier is discarded.

Chær. Do you take care that my Brother, wherever he is, may hear of this as soon as possible.

Parm. I'll go see for him at home.

Thr. Do you now question, *Gnatho,* but that I am ruined for ever?

Gnat. I make no manner of doubt of it.

Chær. (*To himself.*) Where shall I begin first, or whom commend most? Him, who gave me the Advice how to act, or myself; who had the Courage to venture upon it? Or, shall I praise Fortune, who conducted all, and made so many important Circumstances fall out so seasonably in one day? Or the easy Indulgence of my Father? O *Jupiter* grant, I beg of you, the Continuance of these Blessings.

ANNOTATIONS.

We are to suppose, that when the old Man went in to *Thais,* to prevent the Mischief he fancied threatned his Son, he was there made acquainted with every thing, and finding the young Lady a Citizen of Family, and *Chærea* distractedly in love with her, consented to the Marriage. *Chærea* who desired nothing so much, comes here, out from *Thais,* with great Exclamations of Joy. *Parmeno,* who expected the severest Treatment, wonders to hear himself addressed as one, who had done him the greatest good Offices : being at last informed of what had happened, he is sent to give

Phædria

ACT

ACTUS V. SCENA IX.

ARGUMENTUM.

Chærea juveniliter exultat, quod Pamphilam permissu parentis sit uxorem habiturus. Dein & laus Thaidis continetur.

CHÆREA, PARMENO, GNATHO, THRASO.

O Populares, ecquis me vivit hodie fortunatior?
Nemo hercle quisquam: nam in me planè Di potestatem suam [moda.
Omnem ostendêre, cui tam subito tot contigerint com-
PA. Quid hic lætus est? CH. ô Parmeno mi, ô mearum voluptatum omnium [gaudiis?
Inventor, inceptor, perfector! scin' me in quibus sim
Scis Pamphilam meam inventam civem? PA. audivi. CH. scis sponsam mihi?
PA. Bene, ita me Dii ament, factum. GN. audin' tu, hic quid ait? CH. tum autem Phædriæ
Meo fratri gaudeo amorem esse omnem in tranquillo: una est domus:
Thais patri se commendavit: in clientelam & fidem
Nobis dedit se. PA. fratris igitur Thais tota est. CH. scilicet. [foras.
PA. Jam hoc aliud est, quod gaudeamus: miles pellitur
CH. Tum tu, frater, ubi ubi est, fac quamprimum hæc audiat. PA. visam domi. [petuo perierim?
TH. Numquid, Gnatho, tu dubitas, quin ego nunc per-
GN. Sine dubio, opinor. CH. quid commemorem primum, aut laudem maxume? [qui id ausu' sim
Illum qui mihi dedit consilium ut facerem; an me;
Incipere? an fortunam collaudem, quæ gubernatrix fuit, [clusit diem? an
Quæ tot res, tantas, tam opportunè in unum con-
Mei patris festivitatem & facilitatem? ô Jupiter,
Serva, obsecro, hæc nobis bona.

ORDO.

CH. O *Populares ecquis homo vivit hodie fortunatior me? hercle nemo quisquam; nam Dii planè ostendêre omnem suam potestatem in me, cui tot commoda tam subito contigerint.* PA. *Propter quid est hic lætus?* CH. *O mi Parmeno, O inventor, inceptor, perfector, omnium mearum voluptatum! Scisne me in quibus sim gaudiis? Scis meam Pamphilam esse inventam civem?* PA. *Audivi.* CH. *Scis illam esse sponsam mihi?* PA. *ita Dii ament me, bene factum.* GN. *Audisne tu, quid hic ait?* CH. *Tum autem gaudeo amorem omnem esse in tranquillo meo fratri Phædriæ: domus est una: Thais commendavit se patri: dedit se nobis in clientelam & fidem.* PA. *Igitur Thais est tota fratris.* CH. *Scilicet.* PA. *Hoc jam est aliud, propter quod gaudeamus; miles pellitur foras.* CH. *Ubi ubi, frater est, fac audiat hæc primum.* PA. *Visam domum.* TH. *Gnatho, numquid tu dubitas quin ego nunc perierim perpetuo?* GN. *Opinor, sine dubio.* CH. *Quid primum commemorem, aut maxime laudem? Illumne, qui dedit consilium mihi, ut facerem? An me, qui sim ausus incipere? An collaudem fortunam, quæ fuit gubernatrix: Quæ conclusit tot, tantas que res tam opportunè in unum diem? An festivitatem & felicitatem mei patris? O Jupiter; obsecro, serva hæc bona nobis.*

ANNOTATIONS.

Phædria an account of the good news.

[8] *Amorem esse omnem in tranquillo.* A Metaphor taken from a calm and unruffled Sea (in speaking of which the word *tranquillus* is almost always used), and applied here with great Propriety; because there is nothing more common with Poets, than to compare the Fickleness and Instability of a Mistress, to a stormy tempestuous Sea. So *Horace* Carm. I. 5. 5.

> *Simplex munditiis! heu, quoties fidem*
> *Mutatosque deos flebit; & aspera*
> *Nigris æquora ventis*
> *Emirabitur insolens;*
> *Qui nunc te fruitur credulus aurea.*

ACT V. SCENE X.

ARGUMENT.

Phædria *informed of every thing is filled with Joy. The Soldier too, at the Intercession of the Parasite, is admitted to share of* Thais's *Favours, which concludes the Play.*

PHÆDRIA, CHÆREA, GNATHO, THRASO.

Phædria. GOOD Heavens, what incredible things has *Parmeno* just now told me! But where is my Brother?

Chær. Just at hand.

Phæd. I'm quite transported.

Chær. I verily believe it. No one, Brother, deserves better to be loved, than this *Thais* of yours, she has so greatly obliged all our Family.

Phæd. Hey! Do you commend her too to me?

Thr. I'm undone: the less Ground I have to hope, the more I am in love. For Heaven's sake, *Gnatho*; all my Hope is in you.

Gnat. What would you have me do?

Thr. Obtain for me, either by Entreaties or Money, that I may share a little of *Thais*'s Favours.

Gnat. 'Tis a hard Task.

Thr. If you set about it in good earnest, I know what you can do. Obtain but this for me, and ask what Gift or Reward you please, you shall have it.

Gnat. Say you so?

Thr. I positively promise.

Gnat. If I do it then, I desire, that your House, whether you are present or absent, may be always open to me, and that without Invitation, I may always take my place at your Table.

Thr. Upon Honour it shall be so.

Gnat. I'll set about it then.

Phæd. Whose Voice do I hear, O *Thraso!*

Thr. Your Servant, Gentlemen.

Phæd. Perhaps you don't know what has happened here.

Thr. I know all.

Phæd. How come I then to see you in this quarter?

Thr. I depend upon your Goodness.

Phæd. Do you know what Dependance you have? I tell you, Captain, if I ever after meet you in this Street, it will be in vain to say, *I was looking for another, my business lay this way:* you shall have no Quarter.

Gnat. Hush: this were ungenerous.

Phæd. 'Tis resolved.

Gnat. I did not imagine you were so stout.

Phæd. But you'll find it so. Gnat.

ANNOTATIONS.

This Scene contains the Conclusion of the | passed, comes to look for his Brother, and,
Play. *Phædria*, informed of all that had | spying the Soldier, discharges him from
making

ACTUS V. SCENA X.

ARGUMENTUM.

Phædria, de omnibus rebus certior factus, lætator. Tum etiam
miles parasiti precibus, nonnulla in parte recipitur apud
Thaidem, & ita absolvitur catastrophe utriusque partis fabulæ.

PHÆDRIA, CHÆREA, GNATHO, THRASO,

ORDO

D I voftram fidem ! incredibilia
   Parmeno modò quæ narravit ! fed ubi eft frater?
   CH. præfto adeft.   [ter tuâ
PH. Gaudeo. CH. fatis credo. nihil eft Thaide hac, fra-
Dignius quod ametur? ità noftræ omni eft fautrix fa-
   miliæ. PH. hui !
Mihi illam laudas? TH. perii ; quanto minu' fpei eft,
   tantò magis amo.   5
Obfecro, Gnatho, in te fpes eft. GN. quid vis faciam?
   TH: perfice hoc   [apud Thaidem.
Precibus, precio, ut hæream in parte aliquâ tandem
GN. Difficile eft. TH. fi quid conlibuit, novi te. hoc
   fi effeceris,   [feres.
Quodvis donum, præmium à me optato, id optatum
GN. Itane ? TH. fic erit. GN. fi efficio hoc, poftulo
   ut tua mihi domus,   10
Te præfente, abfente, pateat, invocato ut fit locus
Semper. TH. do fidem futurum. GN. accingar. PH.
   quem hic ego audio ?   [fient,
O Thrafo. TH. falvete. PH. tu fortaffe, quæ facta hic
Nefcis. TH. fcio. PH. cur te ergo in his ego confpicor
   regionibus ?
TH. Vobis fretus. PH. fcis quàm fretus ? miles, edico
   tibi,   15
Si te in plateâ offendero hac poft unquam, quod dicas
   mihi,   [haud fic decet.
Alium quærebam, iter hac habui: periifti. GN. eja,
PH. Dictum eft. GN. non cognofco voftrum tam fu-
   perbum. PH. fic erit.

ORDO

PH. D II voftram
fidem ! quæ
incredibilia Parmeno
modò narravit.mihi !
Sed ubi eft frater ?
CH. Adeft præfto.
PH. Gaudeo. CH.
Credo fatis. Nihil,
frater, eft dignius
quod ametur; bac tua
Thaide ; ita eft fau-
trix omni noftræ fa-
miliæ. PH. Hui!
laudas illam mibi ?
TH. Perii ; quanto
eft minus fpei mibi,
tanto magis amo. Ob-
fecro, Gnatho, mea
fpes eft in te. GN.
Quid vis ut faciam ?
TH. Perfice hic pre-
cibus, aut precio, ut
tandem hæream in
aliquâ parte apud
Thaidem. GN. Eft
difficile. TH. Novi
te, fi quid culibuit,
perficere poffe ; fi
effeceris hoc, optato
quodvis donum vel
præmium à me feres
id optatum. GN.
Itane ? TH. Erit fic.
GN. Si efficio hoc,
poftulo ut tua domus
pateat mihi, te præ-
fente vel abfente ; ut
femper fit locus mihi

invocato. TH. Do fidem hoc futurum. GN. Accingar. PH. Quem ego audio hic ? O Thrafo.
TH. Salvete. PH. Fortaffe tu nefcis, quæ fint facta hic. TH. Scio. PH. Cur ergo ego confpicor te in his regionibus ? TH. Fretus vobis. PH. Scifne quàm fretus ? miles, edico tibi, fi
unquam poft offendero te in hac plateâ, quod dicas mibi, Quærebam alium, habui iter hac :
periifti. GN. Eia, haud decet fic. PH. Eft dictum. GN. Non cognofco veftrum tam fuper-
bum. PH. Sic erit.

ANNOTATIONS.

making any Approaches near that Street.
At laft, by the cunning Infinuations of Gnatho, he is received into the Society, and all

ends happily, and to the Content of the feveral Perfons concerned.

18 *Non cognofco* &c. Here we are

R 3   to

Gnat. Hear me first a little. When I have done, if my Proposal pleases, agree to it.

Phæd. Let us hear.

Gnat. Do you retire from us a little, *Thraso.* First, I would have you both be verily perfuaded, that whatever I do in this cafe, is wholly for my own Sake. But if the fame is alfo for your Advantage, it will be imprudent not to comply with it.

Phæd. What is it then?

Gnat. I would have you to let the Captain, your Rival, make one amongft you.

Phæd. What! One amongft us!

Gnat. Only confider. You, *Phædria,* live at a very free Rate with your Miftrefs, and feaft high. It is but little, that you can afford to give, and *Thais* muft receive a great deal; to be able to carry on her Amour with you, without putting you to too great an Expence. For all this, no one can be more convenient, or more to your Wifh, than the Soldier. For firft he has enough to give, and no one gives more liberally. He is a Fool, an Ideot, a dull Wretch, fnores Day and Night: nor need you be afraid of your Miftrefs's falling in love with him, you may have him difcarded when you will.

Phæd. (to *Chærea.*) What had we beft do?

Gnat. Befides, there is another thing, which, I think, yet more than all the reft, no one entertains better, or with more Generofity.

Phæd. A hundred to one, but we may have occafion for this Fool in fome fhape or other.

Chær. I'm of your Mind too.

Gnat. You judge right. But I have ftill one Requeft to make, that I may be admitted into your Fraternity; this is what I have all along aimed at.

Phæd. We admit you.

Chær. And frankly too.

Gnat. And I, in requital, *Phædria* and *Chærea,* give him up to be fleeced and derided by you as much as you will.

Chær. Agreed.

Phæd. He deferves it.

Gnat. *Thraso,* you may advance towards us when you will.

Thr. Pray, how do Matters ftand?

Gnat. How? they did not know you. But when I had informed them of your good Qualities, and given you thofe Praifes, which your Actions and Virtues deferve, I obtained all.

Thr. You have done well. Gentlemen, I return you Thanks. I never yet was in any Place, where all People did not love me mightily.   *Gnat.*

ANNOTATIONS.

to fupply, as *Donatus* obferves, *ingenium, ani-* | this Paffage, it muft be obferved, that *pro-pium merum, induftum,* or fome fuch Word. | *pinare* was faid, properly, of thofe, who af-3° *Hunc comedendum & deridendum vobis* | ter they had drank themfelves, gave the Cup *propino.* To enter into all the Elegance of | to him, whofe Health they had drank.

Gn. Prius audite paucis: quod cùm dixero, si placuerit,
Facitote. Ph. audiamùs. Gn. tu concede paulùm istuc.
   Thraso. 20
Principio ego vos ambos credere hoc mihi vehementer
   velim, [mea.
Me, hujus quidquid faciam, id facere maxumè causâ
Verùm si idem vobis prodest, vos non facere inscitia est.
Ph. Quid id est? Gn. militem ego rivalem recipiun-
   dum censeo. Ph. hem, [Phædria, 25
Recipiundum? Gn. cogita modo. tu herclè cùm illâ,
Et libenter vivis, etenim bene libenter victitas.
Quod des paululum est; necesse est multum, accipere
   Thaidem,
Ut tuo amori suppeditare possit sine sumtu tuo; ad
Omnia hæc magis opportunus, nec magis ex usu tuo,
Nemo est. principio & habet quod det, & dat nemo
   largius:
Fatuus est, insulsus, tardus, stertit noctes & dies:
Neque tu istum metuas ne amet mulier: pellas facile,
   ubi velis. [vel primum puto;
Ph. Quid agimus? Gn. præterea hoc etiam, quod ego
Accipit homo nemo meliùs prorsum, neque prolixius.
Ph. Mirum, ni illoc homine quoquo pacto opus est.
   Ch. idem arbitror. 35
Gn. Rectè facitis. unum etiam hoc vos oro, ut me in
   vostrum gregem [pimus.
Recipiatis. satis diu hoc jam saxum volvo. Ph. reci-
Ch. Ac libenter. Gn. at ego pro illoc, Phædria, &
   tu Chærea, [Ch. placet.
Hunc comedendum & deridendum vobis propino.
Ph. Dignus est. Gn. Thraso, ubi vis, accede. Th.
   obsecro te, quid agimus? 40
Gn. Quid? isti te ignorabant. postquam eis mores
   ostendi tuos,
Et collaudavi secundum facta & virtutes tuas,
Impetravi. Th. bene fecisti. gratiam habeo maxumam.
Nunquam etiam fui usquam, quin me omnes amarent
   plurimùm. 44

Gn. Prius audite paucis, quod cùm dixero, si placuerit, facitote. Ph. Audiamus. Gn. Tu, Thraso, concede istuc paulùm. Principio ego vehementer velim vos ambos credere mihi hoc, ut quidquid Eujus rei ego facio, me facere id maxumè meâ causâ. Verùm si idem prodest vobis, inscitia est si vos non facere. Ph. Quid est id? Gn. Ego censeo militem rivalem esse recipiundam. Ph. Hem, recipiundum? Gn. Modo cogita. Tu herclè, Phædria, & vivis libentur cum illâ, etenim victitas bene libenter. Quod des paululum, necesse est Thaidem accipere multum; ut possit suppeditare tuo amori sine sumtu. Nemo est magis opportunus ad omnia hæc, nec magis ex tuo usu. Principio & habet quod det, & nemo dat largius. Est fatuus, insulsus, tardus, stertit noctes & dies, neque metuas ne mulier amet istum: facile pellus, ubi velis. Ph. Quid agimus? Gn. Præterea hoc etiam, quod ego puto vel primum, nemo homo accipit meliùs prorsum, neque prolixius. Ph. Mirum ni opus est illoc homine quoquo pacto. Ch. Ego ar-

bitror idem. Gn. Facitis rectè. Ego etiam oro vos hoc unum, ut recipiatis me in vestrum gregem. Jam satis diu volvo hoc saxum. Ph. Recipimus. Ch. Ac libenter. Gn. At ego, Phædria, & tu, Chærea, pro istoc, propino hunc comedendum & deridendum vobis. Ch. Placet. Gn. Thraso, accede ubi vis. Th. Obsecro te, quid agimus? Gn. Quid? Isti ignorabant te. Postquam ostendi tuos mores eis, & collaudavi te secundum tua facta, & tuas virtutes, impetravi. Th. Fecisti bene: habeo maximam gratiam tibi. Ego nunquam fui etiam usquam, quin omnes amaverint mi plurimum.

ANNOTATIONS.

The Pleasantry, therefore, of the Passage (usual signification of the Word, which was) consists in this, that Gnatho (though) the also only to express Drinking, and im-

Gnat. Did not I tell you, that he was a perfect Master of the *Athenian* Elegance and Politeneſs?

Phæd. He perfectly anſwers the Character you gave him. Come along with us. *(To the Spectators.)* Farewel, and give us your Applauſe.

A·N·N·O·T·A·T·I·O·N·S.

ploys it, in ſpeaking of a thing ſolid; which was given to be eat. *Plato*, in like manner, | ſays of *Saturn*, that *he drank up his Children*, inſtead of, that *he devoured them.*
Muretus

T H E

Gn. Dixin? ego vobis in hoc esse Atticam elegantiam ſ
Ph. Nil præter promissum est. Gn. ite hac. Vos valete,
   & plaudite.

C A L L I O P I U S R E C E N S U I.

Gn. Dixine ego vo-
bis Atticam ele-
gantiam esse in hoc ?
Ph. Nil eſt præter
promiſſum: Gn. Ita
hac. Vos valete.

& plaudite.

A N N O T A T I O N S.

Muretus is, therefore, guilty of a Mistake, | reading *præbeo* for *propino*. Dacier.
in pretending to correct this Passage, and |

P U B L I I

TERENTII

HEAUTONTIMORUMENOS.

TERENCE's

HEAUTONTIMORUMENOS

THE

HEAUTONTIMORUMENOS.

OF

TERENCE.

The TITLE,

THIS PLAY WAS EXHIBITED AT THE MEGA-
LENSIAN GAMES, WHEN L. CORNELIUS LEN-
TULUS, AND L. VALERIUS FLACCUS WERE
CURULE ÆDILES. IT WAS ACTED BY THE
COMPANIES OF L. AMBIVIUS TURPIO, AND
L. ATTILIUS PRÆNESTINUS. FLACCUS,
THE FREED MAN OF CLAUDIUS, COMPO-
SED THE MUSICK. IT IS FROM THE GREEK
OF MENANDER. IT WAS ACTED THE
FIRST TIME WITH UNEQUAL FLUTES,
AFTERWARDS WITH TWO RIGHT HAND-
ED FLUTES. IT WAS ACTED ALSO A THIRD
TIME, UNDER THE CONSULSHIP OF TI,
SEMPRONIUS AND MARCUS JUVENTIUS,

ANNOTATIONS.

We have very little to say by way of Remark upon this Prologue, be-cause every thing in it may be suffi-ciently understood from what has been said upon the two foregoing.

The most material Circumstance in it is, that as it was several times acted, so the Musick that accompa-nied it was different. From this we learn, that in composing the Mu-sick,

P. TERENTII

HEAUTONTIMORUMENOS.

TITULUS seu DIDASCALIA.

ORDO.

ACTA LUDIS MEGALENSIBUS, L. CORNELIO LENTULO, L. VALERIO FLACCO, ÆDILIBUS CURULIBUS. EGERE L. AMBIVIUS TURPIO, L. ATTILIUS PRÆNESTINUS. MODOS FECIT FLACCUS CLAUDI. GRÆCA EST MENANDRU. ACTA PRIMUM TIBIIS IMPARIBUS, DEINDE DUABUS DEXTRIS. ACTA ETIAM TERTIO, TI. SEMPRONIO, M. JUVENTIO COSS.

HÆC comœdia fuit acta ludis Megalensibus, L. Cornelio Lentulo, L. Valerio Flacco Ædilibus Curulibus. L. Ambivius Turpio, L. Attilius Prænestinus egere. Flaccus Libertus Claudii fecit modos. Est Græca Menandru. Acta fuit primum tibiis imparibus, deinde duabus dextris. Ac-

ta fuit etiam tertio, Ti. Sempronio, M. Juventio consulibus.

ANNOTATIONS.

sick, Regard was not had so much to the Nature and Genius of the Play, as to the Occasion on which it was acted, whether of Mirth, Sadness, or Religion. But as all these things have been explained at large, in what we have said relating to the Music of the *Roman* Stage, I refer to that for full Satisfaction. It is not easy to determine the Time of its first and second Representation, because the Consuls are not nam'd; but it was acted, we are told, the third Time, when *Tiberius Sempronius Gracchus*, and *Marcus Juventius Thalma*, were Consuls; which happened in the 590 Year of the City, and 163 Years before the Birth of Christ, three Years after the first Representation of the *Andrian*.

M.

The ARGUMENT to the HEAUTON-TIMORUMENOS, *from* MURETUS.

CHREMES gives command to his Wife, big with Child, that if she should be delivered of a Girl, she should immediately kill it. For so little Humanity was there in the Manners of the Ancients, that altho' there are none even among the most savage Brutes, but discover a Fondness for their Young, yet they, when they had no mind to bring up Children, thought it lawful to expose or destroy them immediately after the Birth. Sostrata, being brought to Bed of a Girl (as the Mother has generally more of Softness and Tenderness in her Nature) could not bear to take away its Life, but gave it to a certain poor Woman of Corinth, whose Name was Philtera, to be exposed, and, through a piece of female Superstition, taking a Ring from her Finger, ordered her to expose it along with the Child. This, which at the time when it was done, might look like Folly, yet, afterwards, saved the Girl; for by means of this Ring she came to be known by her Relations. The old Woman, upon receiving the Child, names her Antiphila; and educates her as her own; when she was grown up, and believed by every body to be this old Woman's Daughter, Clinia, the Son of Menedemus, fell desperately in love with her, insomuch, that he lived with her in such a manner, as if she had been his Wife; which, when his Father knew, he took it so ill, that by constantly chiding his Son, he drove him to fly into Asia, to serve in the Wars under the King of Persia. Then he, who had been so uneasy at his Son's Love, began to be much more uneasy at his Absence. Therefore, to punish himself for that unseasonable Severity, which had forced his Son to abandon his native Country, he sells his House, Furniture, and Slaves, except such, as might be useful to him for labouring in the Country, and purchases a large Farm, and, from Morning to Night, not only holds his Servants employed, but also fatigues himself beyond all Bounds; he's now in his sixtieth Year. After Clinia's Departure, Philtera, who, as we have observed, was reputed the Mother of Antiphila, died. Clinia, after an Absence of three Months, no longer able to support the Impatience of not seeing his Mistress, returns, but not daring to appear before his Father, as dreading his former Severity, he is entertained by Clitipho, the Son of Chremes, with whom he had lived in the greatest Friendship from a Child. Clitipho overjoyed at his Companion's Return, tho' it was now late, sends Syrus and Dromo, two Slaves, into the City, to bring Antiphila to her Lover. That very Day Menedemus had discovered to Chremes, how desirous he was to have his Son come back, insomuch, that at first, Chremes, when he understood that Clinia was returned, thought of sending immediately to let his Father know. However, he delay'd till next Day, because Syrus thought it would answer better. This Syrus was a Slave of great Cunning, and a daring Temper, who being sent for Antiphila, brought also Bacchis along with him.

M. Aur. Mureti ARGUMENTUM.

CHREMES Sostratæ uxori gravidæ imperat, si puellam pareret, ut eam statim interficeret. Fuit hæc immanitas in veterum moribus, ut, quum fera nulla sit, quæ fœtus suos non diligat, ipsi quam alere nollent liberos, eos recens natos, aut interficere, aut exponere fas sibi tarent. Sostrata puellam enixa (ut est maternus semper animus clementior) vitam ei adimere non sustinuit: sed pauperculæ cuidam anui Corinthiæ, Philteræ nomine, exponendam dedit: eamque, muliebri quadam superstitione, annulum, ae digito detractum suo, jussit, ut una cum puella exponeret. Id, quod tum stulte factum videri poterat, postea puellæ saluti fuit; ejus enim annuli ope tandem agnita est a suis. Anus acceptam puellam Antiphilam nominat, educaique ut suam. Eam, quum adolevisset, anusque illius filia putaretur, Menedemi filius Clinia perdite amare cœpit, prope jam ut pro uxore haberet: quod ubi rescivit pater, ita violenter tulit, ut filium, assiduitate jurgandi, clam militatum in Asiam abire coegerit. Tum vero qui filii amorem iniqua animo tulerat, multo iniquiore ejusdem absentiam ferre cœpit. Itaque, ut de se supplicium absenti filio daret, qui eum sævitia sua exegisset ex ædibus, ædes, supellectilem, familiam vendit, præter, qui servi ad opus ruri faciundum utiles erant: ingentemque sibi agrum comparat, ubi a prima luce ad noctem non servos modo exerceret, verum etiam homo sexagenarius, senectutem miseris modis excruciaret suam. Profecto Clinia, Philtera quæ, ut dixi, Antiphilæ putabatur mater, extremum vitæ diem morte confecit. Clinia, quum jam menses tres abfuisset, amicæ desiderio reversus, non ausus est patri se in conspectum dare, antiquam illius asperitatem veritus, sed ad Clitiphonem, Chremetis filium, divertit, quicum magna ipsi a puero familiaritas intercesserat. Clitipho, sodalis reditu lætus, Syrum & Dromonem servos (jam autem advesperascebat) in urbem, ad arcessendam Antiphilam mittit. Exposuerat eo ipso die Menedemus Chremeti, quanto sibi desiderio esset filius; parum ut abfuerit, quin Chremes, ubi primum de reditu Cliniæ accepit, mitteret qui ei nunciaret: continuit tamen se in diem posterum, quod ita magis e re illius fore conferet Syrus, summa servus & audacia, & astutia; qui quum Antiphilam tantum arcessere jussus esset, etiam Bacchidem adduxit. Erat

hæc

him. She was a Courtezan of a bold, haughty, and expensive turn, with whom Clitipho *had some time before fallen in love. Now to conceal the Matter from* Chremes, *they concert this Project, that* Bacchis *should pass for* Clinia's *Mistress, and* Antiphila *for one of her Maids. Next Day, early in the Morning,* Chremes *goes over to* Menedemus, *and tells him of his Son's Arrival. He almost transported with Joy, wants to see and embrace his Son immediately, and give him the full Possession and Liberty of all he had. But* Chremes *counsels him to beware of doing any thing rashly, For by this means, says he, you'll ruin both him, yourself, and your Fortune; and at the same time recounts the Inconveniencies that might happen, if he discovered himself to be of so soft and easy a Disposition. For that* Clinia's *Mistress (whom he fancied to be* Bacchis) *was not in a mean Condition, or to be satisfied with a little, as formerly, but expensive, glittering with Jewels and Gold, and attended by a numerous Croud of Servants. One single Night, says he, has almost reduced me to want, and it will be vain in you to fancy, that you will be able to support the Expence, if you have her constantly to furnish out in all her Follies. What I would have you do, is this; receive your Son kindly and frankly; but conceal your Knowledge of this his Weakness, and if he endeavours, at any Time, by little Artifices, to have wherewith to supply his Mistress, suffer yourself to be deceived: for this will be a sure way of retaining him with you, and also be less expensive to yourself. This was* Chremes's *Advice, not aware, as is often the Case, that he saw clear enough abroad, but was blind at home. For* Syrus *was, in the mean time, hatching a Project, how he might cozen* Chremes *out of ten Minæ, which he had promised to procure for* Bacchis. *As he is busy in contriving with himself,* Chremes *takes him aside, and addressing him with an Air of Kindness, encourages him to think of some Project against* Menedemus. Syrus *whispers to him a Story, which he had invented to serve the present turn, that an old Woman of* Corinth, *the Mother of* Antiphila, *for so she was reputed to be, had borrowed a thousand Drachms of* Bacchis, *and that, she being since dead, the Girl was left as a Pledge for the Money. While these Things are doing,* Sostrata *happened to know her Ring, and by that means came to discover that* Antiphila *was her Daughter. Transported with Joy, she relates all to her Husband, who, though he pretends to chide her, is yet himself highly pleased at recovering his Daughter. And now every thing had been quiet, but for* Bacchis. *Ten Minæ were to be got for her, by any Means, and there was some Danger too, lest* Chremes *might come to find out, that she was his Son's Mistress. To prevent this, the daring* Syrus *forms a Project of discovering to both the old Men the Matter as it really was, and, at the same Time, fairly extricate himself from so perplexed and entangled a Business. First, therefore, says he, to* Chremes, *I have found a way of obtaining the Money from* Menedemus. *Let us pretend, that this* Bacchis *is your Son* Clitipho's *Mistress, and beg that he will suffer her to be a few Days at his House, and conceal it from you. Besides,* Clinia *shall pretend, that he is fallen*

deeply

hæc *inuetria* *procax*, *potens*, *fumptuofa*, *nobilis*, cujus *fe amore haud*
ita *pridem irretierat* Clitipho. *Quo* autem res Chremem. lateret, hoc.
confilium *capiunt*, ut *Bacchidem* quidem amicam Cliniæ, Antiphilam
vero *quam fit* illius ancillis, *effe fimularent.* Poftridie mane. Chremes ad
Menedemum diluculo proficifcitur, & rediiffe Cliniam nuntiat. Ille
gaudio amens, filium jam jam *videre*, jam jam *amplecti*, jam jam *& fe*
fuaque omnia permittere cupiebat. At Chremes, Cave, inquit *fatuus*,
hoc enim modo, & te, & eum, & rem una perdideris tuam; *fimul* ei
oftendit quod incommoda capturus fit, fi tam molli effe fe, tamque infracto
animo oftenderit. Cliniæ amicam (eam enim Bacchidem exiftimabat),
non jam pauperculam effe, aut parvo contentam, ut antea; fed fump-
tuofam, gemmis atque auro collucentem, cum familia numerofiffima. Unde
inquit mihi nox tantum non paupertatem attulit, nedum tu te. cenfeas
oneri ferendi fore, fi te illi perpetuo fumptibus fuppeditare oporteat.
Quin tu ita potius agito : Humane quidem & comiter excipito. filium,
iftum tamen tam impotens illius defiderium occultum habeto ; tum fi ille,
quod amicæ det, ut habeat, machinam adverfum te aliquam ftruet,
falli te finito ; ita & eum commodius retinebis apud te, & fumptuum minus facies. Hæc Chremes, nefcius (ut funt humana) oculatum fore
effe fe, cæcum domi. Interea enim meditabatur Syrus, decem minas,
quas Bacchidi pollicitus erat dare, eos quomodo illi à Chremete ipfo con-
ficeret ; jamque inibi erat, quum eum Chremes acceptum blande compellat, hortaturque, aliquam ad Menedemum fallaciam moliatur. Inje-
cit in fermone. Syrus mendacium a fe pro tempore confictum : anum Co-
rinthiam, Antiphilæ (ita enim putabatur) matrem, mille drachmarum mutuo accepiffe à Bacchide, ea mortua, puellam pro pecunia illa
arrhaboni reliCtam. Dum hæc aguntur, annulum fuum agnovit Softrata, ejufque judicio, Antiphilam filiam fuam effe cognovit. Gaudio
exfiliens, omnem rem defert ad virum, qui, ea leviter objurgata, re-
pertam tamen filiam, ipfe quoque gavifus eft. Jam omnia in tranquillo
erant ; abfque Bacchide fuiffet. Sed & illi quoque modo excudendæ
erant decem argenti minæ, & periculum erat, ne aliqua eam Chremes
filii amicam refcifceret. Ibi Syrus audax confilium init, quomodo &
utrique feni rem, ut erat, patefaceret, & commode fe e tam impedito negotio expediret. Primum igitur Chremeti, Repperi, inquit, quomodo argentum a Menedemo eripiam : dicemus ei, Bacchidem hanc tui Clitiphonis amicam effe : orabimufque ut eam domi fuæ dies aliquot effe patiatur ;
teque id celatum velit. Porro Clinia filia tua, quæ modo reperta eft,

deeply in love with your Daughter, lately discovered, and beg her for a Wife. What then? why, he will ask Money from his Father, to buy Ornaments for the Wedding, and then will give the Money to Bacchis. *By this time,* Bacchis, *by the Advice of* Syrus, *had passed over to* Menedemus, *and carried her whole Train along with her.* Chremes *did not, at first, approve of this Project: but, says* Syrus, *You can't honourably avoid paying down the Money, for which your Daughter was given in Pledge. Well, says* Chremes, *I will pay it, and contentedly too. Give it then, resumes* Syrus, *to* Clitipho, *and let him carry it to* Bacchis; *for, by this means* Menedemus *will the more easily be deceived into the Belief, that she is his Mistress. Let it be so then, replies* Chremes, *and immediately tells down the Money to* Clitipho, *that he may carry it to* Bacchis. *Meantime, the whole Plot is discovered.* Chremes *raging, and full of Indignation, threatens to make severe Examples of them. At length, after giving his Consent to the Match of* Clinia *with* Antiphila, *softened partly by the Intercession of* Menedemus, *partly by the Intreaties of his Wife, he forgives them.* Clitipho *promises, that he will abandon all Courtezans, and marry. This is remarkable here, that as in other Plays, the Plot exhibited takes up no more than one Day, so in this, we are under a Necessity of supposing two Days taken in.*

PER-

ARGUMENTUM.

*formam fibi complacitam effe dicet, eamque petet uxorem. Quid tu,
pecuniam, inquit, petet a patre fuo, qui novæ nuptæ ornamenta co-
emat : eam pecuniam numeraturus eft Bacchidi. Jam autem ad Menedemum, Syri hortatu, tranfierat Bacchis, & eo pompam omnem fuam
tranfduxerat. Chremes, primo non fatis confilium illud probare : at illam certe, inquit Syrus, pecuniam, pro qua filia tua oppofita erat pig-
nori, quin diffolvas, facere honefte non potes. Ego vero, inquit Chremes,
& libentur quidem. Immo vero, infit Syrus, dato eam Clitiphoni, qui
ad Bacchidem deferat : ita enim facilius credet Menedemus, eam illius
effe. Sit ita fane. Numeratur a patre Clitiphoni pecunia, quam ad meretricem perferret. Interea tota res detegitur : indignari Chremes, &
fremere, & minitari fe omnia atrociffima exempla editurum. Tandem,
quum prius Antiphilam Cliniæ collocaffet, partim Menedemi, partim
uxoris precibus delinitus, ignofcit. Clitipho fe, relictis meretriciis amoribus, uxorem ducturum pollicetur. Quum autem cæterarum fabularum argumentum uno die contineri foleat, hujus non nifi biduo expli-
cari poteft.*

S 2   DRA-

PERSONS of the PLAY.

The PROLOGUE.
CHREMES, an old Man, the Father of *Clitipho* and *Antiphila*.
CLITIPHO, a Youth, the Son of *Chremes*.
MENEDEMUS, an old Man, the Father of *Clinia*.
CLINIA, a Youth, the Son of *Menedemus*.
SOSTRATA, the Wife of *Chremes*.
ANTIPHILA, the Daughter of *Chremes* and *Sostrata*, and *Clinia*'s Mistress.
BACCHIS, a Courtezan, *Clitipho*'s Mistress.
The NURSE to *Antiphila*.
PHRYGIA, one of *Bacchis*'s Maids.
SYRUS, *Clitipho*'s Servant.
DROMO, *Clinia*'s Servant.

MUTES,

ARCHONIDES, an old Man.
CRITO, an old Man.
PHANIA, an old Man.
PHANOCRATES, an old Man.
PHILTERA, an old Woman.
SIMUS, an old Man.

SCENE, A Village in the Neighbourhood of *ATHENS*.

The

DRAMATIS PERSONÆ.

PROLOGUS.
CHREMES, *senex, pater Clitiphonis & Antiphilæ.*
CLITIPHO, *adolescens, filius Chremetis.*
MENEDEMUS, *senex, pater Cliniæ.*
CLINIA, *adolescens, filius Menedemi.*
SOSTRATA, *uxor Chremetis.*
ANTIPHILA, *filia Chremetis & Sostratæ, amica Cliniæ.*
BACCHIS, *meretrix, amica Clitiphonis.*
NUTRIX *Antiphilæ.*
PHRYGIA, *ancilla Bacchidis.*
SYRUS, *servus Clitiphonis.*
DROMO, *servus Cliniæ.*

PERSONÆ MUTÆ.

ARCHONIDES, *senex.*
CRITO, *senex.*
PHANIA, *senex.*
PHANOCRATES, *senex.*
PHILTERA, *anus.*
SIMUS, *senex.*

SCENA, *Pagus suburbanus.*

2

The P R O L O G U E.

A R G U M E N T.

This Discourse, which is not strictly according to the Law of Prologues, is intended against Luscius Lanuvinus, *informs the Audience of what it was necessary for them to know, aims at disposing them in the Poet's Favour, and removes every thing that might thro' Mistake be objected against him. The chief Design is to prevail with the Audience to give a fair and quiet Hearing, the strongest Incentive to great Genius's to exert themselves for the Entertainment of the Public.*

TO prevent any here from wondering why the Poet has given to an old Man a Part, that more properly belongs to Youth: I will first clear up that Point, and then inform you of the Cause of my Appearance now.

I am this Day, to present the Self-Tormentor, a Comedy preserved intire from a single *Greek* Original, but with this Variation, that there is here a double Plot, which was but simple in the *Greek*. I have told you then, that it is a new Play, and of what kind it is, and would tell you, also, who wrote it, and the Name of the *Greek* Author, were I not persuaded, that the greatest Part of you know it already. I will now inform you, in few Words, why I have studied these Parts.   The

A N N O T A T I O N S.

[1] *Ne cui sit vestrum.* It is a great misfortune in explaining this Play, that we want the Assistance of *Donatus,* who has left us nothing upon it, or, indeed, as I am rather apt to think, whose Remarks are lost: for in him we often find the true ancient Reading, which had been defaced by after Transcribers, whereas in this Play, we have no other Helps, than what is to be collected from ancient Copies. And that this is no small Disadvantage appears from hence, that we meet with more Difficulties, from the Incorrectness of the Text in this, than in any other of *Terence's* Comedies.

Ibid. *Cur partes seni poeta dederit.* Viz. The Part of repeating the Prologue. We shall better understand the Custom of the Ancients, in this respect, by attending to the two following Quotations. The one from our own Poet; *Adelph.* Pro. Ver. 22.

Dehinc ne expectetis argumentum fabulæ,
Senes, qui primi venient, hi partem aperient,

In agendo partem ostendent.

The other from *Plautus,* Trin. Pro. Ver. 16.
Sed de argumento ne expectetis fabulæ,
Senes, qui huc venient, hi rem vobis aperient.

Here it is evident, that the Prologue was not repeated by those Actors, who appeared first upon the Stage, to begin the Play, but by others, commonly young Men, as more likely to gain over the Audience in favour of the Poet. *Terence,* therefore, here, acted contrary to the common Custom of Poets, in assigning the Part of the Prologue to *Ambivius,* himself, the Master of the Company, and at that time very old.

[3] *Id primum dicam, deinde quod veni eloquar.* Criticks observe here, that *Terence* contradicts himself, because the Speaker of the Prologue begins with the Reason of his coming, and afterwards shews how he had that Part assigned him. Hence *Guyetus* and *Palmerius* invert the Order of the Words, and read, *Id dicam deinde : primum quod veni eloquar.* But all this proceeds from their mistaking the Poet's Design. For what follows after this, to the tenth Verse, is only a general Account of the Play, to give the Audience some notion of it, and ought to be regarded as a Parenthesis. Thence to the sixteenth Verse, he discharges the first Part of his Promise, and, from that to the End, tells the Reason of his coming.

This

4 2

PROLOGUS.

ARGUMENTUM.

*Hæc oratio, quæ legem prologi non servat, in Luscium Lanuvinum
stringit aculeos, docet auditores, Terentio benevolentiam parat,
& objecta diluens, utitur statu absoluto: id petens, quod ho-
nestum habetur imprimis, & civili disciplinæ conducit, quæ ingenia pro communi utilitate nutrit ac fovet.*

NE cui sit vostrûm mirum, cur partes seni
Poeta dederit, quæ sunt adolescentium:
Id primum dicam: deinde, quod veni, eloquar.
Ex integrâ Græcâ integram comœdiam
Hodie sum acturus Heautontimorumenon;   5
Duplex quæ ex argumento facta est simplici.
Novam esse ostendi, & quæ esset. nunc, qui scripserit,
Et cuja Græca sit, ni partem maxumam
Existimarem scire vostrûm, id dicerem.   9
Nunc, quamobrem has partes didicerim, paucis dabo.

ORDO.

NE sit mirum cui vestrûm, cur poeta dederit seni, partes quæ sunt adolescentium: dicam id primum: deinde eloquar propter quod veni. Ego sum acturus hodie Heautontimorumenon, integram comœdiam ex integrâ Græcâ; quæ tamen est facta duplex ex simplici argumento. Ostendi hanc comœdiam *esse novam, & quæ esset:* nunc dicerim *id; qui scripserit, & cuja Græca sit, ni existimarem maximam partem vestrûm scire* id jam. *Nunc, dabo paucis, quamobrem didicerim has partes.*

ANNOTATIONS.

This I take to be the real Explication of this obscure Passage; but as *Bentley's* Conjecture, here, is very singular and curious, I shall lay it before the Reader at length, that he may be the better able to form a Judgment of it. After mentioning the Change in the Reading, as before remarked, offered by *Guyetus* and *Palmerius*, and the Reasons they give for it, he adds; that they, who expect to meet with what he intends, by *eloquar quod veni*, In the Prologue, can scarce think otherwise, but it is a great Error to fancy so. The Persons, who pronounced the Prologue, immediately afterwards retired, to make way for the old Men, who were to begin the Play. On the other hand, *Ambivius*, who speaks the Prologue here, is again to appear in the first Scene, in the Character of *Chremes*, nor does he quit the Stage. This, therefore, is what *Ambivius* would say: I am first to tell you, why the Poet has made choice of me, rather than a young Man to speak the Prologue, and this is what he does all along: that as being an old Player, known and acceptable to the People, he might plead the Poet's Cause, against those who endeavoured maliciously to detract from his Merit. *Deinde, quod veni, eloquar.* This is the second Part, and refers to what he was to do as an Actor. For immediately after pronouncing the Prologue, the other Actor, who personated *Menedemus*, entering, begins:

Quamquam hæc inter nos nuper admodum notitia est.

5 *Heautontimorumenon.* The Title of the Play is of *Greek* Derivation, ἑαυτὸν τιμωρούμενος; and signifies one, who punishes himself, a Self-Tormentor, in allusion to what the unhappy Father says; *illi de me supplicium dabo.* This Play seems to have been very much esteemed by the Ancients, and that they thought the Poet had succeeded well, in painting the Distress of the unfortunate Father, appears evidently from these Lines of *Horace.* Sat. L. 1. S. 2. ver. 20.

——— *Ita ut pater ille, Terenti
Fabula quem miserum gnato vixisse sigurgato,
Inducit, non se pejus cruciaverit, atque
bic.*

6 *Duplex quæ ex argumento facta est simplici.* This Passage has given a world of Trouble to the several Commentators on *Terence. Julius Scaliger* has fallen into the extravagant Conceit, of the Comedy's being here called *double,* because of its being acted at two different Times, the two first Acts in the Evening, and the three last the Morning following; by which means it became, as it were, two Plays, Instead of one. But without having recourse to such far-

The Poet meant, that I fhould be an Envoy to you, and not bare-ly the Speaker of a Prologue. He refers it to you to judge of the Piece, and employs me as an Advocate to plead his Caufe. But this Advocate can move you no farther by this Eloquence, than he has been able to think happily, who compofed the Speech which I am now to repeat to you: for as to the Rumours that have been fo in-duftrioufly fpread by a Set of Men, who envy his Fame, that he has taken in, and huddled together a great Number of *Greek* Plays, to make a few *Latin* ones; this he, by no means, denies: nor does he repent of it, but thinks it likely he may do it again. He has the Example of our beft Poets, and looks upon that Example as a fuf-ficient Authority to juftify him in doing, what they have done before him. Then as to what an old malicious Bard objects, that he has, but of late, fuddenly turned his Thoughts to this ftudy of Harmony, and the Poetic Art, fupported rather hy the Genius of his Friends, than his own natural Talents; your Judgment and Opinion fhall de-termine. Therefore, I earneftly beg of you all, that you will not fuffer the Suggeftions of the malicious to prevail over thofe of the fair and candid Judge. Be impartial, and encourage the Attempts of thofe who endeavour to entertain you with new and faultlefs Plays. *I fay faultlefs,* that the Bard, who lately made the People give

ANNOTATIONS.

far-fetched Notions, we may obferve, that as there are two young Men introduced into the Plot, with each his Miftrefs, Father, and Servant, this makes the Argument dou-ble; whereas in the Original of *Menander*, there was probably but a fingle Plot.

13 *Sed hic actor tantum poterit à facun-diâ,* &c. There are various ways of ex-plaining this Paffage. Some will have it: *Tantum actor à facundiâ poteft, quantum poëta ab inventione;* and think it a Sign of Judgment in the Poet, to bring in an Actor and efpecially an old one, fpeaking thus of himfelf, in a conceited boafting Strain. But to me, this does not feem fo natural. *Am-bivius* had told the Audience, that he came to plead for the Poet; but at the fame time, in a way of Pleafantry, and to difpofe the Audience to be more attentive, he gives them to underftand, that the Speech he was to make, was of *Terence's* own compofing, and that, therefore, 'tho' he feemed to be the Speaker, yet he no farther influenced the Audience in his favour, than as he had been able to think happily in his own Defence. *Bentley*, indeed, is pleafed with neither of thefe Interpretations, and propofes an A-mendment of the Text thus:

Veftrum judicium fecit, me actorem dedit:
Si hic actor tantum poterit à facundiâ,
Quantum ille potuit cogitare commode,
Qui oratione hanc fcripfit, quam dicturus fum.
According to this, *Ambivius* fpeaks modeft-

ly enough of himfelf, and very refpectfully of the Poet. I, fays he, am to act this Play, nor is there any Fear of its Succefs, or Danger of trufting to your Judgment, if my Endeavours to fet it off by proper Action and Addrefs, equal the Merit and Induftry of the Author. *Si hic actor tantum poterit à facundiâ, hoc eft, à voce, pronuntiatione, geftu, quantum ipfe auctor ab inventione & arte.* For, in fact, it often happens, that a bad Actor damns a good Play, and a good Actor faves an indifferent one, By this In-terpretation, we are further under a Ne-ceffity of referring the laft Line, *Qui orationem hanc fcripfit, quam dicturus fum,* not to the Prologue, but to the Part he was afterwards to act in the Character of *Chremes.* Undoubtedly, fays *Bentley*, this fagacious Player forefaw, that the firft Act would meet with uncommon Applaufe, the Thoughts being fo natural, and the Style fo correct, that no-thing can equal it: and, indeed, according to the Teftimony of *Auguftine,* when that Verfe, *Homo fum, humani,* &c. was firft repeated in the Theatre, it was followed with the loudeft Acclamations of Praife. Thus the Reader may fee at once the feveral Opini-ons; I have followed the common Read-ing, and given the Interpretation of it, which I thought moft natural and unforced.

16 *Nam quod rumores diftulerunt malevoli.* Here he begins to give the Reafons of his coming, as he had before promifed, *viz.* that he

Oratorem esse voluit me, non prologum:
Vestrum judicium fecit: me actorem dedit.
Sed hic actor tantum poterit à facundiâ,
Quantum ille potuit cogitare commodè,
Qui orationem hanc scripsit, quam dicturu' sum. 15
Nam quod rumores distulerunt malevoli,
Multas contaminasse Græcas, dum facit
Paucas Latinas: id factum esse hic non negat,
Neque se id pigere, & deinde facturum autumat.
Habet bonorum exemplum: quo exemplo sibi 20
Licere id facere, quod illi fecerunt, putat.
Tum quod malevolus vetus poeta dictitat,
Repentè ad studium hunc se applicasse musicum,
Amicûm ingenio fretum, haud naturâ suâ:
Arbitrium vostrum, vostra existimatio 25
Valebit. quare omnes vos oratos volo,
Ne plus iniquûm possit quàm æquûm oratio.
Facite æqui sitis, date crescendi copiam,
Novarum qui spectandi faciunt copiam

Poeta *voluit me esse oratorem, non prelogum: fecit judicium vestrum: dedit me actorem. Sed hic actor tantum à facundiâ, quantum ille, qui scripsit hanc orationem, quam sum dicturus, potuit cogitare commodè. Nam quod malevoli distulerunt rumores, eum contaminasse multas fabulas Græcas, dum facit paucas Latinas: hic non negat id esse factum, neque se pigere, & autumat se facturum hoc idem deinde. Habet exemplum bonorum: quo exemplo putat sibi facere id, quod illi fecerunt. Tum quod malevolus vetus poeta dictitat, hunc*

repentè applicavisse se ad studium musicum, fretum ingenio amicorum, haud suâ naturâ: vestrum arbitrium, vestra existimatio valebit. Quare volo vos omnes esse oratos, ne oratio iniquorum hominum possit plus quàm oratio æquorum. Facite ut sitis æqui; date copiam crescendi iis, qui faciunt vobis copiam spectandi novarum fabularum.

A N N O T A T I O N S.

he might refute the Cavils, and malicious Insinuations of the Poet's Adversaries. The Particle *nam* has not here any relation to what precedes, it is merely what we may call a Particle of Transition, serving to introduce a Sentence. *Rumores differre*, is an elegant way of speaking, and very much in use, instead of *in diversum disseminare, spargere, divulgare.*

17 *Multas contaminasse.* See the Prologue to the *Andrian.*

23 *Ad studium hunc se applicasse musicum.* By *studium musicum*, we, are here to understand the same as what we mean by the *Belles Lettres*, or *Polite Learning.* If we confine it to Poetry, it may be conceived the Study of Harmony and Versification. The following Quotation from *Quintilian* will serve to illustrate it. *Instit.* Orat. Lib. 10. *Nam quis ignorat, musicen, ut de hac primum loquar, tantum illis jam antiquis temporibus non studii modo, verum etiam venerationis habuisse, ut iidem musici, & vates, & sapientes judicarentur.*

24 *Amicum ingenio fretum. Scipio* and *Lælius*, who were the Poet's great Patrons, and supposed to have a hand in the Composition of his Plays. This will be more fully spoken to, in the Prologue to the *Adelphi*, under these Lines:

Nam quod isti dicunt malevoli, homines nobiles Eum adjutare, assidueque una scribere; Quod illi maledictum v. hemens esse existimant, Eam laudem hic ducit maximam, cum illis placet, Qui vobis universis & populi placent.

25 *Arbitrium vestrum, vostra existimatio valebit.* The Poet who thought it no dishonour to be supposed to live in Friendship and Familiarity with such great Men as *Scipio* and *Lælius*, takes no Pains to refute this Cavil, but only says: *arbitrium vostrum est, vostra existimatio.* Which may be either interpreted, *I leave it to your Judgment, whether there is a Probability of his having such Assistance;* or, *whether it can be any just Reproach to him, or detract from his Merit.*

29 *Novarum qui spectandi faciunt copiam.* We meet with many Examples of this manner of Speaking in the best Authors, which may be thus supplied, *qui faciunt copiam spectandi* spectaculi, *or* spectaculum *novarum fabularum.* Or this Gerundive *spectandi* may be considered as put here instead of the Verbal *spectatio, visio:* as if the Poet had said, *Qui vobis faciunt copiam spectationis, visionis novarum.*

30 *Ne ille.* Let not *Lanuvinus* fancy, that this

give way to a Slave, running along the Street with all his Might, may not imagine I fpeak of him : why fhould the Poet trouble himfelf to defend a Fool ? he will expofe yet more of his Faults, when he of-fers any new Plays, unle:s he ceafes thefe impertinent Cavils. Attend with candid Minds, and fuffer me unmolefted to act this Play of the quiet and peaceable kind : that the Parts of a running Slave, an en-raged old Man, a guzzling Parafite, an impudent Sycophant, and greedy Pimp, may not always fall to the Share of an old Man, to be reprefented, with the utmoft Expence of Voice, and a World of Fa-tigue. For my fake be induced to think that this is a juft Demand, that fome Part of the Toil I undergo, may be leffened to me. For fuch as now write new Plays, have no regard to my Age. If it is painful and difficult to reprefent, they apply to me ; if eafy, they carry it to another Company. In this Piece, the Style is pure and unaffected, try how I am able to acquit myfelf in both Characters. If I never covetoufly prized my Art too high, but always accounted it the greateft Gain, to contribute all in my power to your Diverfion, eftablifh a Precedent in me, that may encourage our Youth to aim rather at your Entertainment, than the pleafing of themfelves.

ANNOTATIONS.

this is faid in excufe of him, who, indeed, prefented the People lately with a new Play, but far from being without Defects; for its greateft Merit was that of a Slave running with all his Might; and the People making way for him. *Ne ille pro fe dictum exiftu-met*, is therefore to be confidered as ftand-ing in Connexion with *fine vitiis*. After *Terence* had faid ; *Give by your Applaufe Courage to Poets, who endeavour to entertain you with new Plays*: to prevent *Lufcius* from imagining, that he was comprehended in the Number, which was far from his Defign, he adds *fine vitiis*, without Defects ; which were chargeable in great Numbers upon *Lufcius's* Pieces, as he immediately af-terwards inftances.

31 *Qui nuper fecit fervo currenti in via*, &c. Where is the Fault here, to make the People give way to a Slave running in hafte? Slaves and Parafites, often in Plays, threaten any, if they ftand in their way. Witnefs that well-known Paffage in the *Amphitryo* III. 4. where *Mercury*, under the Form of a Slave, fays :

Concedite, atque abfcedite, omnes, de via de-cedite :
Nec quifquam tam audax fuat homo, qui obviam obfiftat mibi.
Nam mibi quidem, hercle, qui minus liceat deo minitarier

Populo, ni decedat mibi, quam fervu'o in comædiis ?
And the Parafite, *Capt.* Act. 4. 2. 11.
Eminor, Interminorque, ne quis mi obfiterit obviam,
Nifi qui fat diu vixiffe fefe homo arbitra-bitur.
What are we, therefore, to fay of this Paffage ? the Sentence that follows, is ftill more intricate and perplexing. *Cur infano ferviat ?* What can this mean, or how does it adhere to what goes before ? Two Con-jectures may be offered to folve thefe Dif-ficulties. The firft is that of *Dacier*, and the more general Explication ; that the Action of his Piece confifted chiefly in this ; inftead of painting Manners, and conducting a regular Plot, he amufed himfelf in thefe Trifles : therefore it is added, *Cur infano fer-viat? Cur Terentius poeta malevoli, hominis infulfi & infani, commedis ferviat ?* *Cur, cum à theatro crefcendi copiam poetis petat, da Lufcio inter eos cogitet ?* The other Explica-tion is that of *Perizonius*, in which he is fupported by *Bentley*, who inftead of *deceffe*, reads *dixiffe*.

Qui nuper fecit fervo currenti in via
Populum dixiffe, Cur infano ferviat ?
This then, according to them, was the Fault of *Lanuvinus*, that he brought the People upon the Stage fpeaking to a Slave :

for

Sinc vitiis : ne ille pro fe dictum exiftumet,　　　30
Qui nuper fecit fervo currenti in viâ
Deceffe populum. cur infano ferviat ?
De illius peccatis plura dicet, cùm dabit
Alias novas, nifi finem maledictis facit.
Adefte æquo animo : date poteftatem mihi,　　　35
Statariam agere ut liceat per filentium :
Ne femper fervus currens, iratus fenex,
Edax parafitus, fycophanta autem impudens,
Avarus leno, affiduè agendi fint feni
Clamore fummo, cum labore maxumo.　　　40
Meâ caufâ, caufam hanc juftam effe, animum inducite,
Ut aliqua pars laboris minuatur mihi.
Nam nunc novas qui fcribunt, nihil parcunt feni :
Si quæ laboriofa eft, ad me curritur :
Sin lenis eft, ad alium defertur gregem.　　　45
In hac eft pura oratio. experimini,
In utramque partem ingenium quid poffit meum.
Si nunquam avarè precium ftatui arti meæ,
Et eùm effe quæftum in animum induxi maxumum,
Quàm maxumè fervire voftris commodis ;　　　50
Exemplum ftatuite in me, ut adolefcentuli
Vobis placere ftudeant potiùs, quàm fibi.

*nunc fcribunt novas fabulas, nihil parcunt feni : fi quæ eft laboriofa, curritur ad me : fi eft lenis,
defertur ad alium gregem. In hac comœdia oratio eft pura, experimini quid meum ingenium poffit in utramque partem. Si nunquam ftatui avarè precium meæ arti, & induxi in animum eum
effe maximum quæftum, fervire quàm maxime veftris commodis : ftatuite exemplum in me, ut adolefcentuli ftudeant potiùs placere vobis, quàm fibi.*

A N N O T A T I O N S.

for altho', in Comedy, it was ufual enough
for à Slave to addrefs the People, or an Actor
the Spectators, yet no Anfwer was ever made.
Plautus Capt. Prol. ver. 10.
　Jam hoc tenetis ? optumum'ft.
　Negat, hercle, ille ultimus : accedito :
　Si non ubi fedeas, locus eft : eft, ubi am-
　　bules.
　Ego me tua caufa, ne erres, non rupturus
　　fum.
Had *Plautus* introduced any one anfwering
from the Pit this Speech of the Player, he
would have fallen into the fame Blunder as
Lufcius Lanuvinus here.

36 *Statariam.* Comœdiam fcilicet, feu fabulam, to which what they call'd the *motoria*
was oppofed. The former was calm and
peaceable, the other full of Action and Difturbance. Both thefe are originally derived
from the *Greek* Comedy, in which were
μίλη ςάσιμα and παρωδικά, i. e. *verfus fta-
tarii & motorii,* which the Chorus either
fung without ftirring from their Place, or
with Dancing, and all the Violence of Ge-

fture. This Comedy then is of the peaceable kind, we meet in it with but little Hurry and Agitation, only a Father, who af-
flicts himfelf for having obliged his Son to
run away.

46 *Pura oratio.* The Purity of Style is
remarked by Cricticks eminently to diftinguifh this Play. The Poet finding that it
was without Action; which might have occafioned fome Prejudice againft it, endeavours
to make Reparation in this other way.

47 *In utramque partem.* That is, in
acting thefe Pieces of different Characters,
whether the peaceable kind, or thofe full of
Action.

51 *Ut adolefcentuli.* The Words may refer
either to Poets or Actors, but more probably
to Actors. *Ut adolefcentuli biftriones poftbac
meo exemplo potius ftudeant fervire veftris commodis, quam fuis, veftramque judicium ante-
ponant fuo quæftui. Statuite exemplum ;* is
here taken for a favourable Example to encourage.

P.

TERENCE's
SELF-TORMENTOR.

ACT I. SCENE I.

ARGUMENT.

Chremes, *observing that* Menedemus *fatigued himself, beyond what was reasonable, with labouring at his Farm, addresses him, enquiring with some Earnestness the Cause of his going so far beyond what his Age seemed to allow.* Menedemus, *answering, tells him that the Cause was his Son's Absence, whom he had forced away by ill Usage, and now desired to see again with the utmost Impatience.*

CHREMES, MENEDEMUS.

Chremes. ALTHOUGH, *Menedemus,* this our Acquaintance is but of short standing, and began only upon your buying a Farm in this Neighbourhood, nor was there indeed, almost any other tye between us : yet either your Virtue, or your being my Neighbour, which I hold in the next Rank to Friendship, makes me take the Liberty of telling you frankly, that you seem to me to live in a Manner, that is not agreeable either to your Age or Fortune. For in the Name of Heaven and Earth, what would you have ? Or what can be your Aim ? you are full Sixty, or rather more, as I guess. No one, in this Country, has a Piece of better Land, or that yields more : you are well stocked with Slaves, and yet toil with the same Assiduity, as if you had not one. I never

go

ANNOTATIONS.

Clinia, as we have seen in the Argument, being greatly enamoured with *Antiphila,* drew upon himself his Father's Resentment, which affected him so much, that to avoid his continual Reproaches, he fled into *Asia,* to serve in the Armies of the King of *Persia.* His Father, after his Departure, gave as much way to Remorse, as formerly he had done to his Resentment, and, to make some Reparation to his Son, for the Hardships he had reduced him to, sells off his House, Furniture, and Slaves, purchases a Farm within a few Miles of *Athens,* and resolves to labour without intermission, denying himself every Pleasure; and using all means to increase his Estate, for the sake of his absent, and as he supposed, unfortunate Son. It happened, that *Chremes* had a Farm in the Neighbourhood, and had often observed *Menedemus* to fatigue himself, beyond what either his Estate seemed to require, or his Age would allow. He is, therefore, introduced here, addressing him in a friendly way, and enquiring into the reason of this unusual Behaviour, frankly professing an Esteem and Value for him, and Willingness to assist him with his Advice, or even Fortune, in whatever might occur to make him easy. This naturally brings on a free and unreserved Conversation, in which *Menedemus* lets him into the whole Story of his Misfortune. Thus the Spectator is made acquainted in the most simple, natural, and unaffected Manner, with what it was necessary for him to know ; sees the Plot, by degrees, begin to be formed, and has his

Curiosity

P. TERENTII
HEAUTONTIMORUMENOS.

ACTUS I. SCENA I.

ARGUMENTUM.

Menedemum excruciantem se in agro laboribus, Chremes alloquitur; sedulo causam inquirens, cur præter ætatem ille id faciat suam. Respondens Menedemus, sui mæroris causam dixit esse filii abitionem, quem jurgiis & contumeliis domo ejectum, impotentius desiderat.

CHREMES, MENEDEMUS.

Q UANQUAM hæc inter nos nuper notitia
admodum est,
Inde adeo, quod agrum in proximo hîc mercatus
Nec rei fere sane amplius quidquam fuit :
Tamen vel virtus tua me, vel vicinitas.
Quod ego in propinquâ parte amicitiæ puto,
Facit, ut te audacter moneam, & familiariter,
Quod mihi videre præter ætatem tuam
Facere, & præter, quam res te adhortatur tua.
Nam, proh Deûm atque hominum fidem! quid vis tibi?
Quid quæris? annos sexaginta natus es,
Aut plus eo, ut conjicio, agrum in his regionibus
Meliorem, neque precii majoris nemo, habet :
Servos complures. proinde quasi nemo siet,

ORDO.

Cн. Q Uanquam,
Menede-
me, hæc rotitia in-
ter nos est admodum
nuper, inde adeo, quòd
mercatus es agrum hîc
in proximo ; nec sa-
ne fuit quidquam rei
fere amplius : tamen
vel virtus tua, vel
vicinitas, quod ego
puto in propinquâ
parte amicitiæ, fa-
cit me, ut moneam
te audacter, & fa-
miliariter, quod vi-
deris mihi facere præ-
ter tuam ætatem, &
præter quam tua res

adhortatur te. Nam, proh fidem deorum atque hominum! Quid vis tibi? Quid quæris? Et natus annos sexaginta aut plus eo, ut conjicio. Nemo in his rigionibus habet agrum meliorem, neque majoris precii: habes complures servos. Proinde quasi nemo fiet.

ANNOTATIONS.

Curiosity and Anxiety raised in behalf of the several Persons concerned.

+ *Vel virtus tua, vel vicinitas, quod ego in propinqua,* &c. By *virtus* here we are to understand, that painful and honest Life which *Menedemus* led. Again we are to observe, that among the several Chains and Links, that hold Human Kind together, Vicinity here obtains the next Rank to Friendship. This exactly agrees with what *Cicero* says, upon the same Subject, in his fifth Book *de Finibus* 23. And as nothing is more pleasing and instructing, than to observe the several Steps and Gradations, by which Society, and the various Conjunctions and Connexions of

Mankind are formed; I shall here, for the sake of the Reader, transcribe that whole celebrated Passage:

In omni autem honesto, de quo loquimur, nihil est tam illustre, nec quod latius pateat, quam conjunctio inter homines hominum, & quasi quædam societas, & communicatio utilitatum, & ipsa caritas generis humani: quæ nata à primo satu, quo à procreatoribus nati diliguntur, & tota domus conjugio & stirpe conjungitur, serpit sensim foras cognationibus primum, tum affinitatibus, deinde amicitiis, post vicinitatibus, tum civibus, & iis, qui publice socii, atque amici sunt : deinde totius complexu gentis humanæ.

go out fo early, or return fo late, but I find you digging, ploughing, or bearing fome Burden. You take no refpite, nor have any regard to yourfelf. I am very certain, you don't do all this merely for your Diverfion. But, perhaps, you'll fay, that you think there is too little Work done: but let me tell you, that if the time you fpend in labouring yourfelf, were employed in overlooking your Servants, your Work would go much better.

Men. Have you fo much leifure from your own Bufinefs, *Chremes*, that you can mind another's, and things that don't in the leaft concern you?

Chrem. I am a Man, and think every thing that regards my Neighbour, refpects alfo me. Look upon what I now fay, either as an Advice, or an Enquiry; that if right, I may do fo too; if not, that I may diffuade you from it.

Men. I find benefit in doing fo; as for you, you may do as you think fit.

Chrem. Can it be for any Man's benefit to torment himfelf?

Men. For mine.

Chrem. If you have any real Uneafinefs, I'm forry for it; but what can this Misfortune be? Or what have you done to deferve fo ill of yourfelf?

Men. Alas!

Chrem. Don't cry: and whatever it is, let me know it. Conceal nothing from me, nor be at all afraid: truft me with it, I fay, I am ready to affift you, either by Confolation, Advice, or my Fortune, if needful.

Men. Would you then know it?

Chrem. Only for the reafon I told you.

Men.

ANNOTATIONS.

[17] *Aut aliquid ferre denique,* We meet with thefe Words differently pointed in different Editions, and thence a great Variation in the Senfe; for fome make *denique* to end the Sentence as here, others to begin a new one: *Aut aliquid ferre. Denique nullum remittis tempus.* In either way, the Senfe is good, but the firft feems to have the jufteft Title to Preference, as it is evidently the Reading that prevailed in *Cicero's* Time, who in his firft Book *de Finibus,* fays, *Terentianus Chremes non inhumanus, novum vicinum non vult fodere, aut arare, aut aliquid ferre denique: non ut illum ab induftria, fed ab illiberali labore deterreat. Donatus* too confirms the fame with this Remark: *Ad Phorm.* I. 2. 71. *More fuo Terentius denique pofuit in fine fenfus. Sic in Heaut. Fodere, aut arare, aut aliquid facere denique; ut fit denique vel deinde, vel ad poftremum.* But there is another Difficulty arifes upon this Paffage; how we are to conceive *Menedemus* employed, when *Chremes* addreffes him.

It is moft likely, that he was returning home from labouring in the Fields, and carrying his Inftruments of Hufbandry with him. This is the more probable, becaufe at the end of this Converfation, it appears they had been all the time within fight of their own Houfes. And in an ancient Manufcript, mentioned by Madam *Dacier,* where there are Figures at the Beginning of the feveral Scenes, that which fronts this, reprefents *Chremes* at a little Diftance from his Houfe, meeting *Menedemus,* who appears to have feveral Inftruments of Hufbandry on his Shoulder.

[20] *At enim me, quantum hic operis fiat, pænitet.* This is the Anfwer which *Chremes* fuppofes *Menedemus* will make to juftify his own Behaviour, and which he therefore here prepares to obviate. The Sentence may be paraphrafed thus: *Pænitet me, quantum operis fiat: dolet mihi tam parum operis fieri: dum tute aras, fodis, omus portas, fervi tui ceffant: plus proficias, fi tute vacuus illos exerceas:*

Attentè tute illorum officia fungere.
Nunquam tam manè egredior, neque tam vesperi 15
Domum revertor, quin te in fundo conspicer
Fodere, aut arare, aut aliquid ferre denique:
Nullum remittis tempus, neque te respicis.
Hæc non voluptati esse, satis certò scio.
At enim, me, quantum hîc operis fiat, pœnitet. 20
Quod in opere faciundo operæ consumis tuæ,
Si sumas in illis exercendis, plus agas.
ME. Chreme, tantumne ab re tuâ est otii tibi,
Aliena ut cures, ea quæ nihil ad te attinent?
CH. Homo sum: humani nihil à me alienum puto. 25
Vel me monere hoc, vel percontari puta;
Rectum est? ego ut faciam: non est? te ut deterream.
ME. Mihi sic est usus: tibi ut opus est facto, face.
CH. An quoiquam est usus homini, se ut cruciet? ME.
   mihi.
CH. Si quid laboris est, nollem: sed quid istuc mali est? 30
Quæso, quid de te tantum meruisti? ME. eheu, [sciam,
CH. Ne lacruma, atque istuc, quidquid est, fac me ut
Ne retice: ne verere: crede, inquam mihi:
Aut consolando, aut consilio, aut te juvero
ME. Scire hoc vis? CH. hac causâ equidem, quâ dixi
   tibi. 35

tute attentè fungeris officia illorum. Nunquam egredior tam manè, neque revertor domum tam vesperi, quin conspicer te in fundo, fodere, aut a-rare, aut denique fer-re aliquid: remittis nullum tempus, ne-que respicis te. ~ Scio satis certò hæc non esse voluptati. At enim (forte dices) I œnitet me quantum operis fiat hîc. Si sumas, quod operis tuæ consumis in fa-ciendo opere, in ex-ercendis illis tu's fer-vis, agas plus. ME. Chreme, esine tantum otii tibi ab tuâ re, ut cures aliena, & ea quæ attinent nihil ad te? CH. Sum homo: puto nihil humani a-lienum à me. Puta me vel monere hoc, vel percontari. Est rectum? ut ego fa-ciam idem: non est? ciam

ut deterream te. ME. Usus sic est mihi: fac tu, ut est opus tibi facto. CH. An est usus cuiquam homini, ut cruciet se? ME. Est opus mibi. CH. Si est quid laboris tibi, nollem dicere amplius: sed quid mali est istuc? Quæso, quid meruisti tantum de te? ME. Eheu! CH. Ne lacrima, at-que fac me ut sciam istuc, quidquid est. Ne retice: ne verere: inquam, crede mibi: juvero te, aut consolando, aut consilio, aut re familiari. ME. Vis scire hoc? CH. Imo, quidem hac causâ, quâ dixi tibi.

ANNOTATIONS.

exercas: ergo, ut tibi parcas, vel res tua te adhortatur.

25 Homo sum: humani nihil a me alienum puto. These Words are an Instance, how much the Sense of any Passage may be mis-taken by those who quote it carelessly, and without consulting the Author himself: for nothing is more common, than to cite these Words as expressing how weak human Na-ture is, and obnoxious to Errors. Whereas, it is evident, that *humanum* here means those Misfortunes and Distresses which happen to us in Life, and which it is the Part of a Friend to concern himself in for our Con-solation. The following Quotation from *Seneca*, Epist. 25. is the best Commentary I can give upon these Words. *Natura*, inquit, *nos cognatos edidit, cum ex iisdem, & in ea-dem gigneret. Hæc nobis amorem indidit mu-tuum, & sociabiles fecit. Illa æquum justum-que composuit. Ex illius constitutione miseriu. est nocere, quam lædi, Et illius imperio pa-*

ratæ sunt ad juvandum manus. Iste versus & in pectore, & in ore sit: homo sum, humani nihil à me alienum puto. Habeamus in com-mune quod nati sumus.

30 Si quid laboris est, nollem. These Words have very much puzzled Commenta-tors, to find out their Meaning. *Muretus*, and some others, frankly own that they are not able to comprehend them. *Guyetus* looks upon them as spurious, and thinks they ought to be rejected. But upon a nearer view we shall find, that the Sense is good, and worthy of *Terence*. *Si quid laboris est* here, signifies no other than *si quid in ani-mo molestiæ est, quod te male habet:* for this Word is often used to expres Trouble, Uneasiness, Discontent. So *Phædrus* I. 30. I.

Humiles laborant, ubi potentes dissident.

Nollem again is an usual Form of expressing one's Desire, that it were otherwise, as if *nollem factum*. The true Sense, therefore,

of.

Men. I'll tell you then.

Chrem. But, mean time, lay aside those Rakes, nor fatigue your-self in this manner.

Men. By no means.

Chrem. What are you doing?

Men. Let me alone, that I mayn't give myself one minute's respite.

Chrem. I tell you, I will not allow it.

Men. Ah! it is not fair!

Chrem. Hey! so heavy too.

Men. No more than I deserve.

Chrem. Now speak.

Men. I have an only Son, a young Man; alas! why do I say I have him: indeed, I had one, *Chremes*, but whether I have him now or not, is uncertain.

Chrem. How so?

Men. You shall know. There is here a poor old Woman from *Corinth*. My Son fell desperately in love with her Daughter, info-much that he lived with her, in a manner, as if she had been his Wife; and all this without my knowledge. When I heard of it, I began to use him roughly, not with the Tenderness due to the weak and unsettled Disposition of Youth, but with Rigour, and the usual Severity of Fathers. I was daily reproaching him: *How do you imagine that you should be suffered to continue any longer in this way, and me, your Father alive; to live with your Mistress, in a manner, as if she was your Wife? You mistake greatly, if you believe so, and do not know me,* Clinia. *I will only have you to be reputed my Son, while you do as becomes you; but if otherwise, I will contrive what course to take with you. All this proceeds from nothing, but too much Idleness: When I was of your Age, I did not give up my mind to Love, but, to avoid Poverty, went and served in* Asia, *and there acquired both Riches, and the Reputation of Courage.* In fine, it came to this; the young Man, by hearing the same things so often, and with an Air of Severity, was quite overcome. He imagined, that both by reason of my Age, and the love I had for him, I must know more, and see clearer, in what regarded his Advantage, than himself. He is gone into *Asia, Chremes,* to serve there under the *Persian* King.

Chrem. What do you tell me?

Men. He went without my knowledge, and has now been absent three Months.   *Chrem.*

ANNOTATIONS.

of the Words must be; *If you have any real Uneasiness, I'm sorry for it, and could wish it otherwise.* This appears evidently from what follows, *Sed quid illud mali est?* But what can this Misfortune be, that pushes you on to such a Behaviour?

37. *Ne labora.* From this, several contend that *Chremes* must have come upon *Menede-*

mus, as he was labouring in his Ground, But as this could not possibly be the Case, from what we have above observed, we are under a Necessity of explaining *ne labora,* with reference to the Instruments of Hus-bandry he carried. *Don't fatigue, and toil yourself so, by bearing this heavy Burden.* This, moreover, agrees with what *Chremes*
soon

ME. Dicetur. CH. at istos rastros interea tamen
Appone, ne labora. ME. minime. CH. quam rem agis?
ME. Sine me, vacivom tempus ne quod dem mihi [facis.
Laboris. CH. non sinam, inquam. ME. ah, non æquom
CH. Hui, tam graves hos, quæso? ME. sic meritum
est meum. 40
CH. Nunc loquere. ME. Filium unicum adolescentulum
Habeo. ah, quid dixi? habere me? imo habui, Chreme.
Nunc habeam, necne, incertum est. CH. quid i'a istuc?
Est è Corintho hic advena anus pauperculâ [ME. scies.
Ejus filiam ille amare cœpit perduè, 45
Prope jam ut pro uxore haberet. hæc clam me omnia.
Ubi rem rescivi, cœpi non humanitùs,
Neque ut animum decuit ægrotum adolescentuli,
Tractare, sed vi & viâ pervolgatâ patrum.
Quotidie accusabam : hem : tibine hæc diutiùs 50
Licere speras facere, me vivo patre,
Amicam ut habeas prope jam in uxoris loco?
Erras, si id credis, & me ignoras, Clinia.
Ego te meum esse dici tantisper volo, 54
Dum, quod te dignum est, facies : sed si id non facis,
Ego, quod me in te sit facere dignum, invenero.
Nullâ adeò ex re istuc fit, nisi ex nimio otio.
Ego istuc ætatis non amori operam dabam,
Sed in Asiam hinc abii propter pauperiem, atque ibi
Simul rem & gloriam armis belli repperi. 60
Postremò adeò res rediit : adolescentulus
Sæpe eadem & graviter audiendo victus est :
Putavit me & ætate & benevolentiâ
Plus scire, & providere, quàm seipsum sibi. 64
In Asiam ad regem militatum abiit, Chreme. [tres abest.
CH. Quid ais? ME. clam me est profectus : menses

ME. Dicetur. CH. Attamen interea appone istos rastros, ne labora. ME. Minime. CH. Quàm rem agis? ME. Sine me ne dem mihi aliquid tempus vacivum laboris. CH. Inquam, non sinam. ME. Ah, facis non æquum. CH. Hui, quæso tractas hos tam graves? ME. Sic est meum meritum. CH. Nunc loquere. ME. Habeo unicum filium adolescentulum. Ah quid dixi? me habere filium? Imo habui, Chreme: nunc habeam, necne, est incertum. CH. Quid ita istuc? ME Scies. Est hic anus paupercula, advena è Corinthe: ille cœpit amare filiam ejus perditè, ut jam prope haberet eam pro uxore. Hæc omnia sunt facta clam me. Ubi rescivi rem, cœpi tractare eum non humanitùs, neque ut decuit tractare ægrotum animum adolescentuli; sed vi, & viâ pervolgata patrum : accusabam quotidie : hem, speresne licere tibi facere hæc diutius, ut habens ami-

cam prope jam in loco uxoris, me patre vivo? Clinia, si credis id, erras, & ignoras me. Ego tantisper volo te dici esse meum, dum facies, quod est dignum te: sed si non facis id, ego invenero, quod sit dignum me facere in te. Istuc adeo fit ex nullâ re, nisi ex nimio otio. Ego istuc ætatis non dabam operam amori; sed abii hinc in Asiam propter pauperiem, atque repperi ili armis simul rem, & gloriam belli. Postremo adeo res rediit ad id: adolescentulus est victus audiendo sæpe eadem, & graviter: putavit me & ætate & benevolentiâ scire & providere plus, quam se ipsum sibi: abiit in Asiam ad regem militatem. CH. Quid ais! ME. Profectus est clam me; abest tres menses.

ANNOTATIONS.

soon after says upon his Friend's Compliance. *Hui, tam graves hos,* to which we must supply *rastros portas?*

47 *Cœpi non humanitus.* Here he endeavours to satisfy Chremes, that he justly exacted Punishment of himself, because when he understood that his Son was in love, he did not use him gently, and with proper Allowance for his Age, and the Prevalence of Passion, but roughly, and in the Method of a rigid Father. He then repeats some of the Reproaches and severe Rebukes, wherewith he was won't to teaze him : *Ego te meum esse dici tantisper volò, dum, quod te dignum est, facies.* You shall be called mine, only while you behave as becomes you ; but if otherwise, I'll contrive to treat you as you deserve. *Eugraphius.*

53 *Me ignoras.* This Verb has a twofold Signification ; for either it respects a

Chrem. You are both to be blamed : yet this Step he has taken, shews great Modesty of Disposition, and a manly Spirit.

Men. When I understood it from those, whom he had made acquainted with his Design, I return home forrowful, my Mind almost distracted, and restless thro' Grief. I sit down : my Servants flock about me : pull off my Sandals : some I see hastening to lay the Cloth, and get Supper ready; and in fine, every one doing his utmost to please me, and soften my Chagrin. When I observed all this; I began to think with' myself, *What ! Are so many anxious and concerned on my account only, to give me Content ? Shall so many Maids be employ'd to prepare Clothes for me ? Shall all this great Expence be for me alone ? But my only Son, who ought to share in it equally, or rather more, as being of an Age fitter to relish these Enjoyments; him, poor Youth, have I driven from me, by my Severity. I think no Calamity too great could happen to me, were I capable of doing it ; and, therefore, while he lives in Penury abroad, banished his Country by my Severity, I'll revenge his Wrongs upon myself; labouring, scraping together, saving, and laying up for him.* This I set about immediately ; I leave nothing in my House, neither Dish nor Garment, but heaped all together. I sold all my Men and Maid Servants, excepting such as by working in the Country could easily pay the Expence of keeping: I also wrote over my Door, *a House to be sold.* I got together about fifteen Talents, and bought this Piece of Land : here I employ myself constantly. I fancy, *Chremes,* that I do my Son a less Injury, by making myself unhappy ; and that it is not lawful for me to taste of any Pleasure, till he return hither safe to share it with me.

Chrem. I see that you are naturally of an indulgent Temper towards your Children, and he too, I persuade myself, is dutiful, if managed rightly, and with some Grains of Allowance. But neither of you seem rightly to have known one the other, which is almost always the case where Differences happen. You never let him know, how much you loved him ; and he never dared to put that Confidence in you, which ought to subsist between Children and their Parents. Had this been done, the present Misfortune would have never happened.

Mem.

Cн. Ambo accufandi : etfi illud inceptum tamen
Animi eſt pudentis fignum, & non inſtrenui.
Me. Ubi comperi ex iis, qui fuere ei confcii,
Domum revortor mœſtus, atque animo fere   70
Perturbato, atque incerto præ ægritudine.
Adfido : accurrunt fervi : foccos detrahunt :
Video alios feſtinare, lectos ſternere,
Cœnam apparare : pro fe quifque fedulò
Faciebat, quò illam mihi lenirent miferiam.   75
Ubi video hæc, cœpi cogitare ; hem, tot mei
Solius foliciti funt causâ, ut me unum explent ?
Ancillæ tot me veſtiant ? fumtus domi
Tantos ego folus faciam ? fed gnatum unicum,
Quem paritur uti his decuit, aut etiam ampliùs,   80
Quòd illa ætas magis ad hæc utenda idonea eſt,
Eum ego hinc ejeci miferum injuſticiâ meâ.
Malo quidem me dignum quovis deputem,
Si id faciam. nam ufque dum ille vitam colet
Inopem, carens patriâ ob meas injurias,   85
Interea ufque illi de me fupplicium dabo,
Laborans, quærens, parcens, illi ferviens.
Ita facio prorfus. nihil relinquo in ædibus,
Nec vas, nec veſtimentum : conrafi omnia.
Ancillas, fervos, nifi eos, qui opere ruſtico   90
Faciundo facilè fumtum exercerent fuum,
Omnes produxi ac vendidi. infcripfi illico
Ædes mercede : quafi talenta ad quindecim
Coegi : agrum hunc mercatus fum : hîc me exerceo.
Decrevi, tantifper me minus injuria,   95
Chreme, meo gnato facere, dum fiam mifer ;
Nec fas effe ullâ me voluptate hîc frui,
Nifi ubi ille huc falvus redierit meus particeps.
Cн. Ingenio te effe in liberos leni puto, &
Illum obfequentem, fi quis rectè aut commodè   100
Tractaret. verùm neque tu illum fati' noveras,
Nec te ille. hoc ibi fit, ubi non verè vivitur.
Tu illum nunquam oſtendiſti quanti penderes,
Nec tibi ille eſt credere aufus quæ eſt æquom patri.
Quòd fi effet factum, hæc nunquam eveniffent tibi. 105

Side gloss column:

Cн. *Ambo vos eſtis accufandi : etfi tamen illud inceptum eſt fignum animi pudentis, & non inſtrui. Me. Ubi comperi ex iis, qui fuer: confcii ei, quid effet factum : mœſtus reve tor domum, atque animo ferre perturbato, atque incerto præ ægritudine : Adfido, fervi accurrunt, detrahunt foccos. Video alios feſtinare, alios ſternere lectos, apparare cœnam : quifque faciebat fedulo pro fe, quo lenirent illam miferiam mibi. Ubi video hæc, cœpi cogitare : Hem, tot funt fel:cit: cau:a mei folius, ut expleant me unum ? tot ancillæ veſtiant me ? ego folus faciam tanto: fumtus domi ? Sed quod ad meum gnatum, quem decuit uti bis pariter, aut etiam amplius, quod illa ætas eſt magis idonea ad utenda hæc, ego ejeci eum miferum hinc mea injuſtitia. Quidem deputem me dignum quovis malo, fi faciam id. Nam ufque dum ille, carent patria ob meas injurias, colet illam vitam inopem, interea ufque laborans, quærens, parcens, ferviens illi ; dabo illi fupplicium de me. Ita facio prorfus : relinquo nihil in ædibus, nec vas, nec veſti-*

Lower prose paraphrase:

mentum : corrafi omnia, ancillas, fervos, nifi eos, qui facile exercerent fuum fumtum in faciundo opere ruſtico : produxi ac vendidi omnes : illico infcripfi ædes mercede : corgi quafi ad quindecim talenta : fum mercatus hunc agrum : exerceo me hîc. Decrevi, Chieme, me facere tantifper minus injuria meo gnato, dum fiam mifer : nec effe fas, me frui hîc ulla voluptate, nifi ubi ille meus particeps redierit huc falvus. Cн. Puto te effe leni ingenio in liberos, & illum effe obfequentem, fi quis tractaret cum rectè aut commodè. Verùm neque tu fatis noveras illum, nec ille fatis noverat te. Hoc fit ibi, ubi non vivitur verè. Tu nunquam oſtendiſti quanti penderes illum : nec ille eſt aufus credere tibi ea, equæ æquum eſt credere patri. Quod fi effet factum, hæc nunquam eveniffent tibi.

ANNOTATIONS.

fperate Courſes. *Inter utrumque* (fays Se-|*rum, ut modo frenis utamur, modo ſtimulis.*
nca) regendus eſt animus inſtitutione libero-

T 2   119 Dionyſia

Men. That's the cafe, I own: but then I am moft to blame.

Chrem. Well, *Menedemus*, I yet hope for the beft ; and perfuade myfelf, that he'll be here fafe ere long.

Men. Heaven grant it may be fo!

Chrem. It will. Now, if it is convenient, as the Feaft of *Bacchus* is celebrated here To-day, I fhould be glad of your Company at my Houfe.

Men. I cannot.

Chrem. Why ? Pray, Sir, have fome little Regard for yourfelf: 'tis what even your abfent Son defires of you.

Men. It is not at all juft, that I, who have forced him upon Hardfhips, fhould fhun them myfelf.

Chrem. Is that your Refolution ?

Men. It is.

Chrem. Well, fare you well.

Men. And you.   [*Exit.*

Chrem. (*Alone.*) He has forced Tears from me, and I pity him from my Soul. But as the Day is far gone, I muft put my Neighbour *Phania* in mind to come to Supper : I'll go fee if he be at home.——— There was no need of reminding him, they tell me, he has been fome time at my Houfe already : I myfelf hinder the Guefts ; therefore, I'll in immediately. But what's the Meaning of my Door opening ? Who's this coming out ? I'll retire a little this way.

A N N O T A T I O N S.

110 *Dionyfia bic funt.* The *Athenians* celebrated a great Number of Feftivals in honour of *Bacchus*, but two were particu-larly famous, the one held in the Spring, the other in *Autumn*. The Feftival here referred to was that of *Autumn*, and called *Dionyfia*,

ACT I. SCENE II.

ARGUMENT.

Clinia, returning home from Afia, *is wonderfully folicitous about his Miſtreſs, whom, at his Departure, he had left at* Athens. Clitipho *tells his Father* Chremes, *with great Joy, of* Clinia's *Return.* Chremes *takes occaſion, from what had happened to* Clinia, *to preſcribe the Meaſures of a right Behaviour to his Son, and tells him that he ought to learn, from the Example of others, what may be of greateſt Benefit to himſelf.*

CLITIPHO, CHREMES.

Clit. YOU have no Reafon as yet for thefe your Fears, *Clinia :* they ftay not long ; and I'm certain fhe'll be here To-day,

along

A N N O T A T I O N S.

Clinia and *Clitipho* had liv'd in great Friendfhip and Familiarity together, from their Childhood. *Clinia,* it is evident, had let his Friend into the Secret of his Armour, his

ME. Ita res eſt, fateor : peccam à me maxumum eſt.
CH. Menedeme, at porro rectè ſpero : & illum tibi
Salvum affuturum eſſe hîc confideo propediem.
ME. Utinam ita Di faxint ! CH. facient. nunc, ſi
    commodum eſt,
Dionyſia hîc ſunt hodie ; apud me ſis volo.   110
ME. Non poſſum. CH. cur non ? quæſo, tandem ali
    quantulum
Tibi parce : idem abſens facere te hoc vo't filius.
ME. Non convenit, qui illum ad laborem impellerim.
Nunc meipſum fugere. CH. ſiccine eſt ſentetia ?
ME. Sic. CH. bene vale. ME. & tu. CH. lacrumas
    excuſſit mihi,
Miſeretque me ejus : ſed, ut dici tempus eſt,   116
Monere oportet mè hunc vicinum Phaniam,
Ad cœnam ut veniat. ibo, viſam ſi domi eſt,
Nihil opus fuit monitore : jamdudum domi
Præſtò apud me eſſe aiunt : egomet convivas moror.
Ibo adeò hinc intrò. ſed quid crepuerunt fores   121
Hinc à me ? quiſnam egreditur ? huc conceſſero.

Et tu. Cu. Excuſſt lacrimas mihi, miſeretque me ejus. Sed ut eſt tempus diei, oportet me monere hunc vicinum Phaniam, ut veniat ad cœnam. Ibo, viſam ſi eſt domi. Nihil opus fuit monitore: aiunt eum eſſe præſtò domi apud me jamdudum: egomet moror convivas. Adeò ibo hinc intrò. Sed quid fores crepuerunt hinc à me ? Quiſnam egreditur ? Conceſſero huc.

ME. Fateor, res ita eſt : peccatum eſt maximum à me. CH. At, Menedeme, ſpero id porro eventuum rectè ; & confido illum ſalvum affuturum eſſe hîc tibi propediem. ME. Utinam Dii faxint ita ! CH. Facient. Nunc ſi eſt commodum tibi, Dionyſia ſunt hîc hodie ; volo ut ſis apud me. ME. Non poſſum. CH. Cur non ? quæſo, tandem parce tibi aliquantulum : abſens filius vult te facere hoc idem. ME. Non convenit me ipſum nunc fugere laborem, qui impulerim illum ad laborem. CH. Siccine eſt ſententia ? ME. Sic. CH. Bene vale. ME.

ANNOTATIONS.

nyſia in agris. It may perhaps be aſked, how Chremes comes to ſay, *Dionyſia hîc ſunt hodie,* the Feſtival of Bacchus is celebrated here To-day. The Reaſon, according to Dacier, is this, becauſe the Solemnity continuing ſeveral Days, it was not celebrated at the ſame Time, in all the different Diſtricts and Diviſions of Attica, but To-Day in one Place, To-morrow in another, that thereby People might have the better Opportunity of inviting their Acquaintance and Friends.

ACTUS I. SCENA II.

ARGUMENTUM.

Clinia demum ex Aſia reverſus, mirum in modum ſolicitus eſt de amica, quam abiens Athenis reliquerat. De Cliniæ in patriam reditu, magna cum animi voluptate Clitipho nunciat patri ſuo Chremeti: Chremes ſuo ex Cliniæ vita & moribus vivendi modum præſcribit, capiendumque ex aliis docet exemplum, quod ex uſu noſtro fiet.

CLITIPHO, CHREMES.

NIHIL adhuc eſt, quod vereare, Clinia : haudqua-
    quam etiam ceſſant :
Et illam ſimul cum nuncio tibi hic ego affuturam

quaquam ceſſant : et ſcio illam affuturam hic tibi hodie ſimul cum nuncio.

ORDO.

CL. NIHIL eſt adhuc, Clinia, quod vereare etiam haud-

ANNOTATIONS.

his Father's Severity, and his Deſign of leaving his native Country. After an Ab-

ſence of three Months, not longer able to bear a Separation from his Miſtreſs, and in

along with the Meſſenger you ſent. Only ſhake off this cauſeleſs Anxiety that torments you ſo much.

Chr. (*to himſelf.*) Who's this my Son is talking with?

Clit. But I ſee my Father, whom I wanted of all things; I'll go to him. Father, you come in a very lucky time.

Chr. What's the Matter?

Clit. Do you know this *Menedemus*, our Neighbour?

Chr. Exceeding well.

Clit. Do you know too that he has a Son?

Chr. I heard he was in *Aſia*.

Clit. No, Father, he is here with us.

Chr. What do you tell me?

Clit. I met him coming out of the Ship, juſt then arrived, and brought him with me to Supper; for there has always been a great Intimacy between us, from our very Childhood.

Chr. You tell me what gives me great pleaſure. How I could wiſh that *Menedemus* were invited, that he might make one more of our Company, and receive this unexpected Joy firſt at my Houſe! Nor is it yet too late.

Clit. Have a care what you do; it is not proper, Father.

Chr. Why ſo?

Clit. Becauſe he is not yet reſolved what to do with himſelf: he is but juſt come, and fears every thing: his Father's Reſentment, and how his Miſtreſs may ſtand inclined: he loves her to diſtraction. It was on her account that this Diſturbance, and parting from his Father, happened.

Chr. I know it.

Clit. He has juſt now ſent a Servant into the City to her, and I made our *Syrus* go with him.

Chr. Well, and what ſays he?

Clit. What ſays he? that he is an unhappy Wretch.

Chr. Unhappy! How little Reaſon has he to think ſo? What is there that the World calls good, but he may enjoy? Parents, his Country flouriſhing in the Bleſſings of Peace, Friends, Birth, Relations, Riches. But theſe indeed are all to be eſtimated by the Temper of Mind of him who poſſeſſes them; to him who knows the

A N N O T A T I O N S.

patient to know how it had been with her all that time, he returns, and juſt as he is landing is met by *Clitipho*, who carries him home with him to his Father's. Thence he immediately diſpatches *Dromo* to *Athens*, to enquire after *Antiphila*; and *Clitipho*, to oblige his Friend, orders *Syrus* alſo to go along with him. The impatient *Clinia*, who thought every Moment an Age, is uneaſy at their long Stay, and gives way to a thouſand Fears and Conjectures. *Clitipho* had been endeavouring to perſuade him they were all groundleſs; and, as he is here coming out, ſtill continues his Diſcourſe to him within; but ſeeing his Father, he goes up to h.m, and tells him about his Friend, not knowing that he was ſo well acquainted with his Story. The old Man diſſembles, thinking it beſt that *Clinia* ſhould be kept in fear, till a perfect Reconciliation was brought about. He therefore pretends to blame *Clinia* for ſo raſh a Step, and juſtifies *Menedemus*, as acting from a fatherly Concern;

Hodie, ſcio. proin tu ſolicitudinem iſtam falſam, quæ te
Excruciat, mittas. CH. quicum loquitur filius? CL.
  pater adeſt,
Quem volui. adibo. Pater, opportunè advenis.   5
CH. Quid id eſt? CL. hunc Menedemum noſtrin' no-
  ſtrum vicinum? CH. probè.   [non eſt, pater:
CL. Huic filium ſcis eſſe? CH. audivi eſſe, in Aſiâ. CL.
Apud nos eſt. CH. quid ais? CL. advenientem, è navi
  egredientem illico   [uſque à pueritiâ
Abduxi ad cœnam : nam mihi magna cum eo jam inde
Fuit ſemper familiaritas. CH. voluptatem magnam nun-
  cias.   [hodie eſſet amplius,
Quàm vellem Menedemum invitatum, ut nobiſcum
Ut hanc lætitiam nec opinanti primus objicerem ei
  domi!   12
Atque etiam nunc tempus eſt. CL. cave faxis : non
  opus eſt, pater.   [quid ſe faciat. modo venit :
CH. Quapropter? CL. quia enim incertum eſt etiam,
Timet omnia; patris iram, atque animum amicæ, ſe
  erga ut ſit, ſuæ   15
Eam miſerè amat : propter eam hæc turba atque ab-
  itio evenit. CH. ſcio.   [noſtrum unà Syrum.
CL. Nunc ſervolum ad eam in urbem miſit, & ego
CH. Quid narrat? CL. quid ille? ſe miſerum eſſe. CH.
  miſerum? quem minu' credere eſt?
Quid relliqui eſt, quin habeat, quæ quidem in ho-
  mine dicuntur bona,
Parentes, patriam incolumem, amicos, genus, cog-
  natos, divitias?   20
Atque hæc perinde ſunt, ut illius animus eſt, qui ea
  poſſidet :

ſe: venis modis: timet omnia, iram patris, atque animum amicæ ſuæ, ut ſit erga ſe. Amat eam
miſerè : hæc turba atque abitio evenit propter eam. CH. Scio. CL. Miſit nunc ſervulum in urbem
ad eam, cſ ego noſtrum Syrum una. CH. Quid narrat? CL. Quid ille? Narrat ſe eſſe miſerum.
CH. Miſerum! quem minus eſt credere miſerum? Quid reliqui eſt de iis, quæ quidem dicuntur
bona in homine, quin habeat : parentes, patriam incolumem, amicos, genus cognatos,, divitias?
atque hæc perinde ſunt, ut animus illius eſt, qui poſſidet ea :

Proin tu mittas iſtam
falſam ſolicitudinem,
quæ excruciat te:
CH. Quicum filius
loquitur? CL. Pa-
ter adeſt, quem vo-
lui: adibo. Pater,
advenis opportune.
CH. Quid id eſt?
CL. Noſt'ne hunc
Menedemum noſtrum
vicinum? CH. Probe.
CL. Scis filium eſſe
huic. CH. Audivi
filium ejus eſſe in
Aſia. CL. Non eſt,
pater : eſt apud nos.
CH. Quid ais? CL.
Adduxi eam adveni-
entem, et illico egre-
dientem e navi, ad
cœnam : nam magna
familiarita fuit ſem-
per mihi cum eo jam
inde uſque à pueritiâ.
CH. Nuncias mag-
nam voluptatem.
Quam vellem Mine-
demum eſſe invita-
tum, ut eſſet nobiſ-
cum hodie amplius;
ut ego primus objice-
rem hanc lætitiam ei
nec opinanti domi!
Atque eſt tempus eti-
am nunc. CL. Cave
faxis : non eſt opus,
pater. CH. Qua-
propter? CL. Quia
enim etiam incertum
eſt; quid faciat de

ANNOTATIONS.

cern; concluding with an Admonition to his
Son, to take Example from his Friend, and
not ſuffer Paſſion to prevail againſt his Reaſon.

10 *Voluptatem magnam nuncias.* Chremes
well knew how anxious and uneaſy his Father was, on account of his ſuppoſed Abſence, and therefore receives this News of
his Return with pleaſure; and as he had
the Reaſon of the Joy, which this Account
gave him, very much at Heart, immediately ſubjoins: *Quam vellem Menedemum*
invitatum amplius, ut hanc lætitiam nec opi-
nanti prius objicerem domi! Eugraphius.

11 *Ut nobiſcum hodie eſſet amplius.* Amplius, is here variouſly turn'd by Commentators. *Eugraphius* refers it to *lætitiam :*
Ut non ſuſpicanti, amplius etiam quam ſpe-
ret, hanc lætitiam domi objicerem. Others
make it, *Quam vellem Menedemum amplius*
invitatam. But *Guyetus* ſeems to me to
have hit upon the true Meaning, who explains *amplius præter alios convivas.* How
could I wiſh that *Menedemus* made one more
Gueſt with us To-night, that I might be
the firſt to give him this unexpected Joy at
my Houſe!

21 *Atque hæc perinde ſunt, ut illius ani-*
mus,

the right Use of them, they are good; but to a Man that don't make a right Use of them, they are Plagues.

Clit. Nay, he was always a peevish old Man; and there is now nothing I am more afraid of, than that his Father in his Passion may use him with too much Rigour.

Chr. What, he! But I'll say no more; for it will be the better for my Neighbour that his Son be held in fear.

Clit. What's that you're saying to yourself?

Chr. I'll tell you: however the Case was, he ought to have staid with his Father: perhaps he was a little more severe than suited his depraved Inclinations; he should have taken it patiently: for whom should he bear with, if not with his own Father? Which of the two think you is the most reasonable, that the Father should live after the Son's Humour, or the Son according to the Father's? And as to his pretending that he was too rigorous, there is nothing in it; for the Severities of Parents are almost always the same, where the Son is not quite intolerable: they will not have them to be always whoring, or feasting and carousing; they allow them but little spending Money: yet all this is with a View to render them virtuous. But where the Mind is once entangled by corrupt Desires, it will of necessity *Clitipho*, follow those Counsels that most favour them. 'Tis a known Maxim; *To learn from the Example of others, what may may be to your own Advantage.*

Clit. I believe so.

Chr. I'm going in, to see what we have got for Supper: Do you, as it is pretty far in the Day, take care not to be any where out of the way.

ANNOTATIONS.

...mus, &c. 'Tis certain that the real Enjoyment arising from external Advantages, depends wholly upon the Situation of the Mind of him who possesses them; for if he chances to labour under any secret Anguish, this destroys all Relish, or, if he knows not how to use them for valuable Purposes, they are so far from being of any service to him, that they often turn to real Misfortunes. Those admirable Lines of *Horace*, with some little Variation, may be well applied here:

Non domus & fundus, non æris acervus & auri,
Ægroti domini deduxit corpore fibres,
Non animo curas. Valeat possessor oportet,
Si comportatis rebus bene cogitat uti.

25 *Nam, in metu esse hunc, illi est utile.* There are three different Turns given to these Words by Commentators: *In metu esse hunc Clitiphonem, illi Cliniæ est utile.* Again, *In metu esse hunc Cliniam illi Clitiphoni esse utile;* or *illi Menedimo est utile.* This last is that which I prefer. For, first, it is plain from *Clitipho's* Words, that *Clinia* was in fear: *timet omnia,* say he, *patris iram, &c.* Again, it was natural enough for *Chremes,* observing that the old Man was like to be too indulgent, not to discover this Tenderness, but to hold *Clinia* still in awe, as thinking

ACT

Qui uti ſcit, ei bona ; illi, qui non utitur recte, mala.
CL. Imo ille ſenex fuit importunus ſemper : & nunc
  nihil magis · · ·
Vereor, quam ne quid in illum iratus plus ſatis faxit pater.
CH. Illene ? ſed reprimam me : nam, in metu eſſe
  hunc, illi eſt utile.   25
CL. Quid tute tecum ? CH. dicam. ut ut erat, man-
  ſum tamen oportuit.
Fortaſſe aliquanto iniquior erat præter ejus lubidinem :
Pateretur. nam quem ferret, ſi parentem non ferret
  ſuum ?   [jus vivere ? &
Hunccine erat æquom ex illius more, an illum ex hu-
Quod illum inſimulat durum, id non eſt. nam paren-
  tum injuriæ   30
Uniuſmodi ſunt ferme ; paulo qui eſt homo tolerabilis.
Scortari crebrò nolunt, nolunt crebro convivarier,
Præbent exiguè ſumtum : atque hæc ſunt tamen ad
  virtutem omnia.
Verùm animus ubi ſemel ſe cupiditate devinxit malâ,
Neceſſe eſt, Clitipho, conſilia conſequi conſimilia. hoc
Scitum eſt, periclum ex aliis facere, tibi quod ex uſu
  ſiet.   36
CL. Ita credo. CH. ego ibo hinc intro, ut videam,
  nobis quid cœnæ ſiet.   [longiùs.
Tu, ut tempus eſt diei, vide ſis, ne quò hinc abeas

lerabilis. *Nolunt eum ſcortari crebro, nolunt convivarier crebro, præbent exigue ſumtum ; atque hæc omnia tamen ſunt ad virtutem. Verum ubi animus ſemel devinxit ſe mala cupiditate, neceſſe eſt, Clitipho, eum conſequi conſilia conſimilia. Hoc eſt ſcitum, facere periculum ex aliis, quod ſit ex uſu tibi. CL Credo ita. CH: Ego ibo hinc intro, ut vidcam quid cœnæ ſit nobis. Tu, ut eſt tempus diei, vide ſis (ſi vis) ne abeas aliquo longius hinc.*

A N N O T A T I O N S.

thinking, that by theſe means he would the ſooner bring him to comply with his Father's Will.

³¹ *Paulo qui eſt homo tolerabilis.* Theſe Words have occaſioned great Difficulty to Commentators, becauſe it is uncertain where they are to be referred, whether to the Father or the Son. Madam *Dacier* embraces the firſt, and renders them : *I ſpeak of Fathers who are not quite unreaſonable;* that is, who are neither of too ſevere, nor too eaſy a Temper. Others refer it to Sons, and ſupply ei : *Irjuriæ pa-rentum ſunt firme uniuſmodi, ei, qui eſt homo paulo tolerabilis :* the Behaviour of Parents is pretty much alike to Children who are not quite abandoned ; they will make ſome Allowances, and overlook little Fail-ings, if not carried to Exceſs. I confeſs I am much inclined to favour this Explica-tion ; for *Chremes* ſeems manifeſtly to diſtinguiſh betwixt a Son who is *homo paulo tolerabilis,* and one cujus animus ſemel ſe cupiditate devinxit mala, and is by that means become quite intolerable to his Pa-rents.

ACTUS

ACT I. SCENE III.

ARGUMENT.

Clitipho *remains here alone, complaining of his Father, as is the general Practice of Youth, who always think the Precepts of their Parents irkſome, eſpecially when they adviſe them againſt Love.*

CLITIPHO.

Clit. WHAT partial Judges are Fathers, in regard to all young Men, who think it reaſonable, that, from being Children, we ſhould immediately arrive at all the Prudence and Diſcretion of old Age, nor feel a Bias to thoſe Purſuits and Paſſions, which are in a manner inſeparable from Youth. They meaſure us by their own Deſires, ſuch as they are at preſent, not ſuch as they were formerly: If I ever chance to have a Son, I promiſe he ſhall find me an eaſy and indulgent Father; for I will encourage him to own frankly to me all his Follies, nor will I be backward to forgive them: not like this of mine, who brings out his moral Sentences, by propoſing to me the Example of others. It provokes me beyond all Patience to hear him, when he has drank a little too much, relating his own paſt Exploits. Now he bids me : *Take Example from others, of what may be to your own advantage.* Cunning Fox! little does he ſuſpect how deaf I am to all theſe grave Remonſtrances. The Words of my Miſtreſs make a much greater Impreſſion on me at preſent: *Give me this, and bring me the other thing:* to which I am at a loſs how to anſwer; nor is there living a more unhappy Creature than I. For this *Clinia*, although indeed he has enough upon his hands, yet his Miſtreſs is well and modeſtly brought up, and a Stranger to the Tricks of theſe Town-Jilts. Mine is an imperious, bold, magnificent, expenſive, and haughty Dame: then when ſhe aſks for any thing, Right, ſay I, with an expreſſive Nod, for it were an unpardonable

ANNOTATIONS.

In this Scene *Clitipho* is repreſented as reflecting with himſelf upon what his Father had ſaid. As young Men are apt to repine at every Interruption of their Deſires, imagine themſelves infallible, and can't bear Conſtraint; ſo is that Character exactly drawn here. The Sentiments are natural, and the moſt ſuitable to one of *Clitipho*'s Age and Diſpoſition, that can poſſibly be imagined. He thinks his Father behaved to him without any reaſonable Allowance for the difference of Age; and as he had himſelf loſt all Reliſh for the Enjoyments of Youth, expected his Son ſhould be equally indifferent to them. As he looks upon this to be very unfair, and believed his Inclinations to be no other than what were natural and excuſable at ſuch an Age; he falls immediately upon reflecting how dif-

ferently he would behave were he a Father, and what Allowances he would make his Son; from which, by an eaſy Tranſition, he comes to think of his Miſtreſs, and how he might beſt anſwer her Demands.

3 *Neque illarum affines eſſe rerum. Affines* are properly thoſe who poſſeſs Lands that border upon one another: thence the Word came to be extended in Signification, and take in not only thoſe who were united by Ties of Conſanguinity, but even ſuch as were obnoxious by their Vices. *Affinis ſceleris, ſuſpicionis, turpitudini, culpæ, facinori,* are frequent in *Cicero.*

5 *Ubi adbibit plus paulo. Terence* is full of moral Inſtructions, uſeful in the Conduct of Life. We here learn how exact Parents ought to be in reſpect of their Children. It is not enough that they
give

ACTUS I. SCENA III.

ARGUMENTUM.

Solus hic Clitipho remanſit, qui de patre conqueritur, ut mos eſt adoleſcentium, qui paterna præcepta moleſte ferunt, præſertim cum ab amore dehorantur.

CLITIPHO.

QUAM iniqui ſunt patres in omnes adoleſcentes judices : [ſenes,
Qui æquum eſſe cenſent, nos jam à pueris illico naſci
Neque illarum affines eſſe rerum, quas fert adoleſcentia.
Ex ſuâ libidine moderantur, nunc quæ eſt, non quæ olim fuit.
Mihi ſi unquam filius erit, næ illæ facili me utetur patre;
Nam & cognoſcendi, & ignoſcendi dabitur peccati locus : 6
Non ut meus, qui mihi per alium oſtendit ſuam ſen- tentiam. [rat facinora ?
Perii : is mihi, ubi adbibit plus paulo, ſua quæ nar-
Nunc ait, Periclum ex aliis facito, tibi quod ex uſu ſiet.
Aſtutus ! næ ille haud ſcit, quam mihi nunc ſurdo narret fabulam. 10
Magis nunc me amicæ dicta ſtimulant, Da mihi, atque, Affer mihi. [quam eſt miſerior.
Cui quid reſpondeam, nihil habeo, neque me quiſ-
Nam hic Clinia, etſi is quoque ſuarum rerum ſatagit, attamen
Habet bene ac pudicè eductam, ignaram artis mere- triciæ. 14
Mea eſt potens, procax, magnifica, ſumtuoſa, nobilis.
Tum, quòd dem ei, rectè eſt : nam nihil eſſe mihi, religio eſt dicere.

ORDO.

CL. *QUAM ini- qui judi- ces ſunt patres in om- nes adoleſcentes : qui cenſent eſſe æquum, nos a pueris jam il- lico naſci ſenes, ne- que eſſe affines illa- rum rerum, quas a- doleſcentia fert. Mo- derantur ex ſua libi- dine, quæ eſt nunc, non quæ fuit olim. Si filius unquam erit mihi, næ ille utetur me facili patre : nam locus dabitur ex cog- noſcendi et ignoſcendi peccati, non ero ut meus pater, qui o- ſtendit ſuam ſenten- tiam mihi per alium. Perii : is, ubi adbi- bit plus paulo, quæ ſua facinora, nar- rat mihi ? Nunc ait, Facito periculum ex aliis, quod ſit ex uſu tibi. Aſtutus ! næ ille haud ſcit, quam nunc narret fabulam mihi ſurdo. Dicta amicæ majis ſtimu-*

lant me nunc, Da mihi, atque Affer mihi, cui habeo nihil quid reſpondeam : neque quiſquam eſt miſerior me. Nam hic Clinia, etſi is quoque ſatagit ſuarum rerum, attamen habet amicam educ- tam bene ac pudice, ignaram artis merctriciæ : mea amica eſt potens, procax, magnifica, ſump- tuoſa, nobilis. Tum quod dem ei, rectè eſt, nam religio eſt mihi dicere eſſe nihil.

ANNOTATIONS.

give them good Advice, and point out to them their Duty ; they muſt alſo edify them by their Example, becauſe the leaſt Failing here will not only deſtroy all the Benefit of their Inſtructions, but give too great an Opportunity for Youth to exert that natural Biaſs they have of turning every thing they ſay or do, that contradicts their own Inclinations, into Ridicule.
¹³ *Etſi is quoque ſuarum rerum ſatagit.* Satagit : ſatis rerum ſuarum agit, ſatis occupatus eſt rebus ſuis. This Word was

commonly uſed in ſpeaking of a Man who had more upon his hands than he could well manage. We find it too employed to deſcribe a Man full of Anxiety, running up and down, and in a perpetual Hurry. *Quintil. Lib.* vi. 4. *Afer enim veruſte Mam- lium Suram multum in agendo diſcurſantem, ſalientem, manus jactantem, togani dejicientem & reſonentem, non agere dixit, ſed ſata- gere.*
¹⁶ *Tum, quod dem ei, rectè eſt.* Com- mentators are much divided as to the Senſe

donable Error to let her know I had it not to give. This is a Mifchief I have but of late difcovered; nor does my Father, as yet, know any thing of it.

ANNOTATIONS.

of thefe Words. What feems moft pro- | not always in his power to fatisfy them,
bable is, that *recte eft* is only a mere Eva- | this often puts him to a difficulty how to
fion, where he was unwilling to give a di- | behave. He did not care to own he had no-
rect Anfwer. As *Bacchis* was making | thing, and therefore comes off by this
continual Demands upon him, and it was | Evafion, *recte eft, right:* which, though,
                                               - feem-

ACT II. SCENE I.

ARGUMENT.

Clinia *is under the greateſt Uneaſineſs at the Lingering and Delay of* Antiphila *his Miſtreſs; for the Mind of a Lover is commonly impatient of any Hindrance, however ſmall.*

CLINIA, CLITIPHO.

Clin. HAD all been well in regard to my Love, I know they would have been here long before now; but I fear much, left ſhe may have been feduc'd here in my Abfence. Many things concur to rack my Mind, *and fill me with Suſpicions:* Opportunity, Place, Age, a wicked Mother, under whofe Government ſhe is, and who regards nothing but Gain.

Clit. Clinia!

Clin. Alas! Wretch that I am.

Clit. Have a care, left perhaps any one coming out from your Father, may chance to fee you here.

Clin. I will: but indeed, *Clitipho*, my Mind prefages, I don't know what Misfortune.

Clit. Do you ſtill perſiſt in judging of a thing before you know the Truth of it.

Clin. If no Misfortune had happened, they would certainly have been here before now.

Clit. They will be here prefently.

Clin. But when is this prefently to be? *Clit.*

ANNOTATIONS.

Muretus and *Goveanus* here begin the fecond Act, and are, I think, now pretty much followed, though *Beeclerus* contends, that it ought to begin with the former Scene. But it is evident there, that *Clitipho*, who had been talking with his Father, after his withdrawing, falls into a Train of Reflections upon what had been the Subject of their Converfation. Thefe we muſt fuppofe to follow immediately upon his being left by himſelf without any Paufe

or Stop intervening, otherwife they will lofe all their Beauty and Propriety.

[1] *Si mibi ſecundæ reſ, &c.* We are to remember, that in a former Scene *Clinia* and *Clitipho* had fent into the City to enquire after *Antiphila*, and if poffible bring her to them. *Clinia*, who was impatient to fee her, wonders at their long Stay; and, as Love is apt to give way to Fears and Apprehenfions, fufpects that fome Misfortune muſt have happened. Full of this Anxiety and

Hoc ego mali non pridem inveni : neque etiamdum
scit pater.

pater etiamdum scit.

	Ego non pridem in-
	veni hoc mali : neque.

ANNOTATIONS.

seemingly a Consent, was in reality just
nothing at all, as it implied no positive
Promise,

7 Hoc ego mali non pridem inveni. Some
explain this of his want of Money, but it

is more agreeable to the whole Train of the
Discourse, to refer it to his Mistress, whose
constant Demands, and his being unable to
supply them, was a Misfortune he had but
lately discovered.

A.

ACTUS II. SCENA I.

ARGUMENTUM.

Clinia cessatione & mora Antiphilæ amicæ nimium torquetur,
solet enim amantis animus, omnis moræ, quamtumvis brevis,
impatientior esse.

CLINIA, CLITIPHO.

ORDO.

SI mihi secundæ res de amore meo essent, jamdudum
    scio,   [corrupta sit.
Venissent : sed vereor, ne mulier, me absente, hîc
Concurrunt multæ opiniónes, quæ mihi animum ex-
    angeant :   [mala,
Occasio, locus, ætas, mater, cujus sub imperio est,
Cui nihil præter precium jam dulce est. CLIT. Clinia.
    CLIN. hei misero mihi !   5
CLIT. Etiam caves, ne videat forte hinc te à patre
    aliquis exiens ?   [præsagit mali.
CLIN. Faciam. sed nescio quid profecto mihi animu'
CLIT. Pergin' istuc prius dijudicare, quàm scis, quid
    veri siet ?   [aderunt. CLIN. quando istuc erit ?
CLIN. Si nihil mali esset, jam hîc adessent. CLIT. jam

ORDO. CLIN. *SI res es-*
sent, se-
cundæ mihi de meo
amore, scio, nuncii
venissent jamdudum :
sed vereor, ne mulier
sit corrupta his, me
absente. Multæ opi-
niones concurrunt, quæ
exangeant animum
mihi ; viz. occasio,
locus, ætas, mater
mala, sub imperio
cujus est : cui jam
nihil est dulce, præ-
ter precium. CLIT.
Clinia. CLIN. Hei
mihi misero! CLIT.
Etiam caves, ne for-

te aliquis exiens hinc a patre videat te ? CLIN. *Faciam sed profecto animus præsagit mihi nescio*
quid mali. CLIT. *Pergisne dijudicare istuc, priusquam scis quid veri sit ?* CLIN. *Si esset nihil*
mali, jam adessent hic. CLIT. *Aderunt jam.* CLIN. *Quando istuc jam erit ?*

ANNOTATIONS.

and Care, he is seen here to come out of
Chremes's House, and looking round him,
if possibly he might discover the Servants
coming back. Clitipho follows immediately
after, and cautions him to take care how
he exposed himself in that Place, lest peradventure he might be seen by some of his
Father's Domesticks.

4 *Occasio, locus, ætas, mater.* Clinia
here mentions the four things that tended
chiefly to beget his Suspicions. *Opportunity.*
His Mistress was wholly by herself, and

had no one to watch over her Conduct.
Place. The City of Athens, full of Debauchery, and where young Women were
daily exposed to Temptations. *Her Age ;*
She was then, young, had but little Experience, and was therefore the more in danger from deceitful Betrayers. *Her Mother,*
avaricious, and corrupt, one who would
make no scruple to sacrifice her Daughter's
Honour to her own covetous Designs. *Da-*
cier.

7 *Præsagit.* Cicero has fully explained
the

Clit. You don't confider that it is a great way off; and you know the Nature of Women before they are comb'd and powder'd out, 'tis an Age.

Clin. O, *Clitipho*, I am afraid.

Clit. Courage: yonder come *Dromo* and *Syrus* together; they are juft at hand.

ANNOTATIONS.

the Force of this Word in his firft Book *de* | *volunt : et fagaces dicti canes.* Is igitur,
Divinatione 31. *Sagire enim, fentire acute* | qui ante fagit; quam oblata res eft, dicitur
eft : ex quo fagæ anus, quia multa fcire | præfagire, i. e. futura ante fentire.

Thus

ACT II. SCENE II.

ARGUMENT.

Clinia *underftands from* Syrus, *that* Antiphila *had behaved with great Modefty in his abfence, which gives him inexpreffible Joy.* Bacchis, Clitipho's *Miftrefs, is alfo brought to Supper, and in the mean time things are fo contrived, that fhe fhall pafs for* Clinia's *Miftrefs.*

SYRUS, DROMO, CLITIPHO, CLINIA.

Syrus. SAY you fo?

Dro. It is fo indeed.

Syr. But mean time, while we are chatting, the Women are left behind.

Clit. Here's your Miftrefs for you, *Clinia*, do you hear?

Clin. Yes, I do hear now at laft, and fee, and am happy, *Clitipho.*

Dro. No wonder: they are fo incumber'd: they bring a Troop of Maids along with them.

Clin. Confufion! how comes fhe to have Maids?

Clit. Do you afk of me?

Syr. We ought not to have left them; they bring Things of Value with them.

Clin. Heavens! *Syr.*

ANNOTATIONS.

This Scene contains the unravelling of all thofe Sufpicions, of which *Clinia* is fo full in the foregoing: it alfo introduces a new and unexpected Event; for *Syrus*, who had gone only to accompany *Dromo*, and affift him in his Charge, by the way takes it into his head to go to *Bacchis*, *Clitipho*'s Miftrefs, and as he chanced to come upon her at a lucky Minute, prevails with her to go along with *Antiphila*, to her Gal- | lant's Father's; and they had contrived among themfelves, that fhe fhould pafs for *Clinia*'s Miftrefs, and *Antiphila* for one of her Maids. All this was tranfacted without *Clitipho*'s knowledge, and therefore, when he hears that *Bacchis* was come, he is in great Surprize, and not fatisfied with *Syrus*'s Project, who reveal'd it to him but in part, he is at firft greatly enraged, but then Defire and Paffion intervening, as he

was

CLIT. Non cogitas hinc longulè esse ? & nosti mores mulierum :

Dum moliuntur, dum conantur, annus est. CLIN. ô Clitipho, [ro ; unà adsunt tibi.

Timeo. CLIT. respira : eccum Dromonem cum Sy-

timvo. CLIT. *Respira : eccum Dromonem cum Syro ; una adsunt tibi.*

CLIT. Non cogitas eos esse longulè hinc ? E: nosti morei mulierum : dum moliuntur, dum conantur, est annus. CLIN. O Clitipho,

ANNOTATIONS.

Thus *Plaut.* Aul. II. 2. 1.

Præjogicbat mihi animus frustra me ire, quum exibam domo.

11 *Dum moliuntur, dum conantur. Moliri* is properly to begin any great Work or

Undertaking ; hence *dum moliuntur* here may be very properly explained with *Marfus, dum se præparant multiplici cultu, ædificant formam variis rebus.*

ACTUS II. SCENA II.

ARGUMENTUM.

Clinia ex Syro intelligit, se absente pudice admodum vixisse Antiphilam, qua ex re, ingenti gaudio perfunditur : Bacchis Clitiphonis amica, ad cœnam adducitur; quæ tamen interim fingitur esse amica Cliniæ.

SYRUS, DROMO, CLITIPHO, CLINIA.

AIN' tu ? DR. sic est. SY. verùm intérea dum sermones cædimus,

Illæ sunt relictæ. CLIT. mulier tibi adest, audin' Cliniá?

CLIN. Ego vero audio nunc demum, & video, & valeo, Clitipho. [gregem

DR. Minimè mirum : adeò impeditæ sunt : ancillarum Ducunt secum. CLIN. perii. unde illi sunt ancillæ ? CLIT. men' rogas ?

SY. Non oportuit relictas : portant quid rerum ; CLIN. hei mihi !

ORDO.

A Isni in ? DR. Sic est. SY. Verùm interea, dum cædimus sermones, illæ sunt relictæ. CLIT. Audisne, Clinia ? Mulier adest tibi ? CLIN. Ego vero nunc demum audio, & video, & valeo, Clitipho. DR. Minimè mirum : eas esse relictas sane

adeo impeditæ ; ducunt gregem ancillarum secum. CLIN. Perii. Unde sunt ancillæ illi ? CLIT. Rogasne me ? SY. Non oportuit eas fusse relictas ; portant quid rerum. CLIN. Hei mihi !

ANNOTATIONS.

was unwilling to lose so fair an Opportunity of enjoying his Mistress, he at last submits, and gives himself wholly up to the Management of *Syrus.*

1 *Ain' tu ?* This Scene begins somewhat abruptly, and introduces *Syrus* and *Dromo* as continuing a Conversation which had been already begun. We may naturally enough suppose, that *Dromo* had been telling *Syrus* some of the Adventures that had befallen his Master and him during their Stay in *Asia,* and as several surprizing Accidents might have happened in that time,

hence at the Relation of some of them, *Syrus* here asks with an Air of Surprise. *ain' tu ?*

Ibid. *Dum sermones cædimus.* The manner of speaking here used is very remarkable, *cædere sermones,* to converse, chat, or discourse alternately. It is borrowed from the *Greeks,* with whom κόπτειν and τέμνειν λόγους is very frequent. *Nonius,* among other Meanings of the Word *cædere,* observes, that it sometimes is put for *commisceo,* which Signification agrees very well with the Use of it here.

5 *Perii ; unde illi sunt ancillæ ?* The Poet
here

Syr. Jewels, fine Clothes; besides, it begins to be late, and they know not the way. 'Twas mighty foolish in us. Do you, *Dromo* go back and meet them; make haste; why do you stand?

[Exit Dromo.

Clin. Alas! unhappy Wretch that I am, from what high Hopes have I fallen?

Clit. What can this be? What is it that troubles you so much now?

Clin. Troubles me, say you? Don't you hear of her Maids, Jewels, fine Clothes, whom I left here with but one Girl; whence should she have them, think ye?

Clit. Oh! Now at last I begin to understand.

Syr. Bless me, what a Train there is! Our House will scarce hold them, I know it. How much they will eat and drink! How miserable my old Master will be! But here come the Persons I wanted.

Clin. O, *Jupiter!* Where is Sincerity and Honour? While I rashly abandoning my Country, wander like a Fugitive for love of you; you, *Antiphila*, have here enriched yourself, and forsaken me in the midst of these my Troubles. You, for whose sake I am now in the highest Disgrace; and regardless of the Will of my Father; I am now quite ashamed and confounded, that he who so often read me Lectures upon the Manners of these Creatures, should give his Advice in vain, nor, with all his Eloquence, be able to wean me from her; which I am now however resolved to do of myself; but then, when there might have been some Merit in it, I would not: no Creature is more wretched than I.

Syr. He, I perceive, has misunderstood what we were talking of: *Clinia*, you imagine your Mistress quite different from what she is, for her Manner of Life is just as formerly, and her Affection for you continues the same, as far as we could conjecture from what we saw.

Clin. What's that pray? for there is nothing I more earnestly wish at present, than to find these my Suspicions without foundation.

Syr. First, then, that you may not be ignorant of any thing that concerns

ANNOTATIONS.

here artfully introduces *Clinia* as hastily taking up a wrong Notion of his Mistress, and applying to *Antiphila* what regarded *Bacchis*; for all this Attendance and *Apparatus* of Ornaments belonged to her. By this he has an Opportunity of setting before us, in a yet stronger Light, his Fears, Suspicions, and Distraction of Mind; all which gives the Reader a very natural Picture of a Man deeply in love: moreover, it makes way for that beautiful Description which comes in afterwards, of the manner of *Antiphila's* employing herself during her Lover's Absence.

7 *Aurum, vestem.* *Syrus* seems to say all this by chance, and without design, but the Poet artfully turns them to augment *Clinia's* Fears and Suspicions, and make the Spectators sensible how much his Happiness depended upon finding his *Antiphila* faithful and innocent.

12 *Vah, nunc demum intelligo.* The Poet industriously protracts this Error of *Clinia*, nor does even *Clitipho* here endeavour to abate his Friend's Distress, as had been all along his Study. *Pergin' istuc prius dijudicare, quam scis quid sit?* But here he seems rather to yield to the Arguments by which

SY. Aurum, vestem : & vesperascit, & non noveruntviam.
Factum à nobis stulte est. abi dum tu, Dromo, illis
   obviam.   [de spe decidi!
Propera. quid stas ? CLIN. væ misero mihi, quanta
CLIT. Quid istuc ? quæ res te solicitat autem ? CLIN.
   rogitas quid siet ?   10
Viden' tu ancillas, aurum, vestem ? quam ego cum
   unâ ancillulâ   [mum intellego.
Hìc reliqui. unde esse censes ? CLIT. vah, nunc de-
SY. Dii boni, quid turbæ est ? ædes nostræ vix ca-
   pient, scio.   [miserius ?
Quid comedent ? quid ebibent ? quid sene erit nostro
Sed video, eccos, quos volebam. CLIN. ô Jupiter,
   ubinam est fides ?   15
Dum ego propter te errans patriâ careo demens, tu
   interea loci
Conlocupletasti, Antiphila, te, & me in his deseruisti
   malis,   [minùs obsequens ?
Propter quam in summâ infamiâ sum, & meo patri
Cujus nunc pudet me, & miseret, qui harum mores
   cantabat mihi,
Monuisse frustra : neque potuisse eum unquam me ab
   hac expellere.   20
Quod tamen nunc faciam ; tum, cùm mihi gratum
   esse potuit, nolui.   [videlicet,
Nemo est miserior me. SY. hic de nostris verbis errat
Quæ hìc sumus locuti. Clinia, aliter tuum amorem,
   atque est, accipis.
Nam & vita est eadem, & animus te erga idem ac fuit,
Quantùm ex ipsâ re conjecturam cepimus   25
CLIN. Quid est, obsecro ? nam mihi nunc nihil rerum
   omnium est
Quod malim, quàm me hoc falsò suspicarier. [anus,
SY. Hoc primum, ut ne quid hujus rerum ignores

* SY. Portant aurum, vestem : & vesperascit, et non noverunt viam. Factum est stulte à nobis: tudum, Dromo, abi obviam illis; propera; quid stas ? CLIN. Væ mihi misero, de quanta spe decidi! CLIT. Quid istuc ? Quæ autem res solicitat te ? CLIN. Rogitas quid sit ? Videsne tu ancillus, aurum, vestem ? Quam ego reliqui hìc cum unâ ancillulâ ; unde senses ea esse ? CLIT. Vah, nunc demum intelligo. SY. Dii boni quid turbæ est ? Scio, nostræ ædes vix capient : Quid comedent ? Quid ebibent ? Quid erit miserius nostro sene ? Sed video quos volebam ecce eos. CLIN. O, Jupiter ! Ubinam est fides ? Dum ego demens, errans propter te, careo patriâ, interea loci, tu, Antiphila, collocupletasti te, et deseruisti me in his malis: tu, inquam, propter quam sum in summâ infamiâ, et minus obsequens meo patri: cujus nunc pudet et miseret me, cum qui cantabet mihi mores harum meretricum; monuisse me frustra ; neque cum potuisse unquam expellere me ab bâc Antiphila ; quod tamen nunc ipse faciam ; nolui tum, cum potuit esse gratum mihi. Nemo est miserior me. SY. Hic videlicet errat de nostris verbis, quæ sumus locuti hìc. Clinia, accipis tuum amorem aliter atque est. Nam et vita est eadem, et animus ejus est idem erga te ac fuit, quantum cepimus conjecturam ex ipsâ re. CLIN. Obsecro, quid est ? Nam nunc est nibil omnium rerum, quod malim mibi, quàm me suspicari boc falso. SY. Intellige boc primum, ut ne ignores quid rerum bujus: anus,*

ANNOTATIONS.

which *Clinia* is persuaded that his Mistress must have been seduced during his Absence ; and this is the more diverting in *Clitipbo* because he does not in the least suspect that it is his own Mistress, and not *Clinia's*, that is here describ'd.

15 *O Jupiter, ubinam est fides ?* Nothing can be more moving or expressive than this Complaint, wherein we see the Lover brought to the very Brink of Despair, for it

was necessary to carry the Mistake as far as possible, before he should be undeceived. We are to suppose his Words too accompanied with Gestures equally expressive of his Grief, till *Syrus*, approaching nearer, perceiving the Error, clears *Antipbila* of these unjust Suspicions, by the long and elegant Account of her which follows.

21 *Cum mibi gratum esse potuit.* This whole Sentence is a little intricate and per-

concerns her, the old Woman, who was formerly fuppofed to be her Mother, was not fo: fhe it feems is dead: this I ch·nced to hear from herfelf, whilft fhe told it the other as we came along.

Clit. Who's that other?

Syr. Patience, *Clitipho:* let me firft finifh what I have begun, and then I'll come to your Queftion.

Clit. Make hafte, then.

Syr. Firft of all, when we came to the Houfe, *Dromo* knocks at the Door: a certain old Woman appeared, who had no fooner o-pened the Door than he rufhed in, and I immediately followed: the old Woman bolted the Door, and then returned again to her Work. Here, *Clinia,* or never might it be known, how your Miftrefs had fpent her time in your Abfence, when we came unexpectedly upon the Woman; for this gave a full Opportunity of judging of her daily Courfe of Life, from whence we have the trueft Infight into People's different Humours and Inclinations. We found her bufily plying her Web, drefs'd in a plain mourning Gown; I fuppofe on account of that old Woman lately dead, without any Ornaments of Gold or Jewels, but like one who was drefs'd only for herfelf; no Varnifh or Paint to fet off her Beauty; her Hair loofe, and fall-ing carelefsly round her Head, in long Ringlets; all was hufh.

Clin. For Heaven's Sake, *Syrus,* don't fill me with a falfe Joy.

Syr. The old Woman was fpinning the Woof, and had a little Girl that fat by her, weaving too, with patch'd Clothes, ill drefs'd, and very nafty.

Clit. If all this be true, *Clinia,* as I make no doubt of it, who is happier than you? Do you mind the fordid, dirty Wench he fpeaks of? This alfo is a great Sign that the Miftrefs is without Blame, when the Confident is fo far neglected; for it is now a Rule with thofe who afpire to the Miftrefs, to begin by bribing the Maid. *Syr.*

ANNOTATIONS.

plex'd. The proper Meaning, however, I take to be this: I am afhamed that my Fa-ther who warned me of the Deceitfulnefs and Bafenefs of thefe Wretches, fhould have fo often counfell'd and admonifh'd me in vain, nor could ever prevail with me to break from her, which however I am now refolved to do, though I would not at that time when it might have effectually gain'd me the old Man's Heart. *Gratum effet,* i. e. *Cum gratiam patris meo obfequio demereri potui.* That this is the proper Interpretation of *gratum* here, appears from the following Verfe of *Phædrus,* where it is ufed in the fame Senfe. Lib. I. 22. 5.

Gratum effet, & dediffem veniam fupplici.

38 *Hic fcire potui.* Nothing can be more juft or happily conceived than thefe fix Lines, which contain a general Rule to di-rect us in forming our Notions of Charac-ters and Perfons. 'Tis certain, that the private Scenes of Life, and thofe Tafks that employ us, when there is no Witnefs of our Conduct, are the fureft Tefts of our real Temper. This is fo agreeable to Rea-fon and good Senfe, that fo grave and judi-cious an Hiftorian as *Livy* proceeds upon the fame Suppofition, where he fpeaks of the Rape committed upon *Lucretia* by *Tar-quin's* Son. Lib. I. cap. 57.

Incidit de uxoribus mentio: fuam quifque laudare miris modis: inde certamine accenfo, Collatinus negat verbis opus effe, paucis id quidem horis poffe fciri, quantum cæteris præftet Lucretia fua. Quin, fi vigor juventæ ineft, confcendimus equos, invifimufque præfen-tes noftrarum ingenia? Id cuique fpectatiffi-mum fit, quod inopinato viri adventu occurre-rit oculis.

52 *Subtemen nebat. Subtemen* is properly that Part of the Web which runs acrofs the Warp, and is driven alternately between its

Threads

Quæ eſt dicta mater eſſe ei antehac, non fuit :,
Ea obiit mortem : hæc ipſa in itinere alteræ   30
Dum narrat, fortè audivi. CLIN. quænam eſt altera ?
SY. Mane, hoc, quod cœpi, primùm enarrem, Clitipho :
Poſt iſtùc veniam. CLIN. propera. SY. jam primùm
    omnium,
Ubi ventum ad ædes eſt, Dromo pultat fores :
Anus quædam prodit : hæc ubi aperuit oſtium,   35
Continuò hic ſe conjecit intro : ego conſequor ;,
Anus foribus obdit peſſulum, ad lanam redit.
Hic ſciri potuit, aut nuſquam alibi, Clinia,
Quo ſtudio vitam ſuam te abſente exegerit :,
Ubi de improviſo eſt interventum mulieri.   40
Nam ea res didit tum exiſtumandi copiam
Quotidianæ vitæ conſuetudinem ;
Quæ, cujuſque ingenium ut fit, declarat maxumè.
Texentem telam ſtudioſè ipſam offendimus,
Mediocriter veſtitam veſte lugubri,   45
Ejus anuis cauſâ, opinor, quæ erat mortua,
Sine auro tum ornatam, ita utì quæ ornatur ſibi,
Nullâ malâ re eſſe expolitam muliebri :
Capillus paſſus, prolixus, circum caput
Rejectus neglegenter. pax! CLIN. Syre mi, obſecro,   50
Ne me in lætitiam fruſtra conjicias. SY. anus
Subtemen nebat : præterea una uncillula
Erat : ea texebat unà pannis obſita,
Neglecta, immunda inluvie. CLIT. ſi hæc ſunt, Clinia,
Vera, ita utì credo, quis te eſt fortunatior ?   55
Scin' tu hanc, quam dicit ſordidatam & ſordidam ?
Magnum hoc quoque ſignum eſt, dominam eſſe extra
    noxiam,
Cùm ejus tam negleguntur internuncii :
Nam diſciplina eſt eiſdem, munerarier
Ancillas primùm, ad dominas qui affectant viam.   60

quæ antehac eſt dicta eſſe mater ei, non fuit mater: ea obiit mortem: forte audivi hoc, dum ipſa narrat alteri in itinere. CLIT. Quænam eſt altera? SY. Mane. Clitiphó, primum enarrem hoc, quod cœpi; poſt, veniam iſtuc. CLIN. Propera. SY. Jam primum omnium, ubi ventum eſt ad ædes, Dromo pultat fores: anus quædam prodit: ubi hæc aperuit oſtium, hic continuo conjecit ſe intro: ego conſequor: anus obdit peſſulum foribus, deinde redit ad lanam. Hic, Clinia, aut nuſquam alibi, potuit ſciri, quo ſtudio exegerit vitam ſuam, te abſente; ubi interventum eſt mulieri de improviſo. Nam ea res tum dedit copiam exiſtimandi conſuetudinem quotidianæ vitæ; quæ maxime declarat, ut ingenium cujuſque fit. Offendimus ipſam ſtudioſe texentem telam viſſitam mediocriter lugubri veſte, opinor, cauſâ ejus anuis, quæ erat mortua, ornatam tum ſine auro, ita uti quæ ornatur ſibi, eſſe expolitam nulla mala re muliebri: capillus erat paſſus, prolixus, rejectus negligenter circum caput. Pax. CLIN. Mi Syre, obſecro te ne fruſtra conjicias me in latitiam. SY. Anus nebat ſubtemen: erat præterea una ancillula, ea obſita pannis, neglecta, immunda illuvie, ea texebat una cum illis. CLIT. Clinia, ſi hæc ſunt vera, ita uti credo, quis eſt fortunatior te? Sciſne tu hanc ancillulam, quam dicit eſſe ſordidatam et ſordidam? Hoc quoque eſt magnum ſignum, dominam eſſe extra noxiam, cum internuncii ejus tam negliguntur: nam eſt diſciplina eiſdem, qui affectant viam ad dominas, munerari primùm ancillas.

ANNOTATIONS.

Threads by the Shuttle: *Subtemen dictum ab eo quod jubeat flamen.* I cannot give a better account of it than by the following Quotation from *Ovid*, where he ſpeaks of the Trial of Skill between *Pallas* and *Arachne. Met.* 6. 54.

*Et gracili geminas intendunt ſtamine telas,
Tela jugo vincta eſt: ſtamen ſecernit arundo:*

*Inſeritur medium radiis ſubtemen acutis;
Quod digiti expediunt, atque inter ſtamina ductum
Percuſſo feriunt inſecti pectine dentes.*

56 *Munerarier ancillas primùm.* This is a never-failing Rule, and ſtrongly recommended to us by the great Maſter in the Art of Love. *Ovid de Arte Amandi.* L. 1. 353.

Clin. Go on, pray, *Syrus*, and beware of endeavouring to gain Favour by deceiving me. What said she when you named me to her?

Syr. When you told her that you was return'd, and that you begg'd her to come and see you, she immediately threw aside her Work, and covered her Face with Tears, in a Manner that made it easy to perceive it was all for love of you.

Clin. As Heaven shall bless me, I know not where I am for Joy, so great was my Fright before.

Clit. But I knew very well, *Clinia*, that there was nothing in it. Well then, *Syrus*, it is now my Turn; come tell me who that other is.

Syr. We bring your *Bacchis* with us.

Clit. How? bring *Bacchis*? Hark ye, Villain, where do you propose to carry her?

Syr. Where to carry her? Undoubtedly to our House.

Clit. What, to my Father's?

Syr. The very same.

Clit. O, the daring Impudence of the Wretch!

Syr. Harkye, Sir, no great and memorable Attempt can be undertaken without Danger.

Clit. Look ye, Sirrah, you want to acquire Fame at my Cost; where the least Slip may prove fatal to me: what will you do then?

Syr. But then, Sir.

Clit. What then?

Syr. If you'll give me Leave, I'll tell you.

Clin. Give him Leave.

Clit. I do.

Syr. This Business now is just as if—

Clit. What the duce does he mean to begin a long round-about Story—

Clin. *Syrus*, 'tis as he says; drop this, and come to the Point itself.

Syr. Absolutely I can hold it no longer; you are many ways injurious, *Clitipho*, nor is it possible to bear with you.

Clit. Nay, he ought to have a Hearing, therefore pray be silent.

Syr. You would love, you would possess your Mistress, and have where-

Sed prius ancillam captandæ nosse puellæ
Cura sit; accessus molliat illa tuos,
Proxima consiliis dominæ sit ut illa vidato;
Neve parum tacitis conscia side jocis.
Hac quoque pollicitis, hanc tu corrumpe rogando;
Quod petis ex facili, si volet illa, feres.

6 *Quid ait, ubi me nominas?* Hitherto we have seen *Antiphila*'s Manner of Life in her Lover's Absence, and that it had been agreable to the strictest Rules of Innocence and Decency; it now remains, that we be inform'd how she stood affected to *Clinia*, and whether her Attachment

here was still the same as formerly. This *Syrus* makes appear by her manner of behaving when he was named to her, and so makes good what he had advanced to *Clinia* in the Beginning.

Nam et vita est eadem, et animus te erga idem ac fuit.

7 *Non sit sine periclo.* After clearing up what regarded *Antiphila*, *Bacchis* comes upon the Stage. *Clitipho*, astonish'd at her being one of the Company, asks *Syrus* hastily, where he meant to bring her; and, still more surprized at his answering *to his Father's*, seems shock'd at his Confidence and Boldness. He, in defence of himself, tells

CLIN. Perge, obfecro te, & cave ne falfam gratiam
Studeas inire. quid ait, ubi me nominas?
SY. Ubi dicimus rediifle te, & rogare utì
Veniret ad te, mulier telam definit
Continuò. & lacrumis opplet os totum fibi, ut   65
Facilè fcires defiderio id fieri tuo.
CLIN. Præ gaudio, ita me Dii ament, ubi fim nefcio:
Ita timui. CLIT. at ego nihil effe fciebam, Clinia.
Agedum viciffim, Syre, dic quæ illa eft altera.
SY. Adducimus tuam Bacchidem. CLIT. hem, quid
  Bacchidem?   70
Eho, fcelefte, quò illam ducis? SY. quò ego illam? ad
  nos fcilicet.
CLIT. Ad patremne? SY. ad eum ipfum. CLIT. ô
  hominis impudentem audaciam! [memorabile.
SY. Heus tu, non fit fine periclo facinus magnum &
CLIT. Hoc vide. in meâ vitâ tu tibi laudem is quæfi-
  tum, fcelus:
Ubi fi paululùm modò quid te fugerit, ego perierim. 75
Quid illo facias? SY. at enim. CLIT. quid enim? SY.
  fi finas, dicam. CLIN. fine.
CLIT. Sino, SY. ita res eft hæc nunc, quafi cum—
  CLIT. quas, malum, abagés mihi.
Narrare occipit? CLIN. Syre, verum hic dicit: mitte:
  ad rem redi.
SY. Enimvero reticere nequeo. multimodis injurius,
Clitipho, es, neque ferri potis es. CLIN. audiendum
  hercle eft: tace.   80
SY. Vis amare: vis potiri: vis, quod des illi, effici.

in mea vita; ubi fi modo quid paululum fugerit te, te ego perierim. Quid facias illo? SY. At enim---CLIT. Quid enim? SY. Si finas, dicam. CLIN. Sine. CLIT. Sino. SY. Hæc res nunc ita eft, quafi cum---CLIT. Quas ambages, malum, occipit narrare mihi? CLIN. Syre, hic dicit verum, mitte: redi ad rem. SY. Enimvero nequeo reticere: es injurius multimodis, Clitipho, neque es potis ferri. CLIN. Hercle audiendum eft, tace. SY. Vis amare, vis potiri, vis effici quod des illi:

ANNOTATIONS.

tells him, that no great and memorable Attempt can be made without incurring fome Danger; a Plea fpecious and good in appearance, and fuited to the Character of that kind of Slaves, who have always a great fhare of Vanity, and affect to give an Air of Importance to their moft trifling Actions.

77 *Ita res eft hæc nunc, quafi cum.* Syrus feems to want here to illuftrate his Defign by a Simile or Comparifon, which, as it does not readily occur, we are to fuppofe him to lengthen out in pronunciation the two laft Words, *quafi cum,* which draws upon him that fmart Reply from his Mafter; *Quas, malum, ambages.*

79 *Enimvero reticere nequeo.* Nothing could ferve better than this, to make us fenfible what a great Mafter of human Life the Poet is, and how well he underftood to paint the Paffions. Syrus knew of what confequence he was to his Mafter, and that as he was intrufted with the Management of his Amours, he would not be willing to fall out with him at the prefent Juncture. This makes him take fo much upon him as he does in the prefent Anfwer; for fervile Natures when they think they have any one in their Power, are peculiarly apt to affect a haughty importunate Air, and fhew of what Confequence they are.

80 *Audiendum hercle eft, tace.* As thefe

wherewithal to make her Prefents, but want to have all thefe Advantages without any Rifk on your fide. You're wondrous wife, truly, if indeed that can be call'd Wifdom, to aim at Impoffibilities; either you muft refolve to take the Hazard with the Enjoyments, or abandon them quite, and run no hazard. Now, confider with yourfelf, which of thefe two deferves the Preference in your Choice; although I know perfectly, that the Project I have form'd is both well contriv'd and fafe: for here you have an Opportunity of having your Miftrefs with you at your Father's without Fear; by the fame means too I fhall be able to procure the Money you have promifed her, to do which you have fo often deafened me with your Inteaties. What would you have elfe?

Clit. If indeed it were fo.

Syr. If indeed I you'll know upon Trial.

Clit. Come, come then, let us hear this Project of yours, what is it?

Syr. We will pretend that your Miftrefs is his.

Clit. Mighty well: but tell me what he'll do with his own? Shall fhe be call'd his too, as tho' one did not bring Difgrace enough upon him?

Syr. Nay, we'll take care to fettle her with your Mother.

Clit. What to do there?

Syr. It were a long Story, *Clitipho*, to tell you why; but be fatisfied, I have Reafon for it.

Clit. Mere Stuff, I can as yet fee no fufficient Caufe why I ought to run this hazard.

Syr. Hold, I have another Expedient, if you diflike this, which I am fure both of you will own to be perfectly fafe.

Clit. Find out fomething of this kind, for Heaven's fake.

Syr. In a Moment. I'll go meet them, and tell them to return home.

Clit. Hah! What did you fay?

Syr. I now rid you of all your Fears, that you may fleep quietly on either fide.

Clit. What fhould I do now? [*to* Clinia,

Clin. You! Whatever appears beft.

Clit. Syrus, but tell me. (to *Clinia*) You advife right. *Clit.*

ANNOTATIONS.

Words are generally fuppofed addrefs'd by Clinia to Clitiple, it occafions fome Difficulty to reconcile them to what the fame Clinia fays a little before to Syrus: Syre, verum hic dicit, ad rem redi: for there he feems to commend Clitipho for interrupting Syrus; and here he is angry with him, becaufe he had interrupted him. But the Reafon of this will eafily appear, by confidering what has been faid in the foregoing Note. For as Syrus could not fmother the Defire of fhewing himfelf to be a Perfon of great Confequence, fo Clinia is for winking at it, and indulging him for the prefent, rather than by an unfeafonable Oppofition to intangle Affairs that appeared already but too intricate and confus'd. We are therefore to fuppofe this addrefs'd to Clitipho with particular Nods and Geftures which he could not but underftand.

86 Etfi hoc confilium, &c. Syrus in the firft Part of his Speech had left it to his own Choice which to prefer, either Pleafure with the Dangers attending it, or to deny himfelf the one rather than be expofed to the other. But as he was unwilling all his Pains and Labour fhould be loft, he here cunningly infinuates that he might indulge himfelf to the

Tuum eſſem in potiundo periclum non vis. haud ſtultè
ſapis :   [contingere.
Siquidem id ſapere eſt, velle te id, quod non poteſt
Aut hæc cum illis ſunt habenda, aut illa cum his
mitt. nda ſunt.   84
Harum duarum conditionum nunc ùtrum malis, vide :
Etſi noc conſilium, quod cepi, rectum eſſe & tutum
ſcio :   [copia eſt :
Nam tua apud patrem amica tecum ſine metu ut ſit,
Tum illi argentum quod pollicitu' es, eadem hac in-
veniam viâ :   [mihi
Quod ut efficerem, orando ſurdas jam aures reddideras
Quid aliud tibi vis? CLIT. ſiquidem hoc ſit. SY. ſi-
quidem ? experiundo ſcies.   90
CLIT. Age, age, cedo iſtuc tuum conſilium, quid id
eſt ? SY. adſimulabimus
Tuam amicam hujus eſſe. CLIT. pulchrè. cedo, quid
hic faciet ſuâ ?   [parum ?
An ea quoque dicitur hujus, ſi una hæc dedecori eſt
SY. Imo ad tuam matrem abducetur. CLIT. quid cò ?
SY longum eſt, Clitipho,
Tibi ſi narram, quamobrem id faciam : vera cauſa eſt.
CLIT. fabulæ :   95
Nihil ſati' firmi video, quamobrem accipere hunc
mihi expediat metum.   [confiteamini
SY. Mane, habeo aliud, ſi iſtuc metuis, quod ambo
Sine periclo eſſe. CLIT. hujuſmodi, obſecro, aliquid
reperi. SY. naxumè :   [hem,
Ibo obviam hinc : dicam, ut revortantur domum. CLIT.
Quid dixti? SY. ademtum ibi jam ſaxo omnem metum.
In aurem utramvis otioſe ut dormias.   101
CLIT. Quid ago nunc ? CLIN. tune ? quod boni.
CLIT. Syre, dic modò.

id : cauſa iſt vera. CLIT. Fabulæ : video nihil ſatis firmi, quamobrem expediat mihi accipere
hunc metum. SY. Mane, ſi metuis iſtuc, habeo aliud, quod ambo confiteamini eſſe ſine periculo.
CLIT. Obſecro, reperi aliquid hujuſmodi. SY. Maxume : ibo hinc obviam : dicam ut rever-
tantur domum. CLIT. Hem, quid dixti ? SY. Jam ſaxo omnem metum ademtum tibi, ut dormias otioſe in utramvis aurem. CLIT. Quid ago nunc ? CLIN. Tune ? Quod eſt boni.
CLIT. Syre, dic modo.

ANNOTATIONS.

the full without fear, for he had laid his
Meaſures ſo well, that his Miſtreſs might be
at his Father's Houſe without Danger of a
Diſcovery ; and he had alſo a ſure Expedient
for obtaining the Money that had been pro-
m ſed to her.

97 Mane, habeo aliud. Syrus is here diſ-
guſted and angry to find a Scheme, which
he had flattered himſelf was well-contriv'd,
ſo lightly thought of by his Maſter. This
Anſwer is therefore a Mixture of Irony and

Indignation, it being his Deſign to go and
order Bacchis to return home : for he ſaw
that his Maſter was not like by any other
means to be rouzed. The Irony is height-
ned by Clitipho's taking what Syrus ſays here
as ſerious.

101 In aurem utramvis otioſe ut dormias.
This was a proverbial Saying, to expreſs that
any one might be quite eaſy and ſecure ; for
auris is here inſtead of latus : ſo that the
proper Meaning is, he might ſleep ſecure on

U 4   either

Syr. Take your Will; you'll in vain wiſh for her To-day again, when 'tis too late,

Clin. You have now an Opportunity, enjoy it while you may; for you don't know whether you will ever have ſuch another.

Clit. Syrus, I ſay.

Syr. Ay, you may bawl, I'll ſtill go on. *(to himſelf:*

Clit. Why truly, *Clinia,* you're in the right. *Syrus, Syrus,* I ſay; ſtay, ſtay, *Syrus,*

Syr. So, now he's warm'd a little, *(to himſelf.)* What do you want? *(to* Clit.

Clit. Return, return.

Syr. Well, here I am: tell me what you would have; by and by you'll pretend you are not pleas'd with this neither.

Clit. Nay, *Syrus,* I throw myſelf, my Love and my Reputation into your Hands. You are the prime Manager, but take care not to deſerve any Blame,

Syr. 'Tis ridiculous, *Clitipho,* for you to give ſuch Advice, as if my Intereſt were leſs concern'd in this Affair than yours; for if any unlucky Accident ſhould fall out to ſpoil our Deſign, you may per-haps be chid a little, but I ſhall not come off without Blows; for which Reaſon you cannot ſuppoſe I will neglect any thing in the Caſe, But beg of him to pretend that this is his Miſtreſs.

Clin Nay, he may be ſure of me. The Caſe is now ſuch, that there is an abſolute Neceſſity for it.

Clit. I deſervedly love you, *Clinia.*

Clin. But Care ſhould be taken that ſhe have her Cue.

Syr. O! ſhe has that perfectly.

Clit. But I wonder how you could prevail upon her ſo eaſily, who is wont to ſlight almoſt every body.

Syr. I came in the critical Minute, which is the grand Article in almoſt every thing; for there I met with a Soldier, ſoliciting ſtrong-ly a Night of her; ſhe managed very artfully, to enflame his Deſire by Denials, and at the ſame time the more to ingratiate herſelf with you. But do you hear? have a Care of giving way imprudently to your Paſſions; you know your Father, how quick he is of Diſcern-ment in theſe Matters, and I well know what little command you have of yourſelf Forbear your double Entendres, your Side-Looks, ſighing, ſpitting, hemming, and ſmiling. *Clit.*

ANNOTATIONS.

either ſide, without fear of being diſturb'd. We have a like Inſtance in *Plautus, Pſeud.* I. I. 121.

> Ps. *Dé iſtac re in oculum utrumvis con-*
> *quieſcito.*
> Cs. *Oculum-utrum, aure in aurem?*
> Pſ. *At hoc pervolgatum eſt minus.*

102 *Syre, die modo; verum.* There is ſome Obſcurity here, ariſing from the Diſ-courſe changing-ſo abruptly from one to another, *Clitipho* put to a Stand, when,

by what *Syrus* threatned, he ſaw himſelf in danger of loſing the preſent fine Opportu-nity, turns to *Clinia,* and ſays: *Quid ego mune?* Who anſwers, *Tune? Quod houi eſt. Clitipho* diſtracted between addreſſing *Syrus* and *Clinia,* replies haſtily: *Syre, dic modo; verum.* Whereas he ought naturally to have ſaid; *Verum, Syre, die modo,* But he is ſo diſturb'd upon ſeeing *Syrus* going a-way, that he begins with recalling him, and afterwards turning to *Clinia,* ſays;

Verum,

Verum. Sy. age modò hodie: ferò ac nequicquam
voles.
Clin. Datur: fruare, dum licet: nam nefcias,
Eju' fit poteftas pofthac, an nunquam tibi.　105
Clit. Syre, inquam. Sy. Perge porro ,tamen iftuc ago.
Clit. Verum hercle iftuc eft.　Syre, Syre inquam,
heus, heus, Syre.　　　　　[dic, quid eft?
Sy. Concaluit. quid vis? Clit. redi, redi. Sy. adfum,
Jam hoc quoque negabis tibi placere? Clit. imo,Syre,
Et me, & meum amorem, & famam permitto tibi.
Tu es judex, ne quid accufandus fis, vide.　　111
Sy. Ridiculum eft, te iftuc me admonere, Clitipho,
Quafi iftic minor mea res agatur, quàm tua.
Hìc fi quid nobis fortè advorfi evenerit,
Tibi erunt parata verba, huic homini verbera.　115
Quapropter hæc res neutiquam neglectui eft mihi.
Sed iftunc exora, ut fuam effe adfimulet. Clin. fcilicet
Facturum me effe; in eum jam res rediit locum,
Ut fit neceffe. Clit. merito te amo, Clinia. [probè.
Clin. Verùm illa ne quid titubet. Sy. perdocta eft
Clit. At hoc demiror, quî tam facile potueris　121
Perfuadere illi, quæ folet quos fpernere!
Sy. In tempore ad eam veni; quod rerum omnium eft
Primum. nam quendam miferè offendi ibi militem
Ejus noctem orantem. hæc arte tractabat virum,　125
Cupidum ut illius animum inopià incenderet,
Eademque ut effet apud te quàm gratiffima.
Sed heus tu, vide fis, ne quid imprudens ruâs.
Patrem novifti ad has res quàm fit perfpicax: -
Ego te autem novi, quàm effe foleas impotens:　130
Inverfa verba, everfas cervices tuas,
Gemitus, fcreatus, tuffis, rifus abftine.

verum. Sy. Age modo bodie : voles fero ac nequicquam. Clin. Occafio datur : fruare dum licet : nam nefcias, an poteftas ejus fit nunquam tibi pofthac. Clit. Syre, inquam. Sy. Perge porro, tamen ago iftuc. Clit. Hercle iftuc eft veram, e Clinia. Syre, Syre, inquam, beus, beus, Syre. Sy. Concaluit. Quid vis? Clit. Redi, redi. Sy. Adfum. Dic, quid eft? Jam quoque negabis boc placere tibi? Clit. Imo, Syre, permitto iftuc, et me et meum amorem, et famam. Tu es judex; vide. ne fis accufandus. propter aliquid. Sy. Ridiculum eft, Clitipho, te admonere me iftuc, quafi mea res minor agatur iftic, quam tua. Si forte quid adverfi evenerit nobis bic, verba erunt parata tibi, verbera buic bomini. Quapropter bæc rei eft neutiquam neglectui mihi. Sed exora iftunc, ut affimilet Bacchidem effe fuam. Clin. Scilicet intellige me effe facturum ita; rei jam rediit in eum locum, ut fit neceffe. Clit. Merito amo te, Clinia. Clin. Verum cavendum eft ne illa quid titubet. Sy. Perdocta eft probe. Clit. At demiror boc, quî potueris tam facile perfuadere illi, 'quæ folet fpernere quefvis! Sy. Veni ad eam in tempore, quod eft primum omnium rerum: nam offendi ibi quendam militem mifere orantem noctem ejus: bæc tractabat virum arte, ut incenderet cupidum animum illius inopiâ, atque eadem effet quam gratiffima. apud te. Sed beus tu, vide fis (fi vis) ne quid imprudens ruas. Novifti patrem quam fit perfpicax ad bas res : ego autem novi te, quam foleas effe impotens : abftine inverfa verba, everfas tuas cervices, gemitus, fcreatus, tuffis, rifus.

ANNOTATIONS.

Verum. Your Advice is right. This Diforder and Confufion of Speech marks ftrongly the Diftraction of his Mind.

109. *Jam boc quoque negabis tibi placere?* Thefe Words are an Interrogation, and to be underftood ironically, which mighty well agrees with the Humour Syrus is in here; who being recalled by repeated Intreaties, rallies Clitipho, that he had not only rejected his Scheme with regard to Bacchis, but

that now he fuppofed he intended alfo to forbid his defiring them to return, as is evident from his faying, *boc quoque.* That we muft fuppofe an Interrogation here, is evident from the Anfwer of Clitipho; *Imo, Syre, et me, et meum amorem, et famam permitto tibi;* q. d. *Nibil negabo earum rerum quas tu fuadebis.*

132 *Gemitus, fcreatus, tuffis, rifus.* I fee no reafon for fuppofing all thefe to be Genitives

Clit. You yourfelf fhall commend me.
Syr. See it be fo.
Clit. I tell you you fhall admire me.
Syr. But how foon the Women are come up!
Clit. Where are they? Why do you hold me?
Syr. You have nothing to do with her at prefent.
Clit. I know I have not when fhe fhall be before my Father, but till then——
Syr. Not a bit the more.
Clit. Let me.
Syr. I tell you I will not.
Clit. But for a little.
Syr. I forbid it.
Clit. A fingle Kifs at leaft.
Syr. Get you gone, if you are wife,
Clit. I go. But what will he do?
Syr. Stay here.
Clit. O happy *Clinia!*
Syr. Walk off.

ANNOTATIONS.

nitives fingular, according to the common | Verfe, and afterwards to make *gemis* t,
Notion. For it feems a very odd manner of | *fcreutus, tuffis, rifus,* Genitives, g 12-
Conftruction to refer *inverfa verba, everfas* | ed by *abftine.* To me they feem 21 to
cervices tuas, to *novi* of the proceeding | be Accufatives plural, govern'd by *ac*-, which

---

ACT II. SCENE III.

ARGUMENT.

Here a Courtezan is compared to a Woman of Virtue, and occafion thence taken to defcribe the Manner of Life of each fort. Bacchis praifes Antiphila's Beauty and innocent behaviour, and pronounces her fortunate. Here too the joyful Meeting of two Lovers is emphatically defcribed.

BACCHIS, ANTIPHILA, CLINIA, SYRUS.

Bacchis. INDEED, my *Antiphila*, I commend, and efteem you
happy, in ftudying to make your Behaviour anfwerable to
your

ANNOTATIONS.

In this Scene, there is a Comparifon be- | felves to every one from whom they expect
tween Women, who attach themfelves to | a Reward. *Bacchis* is compelled to own
only one Man, and continue true to him; and | that the firft are far the happeft, but ex-
common Courtezans, who proftitute them- | cufes in the beft manner fhe can her own
way

CLIT. Laudabis. SY. vide fis. CLIT. tutemet mirabere.
SY. Sed quàm citò funt confecutæ mulieres ?
CLIT. Ubi fûnt ? cur retines? SY. jam nunc hæc non
eſt tua.   135
CLIT. Scio, apud patrem; ut nunc interim. SY. ni-
hilo magis.   [paulifper. SY. veto.
CLIT. Sine. SY. non finam, inquam. CLIT. quæfo,
CLIT. Saltem falutare. SY. abeas, fi fapias. CLIT. eo.
Quid iſtic ? SY. manebit. CLIT. ò hominem felicem !
SY. ambula.

Quæfo, paulifper. SY. *Veto.* CLIT. *Saltem Salutare.* SY. *Abeas, fi fapis.* CLIT. *Eo,*
quid iſtic agat ? SY. *Manebit.* CLIT. *O hominem felicem !* SY. *Ambula.*

CLIT. *Laudabis,*	
SY. *Vide fis.* CLIT.	
Tutemet mirabere.	
SY. *Sed quam cito*	
mulieres funt confecu-	
tæ ? CLIT. *Ubi*	
funt ? Cur retines ?	
SY. *Hæc jam nunc*	
non eſt tua. CLIT.	
Scio, apud patrem;	
at nunc interim. SY.	
Nibilo magis. CLIT.	
Sine. SY. *Inquam,*	
non finam. CLIT.	

A N N O T A T I O N S.

which makes every thing plain, and of eafy
Comprehenfion. Some refer thefe Accufa-
tives to *novi*, and take *abſtine* abfolutely.
I know your double Entendres, Side-Glances,
Sneers, Hems, &c. Take care therefore to
abſtain from them. Qvid, no doubt had
this Place in view where he fays: Heroid
16. 227.

Sæpe dedi gemitus : & te, laſciva, notavi,
In gemitu riſum non tenuiſſe mea.
   Eugrapbius very judiciouſly remarks upon
this Paſſage : Hæc omnia adoleſcentuli faciunt,
quotieſcunque videre, aut videri volunt ab
bis, quas deſidarant. Ita ſub quondam metu,
ut quaſi dum aliud neceſſitate conficiunt, ſic im-
pleant voluntatem.

ACTUS II. SCENA III.

ARGUMENTUM.

Collatio meretricis & honeſtæ virginis, qua vita utriuſque ex-
primitur : Bacchis laudat Antiphilam ob formam & bonos
mores, eamque fortunatam eſſe affirmat. Et hic jucunda
amantium congreſſio ſignatiſſime exprimitur.

BACCHIS, ANTIPHILA, CLINIA, SYRUS.

EDEPOL te, mea Antiphila, laudo & fortunatam
  judico,
Id cùm ſtuduiſti, iſti formæ ut mores confimiles forent :
duiſti id, ut mores forent confimiles iſti formæ :

O R D O.
BA. EDepol, mea
      Antiphila,
laudo te, & judico
fortunatam, cum ſtu-

A N N O T A T I O N S.

way of Life, as being urged to it by Neceſſity, left when Youth is gone, and her
Beauty impaired by Old Age, ſhe may lan-
guiſh under Want, if the prefent Opportunity of making provifion for the Decline
of Life is neglected. We have, likewife, a
moving Defcrption of the meeting of Antipbila and Clinia, after ſo long an Abfence.

¹ Ædepol te, mea Antipbila, laudo. The
Courtezan's Difcourfe here, as it is addreffed
to an honourable and chafte Virgin, contains nothing licentious, or contrary to Decency : but ſhe frankly gives the preference
to a married State, commends Antipbila for
her Virtue and Innocence, and offers ſome
excufe for the Exceffes of Courtezans.

                                        ⁴ Quæ

your Beauty; and, as I hope for Mercy, I should not wonder, if all the Men were in love with you; for your Discourse was to me a plain Indication of your Disposition. And when I now consider in my Mind your Way of Life, and that of all such as are not common to every Pretender; it does not appear in the least strange, that you are so virtuously inclined, and we so unlike you: for 'tis your Advantage to be good; but they with whom we have to do, will not suffer us to be so. For as they love us only for our Beauty, no sooner is that decayed, than they look out for another, so that unless we take care to provide in the mean time for ourselves, we must live abandoned by all the World. But when you have once resolved to pass your Life with one Man, whose Manners and Temper are exactly conformable to your own, they attach themselves to you only: by this mutual Choice you are so firmly united the one to the other, that no Misfortune can happen to disturb your Loves.

Ant. I am little acquainted with others, but know it has been ever my Endeavour, to place my Happiness in what tends most to promote his.

Clin. (Over-hearing) Ah, my *Antiphila*, 'tis therefore that you alone have now brought me back again to my native Country; for while I was absent from you, all the Hardships I was compelled to undergo, were light, compared to the want of your Company.

Syr. I believe it.

Clit. Syrus, I can scarce contain myself. What an Unhappiness it is to be thus deprived of the Liberty of running into this dear Creature's Arms?

Syr.

ANNOTATIONS.

4 *Quale ingenium haberes, fuit indicio oratio.* Although Men of Art, and deep Designs may sometimes wrap themselves up in Disguise, so as to hide their real Purposes; yet 'tis seldom they are so much upon their guard, but that now and then their Speech betrays them. But more particularly in Characters of Innocence, and unaffected Simplicity, such, is that of *Antiphila* here; their Discourse never fails to make a real Discovery of their Inclinations and Temper: and, indeed, this is always the Case, unless when Men, from particular Views of their own, industriously set themselves to deceive. *Cicero,* or whoever else was the Author of the Declamation against *Sallust* observes this Congruity as remarkable to him. Cap. I. *Ea demum magna voluptas est, C. Sallusti, æqualem, & par in verbis vitam agere; neque quidquam tam obscænum dicere, cui non ab initio pueritiæ cum genere facinoris ætas tua respondeat; ut omnis oratio moribus consonet.*

5 *Nos, quibuscum est res, non sinunt.* Virtue is here commended from the Mouth of a Person who had renounced it. *Bacchis* is willing to excuse, in the best manner she can, the Way of Life she was engaged in, and throws the blame of it upon Necessity. This, though the best Excuse that can be offered, is yet in reality but a very frivolous one; for what could hinder *Bacchis* from following at the first the same Course with *Antiphila?*

14 *Hoc beneficio.* Guyetus is for rejecting this Verse as spurious, and confounding the Sense of the rest. But, with a little Reflection, he might have found that what *Bacchis* says here, is this: " Ubi vobis se- " mel decretum est, agere ætatem cum uno " viro, cujus mos maxime est confimilis " vestrum, seu, cui itidem decretum est, " semel ætatem agere cum una muliere : " hi, qui ita animati sunt, applicant se ad " vos. Utrique igitur tali matrimonio " juncti, devincimini ab utrique vero hoc " beneficio, id est, morum similitudine, us- " que adeo, ut nunquam ulla amori vestro " incidere possit calamitas."

16 *Nescio alias.* The Character of *Antiphila* is here finely drawn, and represents Innocence in perfection. There is nothing of

Miniméque, ita me Dii ament, miror, fi te fibi, quif-
que expetit.
Nam mihi, quale ingenium haberes, fuit indicio oratio.
Et cùm egomet nunc mecum in animo vitam tuam
confidero, 5
Omniumque adeò voftrarum,vulgus quæ ab fe fegregant;
Et vos effe iftiufmodi & nos non effe, haud mirabile eft.
Nem expedit bonas effe vobis : nos, quibufcum eft res,
non finunt.
Quippe formâ impulfi noftrâ nos amatores colunt :
Hæc ubi imminuta eft, illi fuum animum aliò confe-
runt. 10
Nifi profpeſtum interea aliquid nobis eſt, defertæ vi-
vimus [viro.
Vobis cum uno femel ubi ætatem agere decretum eſt
Cujus mos maxumè eſt confimilis voftrùm ;. hi fe ad
vos applicant :
Hoc beneficio utrique ab utrifque vero devincimini :
Ut nunquam ulla amori voftro incidere poffit calamitas.15
AN. Nefcio alias : me quidem femper fcio feciffe fedulo,
Ut ex illius commodo meum compararem commodum.
CL. ah. [triam facis.
Ergo, mea Antiphila, tu nunc fola reducem me in pa-
Nam, dum abs te abfum, omnes mihi labores fuere,
quos cepi, leves, [Syre, vix fuffero. 20
Præterquam tui carendum quòd erat. SY. credo. CL.
Hoccine me miferum non licere meo modo ingenium
frui ?

minimeque miror, it Dii amant me, fi quifque expetit te fibi. Nam tua oratio fuit indicio mibi, quale ingenium habere. Et cùm egomit nunc confidero tuam vitam mecum in animo, adeoque veftrarum omnium, quæ fegregant vulgus ab fe: haud mirabile eft, & vos effe iftiufmodi, & nos non effe. Nam expedit vobis non effe bonas. Illi, quibufcum eft nobis res, non finunt nos effe bonas. Quippe a matores impulfi noftrâ forma colunt nos: ubi hæc eft imminuta, illi confirunt fuum animum aliò. Interea nifi aliquid eft profpectum nobis, vivimus defertæ. Ubi femel eft decretum vobis agere ætatem cum uno viro, cujus mos eft maximè corfimilis veftrùm; hi applicant fe ad vos: hæc beneficio vero devincimini utrique ab utrifque, ut nunquam ulla calamitas poffit incidere veftro amori. AN. Nefcio alias: fcio quidem me femper feciffe fedulo, ut comparem meum commodum ex commodo illius. CL. Ah! ergo, mea Antiphila, tu fola nunc facit me reducit in patriam; nam dum abfum abs te, omnes labores, quos cepi, fuere leves mihi, præterquam quod erat carendum tui. SY. Credo. CL. Syre, vix fuffero, non licere me miferum frui hoccine ingenium meo modo?

ANNOTATIONS

of Conftraint or Emulation in her Virtue ; fhe does not at all concern herfelf with what others do, nor is influenced to the Part fhe had made choice of, by any view of the Mi-feries that are apt to overtake Loofenefs and Debauchery, but purely by a natural Byafs and Inclination to what is right.

18 *Ergo, mea Antiphila.* Thefe Words are fpoken by *Clinia* to himfelf, looking earneftly at his Miftrefs, and highly pleafed with the kind Declaration he had juft now overheard her make in his favour. If the Beauty of a Play confifts in reprefenting the Paffions well, and making the Spectators themfelves feel, in fome meafure, what paffes before them, never did Poet fucceed better than *Terence* here. For this affectio-

nate Declaration of *Antiphila*, when fhe had no Sufpicion of her Lover's being prefent to obferve her, and his rapturous Exclamation upon overhearing it, are Scenes too intereft-ing not to raife the tendereft Feelings in Breafts fufceptible of the fofter Paffions.

20 Sy. *Credo.* Cl. *Syre, vix fuffero.*
Hoccine me miferum non licere meo modo in-genium frui ? Tanaquil Faber, in his Expli-cation of this Paffage, differs from all Com-mentators before him. Thefe Words are by them fuppofed to be fpoken by *Clinia*; becaufe, towards the end of the former Scene, *Clitipho* is defired by *Syrus* to walk off. But the above-mentioned Author ob-ferves, that *Clinpho* was of a Temper too amorous to pay fo ready an Obedience, and

that,

Syr. Nay, as far as I can underſtand your Father's Humour, he has not yet done perſecuting you.

Bacc. What Youth is this, who looks ſo earneſtly at us!

Ant. Ah, for Heaven's ſake, hold me.

Bacc. Bleſs me, what is he to you?

Ant. I faint.

Bacc. Heavens! What is it that ſurprizes you ſo, *Antiphila?*

Ant. Is it *Clinia* that I ſee, or not?

Bacc. Whom do you ſee?

Clin. My *Antiphila*, my Life, Heaven bleſs you.

Ant. And you too, my dear, my wiſh'd for *Clinia.*

Clin. How are you?

Ant. Happy to ſee you return ſafe.

Clin. Do I really embrace you, my *Antiphila*, ſo paſſionately long-ed for, ſo dear to my Soul?

Syr. Get you all in, for the old Man has been waiting for you a long time.

ANNOTATIONS.

that, therefore, under pretence of comply-ing he had retired to ſome Corner of the Theatre, where he might ſee and hear *Bacchis*, and that his Impatience at length, getting the better, he breaks from his lurking Place: *Syre, vix ſuffero;* which both muſt have a good Effect upon the Stage, and is perfectly agreeable to *Clitipho's* Character. This Remark may be called ingenious, but will ſcarcely bear Examination. *Antiphila* had ſaid, *Me quidem ſemper ſcio* feciſſe ſedulo, ut ex illius commodo meum comparem commodum. On hearing this Declaration ſo kind, affectionate, and chaſte, *Clinia* breaks out in theſe Words; *Vix ſuffero, Syre: hoccine ingenium frui non poſſe me?* Where *ingenium* muſt be underſtood of *Antiphila. Hoccine ingenium;* this Temper ſo ſweet, ſo chaſte, ſo amiable. As if he had ſaid, *Muſt I thus be deny'd the Liberty of running into the Embraces of this dear deſerving Creature?*

ACT III. SCENE I.

ARGUMENT.

Chremes acquaints Menedemus, *that his Son was returned out of* Aſia, *which gives him inexpreſſible Joy, and makes him re-ſolve to indulge his Son in every thing.* Chremes *earneſtly diſſuades him from this, wiſe in what regards others, but little aware of the Plots of his own Family, and the danger he him-ſelf was in of being over-reached.*

CHREMES, MENEDEMUS.

Chremes. 'TIS now Break of Day: do I forbear to knock at my Neighbour's Door, that he may hear from me firſt of his

ANNOTATIONS.

In this Scene we have a fine Repreſen-tation of the Duty, which one Friend owes another. *Chremes,* in the Beginning of the Play, had profeſſed an Eſteem and Friend-ſhip

Sy. Imo, ut patrem tuum vidi effe habitum, diu etiam
duras dabit.
Ba. Quifnam hic adolefcens eft, qui intuitur nos? An.
ah, retine me, obfecro. [ra! quid ftupes,
Ba. Amabo, quid tibi eft? An. difperii. Ba. perii mife-
Antiphila? An. videon' Cliniam, an non? Ba. quem
vides'? Cl. falve, anime mi. 25
An. O mi exfpe&ate Clinia, falve. Cl. ut vales?
An. Salvom veniffe gaudeo. Cl. teneone te,
Antiphila, maxumè animo exoptatam meo?
Sy. Ite intrò : nam vos jamdudum exfpe&at fenex.

Sy. Imo, ut vidi
tuum patrem effe
babitum, etiam diu
dabit duras portes.
Ba. Quifnam eft
bic adolefcens, qui
intuetur nos? An.
Ab! retine me, ob-
fecro te. Ba. Ama-
bo, quid eft tibi?
An. Difperii. Ba.
Perii mifera! Quid
ftupes, Antiphila?
An. Videone Cli-
niam, an non? Ba.

Quem vides? Cl. Salve, anime mi. An. O mi expectate Clinia, falve. Cl. Ut vales?
An. Gaudeo te adveniffe falvum. Cl. Teneone te, Antiphila, maximè exoptatam animo meo?
Sy. Ite intrò : nam fenex jamdudum expectat vos.

ANNOTATIONS.

Creature? For that *ingenium* is fometimes
thus ufed, is evident from what *Pamphilus*
fays, fpeaking of *Glycery, And.* Act I. 5. 39.
Bene & pudice ejus doctum & eductum finam,
Coactum egeftate, ingenium immutarier?
As to the Genius and Temper of *Bacchis,*
Clitipho himfelf, her Lover, will give the
beft Account of it:
Mea eft potens, procax, magnifica, fumptuefa,
nobilis.
It is evident enough, therefore, that what
pleafed *Clitipho* fo much in *Bacchis,* was her
Form and external Charms, agreeable to
what fhe herfelf fays a little before;
Quippe forma impulfi noftra nos amatores co-
lunt.
All which make it evident, that this Speech

could come only from *Clinia,* which is ftill
further confirmed by *Syrus's* Anfwer: *Ut*
vidi patrum tuum effe babitum, diu etiam du-
ras dabit ; which can be underftood only of
Menedemus, not of *Chremes,* and therefore is
an Anfwer to a Speech of *Clinia's,* not of
Clitipho's.
22 *Duras dabit.* Subaudi *partes aut vices.*
Thus in the *Eunuch,* Act II. 3. 62. *Duras*
fratris partes prædicas.
27 *Teneone te.* This was an ufual Form
among Friends returning from abroad, and
embracing one another after long Abfence.
Plaut. Rud. Act I. 4. 24.
Tu facis me quidem ut vivere nunc velim,
Quando mihi te licet tangere : ut vix mihi
Credo ego hoc, te tenere! obfecro, amplectere.

ACTUS III. SCENA I.

ARGUMENTUM.

Chremes Menedemo nunciat ex Afia rediiffe filium: ex qua re
Menedemus incredibili gaudio perfunditur, & filio pofthac in-
dulgere magis inftituit : quod ei magnopere diffuadet Chremes,
qui plus fatìs foris fapit, non videt de fuo capite agi comitia, &
fæpe in difcrimine effe.

CHREMES, MENEDEMUS.

L Ucifcit hoc jam. ceffo pultare oftium
Vicini, primùm ex me ut fciat, fibi filium

tare oftium vicini, ut fciat primum ex me, filium rediiffe fili?

ORDO.
Ch. H OC cæ-
lum jam
lucifcit. Ceffo pul-

ANNOTATIONS.

fhip for *Menedemus,* and all his Behaviour
hitherto correfponds exactly with it. So foon

he hears of *Clinia's* Arrival, he is for
imparting the News to his Neighbour, as
knowing

his Son's Return? altho' the young Man himself, I know, would not
have me do it. But when I fee my unfortunate Friend fuffer fo much
by his Abfence, can I conceal fo unhoped for a Joy from him, efpecially as the Youth will fuffer no Prejudice from the Difcovery? I
will not do it, for I am refolved to affift the old Man all in my
power : and as I fee my Son united with his Friend and Companion,
and partaking with him in all his Concerns, fo it is fit, that we old
Men fhould do one another all the good Offices we can.

Men. Certainly I am either born of a Temper ftrongly turned to
Unhappinefs, or that Saying which I fo commonly hear is falfe, that
Time allays human Grief: for my Uneafinefs at my Son's Abfence
increafes upon me every day, and the longer he is away from me, the
more I wifh and defire to fee him.

Chr. But I fee him coming out: I'll go and fpeak to him. *Me-*
nedemus, your Servant, I bring you News, which I know you'll be
greatly delighted to hear. *Men.*

ANNOTATIONS.

knowing how agreeable it would be to
him. When to remove *Clinia*'s groundlefs
Fears, he had almoft difcovered the Anxiety
his Father was under for his Abfence, he
fuddenly changes his Mind, as forefeeing that
it would be more for the advantage of his
Friend to fupprefs that ; and now in this
Scene, we have ftill a farther Difcovery of
thefe friendly Difpofitions ; for he is introduced, debating with himfelf, whether he
fhould difcover to *Menedemus,* that his Son
was returned, and tho' he knew the young
Man was unwilling he fhould, yet refolves
upon it, becaufe it was neceffary to the quiet
of his Friend, and would do *Clinia* no real
hurt. In the progrefs of the Scene, his
Friendfhip appears ftill more. He had entertained *Bacchis,* the Evening before, under
a Notion, that fhe was *Clinia*'s Miftrefs.
Her expenfive Temper alarmed him, as
forefeeing that *Menedemus*'s Fortune would
foon be confumed, if care was not taken to
prevent it. Thefe Thoughts poffeffed him fo
much, that he could not even fleep, but fpent
the whole Night in contriving what would
be the moft expedient Courfe for his Friend
to follow. Full of thefe Cares, he rifes very
early, and knocks at his Neighbour's Gate,
refolved to inform him of all he knew, and
offer him his Advice.

¹ *Lucifer hoc jam.* *Chremes* fays this,
pointing up to the Heavens, and cafting his
Eyes round him on every fide ; fo that in
this Mode of fpeaking, *hoc* refers to *cælum,*
which muft be fuppofed to be underftood :
as in the *Curculio* of *Plautus,* Act. I. 3. 26.
Nam hoc quidem ædepol haud multo poft
luce lucebit.

From this *Scaliger,* in his Poetics, and after him, Madam *Dacier* contend, that this

Comedy was exhibited in feparate Parts, and
at different Times. The two firft Acts, in
the Evening, after Sun-fet, and the three laft
next Morning, at Day-break. The Interval between the fecond and third Acts is
filled up by the Supper, which *Chremes* gives
his Guefts on that Night of Mirth, and
Feftivity. The Feaft celebrated at this
time excufed the Liberty which *Menander*
took, of dividing his Play in this manner ;
and *Terence* was not obliged to make any
change in the conduct of the Plot, becaufe
as thefe Comedies were alfo exhibited among
the *Romans,* on occafion of thefe folemn
Feftivals ; *Terence* feems to have had an
equal Pretence, for following this Divifion.
Eugraphius, indeed, in his Commentaries
on this Piece, obferves that it is without
Example. His Words are : " Notandum
" ex hac comœdia, quod in nulla alia licet
" reperiri, ut biduum tempus in comœdia
" fit. Omnes enim uno die actus fuos expli-
" cant ex eo ipfo quo cuncta effici poffunt,
" ut aut nuptiæ celebrentur, aut cognitio fiat
" expofita, aut aliquid horum. At hic bidui
" rationem verfari intelligimus. Ergo dix-
" it : *Lucifcit hoc.*" But in this *Eugraphius,*
is certainly miftaken : for *Ariftophanes* has
followed the fame Cuftom, as appears by
his *Plutus,* the two firft Acts of which were
exhibited in the Evening. and the three laft,
the Morning enfuing ; the Interval between
the fecond and third Acts being filled up by
the Voyage of *Plutus* to the Temple of
Æfculapius, where he paffes the Night.
Did we know the precife Hour, at which
the Play begins in *Ariftophanes,* we fhould,
no doubt, find that he did not exceed the
Rule of twelve Hours; which Space ought
to limit the Duration of an Action brought

. upon

Rediiſſe? etſi adoleſcentem hoc nolle intellego.
Verùm, cùm videam miſerum hunc tam excruciarier
Ejus abitu, celem tam inſperatum gaudium,
Cùm illi pericli nihil ex indicio ſiet?
Haud faciam: nam, quod potero, adjutabo ſenem,
Item ut filium meum amico atque æquali ſuo
Video inſervire, & ſocium eſſe in negotiis.
Nos quoque ſenes eſt æquom ſenibus obſequi. 10
ME. Aut ego profectò ingenio egregio ad miſerias
Natus ſum, aut illud falſum eſt, quod volgò audio
Dici, diem adimere ægritudinem hominibus:
Nam mihi quidem quotidie augeſcit magis
De filio ægritudo; & quanto diutiùs 15
Abeſt, magis cupio tanto, & magis deſidero.
CH. Sed ipſum foras egreſſum video: ibo, adloquar.
Menedemè, ſalve: nuncium apporto tibi,
Cujus maxumè te fieri participem cupis.

*etſi intelligo adoleſ-
centem nolle hoc; ve-
rum, cum videam
hunc miſerum tam
exeruciari abitu ejus,
celem gaudium tam
inſperatum, cùm ni-
bil pericli ſit illi filio
ex indicio? Haud
faciam: nam adju-
tabo ſenem, quod ro-
tero, idem ut video
filium meum inſervire
ſuo amico atque æ-
quali, & eſſe ſocium
ei in negotiis; æ-
quum eſt quòque nos
ſenes obſequi ſenibus.
ME. Profectò, aut
ego ſum natus ingenio
egregio ad miſerias,
aut illud eſt falſum,
quod audio vulgo di-*

*ci, diem adimeri ægritudinem hominibus. Nam quidem ægritudo de filio augeſcit magis mihi quo-
tidie; et quanto diutius abeſt, tanto magis cupio, et magis deſidero eum. CH. Sed videt ipſum
egreſſum foras: ibo, alloquar. Menedeme, ſalve: apporto nuncium tibi, cujus maximè cupis te
fieri participem.*

ANNOTATIONS.

upon the Theatre. At leaſt it is certain, that *Terence* does not paſs theſe Bounds here, and that he is no leſs regular in this, than in every thing elſe. The Houſe opens at eight o'clock. The two firſt Acts take up about two Hours, and the Interval between the Parts may, perhaps, be ſix or ſeven. The third Act begins as ſoon as it is Day-break; for this *Terence* himſelf takes care to let us know, by making *Chremes* ſay, *lu-ciſcit hoc jam.* Thus the three laſt Acts, which could not take up above three Hours in the Repreſentation, were ended before ſeven o'clock. But there is one thing, that well deſerves our Notice here; and that is, that what paſſes in this long Interval, enters into the Action, and makes a Part of it in this Play, as well as in *Ariſtophanes.* It is during this Space, that *Chremes* obſerves the indecent Liberties which *Clitipho* takes with *Bacchis.* Had the Critics but attended to this Circumſtance, it might have ſaved them the Exclamation of *vaſta et hians, et ina-nit comœdia eſt.* How unjuſt is this Accu-ſation, when what they call unactive and time loſt, *vaſtum et hians,* has a neceſſary Connection with the Subject, and is, in-deed, the Foundation of ſome of the follow-ing Scenes. Had *Terence* divided his Piece, in ſuch manner, that the intervening Space had no Connexion with his Subject, that, indeed, had been ridiculous and inſupportable. Were we to take a Play of *Congreve's,* or any of our modern Poets, and act Part of it one Day, and the reſt the next, what could be more prepoſterous? But *Terence* and *Menander* were too great Maſters of juſt Writing, to take ſuch unjuſtifiable Li-berties as theſe; they underſtood too well the Rules of the Theatre, to contradict them ſo notoriouſly. Indeed, our modern Poets might, if they thought it needful, find Op-portunities of copying with a good Grace Precedents ſo unexceptionable, and even ſometimes lay themſelves under a neceſſity of doing it; though at the ſame time, it muſt be owned, that it requires great Ad-dreſs and Judgment.

11 *Aut ego profecto ingenio egregio ad miſe-rias.* As the chief Diſtreſs in this Comedy is that of *Menedemus,* ſo the Poet has taken care to repreſent it in ſuch a Light, as he thought would make the ſtrongeſt Impreſſion upon the Imagination. In the firſt Scene, the Reader finds himſelf wonderfully moved with the Repreſentation there given of *Me-nedemus's* conſtant Uneaſineſs for his Son's Abſence; and by the manner of his Ap-pearance here, we are made to underſtand, that theſe diſturbing Thoughts perpetually haunted him. For he comes out ſpeaking of his Son, and deſcribing his Anxiety as ſtill growing upon him; inſomuch, that this Idea is ſeen wholly to poſſeſs his Mind, which is incapable of indulging any other Reflection.

13 *Diem adimere ægritudinem hominibus.* This is a common Obſervation, and found

Men. What have you heard any thing about my Son, *Chremes*?

Chr. He is alive and well.

Men. Where is he, pray?

Chr. At home here with me.

Men. My Son?

Chr. Yes, your Son.

Men. Is he returned?

Chr. For certain.

Men. My *Clinia* returned!

Chr. Don't I tell you he is?

Men. Let us go: carry me to him, I beg of you.

Chr. He does not care that you should know yet of his Return, and shuns your sight from a Remembrance of his Offence; nay, he doubteth whether your former Severity may not rather be increased.

Men. And did not you tell him in what Temper I was?

Chr. No.

Men. Why, *Chremes*?

Chr. Because it would be unhappy both for yourself and him, if you discover yourself to be of a Temper so indulgent and yielding.

Men. I cannot help it: I have already been too rigorous a Father.

Chr. Ah, *Menedemus*, you run too much into Extremes in both, either by being too profuse, or too sparing. You will fall into the same Error by the one, as by the other. Heretofore, rather than suffer your Son to visit a young Girl, who was then contented with a little, and to whom almost any thing was acceptable, you frightened

him

ANNOTATIONS.

to be just by long Experience, Insomuch that where we mean to express any very great Degree of Grief, we always describe it as such, that not even Time can mollify. Thus, *Cicero* to *Atticus*, Lib. 3. Ep. 15. *Diet autem non modo levat luctum hunc, sed etiam auget. Nam cæteri dolores mitigantur vetustate, hic non potest non & sensu præsentis miseriæ, & recordatione præteritæ vitæ quotidie augeri.*

20 *Num quidnam de gnato mea audisti, Chreme? Terence* discovers uncommon Judgment, in preserving his Characters in their full Force. *Menedemus*, whose Thoughts are taken up wholly about his Son, when he hears of joyful Tidings, immediately enquires, whether they relate to him, as thinking nothing else worthy his Notice.

22 *Clinia meus venit?* These Repetitions here, in the mouth of *Menedemus*, speak the Justness of the Poet's Genius, and how well he understood the Language of the Passions. Nothing could come more naturally from a Heart divided between eager Wishes, Impatience, and Joy mixed with Distrust. I persuade myself, it will give the Reader a sensible Pleasure, to compare what is here said with that incomparable Passage in *Plau-*

tus, Cap. 4. 2. 92. which I shall therefore quote at length.

" ER. Nunc hanc lætitiam accipe à me,
" quam fero: nam filium
" Tuum modo in portu Philopolemum,
" vivum, salvum, & sospitem
" Vidi in publica celoce, ibidemque illum
" adolescentulum
" Alium una, & tuum Stalagmum servum,
" qui aufugit domo,
" Qui tibi surripuit quadrimum puerum
" filiolum tuum.
" HE. Abi in malam rem, ludis me.
" ER. Ita me amabit sancta Saturitas,
" Hegio, itaque suo me semper condeco-
" ret cognomine,
" Ut ego vidi. HE. Meum gnatum? ER.
" Tuum gnatum, & genium meum.
" HE. Et captivum illum Alidensem? ER.
(" Μάτον Απόλλω. HE. Et servulum
" Meum Stalagmum, meum qui gnatum
" surripuit? ER. Νή τὰν Κόραν.
" HE. Jam diu? ER. Νή τὰν Πραινέςην.
" HE. Venit? ER. Νή τὰν Σιγναν.
" HE. Certon? ER. Νή ταν Φρυσινῶςα.
" HE. Vide sis. ER. Νή τὸ Αλάτριςι.

And

ME. Num quidnam de gnato meo audifti, Chreme? 20
CH. valet, atque vivit. ME. ubinam eft, quæfo? CH.
apud me domi [ME. Clinia
ME. Meus gnatus? CH. fic eft. ME. venit? CH. certè.
Meus venit? CH. dixi. ME. eamus, duc me ad eum.
obfecro.
CH. Non volt te fcire fe rediiffe etiam, & tuum
Confpeĉtum fugitat ob peccatum. tum hoc timet, 25
Ne tua duritia antiqua illa etiam aduaĉta fit.
ME. Non tu ei dixifti, ut effem? CH. non. ME. quam-
obrem, Chreme?
CH. Quia peffumè iftuc in te atque in illum confulis,
Si te tam leni & viĉto effe animo oftenderis. [ah, 30
ME. Non poffum: fatis jam, fatis pater durus fui. CH.
Vehemens in utramque partem, Menedeme, es nimis,
Aut largitate nimiâ, aut parfimoniâ.
In eandem fraudem ex hac re, atque ex illâ, incides.
Primùm olim potiùs, quàm pàterere filium
Commeare ad mulierculam, quæ paululo 35

*Quia peffimè confulis iftuc in te atque in illum, fi oftenderis te effe tam leni & viĉto animo. ME.
Non poffum : jam fui fatis, fatis durus pater. CH. Ab, Menedime, es nimis vehemens in utramque partem, aut nimia largitate, aut parfimonia. Incides in eandem fraudem ex hac re, atque ex
illa. Primum olim, potius quam paterere filium commeare ad mulierculam, quæ erat tum contenta
paululo,*

ME.	*Num audifi*
	quidnam de meo gna-
	to, Chreme? CH.
	Valet, atque vivit.
ME.	*Quæfo, ubi-*
	nam eft? CH. Do-
	mi apud me. ME.
	Meus gnatus? CH.
	Sic eft. ME. *Venit?*
CH.	*Certè.* ME.
	Meus Clinia venit?
CH.	*Dixi.* ME.
	Eamus, obfecro, duc
	me ad eum. CH.
	Non etiam, vult te
	fcire fe rediiffe, &
	fugitat tuum con-
	fpeĉtum ob peccatum.
	Tum timet bcc, ne ar-
	tiqua illa tua duri-
	tia fit etiam adauĉta.
ME.	*Non tu dixif-*
	ti ei, ut effem? CH.
	Non. ME. *Quam-*
	obrem, Chreme? CH.

ANNOTATIONS.

And, indeed, in all fudden Emotions of the Mind, arifing from the Joy of hearing any thing agreeable, we are apt to repeat our Enquiries, either to be fure that we have not miftaken the Matter, or for the Pleafure of hearing what is fo agreeable to us again and again confirmed. We have another Inftance of this, in our own Poet, which can fcarce fail to make an Impreffion on every one that reads it ; where *Chærea* in the *Eunuch,* telling *Parmeno* how he came to lofe fight of the Virgin, he was looking for with fo much Impatience, is agreeably furprized to find that that Slave knew her. Aĉt 2. 3. 57.

---- CH. *Noftin quæ fit? dic mihi :*
Aut vidiftin? PA. *Vidi, novi : fcio quo ab-*
ducta fit.
CH. *Ebo, Parmeno mi, noftin'?* PA. *Novi.*
CH. *Et fcis ubi fiet?*

27 *Non tu ei dixifti, ut effem?* Hitherto *Chremes* had endeavoured to comfort *Mene-demus* under his Troubles, but now comes the time for Counfel and Advice. The Poet, in this too, hath acquitted himfelf in the beft manner. The real Intereft of *Me-nedemus* 's confulted, without any prejudice to the Son, and the Advice given is worthy a Friend who was at the fame time a Man of Years and Experience. There is this far-ther worthy of Notice, in what happens to

Chremes in the Courfe of the Play, that he who advifes with fo much fatherly Prudence, how to behave towards a Son, fufpected to be wild and extravagant, amidft this Care to prevent the Uneafinefs of his Friend, is not aware of the Mifchiefs that threaten himfelf. So that it will, perhaps, be im-poffible to meet with an Example handled with more Delicacy and Juftnefs; where Men difcover Pentration in what relates to others, but are blind with regard to them-felves. *Bæclerus.*

29 *Si te tam leni & viĉto effe animo oftende-ris.* A Father ought fometimes to foften and abate of his Authority, but never quite to give it up ; for this is not only an Injury to himfelf, but pernicious alfo to him, to whom th's ill-judged Indulgence is granted. *Chremes,* to avoid the Appearance of a Re-proof, endeavours to make him fenfible of the Error he was going to commit, in the fofteft Terms. It will be dangerous, fays he, to fhew yourfelf, *animo tam leni & victo,* which at the fame time, that it is a Fault we ought to correct, is alfo a Fault that proceeds from Excefs of Good-nature, and which few would think it a Reproach to be charged with.

32 *Aut largitate nimia, aut parfimonia.* Here was the time to make *Menedemus* fen-

X 2 fible

him away. She, compelled by Necessity, began afterwards to get a Livelihood, by making herself common : now, when she can't be kept without a vast Expence, you would give all he wants for to let you know how finely she is fitted out for the ruin of her Admirers; first she carries at her Heels above half a score Waiting-Maids, loaden with Garments of Gold and Silver, insomuch, that had she a *Persian* Governour for her Galliant, he could not support the Charge; much less can you pretend to do it.

Men. What, is she at your House too?

Chr. She at my House, say you? I have felt it sufficiently. I have given one Supper to her, and her Retinue, but were I to give her another such, I must be ruined. For, to pass by other things, how much Wine did she destroy, in barely tasting and spurting it about, telling me, This, Father, is rather too rough; see, pray, for a milder kind. I pierced every Cask and Vessel I had, all my Servants were employed, and this but a single Night. What do you imagine will become of you, whom they will prey upon daily? As Heavens shall bless me, I sincerely pity your Condition.

Men. Let him do what he will, take, consume, and squander away; I'm resolved to bear it all, so I have him but with me.

Chr. If you are absolutely resolved to do so, I think it of great moment to make him believe he has all these things without your knowledge.

Men. What shall I do?

Chr. Any thing, rather than what you have in view at present. Pretend to give him it at the Intercession of some other; suffer yourself to be imposed upon by the Artifices of a Servant. Altho' I am sensible they are upon this Scent already, and contriving privately

ANNOTATIONS.

sible of the Error he was like to fall into, and there is this further remarkable in what *Chremes* says, that it contains one of the best Maxims for the Conduct of Life. For too much Rigour in a Father, or too much Indulgence are equally dangerous. Regard ought always to be had to the Circumstances of Things, and the Temper of the Person. It was, by not observing this Rule, that *Menedemus* brought so much Trouble upon himself. When a moderate Liberality would have made his Son happy, whose Demands were not very great, he, by his Severity, drove him to Despair. And now running into an Extreme equally blameable, he would quietly suffer him to squander away his whole Fortune.

39 *Intertrimento.* This is a Word used originally in the Fusion of Metals, for what in melting degenerated to a Calx, and would not reunite, was called properly *Intertriinentum.* Of this we have an Example in *Livy*, Lib. 32. 2. "Id (*argentum*) quia probum "non esse quæstores renunciaverant, experi-

"entibusque pars quarta decocta erat, pecu-"nia Romæ mutua sumta, *intertrimentum* "argenti suppleverunt." Hence it came to stand for any Loss a Man might sustain, particularly in his Fortune.

43 *Satrapes si fiet amator.* Satrapes is originally a *Hebrew* Word, but in use too among the *Persians*, who gave this Title to their Governours of Provinces. These were generally very rich, and so many petty Kings in the eastern Nations.

48 *Pitissando.* Pitissare, is a Word originally *Greek*, and properly signifies the spurting of Wine out of the Mouth, when it hath been taken in to make trial of its Taste. It is, what we call, a Verb of Imitation, for its Sound in pronouncing resembles very much the Noise made by that Action.

51 *Relevi dolia omnia.* Linere was properly to secure the Mouth of any Vessel with Pitch, Rosin, or Wax, to prevent Air's getting in, to the prejudice of what might be contained in it; and as this was never
omitted,

Tum erat contenta, cuique erant grata omnia,
Proterruisti hinc. ea coacta ingratiis
Post illa cœpit victum volgo quærere.
Nunc, cùm sine magno intertrimento non potest
Haberi, quidvis dare cupis. nam, ut tu scias,   40
Quàm ea nunc instructa pulchrè ad perniciem siet ;
Primùm, jam ancillas secum adduxit plus decem,
Oneratas veste atque auro. satrapes si siet.
Amator, nunquam sufferre ejus sumtus queat :
Nedum tu possis. ME. estne ea intus? CH. si sit, rogas? 45
Sensi : nam unam ei cœnam atque ejus comitibus
Dedi. quòd si iterum mihi sit danda, actum siet.
Nam, ut alia omittam, pitissando modò mihi
Quid vini absumsit? sic hoc, dicens ; asperum,
Pater, hoc est : aliud lenius sodes vide.   50
Reveli dolia omnia, omnes serias :
Omnes habui solicitos. atque hæc una nox.
Quid te futurum censes, quem assiduè exedent ?
Sic me Dii amabant, ut me tuarum miseritum est,
Menedeme, fortunarum ! ME. faciat quod lubet :   55
Sumat, consumat, perdat : decretum est pati ;
Dum illum modò habeam mecum. CH. si certum est
Sic facere, illud permagni referre arbitror,   [tibi
Ut nescientem sentiat te id sibi dare.   [gitas :
ME. Quid faciam ? CH. quidvis potiùs, quàm quod co-
Per alium quemvis ut des, falli te sinas   61
Technis per servolum. etsi subsensi id quoque,
Illos ibi esse, id agere inter. se clanculùm.

cuique omnia erant grata, proterruisti hinc. Ea coacta ingratiis, post illa, cœpit quærere victum vulgo. Nunc, cùm non potest haberi sine magno intertrimento, cupis dare quidvis. Nam, tu ut scias, quàm ea sit instructa nunc ea sit instructa ad perniciem ; primùm, jam adduxit plus quam decem ancillas, oneratas veste atque auro ; si amator sit satrapes, nunquam queat sufferre sumptus ejus : nedum tu possis. ME. Estne ea intus ? CH. Rogas, si sit ? sensi : nam dedi unam cœnam ei atque comitibus ejus. Quod si iterum cœna danda sit mihi, actum sit. Nam, ut omittam alia, quid vini absumpsit mihi modo pitissando ! Sic dicens : Hoc, pater, hoc est asperum : vide sodes aliud lenius. Relevi omnia dolia, omnes serias, habui omnia solicitos. Atque hæc erat tantum una nox. Quid censes de te futurum, quem exedent assidue ? sic Dii amabunt me, ut est miseritum me tuarum fortunarum, Menedeme ! ME. Faciat quod lubet : sumat, consumat, perdat : decretum est pati ; dum modo habeam illum mecum. CH. Si est certum tibi facere sic, arbitror illud referre permagni, ut sentiat te nescientem dare id sibi. ME. Quid faciam ? CH. Quidvis potius, quam quod cogitas : ut des per quemvis alium, sinas te falli technis per servulum : etsi subsensi id quoque, illos esse ibi, & agere id clanculum inter se.

ANNOTATIONS.

omitted, when any Vessel was filled with Wine, hence it is frequently used for putting up Wine in Casks. *Hor. Od. Lib. I. 20. 1.*

  Vile potabis modicis Sabinum
  Cantharis, Græca quod ego ipse testa
  Conditum levi.

Relinere of consequence signifies to remove this Rosin, or Pitch, which as it was never done, but upon opening the Vessel for use, hence *relevi omnia dolia,* I opened or tapped all my Casks.

  52 *Omnes habui solicitos.* That is, commotos reddidi, variisque ministeriis districtos. For hurrying backward and forward, and a Variety of Services, must always occasion a Solicitude to have them rightly performed. Thus too a Sea tossed by raging Tem-

pests, has this Epithet sometimes given it. *Virg. Geor. 4. 262.*

  Ut mare solicitum stridet refluentibus undis.

  55 *Faciat quod lubet ; sumat, consumat, perdat.* Here we have drawn, in lively Colours, the Picture of a Man hasty, in running from one Extreme to another. The same *Menedemus,* who had formerly, by his Severity, forced his Son to leave him in Despair, is here willing to let him squander away his whole Fortune, rather than be without him. This gives occasion to the Expedient offered by *Chremes,* which comes in very naturally, and insensibly leads to the remaining Part of the Plot.

  62 *Etsi subsensi id quoque, illos ibi esse.*

ly among themfelves. *Syrus* is often whifpering with that Slave of
yours; the young Men lay their Heads together; and it is better
to lofe a Pound this way, than a Penny the other. It is not fo much
the Money we are to Mind at prefent, as how to give it him with the
leaft danger to you and himfelf. For when once he comes to find out
your Foible, that you would rather part with both Life and Eftate,
than be without him; alas! how great an Inlet will be given to Debauchery! nay, to that Degree, as to make you even weary of Life.
For we are all apt to grow worfe by Indulgence. Whatever comes
into his Head, he will have it, without once reflecting, whether what
he demands be right or wrong. It will be impoffible for you to behold with Patience, both your Son and Eftate going to ruin. You'll
deny him Money; he'll immediately have recourfe to the Means,
which he thinks likely to work moft effectually upon you, and
threaten directly to be gone from you.

Men. You feem to fpeak what is truly like to be the Cafe.

Chr. I proteft to you, I have not clofed my Eyes this Night, for
thinking which is the beft Method to reftore your Son to you.

Men. Give me your Hand: and, *Chremes*, I beg of you, that
you will continue thus to ferve me.

Chr. I promife it.

Men. Do you know now, what I'd have you do?

Chr. Tell me.

Men. As you perceived them contriving fome Artifice againft me,
that they haften it. I am impatient to give him all he wants; I
long mightily to fee him.

Chr. I'll take care: but firft I muft find out *Syrus*, and give him
the requifite Inftructions. But who can this be coming out from our
Houfe? Do you ftep hence home, that they may not difcover us con-
certing together. I have a little hindrance of Bufinefs at prefent:
Simus and *Crito*, our Neighbours, have had fome Difpute about their
Lands; which they have referred to my Decifion. I'll go and tell
them, that it will be impoffible for me to attend them To-day,
as I promifed. I'll return again in a Minute.

Men. Pray do. *(To himfelf.)* Good Heavens! that Men fhould
be all fo contrived by Nature, that they are better Judges of what
regards others, than themfelves? Is it, becaufe, in our own Concerns,

This comes in very feafonably, and is an Evidence of the great Judgment of the Speaker. He faw *Menedemus* fo anxious to have his Son with him, that every Delay would be infupportable; and, therefore, to remove this Objection from the Expedient he propofed, he tells him, that it was already in great forwardnefs. *Syrus nofter cum illo noftro fervo confufurrat; & ipfi conferunt confilia adolefcentes.*

vidi meis. We have feen all along, that *Chremes* acts with the moft friendly Views, and it was neceffary for him to make *Menedemus* fenfible of it, that his Advice might have the greater Weight; for we are fcarce able to deny any Thing to a Perfon, when we know he has our good chiefly at Heart. Agreeable to this is *Menedemus*'s Anfwer; *Cedo dextram: perge te oro, idem ut facias, Chreme.*

¹² *Somnum hercle ego hac nocte oculis non*   ⁹⁸ *Aliena ut melius videant & dijudicent quam*

Syru' cum illo voſtro confuſurrat : conferunt
Conſilia adoleſcentes, & tibi perdere   65
Talentum hoc pacto ſatius eſt, quàm illo minam.
Non nunc pecunia agitur; ſed illud, quomodo
Minimo periclo id demus adoleſcentulo.
Nam ſi ſemel tuum animum ille intellexerit,
Priùs proditurum te tuam vitam, & prius   70
Pecuniam omnem, quam abs te amittas filium ; hui,
Quantam feneſtram ad nequitiam peteſeceris !
Tibi autem porro ut non ſit ſuave vivere.
Nam deteriores ſumus omnes licentiâ.
Quodcunque inciderit in mentem, volet : neque id 75
Putabit, pravumne an rectum ſit, quod petet.
Tu, rem perire, & ipſum, non poteris pati.
Dare denegâris ; ibit ad illud illico,
Quo maxumè apud te ſe valere ſentiet :
Abiturum ſe abs te eſſe illico minabitur.   80
ME. Videre verum, atque ita utì res eſt, dicere.
CH. Somnum hercle ego hac nocte oculis non vidi meis,
Dum id quæro, tibi quî filium reſtituerem.
ME. Cedo dextram : porro te oro idem ut facias Chreme.
CH. Paratus ſum. ME. ſcin' quid nunc facere te volo ? 85
CH. Dic. ME. quod ſenſiſti illos me incipere fallere;
Id ut maturent facere : cupio illi dare,
Quod volt : cupio ipſum jam videre. CH. operam dabo.
Syrus eſt prehendendus atque adhortandus mihi.
A me neſcio quis exit. concede hinc domum,   90
Ne nos inter nos congruere ſentiant.
Paulum hoc negoti mihi obſtat : Simus & Crito
Vicini noſtri hîc ambigunt de finibus :
Me cepere arbitrum. ibo, ac dicam, ut dixeram
Operam daturum me, hodie non poſſe his dare.   95
Continuò hîc adero. ME. ita quæſo. Dii voſtram fidem !
Itan' comparatam eſſe hominum naturam omnium,
Aliena ut meliùs videant & dijudicent
Quàm ſua ? an eo fit, quia in re noſtrâ aut gaudio.

Syrus confuſurrat cum illi vuſtro Dromone, conferunt conſilia adoleſcentes, & eſt ſatiùs tibi perdere talentum huc pacto, quam minum illô. Non pecunia agitur nunc, ſed illud, quomodo demus adoleſcentulo minimo periclo. Nam ſi ille ſemel intellexerit tuum animum ; te prius proditurum tuam vitam, & prius omnem pecuniam, quàm amittas filium abs te ; hui, quantam feneſtram feceris ad nequitiam ! Porro autem, ut non ſit ſuave tibi vivere. Nam ſumus omnes deteriores licentia. Volet quodcunque inciderit in mentem, neque putabit idee ſit pravum & rectum, quod petet : tu non poteris pati rem & ipſum perire : denegaveris dare ; ibit illico ad illud, quo ſentiet ſe valere maxime apud te : illico minitabitur ſe eſſe abiturum abs te. ME. Videre dicere verum, atque ita utì res eſt. CH. Hercle ego non vidi ſomnum huc noctis meis oculis, dum quæro id, qui reſtituerem filium tibi. ME. Cedo dextram : porro oro te, ut facias idem, Chreme. CH. Sum paratus.

ME. Sciſne quid nunc volo te facere ? CH. Dic. ME. Quod ſenſiſti illos incipere fallere me, ut maturent facere illud. Cupio dare illi, quod vult : jam cupio videre ipſum. CH. Dabo operam. Syrus eſt prehedendus atque adhortandus mihi. Neſcio quis exit a me. Concede hinc domum, ne ſentiant nos congruere inter nos. Hoc paulum negotii obſtat mihi : Simus & Crito vicini noſtri hic ambigunt de finibus : cepere me arbitrum. Ibo, ac dicam, me non poſſe dare operam his hodie, ut dixeram me eſſe daturum. Adero hic continuo. ME. Fac ita, quæſo. Dii voſtram fidem ! Naturamne omnium hominum eſſe ita comparatam, ut melius videant ac dijudicent aliena ſua ? An ſit eo, quia in noſtra re ſumus præprediti ; aut nimio gaudio,

ANNOTATIONS.

quam ſua ? Menedemus ſays this only in regard to himſelf; for although it be equally true of *Chremes,* yet *Menedemus* did not as yet know him well enough to apply it to

X 4   him

cerns, we are too apt to be byaffed by our Joys or Griefs? This, *Chremes!* now, how much wifer is he for me, than I am for myfelf.

Chr. I have difengaged myfelf, that I might be the more at lei-fure to ferve you,

ANNOTATIONS.

him any; otherwife than as a general Obfer-vation, that in fome meafure regards all Mankind.

202 *Diffolvi me, otiofus operam ut tibi darem.*

While *Menedmus* is wondering with him-felf, that Men are generally fo much wifer in what regards others than themfelves, *Chremes* goes and makes an Excufe to *Simus* and

---

ACT III. SCENE II.

ARGUMENT.

Chremes urges Syrus *to contrive a way of drawing fome Money from* Menedemus, *to fupply* Clinia; *but unfortu-nately he falls into the very Snare he had himfelf contrived, for upon this Occafion all his Cunning and Forefight failed him. Thus we often fee Mifchief return upon the original Contriver.*

SYRUS, CHREMES.

Syrus. WHATEVER way I fet about it, Money muft be found; fome Trap muft be laid for the old Man.

Chr. Was I deceived, when I faid they were upon fome Plot? that Servant of *Clinia*'s, it would feem, is a dull heavy Wretch; and, therefore, that Province is affigned to this our *Syrus.*

Syr. Who's that fpeaks? I'm undone. Did he hear me, I wonder?

Chr. Syrus,

Syr. Hah.

Chr. What are you doing there?

Syr. No very great matter; but I wonder, *Chremes*, how you are up fo early, after drinking fo hard laft Night.

Chr. Not too much.

Syr. Not too much, fay you; why, truly, you've feen, as the Saying is, the Eagle's Age.

Chr. Pfhaw.

Syr. This Wench here, is a good agreeable fort of Woman.

Chr. So, indeed, fhe feems.

Syr. And really has a fine Face.

Chr. Well enough.

Syr.

ANNOTATIONS.

Syrus had fucceeded very well, in making *Bacchis* pafs for *Clinia*'s Miftrefs. She had been there all night, nor had the old Man any Sufpicion of their Project. Here then was one Point gained; but ftill there was another thing wanting to make every body

eafy and contented. *Syrus* had undertaken to obtain for *Bacchis* thirty Pounds. She herfelf began to be impatient, that fhe did not receive it, and *Clitipho* was perpetually teazing him with Importunities to fall upon fome Expedient to procure it. *Syrus*, there-fore,

Sumus præpediti nimio, aut ægritudine ?   100
Hic mihi nunc quanto plus fapit, quàm egomet mihi !
CH. Diſſolvi me, otioſus operam ut tibi darem.

Aut agritudine ? Hic quanto plus nunc ſapit mihi quam egomet ſapio mihi ?

CH. Diſſolvi me, ut otioſus darem operam tibi.

ANNOTATIONS.

and *Crito*, that he could not attend them that day ; after which returning immediately, he tells *Menedemus*, that he had diſengaged himſelf to be the more at leiſure to haſten his Buſineſs ; with which the Scene cloſes,

for both upon this retire. Some read *buic ut operam darem*, ſuppoſing that *Menedemus* had before retired, and that *Chremes* having excuſed himſelf to his two Neighbours, ſays this to himſelf, as he comes from them.

ACTUS III. SCENA II.

ARGUMENTUM.

Inſtigat Syrum Chremes ad fabricam, qua argentum a Menedemo Cliniæ extorqueretur fingendam : ſed ſuo malo, incidit in foveam, quam fecit ; nam hac occaſione ſua ipſius conjectura & ſolertia fallitur. Sic ſæpe videmus malum in auctorem redundare.

SYRUS, CHREMES.

HAC illac circumcurſa : inveniundum eſt tamen
  Argentum, intendenda in ſenem eſt fallacia:
CH. Num me fefellit, hoſce id ſtruere ? videlicet
Ille Cliniæ ſervus tardiuſculus eſt :
Idcirco huic noſtro tradita eſt provincia.   5
SY. Quis hîc loquitur ? perii. numnam hæc audivit ? CH.
  Syre. SY. hem.   [Chreme,
CH. Quid tu iſtic ? SY. rectè equidem: ſed te miror,
Tam manè, qui heri tantum biberis. CH. nihil nimis.
SY. Nihil, narras ? viſa verò eſt, quod dici ſolet,
Aquilæ ſenectus. CH. heia. SY. mulier commoda & 10
Faceta hæc eſt meretrix. CH. ſanè idem viſa eſt mihi.
SY. Et quidem hercle formâ luculentâ. CH. ſic ſatis.

iſtic ? SY. Equidem rectè : ſed miror, Chreme, te ſurrexiſſe tam mane, qui biberis tantum heri. CH. Nihil minis. SY. Nihil nimis narras ? Vero, quod ſolet dici, ſenectus aquilæ eſt viſa tibi. CH. Heia. SY. Hæc meretrix eſt commoda & faceta mulier. CH. Sane eſt viſa eſt idem mibi. SY. Et quidem hercle forma luculenta. CH. Satis ſic.

ANNOTATIONS.

fore, ſeeing it can be deferred no longer, is here brought upon the Stage, determined to make ſome Attempt or other : *Intenderda eſt in ſenem fallacia. Chremes*, who, as we have ſeen before, ſuſpected that there was ſome Project on foot againſt *Menedemus*, and was reſolved to encourage it, overhearing what *Syrus* ſays, applies it immediately to that Notion, and never once imagines, that himſelf is ſo nearly concerned. This makes way for a Converſation managed with great Art and Addreſs on both ſides, and full of

Entertainment to the Reader, who is acquainted with their different Views.

10 *Aquilæ ſenectus.* Probably a proverbial Expreſſion, to ſignify a ſtrong and vgorous Old Age ; for ſome Naturaliſts tell us, that the Eagle never dies of Age, but rather renews her Strength. It is further ſaid, that they live only upon the Blood which they ſuck from their Prey, not being able any other way to feed upon it, by the upper Part of their Beaks growing inward.

13 *Ita*

Syr. Not like the Beauties of old, but very well as times are now; nor do I at all wonder, that *Clinia* is so desperately in love with her: but he has a niggardly, covetous Wretch of a Father; this Neighbour of ours, do you know him? Who, as if he had not a Superfluity of Riches, has forced his Son away for meer want. Don't you know that it is as I tell you?

Chr. How should I but know it? a Fellow that deserves *Bridewell*.

Syr. Who?

Chr. I mean this young Gentleman's Servant.

Syr. *Syrus*, I was in great pain for you.

Chr. Who suffered it to come to this.

Syr. What could he do?

Chr. What could he do? he should have found an expedient, or contrived some Stratagem, whence the young Man might have been supplied with Money to give his Mistress, and saved the morose old Fellow all this Vexation, even in spite of himself.

Syr. You joke sure.

Chr. He ought, indeed, to have done so, *Syrus.*

Syr. How! do you commend Servants, pray, who deceive their Masters?

Chr. When there's a real Necessity for it, I do, indeed, commend them.

Syr. Well said!

Chr. Because it often prevents great Disturbances in Families. As here, this Man's only Son would have remained at home with him.

Syr. (*Aside.*) I don't know, whether he says this in Jest or Earnest, only that he encourages me much to go on with my Plot.

Chr. And what does he wait for now, *Syrus*? What, till his Master is forced away a second time, when he cannot longer support the Charge of this Woman? Is he not contriving some Stratagem against the old Man?

Syr. He's a Fool.

Chr. But you ought to help him for the young Man's sake.

Syr. Nay, I could easily do it, if you desire it; for I know well how to set about it.

Chr. So much the better.

Syr. I don't use to fail in what I undertake.

Chr. Do then.

Syr. But harkve: see that you remember this, if peradventure it should any time happen, as in the Course of human things is not unlikely, that this may be your own Son's Case.

Chr. That I hope will never be.

Syr. And so do I, indeed: nor do I say this now, because I apprehend

ANNOTATIONS.

23 Ita non ut olim, sed uti nunc, sánis bonis. This may either refer to her present Beauty at that Age, compared with what she was in her Youth; Her Form, indeed, is changed from what it was, but still she is very handsome; or, as I am rather apt to think, *Syrus* here

Sy. Ita non ut olim, fed utì nunc, fanè bonâ :
Miniméque miror, Clinia hanc fi deperit.
Sed habet patrem quendam avidum, miferum atque a-
  ridum,   15
Vincinum hunc : noftin'? at quafi is non divitiis
Abundet, gnatus ejus profugit inopiâ.
Scis effe factum, ut dico? Ch. quid ego nefciam?
Hominem piftrino dignum! Sy. quem? Ch. iftunc fer-
Dico adolefcentis. Sy. Syre, tibi timui malè [volum 19
Ch. Qui paffus eft id fieri. Sy. quid faceret? Ch. rogas?
Aliquid reperiret, fingeret fallacias,
Unde effet adolefcenti, amicæ quod daret,
Atque hanc difficilem invitum fervaret fenem.
Sy. Garris. Ch. hæc facta ab illo oportebant, Syre. 25
Sy. Eho, quæfo, laudas qui heros fallunt? Ch. in loco,
Ego verò laudo. Sy. rectè fanè. Ch. quippe qui
Magnarum fæpe id remedium ægritudinum eft.
Jam huic manfiflet unicus gnatus domi.
Sy. Jocone an feriò illæc dicat, nefcio ;   30
Nifi mihi quidem addit animum, quò lubeat magis.
Ch. Et nunc quid exfpectat, Syre? an dum hinc denuo
Abeat, cùm tolerare hujus fumptus non queat? [eft?
Nonne ad fenem aliquam fabricam fingit? Sy. ftolidus
Ch. At te adjutare oportet adolefcentuli   35
Causâ. Sy. facilè equidem facere poffum, fi jubes :
Etenim, quo pacto id fieri foleat, calleo.
Ch. Tanto hercle melior. Sy. non eft mentiri meum.
Ch. Fac ergo. Sy. at heus tu, facito dum eadem hæc
  memineris,
Si quid hujus fimile fortè aliquando evenerit,   40
Ut funt humana, tuus ut faciat filius.
Ch. Non ufus veniet, fpero. Sy. fpero hercle ego
  quoque :

Sy. Non ita ut olim, fed fane bona, utì nunc : minimeque miror, fi Clinia deperit hanc. Sed habet quendam patrem avidum, miferum atque aridum; hunc vicinum noftrum: nofine? At quafi is non abundet divitiis, gnatus ejus profugit inopia. Scis effe factum, ut dico? Ch. Quid ego nefciam? Hominem dignum piftrino! Sy. Quem? Ch. Dico iftunc fervulum adolefcentis. Sy. Syre, timui male tibi. Ch. Qui eft paffus id fieri. Sy. Quid faceret? Ch. Rogas? Reperiret aliquid, fingeret fallacias, unde effet adolefcenti, quod daret amicæ; atque fervaret hunc difficilem fenem invitum. Sy. Garris. Ch. Hæc oportebant fuiffe facta ab illo, Syre. Sy. Eho, quæfo, laudas eos, qui fallunt heros? Ch. Vero ego laudo eos in loco. Sy. Sane rectè. Ch. Quippe qui id eft fæpe remedium magnarum ægritudinum. Jam unicus gnatus manfiffet huic domi. Nefcio dicatne illæc

jo'o an ferio, nifi quidem addit animum mibi, quo lubeat magis fingere fallacias. Ch. Et quid hic fervus expectat nunc, Syre? An dum Clinia denuo abeat hinc, cum non queat tolerare fumptus hujus? Nonne fingit aliquam fabricam ad fenem? Sy. Eft ftolidus. Ch. At oportet te adjutare eum, caufa adolefcentuli. Sy. Equidem poffum facere facile, fi jubes: etenim calleo quo pacto id foleat fieri. Ch. Hercle tanto melior. Sy. Mentiri non eft meum. Ch. Fac ergo. Sy. At heus tu, facito dum memineris hæc eadem, fi forte aliquando evenerit, ut humana funt, ut filius tuus faciat quid fimile hujus. Ch. Spero, ufus non veniet. Sy. Hercle ego quoque fpero ;

ANNOTATIONS.

here inftitutes a Comparifon betwixt the Beauties of former Times, and thofe of the prefent Age: *Ita non eft forma Bacchidis, fateor, ut olim erant formæ ; fed tamen fane bona, ut nunc funt formæ.*

19 *Hominem piftrino dignum. Chremes,* that he might the more cunningly infinuate to Syrus his Willingnefs, that he fhould af-

fift in contriving the Means to cozen *Menedemus* out of the Money they wanted, pretends to be angry with *Clinia's* Servant for his Dulnefs and Want of Contrivance, *hominem piftrino dignum;* and afterwards explains it, *qui paffus eft id fieri.* It was natural upon this for *Syrus* to afk what he could do to prevent it, and this gives *Chremes* an Opportunity

bend any fuch Thing. But happen it or not, you fee what Age he is of. And truly, *Chremes*, if there fhould be occafion for it, I could manage it nobly.

Chr. We'll confider of that, when it is needful : meantime, do you think of the prefent Tafk.

Syr. I never in my Life heard a Mafter fpeak more to the Purpofe, nor could I have imagined I fhould have been thus authorifed to play the Rogue with Impunity. But who's this coming out from our Houfe ?

A N N O T A T I O N S.

tunity to open his Mind to him. *Quid faceret ? Aliquid reperiret, fingeret fallacias.* 43 *Neque eo nunc dico.* It is well judged in *Syrus*, after having faid as much as he thought neceffary to ferve for a good De-

fence afterwards, if he fhould chance to be found out, to endeavour to avert Sufpicions, left the Old Man m ght be put upon his Guard, which would have been a great Obftruction to their Defigns. The Ellipfes ufed

---

A C T III. S C E N E III.

A R G U M E N T.

Chremes *chides his Son, and accufes him of behaving indecently with* Bacchis, *whom he believed to be* Clinia's *Miftrefs.* Syrus *then telling him, that he had fallen upon an Expedient to draw fome Money from* Menedemus, *turns the fraudulent Advice, given by* Chremes, *againft himfelf.*

C H R E M E S, C L I T I P H O, S Y R U S.

Chremes. WHAT can you mean, pray ? What Behaviour is this, Clitipho ? Is this becoming in you ?

Clit. What have I done ?

Chr. Did I not juft now fee you put your Hand into this Courtezan's Bofom ?

Syr. (To himfelf.) All's difcovered : I'm certainly ruin'd.

Clit. What me ?

Chr. With thefe very Eyes I faw you ; don't pretend to deny it. Your Behaviour is injurious and mean, not to keep your Hands to yourfelf. For it is, indeed, the higheft Degree of Bafenefs to receive a Man as your Friend, and deal underhand with his Miftrefs.

How

A N N O T A T I O N S.

Chremes, after parting from *Syrus*, in the laft Scene, went in, and coming unexpectedly upon *Clitipho*, finds him taking fome Li-

berties with *Bacchis*, whom he ftill believed to be *Clinia*'s Miftrefs. Upon which he calls him afide, and expoftulates with him,

on

Neque cò nunc dico, quò quidquam illum senferim :
Sed si quid, ne quid—quæ sit ejus ætas, vides :
Et næ ego te, si usus veniat, magnificè, Chreme, 45
Tractare possim. CH. de istoc, eum usus venerit,
Videbimus quid opus sit. nunc istuc age.
SY. Nunquam commodiùs unquam herum audivi loqui,
Nec, cùm malefacere crederem mi impuniùs
Licere. quisnam à nobis egreditur foras ?   50

neque nunc dico eo, quo senferim illum facere quidquam : sed si quid, nequid, vides, quæ sit ætas ejus : & næ ego possim tractare te magnifice, Chreme, si usus veneat. CH. Videbimus quid opus sit de istoc, cum usus

venerit : nunc age istuc : SY. Nunquam unquam audivi berum loqui commodius : nec unquam fuit tempus cum crederem licere mibi malefacere impunius. Quisnam egreditur foras a nobis ?

A N N O T A T I O N S.

ufed here too are well imagined : *Quo quidquam illum senferim : fed si quid, ne quid.* The Countenance and Action of the Speaker supplies what is wanting ; for to gain his Point the more effectually, we must suppose that he assumes an Air of Confidence and

Security : " What I say now, is not from " any Suspicion that your Son is at present " under such Engagements, but only as con- " sidering his Age, it may possibly happen, " don't wonder, or take it ill, that I assist him, " as you would now have me to assist *Clixia*."

A C T U S III. S C E N A III.

A R G U M E N T U M.

Chremes filium objurgat & immodestiæ arguit, quem ludentem viderat cum Bacchide, quam Cliniæ amicam credebat. Tum Syrus fallaciam de emungendo a Menedemo argento invenisse referens, consilium fraudulentum à Chremete datum, in eum ipsum intendit.

C H R E M E S, C L I T I P H O, S Y R U S.

QUID istuc, quæso ? qui istic mos est, Clitipho ?
  itane fieri oportet ?
CL. Quid ego feci ? CH. vidin' ego te modò manum in
  sinum huic meretrici   [hiice oculis : ne nega.
Inferere ? SY. acta hæc res est, perii. CL. mene ? CH.
Facis adeò indignè injuriam illi, qui non abstineas ma-
  num :
Nam isti quidem contumelia est,   5
Hominem amicum recipere ad te, atque ejus amicam
  subagitare.

 O R D O.
CH. *Quæso, quid istic ? Qui mos est istic, Clitipho ? Oportet ne fieri sita ? CL. Quid ego feci ? CH. E- gone vidi te. modo inferere manum in sinum huic meretrici ? SY. Hæc res est acta ; perii. CL. Mene ? CH. Vidi hisce ocu- lis. ne nega : adeo facis injuriam indig-*

ne illi, qui non abstineas manum : nam quidem ista est contumelia, recipere bominem amicam ad te, atque subagitare amicam ejus.

A N N O T A T I O N S.

on the supposed Injury done to his Friend. Syrus concerned for himself, and the Project he was up in the point of executing, joins with the Old Man in his Reproofs, and both

at least agree that *Clitipho* shall withdraw for some time, and not disturb the Lovers. +, &c. *Facis adeo indigne injuriam illi nam ista quidem contumelia est.* He here accuses

How ſtrangely rude was you laſt Night at Supper ?

Syr. (*Aſide.*) 'Tis but too true.

Chr. How teazing too ! infomuch that, as I hope for Happineſs, I dreaded what might be the Conſequence. I well know the Humour of Lovers, they are apt to reſent highly, even when they don't appear to take any notice.

Clit. But my Friend, Father, has too much Confidence in me, to ſuſpect me capable of any thing of that kind.

Chr. Suppoſe it : yet at leaſt you ought ſometimes to withdraw, and leave them together. Lovers have a thouſand things to ſay and do, which your Preſence is a Check to. I conjecture from myſelf ; for I know not at this time a Perſon in the world, *Clitipho,* to whom I'd venture to diſcloſe all my Secrets. This Man's Rank and Superiority in Life reſtrains me, another I am aſhamed to confeſs to ; left to one I may ſeem weak and fooliſh, and to the other preſuming : which imagine to be his Caſe. For 'tis ours to underſtand when and where Complaiſance ought to take place.

Syr. (*Aſide.*) What ſays he to this ?

Clit. (*Aſide.*) I'm ruin'd.

Syr. (*Aſide to* Clitipho.) Clitipho, theſe are the very Injunctions I gave you too ; you have acted like a diſcreet and prudent Man ! [*Jeeringly.*

Clit. Prithee hold thy tongue.

Syr. Nay, 'tis very true.

Chr. Syrus, I proteſt I'm aſhamed of him.

Syr. I believe it : nor, indeed, without reaſon ; for even I am troubled at it.

Clit. Do you perſiſt ſtill then ?

Syr. Why really I ſpeak my Sentiments.

Clit. Muſt I not come near them ?

Chr. What : is there but one way of being near them ?

Syr. Confuſion ! he'll diſcover himſelf, before I can have procured the Money. *Chremes,* will you hearken for once to a Fool's Counſel ?

Chr. What ſhall I do with him ?

Syr. Order him to withdraw hence ſomewhere.

Clit. Where, pray, ſhould I go ?

Syr. Where ? where you will : only make room for them : go take a walk.

Clit. A walk ! Where, pray ?

Syr. Pſhaw, as if there was no place to walk in. Go this way, that way, where you will.

Chr. He's right ; I think ſo too.

Clit.

ANNOTATIONS.

accuſes *Clitipho* of injuring his Friend ; and to make him the more ſenſible of a Behaviour which he thought baſe, deſcribes it as an Indignity and Affront, and immediately after adds the ſeveral Circumſtances that aggravates it : that it was done to a Friend, to his Gueſt, and to a Lover in preſence of his Miſtreſs.

13 *Ego de me facio conjecturam.* Chremes's Reaſoning here is ſtrong and pathetic, and ſhews, that even among the moſt intimate Friends, a proper Caution and Reſerve ought not

Vel herì in vino quàm immodeſtus fuiſti ? Sy. factum.
   Ch. quàm moleſtus ?
Ut equidem, ita me Dii ament, metui quid futurum
   denique eſſet !   [quæ non cenſeas.
Novi ego amantium animum : advortunt graviter,
Cl. At mihi fides apud hunc eſt, nihil me iſtius fac-
   turum, pater.   [quantiſper.
Ch. Eſto. at certè concedas aliquò ab ore eorum ali-
Multa fert libido ; ea facere prohibet tua præſentia 12
Ego de me facio conjecturam. nemo eſt meorum hodie,
Apud quem expromere omnia mea occulta, Clitipho,
   audeam.   [pudet, 15
Apud alium prohibet dignitas : apud alium ipſius facti
Ne ineptus, ne protervus videar : quod illum facere
   credito.   [que opus ſit, obſequi.
Sed noſtrum eſt intellegere, utcunque, àtque ubicun-
Sy. Quid iſtuc narrat ? Cl. perii. Sy. Clitipho, hæc
   ego præcipio tibi,   [ſodès.
Hominis frugi & temperantis functus officium. Cl. tace
Sy. Rectè ſanè. Ch. Syre, pudet me. Sy. credo : ne-
   que id injuriâ.   20
Quin mihi moleſtum eſt. Cl. pergin' hercle ? Sy. ve-
   rum dico, quod videtur.
Cl. Nonne accedam ad illos ? Ch. cho quæſo, unà
   accedundi via eſt ?
Sy. Actum eſt : hic priùs ſe indicârit, quàm ego ar-
   gentum effecero.   [faciam ? Sy. jube hunc
Chreme, vin' tu homini ſtulto mihi auſcultare ?Ch.quid
Abire hinc aliquò. Cl. quò ego hinc abeam ?.Sy. quò ?
   quò lubet : da illis locum :   25
Abi deambulatum. Cl. deambulatum, quò ? Sy. vah,
   quaſi deſit locus.   [cenſeo.
Abi ſanè iſtàc, iſtorſum, quo vis. Ch. rectè dicit :

pudet me. Sy. Credo, neque id injuria. Quin eſt moleſtum mibi. Cl. Pergin' hercle ? Sy.
Dico quod videtur verum. Ch. Nonhè accedam ad illos ? Ch. Eho quæſo, eſt una tantum via
accedendi ? Sy. Actum eſt : hic indicaverit ſe, prinſquam ego effecero argentum. Chreme, viſee
tu auſcultare mibi homini ſtulto ? Ch. Quid faciam ? Sy. Jube hunc abire aliquo hinc. Cl.
Quo ego abeam hinc ? Sy. Quo lubet : da locum illis : abi deambulatum. Cl. Deambulatum,
quo ? Sy. Vah, quaſi locus deſit : abi ſane iſtac, iſtorſum, quo vis. Ch. Dicit recte : cenſeo.

[margin notes omitted]

ANNOTATIONS.

not to be forgot. Our Actions will not appear in the ſame Light to others, as to ourſelves. Our Paſſions ſometimes blind us, and a ſtrong Byas and Propenſity may make, what another thinks trifling, of the greateſt importance to us. It is for this Reaſon, that a Man of Prudence will not be apt to expoſe all his Weakneſs and Foibles, even to thoſe from whom he expects the greateſt Indulgence ; becauſe however excuſable they may appear to himſelf, he knows that it would be in vain to hope for the ſame Allowance from thoſe who are not equally intereſted.

18 *Quid iſtic narrat* ? What *Syrus* here ſays, breaking in upon the Diſcourſe of the Father and Son, requires a little to be cleared up. He had before ſaid, *acta res eſt perii* : being

Clit. A Curfe upon you, *Syrus*, to thruft me away thus.

Syr. (*To* Clitipho *going.*) Learn you then henceforth to keep thefe Hands to yourfelf. (*To* Chremes.) Don't you obferve? What do you think will become of him, *Chremes*, unlefs you watch him all in your Power, chaftife and admonifh him?

Chr. I'll take care.

Syr. But now, Sir, is the Time to keep an Eye over him.

Chr. Leave that to me.

Syr. You had beft: for every Day he minds me lefs and lefs.

Chr. But what fay you of the Bufinefs I talked to you about fome time ago, *Syrus?* Have you done any thing in it yet? Have you hit upon any Expedient, that you like, or are you ftill as you was?

Syr. You mean the Plot againft *Menedemus:* S't. I've lately fixed upon one.

Chr. A brave Fellow! what is it, tell me?

Syr. I will: but as one thing brings in another——

Chr. What, *Syrus?*

Syr. This is a fad Jade.

Chr. So fhe feems.

Syr. Ay, if you knew all: do but obferve what fhe is now a hatching. There was formerly an old Woman of *Corinth* here, to whom this Harlot had lent thirty Guineas.

Chr. What then?

Syr. She is fince dead, and has left behind her a Daughter, a young Girl, whom fhe bequeathed as a Pledge for this Money.

Chr. I underftand you.

Syr. She brought her here along with her, and fhe is now with your Wife.

Chr. What then?

Syr. She begs of *Clinia* to let her have this Money, and offers him the Girl as an Equivalent; but infifts upon the thirty Guineas *prefently.*

Chr. And does fhe, indeed, infift upon it?

Syr. Hy, is that to be doubted?   *Chr.*

ANNOTATIONS.

being in fear for himfelf, and the Projeft he had concerted. Now, *Quid iftic narrat?* which muft be fo taken, as if *Syrus* approved of what the Old Man had faid, and joined in the Reproof. What can *Clitipho* fay for himfelf now? What has he to anfwer? whence *Clitipho, Perii.* What is he my Enemy too, does he help to fpirit up my Father againft me? And when *Syrus* ftill perfifted, he begs him to be filent; *Tace, fodes.* Others think thefe Words addreffed to *Clitipho, Audis quid iftic (pater tuus) narrat?* Do you hear what your Father fays to you? D.d I not tell you it would be fo?

39 *Fuit quædam anus Corinthia hic.* Syrus pretends, that he had concerted this

againft *Menedemus,* to obtain fome Money of him for this Courtezan. This was fpecious enough, yet *Chremes* is diffatisfy'd with it. However, it is of fervice in the End; for when *Antiphila* was difcovered to be *Chremes*'s Daughter, he could not avoid paying the Price of her Ranfom, and thus out of his own Pocket furnifhed the Money wanting for *Bacchis.*

42 *Arrhaboni.* This Word is originally *Hebrew,* and fignifies a Pledge, or rather what is given in part of Security. The Word moft commonly ufed by Lawyers, is *arrha,* which they diftinguifh from *pignus.* This laft, they tell us, is a Security for tho whole, and to be returned upon difcharging what

Cl. Di te eradicent, Syre, qui me hinc extrudas. Sy.
at tu tibi iftas
Pofthac comprimito manus.   [Chreme, 30
Cenfen' vero ? quid illum porro credis facturum,
Nifi eum, quantum tibi opis Dii dant, fervas, caftigas,
mones ?   [affervandus eft.
Ch. Ego iftuc curabo. Sy. atqui nunc, here, hic tibi
Ch. Fiet. Sy. fi fapias ; nam mihi jam minus minuf-
que obtemperat.   [egifti, Syre ? aut
Ch. Quid tu ? ecquid de illo, quod dudum tecum egi,
Reperifti quod placeat, an nondum etiam ? Sy. de
fallaciâ.   35
Dicis ? ft. inveni quandam nuper. Ch. frugi es : cedo,
quid id eft ?   [nam, Syre ?
Sy. Dicam : verùm, ut aliud ex alio incidit. Ch. quid-
Sy. Peffuma hæc eft meretrix. Ch. ita videtur. Sy.
imo fi fcias—   [Corinthia
Hoc vide, quod inceptet facinus. Fuit quædam anus
Hic : huic drachmarum argenti hæc mille dederat
mutuum.   [fefcentulam : 41
Ch. Quid tum ? Sy. ea mortua eft: reliquit filiam ado-
Ea relicta huic arrhavoni eft pro illo argento. Ch. in-
tellego   [rem tuam.
Sy. Hanc fecum huc adduxit, eaque eft nunc ad uxo-
Ch. Quid tum ? Sy. Cliniam orat, fibi uti id nunc
det : illam illi tamen   [quidem ? Sy. hui, 45
Poft daturam. mille nummûm pofcit. Ch. & pofcit

quod inceptet. Quædam anus Corinthia fuit hic : hæc dederat mille drachmarum argenti metuum
huic. Ch. Quid tum ? Sy. Ea eft mortua ; reliquit filiam adolefcentulam : ea eft relicta huic
arrhaboni pro illo argento. Ch. Quid tum ? Sy. Hanc fecum, eaque nunc eft ad
fuam uxorem. Ch. Quid tum ? Sy. Orat Cliniam, uti nunc det id fibi : ait tamen fe poft ar-
gentum receptum, daturam illam illi. Pofcit mille nummûm. Ch. Et quidem pofcit ? Sy.
Hui,

Cl. Dii eradicent te'
Syre, qui extrudas
me hinc. Sy. At tu
pofthac comprimito
ftas manus tibi. Cen-
fefne vero ?. Quid
credis filum porro
facturum, Chreme,
nifi fervas, caftigas,
mones eum, quantum
opis Dii dant tibi ?
Ch. Ego curabo
iftuc. Sy. Atqui,
here, hic eft nunc af-
fervandus tibi. Ch.
Fiet. Sy. Si fapias
nam jam minus mi-
nufque oltempera mi-
bi. Ch. Quid tu,
Syre ? Egifti ecquid
de illo, quod egi te-
cum dudum ? Aut
reperifti quod placeat,
an nondum etiam ?
Sy. Dicis de fulla-
cia? ft. inveni quan-
dam nuper. Ch.
Frugi es ; cedo quid
id eft ? Sy. Dicam
verum ut aliud ex a-
lio incidit. Ch. Quid-
nam, Syre ? Sy.
Hæc meretrix eft pef-
fima. Ch. Ita vide-
tur. Sy. Imo fi fcias.
Vide hoc facinus,

ANNOTATIONS.

what it was pledged for ; whereas the other
is actually paying in part, to fatisfy till the
whole is cleared. Take this more fully
from *Ifidorus*, Orig. 5. 25. " Intereft in
" loquendi ufu inter pignus & arrham. Nam
" pignus eft quod datur propter rem credi-
" tam, quæ dum redditur, ftatim pignus au-
" fertur. *Arrba* vero eft primum, quod pro
" re bonæ fidei contractu empta ex parte da-
" tur, & poftea completur. Eft enim ar-
" rba complenda, non auferenda. Unde,
" qui habet *arrham*, non reddit, ficut pig-
" nus, fed defiderat plenitudinem." According to this Definition, *arrba* correfponds
to what in our Language is call'd *Earneft*;
but it is to be obferved, that this was only
the Meaning of it among Lawyers, for in
ocmmon Converfation it was often ufed to

fignify a Pledge, and it is in this Senfe, that
we are to take it here.

43 *Eaque eft nunc ad uxorem tuam.* An-
tiphila is foon to appear in a Character of
Importance ; fhe is to be acknowledged for
the Daughter of *Chremes*, and given in Marriage to *Clinia*. It is for this Reafon, that
Terence feperates her from the reft of the
Company, nor lets her be at the Entertainment, where only Courtezans were wont to
appear. He conveys her to *Softrata's* A-
partment, that there may be nothing to
breed Sufpicion, or Reproach her with, and
that an Opportunity may offer of her real
Parentage being known.

44 *Illam illi tamen poft daturam. mil-*
le nummûm pofcit. Thefe Words have
ftrangely perplexed all the Commentators,

Chr. I thought fo. What do you propofe to do now?

Syr. Who I? I'll go to *Menedemus*, and tell him that fhe was taken from *Caria*; that fhe is of a rich and noble Family; and that he will get confiderably by ranfoming her.

Chr. That's wrong.

Syr. Why fo?

Chr. I'll now anfwer for *Menedemus*. I don't choofe to buy her. What can you fay?

Syr. Speak what I wifh for more.

Chr. But there is no occafion for it.

Syr. No occafion!

Chr. No, in reality.

Syr. How is that? I'm furprized.

Chr. I'll foon make you fenfible.—Stay, ftay, what's the Meaning of all this Buftle at our Door?

A N N O T A T I O N S.

on *Terence*; but as it would be tedious to mention their feveral Conjectures, I fhall fatisfy myfelf with explaining it according to the Reading I have followed. *Bacchis orat Cliniam, uti nunc det id argentum fibi : illam tamen Bacchidem poft daturam adolefcentulam Antiphilam illi. Bacchis pofcit mille nummum.* Where *mille nummum pofcit* implies that fhe infifts upon the thoufand Drachma's prefently, and may at the fame time be fuppofed to infinuate that fhe forefaw, if once fhe were in poffeffion of the Money, that the Pledge would never be demanded, and therefore it was no other than an artful way of demanding fo much Money as a Prefent. Some fuch Turn as this is neceffary to reconcile this Demand of the Courtezan with what *Syrus* had faid of her before. *Peffima hæc eft meretrix* : and again, *Vah! vide quod inceptet facinus.* It is true, that *Bentley* offers quite a different Comment upon the Words, but then it is founded upon an Alteration of the Text, that at beft is fupported only by probable Conjecture. However, as what he fays is extremely ingenious, and ferves moreover to give feveral ufeful Hints, I fhall here tranfcribe what I think neceffary to make his Meaning underftood.

"Ego vero cum omnes hujus fallaciæ, " technæ, fabricæ partes confiderarem, & " inter fe conferrem ; ftatim & recta via in " veram hujus loci lectionem deveni : fen- " tentia enim femel reperta, verba fponte " fequebantur. Fingit Syrus, Antiphilam

" arrhaboni Bacchidi relictum effe pro mille " drachmis : Bacchidem, quæ hic Cliniæ " amicæ fingitur, eam fummam à Clinia " præfente pecunia petere : Syrum, ut à " Menedemo hanc fummam auferret, porro " ficturum effe, captam effe à Caria Antiphi- " lam, ditam in fua patria & nobilem ; fi " Menedemus pro captiva eam mille drach- " mis emere velit ; magnum fore mox lu- " crum, cum à parentibus vel cognatis re- " dimeretur : eas mille drachmas Bacchidi " dandas effe : & Antiphilam in domo Me- " nedemi futuram : ubi filius familias Cli- " nia facile & tuto cum ea confuefcere pof- " fet. Hæc fallaciæ hujus fumma eft : ad " quam tamen obtinendam neceffe erat, ut " Bacchis Antiphilam a fe abalienaret, & " Menedemo traderet. Id quoque non co- " miffum à Syro erat, fed mendofa lectio " jam à multis fæculis rem obfcuravit. Re- " vocabo tibi fepultam illam fcripturam."

Quid tum? Sy. Cliniam orat ; fibi ut id. nunc det : illa illi tamen

Poft datum iri mille nummum præf fit. Cn. *Et præf fit quidem?* Sy. Hui, *Dubium id eft? ego fic putavit.* Ch. *Quid nunc facere cogitas?*

" Illa, id eft Antiphila, præf fit, five arrha- " boni fit, oppignoretur, id mille nummum, " five iftas mille drachmas, poft datum iri " illi, id eft Cliniæ five ejus patri. Datum " iri repontmus pro *daturum*, vel ut noftri " omnes uno excepto *daturum*. Sic in An- " dria *deferturum* erat pro *defertum iri*, & " alibi non femel eodem modo peccatum eft.

" A

A C T

Dubiumne id est? CH. ego sic putavi. quid nunc face-
re cogitas?   [tam è Cariâ,
SY. Egone? ad Menedemum ibo: dicam hanc esse cap-
Ditem & nobilem: si redimat, magnum in eâ esse lu-
crum.   [nunc tibi respondeo:
CH. Erras. SY. quid ita? CH. pro Menedemo ego
Nón emo. quid agis? SY. optam loquere. CH. atqui
non est opus.   50
SY. Non opus est? CH. non hercle verò. SY. qui istuc?
miror. CH. jam scies.   [crepuerunt fores?
Mane, mane: quid est, quod tam à nobis graviter

Idnæ est dubium? CH.
Ego putavi sic. Quid
cogitas facere nunc?
SY. Egone? ibo ad
Menedemum: dicam
hanc esse adolescentu-
lam ditem et nobilem
captam è Caria: mag-
num lucrum inesse in
ea, si redimat. CH.
Erras. SY. Quid ita?
CH. Ego nunc respon-
deo tibi pro Menedemo:
non emo; quid agis?
SY. Loquere optata.

CH. *Atqui non est opus.* SY. *Non est opus?* CH. *Hercle vero non.* SY. *Qui istuc? miror.* CH.
Jam sciet. Mane, mane; quid est quod fores crepuerunt tam graviter à nobis?

ANNOTATIONS.

" A *præs sit,* hoc est, compendiose *post* vir-
" gula superne ducta, factum est *poscit.*
" Quid *præs* sit jam notissimum est. Ergò
" pro ista pecunia, isto mulli nummûm,
" *præs* dabitur Antiphila. *Ego sic putavi*
" sunt Syri verba, ut recte codex Bembinus.
" Ego putavi eam prædem fore. PORRO.
" *Præs sit.* CH. *Et præs sit quidem?* Ut
Plautus, Bacc. II. 2. 44.
A. *Nam jam huc adveniet miles.* B. *Et*
miles quidem?

45 *Mille nummûm poscit.* There have been
various Disputes about *mille,* to ascertain its
proper Character in the common Distribution
of Words, or as they are called Parts of
Speech. *Varro,* and all the Grammarians
after him, down to the last Age, make it
(when it is put before a Genitive Plural) a
Substantive indeclinable in the singular Number, and in the Plural declined; *millia, mil-*
lium, millibus; but when it hath a Substantive joined to it in any other Case, they
make it an Adjective Plural indeclinable.
But *Scioppius,* and after him *Gronovius,*
contend, that *mille* is always an Adjective
Plural; and under that Termination of all
Cases and Genders; but that it hath two
Neuters, *hæc mille,* and *hæc millia;* that the
first is used, when one thousand is signified,
and the second, when more than one: and
that where it seems to be a Substantive
governing a Genitive, *multitudo, numerus,*
drachma, pecunia, pondus, spatium, corpus, or
the like, is understood, I own that these
last offer several specious and probable Reasons in support of their Opinion: but whoever will take the pains to consult the accurate *Perizonius,* will, I believe, be rather
inclined to follow the ancient Grammarians.
And, indeed, one does not otherwise know
how to construe this *mille nummûm,* for it
will be hard to supply any Substantive to
mille, that may govern *nummûm* in the Genitive.

50 *Optata loquere. Syrus* chagrined that
the Old Man did not approve of his Expe-
pedient, begs that he will answer more favourably, and not discourage him at once.
Others read *optata loqueris.* You speak your
own Wishes, you make him answer what
you would have him to answer. But this
cannot be the Sense, for *Chremes* had all a-
long shewn to *Syrus,* that he wanted the
Plot to be well laid, and such as might
take. *Dacier.*

Ibid. *Atqui non est opus.* But there is no
need of it. *Chremes* is not allowed here to
explain himself, being prevented by the
coming of his Wife; nor have any of the
Commentators upon *Terence* given themselves
the trouble to do it for him. What seems
most probable to me is this. He finds that
Bacchis makes a Demand of thirty Pounds,
and offers *Antiphila* in pledge for it; a Bargain by which he was sure to lose nothing,
and wherein *Bacchis* could not deceive him,
because the Girl was already in his possession.
It is, therefore, likely he intended to advance the Sum himself, and retain *Antiphila.*
Dacier.

ACT III. SCENE IV.

ARGUMENT.

In this Scene we have the Discovery of Antiphila, *which occasions some Words between the Husband and the Wife. For* Chremes *had ordered the Child to be exposed, if it should prove to be a Girl, which had not been done. After* Antiphila *comes thus to be known ;* Syrus *seeks some other Method of finding the Money he wanted.*

SOSTRATA, CHREMES, the NURSE, SYRUS.

Sostrata. I AM greatly deceived, or this is the very Ring I suspect; that with which my Daughter was exposed.

Chr. What can be the meaning of this talk, *Syrus?*

Sost. What say you, *Nurse?* Do you take it to be the same ?

Nur. I told you immediately when I saw it, that it was the same.

Sost. But have you view'd it well, *Nurse?*

Nur. Oh, very well.

Sost. Go you in then immediately, and bring me Word if she has done bathing yet : meantime, I will wait here for my Husband.

Syr. She wants you: go see what can be the matter : I can't imagine why she looks so grave ; it is not for nothing, I'm in some fear about it.

Chr. What should it be ? Nay, for certain she with all these great Efforts is going to be delivered of some mighty Trifle.

Sost. Ha, my Husband !

Chr. Ha, my Wife !

Sost. I was looking for you.

Chr. What is it you would say ?

Sost. First, I request that you will not imagine I would dare to do any thing contrary to your Commands.

Chr. Would you now have me believe this, though so very incredible ? Well, I believe it.

Syr. This Justification beforehand is certainly a Prelude to some wrong step.

Sost. Don't you remember, that once, when I was big with Child, you told me peremptorily, if it should prove a Girl, you would not bring it up ?

Chr. I know what you have done, you have brought it up.

Syr. That is it, Madam ; you have brought a pretty Expence upon my Master. *Sost.*

ANNOTATIONS.

This Scenes makes a very important Part of the Play, as it contains the Discovery of *Antiphila*'s being *Chremes*'s Daughter. When her Mother gave her to be exposed, she also, according to the Superstition of those Times, gaves a Ring to be exposed with her. The Old Woman, who did not comply with her Mother's Injunctions, but had brought her up at her own Charge, was careful to preserve this Ring, and *Antiphila*, it seems, after her Death, constantly wore it. We have seen that *Terence* had separated her from

ACTUS .III.. SCENA IV.

ARGUMENTUM.

Hæc scena Antiphilæ continet agnitionem, unde jurgium inter virum & uxorem oritur. ·Chremes enim jusserat exponi partum, si ipsa puellam peperisset, quod factum non est. Post agnitam Antiphilam, Syro novum quæritur de invenienda pecunia consilium.

SOSTRATA, CHREMES, NUTRIX, SYRUS.

NISI me animus fallit, hic profectò est annulus, quem ego suspicor, [Syre, hæc oratio ?
Is, quicum exposita est gnata. CH. quid volt sibi,
So. Quid est ? itne tibi videtur ? NU. dixi equidem, ubi mihi ostendisti, illico,
Eum esse. So. at ut sati' contemplata modò sis, mea nutrix ? No. satis. · [mihi nuncia. 5
So. Abi nunc jam intro : atque, illa si jam laverit, Hic ego virum interea opperibor. SY. te volt : videas, quid velit. . [CH. quid fiet ?
Nescio quid tristis est. non temerè est. metuo quid sit.
Næ ista hercle magno jam conatu magnas nugas dixerit.
So. Ehem, mi vir. CH. ehem, mea uxor. So. teipsum quæro. CH. loquere quid velis.
So. Primùm hoc te oro, nè quid credas, me advorsum edictum tuum 10
Facere esse ausam. CH. vis me istuc. tibi, etsi incredibile est, credere ?
Credo. SY. nescio quid peccati portat hæc purgatio.
So. Meministin' me esse gravidam, & mihi te maxumo opere dicere,
Si puellam parerem, nolle tolli ? CH. scio quid feceris : Sustulisti. SY. sic est factum, domina ; ergo herus damno auctus est. 15

ANNOTATIONS.

from the rest of the Company, and placed her with Sostrata ; and when she went to bathe, she gave her this Ring to keep the mean while. Sostrata, after looking at it with some Atte tion, knew it again, and immediately runs with it to her Husband. The Conversation that upon this ensues between them, is so managed by the Poet, as to set both their Characters in the strongest

Light. *Chremes*, tho' apt to be very severe in his Remarks upon his Wife's Conduct, is yet in the main, good-natured, and very ready to forgive. *Sostrata* is very frank in acknowledging her Faults, and behaves with great Submission.

15 *Sic est factum, domina ; ergo herus damno auctus est.* This is the common Reading, and that according to which I have rendered

Soft. Not at all; but there happened to be an Old Woman of Co-rinth here, one far from being contemptible; I gave it to her to ex-pose it.

Chr. O *Jupiter!* can any one be so perfectly stupid!

Soft. Bless me, what have I done?

Chr. Do you ask?

Soft. If I have committed any Fault, my Dear, it was ignorantly.

Chr. That, indeed, I certainly know, whether you own it or not, that every thing you say or do is ignorantly and imprudently, you have been guilty of so many Blunders in this one Affair. For first of all, had you regarded my Orders, the Child should have been dis-patched, and I not imposed upon, with a pretence of her Death, when, in fact, you was taking a probable way to save her. But this I pass over. Pity: a Mother's Fondness: I allow it. But how finely did you provide beforehand! What could be your Design? do but consider: 'tis evident you've betray'd your Child to this Old Woman, either for a common Prostitute, or to be openly exposed to Sale. I believe you thought no matter how it happened, if her Life was but saved. What is to be done with them who know neither Reason, Right, nor Justice; be it for better or worse, profitable or hurtful, who see no-thing but what suits their own Humour?

Soft. My *Chremes*, I own I have done wrong. I'm satisfy'd of it: but I beg, that as you have more Years and Experience than I, you will be so much the more indulgent, that my Weakness may find some Protection in your Justice.

Chr. Well, I will forgive you this Fault; but *Sostrata*, my too easy Temper quite spoils you. But whatever the Case may be, tell me your Motive for acting thus.

Soft. As we Women are always foolishly and wretchedly superstitious;

ANNOTATIONS.

dered the Passage. But as the Sense seems to be somewhat perplexed, several Conjectures have been offered to establish a better Reading. *Acidalius*, upon *Paterculus*, corrects it thus:

Sic est factum: domina ego, herus damno auc-tus est.

This it must be own'd is ingenious, and pro-bably on that account so greatly applauded by *Guyetus*.

Syrus nova domina, Chremes damno, nova scilicet d.tis, auctus &,

But this, tho' proposed with great Confi-dence by *Acidalius*, had not yet the good Fortune to please Dr. *Bentley*, who offers the following as the true Reading:

Sustulisti. Sv. Sic est factum; minor ergo herus damno auctus est.

For *domina*, therefore, he substitutes *minor*. *Herus minor* is *Clitipho*, whose Fortune must be considerably diminished by his Sister's be-ing thus discovered, as her Portion was to

come out of it. It appears that this Read-ing was followed in *Eugraphius*'s Time, as may be gathered from his own Words:

Nova dixit, auctus damno, quod ci cobares puella venerit, quam dedit exponendum; from which it is plain, that he understood this as meant of *Clitipho*.

22 *Intercmtam oportuit.* One cannot avoid being seized with a kind of Horror, to think that, in a Country so polite as *Greece*, Men should be found so blind, so inhuman and barbarous, as to murder their own Chil-dren, without Remorse or Trouble, when they imagined the Interest of their Family required it. We have here a Husband, who because his Wife did not obey the cruel Or-der, tells her she understood neither Reason nor Equity. And yet Philosophy had long before this demonstrated the Horror, not only of these Murders, but even of exposing Children. But Philosophy is always weak and

So. Minimè: fed erat hic Corinthia anus haud impu-
ra, ei dedi.   [infcitiam!
Exponendam. Ch. ô Jupiter, tantamne effe in animo
So. Perii, quid ego feci? Ch. at rogitas? So. fi pec-
cavi, mi Chreme,   [cio,
Infciens feci. Ch. id quidem ego, etfi tu neges, certò
Te infcientem atque imprudentem dicere ac facere
omnia: [meum 21
Tot peccata in hac re oftendis. nam jam primùm, fi
Imperium exfequi voluiffes, interemtam oportuit:
Non fimulare mortem verbis, re ipfà fpem vitæ dare.
At id omitto: mifericordia, animus maternus: fino.
Quàm benè verò abs te profpectum eft! quid voluifti?
cogita: 25
Nempe anui illi prodita ebs te filia eft planiffumè,
Per te vel uti quæftum faceret, vel uti veniret palam.
Credo, id cogitâfti, quidvis fatis eft, dum vivat modò.
Quid cum illis agas, qui neque jus, neque bonum, at-
que æquum fciunt.   29
Melius, pejus, profit, obfit, nil vident, nifi quod lubet?
So. Mi Chreme, peccavi, fateor: vincor: nunc hoc
te obfecro,
Quanto tuus eft animus natu gravior, ignofcentior,
Ut meæ ftultitiæ in juftitiâ tuâ fit aliquid præfidî.
Ch. Scilicet equidem iftuc factum ignofcam: verùm,
Softrata,   [eft, 35
Malè docet te mea facilitas multa. fed iftic quidquid
Quâ hoc occeptum eft causâ, loquere. So. ut ftultæ
& miferæ omnes fumus

So. Minimè; fed
anus Corinthia haud
impura erat hîc:
dedi ei exponendam.
Ch. O Jupiter! tantæmne infcitiam effe in animo? So.
Perii: quid ego feci? Ch. At
rogitas? So. Si pec-
cavi, mi Chreme,
feci infciens. Ch.
Ego quidem feio id
certo, etfi tu neges,
te infcientem & im-
prudentem dicere ac
facere omnia; often-
dis tot peccata in
hac re. Nam jam
primum fi voluiffes
exfequi meum impe-
rium, oportuit eam
fuiffe interemptam:
non fimulare mortem
verbis, fed ipfa re
dare fpem vitæ. At
omitto id: mifericor-
dia, animus mater-
nus: fino. Vero
quam bene eft pro-
fpectum abs te!
Quid voluifti? co-
gita: nempe filia
tua eft planiffime
prodita illi anui abs
te, vel uti faceret
quæftum per te, vel
uti veniret palam.
Credo cogitâfti id,

quidvis eft fatis, dum modo vivat. Quid agas cum illis, qui fciunt neque jus, neque bonum atque
æquum: melius, pejus, profit, obfit, vident nil, nifi quod lubet? So. Mi Chreme, fateor, peccavi: vincor: nunc obfecro te hoc, ut quanto tuus animus eft gravior natu, fit tanto ignofcentior,
ut in tua juftitia fit aliquid præfidii meæ ftultitiæ. Ch. Scilicet equidem ignofcam tibi iftuc factum;
verum, Softrata, mea multa facilitas docet te male. Sed qui quid iftuc eft, loquere qua caufa hoc
eft occeptum. So. Ut nos omnes mulieres fumus ftultæ & miferæ, religiofæ,

ANNOTATIONS.

and unavailing, when oppofed to Cuftoms authorized by long ufage.

23 *Non fimulare mortem verbis, re ipfa fpem vitæ dare.* Simulare mortem verbis refers to the method *Softrata* had taken, of executing her Hufband's Orders, who not having Barbarity enough to murder her Child with her own Hands, gave it to be expofed, for that was properly no more than affecting in Words to put it to death. *Re ipfa fpem vitæ dare;* that is, to leave it the means of Prefervation, by caufing it to be only expofed. For Infants, when expofed, were, for the moft part, by fome chance or other preferved, as we learn from a thoufand Inftances.

29 *Quid cum illis agas.* It is raifing Difficulties to no purpofe, to refer this to Mer-
chants who deal in Slaves, or thofe Women
who make it their bufinefs to feduce the
young and beautiful of their own Sex: they
regard only *Softrata*, and the Imprudence
wherewith *Chremes* charges her, as if he had
faid, " Non poteft cum illis difputari, non
" poffunt erudiri, quorum pectori tanta infci-
" tia ineft, quique affectu feu lubidine animi,
" non ratione & confilio ducuntur."

23 *Quanto tuus eft animus natu gravior, ignofcentior.* This Verfe has always appeared
perplexing to Commentators, infomuch that
fome have ventured to reject it altogether.

tious; when I gave her the Child to expofe it, I pulled a Ring from my Finger, and told her to expofe it at the fame time, that if fhe fhould happen to die, fhe might not be quite deftitute of fome part of our Fortune.

Chr. That was right: by this means you both faved her, and humoured yourfelf.

Soft. This is the Ring.

Chr. Where had you it!

Soft. The young Woman that *Bacchis* brought along with her —

Syr. Ha!

Chr. What fays fhe?

Soft. She gave it to me to keep, while fhe went to bathe. At firft I did not mind it; but upon looking at it, knew it immediately, and came running to you.

Chr. What do you fufpect now, or difcover concerning her?

Soft. I don't know, unlefs you inquire of herfelf where fhe had it, if it is poffible to find it out.

Syr. I'm ruin'd: I fee more Hope here than I defire: if fo, fhe muft certainly be ours.

Chr. Is the Old Woman alive, to whom you gave her?

Soft. I don't know.

Chr. What did fhe fay fhe had done with her?

Soft. Even as I had commanded her.

Chr. Tell me the Woman's Name, that we may inquire after her.

Soft. *Philtere.*

Syr. The very fame: 'tis a wonder if fhe is not found, and I loft.

Chr. *Softrata*, follow me in.

Soft. How has it happened beyond my Expectation? For I was greatly afraid left you might be no lefs fevere now, than formerly, when you ordered me to expofe her.

Chr. A Man often can't do as he would; efpecially, if his Circumftances will not permit it. Now the Cafe is fuch, that I fhould be glad of a Daughter: formerly, 'twas quite otherwife.

ANNOTATIONS.

But without proceeding fo far, we may have a very confiftent Senfe, if we adopt a Reading authorized by feveral Manufcripts, and fome of the moft ancient Editions.

Quanto tuus eft animus natu gravior, ignofcentior tanto fit.

For it is plain, that thefe Words were wanting to compleat the Text, and anfwer to *quanto eft.*

39 *Ne expers partis effet de noftris boris.* The Ancients believed it to be a great Crime, if they fuffered their Children to die without poffeffing any part of their Fortune. It was for this reafon, that their Women, who have always a ftrong Byafs to Superftition, when they gave a Child to be expofed, fent fome Jewel with it, imagining that this difcharged their Claim of Inheritance, and fcreened them from any Reproach of their own Minds. We fee then the Nature of the Superftition of which *Softrata* accufes herfelf here; and this, moreover, is a good Pretence for her to prevent her Hufband from fufpecting that fhe gave the Ring on purpofe to be able afterwards to find out her Daughter, if fhe fhould happen to be preferved. The Order and Import therefore of the Paffage is thus: " Cum exponendam " do filiam illi anui Corinthiæ, detraho an- " nulum de digito, & dico ut eum una cum " puella exponeret, ne expers partis effet de " noftris bonis : quod ego quidem fuperfti- " tione feci ; ut mulieres nos omnes fumus " ftultæ, & mifere religiofæ."

40 *Iftuc recte; confervafti te atque ilum.* There is more to be underftood by thefe Word, than at firft fight we are apt to imagine. *Chremes* anfwers, that by beftowing that

Religiofæ ; cùm exponendam do illi, de digito an-
nulum
Detraho ; & eum dico ut unà cum puellâ exponeret ;
Si moreretur, ne expers partis eſſet de noſtris bonis.
Cʜ. Iſtuc rectè : conſervaſti te, atque illam. So. is hic
eſt annulus.   40
Cʜ. Unde habes ? So. quam Bacchis fecum adduxit
adolefcentulam. Sʏ. hem.   [dum mihi dedit.
Cʜ. Quid ea narrat ? So. ea lavatum dum it, fervan-
Animum non advorti primùm : at poſtquam aſpexi,
illico   [invenis
Cognovi : ad te exſilui. Cʜ. quid nunç fufpicare aut
De illâ ? So. nefcio, niſi ex ipſâ quæras, unde hunc
habuerit,   [volo. 46
Si potis reperiri. Sʏ. interii : plus fpei video, quàm
Noſtra eſt, ſi ita eſt. Cʜ. vivitne illa, cui tu dederas ?
So. nefcio.   [feram.
Cʜ. Quid renunciavit olim feciſſe ? So. id, quod juf-
Cʜ. Nomen mulieris cedo quod ſit, ut quæratur. So.
Philtere.   [Soſtrata, 50
Sʏ. Ipfa eſt. mirum, ni illa falva eſt, & ego perii. Cʜ.
Sequere me intro hac. So. ut præter fpem evenit! quàm
timui malè,   [Chreme.
Ne nunc animo ita eſſes duro, ut olim in tollendo,
Cʜ. Non licet hominem eſſe ſæpe ita ut volt, ſi res non
finit.   [minùs.
Nunc ita tempus eſt mî, ut cupiam filiam : olim nil

cum do illo exponen-
dam, detraho annu-
lum de digito, & di-
co ut exponeret eum
una cum puella, ne,
ſi moreretur, eſſet ex-
pers partis de noſtris
bonis. Cʜ. *Iſtuc rectè;*
conſervaſti te, atque
illam. So. *Is eſt hic*
annulus. Cʜ. *Unde*
habes? So. *Ab ado-*
lefcentula, quam a-
dolefcentulam Bacchis
adduxit fecum. Sʏ.
Hem. Cʜ. *Quid ea*
narrat? So. *Dum ea*
it lavatum, dedit mi-
hi fervandum. Pri-
mum non advorti ani-
mum : fed poſtquam
aſpexi, cognovi illicc:
exilui ad te. Cʜ. *Quid*
nunc fufpicare, aut
invenis de illa? So.
Nefcio, niſi quæras ex
ipſa, unde habuerit
hunc, ſi eſt potis re-
periri. Sʏ. *Interii :*
video plus fpei, quam
volo; eſt noſtra, ſi eſt
ita. Cʜ. *Illane vi-*
vit, cui tu dederas?
So. *Nefcio.* Cʜ. *Quid*
renunciavit te feciſſe
olim? So. *Id, quod*

jifiram. Cʜ. Cedo quod ſit nomen mulieris, ut quæratur. So. Philtere. Sʏ. Eſt ipſa : mi-
rum, ni illa eſt ſalva, & ego perii. Cʜ. *Soſtrata, ſequere me intro hac.* So. *Ut evenit præter*
fpem! quam male timui, Chreme, ne eſſes nunc ita duro animo, ut olim in tollendo. Cʜ. *Sæpe*
non licet hominem eſſe ita ut vult, ſi res non finit : nunc tempus eſt ita mihi, ut cupiam filiam ;
olim cupiebam nil minus.

A N N O T A T I O N S.

that Jewel upon her Daughter, ſhe had done
two things inſtead of one : ſhe had complied
with her own fuperſtitious Notions, and preſerved her Daughter's Life. For fcarce any
one would have taken the trouble to bring
up the Child, but for this Jewel, from which
they, who found her, might naturally conclude, that ſhe might one day be acknowledged and redeemed by her Parents. Confervaſti te, you have fatisfied your own
Mind, in yielding to the Dictates of your
Superſtition. Confervaſti illam, you have
preſerved her Life, by expoſing with her a
Jewel, which induced them, who found
her, to train her up in hopes of obtaining,
fome time or other, a great Ranſom for her.
Dicier.
46 Interii : plus fpei video, quam volo.
Syrus ſays this here, becauſe he faw his
Hopes of deceiving Menedemus quite vaniſh ;

and that, therefore, his Project was come to
nothing. Plus fpei video, quam volo. This,
no doubt, proceeded from his Fear, that if
Antiphila was found to be Chremes's Daughter, Clinia would no longer diſſemble, but
claim his real Miſtreſs, by which Chremes
would difcover all that had been tranſacted
againſt him. But for this unlucky Circumſtance, all went extremely well, for he
made no manner of doubt, that Chremes
would be eaſily prevailed on to pay the thirty
Pounds, as being a very reaſonable Ranſom
for his Daughter.
54 Nunc ita eſt tempus mî. Formerly, ſays
he, when my Fortune was ſmall, I could not
afford to bring up a Daughter; but now that
I am in lauta & bene aucta parte, as Syrus
afterwards expreſſes it, I'am very willing
to have one. This he ſays by way of Juf-
tification, for his former cruel Orders.

A C T U S

ACT IV. SCENE I.

ARGUMENT.

After it had been discovered, that Antiphila *was* Chremes's *Daughter,* Syrus, *full of Anxiety, is endeavouring to find out some other way of getting the Money he wanted.*

SYRUS.

AS far as I can perceive, I'm in a fair way of being routed and broken, my Forces are so hemmed in on every side, by this Accident, unless I can find some way to keep the Old Man from perceiving that this is his Son's Mistress: for as to my Hopes about the Money, or of being able to bubble him, they are all vanished : I shall think it Triumph enough to come off with a whole Skin. I'm almost distracted to see so fine a Morsel thus suddenly snatched from my very Chaps. What shall I do ? What shall I contrive ? I must set out upon a quite new Plan. Nothing is so difficult, but by Industry it may be accomplished. Suppose now I should set about it thus ?—It won't do.—What if thus ?—'Twill be just the same.—But this I believe will do.—No.—Yes, best of all. This is, indeed, the best Thought yet. By *Hercules* I'm of opinion, I shall still recover this same fugitive Money.

ANNOTATIONS.

We have seen in the former Scene, that Syrus was present at the Discovery of *Antiphila's* being *Chremes's* Daughter; he appears too to be not a little concerned at it, as apprehensive that it might be of ill consequence to himself. All the rest being gone in to inquire further of this Ring; he is left alone upon the Stage, full of this Notion, and contriving with himself, how he may best avoid the threatening Danger.

[2] *Ita hac re in angustum oppido, &c.* Op-*pido* is here an Adverb, of the same Import with *valde, much, very much.* This its Signification took its rise first from the Custom of Farmers, who, when they meant to express any large Quantity of Grain, often did it by saying, *Quantum vel oppido satis effet.*

[3] *Latere tecto.* Some refer this to the Custom of punishing Slaves. " *Qui nudi*

" *latera & pendentes cædebantur flagris.*" *Plaut.* Epid I. 1. 63.

Detegetur corium de tergo meo.

But it is more probably a Continuation of the military Allusion. For as Army men hard pressed, regard it as a Victory, in some Cases, it is the General's chief Care to cover the Flanks and Rear, the greatest Danger being from an Attack upon them. Thus, *Cæsar,* B. G. 7. 82. *Veriti, ne ab latere aperto ex superioribus castris eruptione circumvenirentur, se ad suos receperunt.*

[8] *Quin quærendo investigari possit. Investigari,* to be found out by careful tracing, as we do an Algebraical or Geometrical Problem. Hence it comes that the word is so frequently used in this latter Case.

[9] *Quid, si hæc nunc sic incipiam ?* These Deliberations,

ACTUS IV. SCENA I.

ARGUMENTUM.

Poſt agnitam Antiphilam Syrus anxius, quærit novum conſilium
de extorquenda pecunia.

SYRUS.

ORDO.

NISI me animus fallit, haud multum à me aberit
    infortunium :
Ita hac re in anguſtum oppidò nunc meæ coguntur
    copiæ :   [ſenex.
Niſi aliquid video, ne eſſe amicam hanc gnati reſciſcat
Nam quod de argento ſperem, aut poſſe poſtulem me
    fallere,
Nihil eſt : triumpho, ſi licet me latere tecto abſcedere.
Crucior, bolum tantum mihi eſſe ereptum tam ſubitò
    è faucibus.   6
Quid agam ? aut quid comminiſcar ? ratio de integro
    ineunda eſt mihi.
Nil tam difficile eſt, quin quærendo inveſtigari poſſiet.
Quid, ſi hoc ſic nunc incipiam ? nihil eſt. quid ſi ſic ?
    tantundem egero.
At ſic opinor : non poteſt ; immo optumè. euge, ha-
    beo optumam.   10
Retraham hercle, opinor, ad me idem illud fugitivum
    argentum tamen.

NISI animus fallit me, infortunium haud multum aberit à me : meæ copiæ nunc oppidò ita coguntur in anguſtum hac re : niſi video aliquid, ne ſenex reſciſcat hanc eſſe amicam gnati. Nam quod ſperem de argento, aut poſſulem me poſſe fallere, eſt nihil. Triumpho, ſi licet me abſcedere tecto latere ; crucior, bolum tantum eſſe tam ſubito ereptum mihi à faucibus. Quid agam ? Aut quid comminiſcar ? Ratio eſt ineunda mihi de integro. Nil eſt tam difficile, quin poſſit inveſtigari quærendo. Quid, ſi ſic incipiam hoc ? eſt nihil. Quid ſi ſic ? egero tantundem. At opinor ſic : non poteſt : imò optime : euge, habeo optimam rationem. Hercle tamen, opinor, retraham ad me idem illud fugitivum argentum.

ANNOTATIONS.

Deliberations, as they are here repreſented, are extremely natural. They give us the Idea of a Man in danger, and greatly perplexed how to extricate himſelf, and compaſs his Ends. He falls upon ſeveral Methods, and again rejects them one after another, till at laſt one Contrivance offers that pleaſes him. This we ſhall meet with in the following Scenes.

   ¹¹ *Retraham hercle, opinor, ad me, idem*
illud fugitivum argentum. He ſpeaks here of the Money as of a fugitive Slave, whom he was in hopes of being ſtill able to recover. But this Alluſion in the *Greek* of *Menander*, whence it was taken, muſt have been far more agreeable, becauſe the Word χρύσος, which he undoubtedly uſed, ſignifies *Gold* ; and is at the ſame time the Name of a Slave, in *Latin Chryſis.*

ACTUS

ACT IV. SCENE II.

ARGUMENT.

Clinia *rejoices at the Hopes he has of being soon married to* Antiphila, *now known by her Parents, and* Syrus *begs of* Clinia, *that he will continue to call* Clitipho's *Mistress his own.*

CLINIA, SYRUS.

Clinia. HEnceforth can no Misfortune happen to me so considerable as to make me uneasy, so great is the Joy that now breaks in upon me. I'll, henceforth, give myself up entirely to my Father, to be more frugal than even he can wish.

Syr. I was not mistaken, she is discovered, as far as I can understand by his Words here. (*to* Clinia.) I am glad, Sir, that things happen so much to your Wish.

Clin. O my *Syrus!* Pray have you heard of it too?

Syr. Why not heard of it, when I was present all the while?

Clin. Did you ever know any Thing fall out so fortunately?

Syr. Never.

Clin. And let me die if I now rejoice so much for my own sake, as for her's, whom I know to be deserving of the highest Honours.

Syr. I believe it: but now, *Clinia*, let me have a Hearing in my turn; your Friend's Business is also to be thought of and secured, lest the Old Man should come to know any thing about his Mistress.

Clin. O *Jupiter!*

Syr. Have done

Clin. Shall my *Antiphila* then be mine?

Syr. Do you still interrupt me thus?

Clin. What can I do, my *Syrus?* I'm transported; bear with me.

Syr. Why, truly, that I must do.

Clin. We shall be as happy as Gods.

Syr. I see it is taking Pains to no Purpose.

Clin. Speak, I hear.

Syr. But you'll not mind what I say.

Clin. I will.

Syr. We must take care to have our Friend's Business secured:
for

ANNOTATIONS.

Clinia, by this time, had been informed of all that had happened; and that *Antiphila* was found to be *Chremes*'s Daughter. Nothing could fall out more happily for him, than that one, whom he so entirely loved, should prove to be of equal Rank with him, and such as he might marry even with his Father's Consent. He is, therefore, here brought upon the Stage triumphing in his good Fortune. It was not so with *Syrus*. This Discovery was like to prove fatal to him. *Clinia*, he foresaw, would be for claiming his Mistress, and then all must come out. To prevent an Accident so unlucky for him and *Clitipho*, he applies to *Clinia*, that he will not be so far transported by his good Fortune, as to pursue only what appeared best for himself, without any regard to his Friend; but as every thing had now succeeded to his Wish, he will consent to defer his Happiness for a Day, till what respects *Clitipho* shall be put on a right footing. *Clinia*,

ACTUS IV. SCENA II.

ARGUMENTUM.

Clinia exultat, quod agnita Antiphila mox ei nuptura sit, & Syrus Cliniæ consulit, quod amicam Clitiphonis suam esse dicat.

<table>
<tr><td>

CLINIA, SYRUS.

NUlla mihi res posthac potest jam intervenire tanta,
   Quæ mihi ægritudinem afferat : tanta hæc læti-
tia oborta est.
Dedo patri me nunc jam, ut frugalior sim quàm volt.
SY. Nil me fefellit : cognita est, quantum audio hujus
Istuc tibi ex sententiâ tuâ obtigisse lætor.   [verba. 5
CL. O mi Syre, audistin' obsecro ? SY. quidni ! qui
   usque unâ adfuerim.   [SY. nulli.
CL. Cui æquè audisti commodè quidquam evenisse ?
CL. Atque ita me Dii ament, ut ego nunc non tam
   meapte causa   [vis dignam. 8
Lætor, quàm illius ; quam ego scio esse honore quo-
SY. Ita credo : sed nunc, Clinia, age, da te mihi vicissim
Nam amici quoque res est videnda, in tuto ut conlo-
   cetur   [esce.
Ne quid de amicâ nunc senex. CL. ô Jupiter ! SY. qui-
CL. Antiphila mea nubet mihi. SY. siccine me inter-
   loquere ?   [hercle verò
CL. Quid faciam, mi Syre ? gaudeo : fer me. SY. fero
CL. Deorum vitam adepti sumus. SY. frustra operam,
   opinor, sumo.   15
CL. Loquere, audio. SY. at jam hoc non ages. CL.
   agam. SY. videndum est, inquam,

</td><td>

ORDO.

CL. JAM nulla
   tanta res po-
test intervenire mi-
hi posthac, quæ ad-
ferat ægritudinem
mihi : hæc tanta
lætitia est oborta.
Jam nunc dedo me
patri, ut sim fru-
galior quam volt.
SY. Nil fefellit me,
Antiphila est cogni-
ta, quantum audio
verba hujus. Lætor
istuc obtigisse tibi ex
tua sententia. CL.
O mi Syre, obsecro,
andivistine ? SY.
Quidni ? qui usque
unaadfuerim. CL.
Cui audivisti quid-
quam evenisse æque
commodè ? SY. Nul-
li. CL. Atque ita
Dii ament me, ut
ego lætor nunc, non
tam meapte causa,
quam causa illius,
quam ego scio esse
dignam quovis ho-
nere. SY. Credo ita :

</td></tr>
</table>

sed nunc, Clinia, age, da te vicissim mihi : nam res amici est quoque videnda, ut collocetur in tuto,
ne senex nunc sciat quid de amica. CL. O Jupiter ! SY. Quiesce. CL. Mea Antiphila nubet
mihi. SY. Siccine interloquere me ? CL. Mi Syre, quid faciam ? gaudeo : fer me. SY. Hercle
vero fero te. CL. Adepti sumus vitam deorum. SY. Opinor, sumo operam frustra. CL. Loquere, audio. SY. At jam non ages hoc. CL. Agam. SY. Inquam, Clinia, videndum est,

ANNOTATIONS.

Clinia, for some time abandoned to the Excess of his Joy, minds nothing of what *Syrus* says to him, nor answers any other way, than by Exclamations on his good Fortune. But at last recollecting himself, he consents, not without some Reluctance, to what *Syrus* requests of him.

6 *Quidni ? qui usque una adfuerim.* What *Syrus* says here, that he was present all the while, makes it probable, that he went in along with *Chremes* and *Sostrata,* and that of consequence there the third Act ends, according as we have distinguished it. The only Objection that can be made to this, is what *Syrus* says in the fourth Verse of this Scene :

Nibil me fefellit : cognita est, quantum audio hujus verba.

For any one may readily say, that as *Syrus* knew not of *Antiphila's* being discovered to be *Chremes's* Daughter, but by what he overheard *Clinia* say, this is a clear sign he was not personally present at the Discovery. But it is an easy matter to obviate this Difficulty. *Syrus* enters with *Chremes* and *Sostrata,* he hears what *Antiphila* says to them, and seeing how it was like to be, and the Disasters that threatened himself, he has not patience to wait the end, but runs out to think of his Misfortune, and, if possible, contrive some Method to prevent it. *Dacier.*

12 CL. *O Jupiter.* SY. *Quiesce.* We have

for fhould you now go away, and leave *Bacchis* here, our Old Man
will immediately know that fhe's *Clitipho*'s Miftrefs; but if you take
her along with you, it will be juft as much concealed as ever.

Clin. But, *Syrus*, nothing can make more againft my Wedding,
than this. For with what Face can I fpeak of it to my Father?
You underftand me?

Syr. Perfectly well.

Clin. What can I fay, what Excufe can I make?

Syr. Nay, I would not have you diffemble, tell him the whole
Cafe as it really is.

Clin. What is it you fay?

Syr. I infift on it: tell him that you're in love with *Antiphila*, and
want to marry her, and that this other is *Clitpho*'s Miftrefs.

Clin. You afk nothing but what is juft and fair, and may eafily be
done: and I fuppofe you mean that I fhould beg of my Father to
conceal all from the old Gentleman.

Syr. Nay, to tell him directly the whole Affair in order as it is.

Clin. What! Are you fober, or in your Senfes? This is betraying
him with a vengeance; for tell how in this cafe can he be fecure?

Syr. This, indeed, I look upon as a Mafter-piece of Art, here I
can never triumph too much; to have at command that irrefiftible
Addrefs, and fo great a power of Cunning, as to be able to deceive
both, by telling the Truth; fo that when the Old Man tells ours,
that this *Bacchis* is his Son's Miftrefs, he will not believe him.

Clin. But by this, you again deftroy all my Hopes of a Wedding:
for fo long as he believes her to be my Miftrefs, he'll never confent
to give me his Daughter: perhaps you little regard what becomes of
me, fo you can but ferve him.

Syr. What, in the name of Wonder, do you imagine that the
Cheat is to be carried on an Age? 'Tis but for one Day, till I have
finger'd the Money: be eafy, nothing more.

Clin Is that, fay you, fufficient? But fuppofe now his Father
fhould find it out; what muft be done then?

Syr. *What if the Sky fhould fall now,* as the Saying is?

Clin.

ANNOTATIONS.

have here a beautiful Scene of the Joy of
Clinia on the one hand, and the Anxiety of
Syrus on the other. Each fpeaks agreeably
to his Character and Circumftances. It
would have been prepofterous to fuppofe that
Clinia, in fo great a flow of Joy, could attend
to any thing but his prefent good Fortune.
It muft be Importunity and repeated Intreaties in *Syrus*, that will bring him to hearken
to what he fays.

31 *Huic equidem confilio palmam do.* We
are here to fuppofe *Syrus* endued with a
great Share of Penetration. He already underftood the Difpofition of both the old Men,
and what were their feveral Defigns, and
had formed in his Mind the whole Plot he
was going to put in execution. From what
had paffed between *Chremes* and him, he
knew that whatever was faid to *Menedemus*, would with the other pafs for a Story
formed to impofe upon him. So that
when the whole Truth was told to *Menedemus*, were he again to repeat to *Chremes*, it
would gain no credit, as *Syrus* would before
hand inform him, that all this was faid with
no other View, but to make *Clinia* eafy with
his Father. And we find that this accordingly happens, till *Menedemus* at length, by

Reafons

Amici quoque res, Clinia, tui in tuto ut conlocetur :
Nam si nunc à nobis abis, & Bacchidem hîc relinquis,
Senex reiciscet illico esse amicam hanc Clitiphonis :
Si abduxerit, celabitur itidem, ut celáta adhuc est. 20
CL. At enim istoc nihil est magis, Syrë, meis nuptiis
    advorsum :   [SY. quidni ?
Nam quo ore appellabo patrem ? tenes, quid dicam ?
CL. Quid dicam ? quam causam afferam ? SY. quid ?
    nolo mentiare :   [SY. jubeo, 24
Apertè, ita ut res sese habet, narrato. CH. quid ais ?
Istam te amare & velle uxorem ; hanc esse Clitiphonis.
CH. Bonam atque justam rem oppidò imperas & factu
    facilem.
Et scilicet jam me hoc voles patrem exorare, ut celet
Senem vostrum. SY. imo ut rectâ viâ rem narrat ordine
    omnem. CH. hem,   [prodis :
Satin' sanus es aut sobrius ? tu quidem illum planè
Nam qui ille poterit esse in tuto, dic mihi ?   30
SY. Huic equidem consilio palmam do : hîc me mag-
    nificè effero,   [astutiæ,
Qui vim tantam in me & potestatem habeam tantæ
Vera dicendo ut eos ambos fallam : ut cùm narrat senex
Voster nostro, esse istam amicam gnati, non credat
    tamen.   [nam eripis : 35
CL. At enim spem istoc pacto rursus nuptiarum om-
Nam dum amicam hanc meam esse credet, non com-
    mitte filiam.
Tu fortasse, quid me fiat, parvi curas, dum illi consulas.
SY. Quid, malum, me ætatem censes velle id adsimu-
    larier ?   [pliùs.
Unus est dies, dum argentum eripio : pax ! nihil am-
CL. Tantum sat habes ? quid tum, quæso, si hoc pa-
    ter resciverit ?   40
SY. Quid si redeo ad illos, qui aiunt, Quid si nunc
    cœlum ruat ?

filio : hic effero me magnifice, qui habeam tantam vim in me, & potestatem tantæ astutiæ, ut fal-
lam eos ambos dicendo vera ; ut cùm vester senex narrat nostro, istam esse amicam gnati, tamen non
credat. CL. At enim istoc pacto rursus eripis omnem spem nuptiarum ; nam dum Chremes credat
hanc Bacchidem esse meam amicam, non committet filiam : tu fortasse, parvi curas, quid fiat de
me, dum consulas illi. SY. Quid, malum, censes me velle id adsimulari per ætatem ? est unus
dies, dum eripio argentum : pax ! nihil amplius. CL. Habes tantum satis ? quid, quæso,
facies tum, si pater resciverit hoc ? SY. Quid si redeo ad illos, qui aiunt, Quid si cœlum nunc
ruit ?

ut res amici tui collo-
cetur quoque in tuto ;
nam si abis nunc à
nobis, & relinquis
Bacchidem hic, senex
illico resciscet hanc
esse amicam Clitipho-
nis : si abduxeris, ce-
labitur itidem, ut ce-
lata est adhuc. CL.
At enim, Syre, nihil
est magis adversum
meis nuptiis istoc :
nam quo ore appel-
labo patrem ? Tenes
quid dicam ? SY.
Quidni ? CL. Quid
dicam ? Quam cau-
sam afferam ? SY.
Quid ? nolo menti-
are : narrato aperte,
ita ut res habet sese.
CL. Quid ais ? SY.
Jubeo te narrare te
amare illam Anti-
philam, & velle
ducere eam uxorem ;
hanc Bacchidem esse
amicam Clitiphonis.
CL. Imperas rem
oppido bonam atque
justam, & facilem
factu : & scilicet
jam voles me exorare
patrem, ut celet hoc ;
vestrum senem. SY.
Imo ut rectâ viâ
narrat omnem rem
ordine. CL. Hem,
esne satis sanus aut
sobrius ? tu quidem
planè prodis illum :
nam dic mihi, qui
ille poterit esse in tu-
to ? SY. Equidem
do palmam huic con-

ANNOTATIONS.

Reasons that were irresistible, convinces highly pleased with it, and talks of it in so
Chremes that it was the Truth. This boasting a manner.
Scheme, it must be owned, was well con-{ 41 *Quid si nunc cœlum ruat ?* . Clinia
certed, and shewed great Cunning in the could not easily be divested of his Fears ; for
Contriver. No wonder then, if Syrus it is} it is natural, when we have much at stake,
                                                     to

Clin. I am in great Pain about it.

Syr. In great Pain? As if it was not in your own Power to free yourfelf when you will, and difcover all.

Clin. Well, well, let *Bacchis* then be brought over.

Syr. That's right. Here fhe comes.

ANNOTATIONS.

to be very folicitous about it. *Syrus* impatient at fo many Delays, and confident too that there was no Danger, endeavours to make them appear ridiculous and abfurd, and for that Purpofe has recourfe to a Proverb which denoted Fears the moft foolifhly grounded, fuch as only People ignorant in the higheft Degree could give into. It was only the weakeft among Mankind, fuch as underftood nothing of the Frame and Conftitution of Nature, that gave Credit to the poetical Fable of *Atlas*'s fupporting the Heavens on his Shoulders. There is a remarkable Paffage in *Arrian*'s Account of *Alexander*'s

---

ACT IV. SCENE III.

ARGUMENT.

Bacchis *angry, that fhe had not yet received the thirty Pounds, threatens to give them the Slip, and expoftulates with* Syrus. *At length appeafed, fhe and all her Train go over to* Menedemus, *at his perfuafion, there to continue till the Money is procured.*

BACCHIS, CLINIA, SYRUS, DROMO, PHRYGIA.

Bacchis. I 'Faith, *Syrus* has brought me here to a fine Purpofe, with his fair Promifes of thirty Guineas; but if I find that he has now deceived me, he may often in vain come to invite me hither; or after I have promifed and fixed the Time, when he fhall be told for certain, that I am to be here; when *Clitipho* fhall be on the Stretch of Expectation, I'll deceive them, and not come. *Syrus* fhall make Atonement to me with his Back.

Clin. (*To* Syrus.) She promifes you very fair.

Syr. And do you think fhe's in jeft? She'll make her Promifes good, if I don't take care.

Bacc. They fleep: I'll rouze them with a Vengeance. *Phrygia,* did you take notice of *Charinus*'s Houfe, which the Man fhewed us juft now?

Phry. I did.

Bacc. The very next to this here, on the Right-hand?

Phry. I remember.   *Bacc.*

ANNOTATIONS.

Bacchis had been drawn from Town, by a Promife of thirty Pounds, which *Syrus* had made. We have feen that he is contriving how to procure it, and is in hopes of being able to do it foon. *Bacchis*, however, who had as yet heard nothing of it, begins to be impatient, and to rouze them effectually, talks aloud to her Maid *Phrygia*, in the hearing of *Syrus*, pretending as if fhe meant to give them the Slip. *Syrus*, in a great Fright, begs her to call back the Maid, affuring her that he will procure the Money for her inftantly: but that in the mean time, to forward his Project, it was neceffary for her, and her whole Train, to go over to *Menedemus*, which at laft with fome Difficulty fhe yields to.

5 *Clitipho cum fpe pendebit a nil.* Some Manufcripts

CL. Metuo quid agam. SY. metuis? quasi non ea potestas sit tua,
Quo velis in tempore ut te exsolvas, rem facias palàm.
CL. Age, age; traducatur Bacchis. SY. optumè. ipsa exit foras.

Bacchis traducatur. SY. *Optime.* *Ipsa exit foras.*

ORDO:

CL. *Metuo quid agam.* SY. *Metuis? quasi ea potestas non sit tua, ut exsolvas te in quo tempore velis, & facias rem palium.* CL. *Age, age,*

ANNOTATIONS.

Alexander's Expedition, Lib. 4. where he tells us, that some Ambassadors from the *Celta*, being asked by *Alexander*, what in the World they dreaded most? answered; Διδέναι, μήποτε ὁ ἐρανὸς αὐτοῖς ἐμπέσοι, *Vereri, ne cælum in ipsos ruat.* *Alexander*, who expected to hear himself named, was surprized at an Answer, which signified that they thought themselves without the reach of all human Power. For it plainly implies, that nothing could hurt them, unless he would suppose Impossibilities, or a total Destruction of Nature.

ACTUS IV. SCENA III.

ARGUMENTUM.

Bacchis irata ob decem minas nondum troditas, abituram se adsimulat: cum Syro expostulat. Tandem placata, suasu ejusdem cum omni strepitu ac turba transit ad Menedemum, tantisper dum Chremes fallatur.

BACCHIS, CLINIA, SYRUS, DROMO, PHRYGIA.

SATI' pol protervè me Syri promissa huc induxerunt,
Decem minas quas mihi dare pollicitus est. quòd si is nunc me
Deceperit; saepe obsecrans me, ut veniam, frustra veniet.
Aut, cùm venturam dixero, & constituero; cùm is certè
Renunciárit; Clitipho cùm spe pendebit animi; 5
Decipiam, ac non veniam: Syrus mihi tergo poenas pendet. [credis?
CL. Sati' scitè promittit tibi. SY. atqui tu hanc jocari
Faciet, nisi caveo. BA. dormiunt: pol ego istos commovebo. [demonstravit
Mea Phrygia, audistin', modò iste homo quam villam Charini? PH. audivi. BA. proxumam esse huic fundo ad dextram? PH. memini. 10

ORDO.

BA. Pol promissa Syri induxerunt me huc satis protervè, propter decem minas, quas pollicitus est dare mihi. Quòd si is nunc deceperit me, saepe veniet frustra obsecrans me, ut veniam; aut cum dixero et constituero me venturam; cum is renunciaverit certe, cum Clitipho pendebit spe animi; decipiam, ac non veniam: Syrus pendet poenas mihi tergo. CL. Promittit tibi

satis scite, Syre. SY. *Atqui credis tu hanc jocari? faciet, nisi caveo.* BA. *Dormiunt: pol ego commovebo istos.* *Mea Phrygia, audivistine villam Charini, quam iste homo modo demonstravit?* PH. *Audivi.* BA. *Esse proximam huic fundo ad dextram?* PH. *Memini.*

ANNOTATIONS.

Manuscripts have *in spe*, which makes the Sentence fuller and more explicit, and requires the Order of Construction to be thus; *Cum Clitipho pendebit animi, in spe.* *Pendere animi*, is an Expression not unusual among Poets; for so *Plautus*, in his Play entituled *Mercator*,

Obsecro dissolve jam me: nimis diu animi pendeo.

6. *Syrus mihi tergo poenas pendet.* This was always the Punishment threatened to Slaves, and what they too naturally expected, when they offended. So in the *Hecyra, Ac. 2. 33. when Phidetis* endeavours to

Bacc. Run thither in all hafte, the Captain celebrates *Bacchus*'s Feaſt with him——

Syr. What's upon the Wheels now?

Bacc. Tell him that I am kept here very much againſt my Will, but that ſome way or other I'll contrive to give them the ſlip, and come over to him.

Syr. S'death, I'm ruin'd: *Bacchis*, ſtay, ſtay, where do you ſend her pray? Bid her come back.

Bacc. Go, I ſay.

Syr. But the Money's ready.

Bacc. Then I ſtay.

Syr. And you ſhall have it directly.

Bacc. When you pleaſe: do I hurry you?

Syr. But do you know what you are to do tho'?

Bacc. What?

Syr. You muſt go over to *Menedemus*, and carry all your Train with you.

Bacc. What's the Villain about now?

Syr. Who I? I'm coining Money to give to you.

Bacc. Do you think me a proper Perſon to play upon?

Syr. I am ſerious.

Bacc. Have I any Buſineſs there with you?

Syr. No: I want only to give you your own.

Bacc. Let us go then.

Syr. Follow this way: ſoho, *Dromo!*

Dro. Who's that wants me?

Syr. Syrus.

Dro. What's the matter?

Syr. Carry over all *Bacchis*'s Maids to your Houſe directly.

Drom. Why ſo?

Syr. Aſk no Queſtions; let them carry all their Baggage with them too. The Old Gentleman will fancy his Expence leſſened conſiderably by this Riddance. Faith, he little thinks how dear he muſt pay for this ſmall Gain. And you, *Dromo,* if you are wiſe, ſeem to know nothing of what you know.

Drom. You ſhall ſay I'm a Mute.

<hr />

ANNOTATIONS.

draw a Secret from *Parmeno*, which he knew would offend his Maſter, did he know of its being diſcovered, his Anſwer is:

Nunquam tam dices commode, ut tergum *meum*

Tuam in fidem committam.

[11] *Percurre. Curriculo percurre,* is an Expreſſion of the ſame Nature with that of *Plautus,* Aul. II. 2. 4.

Nunc domum properare propero.

Again, Trin. IV. 4. 11.

Curre in piraeeum, atque unum curriculum *face.*

Curriculum is properly the Space marked out to be run over by ſuch as are contending in the Race, and hence *currere curriculo* denotes the greateſt Speed and Swiftneſs in running.

[14] *Mane, mane,* &c. Theſe ſingle Words, ſpoken in haſte, and with great earneſtneſs, ſerve well to mark the great Fright that *Syrus* was in, and accordingly we find he mentions the Money, and promiſes it inſtantly, as one ready to undertake any thing to hinder her from putting her preſent Threats in execution.

[20] *Etiamne tecum hic mihi res eſt?* Sy. *Minime,*

BA. Curriculo percurre: apud eum milesDionyfia agitat.
SY. Quid inceptat? BA. dic me hîc oppidò. effe invitam,
atque affervari :   [venturam.
Verùm aliquo pacto verba me his daturam effe, &
SY. Perii Hercle : Bacchis, mane, mane : quò mittis
iftanc, quæfo ?
Jube, maneat. BA. abi. SY. quin eft paratum argen-
tum. BA. quin ego hîc maneo.   15
SY. Atqui jam dabitur. BA. ut lubet : num ego infto ?
SY. at icin' quid, fodes ?
BA. Quid? SY. tranfeundum nunc tibi ad Menedemum
eft, & tua pompa   [gon'? argentum cudo,
Eò traducenda eft. BA. quam rem agi', fcelus ? SY. e-
Quid tibi dem. BA. dignam me putas, quam inludas ?
SY. non eft temere.   [tuum tibi reddo. 20
BA. Etiamne tecum hîc res mihi eft ? SY. minimè :
BA. Eatur. SY. fequere hac. heus, Dromo. DR. quis
me volt ? SY. Syrus. DR. quid eft rei ?
SY. Ancillas omnes Bacchidis traduce huc ad vos properè
DR. Quamobrem ? SY. ne quæros. efferant, quæ fe-
cum huc attulerunt
Sperabit fumtum fibi fenex levatum effe harunc' abitu.
Næ ille haud fcit, hoc paulum lucri quantum ei dam-
ni apportet   25
Tu nefcis id quod fcis, Dromo, fi fapies. DR. mutum dices

BA. Percurre cur-
riculo : miles agi-
tat Dionyfia apud
eum. SY. Quid in-
ceptat ? BA. Dic
me effe atque affer-
vari hîc oppidò in-
vitam ; vèrum me
effe daturam verba
his aliquo pacto, &
venturam ad illum.
SY. Hercle perii :
Bacchis, mane, ma-
ne; quæfo, quo mittis
iftanc ? Jube, ut
maneat. BA. Abi.
SY. Quin argen-
tum eft paratum,
BA. Quin ego ma-
neo hîc. SY. Atqui
dabitur jam. BA.
Ut lubet : num ego
infto ? SY. At fcif-
ne quid faciendum
eft, fodes ? BA.
Quid ? SY. Tranf-
eundum nunc eft ti-
bi ad Menedemum,
& tua pompa eft
traducenda eò. BA.
Scelus, quam rem
agis ? SY. Egone ?
cudo argentum quod
dem tibi. BA. Pu-

tas me dignam, quam illudas ? SY. *Non eft temere.* BA. *Etiamne res eft mihi hîc tecum ?* SY.
Minime : reddo tuum tibi. BA. *Eatur.* SY. *Sequere hac via ; heus Dromo.* DR. *Quis vult*
me ? SY. *Syrus.* DR. *Quid rei eft ?* SY. *Traduce omnes ancillas Bacchidis huc ad vos properè.*
DR. *Quamobrem ?* SY. *Ne quæras ; efferant ea, quæ attulerunt huc fecum.* Nofter fenex fpe-
rabit fumptum effe levatum fibi abitu harum. Næ *ille haud fcit, quantum damni huc paulum lucri*
apportet ei. Dromo, *fi fapies, tu nefcis id quod fcis.* DR. *Dices me effe mutum.*

ANNOTATIONS.

Minime : tuum tibi reddo. There is fome
difficulty in this Paffage, nor indeed have
almoft any of the Commentators made tolerable Senfe of it. Madam *Dacier* has offered an Explanation that feems to bid faireft
for being received. *Syrus* having propofed
to *Bacchis*, to go over to *Menedemus*; fhe
anfwers : What would you have me go there
for ? Have I any Bufinefs or Concern with
you at his Houfe, or ought I to go there out
of Complaifance to you, becaufe you defire
it ? No, returns *Syrus*, but out of Complai-
fince to yourfelf, becaufe upon your going
over to him depends the Succefs of my Project for getting the Money.

[14] *Sumptum fibi levatum.* To get rid of a
Woman, fo expenfive, with all her Train,
muft, without doubt, be a great eafe to
Chremes, efpecially as he had already complained of the great Charge they put him to.

His Hopes, therefore, feemed well founded :
but he was not at the fame time aware, that
it threatened him with a confiderable Lofs,
as by this means chiefly *Syrus* would be able
to extort the Money he wanted from him.
Eugraphius.

[26] *Tu nefcis id quod fcis Dromo, fi fapies.*
Guyetus looks upon this as fpurious, and taken from the *Eunuch* IV. 4. 54. *Tu pol,*
fi fapis, quod fcis nefcis. Becaufe, fays he,
as *Dromo* a little before afks *quamobrem,* it
would feem as if he knew nothing. But befides that thefe Words are found in all the
antient Manufcripts : *Dromo* might have
feen and heard feveral things that were to be
concealed from his Mafter, though he was
not perhaps acquainted with all ; nor knew
the Reafon of *Bacchis*'s going over to *Me-*
nedemus.

ACT IV. SCENE IV.

ARGUMENT.

Syrus *cunningly obtains of* Chremes *the Money he wanted.* Chremes *again expresses his Concern for* Menedemus, *having heard that expensive* Bacchis, *with all her Train, was gone over thither, fancying her all along to be* Clinia's, *and not his Son's Mistress.*

CHREMES, SYRUS.

Chremes. LET me die, if I am not under the greatest Concern for poor *Menedemus,* that he should thus lie under the heavy Burden of supporting this expensive Woman, and her whole Family; altho' I know he won't be sensible of it for some few Days, so impatient he was to have his Son with him. But when he sees the vast Expence he is daily at, and that there is no Appearance of its coming to an end, he'll soon wish his Son away again.—Oh, here comes *Syrus* very opportunely.

Syr. Do I forbear going up to him?

Chrem. Syrus!

Sy. Ha!

Chrem. How go Affairs?

Syr. I have been wishing for you this long time.

Chrem. You seem already to have done, I don't know what, with the Old Man.

Syr. As to what we were talking of some time ago! No sooner said, but done.

Chrem. Indeed!

Syr. Indeed.

Chrem. I can't, I protest, forbear stroking you. Come hither, *Syrus.* I'll certainly do you some Kindness for this, and willingly.

Syr. But if you knew how cleverly it came into my mind.

Chrem. Pshaw, do you magnify your good Fortune?

Syr.

ANNOTATIONS.

In this Scene we have the Continuation and Success of *Syrus's* Project. *Chremes,* agreeable to his Character of a good-natured friendly Man, is here introduced, expressing his Concern for his Neighbour *Menedemus,* to whose Lot it was now fallen to feel the Weight of this expensive Train; and the more so, as he foresaw that he was like to continue under the Burden for some time. While is thus musing, he perceives *Syrus,* and renews the former Conversation about deceiving *Menedemus;* which *Syrus* gives so artful a Turn to, as to persuade him to give with his own Hands the Money to *Clitipho,* and order him to carry it to *Bacchis.*

3 *Illanccine mulierem alere cum illa familia?* Familia here signifies a Troop of Domesticks; *Grex famulorum famularumque.* A way of speaking very common among the Ancients, as they generally made a great part of their Families. *Sallust* uses it in the same Sense speaking of *Cethegus,* endeavouring by means of his Domesticks and Freedmen to have himself rescued. Bell. Catl. 50. *Cethegus autem per nuncios familiam atque libertos suos, lectos, & exercitatos in audaciam, orabat, uti, grege facto, cum telis ad sese irrumperent.* And *Phædrus* III. 19. 1.

  Æsopus domino solus cum esset familia.

9 *Syrum optume, eccum.* The mutual Artifices

ACTUS IV. SCENA IV.

ARGUMENTUM.

Per fallaciam Syrus ab hero Chremete argentum accipit. Menede-
mi rursum miseretur Chremes ob traductam ad illum cum omni
pompa sumptuosam Bacchidem, quam Cliniæ, non sui filii ami-
cam putat.

CHREMES, SYRUS.

ITA me Dii amabunt, ut nunc Menedemi vicem
Miseret me, tantum devenisse ad eum mali.
Illanccine mulierem alere cum illâ familiâ ?
Etsi scio, hosce aliquot dies non sentiet :
Ita magno desiderio fuit ei filius.   5
Verùm ubi videbit tantos sibi sumtus domi
Quotidianos fieri, nec fieri modum ;
Optabit rursum ut abeat ab se filius.
Syrum optumè, eccum. SY. cesso hunc adoriri ? CH.
   Syre. SY. hem.   [dari.
CH. Quid est ? SY. te mihi ipsum jamdudum optabam
CH. Videre egisse jam nescio quid cum sene.   11
SY. De illo quod dudum ? dictum ac factum reddidi.
CH. Bonân' fide ? SY. bonâ, hercle. CH. non possum pati,
Quin tibi caput demulceam. accede huc, Syre :
Faciam boni tibi aliquid pro istâ re, ac lubens.   15
SY. At si scias, quàm scitè in mentem venerit.
CH. Vah, gloriare evenisse ex sententiâ ?

mihi. CH. *Videre jam egisse nescio quid cum sene.* SY. *Dicis de illo quod dudum ? reddidi dic-*
tum ac factum. CH. *Bonane fide ?* SY. *Bona, hercle.* CH. *Non possum pati quin demulceam*
caput tibi ; accede huc, Syre : faciam aliquid boni tibi pro ista re, ac lubens. SY. *At si scias*
quam scitè venerit in mentem. CH. *Vah ! gloriare evenisse tibi ex sententia ?*

ORDO.

CH. *ITA Dii a-*
mabunt me,
ut nunc miseret me
propter vicem Me-
nedemi, tantum mali
devenisse ad eum,
Alere illaccine mulie-
rem cum illa familia ?
etsi scio, non sentiet
malum hosce aliquot
dies : filius suit ita
magno desiderio ei.
Verum ubi videbit
tantos sumptus quoti-
dianos fieri sibi domi,
nec modum fieri his ;
optabit ut filius abeat
rursum ab se : eccum
Syrum optimè. SY.
An cesso adoriri
hunc ? CH. *Syre !*
SY. Hem. CH. *Quid*
est ? SY. *Jamdudum*
optabam te ipsum dari

ANNOTATIONS.

tifices of these two are set off with all the
enlivening Circumstances of which they are
capable. *Chremes* rejoices to meet with *Syrus,* that of him he might learn how the
Plot against *Menedemus* was managed, and
succeeded. *Syrus* again was no less pleased
to meet with *Chremes,* whom we shall see
afterwards greatly over-reached, without
having the least Suspicion of what was transacted against him.

10 *Quid est ?* This was the common
Form of Answer, when any one heard himself called to by another ; for which Reason
I am apt to think, that they ought to be attributed rather to *Syrus* than *Chremes,* on
which Supposition they must be pointed and
distinguished thus :

—— SY. *Cesso hunc adoriri ?* CH. *Syre.*
SY. *Hem*

*Quid est ? te mihi ipsum jam dudum opta-
bam dari.*

17 *Vah !. gloriare evenisse ex sententia ?*
Nannius and *Guyetus,* both prefer *harislare,*
i. e. *inani divinatione jactus :* because *Menedemus* was not as yet circumvented, but
only a Plot laid for it. But by tracing the
Connexion a little backwards, we may both
be able to ascertain the true Meaning of the
Passage, and make it appear that there is
no Necessity for any Alteration of the Text.
Syrus, in answer to *Chremes* insinuating his
Desire to know what was done with *Menedemus,* he said ; *De illo quod dudum ? dictum ac factum reddidi.* Whence *Chremes*
conjectured that *Menedemus* had been already deceived, according to the Scheme concerted between them : and so much the
more, as *Syrus* afterwards, upon being further

Syr. No really: I speak only the Truth.

Chrem. What is it then?

Syr. Clinia pretended to *Menedemus*, that this *Bacchis* was your *Clitipho's* Mistress, and that he brought her over with him, to prevent you finding it out.

Chrem. Excellent!

Syr. But tell me your real thoughts.

Chrem. Admirable, I say.

Syr. Ay, if you knew all. *(Aside.)* But mark only what a Stroke of Policy's behind. He is to say, that he has seen your Daughter, that he was much taken with her, from the Moment he saw her, and that he would like to have her for a Wife.

Chrem. What, she that's just discovered?

Syr. The same: and he will request his Father to ask her for him,

Chrem. What does all this drive at, *Syrus?* for verily I don't understand it.

Syr. Pho! you're dull, I think.

Chrem. Perhaps so.

Syr. His Father will give him Money for the Wedding, with which Jewels and Clothes——You take me?

Chrem. Are to be bought.

Syr. Right.

Chrem. But I neither give nor contract my Daughter to him.

Syr. No! Why?

Chrem. Do you ask me why? Give her to a Man——

Syr. As you please. I did not mean that you should give her to him for good and all, but only pretend it.

Chrem. I'll pretend nothing. Do you manage your own Plots, so as not to bring me into them. Would you have me contract my Daughter, where I never intend to marry her?

Syr. I imagin'd so.

Chrem. By no means.

Syr. It might well enough be done: and I undertook this Business for no other Reason, than that you so earnestly recommended it to me.

Chrem. I believe it.

Syr. However, *Chremes,* all I do is for the best.

Chrem. Nay, I desire of all Things to have it done, but in some other way.

Syr. It shall: another Method shall be thought of. But as to the Money, which I told you your Daughter owes to *Bacchis,* that must be repaid now. Nor will you, I reckon, evade it by saying, What am I concerned? Was the Money given to me? Did I order it? Could she pawn my Daughter without my Consent? It is a true Saying, *Chremes; The more Law, the less Justice.*   *Chrem.*

ANNOTATIONS.

ther interrogated, answers: *bona fide.* Sy- | pleased, and commended him, could not re-
rus then seeing that *Chremes* was highly | sist the Vanity of endeavouring to heighten
                                                                                    the

Sy. Non hercle verò: verum dico. Ch. dic, quid eft ?
Sy. Tui Clitiphonis effe amicam hanc Bacchidem,
Menedemo dixit Clinia, & eâ gratiâ   20
Secum adduxiffe, ne tu id perfentifceres.   [mo fi fcias.
Ch. Probè. Sy. dic fodes. Ch. nimiùm, inquam. Sy. im-
Sed porro aufculta quod fupereft fallaciæ.
Sefe ipfe dicet tuam vidiffe filiam :   24
Ejus fibi complacitam formam, poftquam afpexerit :
Hanc cupere uxorem. Ch. modónc quæ inventa eft ?
     Sy. eam :
Et quidem jubebit pofci. Ch. quamobrem iftuc, Syre ?
Nam prorfum nihil intellego. Sy. hui, tardus es.
Ch. Fortaffe. Sy. argentum dabitur ei ad nuptias,
Aurum atque veftum quî—tenefne? Ch. comparet? 30
Sy. Id ipfum. Ch. at ego illi nec do, nec defpondeo.
Sy. Non ! quamobrem ? Ch. quamobrem, me rogas ?
     homini—Sy. ut lubet.
Non ego dicebam, in perpetuum illam illi ut dares ;
Verùm ut fimulares. Ch. non mea eft fimulatio :
Ita tu iftæc tua mifceto, ne me admifceas.   35
Egon', cui daturus non fim, ut ei defpondeam ?
Sy. Credebam. Ch. minimè. Sy. fcite poterat fieri :
Et ego hoc, quia dudum tu tantopere jufferas,
Eò cœpi. Ch. credo. Sy. cæterùm equidem iftuc, Chreme,
Æqui bonique facio. Ch. atqui cum maxumè   40
Volo te dare operam ut fiat, verùm aliâ viâ.
Sy. Fiat : quæratur aliud. fed illud quod tibi
Dixi de argento, quod ifta debet Bacchidi,
Id nunc reddendum eft illi. neque tu fcilicet   44
Eò nunc confugies : Quid meâ ? num mihi datum eft ?
Num juffi ? num illa oppignerare filiam
Meam me invito potuit ? verum illud, Chreme,
Dicunt : Jus fummum fæpe fumma eft malitia.

Sy. Non hercle vero) dico verum. Ch. Dic, quid eft ? Sy. Clinia dixit Menedemo hanc Bacchidem effe amicam tui Clitiphonis, & fe adduxiffe eam fecum ea gratia, ne tu perfentifceres id. Ch. Probe. Sy. Dic fedes. Ch. Iratam, nimium. Sy. Immo fi fcias ; fed aufculta porro quod fallacia fupereft. Ipfe dicet fefe vidiffe tuam filiam : formam ejus complacitam fibi, poftquam afpexerit : fe cupere hanc uxorem. Ch. Illane quæ eft modo inventa ? Sy. Eam. Et quidem jubebit pofci. Ch. Quamobrem iftuc, Syre ? nam intelligo nihil prorfum. Sy. Hui, es tardus. Ch. Fortaffe. Sy. Argentum dabitur ei ad nuptias, qui aurum atque veftem—tenefne ? Ch. Comparet ? Sy. Id ipfum. Ch. At ego nec do, nec defpondeo filiam illi. Sy. Non ! quamobrem ? Ch. Rogas me quamobrem ? homini—Sy. Ut lubet. Ego non dicebam, ut dares illam illi in perpetuum, verum ut fimulares. Ch. Simulatio non eft mea : tu ita mifceto tua iftæc, ne admifceas me. Utne ego defpondeam filiam ei, cui non fim daturus eam ? Sy. Credebam. Ch. Minime. Sy. Poterat fieri fcite : & ego cœpi hoc eo, quia tu dudum jufferas me tantopere. Ch. Credo. Sy. Cæterum equidem, Chreme, facio iftuc caufa æqui bonique. Ch. Atqui cum maximè volo te dare operam ut fiat, verum alia via. Sy. Fiat : aliud quæratur. Sed illud quod dixi tibi de argento, quod ifta debet Bacchidi, id eft nunc reddendum illi. Neque tu fcilicet eo confugies : Quid refert mea ? Num argentum eft datum mihi ? Num juffi ? Num illa potuit oppignerare meam filiam me invito ? Illud eft verum quod dicunt, Chreme : Summum jus eft fæpe fumma malitia.

ANNOTATIONS.

the Merit of his Artifice : *At fi fcias quàm fcite in mentem venerit.* Here Chremes checks him : *vah! gloriare ?* Do you boaft of it ? Do you want to make it appear greater than it really is ? No, indeed, fays Syrus, I only fpeak the Truth.

32 *Quamobrem, me rogas ? Homini.* Sub. *In alieno amore occupato.* & *amanti Bacchidem ?* Ei ego filiam darem in feditionem & incertas nuptias ? as before in the *Andrian.*

48 *Jus fummum fæpe fumma eft malitia.* Some read *injuria.* This Saying had paffed

Chrem. I'll not do it.

Syr. Nay, were it allowable in others, it would not be so in you ; for all the World knows you to be a rich flourishing Man.

Chrem. Well then, I'll go and carry it to her myself.

Syr. Nay, rather order your Son to do it.

Chrem. Why so ?

Syr. Because the Notion of being her Gallant, is now transferred to him.

Chrem. What then ?

Syr. Because it will then seem more likely, if he gives her the Money himself, and I too shall be the more easily able to compass my Designs. But here he comes himself. Go, bring out the Money.

Chrem. I go.

ANNOTATIONS.

into a Proverb, to which we have something analogous in our Language in that common Saying ; *The more Law, the less Right. Cicero,* Off. I. 10. *Existunt etiam sæpe injuriæ calumnia quadam, & nimis callida, sed malitiosa juris interpretatione. Ex quo illud, Summum jus, summa injuria, factum est jam tritum sermone proverbium.*

5b *Omnes te in lauta & bene aucta parte putant.* If we adopt this which is the common Reading, *pars* must be supposed to signify the Fortune he had inherited from his Ancestors, and improved by his own Industry. It is certain that this Use of the Word is very uncommon, and almost without Example, which has inclined the greater Part of Commentators, some to reject the Passage altogether, others to propose several Variations of the Text. The most approved is that which substitutes *re* instead of *parte :*

Omnes te in lauta & bene aucta re putant. However, as one would not willingly reject a Reading, in which all the ancient Manuscripts

ACT IV. SCENE V.

ARGUMENT.

Clitipho *returns full of Resentment, but is pacified by* Syrus, *who tells him that the Money was ready, and that* Bacchis *was gone over to* Menedemus. *He instructs him also how he is to behave towards his Father.*

CLITIPHO, SYRUS.

Clitipho. THERE is nothing so easy, but it becomes difficult when we set about it unwillingly. Even this little Walk, far from being fatiguing, has yet made me faint : nor is there any thing I fear more, than that I shall be again thrust out somewhere, and not suffered to come near *Bacchis.* May all the Gods confound thee, *Syrus,* with these your Stratagems and Plots ; for you are always contriving some Mischief of this kind to torment me.

Syr. Get you hence, as you deserve. How near was I to Ruin by your ill-timed Forwardness ? *Clit.*

ANNOTATIONS.

Clitipho, we have seen, in former Scenes, had been ordered to go take a Walk some- where, and leave the Lovers at Liberty. He was obliged to comply, but with great Reluctance,

CH. Haud faciam. SY. imo aliis fi licet, tibi non licet.
Omnes tu in lautâ & bene aucta parte putant.　　50
CL. Quin egomet jam ad eam deferam. SY. imo filium
Jube potiùs. CH. quamobrem? SY. quia enim in eum
　　fufpicio eft
Tranflata amoris. CH. quid tum? SY. quia videbitur
Magis verifimile id effe, cùm hic illi dabit :
Et fimul conficiam facilius ego, quod volo.　　55
Ipfe adeò adeft ; abi, effer argentum. CH. effero.

CH: Haud faciam. SY. Imo fi licet a-liis,: non licet tibi. Omnes putant te effe in parte lautâ, & bene aucta. CH. Quin egomet jam deferam ad eam. SY. Imo potibus jube filium. CH. Quamobrem? SY. Quia enim fufpicio amo-ris eft tranflata in eum. CH. Quid tum? SY. Quia id videbitur effe magis verifimile, cum hic dabit illi : & fimul ego conficiam facilius, quod volo : ipfe adeo adeft : abi, effer argentum. CH: Effero.

ANNOTATIONS.

fcripts and Copies concur, I fhall quote a Paf-sage from *Phædrus*, which may ferve to make appear that *pars* was fometimes ufed in a Senfe not much differing from this. It is in the 18th Fable of his third Book, Ver. 10. Where *Juno* returns this Anfwer to the *Peacock's* Complaint:

Fatorum arbitrio partes funt vobis datæ,
Tibi forma, vires aquilæ, lufcinio melos,
Augurium corvo, læva cornici omnia ;
Omne fque propriis funt contentæ voci-bus.

55 *Et fimul conficiam facilius ego, quod volo.* *Chremes* little fufpected the real In-tent of thefe Words, otherwife he would not have been fo forward in bringing the Money. He underftood it of their Plot againft *Mene-demus.* We are to fuppofe that *Syrus,* when he faid this, turned towards the Spectators, and by fome fignificant Looks and Geftures made them fenfible of his Purpofe, that un-der a fhew of plotting againft *Menedemus,* he was making his own Mafter, the Dupe of his Cunning.

ACTUS IV. SCENA V.

ARGUMENTUM.

Redit Clitipho ftomachabundus, verum a Syro placatur, cum pa-ratum argentum & Bacchidem apud Menedemum effe intelligit : fimulque quibus moribus ac verbis uti debeat, apud patrem, præfcribit.

CLITIPHO, SYRUS.

NULLA eft tam faciles res, quin difficilis fiet,
　　Quam invitus facias. vel me hæc deambulatio,
Quàm non laboriofa, ad languorum dedit :
Nec quidquam magis nunc metuo, quàm ne denuo
Mifer aliquò extrudar hinc, ne accedam ad Bacchidem.
Ut te quidem omnes Dii Deæque quantum eft, Syre, 6
Cum tuo ifto invento, cunique incepto perduint !
Hujufmodi res femper cominifcere,
Ubi me excarnufices. SY. is tu hinc quo dignus es?
Quàm pene tua me perdidit protervitas?　　10

ORDO.
CL. Nulla res eft tam facilis quin fit dif-ficilis, quam facias invitus. Vel. hæc deambulatio, quam non laboriofa, dedit me ad languorem : nec nunc metuo quid-quam magis, quam ne ego mifer denuo extrudar hinc ali-quo, ne accedam ad Bacchidem. Opto quidem ut omnes Dii Deæque, quantum eft, perduint te, Syre, cum ifto tuo invento eumque tuo incepto. Semper comminifcere res hujufmodi, ubi excarnifices me. SY. Is ne tu hinc quo es dignus? Quam pene tua protervitas perdidit me?

ANNOTATIONS.

Reluctance, and highly offended, at Sy-rus, who had made the malicious Propofal.

We have him here returning, and ftill under Difcontent, which breaks out upon Syrus,

AS

Clit. By *Hercules,* I wiſh you had been ruined, for you deſerve no other.

Syr. Deſerve! Nay, 'tis well you told me ſo before you had the Money I was juſt going to give you.

Clit. What would you have me ſay? You went and brought my Miſtreſs hither, whom I am not ſuffered ſo much as to touch.

Syr. Well, I am not angry at preſent: but can you gueſs where your *Bacchis* is now?

Clit. At my Father's, I ſuppoſe.

Syr. No.

Clit. Where then?

Syr. At *Clinia's.*

Clit. I'm ruin'd.

Syr. Have a good Heart: you ſhall preſently carry to her, with your own Hands, the Money you promiſed her.

Clit. Pſhaw, you prattle: where ſhould I have it?

Syr. From your own Father.

Clit. You banter me, perhaps.

Syr. The thing itſelf will ſoon ſhew that.

Clit. Nay: then I'm a fortunate Man indeed! *oyrus,* I love you of all things.

Syr. But your Father's coming out, beware of appearing ſurpriz'd how he comes to do it. Mind your Cue: do whatever he bids you, and ſpeak but little.

ANNOTATIONS.

as ſoon as he comes up to him; but when he bears that the Project had ſucceeded, and that he was juſt then to receive the Money, he changes his Note, and wants again to be in favour with *Syrus.*

14 *Quid igitur dicam tibi vis?* Theſe Words come with a milder Air, and Countenance that ſhews him under ſome Concern for his former Raſhneſs. When he hears that the Money is ready, he changes his Note, and endeavours to excuſe what his Reſentment had prompted him to ſay. What would you have me to ſay to you, who have created me ſo much Trouble, and tantalized me by a ſight of my Miſtreſs, when I am deny'd every other Enjoyment, and now excluded even from that?

16 *Jam non ſum iratus.* This is extremely natural and happy. *Syrus* was aware that he had mortified *Clitipho* extremely, by what he had done, and that one of his impatient Temper could not eaſily brook it. His own Project too had ſucceeded to his Wiſh, and this had put him in extreme good Humour. He had a Satisfaction in thinking he could make *Clitipho* happy,

ACT

CL. Vellem hercle factum: ita meritu'. SY. meritu?
Næ me istuc prius ex te audivisse gaudeo, [quo modo?
Quàm argentum haberes, quod daturus jam fui.
CL. Quid igitur dicam tibi vis? abiisti, mihi
Amicam adduxti, quam non liceat tangere.   15
SY. Jam non sum iratus: sed scin' ubi nunc sit tibi
Tua Bacchis? CL. apud nos. SY. non. CL. ubi ergo?
    SY. apud Cliniam.   [deseres,
CL. Perii. SY. bono animo es: jam argentum ad eam
Quod ei es pollicitus. CL. garris. unde? SY. à tuo patre,
CL. Ludis fortasse me. SY. ipsâ re experibere.   20
CL. Næ ego fortunatus homo sum: deamo te, Syre.
SY. Quâ causâ id fiat: obsecundato in loco.
Sed pater egreditur. cave quidquam admiratu' sis;
Quod imperabit, facito: loquitor paucula.

animo: jam deseres ad eam argentum, quod ei pollicitus ei. CL. Garris. Unde? SY. A tuo patre. CL. Ludis me fortasse. SY. Experibere ipsa re. CL. Næ ego sum homo fortunatus; Syre, deamo te. SY. Sed pater egreditur: cave sis admiratus quidquam qua causa id fiat: obsecundato in loco: facito quod imperabit: loquitor paucula.

CL. Hercle vellem factum: meritus es ita. SY. Meritus? Quo modo? næ gaudeo me audivisse istuc ex te, priusquam haberes argentum, quod sui daturus. CL. Quid vis igitur ut dicam tibi? abiisti, adduxisti amicam mihi, quam non liceat tangere. SY. Non sum iratus jam; sed scisne ubi tua Bacchis sit nunc tibi? CL. Apud nos. SY. Non. CL. Ubi ergo? SY. Apud Cliniam. CL. Perii. SY. Es bono

ANNOTATIONS.

happy, and was at the same Time impatient to acquaint him with his Address and good Fortune. All these together make him forget *Clitipho*'s ill-timed Anger, and accept of his Defence.

(22 *Qua causa id fiat*, &c. This is the Reading found in all ancient Manuscripts and Copies. But as, according to this Order of the Words, it is impossible to make Sense of them, there is a Necessity for admitting the Correction of *Muretus*, who changes the Order of the Lines, and makes that first, which, according to the common Reading, holds the second Place:

Sed pater egreditur, cave quidquam admira-
    tus sis,
Qua causa id fiat: obsecundato in loco:

Quod imperabit, facito: loquitor pau-
    cula.

If this is not admitted, the Sentence halts twice, without any apparent Meaning. For how are we to understand *qua causa id fiat?* or to what Part of *Syrus*'s Discourse does it belong? Again, what has *cave quidquam admiratus sis* to do here? Why this Command and Charge? Are we to fancy *Syrus* assuming the Air and Men of a Philosopher? What could be more ridiculous or absurd in this Place? But by the above Transposition of the Verses, every thing is plain and easy. *Cave quidquam admiratus sis, qua causa id fiat.* Beware of appearing surprized at what your Father does, *viz.* in giving you the thirty Pounds to carry to *Bacchis.*

ACT IV. SCENE VI.
ARGUMENT.

Chremes *brings the Money, and gives it to* Clitipho ; *and after his Departure falls into some Complaints at the Expence he was obliged to be at on his Daughter's account.*

CHREMES, CLITIPHO, SYRUS.

Chremes. WHERE's this *Clitipho* now ?

Syr. I'm here, say.

Clit. Here, Father.

Chr. (*To* Syrus.) Have you told him how it is ?

Syr. I have told him almoſt all.

Chr. (*To* Clitipho.) Take this Money, and carry it.

Syr. Go : why do you ſtand like a Stone ? Why don't you take it ?

Clit. Give it me.

Syr. Follow me this Way quickly. You, Sir, mean Time, will wait for us here a Moment, till we come out again ; for we have nothing to keep us long there.

Chr. (*Alone.*) My Daughter has now got thirty Pounds from me, which I conſider as ſo much paid for her Board. Thirty more muſt follow theſe for fine Clothes ; and then ſhe muſt have at leaſt two Talents for her Portion. How many wrong and unjuſt Things has Cuſtom introduced ! I muſt now neglect other Things to look out for ſome one, on whom I may beſtow the Wealth I have with ſo much Labour acquir'd.

ANNOTATIONS.

Chremes returns with the Money which he gives to *Clitipho,* to tarry to *Bacchis,* who, notwithſtanding the Leſſons of *Syrus,* could not ſtifle his Aſtoniſhment at a Thing ſo unexpected, and to him unaccountable. *Syrus* is, therefore, obliged to quicken, and in a Manner, force him along with him : when the Old Man, left alone upon the Stage, falls into a Train of profound Reflections upon human Life, and the Power of Cuſtom.

11 *Quam multa injuſta ac prava fiunt moribus !* Madam *Dacier* propoſes here a Correction of the Text ; more, indeed, for an Opportunity of making ſome Reflections, that come naturally enough from a Lady, than that there is any real Neceſſity for the Change :

Quam

ACT IV. SCENE VII.
ARGUMENT.

Chremes, *while he imagines that* Menedemus *is deceived by the Artifices of* Syrus, *is himſelf the Dupe of* Syrus *and* Clitipho.

MENEDEMUS, CHREMES.

Menedemus. TO Clinia *within.*) I now think myſelf the happieſt of Men, my Son, ſince I underſtand you are ſo much reformed. *Chr.*

ANNOTATIONS.

Bacchis was, by this Time, gone over to *Menedemus,* and *Clinia* had applied to his Father, to obtain for him *Chremes's* Daughter. The Old Man overjoyed at this ſuppoſed

ACTUS IV. SCENA VI.

ARGUMENTUM.

Chremes argentum adfert, quod det Clitiphoni ; ad postremum que-
ritur de sumtu faciundo filiæ causa.

CHREMES, CLITIPHO, SYRUS.

U BI Clitipho nunc eft? Sy. Eccum me, inque. CL.
   Eccum hîc tibi.
CH. Quid rei effet, dixti huic? Sy. Dixi pleraque'omnia.
CH. Cape hoc argentum, ac defer. Sy. I, quid ftas, lapis?
Quin accipis? CL. Cedo fanè. Sy. Sequere hàc me ocius:
Tu hîc nos, dum eximus, interea opperibere :   5
Nam nihil eft illîc, quod moremur diutiùs.
CH. Minas quidem jam decem habet à me filia,
Quas pro alimentis effe nunc duco datas.
Hafce ornamentis confequentur alteræ.
Porro hæc talenta dotis appofcunt duo.   10
Quàm multa injufta ac prava fiunt moribus ! .
Mihi nunc, relictis rebus, inveniendus eft
Aliquis, labore inventa mea cui dem bona.

quas nunc duco effe datas pro alimentis. Altera decem confequentur bafce pro ornamentis. Porro
hæc appofcunt duo talenta dotis. Quam multa fiunt injufta ac prava moribus! Omnibus aliis
rebus relictis, aliquis eft nunc inveniendus mihi, cui dem mea bona inventa labore.

CH. U Bl nunc eft
   Clitipho?
Sy. Inque, Eccum me.
CL. Eccum tibi hîc.
CH. Dixifti huic,
quid rei effet? Sy.
Dixi pleraque omnia.
CH. Cape hoc argen-
tum, ac defer. Sy. I,
quid ftas, lapis? Quin
accipis? CL. Cedo
fanè. Sy. Sequere me
ocius hac : tu interea
opperibere nos hîc,
dum eximus; nam ni-
hil eft quod moremur
diutius illîc. CH. Fi-
lia quidem habet jam
decem minas à me,

ANNOTATIONS.

Quam multa injufta ac prava, jufta fiunt
moribus !
How many Things, of themfelves unjuft and un-
reafonable, derive an Appearance of Juftice from
Cuftom? I am charmed, fays fhe, with the
Sentiment, and yet more with the Application of it. For in fact nothing can be more
ridiculous, than that when a Father beftows

his Daughter upon a Man, he muft alfo beftow part of his Fortune with her. And as a
certain Evidence, that it is Cuftom only
which gives Sanction to a Practice fo ill-
judged, in the more ancient Times the very
contrary to this was in ufe : Money and
Prefents were given to Fathers, by fuch as
courted their Daughters in Marriage.

ACTUS IV. SCENA VII.

ARGUMENTUM.

Chremes, dum Menedemus credit per Syrum decipi, ipfe per
Syrum & Clitiphonem delufus eft.

MENEDEMUS, CHREMES.

M ULTO omnium me nunc fortunatiffimum
   Factum puto effe, gnate, cùm te intellego
fatiffimum omnium hominum, gnate, cum intelligo te refipiffe.

Me. N Unc puto
   me effe
factum multo fortu-

ANNOTATIONS.

pofed Reformation in his Son, is reprefented
here juft coming out, and talking to his Son
within, telling him that he was now happy

to find him another Man, *Chremes,* who
overhears him, and continues ftill in the Error taken notice of in the preceding Scenes,
   wonders

Chr. How he is miftaken!

Mened. Chremes, you are the very Perfon I wanted. Preferve as you have it now in your Power, my Son, myfelf, and my Family.

Chr. Say: what would you have me do?

Mened. You have found a Daughter To-day.

Chr. What then?

Mened. Clinia wants to have her for a Wife.

Chr. Pray what kind of a Man are you?

Mened. Why?

Chr. Have you forgot already the Trick we talk'd of, that by means of it, Money might be extorted from you?

Mened. I know it.

Chr. That's the very Thing they're about now.

Mened. What faid you, *Chremes?* I have then been miftaken.

Chr. And this *Bacchis,* I warrant, at your Houfe, is *Clitipho's* Miftrefs.

Mened. So they fay.

Chr. And do you believe it?

Mened. Every thing.

Chr. And they tell you that he is defirous of marrying, that when I fhall have contracted my Daughter, you may give Money to buy Jewels, Clothes, and other Things needful.

Mened. That is it certainly, that will be given to his Miftrefs.

Chr. Undoubtedly it is for her.

Mened. Alas, unhappy that I am! My Joys were, therefore, all vain, yet I'd rather any Thing, than be deprived of him again. What Anfwer fhall I carry back from you, *Chremes,* that he mayn't perceive I have found it out, and be uneafy upon it?

Chr. Uneafy! you're too indulgent to him, *Menedemus.*

Mened. Let me go on; I have begun it: continue to affift me, as you have promifed.

Chr. Say then, that we met, and treated about the Match.

Mened. I will: but what more?

Chr. That I'll do every Thing; that I like him for a Son-in-Law; and laftly, if you pleafe, tell him alfo, that I have contracted my Daughter to him.

Mened. Oh! that's what I wanted. *Chr.*

ANNOTATIONS.

wonders at his Miftake, forgetting fo foon what had been contrived between them; and at laft, by entering ferioufly into Converfation with him, endeavours to make him fenfible of the whole Plot, which tho' *Menedemus* is perfuaded to believe, he ftill perfifts in his Refolution, of indulging for the prefent his Son.

10 *Quid dixit, Chreme? erravi.* Commentators are greatly divided as to the manner of reading and diftinguifhing the Speakers in this Paffage. I have followed the *Cam-*

bridge Edition, in which every thing is confiftent, and the Senfe good. But that the Reader may not be Ignorant of what others have alfo conjectured, I fhall here, without entering into any Detail, content myfelf with barely fetting down two Readings that feem to bid faireft for the Author's Meaning. The firft is that of *Heinfius*:

CH. *Ea res nunc agitur ipfa.* MT. *Quid dixti, Chreme?*

Erravi. Sic res acta eft, quanta de fpe decidi!

CH.

Refipiffe. CH. ut errat! ME. teipfum quærebam,
Chreme :
Serva, quod in te eft, filium, & me, & familiam. 4
CH. Cedo, quis vis faciam? ME. inveñisti hòdie filiam.
CH. Quid tum? ME. hanc uxorem sibi dari volt Clinia.
CH. Quæso, quid hominis es? ME. quid? CH. jamne
oblitus es,
Inter nos quid sit dictum de fallaciâ,
Ut câ viâ abs te argentum auferretur? ME. scio.
CH. Ea res nunc agitur ipsa. ME. quid dixti, Chreme?
Erravi. CH. & quidem hæc quæ apud te eft, Clitipho-
nis eft 11
Amica. ME. ita aiunt. CH. & tu credis? ME. omnia.
CH. Et illum aiunt velle uxorem, ut, cùm desponderim,
Des qui aurum ac veftem, atque alia, quæ opus sunt,
comparet.
ME. Id eft profecto: id amicæ dabitur. CH. scilicet 15
Daturum. ME. vah, fruftra sum igitur gavisus miser.
Quidvis tamen jam malo, quàm hunc amittére.
Quid nunc renunciem abs te responsum, Chreme,
Ne sentiat me sensisse, atque ægrè ferat? 19
CH. Ægrè? nimiùm illi, Menedeme, indulges. ME. sine,
Inceptum eft, perfice hoc mihi perpetuò, Chreme.
CH. Dic convenisse, egisse te de nuptiis.
ME. Dicam : quid deinde! CH. me facturum esse om-
nia ;
Generum placere : poftremò etiam, si voles, 24
Desponsam quoque esse dicito. ME. hem, iftuc volueram.

qua funt opus. ME Profecto id eft, id dabitur amicæ. CH. Crede scilicet daturum. ME.
Vah, igitur ego miser gavisus sum fruftra. Tamen jam malo quidvis, quam amittére hunc.
Quid renunciem nunc fuisse responsum abs te, Chreme, ne sentiat me sensisse ejus consilia, atque
ferat ægre? CH. Ægre? Menedeme, nimium indulges illi. ME. Sine; eft inceptum : perfice
hoc mihi perpetuo, Chreme. CH. Dic me convenisse, & te egisse mecum de nuptiis. ME.
Dicam; quid deinde? CH. Me esse facturum omnia; generum placere; poftremo etiam, si voles,
dicito quoque meam filiam esse desponsam. ME. Hem, volueram iftuc.

ANNOTATIONS.

CH. *Immo hæc quidem, quæ apud te eft, Cli-*
tiphonis eft
Amica. ME. *Ita aiunt.* CH. *Et tu credis?*
ME. *Omnia.*
The other is proposed by Madam *Dacier:*
CH. *Ea res nunc agitur ipsa.* ME. *Quid*
dixti, Chreme?
Cu. *Immo hæc quidem, quæ apud te eft, Cli-*
tiphonis eft.
Amica. ME. *Ita aiunt.* CH. *Et tu cre-*
dis? ME. *Omnia.*
This laft differs very little from the *Cam-*
bridge Edition.
13 *Id eft profecto,* &c. *Menedemus* is here
at length convinced that *Chremes* had judged
right of his Son's Difpofitions. And indeed,
putting all that had been concerted between
them together, and comparing them with
Circumftances, as they now offered, it was
impoffible not to come into this Notion, Ap-
pearances were fo ftrongly for it. *Menede-*
mus, who is not here diftinguifhed for his Penetration, but reprefented as a Man of plain
Senfe, would have acted quite out of Character, not to be determined by Reafons fo
probable. And herein the Poet fhews the
Juftnefs of his Genius; that he does not
bring mere Idiots upon the Stage, a Character that could neither entertain nor inftruct,
but Men of natural good Senfe, and otherwife difcreet enough, are deceiv'd by an odd
Concurrence of Circumftances.
21 *Perfice hoc mihi perpetuo.* There is
great Elegancy and Force in this Sentence.

As

Chr. That he may the sooner ask Money of you, and you the sooner give it, according to your Wish.

Mened. 'Tis my Wish, indeed.

Chr. Nay, as far as I can guess, you'll soon have enough of him: but however that may be, you'll give him warily, and by degrees, if you are wise.

Mened. I will.

Chr. Go in, and see how much he wants; I'll be at home, if there should be any occasion for me.

Mened. That's what I wish; for I'll do nothing without acquainting you with it.

A N N O T A T I O N S.

As you have already begun to aid and advise lasting and perpetual; me, continue your good Offices; make them) ʃ

A C T V. S C E N E I.

A R G U M E N T.

The Plot now hastening to a Conclusion, that there may remain no obstacle to the Marriage of Clinia *and* Antiphila; Syrus's *Treachery is discovered by* Menedemus, *who tells* Chremes *the whole Affair in order, and makes it evident to him, that* Bacchis *can be no other than* Clitipho's *Mistress.*

M E N E D E M U S, C H R E M E S,

Menedemus. **I** Know very well, that I'm none of the acutest or quickest-sighted in the World: but this Assistant of mine, this Counsellor, and sage Director *Chremes*, far out-does me. Any of the Names commonly given to Fools, may be applied to me; Blockhead, Stock, Ass, Dolt; but they don't come up to him, for his Folly is beyond expression. *Chrem.*

A N N O T A T I O N S.

Things now begin to put on a new Face. *Menedemus* is, by this time, convinced from unavoidable Circumstances, that *Bacchis* was not a pretended Mistress of *Clitipho's*, but so in reality. - *Menedemus* had no doubt conceived highly of *Chremes*, as a Man of great Acuteness and Penetration, he even owns how far he is superior to himself in Judgment, and how capable to advise him, where trusting to his own Understanding, he was like to be misled. These Comparisons, so much to our own disadvantage, are always irksome and painful, nor can we avoid taking a certain ill-natured Pleasure, in finding a Man, whom we had believed greatly our Superiour, brought down to our Level, or perhaps of a Rank even below us. This

is precisely the Situation of *Menedemus* here. In every Word he discovers his Joy, at finding himself not inferiour to *Chremes*; nay he frankly takes to himself all the Titles of Fool, that he may apply them with Interest to the other. The Conversation afterwards naturally flows from this. *Menedemus* is impatient to discover all to *Chremes*; and he greatly surprized and shocked to find he had been so much imposed upon.

a *Sed hic adjutor meus, & monitor, & præmonstrator Chremes.* These three Words, *Adjutor, monitor, præmonstrator,* are all borrowed from the Theatre, and have here a particular Beauty arising from their figurative Sense, which it is not easy to convey into our Language. *Adjutor* was properly one

CH. Tanto ociùs te ut pofcat, & tu id, quod cupis,
Quàm ociſſimè ut des. ME. cupio. CH. næ tu prope-
Ut iſtam rem video, iſtius obſaturabere. [dicm,
Sed hæc ut ut ſunt, cautim & paulatim dabis,
Si ſapies. ME. faciam. CH. abi intro: vide, quid poſtulet.
Ego domi ero, ſi quid me voles. ME. ſanè volo: 31
Nam te ſcientem faciam, quidquid egero.

CH. Ut tanto ocius
poſcat te, & ut tu,
des quam ociſſime id,
quod cupis. ME. Cu-
pio. CH. Næ tu,
ut ego video iſtam
rem, obſaturabere iſ-
tius propediem. Sed
ut ut hæc ſunt, dabis
cautim & paulatim,

ſi ſapies. ME. *Faciam.* CH. *Abi intro, vide quid poſtulet ; ego ero domi, ſi voles me quid.* ME. *Volo ſane : nam quidquid egero, faciam te ſcientem.*

ACTUS V. SCENA I.

ARGUMENTUM.

Ad exitum jam properante comœdia, Syri fallacia (ut ſcilicet Cliniæ nubat Antiphila) per Menedemum detegitur, qui narrat Chremeti totum negotium ordine, & Bacchidem Clitiphonis eſſe amicam oſtendit.

MENEDEMUS, CHREMES.

EGO me non tam aſtutum, neque ita perſpicacem
eſſe, id ſcio : [Chremes
Sed hic adjutor meus, & monitor, & præmonſtrator
Hoc mihi præſtat. in me quidvis harum rerum con-
venit, [beus :
Quæ ſunt dicta in ſtultum, caudex, ſtipes, aſinus, plum-
In illum nihil poteſt : nam exſuperat ejus ſtultitia hæc
omnia.

ORDO.
ME. EGO ſcio,
id, me non
eſſe tam aſtutum ne-
que ita perſpicacem :
ſed hic Chremes, meus
adjutor, & monitor,
& præmonſtrator,
præſtat mihi hoc.
Quidvis harum re-
rum, quæ ſunt dicta
in ſtultum, convenit
in me, caudex, ſtipes, aſinus, plumbeus : nihil poteſt convenire in illum ; nam ſtultitia ejus exſuperat omnia hæc.

ANNOTATIONS.

one *qui adjuvabat hiſtriones in agendis par-*
tibus ; quod ſeu voce, ſeu geſtibus fiebat.
Phæd. V. 5. 13.
In ſcena vero poſtquam ſolus conſtitit .
Sine apparatu, nullis adjutoribus.
Monitor, qui monebat hiſtriones, ne memoriâ vacillarent in agendis partibus. *Præ-*
monſtrator may be underſtood from the following Lines of *Plautus, Perſ.* 1. 3, 68.
Præmonſtra docte, præcipe aſtu filiæ,
Quid fabuletur, ubi ſe natam prædicet.
4 *Caudex.* Properly the Trunk of a Tree,
by changing *o* into *au,* inſtead of *codex*
making it *caudex,* in like manner, as we
have *cautis* for *cotis. Stipes ſtipitis* too has
the ſame Signification, in which it is diſtinguiſhed from *ſtipes ſtipis,* or rather
ſtips ſtipis ; a Soldier's Pay. Some diſ-
pleaſed with the ſeeming Tautology here,

inſtead of *caudex,* read *cautes,* as afterwards
in Verſe 44, we read, *ni eſſem lapis.* But
there is no need of being ſo nice, as it is
frequent, in Compariſons of this nature, to
expreſs the ſame things in different Words ;
the Idea being thereby imprinted the ſtronger, while the Mind is at the ſame time entertained with Variety. *Plumbeus ;* ſo Sueton.
Ner. 2. *In hunc dixit Licinius Craſſus orator,*
Non eſſe mirandum, quod æneam barbam ha-
beret, cui eſſet os ferreum, & cor plumbeum.
5 *Nam exſuperat ejus ſtultitia hæc omnia.*
This muſt be the true Reading, and not
aſtutia, as ſome have contended ; for it is
evident he means that all the foregoing Titles, however applicable to himſelf, yet came
ſhort of the other's Folly. This may be
made appear from a parallel Paſſage in *Plau-*
tus, Bacchid. V. 1. 1.

Chr. (*To* Softrata *within.*) Prithee, Wife, have done teazing the Gods with Thanks for having found your Daughter again, unlefs you judge of them by yourfelf, and fancy they underftand nothing till it has been told them a hundred times. But meantime, whence comes it that *Syrus* and my Son tarry fo long there?

Mened. Who are they that ftay fo long, *Chremes?*

Chr. Oh *Menedemus!* Are you here? Well, have you told *Clinia* what I faid?

Mened. Every Word.

Chr. What fays he?

Mened. He appeared highly pleafed, like one who really wanted to be married.

Chr. Ha, ha, ha!

Mened. What do you laugh at?

Chr. My Man *Syrus's* fly Tricks came into my mind.

Mened. Did they fo?

Chr. The Rogue has the Art alfo, of teaching Perfons to copy other Mens Countenances.

Mened. You mean that my Son's Joy is only a feint?

Chr. I do.

Mened. The fame came into my mind too.

Chr. Old Sly-boots!

Mened. You'd think fo indeed, did you know more of the Affair.

Chr. Say you fo?

Mened. Do but hear me.

Chr. Stay: I want firft to know how much you have fquandered away: for when you told your Son, that I had confented to the Match; *Dromo*, I fuppofe, immediately gave the Hint, that the Bride muft have Wedding-clothes, Jewels, and Attendants, that you might give him the Money.

Mened. No.

Chr. What! No?

Mened. No, I fay.

Chr. Nor your Son?

Mened. Not a word, *Chremes.* On the contrary, he was very urgent to have the Match concluded to-day.

Chr. You furprize me. How did *Syrus* behave? Did he fay nothing neither?

Mened. Not a word.

Chr. How fo?

Mened. I can't tell indeed; but wonder much at you, who are fo quick in other Peoples Affairs. But that fame *Syrus* has fo admirably copyed your Son's Countenance too, that nobody can in the leaft fufpect this to be *Clinia's* Miftrefs.

Chr.

ANNOTATIONS.

Quicunque ubique funt, qui fuere, quique futuri funt poflhac | *Stulti, ftolidi, fatui, fungi, barbi, blenni, buccones.*

Stlus

CH. Ohe, jam desine Deos, uxor, gratulando obtundere,
Tuam esse inventam gnatam; nisi illos ex tuo ingenio judicas,
Ut nil credas intellegere, nisi idem dictum sit centies.
Sed interim quid illic jamdudum gnatus cessat cum Syro?
ME. Quos ais homines, Chreme, cessare? CH. hem, Menedeme, advenis?
Dic mihi, Cliniæ, quæ dixi, nunciastin'? ME. omnia.
CH. Quid ait? ME. gaudere adeò occepit, quasi qui cupiunt nuptias. [mentem Syri
CH. Ha, ha, hæ! ME. quid risisti? CH. servi venere in
Calliditates. ME. itane? CH. voltus quoque hominum fingit scelus. [ME. itidem istuc mihi
ME. Gnatus quòd se assimulat lætum, id dicis? CH. id.
Venit in mentem. CH. veterator. ME. magi', si magis nôris, putes [mane: priùs hoc scire expeto,
Ita rem esse. CH. ain' tu? ME. quin tu ausculta. CH.
Quid perdideris. nam ubi desponsam nunciâsti filio,
Continuò injecisse verba tibi. Dromonem scilicet,
Sponsæ vestem, aurum atque ancillas opus esse, argentum ut dares.
ME. Non. CH. quid non? ME. non, inquam. CH. neque ipse gnatus? ME. nil prorsus, Chreme.
Magis unum etiam instare, ut hodie conficerentur nuptiæ. [quam? ME. nihil.
CH. Mira narras. quid Syrus meus? ne is quidem quid-
CH. Quamobrem? ME. nescio equidem: sed te miror, qui alia tam planè scias.
Sed ille tuus quoque Syrus idem mirè finxit filium,
Ut ne paulùm quidem suboleat esse amicam hanc Cliniæ.

CH. Ohe, uxor desine jam obtundere deos gratulando, gnatam tuam esse inventam; nisi judicas illos ex tuo ingenio, ut credas illos intelligere nil, nisi idem sit dictum centies. Sed interim quid gnatus cessat jamdudum illic cum Syro? ME. *Chreme, quos homines ais cessare?* CH. *Hem, Menedeme, advenis? Dic mihi, nunciastine Cliniæ, quæ dixi* tibi? ME. Dixi *omnia.* CH. *Quid ait?* ME. *Occepit adeo gaudere, quasi qui cupiunt nuptias.* CH. *Ha, ha, hæ!* ME. *Quid risisti?* CH. *Calliditates servi* mei *Syri venere in mentem.* ME. *Itane?* CH. *Scelus fingit quoque vultus hominum.* ME. *Dicisne id, quod gnatus assimulat se lætum?* CH. *Id.* ME. *Itidem istuc venit mihi in mentem.* CH. *Veterator.* ME. *Magis putes, rem esse ita, si magis noris.* CH: *Ain' tu?* ME. *Quin tu ausculta.* CH. *Mane: expeto scire hoc prius, quid perdideris. Nam ubi nunciasti filio* meam gnatam *esse desponsam, scilicet,* an non verum est, *Dromonem continuo injecisse verba tibi, vestem, aurum, atque ancillas esse opus sponsæ, ut dares argentum?* ME. *Non.* CH. *Quid non.* ME. *Non, inquam.* CH. *Neque ipse gnatus?* ME. *Nil prorsus, Chreme, etiam magis instare unum, ut conficerentur hodie.* CH. *Narras mira. Quid meus Syrus? Ne is quidem* dixit *quidquam?* ME. *Nihil.* CH. *Quamobrem?* ME. *Equidem nescio: sed miror te, qui scias alia tam plane. Sed ille idem, Syrus, mire finxit tuum filium quoque, ut ne* quis *quidem paulum suboleat hanc esse amicam Cliniæ.*

ANNOTATIONS.

Solus ego omnes antideo stultitia, & moribus indoctis.

[13] *Servi venere in mentem Syri calliditates.* *Terence*, through all this Scene, discovers wonderful Addrefs, and a true poetic Genius. *Chremes* is represented in full Security, altogether unsuspecting, and even greatly pleased with the Acuteness and Cunning of his Slave; who could contrive and execute a Plot with so much Art, that *Menedemus*, tho' apprised, was not able to discover the Cheat. All this is done with a View to heighen his Surprize and Astonishment, when he comes to know the Truth, and make him appear to the Spectator in a still more ridiculous Light.

[14] *Voltus quoque hominum fingit scelus.* The Meaning is, that *Syrus* not only lays his Plots well, but also teaches those who are concerned in them, to put on Countenances suitable to the several Parts they are to act. For *Chremes* was full of the Belief, that *Clinia* however indifferent he might appear, was enamoured with *Bacchis*, and that his

Chr. What do you fay?

Mened. Not to mention their kiffing and hugging: that I count nothing.

Chr. What can they do more to carry on the Cheat?

Mened. Pifh.

Chr. What is it, pray?

Mened. Hear me only: I have a little fnug Room in the back part of my Houfe; into this a Bed was brought and made up.

Chr. Well, and what followed after this?

Mened. Thither immediately went *Clitipho.*

Chr. Alone?

Mened. Alone.

Chr. I begin to dread.

Mened. Bacchis followed directly.

Chr. Alone?

Mened. Alone.

Chr. I'm ruin'd.

Mened. As foon as they were got in, they fhut the Door.

Chr. And did *Clinia* fee all this?

Mened. See it? Yes; he and I together.

Chr. Bacchis is my Son's Miftrefs, *Menedemus*; I'm undone.

Mened. Why fo?

Chr. I fhall fcarce be able to keep Houfe ten Days.

Mened. What, are you fo concern'd, becaufe he helps his Friend a little?

Chr. Nay, becaufe he helps his Miftrefs.

Mened. If he does.

Chr. Is that a Queftion? Can you fuppofe any Man fo meek and patient, as to fuffer his Miftrefs before his Face to be —— ?

Mened. Ha, ha, ha! Why not? the eafier to deceive me.

Chr. Do you laugh at it? nay, I am now with juftice angry at myfelf. How many things were there, that, had I not been a Stone, might have I difcovered it? How much have I myfelf feen? wretch that I am! But if I live, they fhall fmart for it, for I'll immediately—

Mened. Can't you moderate your Paffion? Have you no regard for yourfelf? Am not I a fufficient Example to you?

Chr. Menedemus, I'm really not myfelf, for Anger.

Mened. For you to talk in that manner? Is it not ridiculous to be

---

ANNOTATIONS.

his defire of being married to his Daughter was no more than a Counterfeit to blind his Father. Hence *Menedemus,* when *Chremes* begins to be convinced of his miftake, retorts upon him his own Words;

Sed ille tuus quoque Syrus idem mire finxit filium.

39 *Quemquamne animo tam comi effe.* Some read *communi,* which feems to have a very peculiar Signification here, and indeed, is frequently ufed by Authors, in a manner, that requires to be minutely explained. *Cicero,* in one

of his Epiftles, fays, Fam. 4. 9. *An, qui in bello, cum omnium noftrum conjunctum effe periculum fuo cerneret, certorum hominum minime prudentium confilio uteretur, cum magis COMMUNEM cenfemus in victoria futurum. Ju- iffe, quam incertis rebus fuiffet?* Upon this *Grævius* has the following Remark: "Communes Latinis dicuntur, comes, aliter civiles, "qui nihil fingulare ac præcipuum fibi tri- "buunt præ aliis, qui non fupra alios cives "fe extollunt, qui funt populares, modefti, "patientes juris legumque communium, qui "non

CH. Quid ais? ME. mitto jam ofculari, atque am-
plexari : id nil puto.
CH. Quid eft, quod amplius fimuletur? ME. vah, CH.
quid eft? ME. audi modò ;
Eft mihi in ultimis conclave ædibus quoddam retro :
Huc eft intro letus lectus, veftimentis ftratus eft. 30
CH. quid poftquam hoc eft factum? ME. dictum ac
factum, huc abiit Clitipho.
CH. Solus? ME. folus. CH. timeo. ME. Bacchis con-
fecuta eft illico. [operuere oftium. CH. hem.
CH. Sola? ME. fola. CH. perii. ME. ubi abiere intro,
Clinia hæc fieri videbat? ME. quidni? unà mecum
fimul.
CH. Filii eft amica Bacchis, Menedeme : occidi. 35
ME. Quamobrem? CH. decem dierum vix mî eft familia.
ME. Quid? iftuc times, quòd operam amico ille dat fuo?
CH. Imo quòd amicæ. ME. fi dat. CH. an dubium
id tibi eft?
Quenquamne animo tam comi effe, aut leni putas,
Qui fe vidente amicam patiatur fuam? ME. ah, 40
Quidni? quò verba facilius dentur mihi.
CH. Derides? merito mihi nunc ego fuccenfeo.
Quot res dedere, ubi poffem perfentifcere,
Ni effem lapis? quæ vidi? væ mifero mihi!
At næ illud haud inultum, fi vivo, ferent : 45
Nam jam—ME. non tu te cohibes? non te refpicis?
Non tibi ego exempli fatis fum? CH. præ iracundiâ
Menedeme, non fum apud me. ME. téne iftuc loqui?

CH. Quid ais? ME. Mitto jam ofculari, atque amplexari puto id nil. CH. Quid eft, quod fimuletur amplius? ME. Vah! CH. Quid eft? ME. Audi modo : eft quoddam conclave mibi retro, in ultimis ædibus : lectus latus eft intro huc, ftratus eft veftimentis. CH. Quid factum eft poftquam hoc? ME. Dictum ac factum, Clitipho abiit Luc. CH. Solus? ME. Solus. CH. Timeo. ME. Bacchis illico confecuta eft. CH. Sola? ME. Solq. CH. Perii. ME. Ubi abiere intro, operuere oftium. CH. Ileni, Clinia videbat hæc fieri? ME. Quidni? fimul una mecum. CH. Bacchis eft amica filii, Menedeme; occidi. ME. Quamobrem? CH. Familia decem dieruin vix eft mibi. ME. Quid? times iftuc, quod ille dat operam fuo amico? CH. Imo, quod dat

operam amicæ. ME. Si dat. CH. An id eft dubium tibi? putafne quenquam effe animo tam comi aut leni, qui patiatur fuam amicam fe vidente? ME. Ah, quidni? quò verba facilius dentur mibi. CH. Derides? ego nunc merito fuccenfeo mibi. Quot res dedere, ubi, ni effem lapis, foffem perfentifcere? Quæ vidi? Væ mifero mibi! At næ, haud ferent illud inultum, fi vivo: nam jam---ME. Non tu cohibes te? Non refpicis te? Non ego fum fatis exempli tibi? CH. Menedeme, Non fum apud me præ iracundia. ME. Tene oportet loqui iftuc?

ANNOTATIONS.

" non fuo in omnibus utuntur confilio, fed " & aliorum civium hominumve." This Senfe of the Word he illuftrates by Quotations from Suetonius, Pliny, and Cornelius Nepos. I fhall fatisfy myfelf with one, from Pliny's Panegyrick upon Trajan, where he defcribes the Prince, as bringing himfelf down to a level with his Subjects, and appearing in public without that Pomp and Affectation, whereby his Predeceffors had, in a Manner, cut themfelves off from all Society and Communication with their Subjects. Paneg. Cap. 24. " Ante te principes, " faftidio noftri, & quodam æqualitatis metu, " ufum pedum amiferant : illos ergo hume- " ri cervicefque fervorum fuper ora noftra ; " te fama, te gloria, te civium pietas, te li- " bertas, fuper ipfos principes vehunt, te ad " fidera tollit humus. Ita communia, & " confufa principis veftigia." Hoc eft, addit Grævius; Incedis ut alii cives, pedibus nimirum, non equo, aut in lectica vectus. From this, it is eafy to conceive how communis may be made to fignify one of an eafy Temper, condefcending to his Friend, and willing to poffefs every thing in common with him. This, however it may fometimes happen in other things: Chremes, with reafon, denies ever to take place in the cafe of a Miftrefs.

+ Quidni? Quò verba facilius dentur mihi. Menedemus, notwithftanding all the obligations

A a 3

giving Advice to others, to be wife abroad; and yet can do nothing for yourfelf?

Chr. What fhall I do?

Mened. What you faid I was fo much to Blame for not having done. Let him fee that you are his Father, one with whom he may venture to truft all his Secrets, and from whom to afk whatever he wants; left, perhaps, he fhould apply elfewhere, and leave you.

Chr. Nay, let him go any where for me, rather than here, by his Debaucheries, bring his Father to want. For if I go on to fupport him in his Extravagances, *Menedemus*, that will, indeed, foon reduce me to the Rake and Harrow.

Mened. How many Inconveniencies will you bring upon yourfelf, if you don't take care? You'll fhew yourfelf a rigid Father, and pardon him at laft; nor will even that quite reconcile him to you.

Chr. Oh! you can't conceive how much I'm vexed.

Mened. As you pleafe. But what fay you to the Propofal I have made, of your *Antiphila*'s marrying my Son, unlefs you have another you like better in your Eye?

Chr. Nay, both the Son-in-Law; and the Alliance pleafe me much.

Mened. What Fortune fhall I fay you intend to give your Daughter? Why are you filent?

Chr. Fortune?

Mened. Yes.

Chr. Ah!

Mened. Don't be in any Pain about it, *Chremes*, however little you defign her. Her Fortune fhall make no difference between us.

Chr. I defigned her, indeed, two Talents, which I thought enough for my fmall Eftate. But if you regard either me or my Son's Welfare, there is a Neceffity for faying that I have fettled all I have upon her for a Fortune.

Mened. What are you about?

Chr. Pretend to wonder at it, and afk him what can be the Reafon of my doing fo.

Mened. And to fay Truth, I can't conceive the Reafon for your doing it.

Chr. Why I do it, to check his Mind, borne away wholly at prefent by Luxury and Debauchery, and reduce him fo low that he may'nt know where to turn himfelf.

Mened. What can you Defign?

Chr. Let me alone; and fuffer me to have my own way in this.

Mened. I do: but is it really your Defire? *Chr.*

ANNOTATIONS.

Obligations he was under to *Chremes*, who had advifed and aided him in fo friendly a Manner, cannot here forbear indulging the malicious Pleafure of triumphing over his Friend. To exalt himfelf above a Man, whom he before believed greatly his Superior, was too bewitching a Victory for him not to glory in. Every one perceives, at firft Sight, how natural, and fuited to the common Paffions of Mankind, this Behaviour of *Menedemus* is. The Poet, it is true, defigns him for a Character of Good-nature, but to have carried it fo far as to neglect the prefent Advantage, or avoid mentioning any Thing to mortify

Nonne id flagitium eſt, te aliis conſilium dare,
Foris ſapere, tibi non poſſe te auxiliarier ?   50
Ch. Quid faciam? Me. id, quod me feciſſe aiebas pa-
Fac te patrem eſſe ſentiat : fac ut audeat   [rùm :
Tibi credere omnia, abs te petere & poſcere,
Ne quam aliam quærat copiam, ac te deſerat.
Ch. Imo abeat potius multo quovis gentium,   55
Quàm hîc per flagitium ad inopiam redigat patrem :
Nam ſi illi pergo ſuppeditare ſumtibus,
Menedeme, mihi illæc verè ad raſtros res redit.
Me. Quot incommoda tibi in hac re capies, niſi caves ?
Difficilem oſtendes te eſſe, & ignoſces tamen   60
Pòſt, & id ingratum. Ch. Ah, neſcis quàm doleam.
          Me. Ut lubet.
Quid hoc, quod volo, ut illa nubat noſtro ? niſi quid eſt,
Quod mavis. Ch. imo & gener & affines placent.
Me. Quid dotis dicam te dixiſſe filio ? [Me. Chreme,
Quid obticuiſti ? Ch. dotis ? Me. ita dico. Ch. ah !
Ne quid vereare, ſi minu' : nil nos dos movet.   66
Ch. Duo talenta pro re noſtrâ ego eſſe decrevi ſatis :
Sed ita dictu opus eſt, ſi me vis ſalvom eſſe, &.rem, &
filium,   [agis ?
Me mea omnia bona doti dixiſſe illi. Me. Quam rem
Ch. Id mirari te ſimulato, & illum hoc rogitato ſimul, 70
Quamobrem id faciam. Me. quin ego verò, quam-
obrem id facias, neſcio.   [ſciviâ
Ch. Egone ? ut illius animum, qui nunc luxuriâ & la-
Diffluit, retundam, & redigam, ut quò ſe vortat ne-
ſciat.   [mihi morem. Me. ſino.
Me. Quid agis ? Ch mitte, ſine me in hac re gerere

*Quid obticuiſti ? Ch. Dotis ? Me. Ita dico. Ch. Ah. Me. Chreme,
ne vereare, quid, ſi
dixeris minus : dos nihil movet nos. Ch. Ego decrevi duo talenta eſſe ſatis pro re noſtra. Sed
ita eſt opus dictu, ſi vis me, & rem; & filium eſſe ſalvum; me dixiſſe omnia mea bona doti illi.
Me. Quam rem agis ? Ch. Simulato te mirari id, & ſimul rogitato illum, hoc, quamobrem faciam id. Me. Quin ego vero neſcio quamobrem facias id. Ch. Egone ? ut retundam animum
illius, qui nunc diffluit luxuria & laſcivia, & redigam ut neſciat quo vertat ſe. Me. Quid agis ?
Ch. Mitte, ſine me gerere morem mihi in hac re. Me. Sino :*

Nonne id eſt flagiti-
um, té dare conſilium
aliis, ſapere foris, te
non poſſe auxiliari ti-
bi ? Ch. Quid faci-
am ? Me. Id, quod
aiebas me parum fe-
ciſſe. Fac ſentiat te
eſſe patrem : fac ut
audeat credere omnia
tibi, petere & poſcere
abs te, ne quærat
quam aliam copiam,
ac deſerat te. Ch.
Imo multo potiùs abeat
quovis gentium, quàm
hîc per flagitium re-
digat patrem ad in-
opiam. Nam ſi per-
go, Menedeme, ſup-
peditare ſumtibus illi,
verè illæc res redit
mihi ad raſtros. Me.
Quot incommoda ca-
pies tibi in hac re,
niſi caves ? oſtendes
te eſſe difficilem, &
tamen poſt ignoſces,
& id erit ingratum.
Ch. Ah, neſcis quam
doleam. Me. Ut lu-
bet. Quid dicis ad
hoc, quod volo, ut illa
tua Antiphila nu-
bat noſtro filio ? niſi
eſt quid, quod mavis.
Ch. Imo & gener
& affines placent.
Me. Quid dotis di-
cam filio, te dixiſſe ?
ne vereare, quid, ſi
dixeris minus : dos nihil movet nos. Ch.

ANNOTATIONS.

mortify *Chremes* farther, or increaſe his Chagrin, would have been overſtraining the
Point. *Terence* had too juſt a Genius to a-
muſe himſelf in drawing Characters altogether perfect, or chimerical ; his aim is to
paint real Life, Good-nature mixed with
human Paſſion and Infirmities.

65 *Ah!* After *Menedemus* had demanded
of *Chremes*, what Portion he intended for
his Daughter, the Father deliberates for
ſome time, not ſo much, indeed, about her
Portion, as the Manner of correcting and

reforming his Son. The other thinking he
was in Pain, left, intending leſs than was
probably expected, the Offer might not be acceptable, encourages him to name it, whatever it was ; ſince having enough of his own,
he did not much mind what Fortune his
Daughter-in-law brought with her. But
Chremes undeceives him, by naming the Sum
he intended, and at the ſame time opening
his Reſolution with reſpect to his Son.

74 *Mitte, ſine me in hac re gerere* mihi
morem. Me. *Sino. Fune, vis ?* Ch. Ita
          Me.

Chr. It is.

Mened. Be it fo then.

Chr. And. now you mày tell *Clinia* to make ready, and fend for his Bride. As for *Clitipho*, I'll give him a Lecture, fuch as Children ought to hear from a Parent: but *Syrus*—

Mened. What will you do with him?

Chr. Do with him? If I live, I'll drefs and curry his Hide for him fo effectually, that he fhall remember it to the laft Day of his Life. A Rafcal! to imagine that I was a fit Perfon to make game of. As I hope to live, he would not have dared to ferve a poor friendlefs Widow, as he has ferved me.

ANNOTATIONS.

Mr. *Fiat.* As this, which is the common Reading, is obfcure, and makes a very uncertain and perplexed Senfe, I cannot forbear mentioning the ingenious Conjecture of Madam *Dacier*, who thinks, that inftead of *fino*, we ought to read *fine*, and taking it from *Menedemus*, add it to what *Chremes* fays, as if he redoubled the Requeft; thus:

Mr. *Quid agis?* Ch. *Mitte: fine me in hac re gerere mihi morem: fine.*
Mr. *Itane vis?* Ch. *Ita.* Mr. *Fiat.*
" Mr. What are you about? Ch. Let me
" alone. Allow me in this particular to have
" my own Will. Allow me I fay, Mr.
" Are you then determined? Ch. I am.
" Mr. Well: I have done." For it is ridiculous

ACT V. SCENE II.

ARGUMENT.

Chremes feverely chides his Son Clitipho, *on account of his Miftrefs, and that with defign to better him by his Admonitions, that cafting off* Bacchis, *he may marry. This Scene, moreover, contains the cunning Device of* Syrus, *by which the Cataftrophe of the Fable is much haftened.*

CLITIPHO, MENEDEMUS, CHREMES, SYRUS.

Clitipho. PRAY is it really fo, *Menedemus*, that my Father has fo fuddenly caft off all the Concern of a Parent for me? For what Crime? What heinous Fault alas have I been guilty of? Moft young Men have done the fame.

Mened. I know this muft be much more terrible and fhocking to you, to whom it happens: but even I am no lefs uneafy at it, who know not, nor can give any other Reafon for my Concern, than that from my Soul I wifh you well.

Clit. Did you not fay that my Father was here?

Mened. There he is!

Chr. Why do you blame me, *Clitipho?* whatever I have done in this

ANNOTATIONS.

There is fome Difficulty here to defend the Conduct of the Poet, who is charged with an unpardonable Overfight. *Chremes* had but juft done fpeaking with *Menedemus*, who quitted him the Moment before, and

here we find *Clitipho* informed of every thing his Father had refolved upon to his Prejudice. This, lay they, is a great Blunder, for what is fuppofed to pafs in the Interval between thefe two Scenes, is fufficient to fill up the

Space

Itane vis? CH. ita. ME. fiat. CH. ac jam, uxorem
  ut accerſat, paret.   75
Hic ita, ut liberos eſt æquum, dictis confutabitur.
Sed Syrum—ME. quid eum? CH. egone? ſi vivo, a-
  deò exornatum dabo,
Adeò depexum, ut, dum vivat, meminerit ſemper mei:
Qui ſibi me pro deridiculo ac delectamento putat.
Non, ita me Dii ament, auderet facere hæc viduæ mu-
Quæ in me fecit.   [lieri, 8c

depexum, ut, dum vivat, ſemper meminerit mei: qui putat me ſibi pro deridiculo at delectamento.
Ita Dii ament me, non auderet facere viduæ mulieri, hæc quæ ſerit in me,

visne ita? CH. Ita.
ME. Fiat. CH. A:
jam, Clinia paret,
ut accerſam uxorem;
hic Clitipho confu-
tabitur dictis, ita ut
æquum eſt liberos eſſe.
Sed dabo Syrum—
ME. Quid dabis
eum? CH. Egone?
Si vivo, dabo eum
adeo exornatum, adeo

ANNOTATIONS.

diculous to fancy that *Menedemus* ſays *ſino*, before he aſks whether his Reſolution was fixed. *Itane vis?*

79 *Ut liberos eſt æquem.* *Chremes* is quite againſt puniſhing Children with Stripes; and with reaſon, for that is treating them like

Slaves. Blows are only to correct, where Remonſtrances fail; beſides, that they check a freeSpirit, and are apt to make the Temper mean and ſervile. See what *Micio* ſays upon this Subject, in the firſt Scene of the *Adelphi.*

ACT V. SCENE II.

ARGUMENTUM.

Pater Clitiphonem filium objurgat propter amicam: idque adeo fit, ut admonitus redeat in viam, &, Bacchide relicta, uxorem ducat. Continet hæc ſcena callidum Syri conſilium, quo cataſtrophen, id eſt, exitum eventumque negotii machinatur.

CLITIPHO, MENEDEMUS, CHREMES, SYRUS.

ITANE tandem quæſo eſt, Menedeme, ut pater
  Tam in brevi ſpatio omnem de me ejecerit animum
  patris?   [miſi miſer?]
Quodnam ob facinus? quid ego tantum ſceleris ad-
Volgo faciunt. ME. ſcio tibi eſſe hoc gravius multo ac
  durius,   [neſcio; 5
Cui fit: verùm ego haud minùs ægrè patior id, qui
Nec rationem capio, niſi quòd tibi bene ex animo
  volo.   [incuſas, Clitipho?
CL. Hic patrem eſſe aiebas? ME. eccum. CH. quid me

ORDO.
CL. MEnedeme, quæſo, i-
tane eſt tandem, ut pater in jam brevi ſpacio ejecerit omnem animum patris de me? Ob quodnam facinus? Quid tantum ſceleris ego miſer admiſi? Adoleſcentes vulgo faciunt. ME. Scio hoc eſſe multo gravius ac du-

rius tibi, cui fit: verum ego patior id haud minus ægre, qui neſcio, nec catio rationem, niſi quod volo bene tibi ex animo. CL. Aiebas patrem eſſe hic? ME. Eccum. CH. Quid incuſas me, Clitipho?

ANNOTATIONS.

Space commonly allowed between two Acts. To ſet this in a clear Light, we are to remember that *Menedemus* leaves *Chremes* to go and ſpeak with *Clitipho.* He juſt enters the Houſe, and in two Words tells him what his Father had done; deſiring no doubt at the ſame time to go out and try to pacify his Fa-

ther, who was at the Door. This may be collected from Ver. 7. His patrem eſſe aiebas? *Chremes*, meantime, walks up and down upon the Stage, wa ting till his Son and *Menedemus* ſhould come out, for he was impatient to know how his Son would brook this late Step he had taken; as is evident from Ver. 70,
of

this Cafe, you and your Imprudence have occafioned it.. When I found you to be negligent and thoughtlefs, and that prefent Pleafures wholly fway'd you, without any regard to what might happen afterwards, I took the Courfe that appeared neceffary to fecure you from want, and my Eftate from ruin. For feeing that your own Folly rendred it unfit to name you my Heir, whom Nature firft dictated, I made over and entrufted all to your next Relations. There, *Clitipho*, you will always find a Remedy for your Indifcretions, Food, Clothing, and Roof to lie under.

Clit. Wretch that I am!

Chr. 'Tis better, than by making you my Heir, to give all to *Bacchis*.

Syr. I'm ruined irrecoverably. What Mifchiefs have I, before I was aware, been the unhappy Caufe of?

Clit. Would I were dead!

Chr. Learn firft, pray, what it is to live. When you have tried that, if Life difpleafes, then defire to die.

Syr. Sir, will you give me leave?

Chr. Speak.

Syr. But in fafety?

Chr. Speak.

Syr. What Folly and Madnefs is this, that my Faults fhould be imputed to him?

Chr. Have done. Don't you meddle in the Affair. Nobody accufes you, *Syrus.* You have no need to look out either for a Sanctuary, or one to plead for you.

Syr. What's your defign?

Chr. I am angry with neither you nor him, nor ought you to be angry with me for what I do.

Syr. He's gone—I wifh I had afked him—

Clit. What, *Syrus.*

Syr. Where I am to eat, now that he has caft us off. You, I underftand, are entailed upon your Sifter.

Clit. Is it come to this then, that I am in danger even of ftarving, *Syrus?*   *Syr.*

ANNOTATIONS.

of the preceding Scene, where he fays to *Menedemus*, *Id mirari te fimulato, & illum bee rogitato fimul, quamobrem id faciam.* Thus there is ftill one upon the Stage, nor is the Courfe of the Play interrupted, becaufe the Spectators too wait, knowing that *Menedemus* is to return immediately. The Scene itfelf, juft before *Menedemus's* Houfe, gave both *Menander* and *Terence* the Opportunity of connecting the Scenes in this manner; a thing frequently done by Poets; and very natural in the prefent Inftance.

6 *Quidquid ego hujus feci, tibi profpexi, & juftitiæ tuæ.* Here the Father acts according to what he had before promifed: *dictis*

confutabitur. Here, indeed, the Poet has given a notable Example, how much more prevalent Reafon urged with a Fatherly Concern is, than Paffion and Vehemence. *Chremes* takes a middle way between the too great Severity of *Demea*, and the overftrained Indulgence of *Micio.* He endeavours to make his Son fenfible of his Error, by fhewing him the prefent Infamy that attended a Courfe of Debauchery, and the future Ruin wherewith it threatned him. Thefe Remonftrances we find have the wifhed for Effect; the young Man is afhamed of his Folly, and refolves to change for the better.

13 *Abii ad proxumos tibi qui erant.* The
Order

Quidquid ego hujus feci, tibi profpexi, & ftultitiæ tuæ.
Ubi te vidi animo effe omiffo, &, fuavia in præfentia
Quæ effent, prima habere, neque confulere in longi-
    tudinem ;   10
Cepi rationem, ut neque tu egeres, neque ut hæc
    poffes perdere.
Ubi, cui decuit primo, tibi non licuit per te mihi dare,
Abii ad proxumos tibi qui erant, eis commifi & credidi.
Ibi tuæ ftultitiæ femper erit præfidium, Clitipho.
Victus, veftitus, quò in tectum te receptes. CL. hei
    mihi !   15
CH. Satius eft, quàm teipfo herede hæc poffidere Bac-
    chidem.
SY. Difperii : fceleftus quantas turbas concivi infciens !
CL. Emori cupio. CH. priùs, quæfo, difce quid fit vi-
    vere :
Ubi fcies, fi difplicebit vita, tum iftoc utitor.
SY. Here, licetne ? CH. loquere. SY. at tutò ? CH.
    loquere. SY. quæ ifta eft pravitas,   20
Quæve amentia eft, quod peccavi ego, id obeffe huic ?
    CH. ilicet,   [tibi,
Ne te admifce : nemo accufat, Syre, te : nec tu aram
Neque precatorem paráris. SY. quid agis ? CH. nil
    fuccenfeo,   [mihi.
Nec tibi, nec huic ; nec vos eft æquum, quod facio,
SY. Abiit. vah, rogâffe vellem. CL. quid, Syre ? SY.
    unde mihi peterem cibum :   25
Ita nos alienavit. tibi jam effe ad fororem intelligo.
CL. Adeon' rem rediiffe, ut periclum etiam fame mi-
    hi fit, Syre ?

Quidquid hujus egi, feci, profpexi tibi, & tuæ ftultitiæ, Ubi vidi te effe omiffo a-nimo, & habere ea prima, quæ effent fu-avia in præfentia, neque confulere in longitudinem : cepi rationem, ut neque tu egeres, neque ut poffes perdere hæc. Ubi non licuit mihi per te, dare tibi, cui primo decuit, abii ad prox-imos qui erant con-fanguinei tibi, com-mifi & credidi mea bona eis : ibi erit femper præfidium tuæ ftultitiæ, Clitipho, victus, veftitus, quo receptes te in tectum. CL. Hei mihi. CH. fatius eft quam, teipfo hærede, Bacchidem poffidere hæc. SY. Difperii : quantas turbas ego fcelchtas infciens concivi ! CL. Cupio emori. CH. Quæfo, difce prius quid fit vivere. Ubi fcies, fi vita difplice-bit, tunc utitor iftoc. SY. Here, licetne ? CH. Loquere. SY. At tuto ? CH. Lo-quere. SY. Quæ eft ifta pravitas, quæve

amentia eft, id quod ego peccavi obeffe huic ? CH. Ilicet : ne admifce te : nemo accufat te. Syre : nec tu pararit aram, neque precatorem tibi. SY. Quid agis ? CH. Nil fuccenfeo, nec tibi, nec huic ; nec æquum eft vos fuccenfere mihi ob quod ego facio. SY. Abiit, vah, vellem rogâffe. CL. Quid, Syre ? SY. Unde peterem cibum mihi ; ita alienavit nos. Jam intelligo effe cibum tibi ad fororem. CL. Remne rediiffe adeo, ut fit periculum mihi etiam mori fame, Syre ?

ANNOTATIONS.

Order of Right in Succeffion is here obferved, nor was this without Defign in the Poet. For *Chremes* would appear to his Son, and to act with the ftricteft regard to Juftice. When he found that Prudence required he fhould not leave his Fortune at the Difpofal of his Son, who had, indeed, the firft and beft Right to it, he went to the next in Blood, his Sifter. Yet they were beftowed with fuch Reftrictions, as to make it in a Manner on-ly a Truft. *Commifi,* I have committed them to her Management ; *credidi,* I have entrufted them to her, that you may want for nothing neceffary, without having it in your Power to fquander away all.

[1]⁸ *Prius quæfo, difce quid fit vivere.* A moft ufeful Counfel, and moft happily ap-plied ; in oppofition to the rafh and extrava-gant Wifh of a young Man, who not know-ing the Value of Life, nor the real good Purpofes it may be made to ferve, can heed-lefsly throw away Life, becaufe of fome check in his little and vain Purfuits. *Lac-tantius* quotes it with Approbation, Lib. 3. 18. *De vita quereris : quafi vixeris, aut un-quam tibi ratio confiiterit, cur omnino fis na-tus. Nonne igitur tibi verus, ille, & commu-nis omnium pater Terentianum illud jure increpa-verit ? Prius difce, quid fit vivere.*

[2]³ *Nibil fuccenfco nec tibi, nec huic ;* nec vos eft

Syr. While there is Life, there is Hope.

Clit. What Hope?

Syr. That we shall have good Stomachs.

Clit. Do you Joke in a Matter so serious, nor offer to assist me with your Advice?

Syr. Nay, I am now thinking of that, and was so all the while your Father was speaking: and as far as I can guess ——

Clit. What?

Syr. You will have it ere long.

Clit. What is it then?

Syr. 'Tis this: I don't take you to be their Child.

Clit. How's that, *Syrus?* Are you mad?

Syr. I'll tell you what's come into my Mind; judge you of it yourself. While they had none but you, while no other Joy affected them more nearly, they indulged you, and gave you whatever you wanted; but now that a real Daughter is found, they have found also a Pretence for casting you off.

Clit. The Thing is not unlikely.

Syr. Do you imagine he'd be really so angry for this small Fault?

Clit. I can't think it.

Syr. There is another thing too: Mothers are always Advocates for their Son's Faults, and take part with them against the Father. 'Tis not so here.

Clit. Very true: what can I do therefore, *Syrus?*

Syr. Let them know your Suspicion, and tell your Mind freely. If it is false, you'll soon soften them to Pity; if true, you'll know your own Parents.

Clit. You advise me right; I'll do it.

Syr. (*Alone.*) This Thought came very fortunately into my Mind; for the less Hope my young Gentleman has, he will be the readier to make peace with his Father upon his own Terms. Nay, 'tis possible he may even consent to marry, but no Thanks to *Syrus*—But what's this now? I see the Old Man coming out: I'll make off. I wonder he did not order me to be trussed up immediately for what's already past. I'll to *Menedemus* directly, and make sure of him for my Advocate; for I can put no Trust in our Old Man.

ANNOTATIONS.

est æquum, quod facio mibi. However provoked *Chremes* might be against *Syrus*, he here dissembles it, because he would seem to act, at present, not thro' Anger or Passion, but from Prudence. He wants, if possible, to reform his Son by the softer Methods of Persuasion; and no doubt he remembred, that he himself had spirited up *Syrus* to the Fallacy, which to discover, and that his own Counsel had been turned against him, must make him appear ridiculous. He, therefore, wisely defers giving way to his Resentment against *Syrus*, till a fitter Opportunity should offer.

44 *Namque adolescens, quam in minima spe situs erit.* We are to admire *Syrus's* Prudence and Address in the present Case. His whole Aim is to make up *Clitipho's* Peace, and bring his Father to better Temper. He could think of nothing more likely to effect this, than by making *Clitipho* feign that he did not believe himself to be *Chremes's* Son. But as there is a great difference between the Behaviour of one who acts from the real Persuasion of a thing, and one who knows that he uses it only as a Pretence; *Syrus* knew the Man too well to trust

Sy. Modò liceat vivere, est spes. Cl. quæ? Sy. nos
  esurituros satis.   [adjuvas?
Cl. Irrides in re tantâ, neque me quidquam consilio
Sy. Imo & ibi nunc sum, & usque dudum id egi, dum
  loquitur pater :   30
Et, quantum ego intellegere possum—Cl. quid? Sy.
  non aberit longiùs.
Cl. Quid ergo? Sy. sic est : non esse horum te arbi-
  tror. Cl. quid istuc, Syre?
Satin 'sanus es? Sy. ego dicam, quod mihi in mentem :
  tu dijudica.
Dum istis fuisti solus, dum nulla alia delectatio, [filia 35
Quæ propior esset, te indulgebant, tibi dabant : nunc
Postquam est inventa vera, invenia est causa, quâ te
  expellerent.   [lum iratum putas?
Cl. Est verisimile. Sy. an tu ob peccatum hoc esse il-
Cl. Non arbitror. Sy. nunc aliud specta : matres om-
  nes filiis
In peccato adjutrices, auxilio in paternâ injuriâ
Solent esse : id non fit. Cl. verum. quid ergo nunc
  faciam, Syre?   40
Sy. Suspicionem istanc ex illis quære : rem profer pa-
  làm.   [cito, aut
Si non est verum, ad misericordiam ambos adduces
Scibis cujus sis. Cl. rectè suades : faciam. Sy. sat rectè
  hoc mihi in   [mâ spe situs erit,
Mentem venit : namque adolescens, quàm in mini-
Tam facillimè patris pacem in leges conficiet suas. 45
Etiam haud scio an uxorem ducat, ac Syro nil gratiæ.
Quid hoc autem? senex exit foras : ego fugio. adhuc
  quod factum est,
Miror non jussisse illico me arripi. ad Menedemum
  hinc pergam.   [habeo.
Eum mihi precatorem paro : seni nostro fidei nihil

Quære istanc suspicionem ex illis : profer rem palam. Si non est verum, cito adduces ambos ad
misericordiam, aut scibus cujus scis. Cl. Suades recti : faciam. Sy. Hæc venit mihi in mentem,
satis rectè : namque adolescens, quam erit situs in minima spe, tam facillimè conficiet pacem patri :
in suas leges. Haud scio an etiam ducat uxorem, ac nil gratiæ Syro. Autem quid est hoc? senex
exit foras : ego fugio. Miror eum non jussisse me illico arripi, ob quod adhuc est factum. Pergam
binc ad Menedemum. Paro eum precatorem mihi : nam habeo nibil fidi nostro seni.

ANNOTATIONS.

trust him with the secret, and, therefore, | redouble her Importunities with her Husband
begins by making him the first Dupe. By | to cancel what he had done. And the young
this two good Ends were answered at once. | Man himself too, thus reduced to the brink
Chremes, alarmed at his Son's entertaining | of Despair, would be the readier to comply
such a Notion, would the sooner relent, and | with whatever his Father might require as
especially the Mother would be stattled, and | the Condition of his Reconciliation.

ACTUS

ACT V. SCENE III.

ARGUMENT.

Sostrata expostulates with her Husband, and anxious for her Son, admonishes Chremes *not to persist in his Design of disinheriting* Clitipho. *But* Chremes *checks her unjust Reproaches, inveighing bitterly against his Son's Disobedience and Debaucheries.*

SOSTRATA, CHREMES.

Sost. INDEED, Husband, if you go on thus, you'll be the cause of some Mischief to your Son; nor can I wonder enough how so extravagant a Fancy should come into your head.

Chr. Oh! You will then still be the Woman? Did I ever in my Life resolve upon any thing, but I found you bent to thwart me in it? And yet were I to ask you what's amiss, or what's the reason of acting thus; you don't know in what it is that you so confidently oppose me, Fool.

Sost. I not know!

Chr. Nay, you know it, I grant, rather than be forced to hear all over again.

Sost. Oh! 'tis unjust to expect I should be silent in an Affair of this Importance.

Chr. I don't desire it: Speak: I'll do it nevertheless.

Sost. You will?

Chr. For certain.

Sost. You don't see what Mischief is like to come of it; he suspects himself a Foundling.

Chr. A Foundling! Say you so?

Sost. He certainly will, Husband.

Chr. Own it.

Sost. Au, bless us! be that the Lot of our Enemies. Shall I own a Son not to be mine, who is really mine?

Chr. What! Are you afraid that you can't convince him he's your own when you please?

Sost.

ANNOTATIONS.

There is still the same Objection to this Scene, as the former; and, indeed, with more Appearance of Reason. For here *Clitipho,* full of the Suspicion that *Syrus* had filled him with, runs to his Mother, complains of his Father's Severity, and declares that he no longer believes himself to be their Child. *Sostrata* alarmed at what she hears from her Son, goes in quest of *Chremes,* to expostulate with him. What a long Interval must we allow here between the two Scenes? This has given occasion to some to conjecture that what *Sostrata* says here, does not pro- ceed from any Conversation with her Son, but is only what her own Mind suggests he would naturally be apt to fancy from his Father's rigorous Behaviour. We shall enter more fully into the Grounds of this Supposition, in some of the following Notes. I shall be satisfied with observing here, that in this Scene, the Poet very happily paints the Tenderness, Anxiety, and Concern of a Mother for her Son, and the morose Obstinacy of a Husband, who persuaded that every thing he does is right, and imagining himself of superior Understanding; despises every

ACTUS V. SCENA III.

ARGUMENTUM.

Sostrata cum marito expostulat, & pro filii salute plus æquo soli-
cita monet maritum, ne pergat exhærédare filium : at maritus
contra falsis objurgatiunculis eam refutat, in ipsius inobedienti-
am & mores acerbe invehens.

SOSTRATA, CHREMES.

PROFECTO, nisi caves, tu homo, aliquid gnato
  conficies mali :
Idque adeò miror, quomodo   [vir, potuerit.
Tam ineptum quidquam tibi venire in mentem, mi
CH. Oh, pergin' mulier esse ? nullamne ego rem un-
  quam in vitâ meâ
Volui, quin tu in eâ re mihi advorsatrix fueris, So-
  strata ?   5
At si rogitem jam, quid est quod peccem, aut quam-
  obrem id faciam, nescias,   [nescio ?
In quâ re nunc tam confidenter restas, stulta. So. ego
CH. Imo scis potiùs, quàm quidem redeat ad inte-
  grum eadem oratio.
So. Oh, iniquos es, qui me tacere de re tantâ postules.
CH. Non postulo. jam loquere. nihilo minùs ego
  hoc faciam tamen.   10
So. Facies ? CH. Verum. So. Non vides quantum
  mali ex eâ re excites ?   [certè sic erit:
Subditum se suspicatur. CH. subditum ! ain' tu ? So.
Mi vir. CH. confitere. So. au, obsecro te, istuc ini-
  micis siet.
Egon' confitear meum non esse filium, qui sit meus ?
CH. Quid metuis ? ne non, cùm velis, convincas
  esse illum tuum ?   15 So. Facies ? CH.

ORDO.

So. PRofecto, tu homo, nisi caves, conficies aliquid mali gnato : a-deóque miror id, quo-modo quidquam tam ineptum potuerit ve-nire tibi in mentem, mi vir. CH. Oh, pergisne esse mulier ? Egone unquam volui nullam rem in mea vita, quin tu fueris adversatrix mihi in ea re, Sostrata ? At si jam rogitem, quid est quod peccem, aut quamobrem faciam id : tu stulta nescias, in qua re nunc restas tam confidenter. So. Ego nescio ? CH. Imo scis potius, quam quidem eadem oratio redeat ad integrum. So. Oh, es iniquus, qui postules me tacere de tanta re. CH. Non postulo, jam lo-quere, tamen ego ni-hilo minus faciam hoc.

Verum. So. Non vides quantum mali excites ex ea re ? Suspicatur se subditum.
ditum ! Aisne tu ? So. Certe erit sic, mi vir. CH. Confitere. So. Au, obsecro te, istuc sit ini-
micis. Egone confitear filium non esse meum, qui sit meus ? CH. Quid metuis ? Ne non convincas
illum, cum velis, esse tuum ?

ANNOTATIONS.

every thing his Wife can say, as trivial and
below his Notice.

[11] *Subditum se suspicatur.* It is upon
this Verse, that the great Dispute arises as
to the manner of *Sostrata's* here opening
her Mind to her Husband ; whether she
speaks only her own Suspicions, or what she
had heard from her Son. *Tanaquil Faber,*
and several Commentaters before him, maintain the former, in which they are supported
by Madam *Dacier.* Her Words are : " In

" the Original we read, Clitipho *suspect'r*
" that he is no Child of ours. But, as my
" Father has observed, this would be a ve-
" ry considerable Error, and such as *Te-*
" *rence* was not capable of ; for he is won-
" derfully exact in the Conduct and Dis-
" position of his Plays, and, indeed, this is
" what all the Ancients admire and praise
" him for. It is but just now, that *Syrus*
" gave *Clitipho* this Notion of his being an
" Alien. The Time will not allow him to
                  " have

Soſt. Becauſe I have lately found a Daughter?

Chr. No: but what is ſtill a more convincing Proof: you will eaſily prove that he is your Son, he's ſo like you in Temper: for he reſembles you to a Tittle; nor do I know of one ill Quality in him, but you have the ſame. Beſides, there's nobody but yourſelf could have given birth to ſuch a Son. But here he comes himſelf, how mighty grave he looks! you may eaſily judge by ſeeing him.

ANNOTATIONS.

" have yet gone in queſt of his Mother to
" communicate this Suſpicion; for at the
" Minute of his retiring, *Chremes* and *So-*
" *ſtrata* appear upon the Stage; continu-
" ing the Diſpute they had had within doors.
" This Paſſage is, therefore, of the great-
" eſt Importance, and as only the changing
" of a ſingle Letter is ſufficient to make all
" plain, we may thence judge what Exact-
" neſs and Application is required in reading
" the Works of the Ancients. It is certain,
" that *Terence* wrote *ſuſpicetur*, and not
" *ſuſpicatur*. This *ſuſpicetur* changes the
" thing entirely. It is now no more than
" a Conjecture, inſtead of what it was be-
" fore a poſitive Affirmation. *Soſtrata* ap-
" prehends, that *Chremes*'s rigorous Beha-
" viour to *Clitipho* might make him ſu-
" ſpect that he was not their Child. Nor
" was this Apprehenſion, in a Mother, to
" be wondered at, eſpecially in an Age,
" when it was ſo common to expoſe Chil-

" dren. But not to detain the Reader with
" far-fetched Proofs, what follows imme-
" diately after in the ſame Verſe, puts the
" Matter beyond Diſpute. For *Soſtrata*
" ſays: *Certe ſic erit, mi vir. It will cer-*
" *tainly be ſo, Husband.* Had ſhe ſaid *ſuſpi-*
" *catur* ſhe muſt have continued to ſpeak
" in the preſent Tenſe: *ſic eſt.* But as ſhe
" uſes here the future, it is a certain Sign
" that ſhe had only declared her Appre-
" henſions." This, I think, is the Sum of
what can be urged in defence of that Conjecture; in anſwer to which I obſerve, that
the long Interval neceſſary to be ſuppoſed betwixt this Scene and the other, may be accounted for in the ſame Manner as at the
Beginning of the preceding Scene. Again,
it is not natural to ſuppoſe that the Poet
would make *Syrus* inſtil a Notion into *Cli-*
tipho's Head, and then introduce *Soſtrata*, as
apprehending that theſe would be his Suſpicions, before ſhe had ſeen her Son, and heard
them

ACT V. SCENE IV.

ARGUMENT.

In this Scene is ſeen the Indulgence and Tenderneſs of a Mother, and the Rigour and Severity of a Father. Clitipho addreſſes his Mother, begging that ſhe will inform him who are his real Parents; at which ſhe is extremely uneaſy. Chremes chides his Son with great Bitterneſs.

CLITIPHO, SOSTRATA, CHREMES.

Clit. IF there ever was a Time, Mother, when you took Pleaſure in me, or delighted to call me your Son, I beg you will now remember it, and pity me in this Diſtreſs. What I want and deſire is, that you will inform me of my real Parents.

Soſt.

ANNOTATIONS.

This Scene is a Continuation of what was
begun in the foregoing. *Clitipho* comes up,
and perſiſts in demanding of his Mother, that
ſhe would tell him his real Parents. *Chremes*

interrupts that Diſcourſe, and chides his Son
in the bittereſt Terms for his Debaucheries;
but at the ſame time with ſuch Strength of
Reaſon, and ſo lively a Deſcription of the Infamy

So. Quòd filia eſt inventa ? CH. Non ; ſed, quo ma
   gi' credendum fiet,
Id, quòd eſt conſimilis moribus,   [probè :
Facilè convinces ex te natum : nam tui ſimilis eſt
Nam illi nihil vitii eſt relictum, quin fit & idem tibi :
Tum præterea talem, niſi tu, nulla pareret filium. 20
Sed ipſe egreditur, quàm-ſeverus ! rem cùm videas,
   ſenſeas.

Su. *Quod filia eſt inventa ? Ch. Non, ſed id, quo fit magis credendum, facilè convinces eum eſſe natum ex te, quod eſt conſimilis tibi moribus : nam eſt ſimilis tui probè : nem nihil vitii eſt relictum illi, quin & idem fit tibi :*

tum præterea, nulla, niſi tu, pareret talem filium. Sed ipſe egreditur, quam ſeverus ! cenſeas rem cùm videas.

ANNOTATIONS.

them from him, There is ſomething trifling in this, and below the Genius of *Terence*. Beſides the Converſation in the next
Scene begins, as if *Clitipho* there only repeated a Requeſt, which he had been making before. As to what ſeems to carry the
greateſt Air in favour of that Suppoſition,
Certè fic erit, mi vir, ſome of the beſt Copies
have *certe inquam, mi vir*. Which I make
no doubt is the true Reading.

[16] *Quid filia eſt inventa ?* There is ſome
Difficulty in This Place, nor does it appear
at firſt Sight, why *Soſtrata* makes this Suppoſition. The moſt common Explication
given by Commentators is this ? Shall I,
therefore, eaſily convince him, that he is my
Son, becauſe our having ſo lately found a
Daughter is an evident Proof, that I have
not been barren ? But this does not at all
appear ſatisfying. It is more probable, that
Soſtrata means ; Do you pretend that I ſhall
find it eaſy to convince *Clitipho* of his being

my Son, becauſe of his reſembling our
Daughter ſo lately found ? What follows,
makes it probable that Reſemblance is here
meant ; for *Chremes* immediately anſwers :
No, but becauſe he reſembles you.

[20] *Quam ſervus ! rem cum videas, cenſeas*,
Terence here imitates a Verſe of *Plautus*,
Caſ. III. 2. 32.
    Sed eccum incedit, at, quam aſpicias triſtem,
        frugi cenſeas.
For *triſtis* here, in *Plautus*, is of the ſame
Import with *ſeverus*, in *Terence*. Or perhaps
it may be an Interrogation. *Rem cum videas, cenſeas ?* H. e. *Credas ex ſeveritate, quam
præ ſe fert, itá rem eſſe ?* It is, indeed, difficult to fix upon any Thing with Certainty,
as the Words are undetermined, and may admit of a Variety of Meanings. What I
think offers moſt naturally is : *How grave
he looks ? To behold his Air and Aſpect*, you'd
think he were ſo really. Rem cum videas, inſtead of *faciem cum videas*.

ACTUS V. SCENA IV.

ARGUMENTUM.

*In hac ſcena matrum indulgentia ac facilitas ; patrum verò ſe-
veritas oſtenditur. Clitipho cum matre colloquitur, ſuos ſibi
parentes commonſtrari cupiens : qua oratione illam admodum
reddit ſolicitam. Chremes contumelioſe filium objurgat.*

CLITIPHO, SOSTRATA, CHEMES.

SI unquam ullum fuit tempus, mater, cùm ego vo-
   luptati tibi
Fuerim, dictus filius tuus tuâ voluntate, obſecro [mei.
Ejus ut memineris, atque inopis nunc te miſereſcat
Quod peto & volo, parentes meos ut commonſtres mihi.

ORDO

CL. SI fuit un-
   quam ullum
tempus, mater, cùm
ego fuerim voluptati
tibi, dictus filius tu-
us tua voluntate, ob-
ſecro ut memineris

*ejus, atque ut nunc miſereſcat te mei inopis : quod peto & volo eſt, ut commonſtres meos parentes
mihi.*

ANNOTATIONS.

famy of his Behaviour, as convinces him
how much he had been in the wrong, and

makes him aſhamed of himſelf, and his
own Actions.

Soft. For Heaven's Sake, my Child, let not such a Notion enter your Mind, that you are any other Person's Child but ours.

Clit. I am.

Soft. Alas! Is this what you want to know, pray? May Heaven as sure grant you to out-live us both, as you are our Child: and if you have any Regard for me, beware of letting me ever hear such a Word from you again.

Chr. And if you stand in any Awe of me, take care how I find in you these Manners.

Clit. What Manner?

Chr. If you want to know, I'll tell you. You are a trifling, idle, cheating, drinking, whoring, spendthrift Fellow. Believe this, and believe that you are our Son.

Clit. This is not proper Language from a Parent.

Chr. Had you issued from my Head, as they tell us *Minerva* did from *Jove's*, I would not the more for that, *Clitipho*, suffer myself to be disgraced by your infamous Debaucheries.

Soft. The Gods forbid!

Chr. I know not what the Gods will do, but shall take care myself to do all in my Power to prevent the worst. You seek after what you have, Parents: but are not in the least solicitous about what you most want; how to obey your Father, and preserve what his Industry has acquired. Had you not the Assurance deceitfully to bring before my Eyes, and into my very House—I'm asham'd to repeat the filthy Word in your Mother's Presence; but you were not in the least asham'd to do the Thing.

Clit. Alas! How am I now entirely dissatisfied with myself? How
much

ANNOTATIONS.

¹⁰ *Gerro.* *Gerro*, ut *Servius* dicit, à *ge-rendo:* unde *nugigerulus,* qui nugas gerit; vel, ut *Nonius* & *Festus,* à *gerris,* nam *gerræ* sunt nugæ & ineptæ, sic dictæ, ut *Festus* refert, quod quum Athenienses Syracusas obsiderent, & crebro *gerras* poscerent, irridentes Siculi *gerras* clamitabant, quum *gerræ* prius dicerentur, ut idem *Festus* ait, crates vimineæ. Propter illam irrisionem Siculorum factum est, ut *gerræ* pro nugis & contemptu dicantur. Hinc *congerro: qui easdem exercet nugas.* Calphurnius.

Helluo, vorax. Insatiabilis, inquit *Servius,* seu immoderate bona sua consumens. Forte ab antiquo *belus,* h. e. holus, quod notat omnis generis dapes. Unde helluo librorum dicitur omnes libros legens, & quasi devorans.

¹¹ *Ganeo.* *Isidorus,* Lib. 10. *Ganeo;* luxuriosus, & tanquam in occultis locis & subterraneis, quæ ganea Græci vocant. *Damnosus,* i. e. damni quidquid tuis parentibus afferens, ut jam fecisti, extorquendo à me per servum decem minas Bacchidi.

¹² *Non sunt hæc parentis dicta.* These Words are commonly given to *Clitipho;* but Madam *Dacier* thinks, that they come more properly from *Sostrata;* a Conjecture I am much inclined to favour.

Non, si ex capite meo sis natus. Here we have the Style somewhat more elevated and raised than is usual in Comedy. This proceeds from the Passion of the Speaker, which as it warms the Soul, suggests at the same time Expressions and Sentiments more noble than those which are apt to offer themselves, when the Mind is cool and calm. Hence *Horace,* in his Art of Poetry;

Interdum tamen & vocem comædia tollit,
Iratusque Chremes tumido delitigat ore.

" Sometimes Comedy too raises it Voice,
" and *Chremes* provoked, speaks in a high
" Strain of Indignation."

¹⁵ *Dii isthæc.* *Sostrata,* whose Character has in it a strong Tincture of Superstition, always has recourse to the Gods. She wishes that they may give a favourable Turn

to

So. Obfecro, mi gnate, ne iſtuc in animum inducas
  tuum, 5
Alienum eſſe te. CL. ſum. So. miſeram me ! hoc-
  cine quæſiſti, obſecro ? [natus es :
Ita mihi atque huic ſis ſuperſtes, ut ex me atque hoc
Et cave poſthac, ſi me amas, unquam iſtuc verbum
  ex te audiam. CH. at [tiam.
Ego, ſi me metuis, mores cave in te eſſe iſtos ſen-
CL. Quos ? CH. ſi ſcire vis, ego dicam ; gerro,
  iners, fraus, helluo, 10
Ganeo, damnoſus. crede : & noſtrum te eſſe credito.
CL. Non ſunt hæc parentis dicta. CH. non, ſi ex
  capite ſis meo [magis
Natus, item ut aiunt Minervam eſſe ex Jove, eâ cauſâ
Patiar, Clitipho, flagitiis tuis me infamem fieri.
So. Dî iſtæc prohibeant. CH. Deos neſcio : ego,
  quod potero, ſedulo. 15
Quæris id, quod habes, parentes : quod abeſt, non
  quæris, patri [nerit.
Quomodo obſequare, & ſervis quod labore inve-
Non mihi per fallacias adducere ante oculos ? pudet
Dicere hac præſente verbum turpe : at te id nullo
  modo
Facere puduit. CL. eheu, quàm nunc totus diſpliceo
  mihi ! 20

So. Obſecro, mi gna-
te, ne inducas iſtuc
in tuum animum, te
eſſe alienum. CL.
Sum. O me miſeram !
quæſiſti boccine, ob-
ſecro ? Ita ſis ſuper-
ſtes mibi atque buic,
ut es natus ex me at-
que boc : et cave, ſi
me amas, ut ego un-
quam audiam iſtuc
verbum ex te poſthac.
CH. At ſi metuis
me, cave ego ſentiam
iſtos mores eſſe in te.
CL. Quos ? CH.
Si vis ſcire, ego di-
cam: es gerro, iners,
fraus, belluo, ganeo,
damnoſus, crede hoc,
et credito te eſſe noſ-
trum. CL. Hæc non
ſunt dicta parentis.
CH. Non, ſi ſis na-
tus ex meo capite, i-
tem ut aiunt Miner-
vam eſſe natam ex
Jove, magis ea cau-
ſa patiar, Clitipho,
me fieri infamem tuis
flagitiis. So. Dii
prohibeant iſtæc. CH.

Neſcio Deos ; ego prohibebo ſedulo, quod potero. Quæris id, quod babes, parentes : non quæ-
ris, quod abeſt, quomodo obſequare patri, et ſerves quid invenerit labore ? An non auſus es ad-
ducere mibi ante oculos per fallacias ? Pudet dicere turpe verbum hac præſente : at nullo modo
puduit te facere illud. CL. Eheu, Quam ego totus nunc diſplicco mibi !

ANNOTATIONS.

to theſe Diſorders in the Family. *Dii iſtæc in melius vertant,* or *probibeant.* But *Cbremes,* without giving her time, haſtily interrupts her, *neſcio Deos.* Theſe Words have, by moſt Commentators, been explained in a manner, very injurious to the Poet. *Dionyſius Lambinus,* in that fine Letter which he writes to *Cbarles* IX, charges *Terence* with Impiety. But upon conſidering the Words candidly, it will appear that the Poet only makes *Cbremes* ſpeak here like a Man of Senſe, and not as one of the Vulgar. He means, that it did not belong to him to pretend to know the Will of the Gods. His Buſineſs was to take all the Precautions that Reaſon and Prudence ſuggeſted, and leave the Diſpoſal of the reſt to Providence, which thus far expected our Care, but did not require of us to dive into its Myſteries. This is a way of thinking, very common among the great Authors of Antiquity. *Saluſt* Cat. 56. *Non votis, neque ſuppliciis muliebrus auxilia Deorum paran-tur : vigilando, agendo, bene conſulendo, proſ-*

pere omnia cedunt. Ubi ſocordiæ tete atque ignaviæ tradideris, nequicquam Deos implo-res ; irati infeſtique ſunt. And *Livy* Lib. 22. 5. *Nec enim inde votis, aut implo-ratione Deûm, ſed vi ac virtute evadendum eſſe.* The Sentiment here is exactly ſimilar in every reſpect, and at the ſame time ſet in ſo clear a Light, that it is impoſſible to miſtake the Meaning of it. The Vulgar, indeed, might fancy that Importunity and Supplications were ſufficient to procure the Interpoſition of the Gods ; but Men of truer Judgment knew, that as the Gods had given us Faculties to provide for ourſelves, and ward off Misfortunes ; ſo the only way to obtain their Aſſiſtance, was by exerting thoſe Faculties, which they had given us for our Defence. Take this from *Plautus,* Ciſtell. I. 1. 53.

  Gy. Dii faxint. Lx. *Sine opera tua nil Dii*
    borunt facere poſſunt.

[18] *Pudet dicere bac præſente verbum turpe.* Both *Greeks* and *Romans* behaved with

ſo

much afhamed? Nor can I now refolve which way to fet about paci-
fying and reconciling him.

ANNOTATIONS.

fo much Refpect towards their Women, that | coming Word to efcape them in their Pre-
they never fuffered an undecent or unbe- | fence. Both Religion and Politicks required,
                                                       that

ACT V. SCENE V.

ARGUMENT.

By the Interpofition of Menedemus, *after fo much Difturbance
and Confufion, every thing is made quiet and eafy. The
Daughter of* Archonides *is deftined to be* Clitipho's *Wife
with his own Confent.* Chremes *is moreover prevailed with
to forgive* Syrus.

MENEDEMUS, CHREMES, CLITIPHO, SOSTRATA.

Menedemus. IN reality, *Chremes* torments the Youth too much, nay,
        even inhumanly. I am, therefore, come out, if po●●●,
to make up the Breach. And here I fee they are very fortunately.

Chr. Oh *Menedemus*, why don't you order my Daughter to be
fent for, and confirm the Settlement I have made upon her?

Soft. Hufband, I befeech you not to do it.

Clit. Father, I beg of you that you will forgive me.

Mened. Forgive him, *Chremes*: let them prevail upon you.

Chr. What! Shall I knowingly, and with my Eyes open, make
over all I have to *Bacchis*? I'll never do it.

Mened. Nay, we would not fuffer it.

Clit. Father, if you defire that I fhould live, forgive me.

Soft. Do, my *Chremes*.

Mened. Do, pray: don't be fo obftinate.

Chr. What's the meaning of all this? I fee you will not fuffer me
to go on with this, as I at firft intended.

Mened. You do now as becomes you.

Chr. But I will do it only on this Condition, if he does what I
think it highly reafonable he fhould.

Clit. Father, I'll do any thing, command me.

Chr. I'll have you to marry.

Clit. Father!

Chr. I'll hear nothing.

Mened. I'll undertake for him; he fhall do it.

Chr. But I hear nothing from himfelf.

Clit. I'm ruin'd.

Soft. What, do you hefitate, *Clitipho?*   *Chr.*

ANNOTATIONS.

In this Scene we have the Play concluded, | length foftened, and agrees to pardon him
to the mutual Satisfaction of all the feveral | upon Condition that he will have done with
Perfons concerned in it. *Menedemus* inter- | the Follies of Youth, and marry; which at
pofes as a Mediator between the Father and | laft, with fome Difficulty, he is brought to
Son; *Clitipho* himfelf too fhews fo much | confent to.
concern for what is paft, that *Chremes* is at | 3 *Cur non acterfi fi jubet filiam, & quod do-*
                                                 iii

Quàm pudet! neque, quod principium incipiam ad placandum, scio.

dum eum.

Quam pudet! neque scio quod principium incipiam ad placan-

ANNOTATIONS.

that they should always before them, shew the strictest Regard to Decorum and Politeness.

ACTUS V. SCENA V.

ARGUMENTUM.

Menedemi interventu, post tantas turbationes, tranquilla fiunt omnia. Archonidis filia Clitiphoni volenti uxor datur. Syrę a Chremete ignoscitur.

MENEDEMUS, CHREMES, CLITIPHO, SOSTRATA.

ENIMVERO Chremes nimis graviter cruciat adolescentulum, [optumè
Nimisque inhumanè. exeo ergo, ut pacem conciliem.
Ipsos video. CH. ehem, Menedeme, cur non accersi jubes [secro
Filiam, & quod dotis dixi, firmas? So. mi vir, te ob-
Ne facias. CL. pater, obsecro ut mî ignoscas. ME.
da veniam, Chreme.   5
Sine te exorent. CH. egon' mea bona ut dem Bac-
chidi dono sciens?   [vivom vis pater,
Non faciam. ME. at nos non sinemus. CL. si me
Ignosce. So. age, Chremes mi. ME. age, quæso,
ne tam obfirma te, Chreme.   [pertendere.
CH. Quid istuc? video non licere ut cœperam, hoc
ME. Facis ut te decet. CH. eâ lege hoc adeò faciam,
si facit id,   10
Quod ego hunc æquom censeo. CL. pater, omnia fa-
ciam: impera.   [ME. ad me recipio:
CH. Uxorem ut ducas. CL. pater. CH. nihil audio.
Faciet. CH. Nil etiam audio ipsum. CL. perii. So.
an dubitas, Clitipho?

ORDO.

ME. *Enimvero Chremes cruciat adolescentulum nimis graviter, nimisque inhumane. Ergo exeo, ut concilem pacem. Video ipsos optime.* CH. *Ehem Menedeme, cur non jubes filiam accersi, & firmas quod dotis dixi?* So. *Mi vir, obsecro te, ne facias.* CL. *Pater obsecro ut ignoscas mihi.* ME. *Da veniam, Chreme; sine ut exorent te.* CH. *Egone? ut sciens dem mea bona dono Bacchidi? non faciam.* ME. *At nos non sinemus.* CL. *Pater, si vis me vivum, ignosce.* So. *Age, mi Chremes.* ME. *Age quæso, Chreme, ne tam obfirma te.* CH.

Quid istuc? video non licere pretendere hoc, ut cœperam. ME. *Facis ut te decet.* CH. *Eiam adeo hoc ea lege, si facit id quod ego censeo esse æquum hunc facere.* CL. *Pater, faciam omnia, impera.* CH. *Ut ducas uxorem.* CL. *Pater.* CH. *Audio nihil.* ME. *Recipio eum ad me; facit.* CH. *Nil audio ipsum respondentem.* CL. *Perii.* So. *An dubitas, Clitipho?*

ANNOTATIONS.

tis dixi, firmas? There are two Ends answered by this Speech of *Chremes.* First, at the Conclusion of the Play, the Marriage of his Daughter is promoted, and here represented as agreed upon and settled; and *Clitipho,* who was already ashamed of himself, is put upon begging to be restored to his Father's Favour, which he obtains upon the Condition of changing his Manner of Life. For nothing could have more effectually tended to rouze *Clitipho,* and make him earnest and importunate in the Demand, and willing to comply with whatever Conditions his Father might require, than *Chremes*'s thus insisting upon having the late Deed, whereby he disinherited his Son, confirmed. 'Tis therefore, that he so earnestly begs to be forgiven. *Pater, obsecro, mihi ignoscas.* And soon after, *Si me vivum vis, pater, ignosce.*

13 *Nil etiam audio ipsum.* Guyetus explains

Chr. Nay, juft what he will.

Mened. He'll do every thing.

Soft. This at firft, while you yet know nothing of it, may feem a hard Condition; but when you underftand a little better, it will become eafy to you.

Clit. I'll do it, Father.

Soft. My Son, I have a fine Girl in my Eye for you, one that you can't mifs to love, our Neighbour *Phanecrata*'s Daughter.

Clit. How! That red-haired, grey-eyed, wide-mouthed, hooknofed Wench? I can't think of it, Father.

Chr. Hy, hy, how nice he is? You may guefs what his Mind has been running upon.

Soft. I'll name another to you.

Clit. Nay, fince I muft marry, I know one myfelf that will do,

Soft. Now, Son, I commend you.

Clit. *Archonides*'s Daughter.

Soft. A very good Choice!

Clit. Father, I have ftill one Favour to afk.

Chr. What?

Clit. To pardon *Syrus* what he has done for my fake.

Chr. I will, *(To the Spectators.)* Farewel, and give us your Applaufe.

ANNOTATIONS.

plains this, *Nihil adhuc audio ipfum refpondere ad ea quæ propofui.* But we are to confider the Words as more immediately an Anfwer to what *Menedemus* had faid: *Ad me recipio; faciet:* for here the Old Man undertakes, and promifes for him. But replies *Chremes, I hear nothing from himfelf; he makes no Promife;* where we are evidently to fupply *mibi polliceri.* Hence *Clitipho* feeing the Dilemma, to which he was reduced, that he muft either engage to marry, or forfeit his Father's Kindnefs, in a Sentence or two

after, makes this Promife: *faciam, pater.*

[17] *Rufamne illam virginem?* What that red-haired Virgin? For red Hair feems to have been a Thing equally difliked among the Ancients as by us.

[18] *Cefiam.* The fame Colour of Eyes feems to be here intended, as what *Plautus,* Curc. I. 3. 35. calls in Contempt *noĉturnos oculos.*

Sparfo ore. Id eft: *ore late diduĉto.* Vel, ut quidam volunt, potius vultu lentiginofo.

[19] *Heia, ut elegans eft! credas animum ibi*

CH. Imo utrum vult? ME. faciet omnia, So. hæc, dum incipias, gravia funt,

Dumque ignores: ubi cognôris, facilia. CL. faciam, pater. 15

So. Nate mi, ego pol tibi dabo illam lepidam, quam tu facilè ames, [nem,

Filiam Phanocratæ noftri. CL. rufamne illam virgi-Cæfiam, fparfo ore, adunco nafo? non poffum, pater.

CH. Heia, ut elegans eft! credas animum ibi efle.

So. aliam dabo.

CL. Quid iftic? quandoquidem ducenda eft, egomet habeo propemodum,

Quam volo. So. nunc laudo te, gnate. CL. Archo-nidi hujus filiam. [CL. Syro ignofcas volo,

So. Perplacet. CL. pater, hoc nunc reftat. CH. quid ? Quæ meá caufá fecit. CH. fiat. Vos valete, & plaudite.

CALLIOPIUS RECENSUI.

pemodum babeo quam volo. So. Nunc laudo te, gnate. CL. Filiam bujus Arcbonidi. So. Perplacet. CL. Pater, hoc reftat nunc. CH. Quid ? CL. Volo ignofcas Syro ea quæ fecit mea caufa. CH. Fiat. Vos valete, & plaudite.

A N N O T A T I O N S.

ibi effe. This whole Paffage is to be under-stood ironically. Quam faftidiofus formarum arbiter! quem fi fpectes, credas, animum ad uxorem appulfurum effe. Qui enim tam pro-feffum ageret formarum cenforem, nifi ali-quam magno è numero electurus?

21 Arcbonidi bujus filiam. Arcbonidi for Arcbonidis, as is frequent among the Anci-ents; thus we meet with Acbilli for Acbillis, and Perfi for Perfis. Hujus, i. e. noftri vi-cini, of this our Neighbour.

22 Perplacet. Softrata only anfwers here, whereas it might naturally be thought, that Chremes ought rather to have expreffed his Approbation. But the chief thing aimed at, is to bring Clitipbo to confent to marry; after which the Poet does not think it any wife neceffary to inform us of all the further Parti-culars; for, as at the Conclufion of the An-drian, Intus tranfigetur, fi quid eft, quod reftet.

The End of the FIRST VOLUME.

BOOKS printed for EDWARD and CHARLES DILLY.

For the Ufe of Schools and Private Gentlemen.

1. THE Whole WORKS of HORACE, tranflated into Englifh Profe, as near as the Propriety of the two Languages will admit; together with the original Latin, from the beft Editions, wherein the Words of the Text are ranged in their Grammatical Order, the Ellipfes carefully fupplied, the Obfervations of the moft valuable Commentators both ancient and modern reprefented, and the Author's Defign and beautiful Defcriptions fully fet forth in a Key annexed to each Poem; with Notes Geographical and Hiftorical. Begun by DAVID WATSON, M. A. Revifed, carried on, and publifhed, by S. PATRICK, LL. D. Editor of Ainfworth's Dictionary, &c. The Fourth Edition, in Two Volumes Octavo, Price bound 10 s.

N. B. The great Care and Pains taken by Dr. Samuel Patrick, both in HORACE and TERENCE, have rendered them the moft ufeful Books of any in their Kind ever yet publifhed; Horace being not only the moft literal Profe Tranflation that has ever yet appeared, but befides, it has the various Readings of Dr. Bentley, and Dr. Douglafs's Catalogue of near Five Hundred different Editions of Horace, with their Sizes and Dates; alfo many curious Notes and Obfervations, not to be met with in any other Tranflation of Horace: Together with the Life of Horace, and a critical Differtation on his Writings: All of which has made the Demand fo large, that in a very few Years feveral Thoufands have been printed and fold.

2. GRÆCÆ GRAMMATICES RUDIMENTA, Ordine Novo ac Facillimo Digefta: Or, A NEW GREEK GRAMMAR. Wherein the Declenfion of Nouns, and Conjugation of Verbs, are difpofed in a new, eafy, and diftinct Method. By THOMAS STACKHOUSE, A. M. Price bound 2 s 6 d.

N. B. Extract of a Letter from the Rev. Dr. Gregory Sharpe to the Author.— " Every Attempt to promote the Knowledge of a Language, fo ufeful in " every Branch of Science and Literature, is very commendable: Your new " Method, in particular, will deferve the Attention of thofe who are en- " trufted with the Education of Youth, as it is more eafy and expeditious " than that of moft other Grammarians."

3. A NEW SPELLING BOOK, intituled, The Child's BEST INSTRUCTOR in SPELLING and READING: Wherein Words of feveral Syllables are fo divided, that the Sound of each Syllable, when joined together, fhall lead the Scholar into a true and correct Pronunciation of every Word. The Whole carefully revifed, corrected, and improved by the Author, JOHN GIGNOUX, Teacher of the Englifh Language.

A New Edition, (being the Fourth).

To which is now added,

A COMPENDIOUS ENGLISH GRAMMAR; alfo a copious Table of Proper Names of Perfons, Places, and Things, collected from the Holy Scriptures, &c. each Word properly divided and accented according to the original Pronunciation. Price bound 1 s. with a handfome Allowance to all Schoolmafters.

N. B. Foreigners and Natives, who are defirous to attain a correct Pronunciation of the Englifh Language, by making ufe of this Spelling-Book cannot fail of meeting with Succefs.

www.ingramcontent.com/pod-product-compliance
Lightning Source LLC
Chambersburg PA
CBHW020236110726
47898CB00004B/1284